T0381066

Quest For The Sword Of Anthrowst
By *Katrina Mandrake-Johnston*
World of Zaylyn

Enter the World of Zaylyn. This is a world filled with strange creatures, magic, and mystery. In this book, you will be introduced to several characters, many of which you will learn more about in later books. This story revolves around a particular group, who through peculiar circumstances, find themselves partaking in a quest for the Sword of Anthrowst.

This is a world filled with many different races: humans, elves, dwarves, fairy folk, centaurs, dragons, dragon-like humanoids, goblins, trolls, shape-shifters, and many others yet to be discovered. With warriors, thieves, wizards, treasure, magic, strange creatures, danger, and adventure, this world is never dull.

Evil, malicious creatures have entered this world to do the bidding of an insane wizard. Can this horrible man control these beasts as he believes, and for what purpose?

Vordin, a teenaged boy, narrowly escaped the fate of his village as the creatures slaughtered everyone there, including his parents. Vordin is told by a tiny fairy queen, whose race had always been thought of as myth, that the evil wizard had to be slain by the Sword of Anthrowst in order to send the creatures back to where they came from.

Two thieves, an elf named Candra and Dendrox her human companion, join Vordin in the quest as does an amateur wizard named Weena. The mysterious being they encounter, half human and half spider, is she friend or foe?

When a dwarf, Nodwel, pleads for their help, they find themselves on a rescue mission to a small village under attack by these same creatures. Nodwel's group had been at the village when it had been attacked and he greatly fears for their safety and that of the villagers.

Will any of Nodwel's companions be alive? Were they able to hold the beasts back long enough for Nodwel to return with help? Is it even possible to defeat these beasts? Will there be anyone left to save by the time they arrive? Will they fall prey to the horrid evil monsters as well, trapped in a malicious web of spells and ripped to pieces by huge dagger-like teeth and claws?

Is this quest simply impossible? How are they to even find this sword, wherever it may be, and the wizard for whom they only know a name?

This group find themselves in many different and exciting situations, wondering if they will even live long enough to find the sword or even discover where it is.

Among their encounters are a mischievous fairy queen and her followers, many vicious monsters, giant spiders within ancient underground passages, bounty hunters after the two thieves, plus so much more. Could there be bandits within the forest, and perhaps even a werewolf lurking about as a few believe?

Meanwhile, a romance begins to stir, as well as a vicious jealousy.

But, worst of all for this little group of adventurers, is the presence of a mysterious and evil vampiric being with immense power, called simply The Black Shadow.

Could he have something to do with this group coming together? If so, what purpose does he intend for them? He wants them to complete their quest and save Zaylyn from the evil wizard and his army of creatures, but why, especially when he could easily take care of the problem himself?

* *

The World of Zaylyn is an elaborate mystical place, and I hope you enjoy exploring it through this and many more books. Enter the World of Zaylyn website at: www.webspawner.com/users/worldofzaylyn

Order this book online at www.trafford.com
or email orders@trafford.com

Most Trafford titles are also available at major online book retailers.

Print information available on the last page.

ISBN: 978-1-4120-8930-2 (sc)

Trafford rev. 05/20/2019

www.trafford.com
North America & international
toll-free: 1 888 232 4444 (USA & Canada)
fax: 812 355 4082

Welcome to the World of Zaylyn by Katrina Mandrake-Johnston.
****
THE WORLD OF ZAYLYN SERIES
****
BOOK #1 = = > Quest For The Sword Of Anthrowst

See website for order information and special features.
****

(World of Zaylyn website = http:// www.webspawner.com/users/worldofzaylyn)

****

<Zaylyn ><Quest For The Sword Of Anthrowst ><By Katrina Mandrake-Johnston >   <Ch 1> < 1 >

CHAPTER 1 =   VORDIN

Vordin was fifteen and an only child. He had a mother and father who loved him dearly and they lived a happy and peaceful life together in the village of Nilnont. One day that happiness violently ended.

On this day, Vordin had spent most of the morning in his room trying to solve his latest puzzle box which he received the month before. He was wearing a grey tunic with his brown pants and a well-worn pair of brown leather shoes. His hair was a light brown and he wore it long at shoulder length. As usual, his hair was tied back at the base of his neck with a strip of leather.

As Vordin went about his usual activities, he was unaware such horrors existed and that such an ordinary day could bring such terror and so abruptly.

Vordin had been at the edge of the forest on the hilltop, when it had happened. Just below him, at the bottom of this small hill lay his village, Nilnont. He had been passing the time away as he waited for his mother to finish preparing dinner. He had made a nuisance of himself by snatching samples of the whipped potatoes with his finger and had been sent out of the house until the dinner was ready.

It had been a warm and pleasant day, still being the beginning of autumn. Sunset was approaching and Vordin had been watching the horizon. He could see the road which made its way over the grassy hills and then up to Nilnont. He knew that this road also continued up through the forest, eventually winding up and over the mountains into the valley beyond. Dee'ellkka Valley was its name.

The vibrant colors of the sunset were incredibly beautiful. There were wonderful shades of red, orange, pink, and yellow. He had said to himself that he ought to come up to the hill more often to watch the sunset, but he knew that he would probably be too preoccupied with other things to actually do so. Then, as he watched, he had noticed a black mass which appeared to flow over the hills out from the horizon.

He hadn't known what to think of it, his mind puzzling over what he was seeing. As the mass got closer, he had realized that he was not seeing one large mass, but many black shapes.

***

Something was heading toward Nilnont. Confused, he stood up, his eyes staring.

He watched the shapes approach and then he heard the awful shrieking howls. Whatever these creatures were, Vordin was sure that they had a malicious intent. Shouts came from the village. People started to run about grabbing what weapons they had. Panic welled up inside him. He was in danger. Everyone was in danger.

The howls grew louder and louder as the creatures got closer. They were moving fast. Vordin's mind was racing. A story he had been told came out of memory.

"Like demons they are, created with evil intent. They are filled with hate and malice. They revel in pain and suffering. They will bring death. A hollow tree can be a savior. The tree was once alive. You will be a being within a being. They will not see you. As a child within the womb of its mother cannot be seen directly, so shall you be hidden from sight."

He could remember asking many questions about this and why the mysterious man in black from the story had said these things. The storyteller, Rasindell, had replied that he too had been puzzled when these words had been spoken to him long ago, as this had been a true story. He told him that

<Zaylyn ><Quest For The Sword Of Anthrowst ><By Katrina Mandrake-Johnston >   <Ch 1> < 2 >

when he had heard the shrieking howl and saw the black shape, he knew to follow the advice no matter how strange it had been.

Vordin was afraid. There just happened to be a hollow tree on the edge of the forest where he stood. He looked at his village, then the approaching creatures as they neared the edge of the crop fields just outside the village, and finally to the hollow tree. The fear was too great. He wanted his parents. He wanted to run. He wanted to live. There didn't seem like there was any time to act. The creatures seemed so close. There was safety in the tree. It had to be true. He went over to it and frantically searched for a way inside. He found an opening and crawled in.

As he wriggled around trying to situate himself better, he couldn't help but wonder what the creatures looked like. It sent waves of fear and panic throughout his body as he imagined visual images to fit the malicious noises the beasts made.

He could hear people screaming. His face was wet with tears.

"They'll be okay," he told himself, "My parents… They'll escape. I know they will. Somehow they'll be safe." He was too frightened to move a single muscle. "What if they don't try to escape? What if they stay, hoping that I will come back?" he asked himself, "They must be so worried. They'll wait for me and they'll be killed, and it will be my fault. There wasn't enough time… It would be impossible to escape the village… No, they'll hide. They'll be safe… But the story spoke as if it didn't matter if people hid… as if the creatures could somehow see exactly where all living things were and that the only hope was to hide within something that had been living, or once was or something like that. I'm just assuming that these are the same creatures too. My imagination runs wild sometimes. I don't really know what these beasts are or what they look like, so how can I tell? There are some pretty tough people in my village, my father included. They'll fight them off, and all will be well."

He knew that his feeble thoughts of comfort weren't going to fool himself away from all the things he was dreading. He knew things had to be much worse, and if it were these 'demon' creatures like he thought, he knew that no one in his village would be able to survive, including his parents. He also knew that he could perish very easily along with them if this hollow tree trick didn't work.

Vordin thought about all the times he had been unkind to his parents, every time that he had lied to them, and all the times he hadn't really appreciated all that they had done for him. He cried and cried, knowing that he would never be able to tell them that he was sorry and how much he really loved them. He thought about all the happy times that he had spent with them and how he would never get to see them again. "They'll be okay," he lied to himself, "Everything will be fine."

He cried until it felt hard to breathe and his stomach ached. His eyes stung from rubbing his tears away with his dirty hands. Now all that was left for him to do was wait in the darkness of the tree and listen helplessly to all the horrible sounds coming from his village.

***

These horrid beasts had come to prey on the village of Nilnont. The crop fields were reduced to ash, as the creatures invoked spells of fire breath upon themselves enabling them to expel magical flames from their throats. The villagers' homes were burned and smashed. The animals of the village had been helpless, having no choice but to face the evil onslaught as their bodies were torn to shreds. The frantic screams of the villagers and the evil howls and shrieks of the creatures filled the night air. The creatures killed without mercy.

These innocent people could hold no hope of salvation from these foul beasts. Some villagers, the lucky ones, were killed before being feasted on, while the unlucky ones were eaten alive as they watched chunks of their own flesh being devoured before them by huge gnashing teeth. The ground was heavily stained with blood. Everyone was slaughtered.

***

Vordin listened from his hiding place to the horrors that were happening. As the screams quickly ceased, he feared that he had become the sole survivor of his entire village. He desperately hoped that these terrible evil creatures would creep back to wherever they came from when morning arrived. Dawn was far away, as the night was still young. Still, it gave him something to focus on. He would wait for the sun to rise. He told himself that things would be better then, all he had to do was wait. He

<Zaylyn ><Quest For The Sword Of Anthrowst ><By Katrina Mandrake-Johnston >   <Ch 1> < 3 >
could do that.

Why these 'demon' creatures would overlook him if he were hidden inside a tree, he didn't really understand. He desperately tried to remember the story he had been told, wondering if it were in fact these same creatures as he had thought.

Slowly, bit-by-bit, the story began to come back to him...

It had been around the time when Rasindell had first begun to learn magic. He had met a woman whom also was studying magic. They would spend hours together practicing their new spells and became quite good friends.

Unknown to Rasindell, she had an admirer. She was not interested in this other man at all, as he was known to practice dark and evil magic.

Unfortunately, this evil wizard had laid claim to her in his own twisted mind. When he discovered the friendship she and Rasindell had, he was furious. He could see that Rasindell and the woman were clearly interested in each other and perhaps even falling in love. The wizard left to hunt the two of them down and exact his revenge, for in his mind she had betrayed him.

This evil wizard discovered them in a rocky yet forested area where they had been practicing their spells. The wizard had come across them during their first kiss and had caught them unaware.

"How dare you!" he had screamed at her.

She tried to explain, yet again, to the delusional man that she was not interested in him and that there was no relationship between them as he imagined. She explained that she was in love with Rasindell and not him.

This just infuriated the evil man further. In his rage, he summoned a Killnarin, using very strong magic to do so. The beast easily slipped into this world using the incredible hate this man possessed as a conduit from its world into Zaylyn.

As the foul beast emerged from what looked like a tear in the very air around them, it growled maliciously. Its body was a deep black and it looked wet and slippery. This beast looked similar to a salamander, but with six clawed legs and a huge mouth of sharp jagged teeth. Its eyes were completely black and it never took its gaze off the woman.

"What have you done?!" she asked the wizard in terror, "It will kill us all!"

"As long as you die, I do not care," was his cold and heartless answer.

Vordin remembered that Rasindell had a very difficult time speaking of this and had never told him the name of the woman or the evil wizard.

The Killnarin pounced onto the woman as a cat would a mouse, killing her instantly with its dagger-like claws. There was nothing he could have done. If he could have given his life to save hers, he would have, but everything had happened so fast. Even in his grief, Rasindell knew that remaining where he was meant his death as well.

Next the Killnarin turned on the wizard that had summoned it. His death was slow and painful. Rasindell had taken this opportunity to run as fast as he could into the forest, trying to escape the terrible beast, as it would surely come after him.

Within the forest, he was stopped by a mysterious man dressed all in black and wearing a hooded cloak. Rasindell could not see his face, as it was cast in shadow beneath his hood. There was something about this figure that had made Rasindell very nervous, although he didn't know exactly why.

"Like demons they are, created with evil intent," said the man in a calm soothing voice, speaking of the Killnarin, "They are filled with hate and malice. They revel in pain and suffering. They bring death. A hollow tree can be a savior. The tree was once alive. You will be a being within a being. They will not see you. As a child within the womb of its mother cannot be seen directly, so shall you be hidden from sight."

Rasindell immediately questioned this mysterious man about what he had told him, fearing that the beast was close behind.

"Their vision is different from ours," he explained, "They can see the life force of others.

Therefore, it matters not where you hide, as they can see within and beyond what we see. Your only hope is to mask your life force with that of another. It does not matter whether the tree is alive or dead and hollow. The fact that it once was alive and had a life force of its own is what is important."

"Where am I to find a hollow tree?" Rasindell asked, frantic to try anything at all to save his life, "The chances of finding one are so slim and then of finding one large enough to conceal me within are even less!"

The man directed him over to a large tree. Rasindell was about to protest that this tree was in good health and not at all hollow, when the mysterious figure pushed him gently forward into the tree as if it had been made of air.

When the Killnarin came into the area a few moments later, its large head moved back and forth searching for any sign of Rasindell. Rasindell tried to understand how he could be standing within a solid tree as he was, but couldn't come up with an explanation. The Killnarin couldn't see him; he was sure of it.

The mysterious man in black stepped forward toward the Killnarin. The creature actually seemed to fear him. The Killnarin reared up until it was standing on its back four legs reminding Rasindell of a centaur he had once met. The creature swiped at the air in front of it and snapped its massive jaws toward the man in black, but dared not approach him. The mysterious figure just stood there making his presence known.

The Killnarin finally dropped its upper body back down to the forest floor again, the ground shaking with the impact. It let loose a terrible shrieking howl in defiance. It stomped around as if it were trying to decide what to do, and then a tear in the air appeared as before. The tear looked similar to the distortion heat from a fire makes in the air, if you look at it a certain way. Rasindell had expected yet another Killnarin or some other terrible beast to enter their world through the portal. To Rasindell's surprise, the Killnarin instead left the world of Zaylyn, returning to wherever it had come from.

Once the Killnarin was gone, the mysterious man helped Rasindell out of the tree, and then he leapt up into the sky and disappeared from sight. Rasindell decided to build a home for himself and devote the rest of his life to magic. Having lost his one and only love, he had nothing else.

"*Could the mysterious man in the black hooded cloak be The Black Shadow?*" Vordin asked himself, "*The Black Shadow is supposed to be an incredibly powerful and evil being. I have heard awful things. Things that one could only imagine in the worst of nightmares. Surely it cannot be the same person. Perhaps I am remembering the story wrong.*"

Inside the hollow tree, it was damp and cold. For once, he was thankful for his short height and thin frame as these qualities allowed him to maneuver into his chosen hiding spot and therefore were responsible for saving his life.

He could feel bugs starting to crawl through his hair. It got to the point where he couldn't tell if it were some of his own hair that had made its way down inside the collar of his shirt or if it were some creepy insect squirming about. The wood was damp and had an earthy smell to it. Many times his hands found themselves sliding over slimy bits of fungus. Vordin wanted to get out of his cramped position and stretch, but he knew that he couldn't take the risk.

He continued to wait. He could smell the burning remains of the village from where he was. Luckily, he was far enough away to not have to worry about his tree catching fire. Vordin waited and waited, and finally the crackling fires became nothing more than smoldering embers.

After dawn, he emerged with great caution. The morning sun's rays were warm and bright. From where he stood at the crest of the hill at the edge of the forest, he could see the grassy hills rolling into the horizon. The road made its way up and over these hills until it reached Nilnont. There was no sign that the creatures had remained or where they might have traveled to afterwards.

He did not want to look at his village. He did not want to see the destruction. He knew it had happened, but if he didn't look at it, he could pretend that everything was fine.

Before this day, Nilnont was a happy and lively place. The small buildings had thatched roofs and the walls were made from stone. Nilnont's buildings had been constructed in this fashion for centuries.

<Zaylyn ><Quest For The Sword Of Anthrowst ><By Katrina Mandrake-Johnston >   <Ch 1> < 5 >

When a new building or home was to be built, it became a village project and everyone contributed in some way or another.

Almost every house had a garden of flowers, and it was a beautiful and peaceful place to live. Nilnont was known for its pottery. Some would be handcrafted for every day use and some would be made with artistic designs and paintings for decoration. On the rare occasion that travelers came to stop at Nilnont, they would always marvel at the quality and beauty of the pottery that the village produced.

It had been his village and his home. Finally, he made himself look down to Nilnont. He could see now that it had been reduced to smoldering piles of rubble and debris.

"My parents are somewhere down there. Everything is destroyed. Everything and everyone is gone. Everyone's dead. No one could have survived. My parents are dead," he tried to explain to himself.

He turned his eyes away from it. He stared at the road, following with his eyes as it continued past Nilnont and up into the forested hills to eventually lead into the mountains.

Vordin had never been to Dee'ellkka Valley, as the trek over the mountains was a long and strenuous one. It was rumored that trolls and dragons inhabited the mountain range, although few had ever seen them.

Vordin reluctantly returned his gaze toward Nilnont again, and then he forced himself to travel down to it. One of the persuasions he told himself was that perhaps he would find some survivors. He would rescue them and be a hero. Deep down, he knew that he would not, but he bravely continued.

He now stood at the edge of his village. There was nothing left of what he had called home. There was an eerie silence which emphasized the fact that he was alone. Everyone was gone. Nothing in the village had survived except for him.

Even though he expected the worst, he wanted to run desperately toward his house, to look for his parents and to see if they were all right. The fear and shock of what had happened and the sight of the devastation in front of him held him back.

At the edge of the village, from where he was standing, he saw the blackened and crumbling walls of many homes and buildings. He saw charcoaled remains of various pieces of wood furniture scattered about in the rubble. The street appeared empty from where he stood, but he knew there would be bodies. It was so very quiet. Usually, he would be able to hear the livestock in their pens at the far side of the village, but there was nothing. The crops were now blackened earth.

The winds changed and the foul stench of burnt flesh reached his nose. He felt numb and emotionless. It was almost as if his body wouldn't accept the devastation in front of him as being real.

After many unsuccessful attempts, he finally was able to force himself to slowly walk down the street. As he walked, he was conscious of every reluctant step and of every tiny detail that he beheld.

He tried desperately to hold his sanity together as he passed the body of a middle-aged man lying face down in the gravel, a large pool of blood beneath him. The crackling embers seemed to taunt him, as if they knew all that had been taken from him and they had remained to gloat.

He felt empty. He thought he should feel at least something, but he just felt hollow and empty. It was as if it were impossible for him to be seeing all of this. It somehow couldn't possibly be real.

He walked past the remnant of a house. Its garden of roses had been trampled along with the white miniature fence that surrounded it. The thatched roof was in ashes. Several of the stone walls had been bashed in, obviously by the incredible strength of these creatures. Vordin could see the destruction inside. Then he noticed the lifeless hand still reaching desperately for the sky beneath the rubble.

He moved quickly past with a lump in his throat as he imagined that it could have been him caught under the rubble like that. Guilty thoughts entered his mind as he passed more and more bodies and severed limbs among the debris and what was left of the houses and buildings.

"Why should I be the one to survive," he thought, *"I hid like a coward while everyone else died."*

He couldn't help noticing that many of the dead strewn about were young children. *"I should have stayed. Maybe I could have saved some of the children,"* and then disgusted with himself he thought, *"I'm a selfish coward. I was frightened. I panicked. I ran and hid. I should have tried to help. I could have brought someone with me. I could have saved at least one child. There was enough room in the*

<Zaylyn ><Quest For The Sword Of Anthrowst ><By Katrina Mandrake-Johnston >   <Ch 1> < 6 >
tree for that."

Vordin now approached the side street where his home should be. He hoped that by some miracle it still stood there intact, with his loving parents alive and well inside. He knew that this could never be true.

He could now see the smoldering remains of his home. The walls and roof had been torn down. Everything that had not been burned, had been smashed or ripped to pieces.

"Mother… Father…" he whispered, and such a combination of fear, anguish, and panic welled up inside him so strong that he would have never believed someone could feel that way.

Without thinking, he blindly made his way toward what was left of his home through the debris and mangled corpses. When he reached his goal, he rummaged around frantically in the rubble without purpose. Vordin suddenly recoiled at the sight of a charred severed arm. At the same time, a wave of reality and clarity was shocked into him. He recognized his father's ring on the burnt and blistered flesh.

"No…" he choked out, "Father… No…"

He looked away with freshly shed tears streaming down his face. That was when he saw the leg of his mother beneath a pile of debris.

"Mother…" his voice said, "I'll help you. Don't worry. I'm here now. I'll help you. I'm here."

He began uncovering her in a desperate hope that she might still be alive. Upon discovering that her head was missing, he just sat there staring blankly into the ashes. His mind was fighting against itself, not wanting to accept the fact that this was real and had actually happened.

As he sobbed heavily, images of his mother and father kept flashing through his mind along with images and memories of his entire family, his home, the village, and the people that lived there. He sat there alone and distraught for most of the day.

As he mindlessly gazed about him, he happened upon a broken piece of mirror. He held it up and looked at the face which was reflected back to him. He knew it was him. It was his square jaw; the same as his father's. He could see his dark brown almond-shaped eyes and his full lips; the same that his mother had. The face was his, but it seemed unfamiliar to him now. It was a jumble of features from people he would never see again.

His mourning turned into a helpless frustration. That frustration turned into anger. In his rage, he made a hasty vow that his family's death would not go unavenged. Then he admitted to himself that for him to pursue vengeance would be impossible and deadly.

He staggered away from the village in the late afternoon. He would have to find shelter and if Rasindell's old home still stood, it would be the best place for him. Also, he hoped that it would give him some emotional comfort. Being around his village and dead parents only brought him incredible distress. He needed to be somewhere familiar and to be somewhere untouched by this massacre.

Vordin walked along an overgrown path which would eventually lead him deep into the forest and to the old hut. As he walked, his thoughts wandered back to his childhood. He had always been mature for his age and therefore didn't really fit in with the other children and their games. He usually played alone with toys, crafts, and other small projects. He was more interested in puzzles and games that challenged his mind, rather than the physical games and activities that most of the other children enjoyed.

Vordin had often ventured deep into the forest against his parents' wishes. He had known by heart the way to the old storyteller's hut. Vordin had often crept out to the hut after dark just to hear the wondrous stories he had to tell. Rasindell had become his only friend.

To see the warm welcoming glow coming from Rasindell's wooden hut had always been well worth the journey through the dark and gloomy forest. Rasindell, expecting him as usual, would often step out awkwardly to greet him wearing his light grey tattered robes and leaning on a gnarled and twisted cane. The wizard would wait patiently as Vordin made his way down the forest path and into the clearing where his home was situated.

Vordin remembered how the old man's grey eyes seemed to sparkle with excitement at yet another

<Zaylyn ><Quest For The Sword Of Anthrowst ><By Katrina Mandrake-Johnston >   <Ch 1> < 7 >
chance to have someone to share his wondrous tales with. Vordin could remember wishing that he too had eyes of a mystical color instead of his plain brown eyes.

Rasindell's round wrinkled face always wore an inviting smile. The wizard would greet Vordin at the door often and beckon the boy inside with a callused hand. He could remember how the hut would smell of potions, spices, and mystical powders.

Rasindell had been a heroic adventurer in his younger days and then had become an expert wizard as he grew into old age. He had become a lonely old man after his full and exciting life, and Vordin was glad that he had been able to spend the time he did with him.

Rasindell was an old man, and when his time had come to die, Vordin had been there for him. He sat there as the old man spoke his last words. Rasindell had pulled him close and spoke of how he had been cursed long ago. He had said that this curse was one of the reasons that he had started to learn magic, in hope that one day he might stumble on a way to break it. He was cursed to recite the legends of their world, Zaylyn, for all eternity after his death. Rasindell had told him that becoming a storyteller to him and seeing the joy and excitement that he could bring with a few words, that his curse had actually become a blessing to him.

Then Rasindell had died and Vordin returned home. After that, he never returned to the hut. He had never spoken of Rasindell, not even after he had passed away. The wizard had been his secret. Vordin now knew that he should have told someone. He had been a small child. He hadn't known how to react to his friend's death.

The old man had always said to remember the stories for the knowledge hidden in them might one day save his life. This was how Vordin had survived. He hid inside a hollow tree as in Rasindell's stories, and he had lived.

The path he had been following soon became non-existent to the point where he found himself stumbling over fallen logs and had brambles and bushes constantly scratch at his legs and arms. His skin itched and several large scrapes and scratches had begun to bleed.

The light began to fade and it became even more difficult for him to travel. He was lost, but he struggled on in the direction he thought Rasindell's old home lay. He was sure that it had not taken so long to reach the hut as a child. He wondered if the creatures would return.

After detangling his hair from a tree branch, Vordin stopped to rest. The sunlight had been replaced by the pale glow of the moon. He smoothed his hair as best as he could with his hands and re-tied the leather strip holding it.

The air was damp and cold. He was scraped and bruised from trying to maneuver through the thick brush in the dark. He had no idea of where he might be now, and he felt and knew that he was extremely vulnerable. The woodland creatures made eerie sounds, which only put him more on edge. He also expected at any moment to come across one of the horrid beasts that had attacked his village.

He figured that it was best to keep moving. As he continued to scramble through the vegetation once more, he heard the loud crack of a branch breaking. Vordin froze, afraid even to breathe. He heard nothing but the gentle night breeze through the trees for a few moments, and then from behind him came a deep bellowing laugh. Vordin spun around to face his unknown adversary, but there was no one to be seen. He heard footsteps and could not tell from which direction they came. His eyes darted around frantically in the dark, as his heart pounded hard in his chest. Then another deep laugh filled the air around him.

Vordin panicked, knowing the damage these beasts could inflict, and he frantically stumbled his way through the brush and brambles in the dark as quickly as he could. His leg had become caught between two logs, and as he fell, he felt the bone in his leg snap. The pain rushed through his entire body and in his agony he cried out.

He struggled in his helpless state, but to no avail. He heard the malicious laughter again as the footsteps quickened and started to move toward his location.

<World of Zaylyn ><Quest For The Sword Of Anthrowst ><By Katrina Mandrake-Johnston ><Ch 2>

CHAPTER 2 = THE FAIRY QUEEN

<Zaylyn ><Quest For The Sword Of Anthrowst ><By Katrina Mandrake-Johnston >   <Ch 2> < 8 >

Suddenly a beast appeared out of nowhere to stand in front of him. The incredible pain in his leg began to numb slightly as his body reacted to the shock of the broken limb. All Vordin could do was stare, his dark brown eyes wide in amazement and fear at this foul creature.

It stood upright on short legs ending in clawed feet. Its body was covered in a golden brown fur except for its feet, hands, and face. Its overly long arms hung almost to the ground and the claws could easily tear a person apart. On top of its massive head were long pointed ears. The creature was just standing there looking with bulbous blood red eyes at the crippled adolescent. A long and tubular green tongue lay in a gaping mouth of jagged teeth. Large quantities of drool dribbled from its mouth down into its fur. The wrinkled skin of its short snout wiggled as it sniffed the air with its four nostrils.

Vordin was terrified and suffering horrible pain from his leg. It opened its jaws and a low growl resounded from its throat. The revolting stench of its breath and body made him gag. It snapped its jaws in the air in front of his face and he could feel the hot steamy breath on his face and neck.

Just when he thought the beast would rip its teeth viciously into his flesh, it started laughing hysterically. The laughter rumbled and gurgled deep in its throat and then gradually became a high-pitched giggle. The creature started to emit brilliant colored sparks of light from its body until the beast was transformed entirely into many glowing lights.

Each spark of light trailed a hue of color as it darted about wildly in the air. Vordin now realized that each spark ridiculed him with its laughter. It was obvious that they thought their cruel prank to be absolutely hilarious.

A larger spark grew to about the size of a small apple and hovered in front of his face. This delicate creature now before him had the wings of a beautiful butterfly and the body of a young girl. This small being wore a tiny dress made of pink flower petals and a tiny crown of silver rested on her head. Her light blue hair floated about her on the gentle breeze that her wings created, and she glowed with a beautiful lavender light. Her eyes were a deep purple, and her pale white skin glittered and sparkled. The fairy gazed upon him in curiosity for a moment and her manner seemed to show power, wisdom, and a hint of childish humor. She put a finger to her rosy lips and the laughter ceased.

She then asked in a high-pitched voice, "Did we frighten you?" She giggled slightly and then continued, "You don't seem as if you are very dangerous. Shall I fix your leg?"

The fairy queen closed her eyes and cupped her hands upward above her head. In her concentration, she slowed the beating of her wings to an extremely slow rate, somehow managing to still stay afloat. As Vordin watched, a lavender mist began to drift slowly upward from her hands and then encircled around Vordin's body. The pain from his injury slowly began to fade. He floated free of the logs which had entrapped his broken limb and then he drifted back down to the ground. The mist then concentrated around his leg and he felt the bone right itself in one violent jerk. Soon Vordin was completely healed, including even his tiny cuts and bruises.

He stood and the fairy queen rose up to meet his eye level once more.

"You are one of great luck to have escaped the fate of your village," the fairy queen said to him, "The one responsible for this evil deed is Dranngore. He is the one who rules over the creatures that killed your village. Beware the night, as that is when they enjoy their hunt; under the cover of darkness. Do not be fooled, as this does not mean the daylight will provide you with safety from them. These creatures are not natural beings. They are Killnarin. They have six limbs, as do centaurs. They are hairless with black, oily skin. They have razor sharp claws and teeth. They are strong. They can cast magic on both mind and body. They are 'demon' creatures, summoned with evil intent. They will revel in the pain, suffering, and torment that they will cause, even delaying a kill to prolong it. Their magical source of life extends from Dranngore. Destroy the wizard Dranngore with the Sword of Anthrowst and all shall be well. Farewell human."

Then without hesitation, she darted quickly away with all her fairy subjects following.

So Vordin was left standing in the dark with many unanswered questions. He continued to scramble through the forest and he figured that by now he must have traveled very deep into it. Vordin crawled over and under fallen logs and fought his way through the thick brush until he stumbled into a clearing.

<Zaylyn ><Quest For The Sword Of Anthrowst ><By Katrina Mandrake-Johnston >   <Ch 2> < 9 >

He tripped and landed on dark green grass illuminated by the light of a full pale moon. The grass was cool and lush. As he picked himself up, his gaze fell on a small decrepit log hut.

With great relief, he realized from his childhood memories that this was Rasindell's old home. When Vordin reached the damp rotted door of the hut, he opened it wondering if the roof would collapse or not. Vordin took the risk and stepped into the blackness.

He slowly moved across the floor, sliding his feet across the ground trying to detect anything that might be in his way. Cobwebs clung to his face and as he tore them away, he began to think he had made a very foolish choice. His eyes strained into the darkness as he told himself, "*There could be other creatures who have also taken shelter in this hut. What am I doing? I could be walking into a pair of hungry jaws right this minute!*"

The clouds shifted and moonlight began to filter through several large holes in the roof, illuminating the room enough for Vordin to see that there was no apparent danger.

Then there came a sound above him. As he looked up, an immense spider, about the size of a dinner plate, dropped down to land on his face. Vordin immediately froze. He fought desperately with the instinct to jump around madly in panic trying to fling the thing as far away from him as possible.

He stared in horror at the hairy legs and fangs positioned just above his eyes. He could see the roof, and through the holes, patches of the night sky overhead. He tried to focus on the roof instead of the spider, as the fear was almost completely consuming him.

"*Don't move,*" he pleaded with himself, "*Don't move! The thing will sink its fangs into you if you move!*"

The thought sent a shiver throughout his body and the panic intensified. He felt it slowly moving its legs gently against his vulnerable skin. His heart was pounding wildly.

"*Don't move,*" his mind shouted at him, "*Please, please, don't move! What can I possibly do?! Even my breathing, as shallow as it is right now, might make it attack!*"

Then he thought he ought to do something now, before it got a chance to bite him, but the fear was too great. "*Get off me! Get off me!*" he screamed inside his mind.

Vordin then heard the flap of wings and the cry of an owl. The spider remained balanced on the boy's face, continuing to caress his skin with its many legs as it kept repositioning itself. The owl, now through an opening in the roof, soared through the air with its sharp talons outstretched to snatch the spider from his face.

"*Please no! No! No! This thing's surely going to bite me, and if that doesn't happen, the owl's talons will rip my face to shreds!*"

The owl was closing in on him fast, and he had to make a decision.

His arm seemed like a separate entity as it slowly and calmly picked up the spider by its mid-section and removed it. The owl continued its dive toward Vordin's face. He winced, helpless against the attack. The bird came extremely close to him with its talons, but then pulled up at the last moment seeing that its meal had vanished. Vordin felt the rush of air against him and he watched the brown and white owl fly up into the rafters where it perched. Its large yellow eyes began searching hungrily for the spider.

He felt something wriggle between his fingertips. For a moment, he had forgotten that he still held the large spider. He recoiled in terror and disgust, dropping the spider to the ground. It scurried toward a small crevice in the wooden floor to find refuge.

Vordin shuddered and felt a cold chill all over his body. He was amazed that the spider's fangs hadn't been imbedded in his skin. He shuddered again and wiped frantically at his face where the spider had been. It felt like it was still there; his face having an itchy, tickled feeling. He couldn't believe that the ordeal was over now and that he had gotten through it unharmed.

The spider was almost to the crack in the floor now. The owl dove down for another attack. As the spider crawled into the hole, the owl landed beside it and managed to sever a piece off one of the spider's legs. Then finding that its attempts to pry its meal out of the hole were futile, the owl flew off through the roof and into the surrounding forest.

Vordin slowly made his way over to what he thought would be the fireplace. There had been a

<Zaylyn ><Quest For The Sword Of Anthrowst ><By Katrina Mandrake-Johnston >   <Ch 2> < 10 >

small table on which Rasindell had kept a lantern. He hoped that the lantern was still there and intact. Reaching the now dilapidated table, he rummaged through the dust-covered debris and eventually he touched cool metal. He turned the object over and over in his hands until he felt a small clasp on one side.

As he opened the front of the metal box, the room was immediately illuminated by a strong glow coming from inside. How he had overlooked the makeup of this arcane and incredible device as a child, bewildered him. Upon further examination, he discovered that although it had been used as a lantern, it was in fact a flask containing a mysterious glowing potion in an elaborate metal case. There was no heat produced by the flask, and there was a metal handle in the top of the case so it could be handled easily. The purpose of the case was obviously to hide the glow of the potion when light was no longer needed.

Vordin looked around the now dimly lit room finding it cluttered with debris and covered in a film of dust. The windowless, one-roomed cabin had only one door leading to the outside and he knew that he should barricade it for the night. Beside the fireplace was a small but sturdy trunk. After dragging the heavy object to the entrance, he realized that the decayed wood of the door wouldn't be that difficult to break through but figured that it would have to suffice.

In one corner of the room was a straw mattress, and in the center of the room was a small table with a chair neatly tucked beneath. Beside the fireplace, on the left side, was a large cauldron, and on the right side, close to where he had found the lantern, was a pile of logs meant for the fire.

Vordin closed his eyes and tried to remember how inviting this old hovel had once been when the fire was roaring, making the shadows dance playfully on the walls. Rasindell would tell his tales of adventure and mystery with a smiling wrinkled face. The cauldron would bubble with a spicy stew or with a mysterious concoction. He remembered Rasindell's home as being warm and cozy with almost a friendly life of its own. Now as he examined his surroundings, he found himself in a cold and undesirable place.

He set the mysterious lantern on the table in the center of the room, and he proceeded to examine the trunk. The lid of the trunk opened easily and Vordin lifted out two thick grey blankets which he placed on the floor beside him. Under these blankets was an empty brown leather backpack and beside this was a wooden bowl, a small wooden spoon, a small dagger, a large wooden spoon for the cauldron, and also a small cracked mirror.

He picked up the mirror and took a look at himself. His hair was filthy and hung loosely at his shoulders, his hair tie lost. His eyes showed every bit of the hollowness he felt. He looked sickly, his skin paler than it should have been, and completely exhausted.

He replaced the mirror, and then he looked down at his clothing. His clothing and shoes were covered in patches of dirt and debris from the forest, but he found he no longer cared about his appearance. He removed the backpack and the dagger and then he closed the lid of the trunk.

He carried the blankets over to the straw mattress and laid them over it. Exhausted, he climbed under the top blanket and was soon fast asleep with the tiny dagger beside him and the backpack on the floor.

A dream came to him...

Vordin stood on the edge of his village. The warm afternoon sun felt good on his skin. The air smelled sweet with the fragrance of roses. A crow cried out from somewhere above, and as he looked up to the clear blue sky, he caught a glimpse of the bird as it beat its black wings against the wind. He walked down one of the busy dirt roads in the village. An old woman wearing a cheerful smile on her face was sitting on her porch with a clay pot in front of her. Her white hair, ruffled by the breeze, was tied back in a loose knot. Vordin watched as she took a small brush, dipped it into a small jar of dark red paint, and began to paint an intricate design onto the surface of the pot. She had a beautiful bed of bright red roses growing in the front garden with a white miniature fence surrounding it. He had seen her before, but he couldn't remember her name.

"Hello there! Vordin is it? Enjoying the day are you?" said a middle-aged man as he walked past.

<Zaylyn ><Quest For The Sword Of Anthrowst ><By Katrina Mandrake-Johnston >   <Ch 2> < 11 >

He had short black hair which had started to grey. His round happy face smiled at him. He had seen this man before too, but he couldn't remember when or who he was.

A small child laughed cheerfully and then several others. A black cat chased a butterfly. Vordin walked past several houses and shops. All of them were busy with life.

Then, he came to his own home. He couldn't remember a time when it had looked more inviting. The light blue flowers in the flowerbed were blooming and brought to him the smell of home. He stepped up to the front door. Something was cooking and the smells coming from the house were wonderful. His mother would be home and his father would be too in a short while for dinner. He opened the door and stepped into the warm cozy kitchen.

"Vordin, there you are!" his mother exclaimed when he entered the house, "I've been calling you for some time now. Dinner's almost ready. We're having stew. Would you mind setting the table dear?"

Vordin went to the cupboard and took the dishes from their place and began setting the table. His mother was wearing her light blue dress. It was the one with the pink flowers. She only wore this dress on special occasions. Her white apron was tied around her waist. She gave him a look that was warm and loving. Her reddish-brown hair shone in the firelight.

"Okay, look out now. This is very hot," she warned him as she set the stew pot on the table. She then gave him a concerned look. "Are you okay honey?" asked his mother, "You look a little pale." She felt his forehead. Her touch was warm and soft.

The door opened and Vordin's father entered the house. "How's my boy? Oh, that smells absolutely wonderful, Hun. I'm just going to wash up a bit and change my clothes," he said leaving the kitchen and went into the bedroom.

"Come sit down, dear," she said as she sat at the table and poured glasses of water for all three of them.

Vordin sat in his chair and took a sip of the water. It was deliciously fresh and icy cold. The smell of the stew made his mouth tingle with anticipation of the hot and juicy meat and the hearty vegetables. A large bowl of whipped potatoes was on the table... and he could see where he had swiped a taste earlier. He noticed that there was also a large loaf of warm crusty bread on the table and a plate of butter. A small knife was laid beside the plate and the flames from the fire danced in their reflection along the length of the metal.

Vordin's father returned, and they began their meal. The food was delicious, better than he could ever remember. He let the flavor of each mouthful linger a few moments before he swallowed. It was as if the creatures had never...

Suddenly, his parents vanished. Their plates were still on the table; their meals half eaten. He swallowed the bit of bread he had been chewing, but it felt like it had lumped in his throat.

The fire in the hearth slowly died out and now the only light in the room was the sunlight coming through the window. He wanted the smiling faces of his mother and father to return. There was a place deep down inside him that knew they wouldn't and in that spot it felt empty, cold, and hurt.

Vordin got up from the table. There was complete silence in the room. It was an eerie silence. Vordin left the house and stepped outside.

Silence. Nothing stirred. The streets were empty. The wind whistled through the trees and shrubs. The wind was cold and bitter.

He heard the cry of an eagle. Darkness fell over the village as if someone had pulled a black blanket up over it. He heard a scream. He heard a blood-curdling howl. Then there were more screams, panicked cries, and frightened words spoken to loved ones. It was everything he didn't want to hear.

He couldn't see anyone around him, but he could feel the presence of many. He could almost feel the hot breath of the beasts upon his skin. Tortured screams and fierce bellowing howls echoed in his ears...

He awoke from a restless sleep. He could see through the roof that the day was already half over.

<Zaylyn ><Quest For The Sword Of Anthrowst ><By Katrina Mandrake-Johnston >   <Ch 2> < 12 >

He had slept clear through most of the day, which disturbed him greatly, for with the night came the possibility that the creatures might return.

<World of Zaylyn ><Quest For The Sword Of Anthrowst ><By Katrina Mandrake-Johnston ><Ch 3>

CHAPTER 3 = LORENTA

His stomach grumbled at him. Vordin got up from the mattress and left the cabin. The air was fresh outside and he breathed in deeply. His body ached and felt stiff. Birds sang happy songs and insects buzzed from bush to bush. This place had a peaceful atmosphere and he was glad for it.

Lying down, he stretched himself out on the cool grass with his hands behind his head and looked up to the blue sky. The last time he had been here, he had been only seven years old. Now, it was eight years later and things here hadn't really changed all that much.

He thought about Rasindell and realized how much he missed his old friend. Now was a time when he wished most that the old man was still here and alive. The night that Rasindell died, Vordin had been so very frightened.

"*What's a kid supposed to do?*" Vordin thought to himself as he remembered that night, "*I had thought about burying him, but that would have been impossible. I couldn't have dug a grave very well and then there was the task of dragging the body to it. I didn't want to have to do that to my friend. I just left him there and went home. That's all I could have done. That's probably how he would have wanted it. If he hadn't been so secretive, things would have been different. I don't think a single person except for me even knew about him and his cabin here in the woods. Why aren't there any bones? Surely after all these years, there would be something. Maybe some animals had carried bits of him off into the woods until there was nothing left. What a horrible thing to imagine, what's wrong with you? Maybe being a wizard, he just magically disappeared. There, now that's a better explanation. Oh stop it, what a stupid thing to be thinking about.*"

Noticing a bush with clusters of ripe red berries growing on it, he got up and walked over to it.

"*What a great idea,*" he said to himself with sarcasm, "*Eat some poisonous berries and die. Then maybe some animals will drag pieces of you away over the years until there's nothing left.*"

He left the berries on the bush and roamed around the surrounding forest in hope of finding food, as it had been over a day, almost two now, since he had eaten anything.

The daylight had begun to fade. His efforts at finding food were useless. He felt incredibly weak, cold, and extremely exhausted. His stomach ached with hunger and his mouth was dry with thirst. He entered the cabin once more.

The lantern was still glowing brightly from where he had left it on the table. He crawled under the blanket and tried to figure out a course of action. He was still puzzling over what the fairy queen had said to him.

Through the roof, he could see that the sun had set and he became annoyed at how quickly the day had passed him by. Then out of the corner of his eye, he thought he saw something stir on the floor.

Vordin noticed that the huge spider was slowly crawling out of the crevice in the wooden floorboards. He had completely forgotten about it when he had laid down to rest the night before and was amazed that he had remained safe during his slumber. The thought of the thing crawling over his skin again sent shivers down his back.

He found the small dagger and held it tightly in his hand wondering how he would catch or kill the thing. Vordin watched the spider very closely as it crawled to the middle of the room. Vordin noticed that the lower half of one of its front legs on its right side had been severed by the owl. It was a wolf spider, greyish in color, and Vordin had seen many of them before. They were normally small, but once he had seen one that was so large that it was near half the size of his fist. This one before him was monstrous. The spider's large round eyes seemed to be watching him as well. He did not want it to scurry off into some unknown location where it could jump out at him unexpectedly.

He thought about maybe crushing the huge spider with the cauldron, but he realized that by the time he reached it, the spider would be long gone and the cauldron would be too heavy and clumsy to

<Zaylyn ><Quest For The Sword Of Anthrowst ><By Katrina Mandrake-Johnston >   <Ch 3> < 13 >

accomplish the deed. To attack it with the tiny dagger was absolutely ridiculous. So he decided to throw the blanket over the spider, thus trapping it underneath, and then crushing it under his shoe. He sat up and held the blanket ready.

Just before he was about to execute his plan, mysteriously, the body of the spider was instantly engulfed in magical green flames. The spider's body seemed to melt into a thick black puddle under the flames, and then, while Vordin sat on the mattress in utter amazement, the puddle slowly increased in size. The black mass traveled upward from the puddle and eventually formed into a humanoid shape.

As the emerald flames subsided, Vordin now saw the figure of a beautiful young woman before him. She was a few inches taller than Vordin, and black web-like robes clothed her slender form. Her long dark brown hair fell gently below her shoulders, and she had smooth pale skin. As the woman took a step closer to him with a dainty bare foot, he could see that she moved with great agility and grace. With her beautiful light brown eyes, she gazed at Vordin slightly puzzled. Then after a moment's hesitation, her pale lips broke into a smile.

She had large curious eyes and they studied his every move and feature.

"Hello," she said in a sweet voice, "Thank-you for saving my life." Vordin did not know what to say to this strange being. The woman continued, "I know you didn't intend to do so, but I thank you anyway. I know that Rasindell probably never spoke of me to you. I think he was a bit ashamed of me, although he would never have admitted this. He probably would have used the potion on a creature more beautiful than I, if he had known the power that it held. He enjoyed your visits so much. I think that he was afraid of what your reaction might be if you knew of me and of my true form. I did not want to stress the friendship between you and him, so I agreed to spend time away from the hut during your visits. He left years ago, and I've remained here ever since in hope that he would some day return. Also, I have nowhere else to go and so far no reason to leave."

"But who are you?" Vordin asked intrigued by this creature's strange story.

"I am Rasindell's daughter," she said as if that would be a sufficient explanation. She curiously felt at her face, tracing her fingertips over her deep-set eyes and high cheekbones, and then over her small round nose, her plump lips, and rounded chin. "Sorry, I have not been in this form for such a long time," she explained.

"What potion? What exactly are you?" he asked.

She sat herself upon the floor with her legs crossed beneath her and smoothed out her wispy black robes. Then she replied, "Years ago, Rasindell gave me my human form through an incredible magic potion that he had acquired in his journeys as an adventurer. He had not known at the time what the potion would do and he had been wary of using it for many years. I guess one day he decided to not let the potion go to waste and poured the contents of the flask onto a large spider which had found its way into his home. I was this spider. Perhaps at the time, he thought the potion would kill or mutilate me in some terrible way, but instead I gained the ability to transform into the form of a human. Rasindell told me that I had transformed immediately into a small child. I discovered that I am able to change my form at will, although only at night, and that I had gained the life span of a human as well. Rasindell from that day on had raised me as if I were his very own daughter. Oh, and as you probably noticed, my size in spider form increased by about ten times."

"That truly is an incredible and elaborate story," he exclaimed with suspicion.

"By the expression on your face, I can tell that you don't believe a word I'm saying," the woman said with extreme disappointment. The excitement in her eyes had vanished and it had been replaced by great despair. "I don't know the real reason why he would not tell you about me, but I suspect it was out of fear," she said to him, "If you had told one of the villagers, they might have come here to destroy me. I am different. Humans don't usually like things that are different."

"If this is all true, then why did you attack me?" he questioned.

She replied despondently, "I would have transformed to escape that horrid owl, but there wasn't time. I dropped down onto you in hope that I could save myself by doing so. Besides, I thought that you might have been Rasindell. You're the first person to come here since he left so many years ago. I am glad to see that you have returned here, Vordin. It's nice to see a familiar face after all this time.

<Zaylyn ><Quest For The Sword Of Anthrowst ><By Katrina Mandrake-Johnston >   <Ch 3> < 14 >
I'm very sorry if I have frightened you."

"Don't you know that Rasindell is dead? He died many years ago," Vordin said with further doubt about her true identity. Why she would not know about the death of her so-called father was even more disturbing.

She was sitting on the floor between him and the door which was still barricaded by the old trunk. He was sitting on the straw mattress with his feet positioned on the wooden floorboards. He still held the small dagger hidden within the folds of the blankets. It was obvious that she could sense his fear. He knew his only defense was to keep her talking, as he was extremely vulnerable against her and had nowhere to run.

"At first, I thought he did die," she said, "but then a strange event occurred that has puzzled me for years. When you left for the village that night, I came back to the hut and found that the old man had finally died. I sat by the fire, not knowing what to do. You had left without discovering that I even existed, and I found myself truly abandoned. After several hours, Rasindell just got up from his resting place and walked out the door as if nothing had happened. If he wasn't dead, then why did he just leave me like that? Was I that much of a disappointment to him? He always said he loved me as if I were his very own child. I don't understand. It doesn't make any sense."

"Did he really just get up and walk out the door?" he asked in amazement, because she had spoken with such sincerity.

"Yes," she replied, her eyes seeming to beg for any explanation that he could give her.

Vordin put aside his suspicions for a moment as he said, "He did speak to me about a curse."

"A curse?" she interrupted.

"He said he was cursed to recite the legends of Zaylyn for all eternity, or rather blessed to do so as he had said. He probably just got up to fulfill his destiny."

She took a moment to ponder Vordin's explanation and then said, "He always told me that one day he would have to leave me, but I always thought he meant in death and not in such a bizarre way."

"I don't understand it either," he admitted.

"I had always hoped you would return. Even though I had never met you then face to face, I had always thought of you as a little brother and part of our strange family." As she spoke, she broke eye contact with him. She knew he did not see it this way and his presence here did not mean her loneliness had come to an end.

Vordin realized that if her strange story was indeed true, he was the only other person besides Rasindell that she had ever known. When Rasindell died, and his visits to the hut had ceased, she had been left in bitter solitude. Vordin found himself truly feeling for her, for he too was now alone. Still, he decided that she couldn't be trusted no matter how convincing she became.

"How old are you now?" she asked.

"Fifteen," he replied.

"It's really been that long?" she paused a few moments, as if this loss of time had saddened her, and then she continued, "I guess that would make me seventeen, or maybe eighteen then. I'm not quite sure. Your village, its name is Nilnont, right?"

"It doesn't matter anymore. It's been destroyed. Everyone is dead," he said in a sullen voice.

Her light brown eyes showed a hint of remorse, as if she understood what he felt and what it was like to loose one's whole world and everything familiar to it.

"Would you like me to light the fire?" she offered.

"Sure," he said.

"I can bring you some food if you like as well. Are you hungry?" she asked.

"Sure," he answered again. He knew that she would have to leave the cabin to do so.

She gracefully moved across the floor and picked up a log by the fireplace. The woman then placed the log in the ashes and stood there waiting. Vordin almost laughed at these ignorant actions. Then to his amazement, the log burst into flames.

"There," she said obviously pleased with herself and the astonished look on Vordin's face, "It still works fine. Rasindell hated to light his own fires. I'm not sure how he did it, but all you have to do is

<Zaylyn ><Quest For The Sword Of Anthrowst ><By Katrina Mandrake-Johnston >   <Ch 3> < 15 >
toss a log in and it will light."

Vordin walked cautiously over to the fireplace and warmed himself by it. "You said something about being able to find something to eat?" he reminded her.

"Oh, of course. I'll be back in awhile then," she said with a cheerful smile.

She displayed exceptional strength as she easily pushed the heavy trunk aside and left through the door. Vordin watched the fire and the shadows dance on the walls as they had so long ago. He listened to the flames crackle and let the heat warm him. He realized that if he were in danger, he wouldn't be able to protect himself. Vordin decided that the only thing he was able to do was to wait for dawn, when she would have to revert back to spider form, and for the chance to escape unseen.

A heavy rain began to fall just as the woman was entering through the cabin door. She approached him with her hands outstretched and cradling a large leaf which held a plentiful amount of wild orange berries. He noticed that she only had a thumb and forefinger on her right hand and realized her missing fingers were the result of the wound caused by the owl's attack.

"Here you are," she said as she handed him the berries.

Vordin accepted her gift and they sat in silence in front of the fire for some time.

I wonder if these are poisonous? Maybe if I taste one, I'll be able to tell. If they are really bitter, I think that it means they are poison. I don't know. I have no clue of how to tell something like that. But what will she do if I refuse to eat them?" he thought to himself.

"Aren't you going to eat?" she asked him.

Vordin popped one of the berries into his mouth. It was slightly bitter, but it tasted all right. The berries weren't poisonous, because he had eaten these same berries before. Rasindell sometimes had a bowl of them for him to snack on during the stories.

He ate the rest of the berries hungrily and wished that there had been more. He noticed how she kept looking sadly at her hand and tried to keep it hidden from sight within the folds of her clothing. Vordin tossed the empty leaf into the fire, and they watched as it sizzled and smoked.

"What's your name?" he asked, realizing he did not yet know it.

"Lorenta," she answered, pleased he had asked.

"It's pretty," he commented and then asked, "Did Rasindell name you?"

"Yes, and thank-you," she said with a smile.

Again there was a long period of silence. The rain beat a soothing rhythm on the roof overhead, and the fire spread its warmth throughout the cabin despite the few large holes in the roof where the rain came in. Soon Vordin had fallen asleep where he sat.

Another dream came to him this night…

Vordin found himself in a dark and damp cavern. Water dripped from stalactites above. A tunnel could be seen to his left and he made his way into it. The tunnel sloped gradually downward and he had difficulty maintaining his footing. As he descended farther, a soft glow steadily increased making it easier for him to see his way.

Eventually the tunnel opened up into another cavern. A pool of lava bubbled up through a fissure in the cavern floor. The heat was intense.

As Vordin approached the pool, a hideous creature arose from the molten rock. It leapt up into the stale air of the cavern and its leathery wings beat the air as lava rolled down its body to sizzle on the rocks below. Its man-sized body was covered in coarse hair and its massive jaws were filled with foul jagged teeth. Its bat-like face turned toward him and it let out a blood-curdling howl. Its beady blood red eyes were fixated maliciously on him and it clenched its sharp talons.

Vordin backed slowly away from the creature, and then he couldn't move. He was trapped in a giant spider web. No matter how hard he struggled, he could not break loose from its sticky embrace. The creature let out a growl that rumbled throughout the cave.

Lorenta came toward Vordin from out of the shadows. She had an evil smirk across her lips. The creature bellowed a wicked laugh and Lorenta joined it in its mirth.

From Lorenta's black cobweb-like robes came forth a horde of tiny spiders. Vordin's struggles were futile against the web, as they swarmed his vulnerable form. Thousands of tiny fangs pierced his flesh, as they crawled up his legs, inside his clothing, and up to his arms and face. Lorenta watched him writhe in pain, with a sneer and a look of satisfaction on her face. He opened his mouth to scream, but no sound came forth as the tiny spiders made their way into his mouth and down his throat…

He awoke early the next morning gasping for air. His mouth tingled with the memory of his nightmare. Lorenta was nowhere to be seen. She had wrapped a blanket around him while he had slept.

He unwrapped the blanket, got up from the floor, and went to the table. Vordin closed the door of the lantern and tossed it inside the backpack. After tucking the small dagger into a little side pocket on the backpack, he slung it onto his back where it rested comfortably. His dream had confirmed his decision to leave before Lorenta returned. He didn't want anything to do with her, no matter what crazy story she had for him.

Vordin then opened the door and stepped out into the cool, crisp, morning air. He heard birds singing their songs in the trees as the sun's rays filtered down through the treetops. He walked through the dew-covered grass as he headed in the direction of the mountains. On the other side of the mountain range was Dee'ellkka Valley and this was the path he had decided on. He did not know what he hoped to find there, but at least now he had some sort of destination to travel toward.

He traveled long and hard through the dense forest. By nightfall, he had emerged into the open and walked until he met the trail-like road that would lead him up into the mountains.

Reluctantly, he decided to stop for the night as it would be difficult to travel in the dark, even with his mysterious lantern. Vordin curled up by the side of the road for there was no place to hide himself from view. He shivered in the cool air and wished that he had remembered to take one of the blankets from the cabin with him. He hoped that his grey tunic and brown pants would offer him some kind of camouflage, but he highly doubted that.

Vordin tried to rest his weary body, for the hike along the mountainous trail would take a lot of endurance. Vordin found himself drifting off to sleep after several hours.

He awoke suddenly to the sound of heavy steps along the road. Vordin stayed low to the ground, as he couldn't detect who or what was coming toward him. A fierce howl resounded through the air that struck great fear in him, as he had heard this same noise at the massacre of his village. He was helpless against this vile beast and he knew it. In a few moments the 'demon' creature would be upon him. He couldn't see the beast from his position where the ground dipped slightly and because he was so low to the ground. Wondering how close his death was, he took the tiny dagger from the pocket of the backpack. Vordin held it tightly and noticed how badly his hand trembled.

"*So, this is it. Fifteen years of life and now it's to be cut short. Looks as if they won't allow anyone to escape. What possible chance do I have? All that's left, is to accept my fate and try to be brave,*" he told himself, trying to force some courage into his last moments, although tears had begun to stream down his face and his whole body was weak with fear.

Before the creature could attack him, a black mass fell from the sky and landed a few feet in front of Vordin. This strange person, who had his back turned to Vordin, wore a black cloak with its hood covering his head. The cloak flapped in the breeze as Vordin stared in amazement. He could see that the mysterious man wore a pair of black pants and had a pair of well-worn black leather boots which came to mid calf.

The man turned his head to look down at the boy who was staring in astonishment at him, but did not utter a single word. His face remained unseen, as it was cast in dark shadow beneath his hood. With a gust of wind, the dark black cloak moved slightly to reveal a sword sheathed in a black scabbard at this man's waist.

The Killnarin shrieked and howled at the sight of this new stranger who had suddenly made his appearance along its path. As this man continued to look at Vordin, in the blackness under his hood, two blood red eyes began to glow until they shone brightly. A low growl emitted from this being's throat as he looked away from Vordin to face the creature.

Vordin did not know what to think of this new situation and wondered if this person were friend or

<Zaylyn ><Quest For The Sword Of Anthrowst ><By Katrina Mandrake-Johnston >   <Ch 3> < 17 >

foe. The Killnarin howled defiantly at this man, but did not approach. The man then spun around and seized Vordin in one arm with an inhuman ease and leapt into the air, soaring away from the beast. Vordin watched as it pranced wildly around in anger and frustration below them.

Vordin was being carried high above the countryside as the man held him firmly in his grip. The black cloak flapped in the wind as they sped through the chill night air. He could see the mountain range below that he had been traveling toward and he wondered what intentions his silent captor had for him.

The stars sparkled above them and the full moon was bright. The forest which Vordin had traveled through and where Rasindell's hut lay, looked smaller than it had felt when he had been struggling through it. He followed the road with his eyes and caught a glimpse of Nilnont far behind them. It looked as if there had only been the one creature and Vordin wondered where all the others had gone.

"*Perhaps, the beast was a scout of some sort. Maybe to check for survivors or maybe they knew that I had escaped them. But those creatures aren't what I have to worry about right now,*" thought Vordin, "*What is he planning to do with me? Does he intend to drop me to my death or does he have something worse in mind?*"

Vordin's legs dangled beneath him. They flew against the wind and as it whipped past them, Vordin found it to be icy cold. They were approaching the mountains and the sight was beautiful. There was snow on the mountaintops, but not much. The night shadows gave the snow a purple glow in places. He had lost track of the road, but he knew it was there, winding its way over the mountains and back down into the valley beyond. The mountains were mainly barren rock, but in places, there were trees and other vegetation. Vordin wondered about the trolls and dragons and where their caves and tunnels might be or if they in fact were just myth after all.

As they continued to fly, he noticed they were now flying at an incline to the mountains and finally they alighted on a mountaintop. The man still held him tightly and Vordin could not struggle free.

There was a dark cave set into the side of the mountain and this is where the man put him. Before the boy had any chance of escape, the man, with an unimaginable strength, rolled a large boulder in front of the cave entrance and Vordin found himself in complete darkness.

Remembering the lantern, he felt around in the backpack until he touched the cool metal of the case. After removing the box, he opened the small door and light filled his tiny prison. He could see that he was trapped within a small area between the boulder and the back wall of the alcove. There was no possible way for him to escape.

Fresh mountain air drifted through a small space between the boulder and the cave wall, and through this, he could see the stars shining in the black sky. He hoped that his captor would return to release him and with good intentions, but feared the worst. Vordin lay on the rock floor pondering the bizarre events that had happened in such a short time. Eventually, he slipped into a deep sleep out of exhaustion.

Lightening flashed and lit up the night sky for a few moments. Thunder roared loud and fierce. A heavy rain, much heavier than the night before, began to fall from above.

***

The tall pine trees, where the mysterious man in black stood now, were dense and made visibility difficult. The Black Shadow looked down at the body of the unknown girl lying on the dark soil. He had lured her out of the village of Dexcsin and into the nearby forest.

She had long beautiful hair, which was of the purest black. She was wearing a thin white gown, and as it became wet, it clung to her shapely form. What blood remained was slowly being washed away by the rain. Her wet, pale face seemed peaceful and it pained him to know she would never awaken.

He averted his gaze, as he could not bear to look at her further. A lump was beginning to form in the back of his throat and he choked it back. He felt guilt, self-hatred, sorrow, pity, frustration, and several other mixed emotions.

He looked up through the treetops to the night sky and let the cold rain wash over his face. He found the sound of the storm soothing and calming. He knew of a place in the forest where he could

<Zaylyn ><Quest For The Sword Of Anthrowst ><By Katrina Mandrake-Johnston >   <Ch 3> < 18 >
find shelter. At sunset tomorrow night, he would return for the boy.

<World of Zaylyn ><Quest For The Sword Of Anthrowst ><By Katrina Mandrake-Johnston ><Ch 4>

CHAPTER 4 = CANDRA AND DENDROX

Meanwhile, as Vordin lay trapped in his rocky prison and the daylight faded, Candra, a twenty-three year old elf, and Dendrox, a twenty-two year old human, had decided to make their camp for the night. They were situated at the tree line, on the other side of the mountain range in Dee'ellkka Valley, where the grassy plain met the forest. There were small patches of grass here and there that had dared to fight for the sun's rays under the shadow of the tall pine trees. Farther into the forest, the smaller vegetation thrived on the light which filtered down from the treetops. Candra noted that although the majority of trees in the forest were pine and cedar, she could also see a few different types among them where the forest was less dense. She wondered if any of them bore edible nuts or if some of the bushes had berries or roots that they could collect.

Candra had wished that they had stopped earlier in the mountains before the rain had started, but she knew well that the edge of the vast forest, where they were now in the valley, would provide better protection than being out in the open. The cool rain washed against her face as she stared into the night sky. Her straight black hair fell a few inches above her shoulders and was wet along with her clothes. To keep her hair from clinging to her face, she tucked it behind her elfin ears.

The rainstorm eventually drizzled out. The smell of wet earth and pine filled the cool autumn air. A cool breeze, fresh and revitalizing, brought with it the pleasant smell of wild flowers.

She was cold and tired, and the warmth of a fire was what she had been looking forward to since late that afternoon. Now everything was too wet to get a fire started. Her feet, in her well-worn brown leather boots, ached from their long journey through the mountain pass.

"Finally, I might have drowned if the rain had continued like that," Candra said jokingly about the rain after it had stopped.

"Not a bad spot for the night," Dendrox commented about their campsite.

They had a clear view of the road from the trees in which they had made their shadowed camp, and if the need came, they could easily move farther into the forest for concealment against an encounter.

Candra could see the mountain range to the west and the dirt road which made its way down the mountain, across the grassy plain, past their position, and into the dense forest. She had been so thrilled at the sight of thick dark green grass on either side of the road when they had gotten to the base of the mountain, that she had taken off her boots and let her sore feet enjoy the cool rain soaked grass for several minutes.

Dendrox, the shy human boy from her childhood, now a young man, went about his preparations for the night and she thought to herself that she had better get started on hers as well before it got too dark to see.

A short bow was slung over her shoulder. With a sigh, the elf placed it on the ground in front of her. The quiver, which was situated on her back with its strap crossing diagonally over her chest, was next to be removed. Candra was thin and wore form-fitting clothes of a dark green color, the same as her eyes. She found, although not a necessity, that wearing close fitting clothes was an asset to her profession as a thief. Her cotton shirt was sleeveless with a v-shaped neckline and the bottoms of her pants she often tucked into the tops of her boots. At her waist, she wore a belt made of brown leather with a plain square metal buckle. She undid her belt and let it drop to the ground along with the two black leather pouches which were attached to the belt on either side of her hips.

"That feels much better. Now to get these boots off my aching feet," Candra commented pulling the boots off.

Dendrox had dark blue eyes and wore his straight dark brown hair at ear length. He had a pair of black pants as well as a navy blue vest over a plain black shirt with long sleeves. On his belt he wore a collection of throwing daggers.

"Yeah, that hike was pretty tiresome. Better to have traveled it in one day like we did though," Dendrox added as he removed his brown leather backpack. He removed its contents: two dark brown

<Zaylyn ><Quest For The Sword Of Anthrowst ><By Katrina Mandrake-Johnston >   <Ch 4> < 19 >

blankets and an empty water skin. He passed one of the blankets to Candra.

"Thanks," she said to Dendrox, "Hey, remind me to get some new boots when we get to town."

"Okay, sure," he agreed.

Candra spread out her blanket on the ground and Dendrox did the same. They were both thankful that the trees had sheltered the ground partially from the earlier rainfall, making the area less damp. Dendrox tossed the empty water skin back into the backpack and then removed the black leather pouch, which rested at the small of his back, and laid it beside the pack on the ground. He almost never parted with his daggers, even to sleep.

"So what do you think happened at that village we passed?" she asked.

"Don't know. Looked pretty bad though," he answered.

"I think we should have stopped there," Candra told him, "We could have gotten a few supplies. Maybe a few survivors could have told us what happened. Aren't you curious? I should have insisted on exploring the village instead of letting you drag me up the mountain trail like that."

"Come on, you saw it," was his reply, "There wasn't anyone still alive. Whatever happened there was awful and I didn't want to stick around to find out what. We're over the mountains now. We're in the valley and hopefully far enough away from danger. Just forget about it, at least for now, we're going to need our sleep tonight."

Soon they both were sitting uncomfortably on their separate blankets trying to rest their weary bodies.

The tall trees cast their shadows over the barren road. The moon above didn't add much to their visibility, the clouds dulling its light. Sight was not one of the senses they would be relying on much tonight and listening to every little sound would make sleep almost impossible, even though they would be taking turns with watch duty.

She knew the ground absorbed body heat and that having the blanket between her and it was the best thing to do. Packing more than one blanket each into Dendrox's backpack would be awkward and take up the room they needed to store any loot they came across, but still, she wished she had another one to drape over her. Her clothing didn't offer her much warmth on nights like these.

"How much farther to the town of Vackiindmire?" the elf asked.

"We'll probably reach it by tomorrow night, Candra. I can hardly wait," Dendrox said with exhaustion.

As she rubbed at her aching muscles, she said, "Yeah, same here."

He said with a sigh, "Just think… a hot bath, a hearty meal, and a good night's sleep in a warm comfortable bed."

"When we get there, I call first on that bath. I'm a lady after all," Candra said with a sly grin.

"Yeah right, we'll see about that one," he chuckled.

She wasn't sure if he were talking about the first bath or the part about being a 'lady', so she just said, "Good-night, Dendrox."

He gave her an annoyed look as he said, "Hey, I thought you were taking first watch."

"Oh you're such a pain," she said with a smile, "I was just seeing if I could get away with it."

"Hey Candra, while you're up, check to see how much gold we have left," he said as he stretched out on his blanket.

"Well, I'm not up," she said unwilling to move, "and besides, I already know that we'll have to do a little pocket searching when we get there. You can scout out the rich folk while I'm soaking in that hot bath."

"Yeah right. I can see it now. Some guy with a fat pouch smells this horrible stench and looks down to see my grinning face staring up at him, with my grimy hand where his gold should be," he said with a hint of sarcasm.

"Ha ha," Candra teased, "Just get some rest."

She lay watching the stars, imagining the huge feast she would be eating after her bath. Woodland creatures scurried through the brush and she tried to stay alert to every sound in order to detect any sign of danger.

<Zaylyn ><Quest For The Sword Of Anthrowst ><By Katrina Mandrake-Johnston >   <Ch 4> < 20 >

The first snore made her jump, as always, with her hand to her bow in a swift reflex. She groaned slightly and sat up checking the forest and its shadows for any movement and listening for any sounds other than his snoring.

"With all that noise, it will either attract danger or more likely scare it away," she thought to herself with a chuckle.

Candra rummaged through one of her pouches and retrieved her last bit of dried meat.

"We desperately need to get to a town. We've already gone through Dendrox's water skin coming over the mountains, and like me, he only has a small amount of food in that pouch of his. I think it might be the last of the cheese he has in there. Yes, he's saving it for tomorrow and he'd be really mad if I took a bite or two of it considering that it's probably all he has left. As tempting as it is, I better not," she thought to herself looking at her tiny portion of dried meat. *"Well my pouches are empty now of both food and gold. I think he has a couple gold coins hidden away in his pouch, but that won't get us very far. It definitely won't be enough to rent a room for the night. This is ridiculous! We shouldn't have headed out so ill prepared. Sure, we expected to just grab whatever we needed along the road when we needed it, but that idea kind of fell through considering that the last and only village that we passed in the area was utterly destroyed!"* she complained as she slowly chewed the meat and hoped that Dendrox was right about reaching Vackiindmire by nightfall the next day.

Her part of the watch was completely uneventful, and when it came time for his watch, she nudged him gently.

"Oh go away," he grumbled, half asleep.

"It's your turn," she said, poking him again impatiently.

"Already?" Dendrox complained.

"Yes already," she said, now annoyed and frustrated, "I can hardly keep my eyes open. Wake up and quit stalling!"

"Okay, okay, I'm up. Go to sleep," he said with a yawn.

"Oh no you don't! Get up," Candra insisted again.

He grunted and said, "I am. I am."

In an angry tone of voice she said to him, "Remember what happened last time you fell back to sleep on your watch?"

"I never," he protested.

"Oh yes you did. The time we stole those damn scissors. The ones with ivory and gold?" she reminded him.

Dendrox paused a moment in thought before he exclaimed, "Oh yeah, I remember those."

Not convinced with his answer, she continued, "I said to leave them, but oh no, you had to have them. Turns out they were magical or something, and we ended up running all over the countryside trying to get away from all those people hired to retrieve the damn things."

"Oh yeah. Whatever happened to those scissors?" Dendrox asked.

"How the hell should I know? You're the one who got rid of them," she said, this time extremely annoyed with him.

"I did?" he asked with a confused look on his face.

"Well they haven't been able to track us since, so you must have," she sighed, "I guess it's best if you don't remember. Now wake up. I'm going to sleep or at least I'm going to try."

"Oh you're such a pain," he bothered, "It's not going to matter much if we both doze off for a bit. The worst thing that'll happen is some animal will start gnawing at your toes."

"You know, you're a real moron when you first wake up. You say incredibly stupid things," she grumbled. Even though she was exhausted and annoyed, she couldn't help but smile at him.

He smiled also and then said, "Yeah, yeah, go to sleep."

"If I wake up and you're snoring away, I'll skin you alive," she threatened jokingly.

"Good-night already," Dendrox sighed.

Finally, she was asleep. *"Like I snore,"* he thought to himself.

Candra had been his best friend ever since he was a kid. She had always had a fiery spirit, was

<Zaylyn ><Quest For The Sword Of Anthrowst ><By Katrina Mandrake-Johnston >   <Ch 4> < 21 >
almost too self-dependant, and was very intimidating even when she wasn't trying to be. The fact that she stood six feet tall, was extremely head strong, and a deadly shot with a bow, didn't help much to make people feel at ease around her either. She loved a good prank and was an extremely good thief. She was the best friend he ever had. Over the years, they had developed unspoken boundaries between themselves and both knew which ones not to cross and how far some of them could be pushed.

"*She should listen to herself snore. It sounds like some dying beast. She'd never admit that she does though. Her snore is definitely worse than mine, if I even snore at all in the first place,*" thought Dendrox.

He brushed off as much debris as he could from his black pants and then he straightened his vest over his shirt as best as he could. He then began fidgeting with one of his throwing daggers waiting for dawn to break.

He looked over at Candra and at her straight black hair lying limply just above her shoulder. He could see at least three leaves and a couple of twigs tangled in it. "*Maybe it is best if she has that bath first, although I wouldn't ever be able to stop her from having one first anyway,*" he sighed. "*Alright, I definitely needed to get more rest than I did,*" he admitted. "*If we keep a low profile in Vackiindmire, we'll probably be able to take the horse drawn carriage that travels between it and the town of Shirkint. Candra would like that. Too bad I wasn't able to take that map with me. Well, okay, let's see what I can remember from it.*"

Dendrox cleared and smoothed out a patch of dirt with his hand. He was thankful that the clouds had dispersed allowing the moon and stars to shine brightly enough for him to see by.

His eyes felt heavy and he yawned sleepily. "*At least this will help me stay awake for awhile. Alright, so this here is the valley.*" Dendrox drew an oval shape in the soil with his dagger.

"*Now on the west side are the mountains we just came over. These rocks will represent the mountains.*" He picked up a few small rocks and placed them on the dirt patch on the edge of the shape he had just drawn.

"*On the eastern side and south edge are high cliffs which act as a barrier between the valley and the sea. These cliffs eventually meet up with the western mountains. The northern edge is the only place where it's open to the sea.*" He picked up a couple small twigs and placed them on the east and south sides of the oval.

"*The forest is quiet large and is situated somewhat in the center of the valley, well just a bit farther south then what would be the center.*" Dendrox grabbed a handful of grass from nearby and placed a bit of it on his map to be the forest.

"*The road goes down from the mountains, through this grassy area at its base, and then continues through the forest. This road would start here, near the southern part of the forest.*" He positioned his dagger near the bottom of his grass pile.

"*We are camped here, on the very edge of the forest, a little distance north from the road, but still keeping it in view. Above the forest, far to the north, are grassy fields and on the eastern side is a lake. A river flows out of this lake traveling south through the forest and then I have no idea where it goes.*" He took his dagger and made wavy lines in the soil to represent the sea, lake, and river.

"*Okay, now below the forest, to the south, is a smaller area of grassy fields before ending at the southern cliffs. In this area, close to the southern cliffs, is the town of Vackiindmire and where we want to go. Oh, and also there is a village, called Dexcsin, and that would be just below the forest, but closer to the mountains than Vackiindmire.*" He placed a couple of rocks to represent the town and village.

"*This road we're about to take, the one that continues out of the mountains, it goes roughly straight through the forest going east for a little more than half way. Then that road will meet up with the main road that runs north up to the town of Shirkint and south to Vackiindmire. There should be a little side road that leads to the small village of Dexcsin just as we come out of the forest on our way to Vackiindmire, but we don't need to worry about that though.*" Dendrox drew the road with his dagger in the dirt.

"*Still have a lot of time to waste, so I might as well fill in the rest of the map.*" He yawned and tried to

<Zaylyn ><Quest For The Sword Of Anthrowst ><By Katrina Mandrake-Johnston >   <Ch 4> < 22 >
keep his eyes open.

"*I think above the forest, at the southern edge of the lake is the village of Leekkar, a road branching off the main road to lead to it,*" he told himself making a line for the road, "*Then if you continue again north along the main road, it branches again and this time to the west back toward the mountains. The village of Torrnell is here.*" He placed a couple of rocks for the villages as he had done with the southern two places.

"*All the way north, at the end of the main road, is the town of Shirkint and beyond that is the sea. I think there is a little side road just before that town which leads to the lakeside and a small boat dock there. I think there's a dock at the village of Leekkar as well. I don't think it's even called a lake when it's joined up like that to the sea. Not really important.*

"*The forest must have been cleared away especially to make the roads, which will make for quick passage through the forest. We should make it to Vackiindmire by nightfall tomorrow, if we keep a steady pace.*

"*Anyway, I have a pretty good idea of what the valley looks like,*" thought Dendrox looking at his completed map, "*I can get us to where we're going. Maybe the maps at Vackiindmire aren't guarded so well against sticky fingers. Perhaps we should forget about trying to steal one and just buy a map. Of course we'll have to steal the money to do so, but that shouldn't be too difficult.*

"*So come morning, we just follow this road into the forest all the way east until it ends and forks north and south. Then follow the road south for awhile until we start coming out of the forest. Then ignore the side road which heads back west leading to the village of Dexcsin and just travel a little more south until we arrive at the town of Vackiindmire.*

"*Okay, that kept me awake for a little while, now what? I really hate watch duty. I don't see the point. If anything happened, we'd wake up in time. Well, maybe not, but still. I just hate being forced to sit here listening to my sleepy brain ramble on about nonsense.*"

The night was a quiet one, with just the occasional rustle of leaves and small night creatures scampering about. Then there was the sharp sound of a twig breaking under a heavy foot. His heart started pounding rapidly in his chest as the adrenalin raced through his body. His eyes frantically searched in the direction that the sound had come from, but saw nothing. He clutched a dagger in his hand. He was quite skilled at dagger throwing, but knew that the darkness would be working against him if an opponent presented himself.

He listened hard for any further sounds of movement for quite some time. Hearing nothing more, he dismissed it as being nothing of importance. He thanked himself for not alerting Candra. He knew that he probably would have never heard the end of it for being spooked by such a trivial thing.

There was another snap of a twig. This time it was closer, but he could not detect any movement within the shadows of the forest. He was getting nervous and the thought of being ridiculed for being a coward by Candra quickly receded to the back of his mind.

"Candra," he whispered frantically.

Her emerald green eyes bolted open with a quick alertness. At seeing the distress in his dark blue eyes, she reached for the bow beside her. She clutched it in her hand, a little disorientated at first, and then took an arrow from the quiver saying, "What is it?"

"A noise from the trees," he said as quietly as he could.

"Where?" she whispered. She moved from the ground up into a crouched position, with bow and arrow in hand, and quickly slung the quiver onto her back.

"There," he said as he gestured toward the trees with his dagger.

"I can't see anything. I can't detect any movement either. Are you sure?" she questioned.

Another snap of a twig sounded. It was closer now and again there was no sign of movement. Candra quickly pulled back the arrow in her bow and held it ready in the direction of the sound.

"Do you think it might be an ambush?" he asked, peering into the forest around them.

"No," she said in a toneless voice, concentrating on the direction the noise had come.

She was well trained in things like predicting the enemy's possible plan of attack, but still he doubted her. He thought to himself, his words dripping with sarcasm, "*It had seemed like a logical*

<Zaylyn ><Quest For The Sword Of Anthrowst ><By Katrina Mandrake-Johnston >   <Ch 4> < 23 >

possibility to consider, but I couldn't question her reasoning, now could I? I wouldn't dare suggest that she may be wrong and should reconsider; I know better than to do that. Candra is way too stubborn to change an idea once it is set in her mind. In most situations she is usually right, having her unspoken reasons why she had made a decision. If you were smart, you'd go along with it and not argue. She says that there's no ambush, so that means concentrate in this direction, but I'm still going to keep an eye out just in case."

He was proud to have her by his side, even though she was often annoying and practically intolerable. He knew she would say the exact thing about him as well. They had a strong bond with each other and that could never be broken no matter how much they quarreled.

"What's taking so long? Where is he, it, she, or whatever the thing is?" Dendrox whispered.

"Be patient," she said in that calm toneless voice again and never let her gaze stray.

Dendrox could see that her fingers were straining to hold the bow ready. He knew she would not break her concentration and hold, no matter what the cost. She was not one to let herself show or accept defeat and failure.

In a low almost inaudible voice she said, "Whoever it is, he's waiting for us to lower our guard. I have to get a better grip. Take the guard for a few seconds."

"Wasn't that what I was doing all this time?" he thought to himself.

It was her way of showing affection for him. She would protect him at all costs to herself. He knew to appreciate this, even though he was well capable of taking care of himself. She was not trying to show incompetence on his part, as most people would probably take it. He knew that he would sacrifice himself for her just as much as she would for him. In fact the reason why they always had trouble maintaining a relationship with someone else, was probably because they were so overprotective of each other. No one could impress 'the best friend' enough to gain approval and could never compete against their friendship. They had a special kind of love for each other.

"Okay, I'm ready again," she said as she stood in her solid stance, with her bow and arrow ready but undrawn. Her fingers ached from holding her bow ready for so long. *"Maybe it wasn't anything at all,"* Candra thought and then she whispered, "If there was someone, they surely would have made their move by now." She looked over to Dendrox and his shorter height of five and a half feet. His hair was a complete mess. She decided, "Whoever it was probably saw that he was no match for us and left."

Dendrox searched his mind for some sort of explanation and then said, "What about someone invisible?"

"What?" she chuckled.

"No, I'm serious. I saw this guy do it once. He was showing off this magic spell he had just learnt. It took him several tries, almost to the point where I thought he was completely nuts, but he did it. It didn't last very long though," he told her.

"You really think so?" she asked as she considered this strange possibility.

"Could be," Dendrox said, "That would explain why we didn't see any movement and why it took him so long to approach."

"If so, he's long gone by now. Check our things. I'll keep watch while you do, just in case," she said in her authoritative voice.

Dendrox nodded and began his search through their belongings as Candra continued to watch for any movement in the surrounding vegetation. "It's not like they'll end up with much," he said to her.

"Just do it," she told him.

"Looks like we'll both have to change our plans. Now there's absolutely no chance of a hot bath, meal, or comfortable bed, no matter how cheap it might be. We've been cleaned out, right under our noses," he reported, "My pouch is gone, along with the last scrap of food which I so carefully had saved for my breakfast, and our last two gold coins."

Candra shrugged at the situation and said, "A couple of thieves getting robbed. How ironic." She tried to hide it, but Dendrox could see the frustration on her face.

He admitted, "Whoever it was, outsmarted us by far and well deserves his prize, but it doesn't make things any easier for us. It's still my watch, so I guess you should get back to sleep."

<Zaylyn ><Quest For The Sword Of Anthrowst ><By Katrina Mandrake-Johnston >   <Ch 4> < 24 >

Dendrox was puzzled that there hadn't been any tracks made by the intruder. He wondered if it were possible for a spell to also hide footprints with magic. There had been no shadow cast by the intruder either, and this he was sure of as he had been watching for fear of an ambush.

They both returned to their blankets. Dendrox wriggled around trying to find a comfortable spot on his blanket that wasn't there. Candra settled back down onto her blanket, a tense look upon her face.

He attempted to lighten the situation by saying, "Oh, and by the way, you do snore."

"I do not," she protested, and he could see the faint glimpse of a smile creep across her pale lips.

<World of Zaylyn ><Quest For The Sword Of Anthrowst ><By Katrina Mandrake-Johnston ><Ch 5>

CHAPTER 5 = THE ROAD

At dawn, Vordin awoke and began to chip away at the tiny opening between the rock wall and the boulder with his dagger trying to free himself. It was pointless, but he felt he had to try.

Candra and Dendrox packed up their things and made their way back to the road which would eventually lead them to Vackiindmire. They had been traveling in silence for quite awhile now, their leather boots treading on the dirt road at a steady pace.

Candra was the first to speak. "We should have been more alert and we should have known better. We both handled the situation poorly. Maybe if we had…"

Dendrox cut her off by blurting out, "Hey, what's done is done. We can't do anything about it now, and considering everything, I think we both did pretty well. The only thing we can do now is learn from the experience and be better prepared for odd situations like that in the future."

"Yeah, okay," she agreed, "It could have been a lot worse, especially if there had been an attack with such a strong advantage against us."

"Exactly, so don't dwell on it. I'm tired, hungry, and irritable, and you are too," he said curtly. Candra was about to protest but then decided against it knowing that it was true. "I suggest," he continued, "that we just concentrate on the road ahead and when we get settled in the town for the night, we can both laugh over all this. It's not as if we could have gotten anything with the gold we had anyway."

After several moments of silence, she said with frustration, "At least we have the decency not to take someone for all they've got. Not even half a gold piece was left for us."

Dendrox, fed up with bickering, remarked, "Hey, I'm the one who skipped my supper last night so I could have something to eat this morning. I hope the guy chokes on it."

"Dendrox, what's that?" Candra asked, suddenly distracted by something in the distance.

"What?" he asked with curiosity.

She pointed ahead of them and replied, "That shape by the side of the road farther up."

Dendrox strained to perceive the object to which she pointed, but finally said, "I can't tell from here."

As they approached the shape, Candra said with alarm, "I think it's a body."

When they reached the area, they discovered that the shape was indeed a body which was lying face down in the grass beside the road. Dendrox nudged the man in the grey robe and brown leather sandals with his boot. There was no reaction.

"He's dead," Candra stated, "You want me to turn him over?"

"Go right ahead," he said.

Dendrox did not have a strong stomach around death. If he was forced to cause it, that was a different story, but he would make every effort he could to avoid being around it. Candra had said once that seeing it probably made him feel his own mortality a little more than he wanted to.

Part of it was the fact that he wouldn't just see a corpse, but think of who it once was. He would imagine how they had lived their life, their loved ones, what they were like, their thoughts and opinions, and all those things that make a person a person. The thought of all that being able to end so abruptly and easily really bothered him.

There was another reason behind this having to do with his grandfather. He had been a young child and his grandfather had been very ill. Dendrox had been visiting him, and being so young, had

<Zaylyn ><Quest For The Sword Of Anthrowst ><By Katrina Mandrake-Johnston >   <Ch 5> < 25 >

been unclear and afraid of what was happening to his grandfather. His mother and father had left the room briefly to talk privately to each other about his grandfather's condition. Unfortunately, as Dendrox nervously stood beside the large oak bed, his grandfather passed away. He stared at the lifeless body. He put out his small hand to touch the hand of his grandfather, thinking that he could perhaps wake him. This is when his grandfather's eyes bolted open, and with a tiny spark of life that had remained, reached out for Dendrox and then fell limp. Dendrox, only a small boy, had been terrified.

Ever since then, he had a fear of the dead, even though he knew better. In the back of his mind, he kept imagining that the body would suddenly jump to life and reach for him. Almost all of his nightmares were those involving the dead coming to life. There was one reoccurring nightmare in which he was situated in a graveyard after dark. He would walk along, past the tombstones and crypts, and then suddenly the dead would erupt out of the soil attacking him with outstretched claws.

He hadn't mentioned this to Candra, as he knew that she would never understand and probably tease him about it. Dendrox looked away as Candra turned the corpse over.

With surprise, she said to him, "Hey, take a look at this!"

"No thanks," he said without hesitation.

"Don't be so foolish. I think this is the guy. Is this your pouch?" she asked him impatiently and then said with annoyance, "Oh would you just look. I'm not about to pry it out of his hands just to show it to you. Quit being such a baby."

Dendrox glanced quickly at the dead man. This man had short blonde hair and his blue eyes were wide open. In both his hands, he clutched a black leather pouch. It was Dendrox's pouch, which had contained their gold and his stolen meal. Immediately, Dendrox felt terrible for making his earlier comment about hoping this man would choke on it.

"So what do you think?" she asked.

"Yes, it's my pouch, and if you haven't noticed, he has an expression of extreme fright. You realize that this is not a good thing, right?" he said to her with a worried look displayed on his pale face.

"No, really?" she said with sarcasm. Candra tugged the stolen pouch loose from the dead man's fingers and searched around inside saying, "I guess you don't want your breakfast, huh?"

"Did you really have to ask?" he said with a somber look.

Candra handed the pouch back to Dendrox and said, "It looks like everything's here that should be and nothing else that could give us a clue as to what happened. Can you search the surroundings? You're way better at that than I am, so I guess I'll be checking the body."

Although her words had been but a feeble attempt at praise and consideration, Dendrox very much appreciated it. He was in fact better than Candra at searching areas for clues. He could track almost anything, which meant looking for and paying attention to all the small seemingly insignificant details that could very well provide him with the information he needed. He headed toward the trees where he figured the man must have come from, and Candra popped the small piece of cheese into her mouth.

After some time, Dendrox came back after his investigation to meet Candra who was standing a fair distance away from the body now so he would feel a little more at ease when speaking with her about his findings.

"What did you find?" she asked him.

"A couple fresh breaks on branches, trampled vegetation, only a few scattered footprints clearly made by him, and that's all. If the Invisible spell hides footprints, he must have been casting it over and over as soon as it ran out. He must have been running and stumbling in the dark from someone or something, although there aren't any tracks made by his pursuer at all, just trampled vegetation. All I can really tell you for certain is that he traveled through the forest and then emerged onto this road only to die while being extremely frightened of something. Everything else I'm just only guessing at," he said disappointed that there hadn't been any further clues.

"Well all that sounds pretty likely. I didn't come up with anything. I say we get to town as quickly as we can. We might have been luckier last night than we realize," she said looking disturbed.

<Zaylyn ><Quest For The Sword Of Anthrowst ><By Katrina Mandrake-Johnston >   <Ch 5> < 26 >

"I agree," he said, as he nodded toward the road, "Candra, I don't like this. Something just isn't right here."

They continued on their way and walked briskly along the road in silence for some time. Candra seemed as if she were hiding something, but he could never really tell with her. Something had her mind preoccupied though for sure.

The forest had become very dense on either side of the road as they continued their journey. Dendrox figured that the village of Dexcsin was just beyond the forested area now to their right, and he thought, *"It probably wouldn't be that long of a hike to get to the village. It would be more difficult and strenuous than the road of course. Trampling through thick forest in hope of coming to the village, by chance alone, is not very appealing though. Candra is unfamiliar to Dee'ellkka Valley, and right now, it seems to be a good thing. Becoming lost as a result of her blind and stubborn determination is not going to benefit us at all. Seeing that man, and having no clue as to why he came to an end like that, is another good reason to stay on the road. Although, perhaps it isn't a good idea. Why had he been traveling through the trees and not by the road in the first place? There had to have been more to him using the Invisible spells. Surely it was not for the sole purpose of robbing us of a few gold pieces. What could be so horrible to make someone die in fright like that? Why didn't she find any wounds or anything on the body? It doesn't make sense."*

"Hey, you look panicked. Are you all right?" Candra asked.

He told her, "Yeah, I'm just a little spooked."

"Yeah, me too," she admitted.

If she were, she would never let it show. He wouldn't tell her about the village. If she knew and wanted to go, he would have to follow.

Again, they traveled in silence for quite some distance. Despite his worries, the warm sunshine added some comfort to both his body and mind.

Candra said looking concerned, "Dendrox, don't you think it's odd that so far we haven't seen anyone since we traveled through the mountains?"

"You're right. I hadn't even thought about that. It is strange," he realized, "You would think that we would at least see someone after traveling as far as we have already."

"Except for that dead man of course," Candra reminded him.

"Thank-you so much for mentioning that again," he said with sarcasm and a grave look on his face.

"Sorry," she apologized.

They continued in silence again for a distance, before Candra said to him, "Dendrox, we're only assuming that man was our intruder last night."

With curiosity, he asked, "What do you mean?"

"I hadn't checked the pouch last night, remember? We don't know when it was taken," she stated.

"So you're saying there's a possibility that it wasn't him last night then, that maybe the pouch wasn't taken during my watch?" Dendrox asked with a puzzled expression, "Maybe in your watch then?"

"It's possible, but probably unlikely," said Candra, and then very worried asked, "I'm pretty sure that I didn't doze off, but what if I did without realizing it?"

"That isn't like you at all," he told her.

"That guy looked as if he was the magical type," she commented after further consideration, "didn't he? So he could have been the one last night, right? Casting his spells?"

"I guess so, but you can't really tell. Let's just hope we make it to town by nightfall. There's no way I want to spend another night out here," Dendrox said dreading the thought.

Now there was a slight tone of anger and anxiety to her voice as she said, "You said for sure we would make it by then!"

"Well, I'm not sure how far it is, exactly," he admitted to her slightly apologetic, as Candra walked quickly ahead of him.

"Walk faster!" she said between clenched teeth, "We're not stopping to rest along the way either!"

<Zaylyn ><Quest For The Sword Of Anthrowst ><By Katrina Mandrake-Johnston >   <Ch 5> < 27 >

She was angry and frustrated, which Dendrox recognized as being a front to hide her fear.

By late afternoon, they were extremely exhausted and faint with hunger and thirst.

Dendrox pleaded, "I have to stop. My feet and legs ache."

"So do mine," she said as she sat down on a log by the side of the road.

She pulled off her boots and let her feet enjoy the coolness of the grass. Dendrox repeated her actions and sighed with relief. Dendrox, as he tended to fidget a lot, picked away at the log with one of his daggers.

"You're going to dull your daggers by fidgeting with them all the time like that," the elf warned. He just shrugged and continued. "We're almost there, right?" she asked him.

"I don't know. We should have been there by now. This road we're on now, connects with the road between Shirkint and Vackiindmire. From there, it's not much farther," he explained.

She told him, "I could really use a drink of water right now."

"Yeah, I know. Me too. I guess we could have tried to collect some of the rainwater last night. Aw, never mind," he said, "It shouldn't be that much farther."

Candra pulled on her boots, adjusted the quiver strapped across her back, and stood up. "Well, let's go then," she said impatiently as Dendrox grumbled and reluctantly struggled to get his boots on once more.

After traveling for quite some distance, Candra muttered, "We're not going to make it by nightfall. Are you absolutely sure that this road connects with the main one between the towns?"

Candra noticed the confused tone to his voice as Dendrox said, "Yes, positive. I don't understand. We should have been to town a long time ago and at least have connected with the other road by now."

Dendrox looked around nervously at the forest around them as the daylight began to slowly fade. He then said, still bewildered, "Hey Candra, take a look over there!"

"What?" she asked, unsure of what he was talking about.

"Over there. That log," he said as he pointed to the side of the road, "It looks like the one we had stopped to rest at earlier."

"So," said Candra.

"No, I mean it looks exactly the same," he explained.

"Don't be silly," she remarked, "Keep walking and maybe we'll make it before it gets too dark to see."

Frustrated with her constant impatience, he insisted, "Just hold on a minute. I want to check it out."

She glared at him and said, "If you want to rest that badly, all you have to do is just say so."

Dendrox ignored her and approached the log, so she sighed and said, "Okay, wait for me."

As Candra approached him and the log, he held out a hand to stop her and instructed, "Don't move any closer or you'll disturb the area."

"Dendrox, you're being ridiculous. To think this is the same log is absurd. Besides, it doesn't look like the same one to me." Then she gave in and said, "Okay, just hurry up then."

As Dendrox carefully inspected and studied the area, he commented, "Something is very, very strange here. This can't be possible. Candra, this is the same log. Unless two people with the same size boots as us came to rest at this log here, and decided to peel away some of the bark with a dagger for something to do in the exact same place I had done when we had stopped earlier, something very odd must be going on here."

"You're absolutely sure?" she said with obvious doubt and ridicule.

"Yes," he snapped back at her.

Angered by his foolishness, she insultingly said, "You realize that I'm really starting to doubt your sanity."

"I'm not fooling around!" he yelled.

She realized she suddenly had an unnaturally large amount of violent hatred toward her friend, for no real apparent reason. She quickly composed herself and said, "I'm sorry, Dendrox. Please don't get

<Zaylyn ><Quest For The Sword Of Anthrowst ><By Katrina Mandrake-Johnston >   <Ch 5> < 28 >

mad. Fine, I believe you. So now what?"

"I don't know. It doesn't make any sense," he said, appearing to also have subdued a sudden surge of anger.

Candra, wanting to get everything out in the open, said, "Dendrox, I didn't tell you before, because I didn't want to make you panic more than you were already."

"What are you talking about? Didn't tell me what?" he asked with a testy look in his eye. He was furious that she had kept something from him figuring he was too weak to handle what might have been vital information. He felt betrayed.

Candra found herself feeling a bit ashamed as she confessed what she had kept from him. "When I checked the man's body," she said hesitating a moment, "Well, there were deep slashes and an enormous bite in his torso. There wasn't much blood, which was odd for such a severe wound, but the little that I saw looked as if it had turned to jelly. It was strange. I didn't know what to think. I don't want to even imagine what kind of horror could do that to a man."

"How could you not tell me something like that?!" he said with astonishment.

"I thought we would be in town soon. You panicked at the sight of the dead body. I didn't want to give you anything more that would cloud your mind and judgment more than it already was," she told him.

Dendrox lost control of the excessive anger that was raging inside him, as it amplified to much more than what it actually was. He blurted out with intense fury, "What is that supposed to mean?! You think I'm weak, don't you?! That I can't handle myself?! That I'm incompetent?! Always second best to you instead of an equal?! To you, everything I think or say is foolish!"

The anger he had felt for her a few moments before was completely gone now, as if it had mysteriously vanished from his mind. Dendrox sat on the log and buried his face in his hands. Candra hesitated, not knowing what to say or how to react to his unexpected outburst.

"This is not at all like him," she thought in puzzlement. "Dendrox, I'm sorry," she said as sympathetic as she could.

He remained silent. She sat beside him on the log. She was as frustrated and confused as he was, but it was obviously taking a greater toll on him than her. She placed her hand on his shoulder in an effort to try to comfort him. This felt extremely awkward to her, but she thought it would help. This surprised Dendrox and he looked up to her face. His face displayed a mixture of confusion and anguish.

"I'm sorry. I don't know what came over me. I had all this violent anger inside of me a minute ago, and now it's completely vanished," he said with sincerity, "I almost wanted to physically harm you." He hung his head and ran his fingers through his hair saying, "I don't know what's going on."

When Dendrox finally looked up at her again, he had such an insane and malicious grin displayed on his face, that it greatly startled her.

"Are you going to be okay?" she asked nervously.

"Yes," he said with a mischievous expression.

Cautiously, she asked him in a calm collected voice, "Then, do you want to go now?"

"What's the point? I'm just going to wait here until that creature comes for me. We can't get to town. It's toying with us, waiting for the dark to conceal its attack. Where do you think everyone is? They're dead, and we're next," Dendrox said in a cheerful voice and grinning.

"You're being crazy," Candra said. She then coaxed, "Let's go, okay?" She was getting worried, as she had never seen him get like this.

Dendrox said defiantly, "No, I'm staying here."

"Come on," she pleaded again.

"I said no, and don't make me say it again," he warned with a wicked look.

"I'll scout ahead and then come back for you. Maybe I'll come to the fork in the road," she said, "We should be close, right?"

He remained sitting calmly on the fallen log as if he were quite comfortable there. "You won't," Dendrox said as he took a dagger from his belt and scraped the dirt from under his fingernails.

<Zaylyn ><Quest For The Sword Of Anthrowst ><By Katrina Mandrake-Johnston >   <Ch 5> < 29 >

"Won't what?" she asked carefully.

"Won't find the fork and probably won't be coming back. It'll be dark soon. It's going to find you." He had spoken in such a calm and definite tone and looked at her in such a way, that it gave Candra the creeps.

"Just stop it. Stop it now! What is wrong with you, damn it!" she said partially afraid, "I'm going to scout ahead, alright? Promise me you'll be here when I get back."

"Okay." His voice was that of someone who didn't care anymore about anything.

His eyes had a wild excited look to them and it made her extremely nervous of him. She took off down the road away from him at almost a running pace.

Her mind was racing, *"This is not like him to act this way. Maybe, it's not even him at all? If I'm supposed to accept all these other crazy ideas, like someone invisible, why not that one too? He was out of sight for awhile back at that body. Dendrox could be dead, all the way back there, and the person sitting on that log could be some horrid creature that has taken his place and is toying with my mind and emotions."* She realized how ridiculous her thoughts had become, and she told herself, *"Now you're the one being foolish this time,"* but still she glanced nervously behind her just in case.

He was still sitting there, grinning at one of his smaller daggers as he flipped it over and over again in his fingers. If she were going to scout ahead far enough and get back to him before dark, she would have to run for part of the way. She also wanted to get as much distance between herself and that dagger as quickly as possible.

Candra broke into a sprint, even though her body ached and her stomach hurt with hunger pains. She ran farther and farther, hoping to see any sign of the fork in the road or of another person traveling along this one.

Just when she was about to give up and head back, she saw what looked to be a person on the road some distance ahead. *"Finally, there's someone else besides us,"* Candra thought to herself. She continued to run as her heart pounded heavily in her chest.

As she got closer, she called out, "Hey!... Excuse me!... I need to speak with you!..." The person had shown no sign that he or she had heard her.

When she had approached even closer, she called out again, "Hello!... I need to speak with you!..."

The man slowly turned around and she cleared the distance between them. Staring at her with wild eyes and with an overly expressed grin, was Dendrox. "No... How could it be? No, it can't..." she stammered, backing away from him.

"Well, I was right, wasn't I? You're right back where you started. Now do you believe me? But don't worry, when it comes for us, I'll protect you," Dendrox told her as he walked back over to the log again. "Come," he said to her, "Sit with me and wait, Candra." He gestured toward the log with both hands and he still had the huge grin on his face.

"No! Listen Dendrox, if that's really who you are, you had better stay away from me. Leave me alone! I'll defend myself if I have to," she said threateningly as she pulled an arrow from her quiver and the bow from her shoulder. "Stay away from me," she insisted.

Dendrox merely sat down on the log and said, "You're the one who's talking like you're crazy. What are you talking about? Of course I'm me. Who did you think I would be? I've just accepted the fact that we're stuck here, and whatever is doing all this, isn't going to get the satisfaction of watching me stumble through its little games. I'm no fool, and I'm not going to be toyed with. If it wants to play, it'll have to do it with my daggers stuck in its gut. Candra, come and sit. All we can do is rest and wait for it to make its move. In the morning, if we still can't get to town, I suggest we travel through the forest to try to find the village of Dexcsin. It should be somewhere on the other side of this part of the forest. If not, at least we'll be close enough that we should be able to find it eventually. We should make our camp for tonight. While you were gone, I piled together some wood. I found quite a few dry pieces. Some are a little damp still in places from last night's rain, but it'll have to do. I think we

<Zaylyn ><Quest For The Sword Of Anthrowst ><By Katrina Mandrake-Johnston >   <Ch 5> < 30 >

should go together to find food though. There's probably a rabbit out there somewhere close. I thought I saw one a bit earlier."

"Are you finished?" Candra said angrily.

"What's your problem?" he asked defensively.

"A village? You just thought to mention that to me now!" she shouted.

"Sorry, I guess we're even," Dendrox said calmly.

She was not satisfied with his complete lack of guilt, but she found it fair enough. She was grateful that the wild frantic look had subdued and his concentration was now focused on the tasks ahead for making camp. The thought of a warm blazing fire was appealing. "You start the fire, and I'll get dinner," she told him, "There won't be enough light to see by if we go together. I'll yell if anything happens, okay?"

She didn't like the idea, but her empty stomach wouldn't let her reconsider her decision. She was still nervous of him and thought it would be a good idea to not go along with his plan, even though it made sense if there was some creature lurking around causing all this as Dendrox thought. "If tonight is going to be as strange and confusing as today has been," she thought, "maybe following what's logical isn't the best thing to do."

She found a rabbit easily and loosed an arrow into it. She was pleased to see the small fire to welcome her back.

"That was fast," he commented, taking the rabbit from her.

Candra spread out her blanket by the fire and collapsed onto it exhausted. Dendrox prepared and cooked the rabbit, as she removed her boots and equipment and began rubbing at her tired aching muscles. The fire felt wonderful. She only wished that it could warm all sides of her at once. She hated to have one side warm while the other side remained away from the fire feeling icy cold.

***

Vordin, in his solitude, had taken a small stone and made it glow indefinitely by applying a few drops from the lantern's flask. It served him no purpose other than to pass the time. When he had become bored with it, he placed the stone into one of the small outside pockets of the backpack.

He had given up on trying to dig his way free. The rock that formed the cave wall was extremely hard and he had only managed to chip away a very small amount. Vordin had spent the remainder of the day listening to the birds singing outside and longing for the freedom they enjoyed. He had watched the daylight fade as the sun set below the horizon. Vordin lay down on the hard rock floor and tried to sleep, as there was nothing else he could do.

<World of Zaylyn ><Quest For The Sword Of Anthrowst ><By Katrina Mandrake-Johnston ><Ch 6>

CHAPTER 6 =   THE CREATURE

Dendrox looked over at Candra, who was sitting on her blanket by the fire, and said to her, "Do you see what I mean, Candra? We can't do anything about being stuck here, so we might as well make the most of it. Panicking isn't going to help things. I already tried that and it didn't work. We have to stay focused and level-headed." She knew his words were really meant for himself rather than her.

"You're exactly right," she reassured him, "I'm starved. Is it almost ready, the smell is making my mouth water."

She watched the roasting rabbit meat cook over the fire. Dendrox had skinned the carcass, stuck a fair sized stick through it, and propped it over the fire. He was sitting in a relaxed position with his forearms resting just above his knees. The firelight illuminated the thick tree trunks around them. Candra could see the road from their camp. To her, it looked so barren and empty. She wondered if they would ever make it to town or see anyone else but themselves. The smoke from the fire billowed up in-between the treetops of the large pine trees into the night sky.

"Be patient, you're always in such a rush. No wonder every time you cook, the food's half raw," he teased.

"This is a good sign," Candra thought, "He seems to be more like himself than before." She questioned, "So whose watch is it tonight?"

<Zaylyn ><Quest For The Sword Of Anthrowst ><By Katrina Mandrake-Johnston >   <Ch 6> < 31 >

"Mine," he said.

"You did the last watch last night though," she stated.

"You're either really confused, or you still think I'm not me. We go by who does first watch, remember? We argued about it practically all night once until we settled on this. You did first watch last night, so I do it tonight," he said and shook his head.

Dendrox sliced off a chunk of meat for Candra with his dagger and tossed it to her. She devoured this as quickly as she could and wiped the grease from her lips with the back of her hand. Soon the carcass had been picked clean between the two of them. Dendrox looked as if he were pondering something.

Candra broke the silence between them by saying, "You know Dendrox, I think this is the most we've ever fought. I know we both have our differences, but we've never acted like this before ever, even considering everything that has happened. I had such an intense anger toward you before that I could barely contain it and there was no apparent reason for it either."

"That was exactly what I was just thinking. Something strange is going on," Dendrox said still deep in thought.

"I'm just saying that I'm really sorry about the way I've been acting," she said with sincerity.

"Yeah, same here, Candra," he told her.

They sat in silence for awhile and then, from behind where Candra was sitting, there came a noise from the trees. As Candra turned around, one of Dendrox's daggers flew past her head and sunk deeply into the shiny black flesh of a huge and hideous creature. It staggered back on its six legs from the pain; each leg on its thick torso equipped with long sharp claws. Dendrox had just saved Candra's life. The creature's large oval eyes were solid black and were set on either side of its huge salamander-like head. Its eyes appeared to be staring at everything all at once, and its short stocky tail moved slowly from side to side.

Candra frantically scrambled along the forest floor to get an arrow and her bow. The creature opened its oversized mouth filled with grotesque teeth covered in a yellowish slime. It howled an unearthly wail that sent shivers down Candra's spine. She now had her weapon. She could see Dendrox reaching for another dagger, and as she turned her upper body up from the ground to face the creature, it lunged toward her. She could never have fired her bow in time... Despite her fear, with the arrow in hand, her aim remained steady, and she drove it deeply into the left eye of the creature. A murky fluid began to drip from it, and as the beast reared up on its back four legs with a squeal and began to scratch at its head around the eye and the protruding shaft of the arrow, another dagger flew through the air to sink into its torso just below its thick short neck.

It now swung viciously at Candra with its clawed front paw, which she desperately tried to dodge. She managed to avoid what surely would have been a fatal blow, but suffered a deep wound to her arm. Blood gushed from the deep gash in thick sticky streams. She winced from the pain but forced herself not to cry out, releasing only a slight whimper. Dendrox threw another dagger into the creature as Candra tried to push herself backwards away from the beast as best as she could. It howled and dropped back down again to all six of its legs and Candra felt the ground shudder beneath her from the weight of the monster. Two more daggers sunk into the beast.

Dendrox could tell that their attacks on the creature so far had been futile. The loss of its eye appeared to only be a mere inconvenience to this creature. It seemed to him that it was waiting for them to become weaponless, so it could hunt them further throughout the forest, enjoying their fear and anguish. *"This has to be its plan,"* he thought, *"because it could have killed us both so easily if it truly wished it. It had been toying with us earlier, I just know it."*

Candra was incapable of firing an arrow in her bow and he only had one dagger left. He decided his only hope was to strike the creature in its remaining eye in hope of blinding it. He thought that at least this would give them a better chance for survival. He could tell that the creature was about to attack again, locking its jaws onto Candra in one deadly thrust of its massive body. He aimed and threw the dagger, hoping it would find its mark and save her.

<Zaylyn ><Quest For The Sword Of Anthrowst ><By Katrina Mandrake-Johnston >   <Ch 6> < 32 >

When the creature roared over and over in a panic, he knew that he had blinded it. Candra was incredibly weak and dizzy from the loss of blood, but on top of this, her vision had begun to blur and she could hardly move. All she was able to do was crawl slowly along the ground trying to desperately get as far away from the creature as she could, as it now stomped wildly about and very easily could crush her to death. The beast stopped, made a guttural sound, and then moved its head back and forth as if it were somehow searching the area. To their horror, it seemed to lock in on them, letting loose a vicious snarl in their direction.

Candra watched with a pale face as Dendrox grabbed a thick burning branch from the fire. As he ran straight at the creature, he drove it into the throat of the beast like a stake. It screamed one last gurgling howl and collapsed finally in death. The foul stench of the creature's scorched flesh made them both gag.

"Candra!" he said in a panicked voice, rushing to her side.

"I'm fine," she said weakly, "It's dead?"

He could see that she was not at all fine. She was always too proud to admit injury and the need for help to the point of being irrational sometimes. "You're bleeding quite a lot, and I don't know what to do," he said frantically.

"I'll be okay. We should get away from this thing," she said weakly, as she fumbled to grab an edge of her blanket and then pressed it to the deep slash in her arm.

"Damn it, you're not thinking clearly! And should you be doing that? What about infection? The blanket is filthy," he said in a panic.

"I have to… stop the bleeding," she said struggling to remain in a sitting position. She looked past him to the road, her vision getting worse, and asked, "What's that… that light?"

Dendrox searched in the direction with his eyes and saw what he thought to be the light of a lantern in the distance.

"It looks like someone's traveling along the road. Wait here," he told her. He ran up to the road and called out, "Hey! Is anyone there! We need help!"

< World of Zaylyn >< Quest For The Sword Of Anthrowst >< By Katrina Mandrake-Johnston ><Ch 7>

CHAPTER 7 =   WEENA

"Is someone there?" a female voice called and the light from a lantern moved to shine in his direction, "I heard horrible frightening noises a few minutes ago."

"Over here. We need help. We were attacked," Dendrox urgently said as a woman hurried toward him.

She was dressed in loose greyish-blue robes that were collected and tied at her waist with a yellow sash. A small cloth bag hung from a cord, which sat loosely above her hips. On her small feet she wore a pair of leather sandals. She was roughly the same height as Dendrox and of an average weight. She had high cheekbones with a small nose and a rounded chin. Her blonde wispy hair fell just below her chin and her eyes were of a bright blue color.

The woman said to him, "I'm so glad I've found someone. I saw that dead body back there and figured I had better get to town as quickly as I could, even if it meant traveling through the night."

"Listen, my friend was wounded by this hideous creature. We killed it, but she's bleeding heavily," he explained to her.

"Dendrox?" Candra called out to him weakly and they both ran over to her.

"My name's Weena," the woman told them, "Can I take a look at your arm?"

Candra removed the blood soaked edge of the blanket from her arm. Surprisingly, the bleeding had slowed and now was oozing from the wound in thick gooey clumps. The elf looked nervously to Dendrox, her vision fading in and out.

Weena continued by saying, "I know magic, although I'm not an expert. I've actually just begun learning it not that long ago. Would you like me to try my healing spell?"

"I don't really… have a choice," Candra said bluntly. Dendrox looked very worried and Candra realized the wound was more serious than she had first thought. Candra looked at Weena apologetically

<Zaylyn ><Quest For The Sword Of Anthrowst ><By Katrina Mandrake-Johnston >   <Ch 7> < 33 >

and said in a kinder tone of voice, "Please, I'll be grateful… for anything you can do."

Candra could no longer hold herself up, the world seeming to swim about around her, and she collapsed backwards to the ground as Weena rushed in to kneel beside her. Weena's bright blue eyes got a vacant look to them and then she began to mouth strange inaudible words. She placed a trembling hand on Candra's arm. Candra felt a burning itch besides the original pain and almost pulled her arm away.

"There, that's the best I can do," Weena told her when the spell was finished. Candra examined her arm, amazed that the bleeding had stopped completely and that the gash had closed slightly. "Here, let me bandage it for you," Weena offered. She removed the yellow sash from the waist of her robes and bandaged Candra's wound as best as she could. Her robes fell loosely now about her as the only thing holding her clothing in place was the cord holding her cloth bag about her waist.

"I'm Candra and that's Dendrox. So, you said your name is Weena?" Candra asked weakly, trying to not give in to the incredible nausea she was feeling.

"Yes," she said, "I'm trying to reach the town of Vackiindmire. You two are the first people I've seen for a long while. There was a man back there who looked as if he had been killed by some strange creature. When I saw that, I decided to travel through the night as well, instead of stopping. Not to mention that entire village back across the mountains. Oh, it was horrible," she said putting a hand to her mouth trying to stifle the emotion, "I didn't think it would be so dangerous to make this trip, but now, I realize I should have paid for an escort." She paused and then added sheepishly, "Well… if I had that much gold, I probably would have. I'm just really relieved to see someone else out here. It was so frightening traveling all alone in the dark, especially after all I've seen." Weena picked up her lantern and as the light shone on the corpse of the creature, she almost dropped it. "Is that it?" she gasped, "This is the creature you spoke of?"

"Yeah, I've never seen anything like it," Dendrox said and then asked, "Have you?"

Weena stepped closer to the beast in curiosity and said, "No. What do you think it is? You're sure it's dead, right?"

"It better be," Candra said as she tried to stand, then decided against it, "Could you retrieve my arrow for me Dendrox, if it's undamaged?"

"Yeah, sure," he said, but he hesitated not knowing how to go about it at first. He grasped the arrow and pulled until it came loose. More of the murky liquid oozed from the creature's eye. He wiped the arrow clean on the grass and tossed it to her. He then retrieved and cleaned his daggers in the same way.

"Thanks," Candra said trying to focus on him as he placed the six daggers back on his belt.

"You okay, Weena? You look a little ill," he commented.

"I'm fine," she said as she held up her lantern for him, "This must be the creature that killed the man and probably had something to do with the massacre of that village. You know… this could be a demon, or a least that's what they've been called."

"You've seen one before then?" Candra asked in amazement.

"Well no, but I've heard stories. This is what they've been said to look like. It's said that they sometimes use magic spells on their prey. Spells such as Confuse, Hallucinate, Hate, and perhaps more, I think."

Dendrox commented, "That would explain our extraordinary day."

"Makes sense," Candra agreed, feeling a little better, "We've been trying to get to town all day, and then found we were traveling the same segment of road over and over and arguing the whole time. Well more than usual. All those insane looks and grins, those weren't natural."

"I have no idea what you're talking about," Dendrox said honestly, "Is that why you were acting so strangely? You were seeing things?"

"Well anyway, I'm glad all that is over now. I didn't know what was real and what wasn't, for the longest time. So, we can all start to think rationally again, right? No more crazy situations?" Candra said looking extremely pale and tired, "I can't handle not being able to trust my instincts."

"You don't think there are more of these things about, do you?" Weena asked them nervously.

<Zaylyn ><Quest For The Sword Of Anthrowst ><By Katrina Mandrake-Johnston >   <Ch 7> < 34 >

"I hope not," Dendrox said, "We almost didn't survive our encounter with this one."

"Do you know how much farther it is to the town, Weena?" asked Candra.

"I've never been there before, but I don't think it would be very far," she answered.

"That's good enough for me. You ready, Dendrox?" Candra said with a strong will to not let her wound inhibit her actions in any way.

"Are you okay to travel?" Dendrox asked with worry.

"I guess we'll find out. I really don't want to stay around here any longer than we have to," Candra said and then struggled to stand.

Weena rushed over to support her. Candra at first was going to refuse her charity, not wanting to appear weak in character, but found herself submitting completely and without protest. Dendrox packed up his equipment and Candra's as well. Then he helped her into her boots, while Weena tried to balance her. Dendrox put on the backpack, then swung Candra's quiver over his shoulder, then her bow, and finally strapped her two pouches to his waist as best as he could. He kicked some dirt onto the tiny fire and stomped it out. Dendrox then walked beside the two women as they all made their way up to the road.

"Dendrox, here, would you be able to take my lantern as well?" Weena asked holding it out to him with her free arm as Candra leaned weakly against her.

"Sure," he said accepting it.

Dendrox walked ahead of them holding the lantern up to light the way. As they traveled, Dendrox was pleased to see that the scenery they were passing was new.

"How's Candra doing?" he asked after they had traveled some distance.

"Not too well. I think we should stop so I can take another look at her condition," Weena suggested.

Candra moaned as if she were extremely ill. As Dendrox shone the light on her, he could see that her face had taken on a sickly pallor. Weena helped her to sit upon the dirt road and she then checked the wound.

"The wound looks like it should heal well. It doesn't look like there's an infection starting, but she has a fever and her color isn't right," she commented.

Candra coughed and thick mucus sputtered from her lips. "Candra examined the dead man when we had come across him. She had said that his blood looked as if it had turned to jelly," he stated, the distress showing in his dark blue eyes, "This is what's happening to her, isn't it? Her blood, it had begun to look odd just before you healed the wound. What do we do? You have to be able to do something! We have to save her, please!"

"Oh, let me think. I came across something like that in my studies once. I think the magic spell Poison might have that effect. I do know that the spell doesn't have the effect natural poisons have, so it could be," she said.

"Could it be that Candra has just lost a lot of blood?" he asked her.

"No, I think it's more than just that. I really do think she might have been poisoned by that creature. You didn't get cut did you?" she asked him with a look of worry.

"No. She's getting worse by the second. Is she going to be okay?" Dendrox asked, truly fearing for his friend's life.

Weena looked at Candra and then to Dendrox saying, "I don't think so."

Dendrox could feel the anger and frustration build up inside him. He felt absolutely helpless and that was something he hated. If it were a physical danger, at least he could do something, but with this he couldn't.

"*At least Weena had been honest about it to both of us,*" he noted to himself, as this was something he greatly respected in a person. The feeling of triumph he had felt after the beast was slain had vanished, as he realized that even in death it might succeed in killing one of them. He wished that he had been the one injured instead of Candra, that way she would be safe.

"I do know a Cure spell, but I don't think it will work. All of my spells are pretty weak. I'm surprised my healing spell even worked at all and on the first try too," she explained to him.

<Zaylyn ><Quest For The Sword Of Anthrowst ><By Katrina Mandrake-Johnston >   <Ch 7> < 35 >

"It's better than nothing. Why didn't you try before? Hurry, before she gets any worse," Dendrox insisted.

"I'm just saying to not get your hopes up. I'll try my best," she said.

She placed her dainty hand to Candra's pale forehead. Weena got the vacant look in her eyes again as she mouthed the strange words of the spell. Dendrox could see Candra's cheeks miraculously get their color back. The glossy look to her eyes faded and her brilliant green eyes sparkled up at him as Weena ended her spell.

"How do you feel? Did it work?" she asked Candra.

"My arm hurts…" she replied, as her head began to clear and her vision gradually started to return to normal, "but that's to be expected from the wound. Nothing else though, except for feeling extremely weak. Thank-you," Candra said to her savior, truly grateful, "You know, I think I'm going to need a couple minutes."

"Yes, of course, you shouldn't push yourself like that," Weena told her, brushing Candra's hair away from her face and checking her temperature.

Weena stayed close by Candra's side until the elf felt well enough to travel once more, and then the three of them continued along the road in the darkness. Candra now walked on her own, but occasionally still needed support from her new companion. She insisted on taking back her equipment from Dendrox, who was glad to be relieved of the extra weight but remained concerned about this. Dendrox still carried Weena's lantern, lighting the way for them as he walked a few paces ahead of the two women.

***

At first Vordin thought the mountain was collapsing around him, but then realized that the huge boulder was moving away from the entrance. Moonlight illuminated the man in the black flowing cloak. He had returned. Vordin, knowing he could not escape this being, waited with fear for his fate to be decided.

"I mean you no harm," said the man in a soothing voice, "I am The Black Shadow, but please, do not fear me."

Vordin did not know what to do. *"If this really is The Black Shadow, I am in the presence of an extremely powerful and dangerous being,"* he thought to himself nervously, *"He's evil, isn't he?"* Vordin just stood there in the cave, afraid to do anything.

"Come," The Black Shadow said to him, "I shall take you into Dee'ellkka Valley."

The Black Shadow came toward the terrified boy, picked him up as he had done the night before, and leapt into the air to fly down from the mountaintop into Dee'ellkka Valley. Vordin could see a trail as they flew above which led down from the mountain to become a road. The night air was cool and refreshing, and by the moonlight, he could see that this road was flanked by deep green grass on either side near the base of the mountain before eventually entering into a dense forest.

They soared over the treetops for some distance before they stopped, landing with their feet upon the dirt road. "There," he said to Vordin, pointing to an area in the trees just off the road.

Vordin was released, and The Black Shadow walked with him over to the area he had indicated. Vordin found the remains of a small campfire and looked to the man confused.

"Over there, in the trees," he said pointing once more.

Upon discovering the body of the creature Dendrox and Candra had fought with, he exclaimed, "This is the kind of creature that attacked my village?"

"Yes," The Black Shadow answered.

"This is the same one that found me along the road?" Vordin asked, remembering the night before and the fear he had felt.

"Yes," he told him, "and it would have killed you. These creatures can be killed, but it rarely happens. This one underestimated its prey. A foul wizard named Dranngore rules over these creatures. Whole villages are being slaughtered at his instruction. Nilnont was the first. Another is under attack tonight. If this lunatic is to be truly stopped, the only means to do so is to slay him with the Sword of Anthrowst. I will not intervene, as it is not my place to do so."

<Zaylyn >< Quest For The Sword Of Anthrowst >< By Katrina Mandrake-Johnston >   <Ch 7> < 36 >

Before Vordin could say a single word, The Black Shadow had him in his grasp again and took flight to soar above the treetops once more. Vordin saw a small light ahead on the road below them, and as they approached closer, he could see that there were three figures traveling along this road carrying a lantern to light their way. They continued to fly through the air, well past them, and eventually Vordin and The Black Shadow came down to land at a fork in the road.

< World of Zaylyn >< Quest For The Sword Of Anthrowst >< By Katrina Mandrake-Johnston ><Ch 8>

CHAPTER 8 =   THE CROSSROADS

The Black Shadow pointed in the proper directions as he said, "Directly to the north is the town of Shirkint and the sea. The sea comes into Seedelle Bay at the northeast edge of the valley and there are high cliffs to the east and south. Because there are high rock formations on three sides of the valley, I magically keep the valley from being cast in almost constant shadow. The village of Leekkar is at the southern edge of the bay. The village of Torrnell is farther north and west, near the mountains and surrounded by grasslands. South along this main road and back west is the village of Dexcsin in a secluded area on the southern edge of the forest. Directly south is the town of Vackiindmire. I must leave now. Rasindell, the storyteller, has used my potion well. Trust her."

"You mean that spider creature, Lorenta? I left her back at Rasindell's cabin," he told him.

"You have a stow away. Trust her," The Black Shadow said as he rose up into the night sky leaving Vordin behind.

Vordin sat down on a large rock by the road. He removed his backpack and looked inside, but found only his lantern. He decided that he would wait for the people he had seen to reach his position.

He had been waiting for only a few moments when someone grabbed him from behind and held a sharp dagger to his throat. A raspy voice whispered frantically, "Give it to me! I want your magic. I need your magic. I've got to have it. You don't understand! Say the words. Say the words! Give me your magic. Give it to me now!"

With the blade pressed dangerously at his neck, Vordin managed to say, "I don't know what you mean! What magic?!"

"You fool! Just give it to me! I need it!" the raspy voice insisted again. Then the man hesitated, the blade still at Vordin's throat, and he looked to his left saying, "No, it's you! You have the magic. You! Give it to me now!" he demanded and the man released Vordin.

Vordin could now see that Lorenta had indeed hidden inside his backpack and must have crawled out when he had been speaking with The Black Shadow. She was standing a few feet away beside a large oak, and before Lorenta knew what was going on, the man had her in his grasp and held his dagger to her throat.

"Now I've got you! You are the one. You will give me your magic now, or you will die! Give it to me! I need it! Do you understand?" he screamed at her.

The man's once white robes were dirty and in shreds. His reddish-blonde hair was dirty and askew. His eyes were wildly insane and full of desperation for this 'magic' he craved so badly. Vordin also noticed the man wore a medallion on a gold chain around his neck. It consisted of a large red jewel encircled by braided gold and silver.

Vordin stood and took a couple of steps toward them, wanting to somehow save Lorenta, but the man said, "Stop! I'll slit her throat! Don't move! I want my magic!" Then to Lorenta he continued, "You're going to give it to me. I need your magic, and I need it right now! Say the words!" Lorenta had an expression of terror and utter confusion on her pretty face. The man reached up and clutched her plump left breast with his grimy hand. He whispered in her ear, "Maybe you'll give me your magic now?" He pressed his body up against her, as he touched and fondled her, and he whispered, "Maybe you think you're going to keep your magic, but I need it. You have to give it to me." He ran his hand down the front of her body to rest on her inner thigh as he continued to press up against her excitedly, while all the time still holding the blade at her neck. "You must have lots of magic. I know you do. I can feel it. You must give me your magic," he whispered again and continued to touch her body. Vordin was desperately trying to think of a way to save her, but was afraid of what this awful man

<Zaylyn ><Quest For The Sword Of Anthrowst ><By Katrina Mandrake-Johnston >   <Ch 8> < 37 >
might do.

Two gigantic spider fangs erupted slowly and silently from Lorenta's cheeks and sank into the man's arm, the one that held the dagger. He screamed in astonishment, fear, and pain. The dagger fell from his hand and landed harmlessly on the ground. She retracted the fangs back into her face and resumed human appearance once more. The man staggered around clutching his injured arm for a few moments until he collapsed dead in the grass beside the road.

She stared at the dead man in wonderment. She looked at Vordin in confusion and said, "I think he was trying to mate with me. Why?" After a moment's hesitation and thought, Lorenta then said, "I was frightened. He was trying to kill me. I've never killed anyone before. I never knew that I could do something like that."

Vordin didn't know what to say to her about this, but he was glad to see her safe. He asked, "How is it that you were able to travel with me all this way? In the cave, when I was searching for my lantern, why didn't I find you then?"

"I don't think this is the appropriate time to be asking trivial questions like this," she said staring at the dead man with a fearful look in her eye, "It's Rasindell's backpack, remember? There's a hidden magical compartment in it that was made especially for me to travel in. You were going to leave me behind. I didn't want to be alone anymore and so I am seeking adventure. I was hoping to do so along side you, but if need be, I will do so on my own. Actually, I'm finding the world a little more harsh than I had hoped, but I will not return to that horrible old hut again."

They heard voices not far off, coming from the eastern road, and saw the approaching light from a lantern. "Please," Lorenta begged, "Help me hide the body."

"There isn't time," was his reply, and as he looked at the man, he noticed that the jewel in the medallion had turned mysteriously from a vibrant red color to pitch black.

"Then please hide me! I'm an ugly and now murderous monster! Do not let these people discover me! This is what Rasindell feared! Please!" she said to him quickly and then suddenly melted back into spider form.

Vordin opened his backpack, holding it so she could crawl in. As soon as she had made it safely inside and he had replaced the backpack onto his back once again, Dendrox, Candra, and Weena came into view.

Dendrox exclaimed as he saw the fork in the road by the light of the lantern, "Candra! It's the fork in the road! We've finally been able to reach it!"

Weena said to her new companions, "I think I see someone standing there."

Candra stated, "Another dead body," as they met Vordin's position. "Who are you?" she asked with suspicion.

"Vordin," he answered nervously.

Weena questioned him in a soft voice, "Where did you come from, and what has happened here?"

"I came from over the mountains. My village was destroyed by some terrible beasts. Was it you that slew the one along the path?" he said not really knowing what to say to these people.

Dendrox eyed him cautiously, "Yes, we killed the beast. Tell me how you came to know this."

"I…" Vordin stammered.

"Tell me how you came to pass us on the road without us seeing you, and how you managed to arrive here so quickly," Dendrox demanded.

"Well…" Vordin said trailing off. He felt his face get hot. He hated this unfeeling interrogation and he knew if he told them the truth that they would never believe it.

"Tell me how this man came to die. Did you kill him? Who are you really?" Dendrox questioned impatiently.

"The Black Shadow brought me here," said Vordin.

"Oh really?" Candra said with a sarcastic smirk.

"He carried me through the air and showed me the dead creature, telling me that these horrible beasts were ruled by an evil lunatic named Dranngore. He said this person could only be slain by the

<Zaylyn ><Quest For The Sword Of Anthrowst ><By Katrina Mandrake-Johnston >   <Ch 8> < 38 >

Sword of Anthrowst. A fairy queen also told me this," Vordin explained as best as he could, "I saw the three of you from overhead. I had been at this spot for only a few moments when this insane man attacked me from behind. He was insisting that I give him my 'magic'. What he meant by this, I have no clue. After a struggle, he met his end. That medallion he has around his neck is a peculiar object though; the jewel was bright red, but when he died, it turned black." Vordin felt ashamed now at how he had doubted Lorenta's unbelievable story so harshly back at Rasindell's cabin.

Weena was the first one to speak, after Vordin had finished his speech, saying, "I've heard something of this."

"Of what?" Candra asked her, astonished that Vordin's bizarre story might hold a bit of truth.

"There is a contest that a group of master wizards hold. Most people are wise to its evil nature now though. When a contestant would prove himself to be highly skilled in magic, he would be awarded an object. In this case, it appears to be this medallion. This object would increase the potency of all the person's magic spells. Then after a few days, the object would start to drain that person's magic. The wizard of this guild, who awarded the poor fool his prize, would slowly gain his or her existing magic spells until all the magic was depleted and then the object would start to drain the very life out of the person's body. The only way the person is able to stay alive is to attack others that have magic ability and drain them of it, killing them in the process. These cursed objects can never be removed from these unfortunate people unless in death. No one must ever possess this medallion or they shall meet the same fate and take several lives with them. The more spells and life these objects collect, the more these wicked and malicious wizards will gain."

"I had no idea. I thought this man was just ranting in his insanity," Vordin commented.

Candra glared suspiciously at Vordin asking, "So what spells do you know?"

"Well, none," he answered nervously.

Weena spoke up quickly in his defense. She suggested, "This man was probably so desperate that he was willing to attack anyone in hope that they knew a spell or two."

"So what's this nonsense about a fairy queen and The Black Shadow bestowing a quest upon you?" Candra said curtly.

"They just told me about him," he protested, "They couldn't possible want me to attempt to slay Dranngore, could they? I'm not a warrior."

"So where is this Sword of Anthrowst supposed to be?" Dendrox asked him.

"They didn't say. I don't even know why they told me. I would have been killed by one of those monsters had The Black Shadow not rescued me," Vordin said to them, his voice wavering with emotion.

Weena looked at him kindly and said, "Why don't you come with us to Vackiindmire. You look like you've been through a great ordeal, whether or not your amazing story is true. This is Dendrox and Candra, and my name is Weena."

Relieved to hear this, Vordin said, "Thank-you so much. I promise not to be much of a burden. Is it alright with the two of you?" he added as he addressed Candra and Dendrox who both wore distrusting expressions.

They looked at each other for a moment and then Candra said, "I don't mind. If you start trouble I can dispose of you in an instant," she teased, but Vordin saw that it was also meant as a very real threat.

"Alright then, Vackiindmire shouldn't be much farther from here," Dendrox said to them all.

"Wait. We have to bury the body," Weena said with a somber face as she looked down at the man.

"But why?" Candra said impatiently, "Let's just go to town. I'm starved, exhausted, and sore."

"The medallion," she reminded them all, "We can't let anyone find it. If anyone puts it on, they'll kill many innocent people and probably end up dying themselves. As soon as they come across someone who knows even just a single magic spell, they'll lose all control and frantically try to absorb the spell into this medallion. Don't you realize that this man would have attacked and killed me if Vordin had not vanquished him?"

At seeing the great importance that this had to Weena, they all proceeded to perform the long and strenuous deed. They dug with their bare hands into the dark soil.

<Zaylyn ><Quest For The Sword Of Anthrowst ><By Katrina Mandrake-Johnston >   <Ch 8> < 39 >

After a few hours, the morning sun rose above the horizon, but they were not nearly finished.

"Is all this really necessary?" Candra asked with a sigh and stopped to rest as her wounded arm throbbed with pain.

"Yes. We're saving lives by doing this," Weena said to her with a smile.

Candra realized that she didn't really care as long as it wasn't her own life that was being put in danger. She wondered that if her own life had traveled a different path, if she would have ended up being more like Weena. She found herself resenting the tough shell she had formed around herself. Her attitude of self-preservation and well-being seemed shallow and selfish when she compared herself to Weena. She had not seen herself as power hungry and bitterly unemotional, as she had heard others joke on occasion, but she saw it now and wondered if it were possible to change. Those characteristics weren't what she wanted to be defined as or known for. It was not who she was.

Candra found herself enjoying the fact that Weena had accompanied them. She didn't see her as being intrusive as she found most other women to be. There was something about being around Weena that made her feel alive and whole. She had noticed the way Weena and Dendrox often exchanged shy glances, and Candra found herself approving.

By early afternoon, the man was laid to rest several feet under the ground. They stomped on the grave to pack the dirt and gathered stones, twigs, and leaves at Weena's suggestion to help hide the grave.

"If we hurry, do you think we might make it by nightfall?" Weena asked Dendrox hopefully.

"Not now, but I think we'll be safe enough being not far off from the town. Besides, there's a horse drawn carriage that travels this road," Dendrox told her and smiled reassuringly.

"Does anyone have any gold?" Candra asked, remembering that they did not have enough even for Dendrox and herself.

"I have a few gold pieces. Unfortunately, I'm afraid it may not be enough for a room and a meal as I had hoped," Weena replied.

"I haven't any," Vordin said with disappointment, but then remembered the glowing rock he had made. He took it out and held it out to them in a closed hand. "I do have this though," he said as he opened his hand and revealed the glowing stone.

"You could fetch a fair price for that, I suppose," Dendrox told him.

"We could be a lot worse off. I guess we shouldn't really complain," Weena said as she considered their situation.

"Let's head out then," Candra said starting off down the road toward Vackiindmire as the others followed, "I'm sure Dendrox and I can scrounge up enough coin for us all from some of the townsfolk there at Vackiindmire." With this being said, both Weena and Vordin realized that the two of them were in fact thieves.

They all traveled in silence, as they were all exhausted.

Vordin exclaimed, as they approached a fork in the road, "Where does that road lead?"

"It probably leads to the village of Dexcsin," Dendrox told him, "Straight ahead is the town of Vackiindmire."

They stopped to rest a moment at this second crossroad where a smaller road branched back west off the main one between the two towns.

Weena had been looking down this new road, when she said, "Hey, look," and pointed. They all turned their eyes toward the road. There was a figure in the distance who was coming toward them.

"We should continue to the town before it gets dark," Candra suggested.

All of them, extremely weary and hungry, agreed to this, and were about to leave, when they heard a man's deep voice calling out to them, "Wait! Please wait!" This burly man who had short, thick legs was now running slowly and awkwardly toward them.

"Come on, whatever he wants can't be very important. Let's just leave," Candra blurted out cruelly.

Weena glared at her and said, "Well I'm waiting here. If you are really so uncaring of others, you can leave without me. Just remember that if I had said the same thing when you were in need of my help, you would not be standing here now." She turned away from Candra with an expression of disgust.

Candra just shrugged and started walking toward Vackiindmire. As she walked, she noticed that Vordin and Dendrox were not following. She continued her stride, miffed that Weena was yet again trying to manipulate the group's decision to what she wanted to do. Candra expected Dendrox to eventually come after her and join her on the way to the town, but he had not moved from his position.

"*I can't go alone! I can't leave him…*" Candra complained to herself with frustration, "*His expression, could it be that he's ashamed of me? Why should he care what she thinks? We helped her to bury the man with the medallion. My debt to her has been repaid. Now we should be on our way to town. We don't owe her anything. Who cares if she's disappointed? So what? We're all going to go our separate ways once we get to town. Why would her opinion be of any importance?*"

But as she continued to walk, Candra knew that she wasn't going to convince herself otherwise. Weena's opinion of her meant more to her than she had realized, and apparently it meant a lot to Dendrox as well. Candra, swallowing her pride, turned around and headed back.

Candra could see that her companions were crowded around a dwarf who was gasping for air after running to meet them. This thirty-seven year old dwarf stood four and a half feet tall and his curly reddish-brown hair was tangled and loosely tied to hang just below his broad shoulders. His scruffy beard ended at his collarbone, hiding his thick short neck. Above his bushy mustache was a large bulbous nose and his two round eyes were a deep brown.

He wore a pair of brown leather boots and dark brown pants. The dwarf also wore a leather jerkin over a light brown shirt, the sleeves ending in a close fit at mid forearm. His strength clearly was found in his stout barrel chest and muscular arms. His short legs contributed to his balance and sturdiness rather than speed. A medium-sized brown leather pouch was attached at his side and a large battle-axe was strapped to his back.

Candra, arriving at their position, came to stand beside Dendrox.

The dwarf had a frantic expression on his broad face, as he said to them all urgently, "Please, I fear that I will not make it to Vackiindmire and back to Dexcsin in time. These terrible creatures attacked there last night killing many of the villagers. My party has remained to protect the survivors. Several of my friends have already died in the attempt. I left to seek reinforcements, but I fear I may already be too late, as night approaches soon. Please, I beg of you, come with me to Dexcsin to try to help these innocent people." He winced in pain and clutched the thigh of his left leg. His brown pant leg was stained reddish-brown as the result of a large gash.

As Weena looked to Candra with a calm expression, Candra offered, "I'll assist you and your companions, to save these villagers."

A smile spread across Weena's pink lips at this. Candra had longed to see Weena smile again at her, as she had feared that she had lost this indefinitely. Dendrox also smiled at her.

Vordin looked worried and he asked, "What kind of creatures were these that attacked the village?"

The dwarf's dark brown eyes looked now to Vordin as he replied, "I'm not sure. I've never seen such horrid beasts in all my life. One of the foul things slashed at my leg, but I had managed to get in a couple of good blows to the beast."

Vordin admired the large and heavy battle-axe that was strapped across the dwarf's back over the leather jerkin. His boots were caked with dried blood and mud. "*The Black Shadow said another village was under attack last night. And this dwarf, he actually fought his way past them! Candra and Dendrox also battled one. Maybe this other village can stand a chance against them if we come to help,*" Vordin thought with hope.

"Did they have six clawed feet and shiny black skin?" Dendrox questioned. Dendrox was glad that he and Candra had not ventured in that direction earlier.

"Yes, but what are they? Do you know?" the dwarf asked.

<Zaylyn ><Quest For The Sword Of Anthrowst ><By Katrina Mandrake-Johnston >   <Ch 8> < 41 >

"We encountered one. We killed it, but I was wounded and poisoned," Candra replied and then gestured toward Weena, "Weena healed and cured me, to which I am eternally grateful."

"You managed to kill one? It seemed near impossible even to cause these creatures the slightest bit of harm. Well this is excellent. It may give us some sort of advantage against them. Are all of you with me then?" the dwarf asked with a hopeful twinkle in his eye and everyone nodded.

"I guess introductions are in order. My name is Nodwel," he said extending a burly hand toward Dendrox.

"I'm Dendrox," he said shaking the dwarf's hand.

"I'm Candra," the elf told him.

"Weena," said the wizard in the greyish-blue robes.

"And I'm Vordin," he said extending his hand to Nodwel and at the same time being careful not to greatly jar the backpack in which Lorenta remained hidden.

"We should leave as soon as possible," Nodwel urged, and the group began the journey to the village of Dexcsin.

<World of Zaylyn ><Quest For The Sword Of Anthrowst ><By Katrina Mandrake-Johnston ><Ch 9>

CHAPTER 9 =   DREAMS IN THE NIGHT: VORDIN

The group traveled quite a distance in silence. Their eyes would stray from the road and occasionally gaze into the dense forest on their right, across the grass covered fields to their left to the high cliffs, and also to the mountain range in the distance ahead.

Darkness was approaching and it was some time before Nodwel reluctantly stated, "We'll have to make camp for the night. There's no chance of making it to the village before nightfall. It will be too dangerous to continue in the dark. This spot here looks as good as any. We'll need a fire and a big one. I want to see these beasts if they decide to make their way over to us. It's doubtful they'll travel this far away from the village, but there's always a chance that they might. I'll start gathering wood for the fire."

"I'll help you," Dendrox offered.

After they returned and the fire they built was burning bright and hot, everyone rested their weary bodies. They were off the road a little way into the forest where the trees were sparse. Grass blanketed the ground and there were a few large rocks scattered about the campsite. The fire was a few feet from the dirt road, so the camp had a good view of the road and fields.

Both Candra and Dendrox had wondered whether this had been a wise choice, for anyone or anything approaching could detect their camp with ease. They did not voice their concerns, however, as they were both tired and confident in their abilities. Also, if a danger presented itself, there were several options for the two of them to make an escape, even if it involved sacrificing some of their newfound companions to do so.

Nodwel eased himself down to sit on one of the boulders beside the fire. It was obvious that his leg was still giving him pain. Everyone else chose to relieve themselves of some of their gear and stretch out on the grass, warming themselves around the fire.

"Do you feel ill or weakened?" Weena asked Nodwel with concern. Nodwel gave her a puzzled look. "Your leg…" she continued, "Candra was poisoned by the wound she received. I was just wondering…"

"Oh, no, not at all. I guess I was lucky," Nodwel replied with a warm smile, "It's pretty shallow. It shouldn't give me too much trouble."

After awhile Nodwel discovered that not any of the others had food or water with them, so he distributed his entire supply of rations among them and they were graciously received and eaten by all.

"I fear for my friends and those poor people," Nodwel said speaking in a solemn voice, "I believe that they are engaged in battle with these creatures at this very moment. I just hope they somehow are able to survive, and that when we arrive, we are able to defeat the creatures or at least drive them away."

"All we can do is try," Candra added.

"I've seen the devastation these creatures are capable of. Across the mountains, my entire village

<Zaylyn ><Quest For The Sword Of Anthrowst ><By Katrina Mandrake-Johnston >   <Ch 9> < 42 >

was slaughtered by these beasts. I was able to survive, so perhaps they have a chance as well," Vordin said trying to inspire a little hope back into the middle-aged dwarf.

Nodwel smiled at him, but Vordin could see the despair that lay behind it. Nodwel, favoring his wounded leg as he sat on the boulder, threw another piece of wood into the fire.

Weena asked him, "Would you like me to try to heal your wound with a magic spell?"

"Well..." the dwarf said hesitating, clearly nervous of magic.

"Oh please," said Weena, "I just want to see if I'm able to. I need the practice, and besides, it probably won't work anyway."

"Oh I guess, it would be all right then," submitted Nodwel.

"Thanks," she said and everyone watched as she held her hand over the wound. With a vacant look in her eyes, she mouthed the strange words of the spell. "Well?" said Weena when she had finished.

"Not a thing," the dwarf answered.

"Oh no. I'm sorry," Weena exclaimed with sympathy.

"Just try it again," Vordin suggested.

Weena shook her head and told him, "I can't use this spell again right away. I have to wait. It's as if the energy used to cast the spell has depleted itself and then it needs time to recharge."

"Oh, I didn't know that," Vordin admitted.

"Weena, that's quite alright that your spell failed," Nodwel said to her and then explained to all of them, "The pain and inconvenience of a wound is a major part of battle. If you have to take the time to endure your injuries, in the next battle you will have learnt to avoid them better. I received this injury because I failed to anticipate my opponent's attack. If magic is always used to heal injuries, your battle skills will never increase. You'll have no motivation to learn to avoid them better."

"Yes, that does have some truth to it," Dendrox agreed.

Weena had been proud of herself when she had saved Candra's life, but now she felt her magic skills weren't of such importance anymore. *"How often does a life or death situation arise like that? Without my magic skills, I am nothing,"* she thought to herself, *"I can't even protect myself if I need to. That horrid man that we buried would have easily killed me. I would not have been able to do anything at all in my defense. Even that complicated Shield spell I have, would not have done any good. And in this case, the moment it was cast, the medallion would have absorbed it, even if it had failed, which it most likely would have. Maybe if I were more like Candra, I would be able to put up some resistance if I were attacked. Maybe what Nodwel had said has a larger truth to it. Maybe I am just a weak and feeble person who is just hiding behind my magic, impressing people with the magnificent show it displays when my spells work. What good is that? Without my magic, I am useless. Even if I were an expert mage, what happens if I have to wait for a spell to recharge? I would be slaughtered if I were in the middle of a battle. I could buy amulets and potions to assist me, but without them I would be helpless. Maybe one of my new companions will be able to teach me to use some sort of weapon. Maybe Dendrox will teach me to use daggers. I like that idea. That will give me an excuse to spend more time with him. I have to admit, he is very handsome. The way he looks at me with his dark blue eyes makes me feel as if my whole body is blushing. Why I find myself so infatuated with him is a mystery to me. He's a thief. We have nothing in common. Candra would be a better match for him, but it appears their relationship is more like that of a brother and sister than of a couple. It's really a shame."* Just then, Dendrox gave her a shy glance and then looked back to the dancing flames of the fire. *"Well, maybe not,"* she thought blushing.

Nodwel addressed the group saying, "We're going to need our rest. We can't allow for a slip in reflexes because of a lack of sleep. I'll volunteer for the first watch."

Nodwel watched over them as they slept. Both Candra and Dendrox were lying on their blankets, while Weena and Vordin were asleep upon the thick grass.

"What am I doing?" Nodwel thought to himself, *"I'm most likely leading these poor people to their deaths. At the first sign of danger, I'm getting these people to safety. I'm not going to be*

<Zaylyn ><Quest For The Sword Of Anthrowst ><By Katrina Mandrake-Johnston >   <Ch 9> < 43 >

responsible for their deaths. Apparently they have already been through quite a lot. Hopefully my friends have everything secured and the villagers will be ready for escape when I return with these meager reinforcements. Hopefully my efforts and those of these generous people before me, will not go unrewarded. I feel as though I am betraying my friends by being here though. Here I am safe from harm or at least so it appears, while at Dexcsin, they are probably at this very moment struggling for their very lives and for the lives of those helpless villagers. I am returning sooner than I would have if I had gone all the way to Vackiindmire, but still I fear that it will not be soon enough."

As Vordin slept, a dream came to him...

He was sitting on a large rock in the middle of a deep and dark pond. Black swirling masses lurked in the depths. Trees loomed around him, surrounding the entire pond.

Tiny sparks of light came at him from the trees. Vordin thought they meant to attack him, but they stopped just in front of him to hover over the water. The fairy queen was among them.

"You must find the Sword of Anthrowst," she whispered, "You must defeat Dranngore, the evil wizard behind these creatures. You must..." Her words were cut short. She and all her tiny subjects met their deaths in the jaws of one of the creatures as it leapt up from the murky waters.

The beast snarled and glared at Vordin, as its claws dug into the stone of his tiny rock island. There wasn't anywhere for him to escape to. The creature's teeth were dripping with drool and fairy blood.

Just when he thought he would join them in their fate, someone grabbed him from behind. It was Lorenta. With incredible strength, she lifted him high into the air above her head and walked along a thin strand of web from the rock to safety among the trees...

He awoke briefly to see Nodwel keeping watch over them like a parent protecting its young. Vordin then drifted off into sleep once more.

<World of Zaylyn ><Quest For The Sword Of Anthrowst ><By Katrina Mandrake-Johnston ><Ch 10>

CHAPTER 10 =   DREAMS IN THE NIGHT: WEENA

As Weena slept, a dream came to her...

She was back in her home village. It was winter and Weena was ten years old. The cold wind beat against the shutters of the schoolhouse. She sat at her small desk with books piled in front of her. She scribbled and drew silly pictures on a piece of paper, not wanting to attend her studies. Weena had been forced to come early to the school as punishment. Her teacher was a drunk and had slipped out to the local tavern for a few drinks. What he had told her was that there were several urgent 'errands' he had to attend to before class. Even he didn't want to be forced to sit here as she was. She had to finish all her assignments and tend to the fire so the schoolhouse would be warm for when the class started. She felt she were being unjustly punished, especially when she couldn't even remember what for. There was a large snowy hill at the back of the schoolhouse and Weena had brought her sled. She tapped at the wood of her desk and then glanced over at her sled.

"I'll just write a bunch of fake answers and then copy off someone else," she decided, *"That fat, stinky, old teacher of mine will be filling his gut with ale right up until class starts. He won't bother to check until later anyway."*

She glanced longingly at her sled again. She scribbled down some answers as quickly as she could. When she was done, she almost bounced with excitement over to her sled and thick dark blue cape. Weena threw her cape over her shoulders and held the sled in her hands.

"Oh damn, the fire will burn out and they'll know I was gone. I'll get in so much trouble. Remember what your brother said: Weena, if you get into trouble again at school... ah well, I can't remember the rest. Anyway, it doesn't matter because I won't get caught."

She stuffed several armloads of wood into the fire. Then she searched throughout the room and threw an assortment of things into the fire as well, anything she thought would make the fire last.

Then Weena skipped gleefully out of the schoolhouse and out to the hill. *"This is the one even the boys are too chicken to go down. Too bad I won't be able to brag about this."*

She followed the course with her eyes: over the many slopes of various sizes, the tricky turns, and then the tiresome hike back up to the schoolhouse. The latter would be worth it though.

Down she went, shrieking with excitement. She flew over the hilltops with the icy wind whipping through her hair. Each turn sent a cloud of powdery snow into the air.

Finally, she stopped. Her breath came out in short pants. The thrill was amazing. She wanted to try it again. Weena grabbed her sled and started to run back up to the school.

She only made it a short distance before realizing it was a lot farther than she had hoped and that walking through snow slows your pace incredibly. She was halfway there when she saw the students entering the schoolhouse. *"Oh well, I'll just say I heard a strange noise outside and went to investigate or something,"* she said to herself.

Weena was nearing the school now, when she smelt a strange odor in the air. Then the school burst into flames. She heard screams and smelled scorched flesh.

She ran toward the school. The doorway collapsed as she reached it. She heard desperate cries for help coming from inside. The windows were foolishly bolted and barred to prevent vandalism. They were trapped. Foul smelling smoke billowed out from everywhere.

"I did this. They know it was me! The fire… maybe something I put in it. I don't know. But it was me! I did it!" she thought in terror and shock. There were more cries for help. *"What can I do?! I'll get blamed for everything!"*

Weena panicked and ran. She hid in the woods, curled up behind a tree. She cried until she couldn't muster the strength to do so anymore.

She didn't know how long she had remained hidden there sobbing. She was frightfully cold and she wrapped her cape around herself with numb fingers. *"Surely I can go back now,"* she told herself, as she was now far too cold to care about any consequences.

As she walked through the trees and neared the schoolhouse, she could see a crowd of people around the remains. She stayed out of sight within the trees. One man was naming off a list of the dead and each name struck her heart with sorrow and guilt. Her brother, her only surviving relative, was named last. He apparently had died looking for her within the burning building during a brave rescue attempt…

Weena awoke with a tight empty feeling inside. Nodwel was warming his hands by the fire. Occasionally, he added more wood from the pile he and Dendrox had gathered earlier. He wore a worried look on his face. The fire crackled and sparks fluttered about in the air.

"Do you want me to take watch?" she asked him.

The sound of her words startled him at first, his hand reaching defensively toward his battle-axe. He then relaxed and said, "Nah, go back to sleep, sweet lass."

At first she thought that the dwarf felt she couldn't do the job, but then realized he had meant nothing by it. He had a lot on his mind and sleep probably was the furthest thing from it right now. "They'll be okay," she told him and rolled over on her side to get back to sleep.

"Thanks," Nodwel said as he tossed another log into the fire.

After a short while, Weena woke again, and this time, Nodwel agreed to let her take over the watch. The dwarf made his way over to the base of a large tree and slumped down against it.

CHAPTER 11 = DREAMS IN THE NIGHT: DENDROX

Dendrox began to dream…

He stood in a forest glade. The sweet fragrance of wild flowers filled the air. The sunlight filtered down through the trees. He could hear birds singing as they fluttered from branch to branch, and there

<Zaylyn ><Quest For The Sword Of Anthrowst ><By Katrina Mandrake-Johnston >   <Ch 11> < 45 >
was the sound of a nearby waterfall.

Just then, something darted out from behind a tree to hide behind another. Dendrox caught a glimpse of pale blue.

Again the person came into view, as she leapt from one tree to the next. Her robes flowed around her as she moved.

Dendrox tried to approach her, and as he did, she giggled and darted away. He tried to follow her, as she danced from tree to tree in an illusive game of chase.

Finally, he lost sight of her. The sound of the waterfall was nearer now, and Dendrox headed toward it. As he approached through the trees, he could see a small lake. Water splashed over a high rock cliff to meet the lake in a bubbling spray.

She was there. Dendrox remained unseen within the tree line. It was Weena. She was beautiful. She gathered her robes about her and bent down to gracefully dip a hand into the water of the lake. She stood up and brushed her blonde hair, which hung just below her jaw line, away from her face to tuck it behind her ear.

She lifted her robes up over her head revealing a thin, blue, gossamer undergarment. He could almost see the smooth creamy skin of her body beneath. She tossed the robes to the ground and waded into the water. There, Weena tilted her head back to wet her hair. She closed her blue eyes, as she enjoyed the coolness of the water.

Dendrox crept down to the lakeside to get a better view. He could see her pale form beneath the water, as it moved back and forth to stay afloat.

Suddenly, she opened her eyes, caught sight of Dendrox, and a smile crept to her lips. Dendrox suddenly felt ashamed for invading her privacy and prepared himself for a proper scolding. Instead, she simply said, "Hello."

Weena glided through the water toward him until she could stand on the lake bottom. Then walking along it came closer and closer to him. Each step she made, revealed more and more of her body, the undergarment clinging to her shapely form. He could see that the water had been quite cold.

She now stood before him on the grassy lakeside. She smoothed back her wet hair. Her creamy skin glistened with moisture. Her bright blue eyes sparkled with excitement. Her soft pink lips parted in a warm inviting smile.

He wanted to touch her, to kiss her; to take her in his arms and hold her close. He thought to himself, "*How can I? How could someone so beautiful, so perfect, be attracted to me? I'm a thief. I'm scum. I take what I want. What do I have to offer her? An empty pouch? A broken heart? She doesn't want me. How could she?*"

She stepped closer until she stood in front of him. Her presence so close made his body ache. He felt his heart quicken and his body grow warm.

Weena ran her fingertips down the length of his arm, and where she had touched him, tingled and felt incredibly hot. Her eyes looked into his, and he felt hypnotized by them.

Then to his amazement, she kissed him. It was a soft, moist, and gentle kiss. Then she put her arms around him and kissed him again, long and hard, with a fierce passion for him that he never imagined could exist.

He held her tightly against him and stroked the small of her back. She was warm despite the chill of the lake, and she was soft. Each kiss from her sent shivers of pleasure down his body. He could feel her warm breath on his skin and it felt wonderful. Every movement she made screamed desire. She looked into his eyes and gave him a sly little smile.

"*She is so beautiful. This can't be happening,*" he said to himself. He ran his hands along her back and kissed her hard again and again.

Then she pulled back and away, making him think that he had done something wrong.

"Hello," said a voice from behind. It was Candra wearing a mischievous grin.

"*Candra, I'm going to kill you,*" he thought with an embarrassed chuckle.

"So, what's going on? Or do I already know?" Candra asked with a cunning smile.

"*I really hope you're enjoying this now, because I'm really going to make you suffer later.*"

There's no way I'm going to let you get away with this one," he sighed to himself.

"Oh, don't mind me," Candra said with her ridiculous grin, "I'm just here for the view. Really, there's the lake, the waterfall, and the trees. It's quite nice," she said almost breaking into laughter at the torment she was putting him through.

"Don't you have somewhere to go?" he asked her, his words showing every bit of annoyance and frustration that he felt.

Candra's smile widened, "Oh no, I've got plenty of time and nowhere to go." She paused a moment and then said, "Thank-you for asking though. You know how I hate to be late."

He thought with a frustrated growl, *"I am really going to hurt you for this, Candra."*

"I'm not interrupting anything, am I? So what were you two doing?" she asked with that same mischievous grin.

"Candra, please shut up and go away! Of course you won't, you're enjoying this torture way too much," Dendrox thought with frustration.

He looked to Weena. *"How am I ever going to apologize for this?"* he asked himself.

Weena smoothed Candra's hair away from her face as she had done when Candra had been injured and poisoned. It had been a simple motherly act before, but now it seemed to be more than that.

Weena turned to him and said, "Dendrox?"

"What?" he asked.

She looked at him with a puzzled expression saying, "Dendrox, wake up."

"What are you talking about? I am," he told her, not wanting to admit that this was a dream.

"Dendrox," she said again.

He grabbed on to her and held her tightly, not wanting to let go, but he felt himself waking up…

"Dendrox… Dendrox…" Weena called sweetly.

He opened his eyes to see Weena's pretty face looking down at him with concern.

"You were breathing pretty heavily. Were you having a nightmare?" she asked innocently.

"Ah, yeah," he said, but couldn't stop the wide grin that spread across his lips. "I'll keep watch if you want to get some sleep," he offered, "You can use my blanket."

"Thanks," said Weena as she accepted the blanket and laid down wrapping it around her. She fell quickly into sleep.

Dendrox sat by the fire. He could see the black starry sky above. The fire crackled. The dwarf was snoring loudly in sitting position against the bark of a large tree. Candra was sprawled out on her blanket, and Vordin was curled up with his backpack beside him.

CHAPTER 12 = DREAMS IN THE NIGHT: CANDRA

As Candra slept, a dream came to her, her memories surfacing…

She was home. She was a small child of nine years. Her father was there. His dark hair was pulled into a short braid at the base of his neck. He was roasting meat over the fire in the hearth. It smelled wonderful. They were a poor family of two, despite how hard her father worked himself in the crop fields. This meat would have to last them the next couple of days. He smiled at his young daughter, his bright green eyes sparkling in the firelight. He was a tall man for an elf.

"Tell me about elves again, father," Candra asked. She loved to hear him talk, even though he would ramble on and on.

"Well, my dear, some elves are very small, anywhere from three to four feet not unlike a lot of the fairy folk I've told you about. Some elves are of a little larger size, anywhere from four to six feet like most humans. And then, some are very tall, anywhere from five and a half to seven feet, like us. The eyes are either slanted or oval and all elves have pointed ears. Some ears are longer than others, but you can always tell if you're looking at an elf by the ears. Well, actually, I think some of the fairy folk have pointed ears as well. Now that there is definitely a race with a lot of variety. With the fairy folk, some

<Zaylyn ><Quest For The Sword Of Anthrowst ><By Katrina Mandrake-Johnston >   <Ch 12> < 47 >

have wings and many are no taller than one or two feet. Candra, you know, I have heard stories of tiny fairies that live in the forests. They're supposed to be so tiny that they appear as little sparks of light. They're also supposed to be awful pranksters, but I think the people that tell these stories drink too much ale and then blame these tiny fairies for their own clumsiness. Or, perhaps people simply see fireflies and are just hoping to see something more, something rare and magical. I think at one time, most of the fairy folk and even our kind used to dwell in the forests, mountainous caverns, in burrows underground, and even on and in the lakes and ponds. Now, so many just live in the towns and villages. It's sad in a way that so many have lost the magical and mysterious quality that we had in our past. Zaylyn is never short of its mysteries, and its strange and exotic people. I would have loved to have the chance to just travel the world and see even a small amount of the wonders it holds, maybe even discover a hidden civilization or who knows what. Alas, all the excitement and adventure I'll ever get to see is an odd-shaped potato in the field. Ah, the meat is done. Could you get the big knife so I can cut it?"

Candra went to the small cupboard, which was almost completely bare, and retrieved their only knife. She placed it on the small rickety wooden table for her father.

"Oh, I need that big plate too," he realized.

Candra went again to the cupboard and retrieved their only plate. She placed it on the table, and her father placed the tiny roast onto it.

"Oh that's hot!" he exclaimed.

He picked up the large knife and was about to carve the meat, when the door burst open. In stepped two burly men. They were covered in filth and smelled foul.

One of them blurted out, "I thought I smelt somethin' good cookin' in 'ere." He pushed his companion aside and stepped up to the table. Then he grabbed the roast with a large dirty hand and bit into it like an apple.

Candra's father stood there in utter astonishment, still holding the carving knife in his hand. Candra immediately despised these crude and selfish ruffians. She yelled angrily at them, "What do you thing you're doing?! Put down our food and get out of our house! Now!"

The two men just laughed at her. The one holding the roast took another bite of the meat with what few teeth he had. The other man, the one with greasy black hair, laughed again and said, "Who's gonna stop us? Not you, little girl, and definitely not this weakling over here." Still laughing cruelly, he asked her father, "Where's yer valuables?"

Her father remained silent. The only thing of value they owned was her mother's necklace. It was the only thing left that they had of hers, and they would not give it up to two selfish scoundrels.

"Y' look like yer hidin' somethin'. Everyone values somethin', whether it be worth money or not. I think ya have somethin' of both, don't you?" the black haired man said with a sly grin of rotting teeth.

"Leave us be," her father spoke up, keeping his voice strong, "We have nothing you want. Your friend here is eating our only thing of value."

"Ah, now I know you be hidin' somethin' for sure now. Beat the girl. That'll get 'im to talk. Then we'll know, won't we?" he smiled wickedly at her father's worried face.

The brown haired man dropped the meat on the table and grabbed the thick wooden club which hung at his side. She would fight back. The man was coming. His club was raised.

The black haired man called, "Don't kill 'er, at least not right away. Just make 'er squeal."

Her father came to her rescue, not by giving the location of her mother's necklace, but by stabbing his daughter's attacker in the back. Neither of the men were expecting this. The large knife had been driven deeply into the man's torso, so far that only the handle protruded. It was not the instantly fatal wound that her father had hoped to inflict, but the man lost the ability to wield his club and Candra was saved.

The black haired man pulled the knife out of his companion's back and snarled angrily at her father. The horribly wounded man made his way over to the door, closed it to any curious eyes, and slumped down against it, wincing in pain. The black haired man still held the carving knife which was dripping with his friend's blood.

<Zaylyn ><Quest For The Sword Of Anthrowst ><By Katrina Mandrake-Johnston >   <Ch 12> < 48 >

"You'll pay for this!" he bellowed. With the bloody knife he stabbed at her defenseless father, striking him in the stomach. Snarling, he then pulled his club from his side. This man's club had sharp metal spikes protruding from the head of the weapon. Then he raised his spiked club and began to beat her wounded father to the ground. He swung again and again.

Candra tried to stop him, but he gave her a vicious kick that sent her small body across the room. She was breathless for a few moments and then each breath after gave her pain. All she could do was sit there as the man continued to smash the very life out of her loving father.

The man had finished. Her father lay dead in a pool of blood.

He searched the house until he found the necklace. He held it up triumphantly and said, "I've found it. This is some prize! Come on, we'll get you healed up."

He helped his companion up and out of the door, slamming it closed behind them. Candra was alone. She made her way painfully across the floor to where her father lay. She couldn't even recognize him. His skull had been smashed open from the heavy and repetitive blows. His face was nothing more than a pulpy mass. She could see the knife that had been thrust into his gut. Several of his bones had been broken as he had tried to defend himself, his body misshapen and bloody. She could look no more.

A dark fury burned inside her. She wanted revenge. She wanted to make them suffer like no other ever had. Her father had taught her to use a bow. She wasn't very good, but she didn't care. She took her bow and a handful of arrows.

Candra left the house and started the hunt for her father's assassins. Her chest ached incredibly. It was definitely bruised and perhaps a couple of ribs had been cracked. The pain just fueled her rage like an internal fire. She would have her revenge.

She thought she had known the direction they had gone, but now she wasn't sure anymore. She had some tracking skills, knowing what sort of signs she should be looking for, but they never did her any good, usually leading her in the wrong direction. She entered the woods at the bottom of the hill.

"Hey you," said a small human boy. He was a year younger than her.

She thought to herself, "*Oh no, it's that annoying kid again.*" She said to him, "Go away! Can't you see I'm busy?" Her words were choked with emotion.

"Don't you want to play?" he asked.

"*He'll ruin everything. I don't have time to play hide-and-seek. I'm on a mission. Besides, he always manages to find me, no matter where I hide,*" she thought. Candra replied, "No, I don't." This time she tried to put more strength into her words, but it didn't work.

"Why not? What are you doing?" he asked her.

"Two men killed my father, and I'm trying to find them. When I do, I'm going to send a million arrows into each of them. Then they'll wish they never came near us," she told him, her words angry and forceful, but her voice trembled.

"Oh…" was all he could bring himself to say.

She thought for a minute and then said, "Dendrox, you're good at finding people. You know, like hide-and-seek. Can you help me find them?"

"I don't know. They really killed your father? This isn't some sort of game?" Dendrox asked, amazed at the thought.

"Yes," Candra replied, this time starting to cry.

"Won't they kill you too if you follow them?" he asked hugging her the way his mother did when he was sad.

"I don't know. They took my mother's necklace too," Candra told him.

"I thought you said that you were really terrible at using a bow. How are you going to send a million arrows into them, if you can't even hit the targeting board?" Dendrox asked her. She sobbed and sobbed. Dendrox offered, "Why don't you come live at my house. I'm sure my mother and father will say it's all right. Then we can practice every day together. I'll come help you, okay? You can practice your bow, and I'll practice my daggers. Then when we're really good, we'll go on adventures. We'll find those two men and then you can fill them full of arrows, and I'll throw some daggers into

<Zaylyn ><Quest For The Sword Of Anthrowst ><By Katrina Mandrake-Johnston >   <Ch 12> < 49 >

them too, okay?"

She nodded, and then drying her tears said, "I thought your mother wouldn't let you play with daggers."

"Well no, but I still do sometimes," he smiled at her, "Anyway, I have to go now. Come on, we'll go practice until we're good enough to beat them. We'll be able to find them eventually."

Dendrox took Candra by the hand and led her to his house. She got to use the spare bedroom across from Dendrox's. She remembered how his parents fussed over her for weeks and how every day they had practiced.

Her dream shifted. It was now years later and they had left for adventure on their own. Visions of the hardships and dangers they went through to gain information about the two men, flashed through her mind until her dream focused on when they had eventually found them.

She had taken her revenge. Their tortured screams filling her ears until it finally gave her a sick feeling of satisfaction. She did not want to be that person she had become that day. It made her shudder each time the memory surfaced of what she had done to them. Both she and Dendrox had been surprised that the two men had kept the necklace all those years.

Candra remembered how they returned to their home village soon after. This was the first and only time she had visited her father's grave. She dug a small hole beside the grave and buried the necklace there. Candra said good-bye to both her parents and headed back to the road to adventure with Dendrox by her side.

They had become thieves themselves and experts at it, as this had been the best way to eventually track the two men down. They needed to associate with the same people, become accustomed to the same kind of life, and with the places they would frequent.

"*Had seeking my revenge really taken over both our lives so completely? Have I, in turn, become exactly what they had been? No, I will never be like them.*" Yes, she and Dendrox were thieves, but for them, it was somehow justified in their minds, as they would only steal from the rich who had plenty to spare. There was never a time they had taken from the poor.

Another dream came to her now, and Candra found herself in the middle of a vast and extremely dense forest. Dendrox was beside her as always.

"Where do you think we are?" she asked him.

Dendrox remained silent. "Dendrox?" she said trying to get his attention.

He started to walk off into the forest, completely ignoring her. "Hey, where are you going?" she asked, as she tried to walk beside him. She found that the trees grew too close to do so, and she was forced to walk behind him.

As Dendrox walked, he would push the branches out of his path, and as he passed, the branches would then fly back to hit Candra in the face. "Hey, Dendrox, watch it," she told him, as she pushed away the offending branches.

Dendrox continued to make his way through the forest, not speaking a single word to Candra. "Is something wrong?" she asked, "Where are you going?" Another branch snapped back at her.

Forest obstacles seemed to appear out of nowhere to bar her path. She made her way over logs, inched her way past brambles, pushed branches out of her way, and stumbled over the rough and rock strewn ground. Dendrox, however, seemed to have an easy path and continued farther and farther away from her. She had to put all her effort into trying to keep up to him.

"Wait!" she called, "Dendrox, please wait! Let me catch up! Dendrox, wait for me!" If he had heard her, he made no acknowledgement of it as he moved farther and farther away. Candra feared that she would lose sight of him and become lost in this terrible forest that seemed to be holding her back and away from him.

She would not lose him! She struggled to catch up to him, but it seemed that the more she struggled to catch up to him, the more strenuous her path became. "Dendrox, please wait!" she called to him, "Dendrox, I'm falling behind! Where are you going?! Wait for me, please!"

Soon she lost sight of him altogether, but she continued on and on. Finally she came to a small

<Zaylyn ><Quest For The Sword Of Anthrowst ><By Katrina Mandrake-Johnston >   <Ch 12> < 50 >

clearing. She stood on one edge of the forest, while Dendrox stood beside Weena on the other.

"Dendrox, why didn't you wait for me?" she asked, quite out of breath. Both Weena and Dendrox had expressionless faces and seemed to stare right past her as if she didn't even exist. "Weena? What are you doing here? Where are we? Do you know? Where are we headed?" Candra asked in confusion.

Weena said nothing. She turned her back on Candra, and so did Dendrox. Then they started into the forest holding hands. "Wait for me!" Candra called in desperation, and she started to cross the grassy clearing to follow them into the woods on the other side.

Suddenly the ground began to shake, and she struggled to keep her balance. The earth in front of her opened up, creating a wide chasm to block her way. There was no way for her to get across. Even if she found a way, it would be too late to find them.

Candra sat down on the grass, knowing that she was helpless. Dendrox was gone. Weena had taken her best friend away from her. She was bitterly alone. She didn't care about holding back her emotions, not here, and she allowed herself to cry. She cried in great heaving sobs. She cried about everything; everything she had held back. She had lost her mother so long ago, and then her father was taken brutally away from her. And when she had taken her revenge, she had lost a bit of herself. Now Dendrox, he had left her too…

Candra awoke. Dendrox was digging at a piece of wood with the tip of a dagger.

"You know, if you keep fidgeting like that, you're going to ruin your blades," she commented.

"Oh, hey," Dendrox said looking down to Candra who was resting on an elbow, "You feel like taking watch now? I'm beat."

"Sure, I don't think I can sleep any longer anyway," she replied.

"Oh, Candra, can I borrow your blanket?" he asked, "I lent mine to Weena."

"Then take it back if you need it," she snapped, the fears from her dream surfacing.

Dendrox gave her a sour look.

She gave in saying, "Okay fine, take mine then."

Dendrox lay down with Candra's blanket and fell asleep. Candra looked from Dendrox to Weena and wondered what might happen to their friendship should their flirtations increase. Candra took her place by the fire.

<World of Zaylyn ><Quest For The Sword Of Anthrowst ><By Katrina Mandrake-Johnston ><Ch 13>

CHAPTER 13 = DREAMS IN THE NIGHT: LORENTA

Lorenta, still hidden in Vordin's backpack, also dreamt…

She found herself back in Rasindell's hut. She was alone and in human form. The place gave her an empty and lonely feeling. Then, Lorenta heard the cry of an owl.

The wood of the roof began to splinter, and then she could see the talons of a gigantic owl. The massive bird tore the roof off the hut as if it had been the lid of a box. A giant yellow eye peered into the room. The owl let out a deafening shriek and tried to widen the opening it had made in order to snatch up its prey. Lorenta was terrified.

Her hand, the one with the severed fingers, was grabbed by someone. It was Vordin. He led her out the door and away from the owl to safety. Her ability to change form had made it possible for the wound to seal itself in both her forms, and Lorenta wondered if there were any other mysteries about herself she was unaware of.

She and Vordin were standing by the side of a road, and there were trees on either side. Before them was the corpse of the man she had killed. In his stiff white hand he clutched the cursed medallion.

"This was not right," she said to herself, *"He was cursed, but I had to act in self defense as anyone would. Rasindell told me stories as a child. Some were of love and romance. That's what I want, not to be groped like some worthless plaything. It's like being poked at with a stick for fun. Eventually, you fight back in self defense, and that's what I did here."*

<Zaylyn ><Quest For The Sword Of Anthrowst ><By Katrina Mandrake-Johnston >   <Ch 13> < 51 >

When she turned around, Vordin had vanished. Then she heard a familiar voice, one she had not heard in a long time. "Lorenta... Lorenta, my child. Come sit by the fire with me. I have another story for you," the voice called to her. It was Rasindell.

She wandered through the forest searching for him. "Lorenta..." he called again. She tried desperately to follow the voice. "I'm here my child... Over here by the fire," he called to her.

She looked and looked but could only see dense and dark forest. She was becoming frantic. She would not lose him again!

Suddenly she fell through a deep hole in the ground and landed in the arms of her father. She was a little girl again and in the warm and cozy home she had known growing up. Rasindell smiled down at her and said, "There you are. I've been waiting all day to see you again."

"I've missed you father," she said and felt tears welling up in her eyes.

"What's the matter, dear? You look as if you are about to cry," he asked his daughter with concern, as he smoothed her dark brown hair. She just shook her head, not knowing what to say. "Okay, I have the perfect story for you tonight. Have I ever told you about how the human-dragons came to be? There are two different kinds: Dragonites and Avygons. Have you heard this one before?" She shook her head. "Okay, now where should I begin? There once was a dragon, long, long ago. She would often fly near the humans, as she was always intrigued with their way of life. Of course, she was always careful not to be seen on her ventures. If she were spotted by the humans, she would be attacked for sure, or at least scare the humans away from where she could watch them."

As she usually asked quite a few questions throughout his stories, Lorenta asked Rasindell, "Why would the humans attack her?" Maybe that's why he kept his storytelling short and simple when he told them to her. With Vordin, his stories were long and elaborate; Vordin usually didn't ask so many questions.

"Why? Well, they were afraid of her," he tried to explain.

"But why were they afraid, if she meant them no harm?" she asked.

"Well, I think it's not a matter of whether she wanted to harm them or not. It's more that she was capable of doing harm," he told her.

Lorenta looked solemnly up at her father's kind face and said, "So, they don't care what her intentions are? If she's dead, there's no possible way for her to do harm? This is their reasoning?"

"I'm afraid so, at least in this case," he told her sadly.

"So, just because I might be able to harm a human, they would want to kill me too? Even though I would never do so? The few times you've taken me with you in the backpack, I've seen horrible things, father. Creatures that could never even threaten a human, being tortured and killed by them as they laugh and make fun. Even the children do it. You can't tell me different, father. If someone saw me in my true form, whether I was capable of harm or not, they would try to kill or injure me. And, they would do this just for the fun. Even a small child would. Humans are horrid things. I don't want to be one." Lorenta was crying now and holding on tightly to Rasindell.

"Dear, I am human. Not all of us are like that. I have to admit a lot of them are, but not all. Don't cry. Come on, let me finish the story. There's a good message in it, and I think it will suit you," Rasindell tried to comfort her.

"Okay," she said wiping the tears away.

"Alright, now where was I? Okay, so this dragon, she would watch the humans from time to time. She would always remain hidden, which was a hard thing to do for a large dragon as she was. Over the years, her random viewings of the humans became more frequent and narrowed to one particular man. She found that she couldn't stand to be away very long. A dragon had fallen in love with a human, as bizarre as that may sound.

"She couldn't stand it any longer. Her dragon heart burned with passion for someone who could never love her. He did not even know she existed. She felt so empty inside. Knowing that she could only watch him from afar, made her sadden more and more each day.

" '*There must be a way,*' she thought to herself, '*If the other dragons knew that I have feelings for a human, they would probably banish me for being insane. But my heart knows different, and I can no*

<Zaylyn ><Quest For The Sword Of Anthrowst ><By Katrina Mandrake-Johnston >   <Ch 13> < 52 >
longer deny it.'

"The dragon had heard tales of an old witch who had strange and powerful magic abilities. She flew to where she was rumored to live and searched for many days by air until she found the small hovel. She landed in front of the entrance. She was afraid, but she did not care. If this was her one chance at the happiness she had imagined each day since she fell in love, it would be well worth it to risk the danger.

"An old woman hobbled out of the dwelling. The witch looked up at the dragon towering over her and called, 'Hey, you up there. What do you want? I don't have much time for visitors. If you have nothing of importance to say, be off with you. You wouldn't be here for any particular reason, would you?'

"At first the dragon was astonished that the witch had spoken to her as if she would a human. She wanted to be human. Then, maybe she could live out the rest of her life with the one she loved. This is what she told the witch.

"A wide, toothless grin spread across the wrinkled face of the witch and she said, 'This is an interesting request. Usually people come to me with small problems. Spoil this man's crops or give someone a headache for three days straight. I won't do anything nasty of course; just things that can be taken as being coincidence, that's all. I don't want anyone hunting me down for who knows what.

" 'But in your case, that would really test my abilities. You truly want this? You do realize that if the transformation works and you become human, that he many not take a liking to you. Just because you love him, doesn't necessarily mean that he will love you.'

" 'I'm willing to take that chance,' the dragon told her.

"So the witch went to work on the task of finding a way to transform the dragon into a human, while the dragon waited patiently for the results.

"Finally, after many days and nights the witch came to the dragon and said, 'I've done it. However, the spell will not last forever. From the moment you dust yourself with this powder, you will become human. You will have five years to remain that way. That's exactly five years, so remember the day and the hour. Hold out your hand, and I shall place the bag of powder into it. It would be a long walk for you to be human now. Good luck.'

"After the witch gave her the powder, she flew gleefully back to her home, clutching the precious bag in her claw. She had to find clothing for when she made her transformation, so that night she swooped down into the village and grabbed a full clothesline.

"When she returned to her cave in the mountains, she waited patiently until early morning. Then the dragon made the transformation, put on some of the clothing, and headed toward the village. There was a small pond along the way, and this is where she viewed her new appearance. Her long hair was a reddish-brown and her eyes were emerald green. Her wings and tail had vanished. She was tiny and frail. Pale smooth skin had replaced her scales. She was human at last.

"As she approached the village, she realized that they would wonder who she was and where she came from. '*I'll say that I had been captured by goblins or Garcs and held captive by them. Then, that I escaped and made my way down here. It will have to do,*' she decided.

"In the village, she told her story and was accepted into their community. As she had hoped, she eventually caught the eye of her beloved. A romance followed and eventually they married.

"Over the years, she almost allowed herself to forget that she was in fact a dragon and that one day she would have to leave her life here and the one she loved. The end of the five years was drawing near. She did not want to tell her beloved that she had to leave. She couldn't bear the heartbreak of telling him why. Even if she could, he would not believe her. She decided it was best just to leave. She would have to go back to watching him from afar.

"The time came to go. She waited for him to leave their home. She had sent him to the market for eggs. She rushed out and started the strenuous climb to the mountaintop where she could make her transformation unseen. Unknown to her, her beloved had seen her leave and, wondering where she was going, had followed her.

"She waited for the change before a steep cliff. It would be perfect for her to take flight from in her dragon form. Her beloved came up the path.

" 'What are you doing? Is something wrong? What's going on?' he asked, not knowing what to think.

" 'Oh no, please,' she begged, not wanting him to see her true form. She wanted him to remember her the way she had been and the wonderful years they had together. Him seeing her as a dragon, would ruin the memories. 'Please, go back home. Hurry! Please, I beg you, do not stay here!'

" 'What are you talking about?' he asked confused, and he came to face her.

"It was too late. The transformation had begun. It was slow at first and then rapidly increased until she was a dragon once more. Her poor beloved, so astonished, backed away from her until he was right near the edge of the cliff.

" 'It's me. This is what I really am, but I am still the one you loved,' she pleaded desperately.

" 'No… How can this be? You're… You're a monster… Keep away from me…' he said staring up at the massive dragon before him.

"She took a step toward him, wanting him to accept her, wanting to comfort him, and afraid of what might happen. Her beloved backed away from her with fear and fell over the edge of the cliff to his death. She could do nothing now but return to her old cave in the mountains."

Lorenta asked, "Can dragons speak the way we do? How could she have told him that it was still her after she had transformed? I can't talk when I'm a spider."

"I suppose I should have mentioned that," Rasindell chuckled, "Dragons speak with their minds to each other and can easily penetrate the mind of a humanoid being with their words if they wish to speak to one. I'm sure this also added to his fear, to hear her voice speaking to him from within his own mind.

"So, anyway," Rasindell continued, "She did not leave her cave for many days, and then it was only out of desperation for food that she did. After some time had passed, she realized that a bizarre miracle had taken place when she had been in human form. She had become pregnant and was pregnant still as a dragon. This became her new joy in life.

"When the time came, she laid her eggs and mothered them with the greatest of care. She had not returned to the dragons after her transformation. They would never accept her young and what she had done.

"The eggs hatched and two different types of offspring emerged. One appeared completely human except for having the wings of a dragon. They grew to become an arrogant race, rarely associating with anyone but themselves. Very few have seen this race, and they are known as Avygons.

"The other type was wingless and also appeared human except for being hairless, having the scales of a dragon, a tail, and claws. Actually, they have normal smooth skin but there are patches of scales scattered randomly along their flesh. I've met a few before. It's hard to describe them really, and their varied eye and skin color are usually more like that of dragons as well. They grew to be a compassionate race and were accepted as a sociable race among the world's population. They are known as Dragonites or human-dragons as they are sometimes called.

"There are a great many wonders in the world and a great variety of people. I've met dwarves, elves, fairies, Garcs, goblins, centaurs, and Dragonites, to name a few. I don't know if my story will help you, child, but a least it made you sit still for once. Okay, run off and play now."

Lorenta hopped off her father's knee and went through the cabin door.

Her dream shifted, and she stepped out into a village. She felt as if she were floating. She moved throughout the village until she came across a crowd situated around a small building.

"We have the foul beast trapped!" one man said triumphantly.

"Burn the evil thing!" someone said angrily.

"It's unnatural! It shouldn't exist! Get rid of it once and for all!" one woman said.

"Who knows what it's capable of? We could all be in danger!" somebody said nervously.

Lorenta could hear a soft sound coming from inside the building. She floated closer. It was singing. The song, which was meant to be a happy cheerful one, held such sadness that it brought tears to her eyes just by listening.

<Zaylyn ><Quest For The Sword Of Anthrowst ><By Katrina Mandrake-Johnston >   <Ch 13> < 54 >

She touched the wall of the building in sympathy and found that she could pass right through it. The villagers continued to rant, as they held their torches and makeshift weapons.

Inside, Lorenta saw a figure sitting on the floor of the small one-room building. The villagers now had set fire to the roof and walls of the place. She could hear cheers and vicious hateful words coming from outside as the building began to burn.

The figure rocked back and forth. It was a woman with a black hooded cloak wrapped about her with the hood drawn up. She had a bundle of something in her arms. Her sad song continued, broken by comforting words whispered to the bundle. Lorenta's heart ached for this poor woman.

She heard a horrible garbled noise coming from the bundle. "Shh, it will be okay. Hush now baby," the woman whispered, but her words were filled with grief.

Smoke began to fill the room. The flames eagerly devoured the wood of the roof and walls. More cheers could be heard. "Burn, you foul thing! Burn!" an old woman cackled.

The heat from the flames was becoming unbearable. Lorenta approached the woman through the smoke-filled room. As she did so, she caught a glimpse of the baby. It was human except for having four bulbous eyes, eight hairy legs, and large curving fangs. Then the woman, her face wet with tears, lifted her head to look up at Lorenta. Lorenta saw her own face beneath the hooded cloak, and then the flames engulfed the three of them…

Lorenta awoke to the darkness of the backpack. Then she drifted back to sleep, realizing that she was no longer truly spider and would never be truly human.

<World of Zaylyn ><Quest For The Sword Of Anthrowst ><By Katrina Mandrake-Johnston ><Ch 14>

CHAPTER 14 = NODWEL'S DREAM
Nodwel also began to dream in his slumber, remembering the events of the day before…

Nodwel stood in the small village of Dexcsin. His companions, tired and hungry, had gone in search of food and lodging for the night. Asdella, Narr, and Dimwar had gone to the general store to buy supplies. Nimdor and Borin had gone to find shelter for the night for them all. There had been no sign or word of the illusive wizard.

Nodwel walked through the village toward the designated meeting place: the well at the center of the village. The forest edged the village to Nodwel's right. He and his companions had made a strenuous journey through those very trees all the way from the road to end up at the village. To his left, past the village crops and animal pens was a grassy plain with high cliffs towering above beyond it. Behind him stretched a road that most likely joined with the one that connected the two towns, Shirkint to the north and Vackiindmire to the south.

Vackiindmire had been their original destination, being the closer of the two, before the wizard had disappeared into the forest. The villagers stared and smiled as he passed them on his way to the well. They obviously didn't get many travelers here, as the village was in an isolated location. One little boy, a human, ran up to Nodwel.

"Are you a dwarf?" he asked, his green eyes wide with excitement.

"That I am," Nodwel replied with a warm smile.

"Can I see your axe?" the boy asked.

His mother came to fetch him. "Come on, honey, don't bother the nice man," she said as she ruffled her son's tawny blonde hair.

"Aw, mother," he protested.

The woman took the boy by the hand and said to Nodwel, "Sorry, I'm sure you're busy," then to her son, "Come on, dear, we have to go home for dinner."

"Oh it's no bother. Good-day ma'am," he said with a nod, and he continued down the dirt street of the village.

When he reached his destination, Nimdor and Borin were there already, obviously successful in their task of finding suitable lodgings. Nimdor waved a welcome to the dwarf. "Any word about our

<Zaylyn ><Quest For The Sword Of Anthrowst ><By Katrina Mandrake-Johnston >   <Ch 14> < 55 >

newly recruited wizard? Has anyone seen him?" Nimdor asked.

"No," Nodwel replied, "What about tonight?"

Borin answered, "We've secured a place for tonight and meals too. Compliments of the village leader and his wife."

"Yes, Bren and Kreasa are their names," Nimdor told him as he leaned on his wooden staff, "The others aren't back yet, but they should be able to get enough supplies to last us until we reach Vackiindmire."

Nimdor was an elf. He was an older man of fifty-five years and his hair, which was as white as bone, hung to his shoulders. The pointed tips of his ears showed through his straight wispy hair, which he always wore loosely about his face. He wore dark green robes, a pair of brown leather boots, and his wooden staff had ornate swirl-like designs carved into it. Nimdor stood five and a half feet, and the features of his face were thin and elongated, especially his nose and chin. His bright blue slanted eyes reflected his patience and wisdom.

Although there were no ranks among this group of friends, the entire group looked to him for leadership. He was adept in Natural magic, but he also had some skill at casting a few Black and White magic spells. Also he was a skilled fighter, and despite his age, Nimdor's thin form was still agile and swift. He could knock a weapon out of a hand or sweep someone off their feet with that staff of his in an instant. Nimdor preferred to use his spells over physical combat though, and probably liked the awe he inspired among his friends every time he cast a spell.

Borin was a thirty-nine year old human and a big man, standing at almost seven feet. His hair was short, black, and had the early signs of greying. His round tanned face had high cheekbones, an average-sized nose, a rounded chin, and had the stubble of a beard starting. Borin's grey eyes always seemed to have an adventurous spark to them, and he always had a large wide smile when he laughed.

For clothing, he wore a light grey cotton shirt with its sleeves ending at his elbows, a brown leather vest with crisscrossing leather strips up the front, and a pair of black pants. His leather backpack was strapped loosely to his back, and at his sides, he had a short sword and a hatchet.

He was more of a woodsman than a fighter. If he hadn't been there to guide them through the forest, they probably would have gotten hopelessly lost. Borin had lost track of the wizard almost immediately, which was strange; it was almost as if he had vanished.

Shortly thereafter, the others came into view. These three humans each were carrying two small sacks of supplies.

Dimwar stood six feet tall and had short auburn hair. His squarish face was clean-shaven and had a prominent jaw line with a cleft chin. He had a small flat nose, a small mouth with full lips, and his eyes were light brown.

He wore a chain mail coat over a black full-sleeved shirt. His black pants had patches of thick leather sewn into them for added protection to his thighs and calves. He found that this added greatly to the ease of movement much more so than the heavier chain mail leggings he used to wear. Dimwar also wore a pair of brown leather gloves and black boots.

Dimwar was an excellent fighter, trained in many different styles and techniques. Oddly, his favorite choice of weapon was a spiked flail, and he could wield it in a most deadly fashion. He also wore a long sharp dagger at his side and a brown leather traveling pouch. His small iron shield, that was plain except for the large spike in its center, was slung over his shoulder by a leather belt.

Asdella was dressed in brown suede, but barely. She wore only a halter-top and a pair of high-cut shorts. Her feet were bare, but she didn't seem to mind the rocky dirt roads of the village. Her skin was tanned, and she had short reddish-blonde hair. She was twenty-six years old and tall for a human, standing near six and a half feet. She had a pretty face, but there was a hardness to her dark brown eyes. There was a light spray of freckles along the bridge of her small nose and cheeks, and under her small mouth was a v-shaped chin.

Asdella was clearly muscular, especially in her arms and legs, but not unattractively so. Her firm stance was always daring and defiant. The only possession she carried was her bare bladed sword. Usually someone else would have to hold on to her food and water, as she refused to carry anything but

<Zaylyn ><Quest For The Sword Of Anthrowst ><By Katrina Mandrake-Johnston >   <Ch 14> < 56 >
her sword.

Narr, a slender twenty-eight year old man, wore a sly smile across his lips, as usual, as he approached the group at the well. He always appeared to be aware of some joke which no one else knew and usually had some snide remark to share. He had a rounded face and stood just over five feet tall. He had eyes of blue and short blonde hair which had a slight wave to it.

Narr always seemed to be annoying at least one member of the group at any given time. Knowing the pride a male dwarf takes in his beard, one of Narr's many torments for Nodwel would be to start bragging about how soft and silky his own hair was. He'd go on saying how the ladies always love a man with fine hair, being able to playfully run their fingers through it. Then he would tease the dwarf about whether or not he would even be able to run a comb through his tangled beard without getting it stuck. Narr would joke about all the different kinds of birds that would just love to use it as the perfect nest, and he would pretend for hours that they were secretly being followed by a whole flock of birds determined to make Nodwel's beard their home. Nodwel knew that all his talk was just in fun to pass the time; otherwise Narr would wake up completely bald and with a black eye or two.

Narr was always joking and talking. It made a long journey seem shorter, which was a blessing, but only to a point as he often got quite annoying. He also had his 'words of wisdom' about how things are or should be and all the silly little things that sound as if they make sense until you think about them.

For clothing, Narr wore a pair of plain dark brown pants and a leather jerkin under which he wore a white long-sleeved shirt. At his waist was a short sword. He wasn't especially skilled with it, but he could manage all right. He was better fighting with his fists after too many drinks were in him. In this, he had a lot of practice, as his mouth and ego tended to get him in trouble quite often.

Nodwel's dream shifted, and he found himself seated at a long, crowded wooden table. The village leader Bren, his wife Kreasa, their two young sons, Nodwel, and his companions all began to eat a hearty meal of roast lamb and vegetables.

Near the end of their meals, a chilling scream was heard through the open window. Everyone fell silent.

Dimwar was the first to react. He stood up quickly from the table, his square jaw continuing to work at a mouthful of meat. His chain mail glistened with the light from the fire. He hesitated a moment. Another strangled cry was heard. Dimwar quickly donned his leather gloves, took up his spiked flail and his small shield, and looked to his companions. He had a worried look in his light brown eyes, and then Dimwar yanked open the door and strode quickly into the night in the direction of the screams.

Asdella got up from the table with a wild excited look in her eyes. She grabbed her sword and standing there in her leathers, which barely covered what needed to be, said to them all, "Someone or something needs to be gutted. I can't let Dimwar have all the fun, now can I? You boys coming?"

"You know I'd follow you anywhere. Who could resist such a view?" Narr said to her with a playful smile.

The others quickly grabbed their gear and headed toward the forested edge of the village. Panic-stricken villagers raced past them trying to herd their family members to safety. When they approached Dimwar's location, they beheld a fearsome sight.

The bodies of at least five villagers were strewn about on the ground. A black six-legged beast was stomping about not knowing what to make of Dimwar. The creature's gaping tooth-filled mouth drooled a slimy liquid.

It took a swipe at Dimwar who blocked the blow with his shield. The force of the blow sent Dimwar staggering back. He swung his flail, striking the beast in a downward motion to the base of its skull. The creature paused a moment, only slightly dazed, and Dimwar got ready for a second attack.

The group was almost at his position, weapons drawn. The beast reared up on its back four legs, and one of its front clawed paws lashed out toward Dimwar. He swung again with his weapon with obvious strength behind it to smash the beast towering over him in the jaw. The flail's blow appeared harmless, and the beast's attack did not falter. The dagger-like claws of the creature slashed clean through Dimwar's neck in one swift and fluid motion.

<Zaylyn ><Quest For The Sword Of Anthrowst ><By Katrina Mandrake-Johnston >   <Ch 14> < 57 >

The group watched in horror as Dimwar's severed head rolled toward them, his body collapsing before the beast. The creature howled in triumph.

Asdella screamed a battle cry and started slashing her sword wildly in the air, and then she leapt forward ready to run at the beast in full fury.

"Asdella! No!" yelled Narr and grabbed her sword arm with both hands, "You'll be killed!"

"Not if I kill it first! Let go of me!" she snarled and wrenched her muscular arm out of his grasp. Borin and Nodwel also grabbed her, and Narr once again attempted to hold her sword arm. "Let go!" she screamed.

Narr, with the help of the other two men, was finally able to pry the sword out of her hand. Nimdor stood nearby ready to cast a spell if the creature attacked them, but the beast seemed to pay them no notice. It gave Dimwar's headless body a swat and pranced idly about. More screams and howling shrieks could be heard elsewhere in the village.

Asdella was dragged away from the scene, as she screamed and struggled. She kicked and even bit her so-called companions. Eventually, they were able to get her back inside the home of the village leader.

Narr bolted the door once they were inside, mainly to keep Asdella from running blindly into battle. Sadly, Nodwel wasn't sure if the insane rage she had shown here was the result from a desire to avenge Dimwar's death or because she had been kept from battle. She seemed to desperately crave battle and confrontation as if it were a necessity of life. Nodwel's dream seemed to pause as he thought about her.

She possessed such a rage, and although she was unpredictable and hard to manage sometimes, she usually proved herself a worthy ally in battle. Asdella tended to go overboard with the number of blows she dealt to her opponent, usually continuing to strike well after the enemy had been slain, completely berserk. Sometimes, she would try to take on an entire group all by herself in a battle that she usually had provoked. She would refuse any and all help from her companions, pushing them away from combat, purely so she could have the thrill of the kill.

She acted as though she were completely invulnerable, but that of course was untrue. Oddly, she seemed to enjoy pain, almost hoping for injuries. Once Nodwel had seen her smearing the blood of the recently slain all over her body in an almost sexual ritual and then go racing into further battle against incredible odds, laughing insanely and grinning maliciously.

Asdella was clearly mad. She was definitely distracting to her opponents as she would enter battle practically unclothed which would especially affect her male enemies, if only for a vital second or two, enabling her to deal a deadly blow. Also, because she made herself so vulnerable without any armour of any kind, she placed doubt in her enemy's mind of exactly what kind of defenses she possessed, perhaps magical abilities or something other that they should be wary of. Of course, she had no protection other than her sword fighting abilities.

Most people are cautious when engaging in a fight, usually feeling out the situation, weighing the odds against them, and so on. Asdella would just lunge in, screaming a battle cry and with that crazy grin of hers. This tended to give her a slight edge, as most were a little shocked by her, not expecting such a ferocious attacker.

Anyone that knew her, quickly realized that one needed to be constantly wary of her and to always be ready with some sort of defense in case out of boredom she decided to give someone a painful jab with her sword. Nodwel had known her for a few years now, and every time he had traveled with her, the time was never an uneventful one, especially if they ended up at a tavern. She loved her ale and was even more violent and nasty when drunk, if such a thing can be imagined.

Nodwel wondered if she even cared that Dimwar had been killed and if she were at all concerned about what was happening outside to the innocent villagers of Dexcsin. What Narr saw in her, Nodwel couldn't tell. Narr was so persistent in his pursuit of her and it was clear that she was definitely not interested in anything other than being comrades in adventure. He would continue to taunt her with his silly little remarks, and she would bicker back. But they seemed to enjoy it, almost a verbal battle between them.

<Zaylyn ><Quest For The Sword Of Anthrowst ><By Katrina Mandrake-Johnston >   <Ch 14> < 58 >

Nodwel often wondered if she considered the individuals in their group as her friends or as just convenient battle partners. One thing he strongly felt though, as crazy as she may be, was that he could trust her, even with his life if the need came.

Nodwel's mind drifted back to the events happening around him.

"They're gone," Borin stated, "Bren and Kreasa with their children."

Nimdor suggested, "They must have fled or more likely are trying to provide some direction in all this insanity being the head figure in this village."

"What are we to do?" asked Nodwel.

Asdella, still being held by Borin and Nodwel, seemed to be calming down. "If I give your sword back, are you going to stick any of us with it?" Narr asked her.

"No," she answered reluctantly and with a glare.

He handed back her sword, and she stood up after the others had released her. "You know, Asdella," Narr smiled at her, "when I dreamt of the day your lips would be pressed up against me, I didn't think it would be so painful." He rubbed at his arm where the red imprint of her teeth could be seen.

"I can't believe Dimwar's gone," Borin exclaimed as he rubbed at his leg where Asdella had given him a nasty kick, "One minute we were all here eating dinner, and the next…"

Narr said, "We have to do something. We can't just stand by while these people are being slaughtered."

"But what the hell is that creature we saw?! I've never seen anything like it before!" Nodwel exclaimed.

No one had an answer.

"I don't really care. Once I kill the lot of them, I'll let you examine one, alright?" Asdella told them, anxious to shed blood.

Borin asked, "Nimdor, what should we do?"

"Well," said the elf, "there are definitely more of these creature about in this place than the one we encountered. We'll need a plan of attack and a plan of defense for these villagers."

"Yeah, hack the things to pieces and tell the villagers to stay out of the way. That's a good enough plan for me," Asdella blurted out.

Finally, out of frustration with her, Borin said sternly, "In case you haven't noticed, Asdella, Dimwar is dead. You know that he was a damn good fighter, probably better than most of us put together. These creatures can't be taken lightly!"

"Do not worry," Nimdor added, "I'm not about to let Dimwar's death be in vain. He was a good man and my friend. I will miss him greatly. We are going to save as many of these people as possible, and then concentrate all our efforts on destroying these terrible beasts, whatever they may be."

Nodwel could see the tension and grief growing in Nimdor's light blue eyes. The elf paused a moment looking down to straighten the cord about his waist on which several small cloth pouches were tied. His action was mainly to hide his emotion from the others. He composed himself quickly and held his staff in front of him, leaning on it slightly with both his hands as he often did.

"Alright then," Nimdor continued, "It didn't seem to be too concerned with us earlier. Therefore, instead of rushing into battle, I say we concentrate on getting these people together and to safety. Having them running around in a panic just makes them easy prey. After that, we can figure out some sort of strategy. Everyone agreed?"

Everyone nodded, including Asdella reluctantly.

Nimdor went on to say, "Okay then, we'll split up. Direct villagers to the center of town. I remember someone saying at dinner that there is a large building used during festivals that is situated around there. It shouldn't be very hard to find. I'll be there. Try to get a rough count on how many of these beasts we're dealing with and try to return as quickly as possible to help build up some sort of resistance against these creatures. I'll use spells to protect and defend in the meantime. I'm not sure how long I'll be able to keep the beasts at bay and unaware of our activities, but I'll do my best. I'm not expecting the villagers to be much help in battle, but we won't know until we get everyone together and

<Zaylyn ><Quest For The Sword Of Anthrowst ><By Katrina Mandrake-Johnston >   <Ch 14> < 59 >

focused. These people are frightened and need direction. If we don't provide all the help we can, they'll be doomed. Alright, let's go. Remember, do not engage in battle if you can help it. We'll have a better chance if we attack together."

Narr added, "Don't worry, I'm not going to go near those things. Look what one of them did to Dimwar and in a single slash from its claws. I don't even want to think of what they could do to us with one of their bites."

Nimdor said to them, "Let's just focus on the plan, alright, for all our sakes. We can't just abandon these people. We at least have some battle experience." He hesitated mournfully a moment before adding, "Besides, it's what Dimwar would have wanted."

Everyone nodded their agreement.

<World of Zaylyn ><Quest For The Sword Of Anthrowst ><By Katrina Mandrake-Johnston ><Ch 15>

CHAPTER 15 = NODWEL'S DREAM: NIMDOR'S PLAN

The dream shifted as he continued to relive the events of the night before. Nodwel found himself standing on a village street with his battle-axe ready. People were screaming and scattering about, dragging their loved ones to what they hoped was safety. He heard children crying and a dog was barking somewhere in the distance.

"Everyone!" Nodwel bellowed, "To the center of the village! We'll try to protect you!"

"Where's my son!" one woman screamed.

Nodwel tried to calm her as best as he could, but she was hysterical. She would draw one of the beast's attention very quickly. As much as he wanted to help the woman, he couldn't afford to start a search for her lost child.

"Find him and get to the center of the village, otherwise we can't help you," he finally told her. He was unsure if what he told her even registered. He didn't have the time to deal with her; it meant more lives would be lost because of it.

When Nodwel finally headed there himself, he had several villagers following him. Several men of the village were determined to fight; anything to protect their families. Some of the women carried small children crying in their arms. Many of the frightened people, unable to locate their missing family members, hoped to find them at the center of the village alive and well. It was heartbreaking, but Nodwel knew he had to keep these people focused. He had to be firm and strong. These people saw him as their only hope right now. Everyone was looking to him for their own strength and for direction.

His dream soon brought him to stand outside the building Nimdor had chosen near the center of Dexcsin. It was a little way north of the village well and its doors faced in the direction of the forest. It was a large community hall that they would use during their festivals and other events. There was a large fire pit here, and as it was a wide spacious area, with the moon bright overhead, visibility was fairly good here. The group had led as many of the villagers they could find still alive into the building.

As the group was directing the last of the villagers into the building, one of the foul creatures saw through Nimdor's deceptions and discovered them. It ran toward them on four legs, its head held high with its two front clawed limbs ready to strike. Nodwel held his axe, and Borin had both hatchet and sword in his hands. Narr, holding his short sword, managed to close the double doors after the last villager had entered and then turned to face the creature along with his companions.

Nimdor and Asdella were closest to the beast, being farthest from the building. It was the elf that the creature decided to attack. It leapt straight for him. He was ready for it, and so was Asdella.

Nimdor cast a ball of fire directly into the face of the creature that was bearing down on him. It stopped, shook its head slightly, and as its solid black eyes became fixated on him once more, it let out a growl from deep within its throat. Asdella's sword struck the beast's side repetitively, as she yelled and screamed in an insane fury. It simply swatted her aside, and then pounced on Nimdor, knocking him down.

Everything happened so fast that Nodwel, Borin, and Narr had no time to react, not that it would have made a difference. Asdella rolled from the ground into a crouch, then ran at the beast and slashed at it again and again, hacking bits of flesh from its torso. Once again seeming to ignore the onslaught

<Zaylyn ><Quest For The Sword Of Anthrowst ><By Katrina Mandrake-Johnston >   <Ch 15> < 60 >

from Asdella, the creature stomped its front leg hard into Nimdor's chest. Bones cracked. The malicious creature howled triumphantly at this and leapt away, escaping down a village street. Asdella, in her unstable anger, started to venture after the beast until she heard Nimdor urgently utter a word.

"No," he managed to say to her.

Asdella stopped, staring off in the direction the beast had gone, and then came to his side, as did everyone else in the group.

"I'm dying friends," he coughed. It was clear that each gasping breath he managed caused him great pain. Foamy blood sputtered from his lips. "Someone... go for... help... Save... these..." he uttered before he died.

"Damn it! No!" Borin yelled with hatred for the horrid creatures.

Narr said frantically, "We're all going to die! First Dimwar, now Nimdor. These things are picking us off one by one! Who's going to be next?! They were our best chance against these things, and they took them both out like they were nothing! I mean, I'm all for trying to help these people, but I say we get the hell out of here now! To hell with the plan! We can't beat whatever these creatures are! Let's run and take as many villagers as we can with us."

"We can't now," Borin said to him, "They'll never make it. You know that! Our best bet is to keep these people together and try to protect them as best we can. Of course, it will be only a matter of time before they tear that building apart, and if that happens, again, we'll try our best to protect them. So like Nimdor said, someone has to go for help. We can't do this on our own."

Nodwel suggested, "We should get inside before another creature comes this way. We don't want to draw too much attention to this place."

"What about Nimdor? Are we just going to leave him here? Shouldn't we bring him inside?" Narr asked.

"We can't. We're trying to give these people hope, remember?" Borin said, his voice cracking with emotion.

At the sound of another howl, Nodwel said, "I really think we should get inside and quickly."

"Let them come! I'm ready," Asdella said defiantly.

"We're not losing you too. Come on!" Nodwel demanded.

"Please," Narr pleaded, "don't do this."

"Alright, fine. I'm coming," she told them.

"Rest well, my friend," Borin said with tears in his eyes.

They all entered the building leaving Nimdor's body where it lay as they had done with Dimwar's.

"Everyone, calm down, please," Borin told the frightened group of villagers, "Try to stay quiet, everyone. We don't want to draw attention here. We are sending someone for help."

Nodwel looked at all the pale faces staring helplessly at them.

"We're all going to die!" one man wailed.

"My son, why isn't he here?! I have to find him! He's still out there somewhere! Let me out! Let me out..." one woman cried as others held her back and tried to calm her, trying to give her hope.

One man, cradling a woman's head in his arms, called out, "My wife, please someone help her! She's losing a lot of blood! Someone, anyone, help her! Please! I'm losing her!"

Children were sobbing along with several of the women and men. Others were just staring blankly in front of them, grief-stricken and paralyzed with fear and the shock of what was happening.

"Where's the elf?! The man with the white hair, the green robes, and staff. Where is he?!" one woman asked, "He's dead, isn't he? He must be dead! Who's going to save us now?!"

Nodwel asked, "Who's going? How far is the nearest town?"

"I'm staying to fight and to kill these horrible things," Asdella said through clenched teeth.

"No," Borin said, "It has to be fair." He took a small piece of string from his backpack and cut it into different sized pieces using the blade of his sword. "Okay, whoever picks the smallest piece goes for reinforcements."

Borin held the pieces up for everyone, and they all chose until he was left with the last. Nodwel had the shorter piece of string.

"It's decided. Good luck old friend," Narr said to him with a pat to the dwarf's shoulder.

"Good luck to all of you," Nodwel told them, "I'll see you real soon, and we'll beat these things."

Nodwel left them and made his way through the village to the beginnings of the road. Just when he thought he would be able to make his escape, Nodwel felt a sharp pain in his leg and stumbled forward. He recovered quickly, however, and turned with his axe ready to strike. The front claw of the beast before him dripped blood… Nodwel's blood.

Its black eyes stared down at him as if daring the dwarf to attack. Nodwel swung his axe and it imbedded itself into the beast's neck, biting into the creature's shiny black flesh. The beast howled in rage. The dwarf swung again. He would not let it beat him. He swung again and again, with as much force as he could muster.

Finally the creature decided to wander off in search of easier prey. Nodwel headed down the road away from Dexcsin, trying to ignore the pain his wound was giving him. He would not let them down. He would return before it was too late… Nodwel felt himself waking up.

CHAPTER 16 = THE ROAD TO DEXCSIN

Nodwel awoke anxious to return as quickly as possible to the village. At dawn, as soon as there was enough light to see by, they headed once again in the direction of Dexcsin. Nodwel led the way, walking in front of the group at a swift and steady pace. Candra and Vordin walked slightly behind him, with Weena lagging behind beside Dendrox.

"So, if time allows, do you think you might be able to show me how to use a dagger?" Weena asked hopefully.

Dendrox smiled at her and nervously brushed his hair back behind his ear. "Yeah, sure. I guess."

"That would be great," she said with enthusiasm.

Dendrox thought a moment to himself and then asked, "Why do you want to learn how to use a plain ordinary dagger when you know how to use magic? Isn't that far greater than any physical weapon?"

"Well yes, sometimes," Weena said and then after hesitating for a moment added, "I just feel as if I'm helpless. My magic isn't as reliable as I would like it to be. Besides, I don't have any offensive spells, and all I have is one defensive; a Shield spell. I guess I'm still bothered by the thought of that man with the medallion. If things went differently and he had attacked me, my magic would have been completely useless to me. Candra can face danger, deal with it, and then not give it a second thought. At least that's how it seems. I don't have that kind of courage. If I knew how to use a weapon, at least I wouldn't feel so insecure," she explained.

Candra smiled to herself at Weena's compliment, as she was listening to Weena's conversation with Dendrox.

Weena's bright blue eyes sparkled up at him, as Dendrox said, "Oh, I see. Well I guess I could teach you a few things. It will take a lot of work and a lot of practice, and even a greater amount of patience. These things don't come easy."

"Don't worry, anyone who has ever been able to learn a spell knows well about patience and the frustration of trying to learn something new. Most give up during the first three days and nights of continuous study, usually giving into sleep. The fourth and fifth days are the worst; trying to concentrate is almost impossible. Oh and there's the really creepy fact that you start to see things out of the corner of your eye. Dark shapes that you can never really get a good look at, but can feel lurking about. It gives me shivers just to think about it. People rarely speak of such things, but I'm sure it's been the reason why a few people I know have quit learning spells all together. They would rather not be aware of mystical creatures which people rarely glimpse, and I know exactly how they feel. You're usually alone when it happens and whether you sense good or evil from whatever being you happen to glimpse, it's very frightening either way. People just say that your mind starts to drift off into dream now and then when you're awake because of the incredible lack of sleep, but I think it's something

<Zaylyn ><Quest For The Sword Of Anthrowst ><By Katrina Mandrake-Johnston >   <Ch 16> < 62 >

more. It could be that part of learning magic is learning to alter your perception of things and to be aware that within and around us is magic that just needs to be manipulated in order to use it. Whatever these beings are, they are connected to it all on some greater level somehow and therefore can only be seen when the perception of things is altered. Well, at least that's what I suspect to be true. Or, the incredible lack of sleep could just be making people go crazy, who knows? If I start to think about how a spell is actually working itself, it just doesn't happen. I guess it would be similar to trying to consciously control your heartbeat. You would have to be concentrating so carefully and the beats would surely end up irregular. Casting a spell is like that. If you try to understand what is happening and concentrate on casting the spell, it just doesn't work right and most often not at all. You just have to relax, clear your mind and sort of let the spell unconsciously work itself. Anyway, what was it that I was talking about?" Her face had grown flushed and hot with embarrassment. "Um, sorry, yes, I'm prepared to work at learning to handle a dagger and would appreciate whatever you can teach me," she said sheepishly, "Sorry, I tend to ramble when I'm nervous." *"Oh yeah, admit that he makes me nervous. That will make a good impression,"* her mind told her sarcastically, *"What's the matter with you? Bla, bla, bla! You're so scared of not having anything to say that you end up talking everyone's ear off."* Weena hesitated before adding, "You know, with all this impending doom and all, it doesn't really put my mind at ease."

Dendrox commented, "I know what you mean. I sure wasn't expecting all this when we first decided to head out to Vackiindmire."

"Why did you travel out this way?" she asked.

He answered with a sly smile, "Let's just say it was a professional necessity. The place we were in started to become less and less tolerant of us and our trade. We had to leave rather quickly."

Candra chuckled to herself at this.

"Oh," Weena said quietly, again being reminded that he and Candra were criminals. She found that this was something that kept slipping her mind.

Vordin was fascinated with the determination Nodwel had shown. *"He clearly has a good heart and is willing to put his own life at risk for another. Well, I guess we all are,"* Vordin thought to himself as he walked with his new companions. Vordin admired the large battle-axe displayed on Nodwel's back once again and tried to imagine the dwarf swinging it madly with his thick and muscular arms at a fierce Killnarin. *"The creature would slash toward his broad chest covered by his leather jerkin and Nodwel would skillfully maneuver out of the way and bury the double-bladed axe deep into the evil beast,"* thought Vordin trying to visualize it in his mind.

Vordin let his gaze fall onto Candra: her creamy white skin, her black hair falling gently about her face, her sparkling emerald green eyes... He found her to be a very beautiful woman. He thought to himself, *"She's like a rose. Beautiful, but if you get too close you'll probably get pricked by the thorns."* Candra still had Weena's yellow sash tied around her arm as a bandage for her wound. Vordin counted eight arrows in her quiver which was strapped tightly to her back. The leather strap of the quiver lay on an angle across her chest between her small breasts. The points of her elfin ears could be seen through her hair. She appeared to Vordin, from what he had seen, as being a cold and heartless person, but he hoped this was not entirely so. He would have to rely on her and the others to protect him when they encountered danger.

Candra looked down at him from the corner of her eye, and Vordin realized he had been staring at her for quite some time now. Annoyed by this, Candra asked abruptly, "Did you want something?"

Vordin, not wanting to admit that he was just admiring her beauty, quickly thought of an excuse and said, "Oh, I was just wondering how your arm is doing. That is where you were wounded by the creature, isn't it?"

"It's fine," she said sharply and returned her gaze to the road ahead.

Vordin, feeling rejected, slowed his pace slightly until he was walking beside Weena and Dendrox.

Weena's clothing fell loosely around her body, as her sash was being used by Candra. Her leather sandals patted against the dirt road and the small cloth pouch at her waist swayed back and forth as she

<Zaylyn ><Quest For The Sword Of Anthrowst ><By Katrina Mandrake-Johnston >   <Ch 16> < 63 >

walked. In her left hand, at her side, she carried her lantern.

Noticing that Vordin was glancing at her more frequently as they walked, she felt the need to say something to break the uneasiness this was creating. "Hello," she said, as she tucked a loose piece of her hair behind her ear.

"Hello," Vordin replied looking into her blue eyes and then said attempting to make conversation, "So, I heard you say you were thinking of learning to use a weapon?"

"I thought it might be a good idea," Weena commented.

"You're lucky, I guess. I don't know how to use magic or a weapon," he told her, and in doing so, felt extremely awkward and foolish.

"That's okay," Dendrox told him, "We were going to use you as bait anyway. Also, if we have to run, you'll slow the creatures up." Dendrox chuckled to himself, as a confused and panicked look crossed Vordin's face. "Relax, I'm kidding," he added, but then thought, "*That's exactly what we might have to end up doing to you. Not that I would want to, but if you get in the way and endanger the rest of us, getting rid of you might be the best thing to do. Candra would leave you here by the road, tell you where to find a town or village, and just walk away. Even if you proved to be of some use to us, she still would rather get rid of you. She's a loner who can't stand to be truly alone. I guess that's my role, to be a loner with her. I'm surprised she hasn't said anything much to insult Weena. Usually, she's fiercely aggressive toward women I take an interest in.*"

Vordin decided to walk to the front of the group and converse with Nodwel, since he was feeling insecure and hoped that the dwarf would be more receptive of him. "How much farther is it?" Vordin asked him.

"We should be there fairly soon I hope," Nodwel replied.

Dendrox was showing Weena how to hold a dagger properly as they walked, and Candra began to feel slightly rejected. "*I know I'm not jealous. It's only Dendrox. He's like a brother to me. He's my best friend. I like Weena. She's a good person. Still, I feel threatened by her... Dendrox would never trade in our friendship for her, right? Besides, she doesn't seem selfish enough to try to ruin such a strong friendship. Weena's already getting all of his attention as it is. He's hardly said a word to me. Plus, he hasn't shown any interest in attempting to catch up to me and include me in their conversation. He would rather walk behind me, and with her. I'm not going to lose him. I'm not going to be cast aside. I know that I'm not perfect, but that's why we're inseparable. We're thieves. We thrive on adventure and danger. We rely on our skill and cunning to survive,*" Candra thought to herself and then slowed her pace until she was beside Dendrox.

"Hi Candra," Weena said grinning.

Candra looked at her with an expressionless face and said calmly, "Hello."

To Dendrox she said cheerfully and in a joking manner, "So, you two are really getting along well. Maybe some day you'll get a little cottage, have a couple kids, maybe do a little farming... Of course I'll visit from time to time as Auntie Candra when I pass by in my travels. I'll bring by some of the loot, maybe part with a couple of jeweled trinkets for the kids and a couple adventure stories." Candra knew this would shock him back to his former self.

Dendrox stopped smiling and his face grew somber. Candra knew he was deep in thought and this pleased her. She told them, "Well, I'll leave you two alone. I'm going to walk ahead and ask Nodwel how much farther the village is." Candra walked quickly to meet Nodwel and Vordin. "How much father is it?" she asked without any real interest in the answer.

Nodwel replied, "We're almost there now."

"Thank-you," she said and resumed her position just ahead of Dendrox and Weena so she could hear what they were saying.

"So, Dendrox, am I holding the dagger right?" Weena asked him.

"Yeah," he said without even a glance toward her hand and the dagger.

"Oh," Weena said with such a sadness and disappointment that Candra felt guilt sneaking up on her.

"*Why did I do that?*" Candra asked herself, "*I put distance between Dendrox and Weena. I hurt*

<Zaylyn ><Quest For The Sword Of Anthrowst ><By Katrina Mandrake-Johnston >   <Ch 16> < 64 >

them both, destroying the happiness they were feeling by spending time together. I'm the one that's selfish. I'm the one who has to have all the attention I can get from him. That's the reason why I feel threatened by her, and it's a terrible one. I like her, and I didn't want to hurt her or Dendrox. I did though, and I can't take back my words. If they start a relationship, it wouldn't really matter. I would be included as a friend to both of them. Also, if she decides to join up with us, the addition of magic to our adventures would be a great asset and a profitable one as well. As long as she learns to be inconspicuous, that is. What he'll do now is just play her for a fool and leave her behind with a broken heart. I couldn't allow him to do that to her, especially now that I know he would be disregarding his feelings about her to do so. He doesn't act like this toward someone where his interest in them is purely physical. I have only been able to have unfeeling and short relationships when I take the time to begin one, but if Dendrox is able to have something more than that and be happy, I'm not going to hold him back."

"So you said that your village was annihilated by these same creatures?" Nodwel asked Vordin.

"Yes," he answered, "Killnarin are what they're called, but that's all I really know about them."

"So the things have a name… What was it again?" inquired Nodwel.

"Killnarin," Vordin answered disheartened, "An evil wizard named Dranngore is supposed to control them and has to be defeated by the Sword of Anthrowst."

"Really? How did you come to know something like this?" Nodwel asked amazed.

"A fairy queen, no bigger than a few inches tall, told me this after I had escaped my village, and also I was told this by The Black Shadow," he answered.

"I wouldn't joke about such things," Nodwel said seriously.

"No, it's all true! I swear!" he told the dwarf.

"Alright, calm down, lad. I believe you," Nodwel assured him.

There was an awkward silence between Vordin and the older dwarf for a few moments, and then Nodwel questioned, "What was the name of your village?"

Vordin was glad that the dwarf was taking an interest in him and not finding him an annoyance and inconvenience as he imagined the rest of the group did. "Nilnont," Vordin replied.

"And that was the village on the other side of the mountain range?" the dwarf asked with a hint of a smile which seemed to welcome Vordin into further conversation.

"Yes. You're the first person to ask the name of my village or anything about it since it happened. I'm the only one left. No one else survived," said Vordin.

"Really?" exclaimed Nodwel with surprise.

"Do any of the others even care about what happened to Nilnont? They know what happened there," Vordin thought feeling hurt, *"Shouldn't they be more sympathetic toward me? I mean, I've lost everything. Everyone is dead. Maybe they just don't know what to say. That must be it. What can anyone possibly say anyway? Any words will just be hollow. Words cannot take the pain I feel away. Words can not undo what has happened."*

"What was your village like, and the people that lived there, what were they like?" Nodwel asked combing his stubby fingers through his beard.

"Well, the village had a few fields of crops. There was corn… several other types of vegetables and grain. Umm, there were several animals: sheep, horses, pigs, and others that I can't think of right now. Quite a few people had cats or songbirds as pets. It was a small village. A lot of people made pottery. There wasn't really anything special about my village or the people in it… Ah… My father… he worked as a butcher and my mother worked at the general store there," Vordin paused with emotion but continued after a few moments, "I didn't have many friends… My best friend growing up was an old hermit who lived in the forest near Nilnont… During the many years after he died, I spent most of my time with my parents and doing puzzles and other little projects like that by myself."

"Interesting… You know, you should be proud of where you come from. Even more so now, since you are the only person remaining to keep those memories alive," Nodwel said to him, "Exactly how did you survive such a brutal onslaught?"

Vordin ignored Nodwel's most recent question, as he had been pondering a disturbing thought.

<Zaylyn ><Quest For The Sword Of Anthrowst ><By Katrina Mandrake-Johnston >   <Ch 16> < 65 >

Vordin abruptly asked, "How exactly did you and your companions arrive at Dexcsin? This is the only road leading to it that I saw, and Vackiindmire would have been a lot closer than this small village. Why would your group travel all the way down to this remote village in the opposite direction of your destination? You were headed to Vackiindmire, weren't you? Weena was the one that first suggested we follow you. Candra, when did you meet her?"

Candra answered, her suspicions growing as well, "Along the road just after we defeated the Killnarin."

Vordin continued, his fear growing, "What if I'm caught in some elaborate lure to dispose of the two thieves that had become a threat to them and me as well being the one that escaped them at Nilnont. Maybe I'm just being paranoid, but I have a good reason to be, and it's nothing personal about you or Weena. If it's true, I shouldn't really be telling you this…" Vordin added slowly backing away from the group.

Candra pulled an arrow from her quiver, and Dendrox seeing her actions, took a dagger from his belt.

"What is it?" Weena asked Dendrox in a frightened voice.

"Be quiet," he said sharply. "Candra, what's going on?"

Candra explained, "Weena and Nodwel might be some of the creatures in disguise leading us into an ambush. Revenge against us and taking care of unfinished business with Vordin, if you know what I mean. Then again, we can't even be sure about him either. How likely is it that they would let someone escape? Nodwel, I could see maybe, but not Vordin. He's unarmed and unskilled; it's too suspicious. Weena came out of nowhere, just when it was convenient for us. Helping me to survive could have been just to gain our trust. Who was that man we buried? It was Weena that had insisted on it. Why was she so eager to trust Vordin? I don't like this one bit. I said we should go straight to Vackiindmire, but she said to follow Nodwel. We are heading to a small village, that would be out of the way and pointless for any group of travelers to go to, and especially when a larger town is closer. There's one road that leads to Dexcsin, right? Why would Nodwel and his traveling companions go there? What do you think, Dendrox? If you are in fact Dendrox."

Everyone was now standing in the middle of the road staring at each other in confusion, and there were also several suspicious and mistrusting glances exchanged. Candra and Dendrox still had their weapons ready. There was a long silence filled with suspicion throughout the group. Vordin wished that he had kept his mouth shut and didn't have such a vivid imagination. He had created chaos.

"This isn't going to get us anywhere," Nodwel exclaimed, "What man are you talking about that you had to bury?"

"Don't change the subject. Who are you?" Candra demanded. She drew the arrow back in her bow and pointed her deadly weapon directly at him a few feet from his face.

"You don't trust anyone, do you?" Nodwel chuckled nervously as he backed slowly away from the arrow, his hands held up to show he didn't want a fight.

Candra replied calmly, "I trust Dendrox." She then hesitated a moment and added, "When I know for sure that it really is him. Damn creatures, I can't trust my own senses or instincts!"

Weena was amazed at how cold Candra could abruptly become, even toward Dendrox which had shocked her the most.

Nodwel explained, "We originally were traveling along the same road leading into Dee'ellkka Valley, probably some time before any of you did. One person in our group, who had just recently joined us, went into the woods when we had made camp. In the morning, when he still hadn't returned, we started to search for him. Someone said that he had heard him muttering something about a pair of scissors. The guy must have been completely insane."

"Go on," Dendrox said, at hearing something about a pair of scissors, and then thought to himself, "*Maybe we're not free of those cursed things. I wish I could remember what I had done with them. Why can't I remember?*"

Nodwel continued, "We looked for him. We couldn't find him and eventually came across the village of Dexcsin, where we all had planned to stay for the night, until the village was attacked by

<Zaylyn ><Quest For The Sword Of Anthrowst ><By Katrina Mandrake-Johnston >   <Ch 16> < 66 >
these creatures. The rest I've already told you."

"We found your friend. He was killed by one of those creatures after stealing my pouch," Dendrox told him.

"I'd hardly call him a friend; we just met him. He just happened to be traveling the same road with us," Nodwel added.

"Oh, how could I have forgotten? I had hidden them in the lining of my pouch! That must be why he had gone for it!" Dendrox exclaimed to himself, *"Things make better sense now. I'll have to check later. Maybe I can find out what's so special about them. It must be something magical."*

"What about you, Weena?" Candra said pointing her arrow toward her now. Weena's magic ability made Candra nervous, not knowing what to expect from her.

Weena protested, clearly afraid of what Candra might do, "Everything I've told you has been true! I've been completely honest with all of you!"

"And you?" she said to Vordin, "Your story was odd to begin with. You're the one that instigated all this paranoia."

"I haven't lied to any of you," he protested.

"How did you escape the creatures?" Nodwel asked once again.

"I hid inside a hollow tree," he told them.

"Why?" Weena asked curiously.

"Rasindell told me to. Well, he really just had just told me a similar story when I was little. Rasindell was an old hermit I used to visit," he explained.

"Rasindell?" Nodwel said pondering the name, "Rasindell… Why does that name sound so familiar?"

"Okay," Candra said putting the arrow back into the quiver and the bow over her shoulder, "This is ridiculous. I'm becoming so paranoid, I can't bring myself to trust my own judgment. I'm even starting to doubt Dendrox's identity again. And I just can't grasp all these crazy illogical happenings with all these weird magic spells and creatures and everything. I'm just going to assume everyone is who they appear to be. And if any of you aren't, I'll just have to kill you. Deal?"

"Yeah," Dendrox chuckled, replacing the dagger back onto his belt.

The group all started toward the village again. After some time had past, Candra was pleased to notice that Weena and Dendrox had resumed their flirtatious manner toward each other once more.

<World of Zaylyn ><Quest For The Sword Of Anthrowst ><By Katrina Mandrake-Johnston ><Ch 17>

CHAPTER 17 = DEXCSIN

Nodwel described his companions to the group, so they could recognize them if they found them, along with stories about them just to pass the time. More and more he feared for them as they neared the village. He found that the more he worried, the more he talked. The others were thankful for it, as it kept their minds from imagining what they would find when they reached Dexcsin.

When they finally entered the village, they immediately noticed the eerie and unnatural silence. As they viewed the destruction and carnage before them, Vordin's mind raced with images of his own village's demise. He found that he had started to form an outer shell toward all the blood, strewn entrails, and the stench of death. It was not that he didn't feel for these people, he just wasn't letting his emotions cloud his mind. He told himself that there was plenty of time to feel for these people later when he wasn't in danger. Perhaps it was the fear that there might still be Killnarin here that kept his emotions at bay and his body alert. In this, he felt he could identify with Candra.

"Candra's feelings must be buried so deeply that no one can seem to find them. I wonder how she came to be like that? Perhaps total cold-heartedness just comes with being a thief. I really shouldn't be so hard on her. She isn't such a bad person. I'm actually quite fascinated with her," Vordin thought. Vordin couldn't fool himself any longer and a cold lump began to form in his throat, as he viewed his surroundings. He had feelings of panic and anguish. *"We shouldn't be here. We're in danger. Not again! I can't be here! I can't see this again!"*

The whole group was just standing there silent and astonished. None of them, except for Vordin,

<Zaylyn ><Quest For The Sword Of Anthrowst ><By Katrina Mandrake-Johnston >   <Ch 17> < 67 >

could have expected the extent of the slaughter before them.

"Oh…" was all Weena could gasp as she witnessed the horrors that had taken place here.

"Hey Candra, and I thought just one dead man was bad, and he was intact," Dendrox said, his face extremely pale as he tried to hold back his nausea.

"Damn it!" Nodwel exclaimed, a look of anguish and helplessness on his broad face. A tear escaped his eye and ran down the side of his bulbous nose and into his reddish-brown beard.

Candra's stomach wanted to violently empty its contents, but she was able to calm the nausea by searching the debris with her eyes for something else to focus on.

Nodwel took charge of the situation finally, and said to them, "Help me search for survivors. It's almost dark. Salvage anything you can find that might be of use to us should the beasts return. We'll have to find some sort of shelter. The creatures may very well decide to return, and I don't think we should assume otherwise."

"If we split up, we'll cover more ground," said Candra.

"I don't want to go alone," Weena commented weakly. She looked to Dendrox with anticipation.

"I'll go with Candra," Dendrox decided.

Candra could see the effect that this decision had on Weena. Candra knew that it was she, not Weena, he would want to be with during this. Candra was kind of an emotional crutch for him. She thought to herself, "*I would never be able to explain that to Weena without making him seem weak. He has an exceptionally strong character, stronger than most people, just not in this aspect. Everyone needs someone to turn to in some way or another when they're faced with a weak point. Even I have times like that. I thought for a long time that I was turning into myself in times of need. Then I realized that I was actually turning to my dead father and finding solace in knowing that his spirit was with me. Then I realized that Dendrox had become very important to me in that aspect as well. I would be devastated beyond capability if anything happened to him.*"

"I'll go alone," Nodwel told them, "I'll try to discover if any of my companions are still alive. I'll know the places they're most likely to be."

"I'll go with Weena," Vordin offered.

"What if something happens? What if we're attacked?" Weena asked filled with worry.

"You have your magic capabilities," the dwarf stated. Nodwel sighed to himself and added, "Use extreme caution. You'll probably find that we won't be far off. It's a small village, so if you two get into trouble, just run," Nodwel instructed Weena and Vordin who both wore expressions of helplessness and despair. He hated to have to say that to them, but he couldn't afford to coddle them. He didn't know how much time they had until another attack, and he feared there would be, as the beasts had obviously attacked two nights in a row so far. He assumed their attack would be at nightfall, as was the first invasion. Also, he didn't want to argue with the thieves trying to get one of them to go with Weena and Vordin, as that would waste more of their precious time to find any survivors and secure themselves for the night. Nodwel said to them all, "There's a well at the center of the village. We'll meet there?"

Everyone agreed. Nodwel left them quickly and headed toward the center of the village. Candra and Dendrox decided to head left to search the south end of the village. Weena and Vordin went right and toward the forested edge of the village to the north.

Weena had made the suggestion that it might be safer for them in that direction. She decided that if they were in danger, they might be able to climb a tree and call for help or signal the others somehow. Weena felt that there was safety among the trees; she felt protected there. She could hide, being blanketed by the foliage. She felt that it was a far wiser decision than being vulnerable out in the open. Vordin had been unsure about this, but went along with her decision.

<World of Zaylyn ><Quest For The Sword Of Anthrowst ><By Katrina Mandrake-Johnston ><Ch 18>

CHAPTER 18 = YARIN

Nodwel rushed to the building where he hoped to find the surviving members of his party and the remaining villagers. Nimdor's plan had failed. The walls had been broken through. He was slightly relieved to see that his companions were not among the dead that he could see, and that the number of

<Zaylyn ><Quest For The Sword Of Anthrowst ><By Katrina Mandrake-Johnston >   <Ch 18> < 68 >
villagers slain wasn't as large as he had dreaded. There was still hope.

"*They must have escaped and hopefully with some of the villagers,*" thought Nodwel, and he tried to think of where they may have fled to. He would look for the general store.

"I'm sorry, my friend," he whispered to the wind as he passed the place where Nimdor had fallen and still lay. "*I should have gotten here sooner... I'm not sure if the help I brought will be of any use. I've probably led them here to meet their doom as well. I don't know what to do, old friend. Where is the hope now? Is there even anyone still alive here? I've failed. Everyone was relying on me, and I've failed them. What was Borin thinking in having a fair pick? Damn him and his bits of string. Send the dwarf, the one with the shortest legs? Now there's a great idea,*" he said to himself sarcastically, "*Oh yeah, he'll be able to cover the distance in no time. Damn it, I could have done a hell of a lot better if I had stayed here. I should have insisted. Narr should have gone. He's the weakest fighter out of all of us and could have traveled a lot faster than my stubby legs could have taken me.*" Then he said to Nimdor, "And you'd have something wise to say to me now, wouldn't you?" Nodwel continued, "*If Narr had gone, the beast that attacked me would have attacked him. I survived, where Narr most likely wouldn't have. Then there would be no help for these people. Well, here's the help, as meager as it is, and there's no one left to save that I can see. The village of Dexcsin is now a graveyard and nothing more. The poor lad, Vordin, he shouldn't have to be seeing this, not after what happened to his own home.*"

Nodwel could still see in his mind the frightened faces of the people that had been huddled together in the hall. All of them had looked to them for help and for some sliver of hope. It was he they were relying on. He was their one chance. He was the one that had been sent. "*Don't worry,*" he imagined them saying, "*We just have to hold on a little longer. Nodwel is coming with help. We'll be saved. We just have to hold on.*" The dwarf wept heavily. He recognized some of the faces within the remains of the building, now cold and lifeless. The worst was seeing the children. Nodwel couldn't remain any longer.

"Nimdor, if there is anyone still alive here, I will save them. That includes the people I've brought here as well. You have my word. I won't let you down. And when all this is over, I shall return and lay your body to rest."

He started walking in the direction of the general store where he hoped he would find some clue as to what happened and where the survivors, if any, might be. His mind continued, as he tried to ignore all the blood and the occasional corpse along his path, "*And don't worry, Nimdor, it will be a funeral as is custom with your elfin kind. Your body burned with that of trees, so the two become as one in the flames, and the ash returns to nature on the wind to watch over it, or something like that. I know it's supposed to be all lengthy and poetic and all that, but I'll do the best I can. For us dwarves, it's mostly centered around the earth rather than trees. You know, from the earth, nourished by the earth, for most housed in the earth, and in the end, back to the earth with burial in it. It's basically the same thing if you think about it, all with having to do with nature, having respect for it, and knowing that everyone is connected to it. And yet there are always arguments started where one race figures that another should abandon their ways and customs and adopt the ways and beliefs of the other. It's silly, really. Nature is made up of many different elements. Why should it be any different when it comes to its people? As for Dimwar, I'm not sure what to do for him. Humans have so many different customs; they really don't have one they call their own. Some bury their dead as the dwarves do, or follow the ways of the elves with fire and scattering of the ashes, or some even send their dead out to sea. I'm sure that there are plenty of customs and beliefs that I have yet to hear of as well. As for your daughter, Nimdor, I don't know how I'm going to bear telling her what has happened. Dimwar had a sister. He told me once the name of the town where she lived, but I cannot seem to remember it...*"

When Nodwel finally reached the general store, he found the door slightly ajar. When he pushed on it, Nodwel found that a feeble attempt had been made to barricade it. With a couple good shoves, he made his way into the small store.

Nodwel now stood inside and saw that a cabinet had been used to block the door. There was a gaping hole in the roof and four bodies were sprawled out on the floor. The counter had been toppled

<Zaylyn ><Quest For The Sword Of Anthrowst ><By Katrina Mandrake-Johnston >   <Ch 18> < 69 >

and various goods were scattered about. One of the dead here had been one of his friends. A Killnarin must have torn through the roof and made its departure the same way. "Rest easy, my friend," he said with grief.

From Narr's head, a large pool of blood had formed. His skull had been smashed in, and Nodwel could see the bits of brain that had been exposed. He had to look away; it was too much for him.

Nodwel closed his eyes, "*Narr, old pal, you could sure make people laugh in rough times. I know you did your best to protect these people and made them smile even though they were facing inevitable peril... I should have been here for you. This is not how it should've ended for us...*" He blinked away his tears and took in a deep breath trying to compose himself.

There was a young woman with long black hair and wearing a light yellow dress. Her left arm had been severed, and she obviously had bled to death. An older man, in a shabby grey robe, bald and with a long white beard, had been disemboweled from a large gash across his belly.

"*This shouldn't have happened. The village of Nilnont, if that was even the first, and now Dexcsin. These people were defenseless and innocent. What mad reasoning is behind this? Why? What possible motive could this wizard Dranngore have? This is just pointless death and destruction; chaos,*" Nodwel commented to himself sadly and with an angry frustration.

A small brown haired boy in a dark blue shirt and grey leggings, was sprawled out beside the old man. The boy had lost both his legs in what looked to be a single bite from one of the creatures. Nodwel thought despondently, "*The poor kid appears to have been crawling toward his mother. This is awful!*"

He looked away and tried to concentrate on finding supplies for the approaching night. He searched the shelves and found enough provisions to last the group at least a day or two. He put the food into two small sacks, which he had found beside the front counter of the store. In a small box, he found five candles that he placed in his own pouch along with a length of rope. Nodwel had hoped to find a flame box, a magical box that produces a small flame each time the lid is removed, but he was unable to find one.

He went over to the cabinet, bringing the two small sacks of food with him. It was made of solid oak and was beautifully made with dragons carved onto the cabinet doors. Nodwel attempted to open the cabinet. The doors opened slightly and then, to his great surprise, were pulled right out of Nodwel's hands to slam shut again.

He again tried to open the doors and this time with more force. The cabinet doors flew open to reveal a small boy shielding his face with his arms and trembling with fear. Greatly surprised and relieved, Nodwel said to the boy, "It's alright. I'm here to help you. I'm a friend." "*Narr, you did it. Your sacrifice has not gone in vain. I won't let you down. I'll get him to safety,*" he promised.

The boy put his arms down and said, "I... I thought you were one of them. One of those monsters."

Nodwel could see that he was an identical twin to the dead boy on the floor. Immediately, he was suspicious of this, but then he thought better of it. Over his thin frail form, the boy had a light grey shirt and brown shorts which came to his knees. A pair of dark brown shoes were on his tiny feet.

"Come on, let's go outside," Nodwel coaxed with a wide friendly grin.

The boy hesitated nervously and then agreed, "Okay," and stepped weakly and cautiously out of the cabinet.

Nodwel knew that the boy would see the death in front of him, but it couldn't be helped. The boy remained silent as he walked slowly out of the store, his head down. The dwarf followed, and once they were outside, Nodwel sat down on the wooden bench there, as did the boy.

"My name's Nodwel. What's yours?" he asked in a friendly manner.

"Yarin," he answered. His eyes were red and swollen. They were brown, the same color as his hair.

Nodwel thought, "*He must have been crying right up until I entered the place. Poor kid.*"

"Narr said someone was going for help. Is that you?" Yarin asked.

"Yes, I'm the one that went for help. I'm with some others, and they'll be meeting us soon up by

<Zaylyn ><Quest For The Sword Of Anthrowst ><By Katrina Mandrake-Johnston >   <Ch 18> < 70 >

the well. One's a powerful wizard. Her name is Weena. Another also escaped the creatures as you did, and his name is Vordin. His village was also attacked. The other two, a man named Dendrox and a female elf named Candra, are expert… 'fighters'," he decided, not wanting to say that they were thieves even though he had heard Dendrox hint at it in his conversation with Weena.

"Oh," Yarin said, as if all Nodwel had said didn't really matter.

"The poor kid. Here I am trying talk up the others and for what? The help I've brought is far too late to save his family. What we needed here was an army, not a handful of adventurers," he thought with a sigh.

Yarin was staring blankly out into the silent village, and Nodwel decided it was best not to attempt further conversation.

<World of Zaylyn ><Quest For The Sword Of Anthrowst ><By Katrina Mandrake-Johnston ><Ch 19>

CHAPTER 19 = ASDELLA

Candra and Dendrox walked side-by-side in-between the buildings. There weren't many bodies visible in this part of the village which Dendrox was thankful for. Dendrox offered to stand guard while Candra checked the houses and shops, but Candra knew the real reason why he had suggested conducting the search in this way. Everywhere she went, she only found the mutilated bodies of innocent people.

She wondered if Dendrox knew. *"Does he realize how much seeing… Does he think it doesn't bother me?! Just because I shelter him as best I can from it, doesn't mean all this death doesn't greatly effect me too. I just have to remain strong… for him… for myself…"*

They soon came across a large Killnarin, dead in the middle of the street. A woman, scantly clad in brown leather was collapsed over the beast. She still clutched the sword that had been thrust into the creature's chest.

Candra thought to herself, *"She doesn't leave much to the imagination dressed like that. It would prove to be most distracting in battle against a man. It certainly would give her an edge. This must be Nodwel's companion, the warrior woman he spoke of."*

Candra knelt down and put her elfin ear to the woman's back. Her skin felt cold. She heard a faint heartbeat. "She's alive!" Candra exclaimed, "I don't want to move her. She doesn't have much time. I don't know what to do. Damn it, where's Weena."

"There's no time to find her," said Dendrox. He placed a hand on the woman's back in an effort to comfort her in her last moments of life.

"Am…" breathed the woman to their surprise. They hadn't thought that she still had it in her to speak, and they realized that she was using her last reserves of energy to do so. "Am… u… let…" she painfully forced out.

Dendrox looked frantically around using his skills to determine where she might have come from to battle the beast before them. He reasoned, *"It must be nearby for her to ask for it."* He turned to Candra saying, "Wait here, Candra." Dendrox then sped away into one of the houses close by.

"It's alright," Candra said stroking the woman's back, "Don't worry. You're strong. You'll make it. Fight and you'll live. Don't give in to death. You're stronger than that."

Dendrox found the body of a small girl lying face down in the house he had entered. An amulet was next to her outstretched hand and deep slashes were in her back. *"If the amulet does have healing properties, those foul beasts made sure that this girl couldn't get to it,"* Dendrox thought with further hatred for the beasts.

He snatched up the amulet and ran back to Candra and the dying woman. He held it in his outstretched hand not sure of what to do, and then said, "Ah, here," and placed the amulet on the skin of her back. To his astonishment the green jewel set into the amulet began to glow. Dendrox immediately was reminded of the cursed medallion and the man they had buried, but he hoped that his thoughts were misled.

When the glow subsided, the woman weakly stood up and the thieves watched in amazement as a large gash in the woman's torso closed, rapidly healing itself until the wound had completely vanished.

<Zaylyn ><Quest For The Sword Of Anthrowst ><By Katrina Mandrake-Johnston >   <Ch 19> < 71 >

Then the woman weakly said to them, "This means the girl is dead, and that the amulet is useless now." She threw the amulet across the street and then looked into the faces of the two thieves saying, "Thank-you. It was the strongest healing spell I've ever seen, but I never expected that I would be the one it would be used on. Once again, thank-you both for saving my life. Did Nodwel send you?"

"Yes, we're with him," Candra replied.

"Wow, you're completely healed. I can't believe that you were seconds away from death just a few moments ago," said Dendrox, amazed at the miracle that had taken place.

"So the girl, she is dead?" she asked him.

"Yes," he replied with sorrow.

"Damn it. I had given her the amulet as a good luck charm. I didn't know what else to do. She was frightened and so I had promised to keep her safe," the woman said. Her words were filled with anger and frustration, but it appeared that she felt only a sense of failure and not really any grief or sorrow for the child. Then her show of anger abruptly stopped as if a switch had been turned off, and she said calmly and plainly, "Even if the amulet had healed her, she would have died soon after anyway."

"I'm Candra, and this is Dendrox," Candra told her.

"Asdella," she said and then spoke with enthusiasm saying, "So Nodwel's around here somewhere, is he? Let's find him. Narr is still alive, as far as I know, and is protecting several of the remaining villagers. Borin might be as well. I have no clue as to how many villagers are still alive or where they might be though. Everyone got separated in all the bloodshed that took place last night. It was a glorious battle. It was a good thing that we sent Nodwel for help the night before last. I'm alive now because of it. After the horrendous struggle for survival that night and the one last night as well when the creatures attacked a second time, well, things looked pretty hopeless. We thought about making an escape during the day, but we soon found out that the creatures were merely lying in wait within the forest. They wouldn't outright attack in the daylight, well, that is unless anyone attempted to leave the village. But less talk and more action. Follow me. Nodwel has probably gone already to the general store. Let me guess, you're meeting him at the well, right?"

"That's right," Candra said with a nod.

Asdella's dark brown eyes had the look of a fierce and unpredictable warrior. Candra and Dendrox both had no problem at all imagining her madly screaming a battle cry and charging wildly into battle, as Nodwel had spoken of during their journey to the village.

Asdella grasped the hilt of her sword, positioned her bare foot against the shiny black skin of the beast, and pulled until the bloody blade withdrew from the corpse. She grinned triumphantly.

She headed toward the well, with Dendrox and Candra following her lead.

<World of Zaylyn ><Quest For The Sword Of Anthrowst ><By Katrina Mandrake-Johnston ><Ch 20>

CHAPTER 20 = THE WOLVES

Weena and Vordin saw death everywhere as they walked.

"It looks like the creatures came from the woods," Vordin commented, "You see here, where it borders this side of the village? At Nilnont, my village, the houses and buildings were burnt to the ground. Nothing was left. Why didn't they do that here?"

Weena suggested, "Well, if they did in fact come out of the forest, it would make sense that they would avoid setting fire to the village. The trees and brush would catch flame as well and destroy their hiding place." She realized that her plan to search this side of the village was perhaps not as wise as she had thought.

"Do you really think that they would even consider that?" Vordin asked her.

Weena replied, "Well, didn't you say that these creatures are controlled by an evil wizard? Anything is possible when magic is involved, at least to some extent. I suspect the creatures are intelligent though. I highly doubt the wizard is in total control of their every action."

"That's frightening," he said, "I mean, right now, they are following whatever horrible plan the wizard has for them, but what if he loses control or they decide to turn on him? Can you imagine these

<Zaylyn ><Quest For The Sword Of Anthrowst ><By Katrina Mandrake-Johnston >   <Ch 20> < 72 >
creatures running loose all over Zaylyn?"

Weena, not watching where she was going, tripped and fell, landing on the hard gravelly dirt which made up the streets within the village. Looking back, the sight of what she had tripped over made her frantically crawl away in revulsion.

She could see the glazed, sunken eyes of the dead man staring straight at her. His lips were dried up against his gums making his teeth more pronounced than they should be. A swollen tongue protruded slightly from his mouth. His skin was a greyish-white. Intestines trailed from a large wound to his gut. Dried blood was on the ground around him and various fluids had seeped out of him. Flies buzzed around and on him, attracted by the putrid stench emitted by his body.

The beasts must have done something to promote such accelerated decay, as it is definitely unnatural. He must have been one of the first people to die here, so close to the forest… Oh my stomach…" Weena thought just before she vomited again and again.

Vordin helped her up, when she had finished, and led her away, approaching a building which appeared to be some sort of shop. They were about to walk around to the front to find a door, when they heard a noise.

As Vordin peered around the corner of the small building, he saw what looked to be a wolf or perhaps a large dog nudging and licking the exposed leg of a young girl. "Wait," he whispered to Weena.

"What is it?" she whispered to him as she also peered out from behind the corner.

They heard the wet tearing sound of flesh being ripped from the bone. The wolf looked up from his meal and sniffed the air in their direction. Its snout was stained red with blood, and it slowly licked its jaws. They feared that they would be discovered, but then it continued to rip the muscle from the girl's leg.

Vordin could see that the girl had been a victim of the Killnarin, as she had large puncture wounds in her torso made by the teeth of the foul beasts. He whispered this to Weena, but it did not seem to put her at ease in the slightest.

"Look what it's doing to that girl's body, that could very easily be us," Weena said and then retched again, but there was nothing left to be emptied, "Let's get out of here before it sees us."

Another wolf, much larger than the first, now approached the body from out of the woods. A deep growl resounded from the throat of the first wolf, as it did not want to share its gruesome prize. The second wolf suddenly looked to the corner of the building where they were, perked up its ears, and growled.

"He's seen us!" Weena whispered frantically, "We'll never be able to out run them, not both!"

The smaller wolf now looked up in their direction. The second wolf seized its opportunity and snatched the little girl's arm attempting to drag her away in his direction. The first wolf, realizing what was happening, snarled at the larger wolf, threatening to attack. It returned a deep growl which made the smaller wolf back away slightly, but it was determined not to give in to the second and clamped its jaws around the bare bone of the leg trying to tug the body away from its rival.

"Come on, let's go," Vordin whispered, "Quickly, but don't run. We don't want to draw attention to ourselves."

Weena nodded, and they both headed toward the center of the village with Weena mentioning that the behavior of the wolves seemed odd somehow.

<World of Zaylyn ><Quest For The Sword Of Anthrowst ><By Katrina Mandrake-Johnston ><Ch 21>

CHAPTER 21 = THE WELL

"So Yarin," Nodwel said to the boy, "shall we head toward the well then? My companions should be heading there by now."

"Sure," Yarin said without emotion.

Nodwel led the small child toward the well at the center of the village, and as they walked, they both tried to keep their eyes from the awful sights around them.

"So, how old are you? I'd guess ten, maybe eleven, years old?" said Nodwel trying to break the

<Zaylyn ><Quest For The Sword Of Anthrowst ><By Katrina Mandrake-Johnston >   <Ch 21> < 73 >
uncomfortable silence surrounding them.

"I'm nine," Yarin answered plainly.

The dwarf couldn't think of anything else to say to the boy. He was trying to pick his words carefully for fear of saying something that would upset the boy any further, as Yarin was already in a very tender and unstable state.

"I like the way the setting sun glints off your axe," Yarin said.

"Yeah?" Nodwel said pleased that he had spoken. *"Yarin's right,"* he thought with worry, *"the sun is setting. We don't have much time left until dark. I hope the others are well, and on their way to the meeting place."*

"We'll be dead by dawn," Yarin stated calmly.

"Don't say that. We'll make it," he encouraged, but he thought, *"You're probably right kid."*

When they arrived at the well, Nodwel exclaimed, "Oh no, what's this?"

Strewn across the ground were several dead spiders. They were huge creatures. Alive, they would have stood about four feet high. Their bodies were about the size of a small child. Each leg was at least two to three inches thick. Nodwel counted four of them. Beside the well and the bodies of the giant spiders, were three dead villagers in front of a small building.

"Stay close to me," Nodwel told Yarin.

"Okay," he said meekly.

Yarin remembered seeing a similar looking spider in one of his picture books. His mother had given the book to him and his brother on their last birthday. She had traveled all the way to Vackiindmire to purchase it for them at a bookstore there.

These spiders looked similar to a tarantula, only much larger. He noticed the tiny brown hairs all over their bodies, almost giving the appearance of fur. Yarin had read that these hairs enabled the spider to sense vibrations. This was how the spider could hear approaching prey and predators.

The numerous eyes of each spider were tiny in proportion to the rest of it. The eyes were clustered close together in a tiny area in the center, positioned over the two large fangs. Being as large as these spiders were, each eye was a little smaller than an egg.

Each spider, in addition to its eight legs, also had two smaller legs in the front that it could use almost like hands to manipulate its food and feel around.

The fangs were tucked neatly under the front of each spider. Yarin thought to himself that the front of the spiders looked almost like two furry fingers that had been curled into a fist, the eyes being between the two knuckles and with the smooth, black, claw-shaped fangs curling underneath at the second knuckle.

Yarin could remember how he and his brother had been fascinated with spiders and insects. That time had passed.

Being wary of the spiders, Nodwel and Yarin approached the small building. It was a home belonging to one of the villagers. Nodwel peered inside the house through the open door and discovered two dead women. He entered and saw that he was in the first of two rooms. This was the kitchen and living area of the home and the second room was a bedroom.

He dragged the bodies out of the house and laid them beside the others, while Yarin watched. After seeing the pale look on the boy's face, he realized, *"Maybe this wasn't such a good idea... Well, he would have seen the bodies anyway when we went inside. I guess I could have told him not to look or something. But then where was he supposed to look? There's death all around us, and now giant spiders added to the mix. I mean, he probably knows more than half the people here in some way or another, but what am I supposed to do? What can I possibly do?"* "Yarin, you okay?" he asked.

Yarin nodded, but he looked terrible and was trembling slightly. His eyes were wide with fear, and he kept looking nervously about, and up to the sky and the quickly fading light.

"Let's get inside, alright? We'll stay here for now and wait for the others," Nodwel said, and then upon further observation of their surroundings, stated, "This house has been somewhat barricaded against the creatures. It looks like Borin's work. Of course, I could be mistaken... Are you sure you're all right?" Nodwel asked with concern.

<Zaylyn ><Quest For The Sword Of Anthrowst ><By Katrina Mandrake-Johnston >   <Ch 21> < 74 >

Yarin just nodded.

The bedroom, which Nodwel could see clearly, was bare except for a bed with a heavy wooden frame. The bed had been raised up to block the only window in the room and could be removed quickly enough in an emergency. In the front room, a large brown couch was turned over and upright against the wall next to the door for use as a barricade if the need came. There was a small wooden chair and table with a few eating utensils scattered about the room.

Nodwel eased the couch down to the floor so Yarin could sit upon it. The boy sat, curling his legs tightly up against his chest until his knees were almost to his chin. Yarin waited silently and patiently, staring out the open door.

Nodwel mentioned, "I can see well in the dark; something I inherited. I'll be able to see if anything comes for us, and we'll have time to escape if we need to. Don't worry, okay?"

Nodwel stood at the doorway and watched for his companions and for any signs of danger. He dreaded the fact that night would soon fall upon them all and that the creatures might return once again.

Nodwel's mind was racing, *"Where are they? They should have been here by now! Okay, I'm getting carried away here. There's still plenty of time before the sun passes below the horizon... But who knows if these creatures are even going to wait until that time? They could be upon us any moment, if they wanted to. Perhaps they are already here? No, I can't be thinking like that. We'll have time. I have no idea how we are going to go about preparing for whatever awaits us during the night, but we'll do our best. If anything, my main goal is to protect Yarin and the others as best as I can."*

Soon Weena and Vordin came into view. "Over here!" Nodwel called out to them.

When Weena saw the spiders, she cried out suddenly, "Oh! They're huge! They're not alive, are they?"

Keeping their distance, Vordin and Weena began to edge toward the spiders, nearing the house where Nodwel was waiting for them. "I've never seen spiders like this before," Weena told Vordin, as she clutched his arm tightly, "I didn't think ones this big even existed... I can't stand spiders. They're absolutely hideous. I squash even the tiniest of them... Would you just look at the fangs on them!"

Vordin felt Lorenta stir in the backpack, as Weena's words had made her uneasy. Weena's grip was intensifying more and more, as they slowly approached where the spiders lay. "They're dead, Weena, relax," Vordin told her.

"Of course they're dead. I can see that," Weena snapped defensively, trying her best to sound brave, "If I thought they were alive, I'd be fleeing in the opposite direction."

"Let me guess. Right now she's imagining one of them coming to life, and is about ready to explode from the terror," he thought to himself with a silent chuckle.

"Do you really think I'd even get this close to these things if I knew that they could just jump up and..." Weena started to say and then let out a muffled whimper and made a frantic dash for the safety of the house.

When she reached the doorway and the dwarf, she suggested, "They must have also attacked the villagers."

Vordin eyed the villagers as he passed them and joined his companions in front of the house. "No," Vordin told her, "Looks like the Killnarin got these ones."

"Still..." Weena said.

Nodwel greeted them with a firm handshake and ushered them both inside. "This is Yarin," he told them.

"Hello," Yarin said looking up at them.

"I'm Vordin," he said with a slight wave to the boy.

"My name's Weena," she told him kneeling down to Yarin's eye level. "You must be the bravest little boy I have ever met," she said with a smile and got the beginnings of one in return.

<World of Zaylyn ><Quest For The Sword Of Anthrowst ><By Katrina Mandrake-Johnston ><Ch 22>

CHAPTER 22 = REUNION

<Zaylyn ><Quest For The Sword Of Anthrowst ><By Katrina Mandrake-Johnston >   <Ch 22> < 75 >

Candra, Dendrox, and Asdella reached the well, and then, locating their companions, entered the small dwelling.

Nodwel, upon setting eyes on Asdella, exclaimed, "You're alive!"

"That I am," she said with a smile.

Nodwel's expression showed joy and relief at discovering at least one of his friends was still alive.

Weena thought to herself, "*I'm so glad for him. It had seemed like he was feeling somehow responsible for the deaths of his friends. No one can be responsible for everyone. No one can protect everyone all the time. He shouldn't put himself down for the loss of his friends…*" then scolding herself she thought, "*Wake up, Weena! Why don't you follow your own advice? You didn't start learning magic for no reason at all. You still feel useless. I can't bring those kids back. They died. I could have done things differently. Maybe if I had acted more quickly instead of hiding in the forest while the school burned, I might have been able to save someone at least, probably more. My brother would still be alive today, of that I'm certain. It was all my fault.*" Tears started to well up in her eyes and then she told herself, "*Oh please, this is not a time to start getting all emotional over the past. Don't show that you're weak, Weena. Be strong like Candra.*"

Asdella gave Nodwel's beard a playful tug and said, "I thought you'd never get back. You missed all the action. I killed one of the beasts. I told you I would."

"You did? And managed it without a scratch, eh? You sure are a fierce one aren't ya?" Nodwel said and nudged her shoulder gently with one of his large fists. This actually looked quite comical, since Asdella was taller than the dwarf by a fair amount.

"I still say the axe is better than a puny sword," he teased.

"Oh really? And why is that, old fool?" she questioned in a playful manner.

"Well," he said pulling out his axe and balancing it in his hands. "Yes," he said grunting to accentuate that the weapon had a fair weight to it. "This here is, I think, about the best weapon there is. It can be used as a bludgeoning weapon to crush a man's skull, or perhaps that of an obnoxious warrior woman," he said with a smile directed at Asdella. "And, it can slice clean through an offending limb, say one holding a puny sword," he added with a wink and continued, "granted the user of the axe has incredible strength in his arms, say that of a handsome dwarf."

"Ah, well, I see little man," Asdella said with a smirk, "But you see, with a sword, I can slice through all the major tendons before that clumsy piece of metal could be wielded, especially if the user of the axe has to chase after me with stubby little legs."

"Really?" he said to her. "*That's Asdella. I'm glad she's as happy to see me, as I am her. Most of the time I don't have the faintest idea of what's going on in that muddled head of hers. Maybe that's a good thing. To tell the truth, I thought she might turn on me, blaming me for not returning quickly enough and for Narr's death and perhaps Borin's too wherever he may be,*" Nodwel thought slightly nervous.

She ignored him now and said, "I'm Asdella," to the unfamiliar faces.

"Oh, I'm sorry," Nodwel apologized, "Introductions are in order. Everyone this is Asdella…"

"I already said that," she interrupted.

He gave her a smirk and continued, "As I was saying, this is Asdella. This little boy here is Yarin. I found him hiding in an oak cabinet at the general store. Do you think that's similar to the way you survived Vordin?" he asked him.

"I don't know. A hollow tree was how I escaped them. The wood cabinet might have had the same effect. I really have no clue," Vordin replied.

The dwarf continued his introductions, "Anyway, this is Vordin. This fine lady is a powerful wizard or sorceress or whatever you want to call it, and her name is Weena."

Weena was about to protest the part about being a 'powerful' wizard, but on second thought, she just politely nodded a greeting to Asdella.

"Yarin, the lady elf there is Candra, and over there is Dendrox," Nodwel told him.

Yarin said meekly to the new arrivals, "Hi." Then he looked up at Asdella and said innocently, "Aren't you cold? Where's all your clothes?"

<Zaylyn ><Quest For The Sword Of Anthrowst ><By Katrina Mandrake-Johnston >   <Ch 22> < 76 >

At this, all she could do was laugh and smile at him. Asdella then noticed that Vordin was intensely studying her nearly naked body and she snapped angrily at him, "What are you looking at?!"

"Oh come on," Nodwel stepped in quickly, "He doesn't mean anything by it and you know it."

Her mood suddenly and drastically changed as she joked, "Well, I guess I can't really blame him. I am extremely beautiful. Oh! And this body is simply exquisite!"

Candra saw that there was a pain buried deep in this woman, surfacing now and then briefly in her words and expression. Candra wondered, *Could she have been abused? From what Nodwel told us of her on our way to Dexcsin, she seems to treat her body as a tool, a distraction to be used in battle, as if it were separate from herself. This insane rage, that Nodwel spoke of, must stem from somewhere. I haven't seen her in battle, but I can sure imagine. She certainly is interesting, but already I'm assuming too much. I really don't know anything about her.*

"Nodwel," Asdella said suddenly somber, "about what you said."

"What?" he asked.

"I killed the beast, but I would be dead now if not for these two passing by," she said gesturing toward Dendrox and Candra. She continued, "I used the amulet. The one that Nimdor used to have. We decided to take what we could and split up, each of us taking a group of villagers. We took what magic items we could find off Nimdor's body, as it was nearby. I took the healing amulet. When the beasts found out where we were, they all attacked together tearing down the very walls to get at us. We figured that we would have a better chance separately as trying to take on all of them together would have been suicide. All those under my care got slaughtered except for a small girl. I had given it to her for protection while I was in battle against the creature that had been following us. I hadn't expected to live and was hoping that she would. It's really good to see you, old friend. Really, it is."

"I see," said Nodwel.

There was a short pause of silence before Dendrox broke in, "Does anyone know where all those dead spiders came from? They're gigantic!"

Asdella shrugged her reply.

"Don't know," Nodwel commented, "It was like this when I arrived here with Yarin."

"Any helpful hints on how to kill these creatures?" Asdella asked them.

"We've discovered that these beasts have a name. They're called Killnarin," Nodwel told her.

Weena added, "Apparently, a wizard named Dranngore summoned them. Whatever purpose he has for these creatures, we are clueless to it. Why he would have them attacking helpless villages is beyond me. Perhaps, the slaughter is simply a reward for the creatures. Or maybe to prepare them for something larger."

Vordin added, "One thing for sure is that the creatures are thorough in making sure no one is left alive to talk about it."

"So, there is a good chance that they'll be back tonight then?" Dendrox asked.

Vordin said, "Well, they did send a scout out after me. They must have come back to Nilnont. I don't know. Maybe they caught my scent or just happened to be searching for anyone that might have escaped them. It found me, and if it weren't for The Black Shadow, I would have been dead for sure."

"The Black Shadow?" Asdella scoffed with disbelief.

Vordin explained, "He brought me over the mountains, showed me the Killnarin that Candra and Dendrox had killed, and told me of Dranngore and the Sword of Anthrowst. A fairy queen also told me of the wizard and the sword."

"You're saying that you met The Black Shadow, that he actually saved your life instead of taking it," Asdella snapped accusingly at him, "and that he spoke to you, and then on top of that, that you met some ancient fairy queen who is thought to exist only in myth and legend?"

"Well, yes, but no one believes me. I didn't think what happened to me would be such a rarity," Vordin admitted.

"Well it would be, if it were true," Asdella snapped in response.

"It is!" Vordin protested, "Why would I lie? What would I have to gain by it?"

"I don't know. You tell me," she continued.

<Zaylyn ><Quest For The Sword Of Anthrowst ><By Katrina Mandrake-Johnston >   <Ch 22> < 77 >

"I…" Vordin started.

"Asdella, leave the poor lad alone," Nodwel told her.

"Okay, yeah, I believe you," she said to Vordin, eyeing him suspiciously, and then her lips spread into a sly smile, "I was just testing you. Maybe it is true. Strange unbelievable things have been known to happen now and then."

"Come on, we have work to do," Nodwel commanded.

"This is our camp for tonight?" Asdella asked.

"It'll have to do. What do you think? Borin's work?" the dwarf asked her.

Asdella eyed the barricaded room and then said, "Could be. He did head off in this direction, last I saw of him. You find his body?"

"No. I did find Narr's though," he said gravely.

"Oh," she said without emotion, but her eyes betrayed her as the sorrow began to build. She finally had to look away from him in an attempt to hide it.

Nodwel was furious with himself, *"Damn it. Think before you blurt things out! You're getting clumsy you old fool. Narr and Asdella had been close. You always saw them teasing each other, flirting every once in awhile. It never amounted to anything, Asdella being so reclusive in her emotions when it came to things like that. But still, there was a certain something between them. Nodwel, you're a damn idiot. She didn't need to know that about Narr. Oh sure, she seems like a killing machine without any emotions whatsoever, but she is still a person and has to have some sort of feelings, even if they are buried way down deep. That's where it's going to hurt her the most."*

Yarin bravely spoke up to the group, "Narr was the one who helped to protect my family. They all were killed, but I survived."

"Well kid," Asdella addressed Yarin, "I guess in the end, Narr and I were more alike than I thought. I was going to be dead for a kid too, but I got a second chance. He didn't." Yarin was confused and wondered if she were still speaking to him or not. She continued, "We used to have many great arguments about things like that, you know? I mean, in what situations we'd be willing to die. Well, I guess you win this one, Narr. I am like you. I do care about something. There, I've said it." She paused and looked around the room. "I'm going for a walk," she decided abruptly.

"Are you crazy?! It's dark now. If those creatures are out there already, you might be killed!" Dendrox told her.

"I am going for a walk," she repeated, and then with a threatening glare, she pushed past him and out through the door.

Nodwel mouthed the words 'Let her go' and then thought, *"See even Asdella has a heart. A cold and icy one, but still it's there. Poor thing. The persistent flirtations from Narr probably was the closest to love she had allowed herself. Nothing can be done about it now. Damn, why didn't I keep my mouth shut. She's probably gone to find him. She needs the visual confirmation; words aren't enough for her. Well, if trouble starts, at least I have a good idea of where she might be. Please, please, let this be a peaceful night."*

Yarin was fascinated by these so-called 'warriors' as the dwarf had called them. A few of them seemed just as weak and frightened as he was, but because of them, he had been saved from the bitter loneliness and helplessness he had felt when hiding in the cabinet. The time he had spent there seemed like an eternity. He felt as if there was hope now, even though he had seen several strong 'warriors' fall before the vicious Killnarin.

Everyone in the party needed sleep, but they all were experiencing the restlessness that fear and danger brings. Nodwel distributed the rations he had collected and discarded the two small sacks. He put Asdella's portion into his own pouch for her when she returned. Everyone ate slowly and silently, except for Yarin who just stared blankly at his share of the bread and cheese.

"Honey, aren't you going to eat something?" Weena asked Yarin.

"My belly feels like it has a big lump in it. I don't want to eat," Yarin said on the verge of tears.

"None of us feels like eating right now, but we need to keep our strength up," she told him.

"I want my mother. I want my brother. I want everything to go back the way it was. I want to be

<Zaylyn ><Quest For The Sword Of Anthrowst ><By Katrina Mandrake-Johnston >   <Ch 22> < 78 >

able to go home," Yarin cried.

Weena took him into her arms and tried to comfort him as best as she could. "Dendrox? Could you pack his food away for him?" Weena asked, "He might feel like eating later."

"Sure, I guess," Dendrox answered.

"Great, now she's got him babysitting. We're all going to get killed," Candra muttered to herself.

Vordin removed his backpack and placed it gently in the corner by the door, where he hoped Lorenta would be safe from clumsy feet. He was unsure whether the magical compartment would protect her against such things. He then sat down beside Yarin and Weena on the couch.

Nodwel motioned for Candra and Dendrox to join him over by the bedroom door. They did so, and Nodwel whispered to them, "As we all well know, those three won't be any help in battle. If anything, they'll just get in the way. These creatures are far too dangerous. For us to be worrying about those three while in battle, might distract us enough to lose our own lives."

"So what do you suggest?" Dendrox whispered.

Candra said coldly, "Just forget about them. If they're of no use and liable to inhibit our own attacks, we don't need them. If they can't fend for themselves, well that's just too bad."

"No one gets sacrificed," Nodwel said angrily, "I wasn't suggesting that. I would never even think of something like that! The whole purpose of us coming here was to save the innocent."

"I don't care anymore," Candra blurted out, "This is insane. We're all going to get slaughtered. If everyone can't make it on their own, good riddance. I'm not about to get killed because I'm coddling someone who's hanging all over me to protect them."

"Well I'm sorry you feel that way. We'll just have to remember that when one of those beasts is gnawing on your leg, okay? We'll just stand there and watch," Nodwel snapped angrily.

"Listen, there's no use in bickering like this. We're all frightened," Dendrox told them, "There's no need for panic." Candra glared at him. "Yes, you're frightened too, Candra," said Dendrox, "even though you won't admit it. We all need to stick together in this or we won't have the slightest chance of survival, Candra, and you know it."

"Okay, fine. So what do you think we should do about them?" Candra asked Nodwel.

"Thank-you. Now as I was saying, they won't last very long if the creatures attack. Yarin survived in that cabinet, but no one but him is small enough to hide in there. We'll have to somehow make our way back to the general store though."

"So, hide the boy. That sounds good. What about the other two?" added Dendrox.

"Well, that's where I need some suggestions," Nodwel said. Then, a guilty look spread across his face as he noticed that Weena, Vordin, and even Yarin, who had reduced his crying to a teary-eyed sniffling, were staring at them blankly. They had apparently heard every word despite their hushed tone.

Weena took Yarin by the hand and walked over with Vordin to where the others were standing. "So we're expendable, Candra?" Weena said in a hurt voice.

Candra didn't let her gaze falter.

"Weena, it's just fear talking," Dendrox told her, trying to keep peace between the two women.

"It would be nice to be able to have some say into our own fates," Vordin told them.

<World of Zaylyn ><Quest For The Sword Of Anthrowst ><By Katrina Mandrake-Johnston ><Ch 23>

CHAPTER 23 = LORENTA EXPLORES DEXCSIN

Meanwhile, Lorenta had escaped the confines of the backpack and crawled out through the open door unseen. Once outside, against the wall of the building and away from the door, she transformed. Lorenta looked up at the moon with human eyes and felt the chill night air against her human skin.

She left the group to their quarrels and walked silently away from the building to explore the village. She knew it would be dangerous, but the excitement led her on. Just being somewhere other than the dreary old hut and woods she had lived in all her life was a thrill. As she wandered, she saw numerous bodies.

The stench of death was everywhere. She covered her nose with her hand and was reminded of

<Zaylyn ><Quest For The Sword Of Anthrowst ><By Katrina Mandrake-Johnston >   <Ch 23> < 79 >

her encounter with the owl at the sight of her missing fingers. In her spider form, it was her wounded front leg with its missing tip and another leg which formed together to create this human arm, so only a thumb and forefinger remained now on her right hand. It was becoming a constant reminder of how lucky she was to be alive and how precious life is.

"*Why,*" she wondered, "*did these creatures kill all these people? It's obvious that they weren't meant for food. It's as if they were killed purely for their entertainment, playing with these people's lives. It goes against the laws of nature. I've seen enough. I'm going back.*"

When Lorenta returned to the area near the well, she saw for the first time the bodies of the giant spiders strewn across the ground. She had been curious about them ever since she first heard the others talking about them, but was nervous about what she might discover. She crept closer to one of the spiders and knelt down beside it.

"*He's huge! I've never heard of a spider reaching this enormous size. My size as a spider increased when I gained my human form, but this is amazing. Where could they have come from?*"

Upon further examination, she noticed a wound along its abdomen. "*This slash was made from a sword! No, this is what I was fearing! The humans attacked them! Why? I didn't see any of the bodies with evidence of spider attacks.*"

Just then she saw a long hairy leg reach up from the well. Then another leg appeared and then another. Lorenta stood up. A giant spider was now standing on its eight legs in front of the well. Spiders aren't usually tolerant of another spider within their territory and most often see the invading spider as being either a threat or food, or both. But she was here as a human and not as another spider. She didn't know what to expect. The spider padded over the earth toward Lorenta.

She stood motionless, afraid of what might happen. It touched her lightly with one of its front legs and then began nudging her toward the well.

Then Lorenta felt as if there were a heavy weight settling into her mind. At first, she was going to fight this invasion into her mind, but then gave in and let it envelope her. To her astonishment, she heard a voice within her head which said, "The creatures… It's safe in the well… Go… Hurry…"

Suddenly an arrow flew through the air, sinking into the abdomen of the spider.

<World of Zaylyn ><Quest For The Sword Of Anthrowst ><By Katrina Mandrake-Johnston ><Ch 24>

CHAPTER 24 =   DISCOVERING LORENTA

Lorenta collapsed to the ground, screams of agony and fear filling and echoing within her head. The spider recoiled from her mind, leaving Lorenta confused and disorientated.

"Damn arm. So much for my aim. Now I'll have to fire yet another arrow just to finish it off," Candra muttered to herself as she pulled another arrow from her quiver.

As Lorenta stood, she could see Candra standing in the doorway of the nearby building. The room behind the elf was filled with the light from Vordin's magical lantern, as it was now dark. Lorenta recognized its strange glow. "*They must be conserving the fuel of Weena's lantern. Good idea,*" she commented to herself.

Her head still felt hazy and it took her a moment to realize what was happening. Candra's sleek form, illuminated by the light behind her, aimed her bow in Lorenta's direction. A slender arrow was between the elf's nimble fingers. The string was held taut, ready to loose the arrow.

"*No… The spider…*" she realized. Unsure of what exactly had taken place during the peculiar communication between herself and the spider, this was the first time that she really noticed the arrow protruding from the creature. She hoped desperately that it wasn't too late to save him.

"No! Don't!" she screamed and leapt in front of the spider. She wasn't sure if this would stop the thief from firing, but she had to do something. She also hoped that Candra had enough control to still have a choice in whether she fired or not, as stopping the arrow with her body wasn't something that Lorenta really wanted.

"What the… Hey! You stupid villager! Can't you see I'm trying to save your pathetic life? Get out of the way!" Candra barked at her.

"What's going on?" Nodwel asked as he stepped into the doorway.

<Zaylyn ><Quest For The Sword Of Anthrowst ><By Katrina Mandrake-Johnston >   <Ch 24> < 80 >

"What is it?" Vordin asked with curiosity as he poked his head into view.

Candra explained as she lowered her bow, "I could have killed the thing with one shot, if my wounded arm hadn't affected my aim so. I would have been able to put more strength behind it too. Looks like it will have to suffer a slow death because of it. I think a mercy kill is definitely in order here, but this damn villager I found keeps getting in the way." Seeing the look of terror on Lorenta's face she told her, "Oh calm down, I wouldn't have hit you. My aim's not that bad, even with my arm in this state."

"Vordin! Do something! Stop her!" Lorenta pleaded, desperately trying to protect the wounded spider.

"Lorenta?" he exclaimed in surprise, as he thought she was still hidden inside the backpack. "What are you doing?" he asked her, coming out of the house.

"Hey, what's going on out there?" Dendrox called from inside, "Yarin's panicking. I don't want to leave the kid."

"It's okay," Vordin called back.

Candra replaced the arrow into her quiver and swung the bow over her shoulder. "Okay, what is it this time?" Candra said giving Vordin a distrusting look.

"How can you possibly know this woman?" Nodwel asked him. His face was stern. "That spider doesn't look as if it will cause us much of a threat anymore, so explain away."

Vordin realized that attempting a lie wouldn't be very useful. He assumed that they would see right through him if he did. He wasn't even very good at telling the truth. "Her name's Lorenta. She's my companion. She's been traveling with me for awhile now. She's a shape-shifter of sorts and she's been riding along in my backpack. Being different, she thought it best that she remain hidden, especially with everything going on like this. Don't worry, we can trust her. At least hear what she has to say," Vordin said with a pathetically hopeful look on his face.

They looked at Lorenta expectantly. Dendrox came to the doorway with Yarin holding on tightly to his hand. Weena peered out from behind Dendrox, deathly afraid of the giant spider.

"Hey, that thing's still alive. You want me to take it out?" Dendrox asked the group.

"No," Lorenta said frantically, "Please, listen! This spider here, he was trying to warn us!"

"Warn us of what?" Candra said in a threatening tone, showing that she wasn't one to be toyed with.

"We must help him!" she begged, "He was trying to lead us to safety! The others were trying to do the same, but were attacked." Lorenta felt hot tears welling up in her eyes as her words seemed to fall on uncaring ears.

"Enough with this nonsense! Candra just saved your life. This is your gratitude? To fabricate this insane story?" Nodwel said to her unkindly. The stress of the past few days had taken its toll on the dwarf who was usually quite friendly.

"No, please. I don't know how, but he spoke to me through some sort of telepathy. Please believe me! We have to help him! Can't you see he's dying?" Lorenta pleaded.

"I've heard enough," Nodwel said with a stern look of intolerance. He crossed his arms and remained in his firm stance. His distrusting gaze did not falter.

Lorenta found herself becoming more and more wary of Vordin's companions. *What if they find out my true identity? Will they treat me in the same manner as this spider here? Kill first and ask questions later? It seems to be human nature to do so. Just look at these others. They were just trying to help these villagers, to take them to safety. Their kind gesture was met with bloodshed. Suddenly I don't feel so bad about my encounter with that 'magic stealer'. He got what he deserved... No, I can't think like that. If I do so, that makes me no better than them. I have to stay in human form as long as possible around them. My life would be in grave danger if they knew. But when daylight returns, I have no choice in my form. What will I do then? I'll just have to overcome that obstacle when the time comes. Oh no, here comes that berserk warrior woman!*

CHAPTER 25 =   KILLNARIN OR GIANT SPIDERS

Asdella came into view, walking slowly toward them.

"Asdella!" Nodwel called to her raising a hand to greet her. "Well, Lorenta, or whoever you are," he said to her unkindly, "Looks like your precious spider is done for now. As soon as she sees that thing, she'll slice and dice until nothing's left. We no longer have a say in it. Go ahead, try to stop her. It will only get her to attack you as well."

"Please… He said that there's safety in the well. They must have an underground lair of some sort," Lorenta said to them.

Asdella approached them calmly and said, "Looks like a trap and she's the lure, but I'd rather face a bunch of giant spiders than those foul demons."

"She must be taking Narr's death worse than I thought. To pass up a battle? Even a wounded and dying creature wouldn't have invoked mercy from her before," Nodwel commented to himself.

"So who's this?" Asdella asked.

Candra repeated what Vordin and Lorenta had told them.

Lorenta pleaded with them again, "We have to hurry! He said the beasts are coming! Who knows how close they are… We have to get down into the well! We have to help him… We can't just leave him here to be killed!"

"We can put it out of its misery," Nodwel told her.

"No! We have to help him!" she protested.

"Looks like we're taking it with us," Asdella commented. Lorenta was surprised to be getting help from the one she expected the least.

"There is no way I'm getting close to that thing," Weena said, her fear showing through, "And I'm especially not going to help carry it down into a well with its fangs so close to my skin."

"Will no one help?" Lorenta asked desperately.

Vordin shook his head. He too was afraid, agreeing with what Weena had said.

Dendrox added, "We'd end up falling down the well ourselves trying to maneuver down a ladder with such a huge load. We aren't even sure if there is a ladder."

"You wouldn't leave one of your own here. You'd find some way of making the journey," Lorenta said with frustration.

The others stood silent.

"Okay, looks like I'm taking the spider down myself then," Asdella spoke up. "Bunch of scared wimps," she joked.

Lorenta felt a wave of relief at Asdella's words. Asdella picked up the giant spider awkwardly, trying to take the weight on her back and keep an arm free as well. She finally got the spider positioned so its wounded abdomen was behind her head, the front of the spider was resting on her lower back, and its many legs were dangling weakly about her. Asdella's left arm was behind her trying desperately to hold the spider in place at its mid-section.

Lorenta had the strength to carry the spider herself, but she didn't want to have to try to explain that to them. Also she never had to climb in human form before. This would be a new and awkward task for her.

"Lorenta, see if someone has a rope and then strap this thing onto me. I think I can manage the climb," said Asdella.

"Sure. Does anyone have a rope?" Lorenta asked timidly.

Nodwel chuckled slightly at the awkward display of Asdella and the giant spider. "You really intend to carry that thing down into that well, don't you?"

"What does it look like?" she said with a mocking smile, "You're the sort to have a rope. So hand it over."

"It just so happens that I found a rope, so here you go," the dwarf said to Asdella, as he took the rope from his pouch and handed it to Lorenta. "You do know that I think you're making a big mistake," he continued to tell Asdella, "That thing's going to bite you, especially where it's wounded and all."

<Zaylyn ><Quest For The Sword Of Anthrowst ><By Katrina Mandrake-Johnston >   <Ch 25> < 82 >

"Yeah, I know, and when has that ever stopped me before? Where's your sense of adventure? You can't have a little adventure without some danger, now can you?" she replied.

Lorenta wrapped the rope around the spider and the woman, at the same time trying her best not to aggravate the wound. She wanted to remove the arrow but feared she would do more harm than good if she made the attempt.

"There," she said as she finished tying the last knot, "But I'm not sure if that's going to hold."

"Well, it's the best we can do," Asdella told her, "Let's go." Asdella peered into the well. It was very dark but she could see that there were metal rungs set into the stone forming a ladder. With Lorenta's help, she lowered herself into the well with the spider. "Someone better have a lantern," Asdella grumbled, "Oh and Nodwel? You found rations, right? Could you grab mine then? Unless you want me stealing yours."

Lorenta lowered herself into the well, after Asdella and her burden.

The remaining group hesitated quite awhile before deciding.

"They're walking into an ambush," Dendrox said, "Even if Lorenta is on our side, she's clearly being tricked."

"We can't just let them face a battle alone," Vordin said to them, "Asdella may be an excellent warrior, but how well can she fight with that spider strapped to her back? Not to mention how quickly the venom will affect her if it bites her. She probably won't be able to survive a bite from that thing. What was she thinking? Does she have a death wish or something? We'll need her in battle if the Killnarin attack again."

"That's Asdella. There's usually no reasoning behind her thinking that I can see. I'm not about to argue with her about her decisions either. I would have better luck trying to move a boulder with a blade of grass," Nodwel told them, "I agree with Vordin though, we can't let them face an ambush alone."

"How well do you know Lorenta anyway? Are you sure she's trustworthy?" Dendrox asked Vordin.

"Well, I haven't known her very long actually, and I know not much more about her than I do any of you. The Black Shadow said to trust her though," answered Vordin.

"Well, that can't be good," said Candra, "But I'm not about to start turning on people again like before. Asdella seems to trust her, and I definitely don't want to make that woman angry by arguing about it." Candra stepped over to the well and called out, "What do you see down there? Does it look safe?"

Asdella called back, "What do you think I see? It's pitch black down here! You're the ones with the lanterns, aren't you? Hurry up! I feel a draft down here. Could be a tunnel."

Yarin pulled at Dendrox's arm. "What is it?" he asked the boy.

Yarin's eyes were wide with fear. "I hear them," he whispered, "The beasts are returning! Quick, we have to hide!"

Nodwel cursed, "Damn it, this is insane! We're wasting time! We'll all be trapped down there! How are we supposed to defend ourselves halfway down a ladder and in the dark? Vordin, give me that magic lantern of yours and hurry." Vordin did what he was asked. "Alright," Nodwel said as he went over to the well and held the lantern over it, "Can you see anything now?"

"Hurry, I hear them too," Vordin said beginning to panic, "It's them. It's the Killnarin for sure. We'll all be killed! Hurry! Are we going into the well or staying here?!"

"Just wait," Nodwel demanded. "Asdella!" he called, "Can you hear me? Can you see anything now with the light? Are you sure that there's a tunnel down there?"

"Yes, I'm sure. I can't tell where it leads, but it does lead somewhere," she answered.

"We should all stick together in this, which means down in that well," Nodwel decided, "Damn it. I still think this is a bad idea."

"I agree that we'll have a better chance fighting off a horde of giant spiders than even a few of the Killnarin," said Candra.

Between spiders and the Killnarin, the well did seem a better choice, but not by much. Everyone

<Zaylyn ><Quest For The Sword Of Anthrowst ><By Katrina Mandrake-Johnston >   <Ch 25> < 83 >
collected their supplies, and Weena lit her lantern with the flame box from her cloth pouch. Then as the howling sounds of the Killnarin began to close in on their location, they all followed Lorenta and Asdella in their descent into the well by the light of the two lanterns.

<World of Zaylyn ><Quest For The Sword Of Anthrowst ><By Katrina Mandrake-Johnston ><Ch 26>

CHAPTER 26 =   THE SPIDERS

Soon they could see the well water beneath them. Also a few feet above the water, they could now see what appeared to be an opening in the rock wall of the well.

"Hey," Asdella called out to the others, "I'm heading into the tunnel." She awkwardly made her way into the opening, being careful of the spider strapped to her back.

"What do you see?" Lorenta asked.

"It looks like a tunnel to me. There's enough room to stand, and it seems wide enough for at least two people to walk side-by-side. It's pretty dark though; I can't tell much from here. If it is a tunnel and if it stays like this for the length of it, we'll have no trouble traveling along it. And if we have to battle some horrible beast, it won't be so difficult to maneuver. Come on, I think it's safe," the warrior woman yelled out to the group and then waited for them to join her.

They discovered that the tunnel they were now in, sloped slightly downward. As they traveled along it, Vordin was reminded of the dream he had back in Rasindell's hut where Lorenta had betrayed him and sent millions of tiny spiders to engulf him. They eventually found themselves in a large chamber with many passages leading off in all directions. Including the short tunnel leading back up to the well, there was a total of eight passageways.

"Untie the rope," Asdella demanded, "I'm getting this thing off me."

Lorenta removed the rope and helped Asdella lower the spider to the stony floor of the cavern. "At least he'll be somewhat safe here. I wish there was something more we could do for him," said Lorenta.

"Besides put it out of its misery?" Dendrox added.

Candra said to Lorenta, "It is cruel to let the thing suffer like this, but I guess its fate lies in your decision. I'm not going to decide for you, when you've become so attached to it. You are a strange one."

Asdella looked around at their surroundings and said, "Okay, now what?"

"Doesn't look like this place is a natural formation," Weena said as she moved her lantern around trying to see better, "Perhaps some of it is, but several tunnels appear to have been cut into the rock. Could be that an ancient civilization once lived here in these underground passages."

The light from the two lanterns only dimly lit the large chamber. She stepped a bit closer, trying to examine the construction of one of the tunnels. "This is such an incredible find! Aren't any of you even a little bit interested? Do you think any of the villagers knew about this place?" she asked the others.

"Ah, curiosity… It can be a deadly thing sometimes," Nodwel muttered. His eyes darted nervously from tunnel to tunnel. Occasionally, his wary gaze fell on Lorenta, who was squatting next to the spider and whispering comforting words to it. "*I don't like this situation one bit,*" Nodwel thought, "*I feel that we may have been led into a trap, even more so now than before we descended into this eerie place. I just have a really bad feeling about this.*"

"Oh… See here? In places where the soil and rock has crumbled… It's been repaired and the weaker points have been strengthened. It appears that this place gets regular maintenance. This is exciting," Weena said getting bolder with her exploration of the chamber.

Dendrox called quietly to her, "Weena, it would be wise not to get away from the group."

"Yeah, okay," she replied, but made no apparent effort to follow the advice, at least not right away.

Yarin was clearly afraid. His eyes were wide as he looked all around him, his fear keeping him alert. Yarin's heart pounded hard and fast in his chest. His ears almost hurt from trying to be aware of every tiny sound. He looked to Lorenta and the giant spider and didn't know what to think. All he knew was that he wanted to be safe and that's not what he felt here. To Yarin, both Asdella and Candra appeared calm and collected, and it was clear that they had not let their guard down, not even for a

<Zaylyn ><Quest For The Sword Of Anthrowst ><By Katrina Mandrake-Johnston >   <Ch 26> < 84 >
second. He could tell that Dendrox was on edge and so was Vordin. The dwarf wore a worried expression and Weena seemed to be oblivious to the fact that there could be danger here.

As Vordin did not want to cause the others to have further mistrust in Lorenta, he said to her only in his mind, with some part of him wishing that she could actually hear him, "*Lorenta, I hope you know what you're doing. To trust these spiders just because they say we should is probably not a good idea. You might have only seen what you wanted to see and not the reality. Perhaps this voice you hear inside your mind is there just because of some desperate need to be accepted. If that's the case, we are dead for sure.*"

Weena called out to them, "The tunnel repairs seem to be held and strengthened with some sort of strange substance. I think it's… web. A lot of it…" Weena quickly realized that this was the last place she wanted to be. Fear led her back to the safety of the group. "We really should get out of here as soon as possible. Maybe it's not as bad as we think up above. We should go back. We really should. We're in a whole nest of these giant spiders!" Weena urged with fright.

Candra told her, "Just relax. There's no immediate danger, at least not yet. Did you find out anything at all? Any bit of information could be helpful."

"Didn't you hear what I said? We are in a large nest of these huge spiders!" Weena explained in disbelief of the elf's words, "The webbing used to fortify the passages, the new and recently laid, suggests that there has to be quite a lot of them! We won't be able to escape! We can't possibly fight our way out, not after they find us! So, before they discover us and realize that dinner has stupidly walked right into their snare, we should leave! Right now! Come on! Please, I can't go all by myself!"

"First you have to calm down," Candra said to her with an annoyed look, "I'm not going back up to the surface, especially if there are Killnarin up there. So what do we know about these giant spiders, besides being large and creepy, with fangs and everything else?"

"I don't know!" Weena began, but then quickly changed her tone noticing the angry glare starting in Candra's eye, "It's peculiar behavior. Spiders don't live in colonies like ants and bees do, at least not that I've ever heard of. When baby spiders emerge from an egg sack, there are a lot of them that scatter, but that clearly isn't the case here."

"What else?" Candra asked.

"Why do you keep asking me all these questions? We're wasting time! We have to get out of here!"

"For one, she's trying to calm you down and stop you from drawing attention to us," Dendrox explained and then added, "Maybe we're dealing with some kind of advanced form of spider. They don't seem like ordinary ones, as we know them. Maybe the spider did communicate with her somehow." He asked Lorenta, "Sorry, what was your name again?"

"Lorenta," she answered remaining in her solemn state. She wasn't pleased with the way the spider, in his critical state, was being ignored. He was most likely their savior, and they were treating him as if his fate didn't matter one way or another. Lorenta added despite her feelings, "Yes, I agree. It is odd behavior."

"I want to leave! I have to get out of here! We all have to get out of here!" Weena said still in a panic, "We are in a nest of giant spiders! Hairy and hideous spiders with fangs the size of daggers, dripping with venom… I feel itchy, like tiny ones are crawling all over me! I have to get out! Which tunnel leads back to the well?"

"Shut up!" Asdella snarled, "Before I make you!"

"I'm sorry, it's just that…" Weena started, shocked at Asdella's intolerance.

"What's that noise?" Yarin asked, his voice choked with fear.

They all paused a moment in silence, trying to hear what Yarin had heard.

"I hear it. It sounds like… like… I don't know, like a drumming sound of some sort, like rain on a rooftop or something like that," said Dendrox.

Candra said, "Whatever it is, I don't like the sound of it."

A moment passed before Lorenta told them, "It's footsteps."

"What?" Vordin asked her.

<Zaylyn ><Quest For The Sword Of Anthrowst ><By Katrina Mandrake-Johnston >   <Ch 26> < 85 >

"Footsteps. There is web within the tunnels, allowing for easy movement through them. What you hear is the sound of footsteps padding along the webbing. There are quite a few of them, and they're coming from all directions." She was able to feel the vibrations of their movements even in her human form. Here, in this, she was more aware of her surroundings as she did not have only her ears to rely on. Lorenta then added, knowing that these next words would be ignored, "I'm sure they mean us no harm."

"Yeah, right," Candra laughed uneasily as she got ready for battle, as did the rest of the group, whether it was to run or fight.

The soft drumming of the footsteps gradually got louder as the spiders approached the chamber.

<World of Zaylyn ><Quest For The Sword Of Anthrowst ><By Katrina Mandrake-Johnston ><Ch 27>

CHAPTER 27 = SPIDER CONFRONTATION

"If they are part of some strange telepathic community, they aren't going to take it lightly that we have one of their members wounded and dying beside us. And it doesn't help that we're responsible for making it that way either," Nodwel said lifting his battle-axe from his back and holding it ready in his muscular arms.

Illuminated by the lantern light, at least one giant spider could be seen at the entrance to each tunnel. Several also came around to guard the short tunnel leading back up to the well, blocking their escape. Their party was surrounded and outnumbered. The spiders did not approach them, and once again there was silence.

"Ambush… This should be interesting," Asdella said with a grin.

"Tell me something," Dendrox asked her, "Which is it? Do you have a death wish? Do you think you're invincible? Or are you just plain nuts?"

"Maybe all three," said Asdella, "Maybe I just got bored and decided to create a situation full of awkward and dangerous obstacles just to see what happens. You know, see if we survive or not. It's all in fun. Don't you find this thrilling enough? We could always throw in a twist. Maybe see what happens if we hack up their friend here a bit. That would make it more interesting, you think?" Her sword was positioned so the blade tip was on the ground and she rested her hands on the hilt. She appeared to be just calmly waiting for something to happen. Dendrox wasn't sure if she were joking or not, so he just left it alone.

"Lorenta," Vordin said as he held the small dagger he had taken from Rasindell's hut, "can't you tell them we come in peace or something?"

"I can't talk to them. I'm not one of them. Even when this one was speaking to me in my mind, I was unable to speak back to him. As far as I know, they can only talk to us or maybe only to me. I don't know," she told him, "I wish I had the answers. I'm just as scared as you, you know. I have no idea what their intentions are."

"Oh great! You could have told us that before!" Dendrox snapped angrily, "You led us all to believe that you could somehow talk to the damn thing!"

"I didn't. I said that he spoke to me, and I told you what he said. I never said that I could speak to him," Lorenta protested.

"It doesn't matter now," Nodwel said to them, "We all made our decision to come down here, whether we had our suspicions or not."

"I'm sorry. I never knew what their intentions were when I suggested we follow," Lorenta apologized, "I just thought that maybe… I wanted to trust them… I wanted to believe that there was some hope, that all was not lost… I do know what the intentions of those 'demons' are, though. They kill and destroy. I'd rather be here with these spiders who perhaps have good intentions than to be slaughtered by those foul beasts."

"I agree, I like our odds better here than up there," Vordin added.

"Are you blind?! Have you not looked around us at the situation here?!" Candra said with a grim face, "We have chosen one death over another. Our odds are better here of receiving a quick and less painful death than above, where I'm sure those creatures would prolong it and torture us as long as

<Zaylyn ><Quest For The Sword Of Anthrowst ><By Katrina Mandrake-Johnston >   <Ch 27> < 86 >
possible before letting us die."

"What are they doing?" Weena managed to say, "Why are they all just standing there?"

Several moments passed. Then, what felt like a heavy weight tried to settle into each person's mind.

"What's going on?" Candra demanded.

"Don't fight it. They're trying to communicate with us. Let them into your mind," Lorenta told them.

"So they can take control and do whatever they want with me? Turn us against each other, so they can watch us kill each other? I'm not going to give up my mind to them," said Candra, "I'm keeping my wits about me and I think I speak for everyone too when I say that."

"I'd have to be pretty trusting to allow something like that, and right now, I am everything but," Nodwel commented.

Dendrox said, "We don't even know what their intentions are, and even if we did, I wouldn't agree to it."

Vordin added, "Yeah, they might be seeking revenge on us for their wounded member. If they want into my head they'll have to force their way in. Sorry, Lorenta."

Yarin crouched down on his knees holding his head, trying to keep them out. Weena placed a hand on his back to comfort the frightened boy.

Weena suggested to them all, "Try to imagine an empty room, and the force trying to enter as one of the walls. Push with your mind against this wall as hard as you can and hold it back. That works for me at least."

"Alright, I'll try that," said Asdella.

"Lorenta? Are you going to let them in?" Vordin asked her.

"I have to try. It's our only way of finding out anything," Lorenta told him, letting the weight settle and envelope her mind as before.

A long silence passed while the spiders spoke to Lorenta, while the others, still wary of a possible attack, waited nervously for a response.

Finally, Lorenta addressed them. "They spoke of the creatures that attacked the villagers. Several spiders came to the surface last night to make an attempt to save some of the people by dragging them down into these underground passages. They were attacked and killed, as we saw, and not by the beasts. The Killnarin continued their attack upon the people and nothing more could be done. A further attempt to help the people was decided as a lost cause, and that no more lives should be lost to their ignorance. This spider here went above tonight against the wishes of the others. He found us, and almost died, and probably will, for his brave and selfless rescue. They really don't trust us."

"They have good reason not to," Weena said.

Lorenta continued, "Anyway, they want us to drop our weapons. We're to go with them and wait until a decision has been made. Apparently their telepathic capabilities have enabled them to evolve into a prospering community much like you would find in any town or village."

"That's all very interesting, but there's no way I'm parting with my weapon," Asdella told her, "I never do."

"Neither am I. I'm the one that shot their friend here with an arrow, remember? As if I want to be weaponless when they learn that little bit of information," Candra said giving Dendrox a nervous glance.

"Well, I'm putting my pathetic little dagger away. It probably won't be of much use to me anyway in a fight," Vordin said tucking the dagger back into the side pocket of his backpack. He looked to Lorenta saying, "I'm hoping that this will be sufficient enough for them. I don't want to part with my only tool and means of defense."

"Don't look to me," Lorenta told them, "I'm just relaying their message."

Several moments passed in silence as the party stood there ready for action. Then, as if from nowhere, thick and sticky net-like webbing dropped down from the ceiling onto all of them. Everyone

<Zaylyn ><Quest For The Sword Of Anthrowst ><By Katrina Mandrake-Johnston >   <Ch 27> < 87 >

was instantly ensnared and the more they struggled, the more helpless they became, eventually falling to the floor of the chamber like wriggling worms. Luckily, Weena's lantern was extinguished in the process, eliminating the possibility of the webbing catching fire.

Several of the giant spiders, obviously the ones that had released the trap, descended down a series of narrow ramps that led from several small platforms near the ceiling of the chamber to the floor.

The spiders then proceeded to separate the struggling adventurers. Vordin's magical flask continued to light their way, although it was of little help to them as they couldn't discern one thing from another, as the spiders were now rolling the tightly bound captives toward the tunnel opposite the one leading up to the well.

Eventually, they stopped in a smaller but spacious chamber. Except for being incredibly dizzy, no one in the group was hurt except for a few minor bruises. Weapons and accessible belongings were stripped from the prisoners and placed in the center of the room. Then each person was pushed into separate alcoves in the rock wall. The alcove openings were sealed by use of the same thick and porous net-like webbing that had been used to capture them. All of the spiders then exited the chamber except one, who remained as a guard at the tunnel entrance which also happened to be the only exit.

Vordin's lantern was on the very top of the pile of their belongings, lighting the room in a dim glow. Vordin was thankful that the flask had not been broken, and found himself wondering if it even could be broken, as it had taken quite a beating. The clasp locking the metal door of the case to its side had held firmly, keeping it open, which he was also thankful for. The last thing he wanted, was to be in the dark as well during all this.

After some time, everyone managed to struggle free as the strength of the web had diminished greatly and most of the webbing had been removed when their weapons and items were taken. Asdella still had her sword, as the spider would have had to free her completely to remove the weapon from her.

Vordin, within his alcove which was only about three feet deep, looked around the circular chamber through the webbing. He could see that there were tiny holes in the ceiling, which let in light and fresh air. These were about the size of a rabbit hole, so they offered no hope of escape. He wondered if small animals ever fell through these holes and decided that this was probably so and partially how these giant spiders obtained their food.

"*Perhaps foolish adventurer for dinner and clumsy woodland animal for dessert. How did we get ourselves into this? What was the point of surviving my village? Instead of going somewhere safe, I foolishly agree to travel down to another village which I know is being attacked by the same creatures that slaughtered mine,*" he said to himself, "*And now I'm here awaiting my death, just as I did in that damn tree! And what about that poor kid? We take Yarin from the one place he might have been safe and drag him down here. There must be a way to escape. I won't just wait here! I have to figure something out.*"

"Is everyone all right?" Nodwel asked.

"I'm scared," Yarin said, his voice full of fear, "What's going to happen to us? Are they going to eat us?"

"Well, that ambush was sneaky, but they're obviously not too smart. This little bit of webbing they've celled us up with can't hold us. I'll have you all out in a second," Asdella said. Her first attempt to break through the webbing was with her sword and then in frustration with her bare hands. She found that she couldn't break the web, no matter how hard she tried. "What's going on? This isn't right!" she exclaimed.

They all tried to free themselves and their efforts had similar results.

"It can't be," Weena exclaimed in amazement, "but it's the only thing that could make sense."

"What?" Candra asked.

"It has to be a spell of some sort. It's the only explanation," she answered.

"How can they possibly cast spells or even know magic in the first place?" Dendrox muttered.

"I don't know. What are they going to do to us? I don't want to die…" Weena said as she started to cry.

"So what? We just wait here and accept whatever fate they decide for us?" Vordin said in

<Zaylyn ><Quest For The Sword Of Anthrowst ><By Katrina Mandrake-Johnston >   <Ch 27> < 88 >
frustration, "Can't you do some sort of counter spell or something, Weena?"

Weena replied between sobs, "I'm nothing. How many times do I have to tell you people that? I'm an amateur. So I got lucky twice. So what? I'm useless. I can't do magic. Not the way you want. Nothing that can help us."

"There has to be some way of escaping," Vordin said.

Dendrox said to him, "And then what? Brave a million giant spiders with all their strength, venom, and speed? Even if we fight our way through, then what? Back up the well to face who knows how many of those foul Killnarin? We have a better chance of survival if we just wait and see what options arise. I have no intention of going out without a fight."

Nodwel added, "What we need is a plan. We need to find out more about these spiders and what their intentions are. Any ideas? Lorenta seems to be our best bet at getting us through this. I agree with Dendrox. There's just too many of them to battle our way free."

Asdella announced, "I'm no good at plans. You know that Nodwel. I'm going to catch some much-needed sleep." Then she said calmly, "Oh and Weena?"

"Yes," she replied, still sobbing.

"Do shut up. I thought you were supposed to be somewhat intelligent," she said to her in an annoyed tone.

Weena tried to stifle her tears, mainly out of fear of angering Asdella.

"Nodwel," Vordin tried to whisper to the dwarf, "How can she take a nap at a time like this?"

"Don't ask. I have no clue either," he replied.

<World of Zaylyn ><Quest For The Sword Of Anthrowst ><By Katrina Mandrake-Johnston ><Ch 28>

<u>CHAPTER 28 = THE SPIRIT</u>

Of course, Asdella could not sleep. Sleep had merely been an excuse to be left alone. She sat upon the cold rock floor with her tormented thoughts of Narr and his horrible death. Even though she tried not to think of him, she couldn't stop herself.

"What did he expect from me? That I would eventually fall in love with him, if he kept pestering me? Sure, he's the type that grows on you after awhile, even to the point where you start to take him for granted. I guess I got used to having him around, that's all. I'm just expecting to have some annoying remark or aggravation from him to put up with, nothing more. Now that he's gone, it doesn't feel right. All the unwanted attention he kept giving me, most of the time I couldn't get rid of him. I should have just given him a good punch in the nose every time he bothered me. I don't know why I could never bring myself to do that. I can't possibly miss him. I just need to get used to the peace and quite of not having him around, that's all. Could I have loved him? Even if I could have brought myself to feel something, then what? A kiss, a touch, for him to be near me... The only emotions I'll ever feel regarding that are hatred, disgust, and a feeling of violation. I would end up hating him. What we had was fine. It was comfortable. But I realize now that it wasn't. I find myself longing for something more now, wishing that there had been something more than the awkward but comfortable distance that I accepted for so long. I'm such a fool. Comfortable? What, that I didn't have to admit that I felt something for him? I should have tried. But it would have ended horribly and I would have lost one of my closest friends. I know it would have ended that way. But can I even call him a friend? I don't really allow myself to have friends, now do I? If you have friends and people close to you, they can be used against you, tortured and killed until you can bare it no longer. Then they win and you lose. But I have lost. What they did to me... What they did to the others... And now my heart is cold, and I am alone even when I am among people I call companions. But for that slim chance that it may have worked somehow for Narr and me... that this ball of hatred might have melted just a little bit... that someone might be able to connect with the inner me, the one that was lost to me so long ago... Perhaps it might have been worth the risk to let him get close. If I could feel something more than this cold and aching hollowness... If there was anyway that I could have somewhat of a normal life... It would have been worth it. I know that now. And now it's too late... I do miss him... And even more now that I can imagine that we could have had something more, like he wanted. I'll probably hate

myself forever for this, for letting my chance slip by."

* *Figures I have to die for you to finally notice me.* *

"Who said that?" Asdella said as she instinctively raised her sword.

"Who said what?" Candra asked, "No one said anything just now."

"We've given up on the plan making for now. Everyone needs rest. Get some while you can," Nodwel added.

Asdella ignored them both. She was sure that she had heard someone speak to her.

* *Looks like you're just replacing one excuse to be miserable with another. You can't love because of your past and now you can't love because the only person you cared about is dead. Is that your excuse?* *

"Show yourself," she demanded.

"Nodwel, is she okay?" Weena asked.

"Asdella?" Nodwel bellowed, hoping that she was merely talking in her sleep and that he would wake her. She made no reply. Then he realized, "*This might be the only way for her to deal with Narr's death: to sleep it off. I shouldn't wake her.*" He told Weena, "I think it's best to leave her alone."

After hearing the voice twice now, Asdella was alert and defensive.

* *You can hear me? Asdella, you can really hear me? It's me! Don't you recognize my voice?* *

"Of course I do. That's why my weapon is drawn. You are not who you pretend to be, and you will die horribly for your choice of disguise. Narr is dead. I saw for myself," she whispered under her breath.

* *I know it must be hard for you, and I'm sorry, but it's me! I can't explain it. I think I might be a ghost or something. It's crazy, I know. You're the only one who can hear me. I can remember dying, I think. You can't see me, can you?* * Narr's voice said to her.

"No, I can't," she whispered very quietly, "You're not one of those damn spiders are you, because I didn't mind any of you much until you tried getting inside my head and started suggesting I part with my sword."

* No, it's actually me, * he tried to convince her.

"You do realize that I want to believe you're real. So… I will accept that by some strange miracle you actually are somehow," she decided, and then made sure her very real and serious threat was made extremely clear to him, "But, you better hope that I don't discover otherwise or my revenge will be violent and messy."

"*I can hear your thoughts,*" Narr told her, "*Maybe it would be a good idea to just think what you want to say, instead of saying it. I think you're making your new companions uneasy.*"

"*Alright,*" she agreed and asked within her mind, "*What's it like then?*"

"*Well, it's hard to explain,*" he told her, "*I don't have a body, so that's bad luck for you, eh?*" Then realizing that his attempt to lighten the situation was an utter failure, he said, "*Yeah, well, everything that has to do with a body is gone, like sight, smells, touch, taste, and things like that. Well, I don't need to eat anything ever again, so I guess my loss of taste won't bother me too much. Okay, it's weird, and I don't really know how I can do this, but I can experience these senses through others. What I think, is that somehow my energy can slip into someone and sort of share experiences. I can hear their thoughts, see through their eyes, experience their emotions, feel what they feel, maybe even taste what they taste. I have yet to try that one. I can sense things. That's how I see and feel. I really don't know how to describe it to you. You know, if you close your eyes and walk towards a wall, you get a weird feeling just before you hit it, and you just somehow know it's there? It's kind of like that. Well, I guess some would hit it without sensing it first, but you know what I mean, right? And I can sense a person's energy. Like if there is someone standing behind you, and you can tell there's someone there and maybe even who it might be without even looking? It's like that, only on a larger and more complicated scale. So far you're the only one that can hear me, or more likely, feel what I want to say. Maybe it's because I have a special connection with you. Can't hide from me now,*" he laughed, "*I can read your every thought. No more cold shoulder treatment for me this time. There's no*

<Zaylyn ><Quest For The Sword Of Anthrowst ><By Katrina Mandrake-Johnston >   <Ch 28> < 90 >

getting rid of me. Oh come on, what do I have to say to get you to smile?"

"*It's just that all this is a little hard for me to accept,*" she admitted.

"*How do you think I feel?!*" he exclaimed, "*This is much harder for me to accept than it is for you! I'm dead! Is this even supposed to be happening to me? I don't have a body, I'm scared, I… I…*" Then Asdella could hear him let out a big breathy sigh inside her mind as he tried to calm himself. He finally said, "*I'm just relieved that I don't have to be alone in this anymore.*"

"*Lucky me,*" she thought sarcastically and not very kindly, "*I'm glad you're still alive in a way, but can't we talk later? All this talking within my head is starting to make it ache terribly.*"

"*Hey, sorry, but this is pretty frightening for me, alright?*" he said starting to get upset with her, "*Plus, I'm thinking my thoughts at you, rather than speaking them, so I'm sorry if I'm rambling on and on. This is all new to me. You have my full attention now, I mean, who else am I going to talk to? No one else can hear me!*"

"*Okay fine. If you need to talk, I'll listen. Just try not to overwhelm me,*" she allowed.

"*Sure, Asdella,*" Narr agreed, trying to subdue the tension he was feeling and keep it from affecting her mind. "*Hey, I'm going to try something,*" he said with a mischievous hint to his voice, "*Tell me if you can feel this.*"

An electric-like shiver ran along the length of Asdella's arm. "*Oh wow, was that you?!*" she exclaimed in astonishment, "*I could almost feel a hand run along my arm.*"

"*Who says it was my hand?*" he joked.

"*Oh stop it,*" she blushed and the corner of her mouth turned up in the beginnings of a smile.

"*Ah, it worked! I knew I could cheer you up,*" he chuckled.

"*It's good to have you back. So, tell me, how exactly do you move about?*" she asked.

"*Well, you know how I said I can sort of sense the presence of other people. I can move within the spaces, but like I said, I can't see things the way you do anymore. Imagine a dark room and everyone in it with a light around them. And I figure that like vision gradually adjusting to the darkness of a room, I have a feeling that as I become more accustomed to my new state, things will become clearer for me. My abilities have already improved quite a lot since I first died. At first, I was completely blind to everything; I couldn't sense or feel anything or anyone. Then I gradually became aware that Yarin was still alive. I'm glad Nodwel was able to find him. Asdella, I just want to stay with you for now, riding in the back of your mind where I feel safe. Alright? I felt so lost before: no one could hear me, no one could see me, no one could touch me. I'm also afraid that if I discover too much about my state, that I might move on to something different and lose you again. You're so incredibly tired, Asdella. Get some sleep. As far as I can tell, things seem safe enough for now.*"

"*Alright,*" she thought to him, as she tried to get as comfortable as possible on the hard rock floor. Then to her surprise, she felt ghostly arms wrap around her, and she felt a sense of comfort that she had not felt since she was a very small child.

<World of Zaylyn ><Quest For The Sword Of Anthrowst ><By Katrina Mandrake-Johnston ><Ch 29>

CHAPTER 29 = YARIN'S DREAM

Meanwhile, Yarin, sitting as quietly as he could on the rock floor of his cell, listened to all that was happening around him. Everyone had their attention drawn elsewhere, and Yarin didn't mind, as he didn't want everyone fussing over him. He wanted to be alone.

"*How did all this happen? A few days ago everything was fine. I was happy. My mother and brother were with me. This is like a horrible nightmare… Maybe I'll wake up soon… I want my mother… I want to see my brother…*" Yarin cried trying not to make much noise, as he didn't want the others to hear. His head ached. His face was wet with tears. And, even though he fought it, he dozed off for the first time in two days.

He began to dream…

His mother and brother were standing beside him in an open field of green grass. The sky was clear blue, and the sun was shining brightly.

<Zaylyn ><Quest For The Sword Of Anthrowst ><By Katrina Mandrake-Johnston >   <Ch 29> < 91 >

Then suddenly he felt himself falling backwards. He was falling down a hole in the earth. As he fell, he could see his family reaching out to him from the top of the hole. Darkness surrounded him as he fell farther and farther away from his mother and brother.

He landed on wood. Large cabinet doors closed in front of him blocking the vision of his family. He pounded on the cabinet doors trying to break them open and to somehow get back up to his family. The doors wouldn't budge.

He heard a voice shouting. It was Narr. He was back in the store. His mother and brother were just on the other side of the heavy wooden doors. He heard the beast tear into the room.

Narr was shouting for them to get back, as he was going to try to hold off the beast. Yarin couldn't see anything. He had to get the doors open! He couldn't let it happen again! He pounded as hard as he could on the doors, but they wouldn't move.

The old man that had been with them let out a painful cry. Then his mother was screaming. A beast was snarling. Narr was shouting. Yarin heard objects breaking. He heard the sound of claws on steel. His brother let out a horrible sound and then there was the sound of something hitting the floor.

Soon there was silence. Narr was dead. His family was gone and so was the old man. Just the beast remained. Yarin could hear its heavy and raspy breathing as it searched for him. Its heavy feet pounded on the floor as it walked. It was close now. Yarin could feel its breath through the doors, it was so close. It was searching for him; it wasn't going to let him escape.

Claws suddenly ripped through the cabinet doors as if they were paper. The creature lunged at him viciously with huge teeth dripping in blood... and Yarin woke up screaming.

<World of Zaylyn ><Quest For The Sword Of Anthrowst ><By Katrina Mandrake-Johnston ><Ch 30>

CHAPTER 30 =   THE TRIAL

"Yarin, are you all right?" Weena asked with great concern.

"I just had a bad dream. I'm okay," he told them.

The spider that guarded the entrance suddenly moved from its position. Another spider entered the chamber and came to stand in front of the cell containing Lorenta.

"I think it's talking to her," whispered Dendrox.

Everyone waited impatiently, and after some time, Lorenta said to the others gravely, "It has been decided, that if the one who was shot with the arrow dies, so shall the one who shot him." Lorenta looked to Candra with a worried look.

Having relayed its message to them, the spider departed, and the guard took its position in front of the tunnel once more.

"Hey, Weena," Candra called, "Can't you use some sort of magic to get us out of here?" Even though she tried to hide it, there was a hint of panic to the elf's voice.

"I know three useless spells: Heal, Cure, and Shield. And they don't work properly," Weena explained, once again on the verge of tears.

Vordin told her, "Use the Heal spell to heal the spider. Why can't you just do that?"

"Yes, do it," Candra said, "Sooner or later they'll discover that it was me that shot the spider."

"There's a slight chance it might work," she replied, "but I'm so incredibly frightened of them. If I have to walk out there, vulnerable and afraid, there is definitely not any chance of the spell working. It takes a lot of concentration to do a spell you know, and the only thing I'll be concentrating on is keeping myself alive."

"I thought you said you have to let a spell work itself or something like that, that you didn't have to concentrate. You told me that it will fail if you try to concentrate on how a spell works," said Dendrox.

"No, that's right. What I meant was, I wouldn't be able to clear my mind enough even to make a feeble attempt at casting it!" she explained, "It's not exactly easy when there is danger everywhere I look!"

Vordin asked, "Well what about that Shield spell? Can't you use it and be protected that way?"

"Okay, say I go out there. What if my Heal spell doesn't work? And it won't, because I won't be

<Zaylyn ><Quest For The Sword Of Anthrowst ><By Katrina Mandrake-Johnston >   <Ch 30> < 92 >

able to concentrate," Weena said in a hurried voice, "The point is, they don't know how slim the chance is of it working. They'll kill me thinking that it's some sort of deception. And if my Shield spell works, all they have to do is just wait until the spell wears off to get at me."

"Lorenta," Nodwel said, "tell them that it's a weak spell. All she can do is try, nothing is guaranteed. I will accompany Weena to provide protection for her."

"I can't speak to them. I can only understand them. I've explained this before," she told them, "In spider form, maybe, but even then I probably wouldn't be able to since I'm not one of them. They behave very differently and speak to me through some kind of mind ability. When I feel them trying to enter, I simply don't resist them. I have no reason to. Then a voice fills my mind."

"Okay, we understand. So you're saying you can change into a spider then?" Dendrox asked, "Vordin said that you were some sort of shape-shifter. So you can change into any form you wish, including a spider?"

They had made their feelings on spiders clear already, but Lorenta didn't care what they thought of her anymore. She was angry, and she refused to hide who she was any longer. Besides, come morning she would not have a choice in the matter. "No, at dawn I will turn back into my true form. I am just the same as these beings you despise. I am a spider who at night can change into a human. I know now, that this has to be a curse. Humans are cruel. Why should you treat me any differently than these spiders here? Just because I appear human to you now? I don't want to pretend anymore. If it means anything, I think their decision is beyond fair. They show mercy now after all the pain and suffering that the villagers gave to them, and they still continue to show mercy to you, Candra. All they want is our help to save the wounded one. Anyway, these spiders truly act more human than they do spider, just without the cruelty and prejudice."

"I don't trust her," Nodwel told the others.

"Oh who cares," Asdella spoke up, "Lorenta's not the threat here. Just use gestures to show that you mean them no harm and that you want to help. Don't seem threatening, and don't show fear. Animals hate that. It makes them nervous. I guess that goes in this situation too. If you don't try, Weena, they'll most likely kill us all, so where's the harm in trying then? Maybe you'll get lucky and save us all, who knows? Of course, there's always the option of fighting our way out, but even I have to admit that the chance of victory trying that, is less than measurable."

Nodwel was surprised, as he had never seen this side of Asdella before and he was sure that not many people had. She was actually weighing the odds of a battle beforehand and giving encouragement to a fellow companion. It was not like her to do so and especially not in the manner she had.

"Don't show fear?" Weena asked letting out a weak laugh, "Yeah right, that is definitely not going to happen." But then Weena said reluctantly, "But I will try. I guess I'm our only hope, right?"

Weena patted the web to get the spider's attention. She put her hands to her breast and then held them outstretched in hope that it would be interpreted that she was willing to help.

As the spider moved slowly toward her, Weena pressed her back up against the back wall of her cell, trembling with fear. The spider began tearing down the web to Weena's prison. Weena whimpered and squealed, her face fear-stricken and with tears running down her cheeks. Vordin was worried that she would faint before she was free.

When the webbing had been removed, the spider stood aside and waited for her to step out. She clung to the back wall, frozen with fright.

"I can't do it," she managed to choke out, "I'm too afraid. It's right there. Right beside me. I can see its fangs… its hairy legs… It's looking right at me with all of its eyes. Help me. Somebody help me," she whimpered.

"He's not going to hurt you. Come on, just go," Lorenta told her.

"I can't move," she hissed at them, "Do something! Keep it away from me! Help me…"

The spider moved one of its front legs slightly, and Weena frantically attempted to clamber up the rock wall behind her in a desperate panic.

The spider moved away from Weena and waited over by the tunnel entrance, giving Weena some much-needed space. Weena calmed down slightly, but not much.

<Zaylyn ><Quest For The Sword Of Anthrowst ><By Katrina Mandrake-Johnston >   <Ch 30> < 93 >

"I can't do this. Please don't make me do this," she whined.

"Weena," Vordin called, "take my lantern with you or else you won't be able to see."

"I'm too afraid to move," she told them again.

"It will be okay," Nodwel said to her, "We're all counting on you."

"He's not going to hurt you. They want you to help, remember?" Lorenta added.

"What happens when I fail? They'll kill me," Weena said.

"No, they won't. They'll bring you back here," Asdella told her, "They said if the wounded one dies, that the one who shot him is going to pay. That means Candra. Isn't that what they said?"

"Oh great, thanks a lot," Candra tried to snarl at her, but her fear was showing. "Weena? Don't fail, okay?" Candra said to her with desperation in her voice, "You can do this, alright? Please do this, and hurry! You're wasting time! The thing's going to be dead before you even get out there, which means so will I!"

"*Damn it, why doesn't she move! It's going to be too late!*" Dendrox screamed at her within his mind and then pleaded, "Weena, don't let this happen. If you're not even going to try..." There was anxiety in Dendrox's voice. "They're going to kill Candra for sure! Most likely all of us!"

"Okay, I'll do it. I'll try," she told them.

She tried to give herself the strength to do what needed to be done. "*I can't let this happen. I sat by, too afraid when the school burned, while my brother... There was time to warn them... to get them out before it was too late. I saw the signs that something was wrong. I smelt the strange odors and knew it had to be something I added to the fire. I could have saved my brother. I could have saved everyone, and all I did was hide and let it happen because I was too scared to do something about it. Even in my dreams I alter what really happened. I try to fool myself into believing that I had no time to help, that I didn't know what was happening, that I didn't know that my brother had gone in to look for me, and worst of all that I wasn't entirely sure of what I had put into the fire. I didn't intend for anyone to get hurt, just to maybe get back at them a little for all the teasing they did and that damn teacher who kept picking on me. I was just angry, that's all. I didn't mean to... But whether I meant to or not doesn't matter. Everyone died and because of me. I can't let that happen again. I have to try and I have to do it now...*" and Weena pushed herself away from the wall and into the room.

She edged slowly toward the pile of their belongings, her eyes falling on all the weapons she couldn't wield. She spotted the box with the glowing flask inside. She retrieved it from the pile, her eyes ever-watchful of the enormous spider and its fangs.

With great effort, Weena forced every reluctant step, bringing her slowly toward the exit and the spider that awaited her.

"*All their encouraging words, and all of them trying to show confidence in me and my abilities. All I see is fear,*" Weena thought to herself, "*I am in this situation alone now, and I will be relying only on myself. All their words are just words without any meaning other than to give me false hope. They all are counting on me. I don't want this responsibility, not when lives are at stake.*"

She hesitated, looking at her imprisoned companions, and Weena was then pushed gently with a hairy leg urging her toward the tunnel entrance. She cringed, a shiver jolting down her spine. She held Vordin's lantern close in front of her with both hands, and held the metal case so tightly that her knuckles were turning white.

Rigid with fear, she slowly entered the tunnel. Words of encouragement continued to be called after her as she walked, and Weena could hear the sound of the spider's many feet patting along the tunnel as it followed her.

When Weena exited the tunnel, she found herself once again in the larger chamber, and by the magical light of the lantern, she could vaguely make out the other passageways that led away from it. Her eyes searched from tunnel to tunnel, longing to find the one leading to the well and her freedom, but she knew being surrounded by numerous spiders as she was, meant there wasn't any chance for escape. She could feel the fear building up inside her to the point where she thought she might actually explode from it. She wanted to run... to escape. She counted four of the spiders between her and one of the tunnels, and she figured that this must be the one leading to the well. Her complete focus was

<Zaylyn ><Quest For The Sword Of Anthrowst ><By Katrina Mandrake-Johnston >   <Ch 30> < 94 >

now on the tunnel before her. Each time she weighed her chances, her mind kept pushing in favor of running. Deep down she knew that the fear was keeping her from thinking rationally.

"*Don't run. Don't run! Whatever you do, you can't run,*" she commanded herself, "*You will be killed, if you run. You can do this. Don't run. The others are counting on you.*"

The one that had led her from the prison nudged her again. Weena jumped and a frightened screech escaped her lips. Some of the spiders around her shifted position slightly, but they did not attack as she thought they might.

She moved forward until she could see the wounded spider. Weena tried to focus on the single spider and the task that lay before her. She would have to concentrate in order to keep the fear from taking her over. Weena approached and she desperately tried to ignore all the spiders that encircled her now with their many eyes watching her every move so intensely. She found that she could not simply ignore their presence and the sound of her heart began to pound loudly in her ears.

Weena tried to compose herself and knelt down beside the wounded spider, making sure to be as far away from its fangs as she could. As she did so, one of its legs twitched and brushed up against her robe. Her whole body jolted with terror and she let out a shriek, which she immediately and desperately tried to muffle.

"*If my spell is going to have any chance of working, I have to get over this fear and fast,*" she commanded herself as she tried to hold back the almost unbearable panic which was erupting inside her. She placed the lantern beside her, noticing how terribly her hands were trembling. "*Okay,*" she told herself trying to remain calm, "*Imagine that in reality the spiders are actually the remaining villagers. They were somehow turned into spiders and have come here to hide from the beasts. It's plausible. There are odder things happening all around, like Lorenta for example if she truly is a spider as she says. Anything is possible, right? They are intelligent and they have a village-like community down here. It makes sense. That's why they are so incredibly different from regular spiders and this would explain their bizarre behavior as well. They must have been human once. This spider here before me could possibly be a small child… an innocent little boy perhaps, with his mother and father standing by terribly worried about him. It is obvious that they are worried for him. His family is depending on me to save him. Why would these 'people' want to hurt me? They were trying to help us and this poor boy was almost killed for doing so. It's our fault and we must help. I am our only hope. I am this child's only hope.*"

A spider nudged her from behind, as she had been kneeling motionless for some time now. This time, it wasn't as frightening for her as before. She saw them as people now and not just a tangle of hairy legs, fangs, and eyes. She found herself, in some part, actually believing her scenario, at least enough to keep herself from going into an uncontrollable panic.

Weena drew in a deep breath and tried to let it out slowly. Her breath quivered as she did so. This was not good, as fear still had her firmly in its grip.

She drew in another breath and tried to focus. She released the air quickly with determination and in that same instant placed her hands around the wound to its abdomen where the arrow was protruding from it.

She closed her eyes, concentrating on what she was trying to do, and then let her mind relax. The spell began to take form. She felt the magical energy bubbling up inside her and then flowing outward as she mouthed the silent words of the spell.

She kept her eyes shut tight, afraid to see whether or not her spell was working. "*This has to work. It's going to work. It needs to work!*" Then she heard the sound of the arrow hitting the rock floor.

Her eyes bolted open in surprise. "*It worked! It worked! I actually did it! I saved him!*"

She watched as her spell slowly closed and healed the wound until just a small bald scar-like area represented the spot where the arrow had struck. Several of the spiders approached her, and after Weena had snatched up Vordin's lantern once more, they led her back to the prison chamber.

A guard came to stand in position at the entrance, and one spider came to stand in front of the cell containing Lorenta.

"Weena?!" Candra asked with worry, "What happened? Did you do it?"

<Zaylyn ><Quest For The Sword Of Anthrowst ><By Katrina Mandrake-Johnston >   <Ch 30> < 95 >

"I healed him! I really did it!" she replied with a grin, although it quickly faded as she looked nervously over at the spider speaking to Lorenta. Weena asked, "What do you think they're going to do with us now? I mean, now that they don't need us to do anything for them."

After the spider was finished communicating with Lorenta, it left the room. The guard stood motionless in his position, forever watchful.

"Well, at least they didn't lock me up again," Weena commented, "That's a good sign, isn't it? Perhaps they will let us go."

"What did it say?" Vordin asked Lorenta.

"Well, they give thanks for saving the life of their wounded member, but they're afraid that if they release us, that they will be attacked," Lorenta replied.

"So, then what's going to happen to us?" Candra asked her, "They can't just leave us here!"

"Most likely they'll use us for food," said Dendrox.

"Don't say that," Nodwel snapped, "Think of the boy!"

"Well it's true. Why shouldn't they?" retorted Dendrox.

"But I helped them. I healed the spider. Why would they want to kill us after we helped them like that," Weena added, nervously rubbing her hands together.

"Nobody helped them," Dendrox answered, "We made the problem, and now we've just undone it to the best we can. They don't owe us anything. Don't you realize that? Did you ever think that they might decide that we are somehow responsible for the deaths of the spiders above as well simply because we are human? What then? We don't know how these things think! You even said it, now that we're of no use to them, now what? We'll all be food for these things, that's what!"

"But I don't want to die," Weena whined, as tears welled up in her bright blue eyes, "Isn't there something we can do?"

"If everyone would just calm down for a minute," Lorenta spoke up, "I have more to tell you. They're going to remove the webbing, but we must stay in this room until they decide what to do with us. If we provoke them, they will defend themselves. They also want to attempt to teach me to speak as they do. I'm going to try to learn, if I am even physically capable of doing so. If I am able to speak back to them, it will be of great help to us."

Nodwel said to them all, "So, I guess all we can do now is wait."

It was only a few moments before a group of spiders came into the chamber and started to remove the webbing.

"You think we should attack? It may be our one and only chance. What do you say?" Asdella asked.

"For one, you're the only one with a weapon right now. Even if we all did have weapons, we wouldn't stand a chance and you know that," Nodwel explained to her.

"No, please don't attack them," pleaded Lorenta, "You'll ruin any chance of us getting out of this alive. Just let me go with them and see if I can learn anything from them. I may be able to save us. You just have to be patient."

Once everyone was free from their cells, Lorenta was escorted out of the chamber.

"Good luck," Vordin called after her.

<World of Zaylyn ><Quest For The Sword Of Anthrowst ><By Katrina Mandrake-Johnston ><Ch 31>

CHAPTER 31 = DARK THOUGHTS

After Lorenta was out of sight, and a spider had taken position as guard in front of the entrance once more, Weena exclaimed, "Why did they release us? That is what they're going to do, right? I mean it's not dinnertime for them, or anything like that, right? I saved that one; they must be releasing us."

"Who cares, at least we're out of those tiny alcoves. Me, I'm getting my weapons as quickly as possible," Dendrox said heading over to the pile of their belongings, as did both Candra and Nodwel right away.

Nodwel, ever wary of the spider, after picking up his battle-axe, next retrieved his pouch.

<Zaylyn ><Quest For The Sword Of Anthrowst ><By Katrina Mandrake-Johnston >   <Ch 31> < 96 >

"My arrows are scattered all over the place," Candra remarked, clearly annoyed.

"Yeah, well so are my daggers, alright?" Dendrox said to her, "Just get your stuff as fast as possible, okay? I don't trust these spiders, and I at least want to have my weapons if I need to defend myself."

The guard watched them with its many eyes as they rummaged through the pile in search of their belongings.

"It appears that it will be quite awhile before Lorenta returns. We should eat now, as we may not get a second chance depending on what they decide for us," the dwarf suggested.

They all agreed and sat down to eat the remainder of their food in silence, by the magical light of Vordin's lantern.

***

"*I can still see her blood on my hands, even though it has been cleansed long ago. The taste of her blood on my lips is still vivid in my memory.*

"*I told her to leave. I couldn't stop myself. I tried to warn her. Why didn't she leave?*

"*I shouldn't have pretended to be something I'm not. I can't possibly have a normal life. I can't have love… only fear and hate. I am a danger to everyone. The closer someone gets to me, the greater the risk to their life. I am a fool to think I can have the simple things in life.*

"*I am a monster. I can't control these evil urges. The closer I get to love or even a simple friendship, the greater the desire to destroy it. The more I try, the stronger the hunger grows within me.*

"*I've tried feeding only a little from several people to take the place of the one or more whole victims I claim in a night… somehow trying to reach some sort of equivalent in hope of sparing lives. I even took the time to heal their wounds and to erase the memory of the attacks from their minds. I've managed to spare a few lives here and there in the past. But when I do this, the hunger is worse than ever, and it's so hard to hold back and stop myself before it's too late. The hunger is never satisfied, and when I try to resist it, the need to feed is almost constant.*

"*Is there any hope that I can be good? To somehow repay the people for the suffering I cause? How can I possibly? There is no way of justifying what I am. I could save lives, stop criminals, punish the wicked. I do sometimes, but that doesn't make a difference when it's weighed against my past deeds.*

"*I have been named many things: God of gods, Bringer of Death, Monster, Demon… There are so many,*" he sighed, "*I am The Black Shadow.*

"*I frighten even myself sometimes knowing what I am truly capable of. That is why I can never lose total control over myself and my evil nature. I must always care. I have all this power and could destroy the world with a single thought if I wished. But what kind of life would I have if I used the full extent of my powers? Is there even a limit to what I can do?*

"*All this power and I can't have love. Maybe it's best if I am denied it. If I love someone, it will give people a way to actually hurt me. They would take out all their fear and rage on her because they can't get to me. But that's not the point.*

"*I can't handle love. For someone to get close, it would be unbearable. The scent of her skin, the warmth of her touch, the soothing rhythm of her heartbeat… the beast in me wouldn't be able to resist. I would take hold and drain the life out of her until there was nothing left. I would try so desperately to hold back, but the hunger wouldn't let me. She would fade away in my arms. I would be alone again and by my own doing. How can someone ever put trust in me when I can't even trust myself?*

"*Such a stupid girl. Couldn't she see that she was in danger? I warned her to leave. It was her choice to stay. It was her fault that it happened. No, I can't allow myself to blame her. I am the monster, not her.*

"*Why didn't she go! Would that really have mattered though? How far would she have gotten? Her scent had excited me. I would have hunted her down no matter how many unsuspecting prey came between us.*

"*What was I thinking? That somehow, in some way, that she could have loved me being the horror that I am? It would have been over as soon as she discovered what I really am. Just my name strikes fear into people. She would have never gotten that close if she had known the full truth… seen the evil*

<Zaylyn ><Quest For The Sword Of Anthrowst ><By Katrina Mandrake-Johnston > <Ch 31> < 97 >

surface beyond a simple feeding…

"*What kind of life could I have given her? One of death and isolation? Living in constant fear that the one she loves could suddenly lose control of himself and take her life away? Well, that's what happened, didn't it?*" A tear ran down his pale cheek under the hood of his dark cloak.

"*I didn't have control. I thought I did. I thought I could control the urges. But the smell of her skin, the warmth of her touch… it was too much for me. The sound of her heartbeat pounding in my ears getting louder and louder, until I couldn't resist any longer, to the point where all I could do was bury my face deep into her warm flesh. And then… bite down and drink long and hard… until she became limp and lifeless in my arms...*

"*Why do I try to have something more? I have to be alone! It's what I deserve!*

"*I should just feed. There is no other reason to come in contact with the people of Zaylyn other than to do that. There's no use in trying to prolong the inevitable. All that happens is that I end up just toying with the victim, trying so desperately to have something more. Whether it be trying to gain affection, friendship, or whatever... when someone gets close, they get hurt. I can't stop it. I've tried.*

"*Am I truly evil? I must be. All the good I try to do doesn't make up for any of it. It can't. Should I just give in and play with these helpless beings as I see fit? Assume that they exist merely for my pleasure? That wouldn't be right.*

"*But so many of them, if they were in my place, would relish in the pain and destruction they could cause. All the suffering… and to them it would be mere fun. Enjoying it because it wouldn't affect them. They wouldn't stop once to think about things from the perspective of the victims.*

"*I know I've caused a lot of pain in the past, but I truly want to help these people now, beyond what I am already providing for those in the valley. I owe it to them. But I have vowed not to use my higher powers and I must keep to that vow.*

"*But, I cannot stand idle while this insane man slaughters entire villages. I feed from these people. I must make sure that my supply doesn't run short. No, that is not the real reason, I can't think like that. I could stop him myself, but I won't. Instead, I will guide the group toward this mad man's defeat. At least it will be more interesting this way. Perhaps I should get more involved with them than I have, or perhaps not.*"

From his perch in a large oak tree, he glided down to the ground. Like a shadow moving across the earth, he silently crept to the nearby cottage. He climbed up the wall of the cottage, a sleek creature of the night, and slipped quietly into the open window. Camouflaged in the darkness of the room, he spied the sleeping figure lying in the bed.

"*What does your mind tell me… Your children sleeping downstairs… You beat them almost to death… More often now than before… You blame them for your drunk of a husband leaving you… You never even wanted your children in the first place… They were just a tool to be used against him to make him stay… I think your sister should have your children instead of having you beat them into their graves. At least this will be doing your children some good whether they realize it or not. But who am I to judge? Is it right to deprive children of their mother, even one as horrible as you? You could change. Things could be different… Stop wasting time!*" his mind screamed at him, "*Feed before you lose control of your actions! You'll slip into a feeding frenzy and end up killing her, the children, and anyone else unfortunate enough to be nearby!*"

He reluctantly approached the bed. "*Perhaps feeding only when it's absolutely necessary is not as wise as I thought. Sure, less people die, but the risk of losing control is greater, and if that happens, the death toll would be much more than a little restricted feeding here and there could ever balance out. Just listen to me, I'm talking about people's lives as if they were meaningless! Like a balancing of numbers and ratios could make it any better. Life is precious, and each individual is unique. I can't just ignore that, slap a number on them, or figure that somehow they deserve it. Saving the lives of three won't make up for the death of one. Nothing can make it somehow all right. The only ultimate solution is my own death. I've even tried that too, unsuccessfully. Am I truly invincible? The least I can do, if I am forced to feed, is try to do some good for the people of Zaylyn as a result of it.*"

There was a sharp pain in his gut and the hunger intensified. He was starting to lose control. The

<Zaylyn ><Quest For The Sword Of Anthrowst ><By Katrina Mandrake-Johnston >   <Ch 31> < 98 >
woman lay before him, unaware that she was in grave danger.

"I'm sorry," he whispered and drained her of her blood and her life.

<World of Zaylyn ><Quest For The Sword Of Anthrowst ><By Katrina Mandrake-Johnston ><Ch 32>

CHAPTER 32 =   ANGER

They idly wandered about the chamber, waiting for Lorenta to return. The spider at the tunnel entrance, who had remained motionless for quite some time now, began shifting its position as if it had become agitated by something.

"Nodwel, what do you think is going on?" Asdella asked calmly.

"Don't know. I say, just be prepared for anything," he answered.

Asdella let out a bit of a snort. "I'm always ready for battle you silly dwarf."

"Do you think we can leave now?" Yarin asked in a meek voice, "I want to leave now."

"So what do we do?" Vordin asked.

"Easy, we wait," Nodwel said calmly, "We simply wait to see what happens, lad."

The guard returned to its motionless state at the tunnel entrance, and the group continued to wait patiently for Lorenta to return as it seemed they had no choice but to do so. Through the small holes in the ceiling of the chamber, they watched the night sky gradually turn to dawn and then high noon. Lorenta still had not returned.

Weena asked, "What do you think they're doing?"

"I have no idea. I just wish they would hurry up," muttered Dendrox, scuffing his boot along the rock floor.

Candra commented, "Yeah, it's pretty near unbearable just sitting here not knowing."

More time passed as they waited impatiently. It was now late afternoon, and there was still no sign of Lorenta.

Suddenly, to everyone's surprise, Asdella put both hands to her head and winced in pain.

"What's wrong?" Weena asked concerned, "Does your head hurt?"

Asdella's pulled at her short reddish hair, clenched her hands into fists, and screamed in rage.

"What the hell's wrong with her?" asked Candra with an insulting look.

"Shut up!" Asdella screamed, "Shut up, shut up, shut up!"

"Who is she talking to? One of us? What the hell did we do?" Dendrox asked defensively.

She bellowed out in rage, "You will never control me! It's my mind! I'm in control. I'm in charge!" Then she ran over to the rock wall and started banging her head against it, the whole time screaming, "Get out... of my... head!"

Nodwel exclaimed, "Asdella! No! What are you doing? Stop! You're going to hurt yourself!"

"Shut up!" she said refusing to stop.

Dendrox muttered, "One too many nuts in her fruitcake."

"What?" Candra snapped at him, "That is the most ridiculous thing I've ever heard!"

"Asdella, I'm just trying to help," said Nodwel.

She stopped banging her head and turned to him, giving him a disgusted look and saying between clenched teeth, "I'm not talking to you! I'm talking to them!"

"To who!" Nodwel demanded as his patience with her was diminishing fast.

Dendrox, insulted by what Candra had said, now said in defense, "Sounded good at the time."

"No it didn't!" the elf said with a scowl.

"To the voices, fool!" Asdella yelled at Nodwel. "Who else?!" she said looking at him as if he were a complete idiot.

"Voices? You know damn well there aren't any voices. Listen, I've had quite enough of your craziness!" Nodwel yelled at her, "I always stick up for you, telling people that you're not a complete lunatic, that all they have to do is get to know you. But it looks like I'm the fool for thinking it. There isn't a sane bone in your body, is there? You treat your friends like enemies, acting like you're so tough, when in reality you are the biggest fool I've ever seen!"

Yarin exclaimed, "Hey, how did that little spider get over there by Weena?"

<Zaylyn ><Quest For The Sword Of Anthrowst ><By Katrina Mandrake-Johnston >   <Ch 32> < 99 >

Vordin and Weena both had been watching the others argue and had not noticed much else. Weena looked down beside her and, in seeing the spider so close to her, immediately reacted in fear by stomping her foot down toward it. Luckily, Vordin reacted quickly. As soon as Yarin said this, Vordin instantly knew what Weena's reaction would be. He shoved Weena as hard as he could, knocking her down just before her foot connected with the spider and was able to save Lorenta's life.

"Hey, why did you push me?" Weena blurted out, and then seeing Vordin's glare, realized what she had almost done. "Oh… I can't believe I almost… It was simply a reaction; I wasn't thinking… If you hadn't been so quick… I can't believe… Hey, wait a minute, why didn't she change to human form? Why'd she sneak up like that?! Of course I would have reacted like that! What was she expecting?"

"It's not night yet! She can't change during the day," Vordin told her, "That doesn't matter. You could have killed her! There's no excuse! Especially after all she's done to try to help."

"Candra," Dendrox said in an annoyed tone, "you always snub everything I say."

She rolled her eyes and hissed at him, "If you didn't say such stupid things, I wouldn't have too."

Nodwel continued, "Running around like that with hardly a scrap of clothing on, bare feet most of the time even! Putting everyone else in danger, running blindly into battle without caring who else gets hurt as a result of it! You don't even care about yourself, and it ends up that it's us that has to do all the reasoning for you and pull you out of certain death situations. Oh, and then you fight us as well for saving you, don't you, as if you want to die! That's it, isn't it?! You crazy lunatic! You want to die, and you don't care who you end up taking with you, friend or foe! Well, I've had enough!"

Sunset had arrived, and Lorenta transformed. The green flames engulfed her spider form and her human form rose up out of it as the flames subsided. Her expression was one of utter hatred.

"You tried to kill me you horrible woman!" she said staring down at Weena who was still on the ground, "What were you going to say? 'Oh oops, sorry' and be done with it?! 'Miss all high and mighty' with your spells, thinking you're better than everyone and most of all me."

Weena stuttered, "No… I… I don't… I didn't mean…"

Lorenta snapped viciously at her, "Oh shut up, you whining insect," and she took a slight step toward her, "You tried to kill me," and she took another step, "The other wizard tried to hurt me."

"What other wizard? The one with the medallion?" Weena asked, her fear growing.

Lorenta continued, "I killed him, and it was so easy too, and he deserved it, the filthy beast. Try to crush me under your shoe?!" She took another step toward Weena who was starting to tremble. "Try to crush me, like I'm nothing?! You horrible self-centered whining bitch! I'll kill you too!"

Vordin grabbed Lorenta and tried to hold her back saying, "Lorenta no! It was an accident! What are you doing!"

"So you're saying that you're perfect, Candra?!" Dendrox glared at her, "Should I recall some of the times you supremely messed up opportunities for us? Gee, there's so many I don't know where to begin."

"Oh, and Asdella," Nodwel continued, "You can carry your own damn supplies, or, you can see how your belly likes going empty."

Candra replied to Dendrox, "You would be dead so many times over if I wasn't there to save you."

"Oh really?" the thief said, "If you weren't always getting in the way…"

"Me?! Ha! That's a laugh," she snapped.

Dendrox gritted his teeth in anger, "Yes, you! I don't need you to protect me! It's you that needs to think that, so you can feel as if you are somehow above me. It's all in your head!"

"Yeah, whatever," she said waving her hand at him as if she were sweeping him and his words away.

This made Dendrox even more furious. "How about I show you how well I can defend myself by pounding your smug arrogant face into a bloody pulp!" he yelled at her raising his fist.

"I'd like to see you try. I'll have you on the ground begging for mercy so fast you won't even know what happened. Oh, and I'm not feeling very merciful right now, so try not to bleed on me too much," she said with a sneer.

<Zaylyn ><Quest For The Sword Of Anthrowst ><By Katrina Mandrake-Johnston >   <Ch 32> < 100 >

"Let go of me, Vordin! You know I'm stronger than you, don't make me throw you off me! I've never been so furious in all my life! She has to pay for what she tried to do to me!"

Weena blubbered, "I didn't mean it… I'm sorry… Keep away from me!"

Nodwel continued to yell angrily at Asdella who was just staring at him in silence, but it was clear that there was a mountain of rage bubbling inside her, and it didn't seem like she was going to hold it back for much longer.

"You're just going to put the rest of us in danger!" Nodwel yelled at her, "We enjoy life, we want to live, and if there's a chance to get out of here alive, we're going to fight for it! I'm not going to let you jeopardize that! Hell, you want to die so badly, let me help you along!" He took his hefty battle-axe into hand and it was certain that he actually meant to fight her.

"You!" Asdella burst out with hatred, "It's all your fault! We should have never trusted you to go for help! You, with your uselessly short stubby legs. You didn't even try to go for help. You just brought back these useless fools, and you took your sweet time about it too while we all were risking our lives! I tried to avenge Dimwar, when that beast took his damn head off, and you pulled me back! You let Nimdor die! You didn't even try to help when he and I were in battle with the other one! You wanted him to die so you could play at being the leader. The girl I tried to save would be alive if you had done your job!"

And her next words were filled with such malice that it almost made Nodwel shudder. "Narr was killed because of you. And the boy he saved was dragged down here into this hellhole. And instead of getting us out, the little tiny speck of a dwarf decides to make his big manly decision to simply wait here for our deaths! Well let me hurry yours along, because the rest of us are done waiting," she snarled pointing the blade of her sword toward his face taunting him to make the first move. "Come on," she barked at him, "You made your little speech. You have the guts to say it. Lets see how much you have to say after I spill them. As I once called you friend, I'll let you take the first move," and then she dared, "The question is are you foolish enough to do it?"

The spider guard, more agitated now than ever, hurried down the tunnel leaving them to their quarrels.

"Look!" exclaimed Yarin with excitement, "The spider is letting us go."

Everyone was too caught up in their own arguments and barely even heard Yarin. The small boy started to edge slowly and nervously toward the tunnel. "Come on! Don't fight. We're free! Let's get out of here," Yarin tried to convince them.

As soon as Yarin reached the tunnel, a Killnarin burst from the shadows of the passageway and clamped its massive jaws onto his frail little body in one fluid snap of the creature's thick muscular neck. All anyone could do was just stare in shock. All their prior heated words instantly became meaningless, their ears filled with the small boy's screams and the sickening sound of his bones snapping within the creature's jaws.

The beast stomped into the chamber, as Weena let out a horrified protracted wail. The beast turned to them and let what was left of Yarin's body drop to the ground in a crumpled heap of mangled tissue, the tiny boy's innocent face white and blood-splattered.

<World of Zaylyn ><Quest For The Sword Of Anthrowst ><By Katrina Mandrake-Johnston ><Ch 33>

CHAPTER 33 = KILLNARIN INVASION

The Killnarin howled defiantly. It swung its head back and forth, gnashing its teeth together, daring the astonished group to attack.

Six spiders immediately rushed into the chamber after the Killnarin and surrounded the creature. The beast was down on all six of its legs and the yellow fluid, which dripped from its deadly teeth, was streaked red with Yarin's blood. As the Killnarin tried to approach the rest of the group, the spiders came to stand between it and the adventurers. Their front legs were raised defensively with their fangs clearly displayed to the beast.

The creature snorted in frustration at this. It quickly reared up and simply batted one of the spiders away with its clawed forepaw. The spider was thrown through the air hitting the wall to the side of the beast where it fell in a crumpled heap near Weena. The Killnarin howled in triumph and started to approach, ignoring the spiders around it and intent on spilling more blood.

By this time, Candra had been able to get an arrow ready, and taking aim, fired it with great speed. Dendrox also threw a dagger toward the beast. Nodwel and Asdella did not approach the Killnarin but had their weapons ready. The attack by the thieves didn't seem to affect the creature except to startle it slightly.

The spiders, taking advantage of this, quickly crawled up onto the Killnarin to bite the creature repeatedly, trying to release as much of their venom into the beast as possible. The Killnarin began thrashing about, knocking the spiders to the ground where the creature could bite and claw at them. One spider was mashed between its huge teeth. Another was crushed under a heavy foot as the creature stomped and thrashed about. It took a forceful swipe at another but managed only to graze its abdomen. This spider, even though it was wounded, still tried to crawl back up onto the Killnarin.

Candra asked them, "Should I let loose another arrow? It seemed to have no effect."

"No, you'll hit one of the spiders," Vordin said to her, "Look, it's working. The beast looks like it's about to collapse."

The creature staggered about until it slumped to the floor, but was still very much alive. The Killnarin, even in its weakened state, still tried to bite and claw at the remaining spiders as they began to hurry out of the room. The wounded spider, however, collapsed just before the tunnel unable to follow and quickly died soon after.

Nodwel and Asdella ran up to the Killnarin and hacked, slashed, and stabbed at the beast's thick resilient hide as they avoided its flailing limbs and vicious mouth of slimy teeth.

While the two warriors fought the beast, Lorenta smiled at Vordin and said, "Vordin, looks like you saved my life again and intentionally this time. First from the owl and now from Weena," and then she apologized to Weena saying, "I'm sorry about what I said earlier."

"I understand," Weena said, knowing what the Killnarin were capable of with their spells.

"It's the beasts," Dendrox added, "They did the same to me and Candra earlier. They make you hate. They don't make you say things you don't mean, just things you normally wouldn't say. They create chaos, destroy friendships, turn people against each other, and try to create as much suffering as possible before they kill you." His voice was sorrowful but was also filled with great hatred of the beasts and a desperate need for vengeance against them all. "All the arguments we just had were all part of its plan to kill Yarin first, as it knew that his death would cause us the most suffering and grief."

"You don't know that for sure," Candra told him.

"After all you've seen?" Dendrox snapped, "You know it's true. And why are they so strong? The ones Nodwel's group encountered were apparently much stronger than the one we killed and so is this one."

"Why won't you die!" Asdella screamed at the beast as she continued to stab at its black oily skin.

"I can't believe he's gone," Weena sobbed, "I can't even bring myself to look." As she said this, she glanced over to where Yarin had fallen. Still upon the ground, she drew her legs up about her, hugged them tightly in her arms, and began to rock back and forth, sobbing miserably.

Lorenta told Vordin, "I learnt to communicate. Well, only a bit. The spider teaching me got distracted suddenly and left saying something about the demons finding a way in, and that is when I returned here to warn everyone. But, I, ah, got distracted." She felt ashamed and knew that what Dendrox had said was true, in some way she had meant what she had said. *I might have had time to warn everyone of the Killnarin, if I hadn't given in to my anger. I might have been able to save Yarin. Now it's too late."*

Nodwel took another swing with his axe at the beast and then dodged the beast's claws as it took a weak swipe at him.

"This isn't right," Weena sobbed, "How could this happen... I can still hear his voice... He can't be dead... We were trying to save him... Everything was going to be okay... I told him everything was going to be okay... He looked up to me... This can't be happening... This can't be real..."

The Killnarin was finally slain. "It's finished," Nodwel announced, and then as he stared at Yarin,

<Zaylyn ><Quest For The Sword Of Anthrowst ><By Katrina Mandrake-Johnston >   <Ch 33> < 102 >
his axe fell from his hand.

Dendrox and Candra retrieved their arrow and dagger, but dared not look at the boy. To Candra's disappointment, she discovered her arrow to be broken. Nodwel picked up his axe; he knew there would be more of them.

"I... No... I was just talking to him; he can't be gone..." Weena sobbed, "It's not right... It can't be real... Yarin, the entire village of people... all gone... All dead... It just isn't possible... Why didn't we listen to him? If we had been paying more attention... We should have made sure that he was safe. He can't just be gone... He just can't be dead, and that's it... He's a little boy. He didn't do anything to anyone..."

Asdella came over to her and shook her violently. "He's gone! Get up and deal with it, or you'll be dead too!" she snapped at her unkindly.

Weena reluctantly got up from the floor and managed to reduce her sobbing to a mild whimpering.

"We've got to get out of here. Right now, or we're as good as dead," Dendrox spoke up.

Weena re-lit her lantern with the flame box from her pouch, and soon everyone was racing down the tunnel with the two lanterns held high lighting the way. To their surprise, the large chamber was empty except for the sticky remains of one spider.

Vordin commented, "This is probably the spider that was guarding our chamber. The two spiders that survived the battle, where do you think they took off to? I'm sure there must be more Killnarin down the other passageways."

Candra said, "The Killnarin had us trapped back there. If it weren't for the spiders and a large amount of luck on our side, we wouldn't have made it out of that room. They could ambush us very easily down here, especially if they attack together. You saw how hard it was to kill that thing, even with the spiders' help. We have no idea where this maze of tunnels leads, or if there even is an exit other than the well."

Lorenta knelt down beside the dead spider and said, "Thank-you for trying to keep us safe. We shall not forget your sacrifice, as well as the others that gave their lives today."

"Should we make an escape through the well then?" Nodwel asked them all.

"We can't just leave the spiders to perish," Lorenta exclaimed, "You were all so eager to risk your lives for the villagers, but when the spiders need your help, you just flee and leave them to fend for themselves?"

"Their only chance is to flee as well," Vordin told her, "You saw how many spiders it took to take down that one Killnarin, and they weren't even able to kill it. If you can tell them to escape, or better yet, ask them if there is an escape route somewhere..."

Weena, who was slowly backing up and staring wide-eyed toward one of the tunnels, interrupted, "We can't go through the well, because here comes one of them through it!"

The others turned their attention to the tunnel that was on the far side of the large chamber.

"I don't see..." Nodwel started.

"Shh, listen," Weena whispered loudly in fright.

A few moments of silence passed as the group listened for what Weena had heard. Then they heard a faint scraping sound and the light sound of pebbles and dirt falling.

"Do you hear it?" Weena whispered, "It's coming down the well. We have to get out of here, now!"

Candra made a dash for her missing arrow, the one that had been shot into the spider, and retrieved it from the floor of the chamber. She held it ready in her bow. Dendrox slipped a dagger into his hand.

Weena said urgently, getting frustrated that they seemed to be ignoring her, "We can't fight it! We have to go! Quickly before it gets into this room! You're wasting time!"

"Where are we going to go?" Asdella barked angrily at her, "At least we know what's here in this room. Do you want to walk into another ambush?"

Nodwel thought to himself, "*Asdella's sure acting strange. She normally runs about, madly trying to kill everything in sight. She's actually making decisions based on reason and not just blind rage. I don't know what it is exactly, but something's very different about her. Ever since she went to see*

<Zaylyn ><Quest For The Sword Of Anthrowst ><By Katrina Mandrake-Johnston >   <Ch 33> < 103 >

Narr's body. Could it be possible that she is somehow under the control of the Killnarin? That would explain how they managed to find us. No, that can't be it. I know it's silly, but it's almost like she's taken on a bit of Narr's personality. I can definitely see it in her now and then. And more so now since the attack of the Killnarin. Could his death have affected her more than I can possibly understand? I don't know. It must be my imagination. I miss him terribly, as I do the others… Nimdor, Dimwar, Borin… and Yarin. How could we have failed so miserably? How could I have failed so terribly? Was Asdella right about what she said? The beasts bring out the worst with their Hate spells, but what we say is all true. Well, at least what we are feeling deep down inside and little things that annoy us from time to time... things we normally wouldn't say because they hurt. Damn beasts mess with you even after they're dead, the evil things."

"Nodwel? Nodwel? You okay? What should we do?" Dendrox asked.

"How am I supposed to know?" the dwarf snapped back and thought, "Don't look to me as if I have all the answers. I never wanted to be a leader in all this."

"Well, I just thought…" said Dendrox.

Weena said to them all in an anxious tone, "Listen, you don't want to leave this room for fear of an ambush? Well look around! We are in a room with who knows how many passages all leading into it. We are standing in the very spot where an ambush would be perfect, am I right?" She paused to see if they were listening to her. "From all sides," she added.

"The wizard's right," said Lorenta, "It would be smart to leave this place. If the creature can communicate with others of its kind, as soon as it sees us, it will alert the others to our location. Others could be on their way already."

"Can you talk to the other spiders?" Vordin asked, "Find out if there is a way out of here?"

"No… I don't know… Maybe. I learnt how to receive messages which was easy, and he explained how the whole things works and a little bit about their history, but we only just started the lesson on how to send out messages to others. He was saving that for last, as it was the longest and hardest to learn. He wasn't even sure if I were going to be physically capable of doing it, but where I have this shape shifting ability, he thought that I might be able to by channeling that magical energy and expanding it."

"Lorenta, just try it! There's no time!" Vordin said to her as he heard a large thud and the scraping of claws on the rock floor.

"It's in the tunnel!" Weena screamed, "We have to run!"

A single spider rushed into the chamber. "Did you call him?" Vordin asked with amazement.

"No, I didn't. But he says for us to get out of here now, as there are more of the creatures and they are slaughtering everyone," Lorenta answered.

The Killnarin walked slowly into the chamber. Its black eyes and skin glistened in the light from the lanterns. It opened its mouth showing its many grotesque slime-covered teeth to the adventurers. The spider rushed to their defense. Lorenta screamed, "No! Don't!"

But it was too late, even if the spider had been able to understand her words. The Killnarin batted the spider aside as if it were nothing. The spider skidded across the floor from the force of the blow and lay broken and dying in a crumpled heap. The beast snarled and returned its focus to the adventurers.

"I think we should run," Asdella said to Nodwel's surprise, as he was expecting her to rush into battle with the beast and endanger them all.

"I hear more of them in the tunnels and they're coming this way," Candra reported.

"Which one do we take?" Weena asked hurriedly.

"Asdella, Borin is here! Take the far left tunnel. Hurry!" Narr said in her mind.

<World of Zaylyn ><Quest For The Sword Of Anthrowst ><By Katrina Mandrake-Johnston ><Ch 34>

CHAPTER 34 =   BORIN

"Follow me! Run! Now! All together!" Asdella commanded, and she darted toward the passageway with Lorenta following right beside her.

"Go! Don't get separated!" Candra yelled and ran after them, pulling Weena along by the hand

<Zaylyn ><Quest For The Sword Of Anthrowst ><By Katrina Mandrake-Johnston >   <Ch 34> < 104 >
with Dendrox running after.

Nodwel and Vordin also headed for the tunnel behind the two thieves and Weena. This is when the creature decided to leap toward them shrieking, as if it had been waiting for the group to make their move. Now it had become an exciting chase and exactly what it wanted. It scurried after them on all six of its legs, snapping its massive jaws in eager anticipation.

"They like fear! They're definitely getting what they want!" Vordin called back to Nodwel.

The dwarf was falling behind. His short legs were holding him back. Nodwel, realizing that there was going to be no chance of him being able to outrun the beast, shouted ahead to Vordin, "Run boy! I might have to hold this thing back!"

"As long as you keep running," Vordin panted, "it will want the chase," he breathed, "If you fight... try to slow it down... it will just kill you swiftly... in order to continue the chase... after the rest of us... Come on..." he encouraged, "We need you... Run! Don't give up!"

Vordin was beginning to lose sight of Dendrox and the others, as he also was starting to fall behind. *"I'm so glad that Nodwel's here. At least he can fight, maybe slow the beast up a little,"* Vordin thought to himself. *"What can I do? Maybe it'll choke on one of my bones,"* he tried to joke with himself, but all he could think about was Yarin and how easily the creature killed him.

Yarin's screams haunted him as Vordin pushed himself to run faster, but he felt his exhausted body refusing him. The light from Weena's lantern was beginning to disappear from sight as the others got farther and farther away. Vordin began to feel the hopelessness and despair take over, and his pace faltered even more so.

"You'll not take me! Not now!" someone bellowed from farther up the tunnel.

"Borin!" Asdella called out at the sound of his voice.

"Borin?" Nodwel exclaimed with surprise, between heavy breaths, and his pace quickened slightly.

The warrior woman bolted ahead and emerged from the passage into the small chamber where she could see Borin engaged in battle with one of the beasts. It was reared up on its back four legs as it slashed madly at him with its claws. The large middle-aged man, wielding both a short sword and hatchet, was a welcome sight to the warrior. She raised her sword and then screaming in a fierce fury at the creature, joined Borin in battle.

His leather backpack was missing and had been replaced by a small leather pouch at his side. His short black hair was wet with perspiration and clung to his round face. His grey shirt and brown leather vest were caked with mud, as were his black pants. His pant leg was torn and a bloody gash on his muscular leg could be seen.

There were torches wedged into crevices in the rock around the room, which Borin must have placed there. The chamber had four passages leading from it. At the north tunnel, Asdella and Borin fought with the Killnarin as it bore down on them both. Lorenta emerged from the east passageway followed by Candra and Weena with Dendrox close behind.

"Be prepared to use your spells," Candra told her breathlessly, "We'll need every advantage we have."

"Yes, I know," the wizard panted heavily, trying to breathe. *"I can't believe anyone could run that fast!"* Weena said to herself, *"No more sweets for me, that's for sure. I guess Candra and Dendrox are used to making a quick get away being thieves and all. Asdella being a warrior and Lorenta a spider, I guess they all can move pretty quickly. Candra practically had to drag me the whole way. Oh, my side hurts. I can hardly breathe. Why did she care so much? I thought her thinking was, if you couldn't keep up, you get left behind. It can't be that she's expecting my magic to work. I'm expendable in her eyes, aren't I?"*

"Dendrox!" Candra commanded, "Asdella and the other will have to battle on their own. We have the creature behind us to worry about! Get ready!" She drew an arrow and pulled it back aiming into the darkness of the tunnel.

"Wait for the others!" Weena yelled in a panic, "You'll hit them! Where are they? They were right behind us, weren't they?"

<Zaylyn ><Quest For The Sword Of Anthrowst ><By Katrina Mandrake-Johnston >   <Ch 34> < 105 >

"I won't miss," Candra said calmly.

Vordin came stumbling into the room and collapsed into Weena's arms, almost knocking her over. His breath was coming out in desperate gasps, but he managed to say, "Nod…" followed by an enormous gasp for air and then, "wel…"

"I see the dwarf," Candra shouted to Vordin's relief, "The creature's right behind."

She loosed her arrow. It flew right past Nodwel, so close that he felt the air rush past his ear. The arrow punched deep into the creature and it howled in pain and rage.

Borin dodged the claws of the attacking beast at the northern tunnel and struck with a well-placed blow to its thick throat. It made a choking noise and stepped back a bit.

Nodwel emerged from the east tunnel and ran right over to join Asdella and Borin in their battle, hoping that the others could hold back the other one at least for awhile.

"Borin!" Nodwel panted, "You're alive!"

"There's an escape tunnel to the west," Borin told them, "The spiders are trying to come up from the south to escape through it. We have to hold this thing back."

"One followed us. We have two to worry about," Asdella told him.

Their creature gnashed its teeth together and dropped down to all six of its legs. Then it came at them viciously with its powerful jaws.

Nodwel came down with his axe on the beast's head, dealing it a mighty blow. All this did was distract it for a second, but it gave enough time for Asdella to ram her sword through its eye and into its skull. Its body twitched and collapsed.

Before they could feel any sort of relief, she yanked her sword free and shouted, "Here comes another behind it!"

From the southern tunnel, a group of five spiders entered the room. They stopped and watched as the warriors engaged in battle with yet another creature from the north passage. Candra shot another arrow and Dendrox managed to throw two daggers at the approaching creature from the east passage, but both were unsure if they had succeeded in wounding the beast.

"Go! This way!" Lorenta shouted, both in speech and in her mind while pointing over to the west tunnel, hoping that they would understand her. The spiders quickly moved over to the west tunnel and disappeared down it into the darkness. "They say they're the last," Lorenta reported.

"Good," Borin shouted, "Follow them. There's another room where we can hold these things off better."

Weena, Vordin, and Lorenta ran after the spiders down the west passage. Dendrox threw yet another dagger at the beast but missed terribly and, having only a few daggers left, ran shortly after. Candra also followed, stopping only twice to loose an arrow toward their beast.

"Go Nodwel, we can handle this one," Borin told him, trying to block the clawed arm with both his short sword and hatchet as the arm bore down on him from above.

Nodwel, knowing that he was slower than the rest, didn't argue and started for the tunnel.

"Next chance we get, we'll go, okay?" Borin said to Asdella.

"I can take this thing. You go," she argued, "This one's not as strong as the first one for some reason."

"We have to go," he told her again.

"*Asdella go! Please! Go and live! Before the other one decides to attack,*" Narr pleaded with her in her mind.

She slashed her sword across the Killnarin's head. It didn't flinch; it just growled at her.

Borin yelled, "Go now!" and they both ran for the tunnel.

The beast they were fighting shrieked at them and climbed over its dead sibling to meet the creature who now emerged from the east passage. Two of Candra's arrows protruded from its left shoulder. Borin looked back as he headed down the tunnel and could see that many more creatures were piling into the room, all eager to pursue them.

Borin stopped, took an amulet from his pocket, and rubbed at it furiously.

"What are you doing?!" Asdella barked at him, "Come on, if you want to flee so badly!"

<Zaylyn ><Quest For The Sword Of Anthrowst ><By Katrina Mandrake-Johnston >   <Ch 34> < 106 >

"It's a Camouflage amulet. I'm hoping it will disguise the tunnel and give us some time," Borin told her. He dropped the amulet on the ground and continued down the passage.

"I see the exit!" Asdella said to him, "The others are there waiting for us."

When they reached the rest of the group, Borin told them, "There's too many. The spiders saved my life, dragging me down into the well before the Killnarin could finish me off, so hopefully, I'll be able to save their lives in return. I owe that to them, especially after all they've told me. If there is any chance that I might be able to trap these creatures here, if only for a short while, it might be enough to save all of you and the spiders as well. Please, you must escape and find a way to defeat these things." He took a bottle from the leather bag at his hip.

"What's that?" Nodwel asked, "What are you going to do?"

"There's too many, friend," he answered, "They'll follow and kill you all. I have to stop them. This is a Blast potion. Nimdor had it. It will collapse and seal the tunnel, maybe even kill a couple of them. Well, at least I hope it will."

"You'll never be able to survive that!" Weena exclaimed.

"I know. Now go," he commanded.

"You can't just kill yourself! There has to be another way! Can't you just throw the potion at them?" Weena asked, extremely upset.

Borin explained, "There's no other way! I have to make sure this works. If I throw it, there's too great a chance of something going wrong. We only have one go at this. I've made my decision. This was my plan before I knew you all were here, and it's definitely not going to change now, now that your lives are at risk as well. Go, please. There's no time to argue about it." The howl of a creature came echoing down the tunnel and it was nearing their position. "Go! The magic of the amulet won't confuse them for long," he yelled as he uncorked the potion, "I'll try to wait until the last moment. Make sure you're all clear."

"I am not going to leave," Asdella said calmly.

Borin said sternly, "Damn it, Asdella, go!"

Candra called to her as she started to shove Vordin and Lorenta out of the tunnel, "Asdella! He's made his decision. Do what the man says!" The sky had already begun to brighten with the coming dawn. The elfin thief turned to Borin and said, "Thank-you. You are an honorable man."

"There has to be another way," Vordin protested.

"Are we just going to abandon him like this?" Lorenta asked.

"Come on," Candra called to the rest, "There's no sense in all of us dying!"

Dendrox and Nodwel made their way reluctantly toward the exit.

"Are you sure you want to do this?" Nodwel asked Borin.

"Nothing you can say will make me change my mind," was his reply.

"I... I could take your place..." Nodwel suggested.

"No! Now take these people out of here!" Borin demanded.

"Weena, come on," Dendrox said to her.

"Asdella," Nodwel said, "Let's go!"

"I'm not leaving him to die! I can save him!" she screamed with fury.

"Now is not the time to have a change of heart, Asdella. Go. Save yourself," Borin told her, "These things have definitely found their way through the magic of that amulet by now. There is no time to argue."

Borin held the bottle ready and waited for the creatures to come. He could see them now. The two wounded creatures were at the front of the group and held up the others in their slowed pace.

"You all go," Weena said to them, "I think I can convince her to follow. If not, I'll leave too."

"You sure?" Dendrox asked her, the deep concern showing in his eyes.

"Yes go," she answered, although she was unsure if this was the right thing to do.

They exited through the opening, and Weena, Asdella, and Borin stood alone as the Killnarin grew nearer and nearer.

"I'm not going to leave him," Asdella said angrily through clenched teeth.

Weena did not want to leave Borin to his death any more than Asdella did, but there was no sense in all three of them getting killed.

Weena, seeing that one of the creatures was moments away from bursting through the tunnel at them, cast her Shield spell hoping that it would be able to counter the Blast potion's magic.

Borin could wait no longer and shattered the bottle. A blinding light filled the tunnel and the force of the blast shot Weena and Asdella backwards out of the tunnel in their protective shield bubble. The spell had been able to absorb the energy of the explosion and saved them from harm, but ended abruptly and they both landed hard on the ground. Weena watched, by the early morning light, as the tunnel entrance collapsed in on itself.

"*We're safe for now,*" Weena said to herself, hugging the ground in utter exhaustion, "*I did it. Asdella's alive.*"

"No! Borin!" Asdella wailed.

Asdella's mind screamed at her, "*Dimwar, Nimdor, Borin... Narr... even Yarin! They're all gone! Why didn't I do something! I'm the one who should have died! I'm expendable, not them!*"

"*I'm so tired,*" Weena's mind said weakly, "*When they said that extending the spell to include another takes a greater toll on the mind and body, they weren't kidding.*" She closed her eyes and let herself rest. "*How could Borin sacrifice himself like that? He's dead. Yarin's dead. This can't be happening! This isn't real...*" and then Weena passed out lying on the rocky ground with a trickle of blood from her nose.

CHAPTER 35 =   SORROWFUL CAMPSITE

Nodwel, Dendrox, Candra, and Vordin all raced toward where Asdella and Weena had fallen. They had been waiting anxiously for the two women to emerge, worried for their survival.

Lorenta was at the bottom of the hill, trying to console the group of agitated spiders.

The tunnel entrance was completely collapsed in on itself; a heavy amount of rock and forest debris barring the passage. If any of the approaching Killnarin survived the explosion, they were now trapped within the spiders' lair.

The tunnel had been situated near the top of a rocky hill and from here they could tell approximately where they were. From the top of the rocky hill, they could see that they were a little way into the western edge of the forest, as the mountain range could be seen not too far away from their location. They could also see that the forest seemed to thin out and that the land eventually turned into grassy plains not far to the south.

"We should get everyone into the cover of the forest," suggested Dendrox, "I feel vulnerable up here in the open like this, especially when those creatures are just on the other side of this rubble."

"I doubt if anything could have survived that blast," Nodwel commented, "including Borin."

"Candra, how's Weena?" Dendrox asked.

"She's alive, but unconscious as far as I can tell," was her answer.

"Do you think she'll be okay?" Vordin asked, greatly concerned that yet another companion might die.

Candra answered, "She'll be fine. Asdella won't say a thing to me, all she'll do is glare."

"She's fine," commented Nodwel, "I agree with Dendrox about getting down into the trees. I say we make camp though and give Weena a chance to recover. I've heard of wizards going through something like this. She's not injured is she?" Candra shook her head. "Yeah, then it must be the magical strain put on her. Saving both herself and Asdella took a lot out of her. Something, by the way, which could have been avoided if someone hadn't been so damn stubborn. Asdella, you both could have been killed! If Weena's spell hadn't worked..."

"Yeah, well Borin's still dead. Just leave me the hell alone," and saying this, she got up, sword in hand, and stomped off into the woods.

"Should she be off all by herself like that?" Vordin asked, "What if something happens?"

"It'll be a good idea just to let her be. She'll find us well enough when she's ready. Let's get

<Zaylyn ><Quest For The Sword Of Anthrowst ><By Katrina Mandrake-Johnston >   <Ch 35> < 108 >
Weena to a safe spot," said Nodwel.

"Lorenta?!" Vordin called suddenly realizing that she wasn't in sight anymore, "Where did she go? She was here a moment ago, wasn't she?" Then realizing, he said, "Oh, it's morning already, she must have changed back into spider form. Yeah, there she is," he said pointing to a smaller spider in among the larger ones. Confused, Vordin asked them all, "How is it possible that it's already dawn?"

No one had an answer for him, but Nodwel told him, "Let's just be thankful for it. The Killnarin seem to be more active during the night. There's only one person that comes to mind when I think of how this is possible, and I'd rather not speak of such things."

Vordin nodded saying, "The Black Shadow."

Nodwel and Dendrox carefully carried Weena down the rocky hill and laid her gently on a soft bed of moss. Then they proceeded to clear an area suitable for making a campfire. Candra and Vordin offered to look for food and headed off into the forest together.

A total of twenty-six giant spiders had been able to escape out of a community of almost two hundred. Lorenta and the group of spiders went off into their own secluded area, and Lorenta once more began her lessons on learning the communication ability.

Nodwel remained silent as he gathered wood for the night. His mind was clearly not on his task, as his face was grief-stricken. He was thinking about friends lost and the boy that would have given their deaths some sort of meaning. But Yarin was gone. Their efforts to save the villagers, the deaths of his friends… it was all for nothing.

"Hey Nodwel?" Dendrox said, but Nodwel was lost in thought and did not hear him at first. "Nodwel?" Dendrox repeated.

"Sorry, you were saying something?" the dwarf asked.

"I was just thinking," he said, "Do you really think it's safe to camp here? You're obviously planning to stay here all day plus the night, right? I mean, sure the tunnel has collapsed in on itself and the creatures probably won't be able to get through, but what's to stop them from still coming after us? Dexcsin is a little way to the east and probably not very far away. They could just come up the well or out another way. We don't know how many went into the tunnels. Several could have remained out in the forest."

"I don't want to move Weena," the dwarf told him, "We all need some recovery time. You saw how much trouble the beast had coming down the well; they'll have the same trouble going up. Besides, I don't want to walk into one of their traps again, especially when they have the ability to manipulate our minds. Yarin's death proves how cunning and effective they can be. It'll be better to camp here."

"Yeah, I agree. It's just that I'm feeling kind of helpless," admitted the thief.

The two men continued their task in silence once more. Dendrox now started to collect kindling, and Nodwel began to chop a fallen log into smaller pieces with his axe. He hated to use his battle-axe in such a manner, but if they were going to be safe during the night, they were going to need a large fire. It wouldn't matter if the blade was a little dull from chopping wood if the creatures caught them unaware because of poor visibility. Besides, he had a whet stone in his pouch. It was about time he tended to its edge anyhow.

Dendrox asked him, "Do you think all this trouble is over us?"

"What do you mean?" asked Nodwel tossing another chunk of wood into their growing pile.

"The Killnarin," he explained, "Do you think they came down into the spiders' lair after us?"

"I don't know. It seems silly to send a whole army of the beasts after the likes of us, don't you think?" replied Nodwel.

"Yeah, it does seem unlikely. So you think invading the tunnels and the village were part of a bigger plan? What would they want with the tunnels?" Dendrox asked.

Nodwel suggested, "Great place for the creatures to hide, prepare for something larger perhaps?"

"Maybe. Then they'll probably want to send a couple after us, just to make sure we can't warn anyone of what this wizard is doing," added Dendrox.

Nodwel chuckled, "Doesn't need to. No one would believe us if we did tell. I think we are just

<Zaylyn ><Quest For The Sword Of Anthrowst ><By Katrina Mandrake-Johnston >   <Ch 35> < 109 >
more of an annoyance than a threat."

After several hours, Candra and Vordin returned. Candra carried two large rabbits and several good sized sticks in order to make a spit once a cooking fire was started. Vordin had a collection of berries and nuts nestled in the front of his outstretched shirt.

Candra wore a triumphant grin on her face as she announced, "We've done well, as you can see. We'll have somewhat of a feast this morning, eh? It's not much of a breakfast, but it's a lot more than we've been getting these past few days."

"How's Weena doing?" Vordin asked.

"Still recovering," said Dendrox, "She could do with some water. You find any?"

"No," Candra answered.

"Hey Vordin, you better let me check that stuff, just in case. Candra's terrible at picking out the poisonous from the good," Dendrox told him.

"Yeah, I'm not so good either," Vordin admitted transferring the berries and nuts to Dendrox's lap.

"You see Asdella at all?" the dwarf asked.

"We sort of went off in the other direction," answered Vordin, "We were kind of nervous about running into her, to be honest."

Candra asked, "Hey Dendrox, you think any of the creatures are going to come this way?"

"I was just talking to Nodwel about that," Dendrox said as he examined a dark purple berry.

The elf said, "By the luck we had with the hunting, it looks like we're safe at least for the moment. I'm pretty sure those damn creatures would scare every living thing out of the area for quite a distance."

Weena opened her eyes and tried to sit up but still felt a bit groggy. Nodwel was busy trying to get the fire started. Vordin went over to Weena and sat down beside her on the moss-covered ground. He held her hand to steady her and felt her forehead.

"I'm fine, just a little dizzy," she told him, "Asdella? She's okay?"

Vordin nodded and said, "She took off on her own for awhile though."

Weena took her hand back as she was feeling better. "How long was I out for?" she wondered.

"Hours. It's still a few hours before noon though," he told her.

Nodwel went about getting the fire started, arranging the wood and with the kindling between. Candra grabbed a dagger from Dendrox's belt as she sat down next to him with one of the rabbits. Dendrox tossed a couple of berries into the trees and then proceeded to examine another handful.

"Oh, Nodwel, I have a flame box. I didn't think of it before, but wouldn't it be a lot faster and easier to use it to light the fire?" Weena said as she took it from her pouch and offered it out.

"Yes, I was about to ask to borrow it actually. I never really liked getting fires started much. I always let someone else do it," he explained. She walked over to the dwarf and handed him the tiny box. "I see you've recovered quite quickly," Nodwel said with a smile.

"Oh, I feel fine now," she told him.

"Really? I've heard that most don't for a day, sometimes two. That's great though, means you're stronger than you think. Here, why don't I show you a few things about starting a fire," he offered.

"*I already know plenty about getting a fire started, don't I?*" she thought with a hollow feeling, forever haunted by the memory of the fire she caused at the school. "Sure. Thanks Nodwel," she said with a weak smile and knelt down beside him in front of what was to be the fire. She was glad it was to only be a small fire, meant for cooking the meat. "*A small one. But that's what my fire was supposed to be at the school, wasn't it, and look what happened there...*"

"See how I've arranged everything here? Now you want to light it in these places and that should get it going," Nodwel instructed, "I'll watch to see if you need any help."

They all remained silent as they went about their tasks, thinking about recent events and about all the many lives that had been lost. Occasionally, Vordin would check Weena's condition but each time she insisted that she was perfectly all right.

After a long drawn out silence, Vordin, no longer able to stifle his emotions, choked out, "Yarin should be here with us."

Everyone had been thinking about the loss of their young companion, about all the innocent people

<Zaylyn ><Quest For The Sword Of Anthrowst ><By Katrina Mandrake-Johnston >   <Ch 35> < 110 >
from the two villages, and the members of Nodwel's group that had given their lives.

"None of this should have happened," Nodwel said.

Candra said, "First Vordin's village, then Dexcsin, then even the spiders' lair. Why? So much death… It doesn't even seem real. I don't even know how to react to all this. I'm just in a state of constant shock."

"He was like me," Vordin said, his face wet with tears, "He was the last of his village… a survivor. He beat the beasts, just like I had. We both escaped them. He should be here. Saving at least someone was the only reason we even went to Dexcsin in the first place. I can't… All I can think is just who's going to be next to die and how much longer I have to live. Whether or not this will be the last time I'll ever hear a bird's song or even feel moss beneath my fingertips like this. Every moment is precious no matter how small. I know this now. I miss my mother and my father. Everyone I ever knew in Nilnont. I just can't take anymore."

Weena had a tear in her eye, "We've all lost people we've cared about. You must be feeling the worst, but everything's going to be okay. We can't lose hope."

"My mother, my father, everyone I've ever known," Vordin sobbed, "And now practically everyone I meet ends up dead as well. At least with Yarin around, I wasn't alone. I'm useless! I can't fight these creatures! At least with Yarin, there was someone like me; someone who had gone through the same thing."

"I'm still amazed that we escaped at all," Dendrox commented, "I didn't think we were going to survive the spiders. But we did. And when the Killnarin attacked, I thought we were all trapped and were surely going to be killed, but we survived. We should be thankful of that."

"And because we are the only ones still alive," Nodwel told them all, "we should do our best to try to prevent anyone else from dying because of those beasts. We owe everyone that much. We may not succeed, but we have to try. We're the only ones that have encountered the Killnarin and lived to talk about it. I hate to say it, but we're probably the only ones that have even a slim chance of stopping these things. Anyone else wouldn't know what they were up against; they wouldn't know what to expect. We can't just sit by while innocent people are in danger, hoping that someone else will defeat them."

"The only way we have any hope of stopping them is to defeat the wizard behind them," said Vordin, "Dranngore was his name. Even if we could kill all the Killnarin, what's to stop him from summoning more?"

"You mean, the ones we killed, the ones Borin gave his life to kill, it could all be for nothing?" Candra asked with shock as she stood up, her face tense with frustration.

"Now can you see why everything seems so hopeless?" Vordin said.

"I doubt the blast did them any harm," commented Asdella, "Nimdor, our friend, cast a fireball at close range right into a Killnarin's face and it didn't even faze it at all."

"No!" Candra said pacing back and forth in front of the fire which was now lit, "It can't be like that! It can't all just be for nothing! We have to get rid of this wizard and end it all!"

"How are we going to do that? We don't even know where he is," said Dendrox.

Candra was getting more and more upset, and she told him, "Well, then we find out where. We have to do something. No one else is going to believe us. It's up to us. And like Nodwel said, we have to at least try. I can't just admit that it's hopeless and that hundreds more are going to be slaughtered."

"Do you think the spiders may know something?" Weena asked.

"We'll have to wait 'till nightfall for Lorenta to change," Vordin told her as he dried his eyes with the back of his hand.

Dendrox asked him, "You're the one that told us about Dranngore. Something about a sword?"

"Yeah, the Sword of Anthrowst. I was told that the wizard can only be defeated with it, if we're going to stop the Killnarin," he answered.

"Well, there we go. We find out as much as we can about the sword and any information there is about the wizard," Weena said trying her best to sound cheerful, but her heart was heavy.

"Alright," Candra said propping a rabbit over the now roaring fire, "So we sort of have a plan now.

<Zaylin ><Quest For The Sword Of Anthrowst ><By Katrina Mandrake-Johnston >   <Ch 35> < 111 >
Travel to Vackiindmire then, and find out information. Sounds good to me." She picked up the other rabbit and began to prepare it for the fire as well.

Dendrox wondered if she were going to hold up to her heroic words when they finally reached Vackiindmire. She was not the type to willingly put herself in danger for someone else if she could help it, and neither was he.

Everyone sat grieving, absentmindedly watching the crackling fire and the cooking meat. Dendrox passed around the nuts and berries.

"I'll save a share for Asdella," Nodwel offered, remembering his harsh words to her when they had been under the spell of the Killnarin in the spiders' lair and feeling regretful of them.

Candra, who was finished with the second rabbit, stuck it on a stick and positioned it over the fire as well. They all ate the nuts and berries in silence waiting for the meat.

Once all the meat was cooked, passed around, and eaten, it was near noon.

Weena had been trying so hard to be strong, but tears were starting to well up in her eyes once more. Vordin noticed this and decided to start up a conversation with her to get both their minds thinking about something other than the tragic deaths and the shock and fear of their escape.

"So what's it like to do magic?" he asked her.

She looked at him with tears in her eyes and he could see that her hands were shaking. "It's pretty complicated," she said softly.

"I'd like to hear," Vordin urged.

"Um, well, the words of a spell have no sound," she told him, calming slightly as she tried her best to explain things to him, "It's as if the sound the words would have made are instead replaced by a magical power. You have to will the words into being. The words themselves are more feelings than actual words. Anyone can speak the syllables, that's easy. You have to feel the sounds in your mind and project the energy they create in you. It's hard to explain, like I said. You have to will the magic to work by concentrating your emotions into what you want to do. Just saying the sounds in your mind isn't enough, you have to put a bit of yourself into it."

Vordin was glad that he was able to get her mind off the recent horrors, even if it were just briefly. "So what are these words? Are they actual words or just magic nonsense words?" he asked.

"It's actually an ancient language. Probably the first language or more likely the language of the spirits or a combination of both perhaps? Anyway, these words have power. It's not language like we define and use today in our speech. It's more meanings than definitions and labels. In language, we have so many labels for one thing. A woman, for example, has the label woman, but also mother, daughter, sister, grandmother, female, person, human, and the list goes on and all these words mean the same individual. Okay, this is more difficult and complicated to explain than I thought. There are words for certain emotions and for objects, but it's not as specific as we have in our language where things have many names and classes for the same thing. Most common examples are 'you' and 'I', and 'physical body' and 'soul'... These are all rough translations of course. Umm... 'hot', 'cold', 'love', 'hate', and different degrees of these. It's all too complicated for me to explain, but in a way, it's simple at the same time. I'm still trying to learn the basics and the whole concept of invoking the feeling and a bit of myself behind these words. The sound of the words are highly tied in with their meanings and purpose. As in with the word 'hate', it will have a harsh sound. The word 'love' will have a soft sound for example. The translation is hard to explain too. Our words are very specific in what they mean, where the words used in a spell are more general and have a broader meaning. A single word can have various meanings depending on how it's used and most importantly the feeling put behind it. Oh, and the way the words are written express both sound and meaning within the strokes and shape of the symbols."

Vordin was having difficulty understanding exactly what she meant, but he was glad for the conversation and it seemed to be helping Weena to calm her emotions. "What made you choose to learn the spells you did?" he asked her.

She answered, "I don't know. I thought they would be something good to learn. That way I could help people, I guess."

<Zaylyn ><Quest For The Sword Of Anthrowst ><By Katrina Mandrake-Johnston >   <Ch 35> < 112 >

"Maybe that's why you've been having such good luck with your spells," he suggested, "When it's really necessary and someone really needs your help, that's when your spells really come through for you."

"I don't know, maybe I should just give up," she sighed, "I'm never going to be a proper wizard. It takes so much effort and patience. I mean, I've studied so long and hard already and haven't even gotten a single spell mastered to where I can rely on their abilities when I need them, and that's with simple first level spells. It takes a lot of skill to perform a spell, and it's not guaranteed to work every time. Wizards usually have magic items along with them and when they need to perform a spell and happen to fail at casting the magic themselves, they can just use a magic item in place of the spell to get the same effect."

"What do you mean?" Vordin asked confused.

"Potions, amulets, powders, globes, things like that. Some wizard I am. I can hardly do a simple spell and can't afford to buy the pricey magic trinkets to back me up. And, I have been put in situations that even the most highly equipped and experienced wizard couldn't have anticipated," she said looking even more upset now than she had before.

"You made it through. You came through for us. You saved lives," he told her.

"Not Yarin's. Not Borin's. If I were a proper wizard, I would cast my spells properly and I would have magic items with me for emergencies," she said with tears in her eyes. Vordin's success at maintaining a pleasant conversation had ended. Weena continued, "How can you say we made it? We came to Dexcsin to try to help the villagers. We found the only person left, an innocent child, and we couldn't even save him. Sure, we survived, but he should have been the one. I would have taken his place if I could have."

"I know what you mean," Vordin said remembering how he had felt when he had returned to his village. Seeing the dead children had given him a horrible hopeless feeling and a feeling of guilt that he had remained safe and alive while they had been forced to suffer. He knew that Weena was probably feeling the same way, as he too again had this same feeling. But he knew that he had to fight it and that Weena had to fight it as well. They had to move on, all of them had too. Many of Rasindell's stories had been meant to teach him this and now he realized this to be true. They couldn't dwell on things that couldn't be changed, not if they were going to stop Dranngore and the Killnarin. "That's the way it happened though, so the most we can do is try to do some good," he said hoping that he could reach her, "We survived, while the others died. Borin sacrificed himself. Don't let it be in vain. We can't just give up. How many other innocent people will perish if we do that?"

"I... I think I need to be alone. I'm going to take a walk," she decided.

"It's not safe, you should stay here," Vordin protested.

"I'll yell if I get into trouble. I'm not going to go far," Weena assured him, "I just need to go."

"Weena, be sure not to wander. Stay close to camp," Nodwel cautioned, as Weena headed off into the forest.

She didn't stop until the campsite was just out of sight. She sat upon the forest floor and let the tears run down her face. *"Why couldn't we save Yarin? Maybe he could have survived if we hadn't come,"* she thought sobbing.

The sun was filtering down through the treetops. The air was cool and crisp, and there was the faint smell of damp earth and pine. Everything was still and quiet. She stood and inhaled a deep breath, but the ache in her chest did not subside. Vegetation surrounded her like protective walls shielding her from everything and everyone.

She had been thinking about what Vordin had said. *"What if these are the last moments we will be alive? Do I really want to be worried about every little thing or do I want to be enjoying what time I have left?"*

A small brown and black bird, not seeming to notice her at all, fluttered down from the sky and landed on the branch of a nearby tree. Its small black eyes darted around its little world and then it opened its black beak and sang a sweet happy song. She watched and listened, and the beginnings of a

<Zaylyn ><Quest For The Sword Of Anthrowst ><By Katrina Mandrake-Johnston >   <Ch 35> < 113 >
smile started to cross her lips. The bird knew nothing of her feelings and of her life, but it seemed to care and to be concerned for her. The bird jumped to another branch and continued its song. Her smile grew, but the ache was deep in her heart and could not be removed so easily. The bird spread its little wings and flew high up into the sky.

Weena stood, and brushing the debris from her robes, stepped away from where she had been sitting and stepped onto a narrow overgrown trail. She didn't think of where it might lead. She moved a slender branch full of lush green leaves aside.

The silence was calming, and she walked slowly along the trail. Her feet moved quietly over the rocks and gravel. Weena took her time, enjoying the natural beauty of her surroundings and she tried to take in every detail. She stopped to touch a leaf, her fingers caressing its surface. She then noticed a fuzzy little caterpillar on the branch of the tree. As it inched along, its body rippled with every movement. She plucked it from the branch and placed it gently in her hand and smiled as its many feet tickled her. She was simply enjoying the fact of being alive. She wondered briefly if this might be a rarity to find one during the early autumn, and then replacing the caterpillar carefully and gently on the branch once more, she continued along the path.

After awhile she stopped, opened her small cloth pouch, and took out her mother's ring. The gems sparkled in the light and Weena slipped it onto her finger. She hadn't worn it for a very long time. It gave her the comfort she needed, and then deciding that she was getting too far away from the camp, she turned around and headed back.

<World of Zaylyn ><Quest For The Sword Of Anthrowst ><By Katrina Mandrake-Johnston ><Ch 36>

CHAPTER 36 =   ASDELLA AND NARR

Asdella had been sitting upon a fallen log for most of the morning now.

"I wonder what they all think of me? That I'm crazy? That I talk to myself because of Narr? That I might turn against them? That I can't be trusted? Wait a minute, since when did I ever care of what they might think? I don't feel like myself anymore. I don't like it. It's Narr… he's invaded my mind and somehow is changing me. At least I think he might be. I hate this. I can't escape him. He's always swimming around in my thoughts… in my private thoughts... Watching my every move. It's not right. Sure, he helped get us out of the tunnels; found Borin to be still alive and told me how to find him. Didn't really matter in the end though, as he's dead now too. I wonder if I'll start hearing him too inside my head. No, I don't think so. But it must have been Narr. He must have been influencing my decisions. It was like I was being held back. I wanted to kill those beasts, make them pay for what they did. Hell, I just wanted to kill something and make everything go away."

"Asdella," Narr's voice said in her mind.

"No, go away!" she yelled out loud.

"What's wrong?" he asked, *"I discovered Borin, told you, came with you all in your escape, and then I've just been exploring the forest trying to learn more about this whole ghost thing. No sign of the creatures in the forest, so that's a help. I've come back to keep you company, if that's okay. I don't like being out there all alone with no one to connect to, at least not like I can with you."*

"Oh joy," she said sarcastically, "You've been staying out of my inner thoughts like you said you would, I hope."

"Of course I have. I said I would, didn't I?" he said defensively.

"You know Narr, you don't seem to joke around as much as you use to," she told him.

"Yeah, I know," he said, *"It's just that I'm trying really hard to adjust to this new ghostly state and it's really confusing and frustrating. There's so much that I wanted to do and wanted to say to people, and now I can't. Well, unless I share the experience through someone else I guess. But it's not the same… it will never be the same. I know so much more than I did before about myself and others now, and I would be able to live my life to the fullest, savoring every moment whether it be good or bad, if I only could."*

"Okay, I think I liked you a lot better when you didn't try so hard to figure things out," Asdella thought to him, *"Maybe you're not supposed to. You used to be so carefree before. What's with all the*

<Zaylyn ><Quest For The Sword Of Anthrowst ><By Katrina Mandrake-Johnston >   <Ch 36> < 114 >

regrets now? You used to be happy. Sure, you used to let loose a couple of snide remarks now and then in fun, but now you're simply just depressing and annoying. And you didn't talk as much. You tend to ramble now. But that could be just because it's thought and not speech. I find that I ramble on a lot when I talk to you in thought. I'm starting to sound like Weena. And why are you so desperate to tell me all these romantic feelings you have for me? It's getting to be really overpowering. I know you're going through this 'analyze your whole life stage' or something like that, but please, give it a rest. You have the rest of eternity probably to do it."

"*Sorry,*" he said, sounding truly hurt by her words.

She asked, "So is Borin around too?"

"*If so, I can't see him or talk to him, but I'm sure he's about somewhere in our world. He had a younger brother. If I were him, that's where I'd be,*" he told her, "*I guess that's why you should make the most out of the time you do have around the people you care about. I've been thinking. You know how ghosts are said to remain about because they have some unfinished business?*"

"Yeah sure," she said, letting her voice show that he again had started doing what she had just complained about.

Narr ignored her tone and continued, "*I don't think that's entirely true. Well, from what I've been experiencing, I think I might have it figured out. Everyone has a soul, and I mean everyone, including the animals, plants, insects, birds, and so on. They live their lives and eventually die, some sooner than others of course. I seem to have two parts to my consciousness. One is me, Narr, the life I just lived recently. The other part is a larger consciousness, like a higher being too large to fit inside a body completely. I see this as my soul, not me Narr as you know, but the entire me, a being existing beyond time and living many, many lives. My soul, my pure self, is judging Narr, the life I lived. I have to explore myself and come to terms with the life I had with this higher knowledge that my soul possesses. When that happens, and I become at peace with myself, I carry on into another life, starting out fresh and renewed. Of course it will be quite awhile for this, and I guess this transition period could seem to be either extreme torment and frustration, a hell of sorts, or as joy and happiness, depending on how you lived your life and how you look at it. I would have liked to have children. I could be watching them grow and experience life right now, living on through them. I have a lot of things in my life that I'm pondering, and there is a lot that I have yet to deal with.*"

"So I'm finding out," she commented impatiently, trying not to think any of the sour remarks she had for him and his non-stop thoughts, because she knew that he would hear her. She had become wary of making him angry, as she was uncertain of what he was capable of. She was worried that he may be able to take complete control over her body and that she would be trapped in some kind of limbo.

Narr continued, "*I'm able to see things from aspects I never thought possible. I can't explain it. I find my happiness in you, Asdella. I'm frightened and alone right now. I need you. Please don't shut me out. I watch you. I feel you. I feel your pain, your sorrow. I want to make you happy. I want to be a part of your life. I can't watch you from afar. The fact that you can hear and feel me just shows how much you really do need me too.*"

"I don't need anyone. You know that. I can handle things myself," she told him, and then as an after thought, "*Except maybe a ghost in my head.*"

"*Just be thankful that I'm just roaming around in your head, although if you would prefer other parts of your body to be haunted, I could arrange it. In fact that sounds like it might be fun. I have some places in mind that could be very interesting,*" he said with the same slyness that Asdella so well remembered.

"Being molested by a ghost isn't my choice in fun," she said with a smirk.

"*At least you couldn't punch me,*" he said with a laugh.

"Lucky you," she said.

He then said in a serious and caring tone, "*Listen, Asdella, part of you is reaching out desperately for help, and so here I am. It's the only explanation for why I can contact you like this as if I was right here beside you. You can't live your whole life hiding from the pain, denying yourself love. I haven't pried into your memories. Those I'm leaving for you to share if you wish on your own accord. But I*

<Zaylyn ><Quest For The Sword Of Anthrowst ><By Katrina Mandrake-Johnston >   <Ch 36> < 115 >

feel that you blame yourself or have this self-loathing for some reason, and all I can say is that you can't punish yourself like this. You don't deserve this isolation no matter how much you think you do. I love you, and I'm not going to let you push me away like you did when I was alive. I'm not trying to force myself on you. I'm just saying that I am here for you. Talk to me if you need to. It's all unconditional. You can tell me anything, and I'll try to understand and help, if you want me too. Besides, it's not like I can go and tell anyone else what secrets you've told me."

"Please just get out of my head. I want to be alone right now. Am I forever cursed now to never be alone with my own thoughts? To have you constantly swimming around in my head? Telling me what to think and forcing your opinions on me all the time? At least before, I had the choice of whether not I wanted to share something. Now you're in there eavesdropping on my inner most thoughts and feelings," she said unkindly, "Am I never to have privacy again?"

"That was not the reaction I expected," Narr said. He was clearly hurt and frustrated by her. *"Figures though, I pour my inner most feelings out to you, and you shoot me down, getting all defensive,"* he said to her, his temper rising, *"Fine. It was hard enough for me to finally open up to you about things. If you think I'm annoying and that I'm violating you, then I will leave you alone! What was I thinking?! I guess everyone was right. You are just a crazy nut! No one can reach you! I was a fool to think that you could feel. Your heart is as cold as ice and as hard as a stone. All that time and life I wasted trying to pursue some sort of affectionate response from you. You aren't capable of it, not even now!"* Asdella simply shrugged. *"Do you even realize how selfish you are? Everything is about you and how things will affect you and you alone. Think about it, you'll see that it's true. Do you even care that that kid died? Was Borin expendable?"*

She refused to provide him with any sort of reaction.

"I'll be around. If you ever come to your senses I might decide to visit you again. Don't expect me to come crawling back."

She slid her bare calloused foot over a smooth stone.

"Things don't exist for your amusement, including people and their feelings. A friend is not just someone who is useful in battle and amusing at times, although you seem to think otherwise. You can't just brush people off and expect things to return to normal when you need something from them. I know you don't care, and you think that you're alone, and that you don't need anyone, and that you don't need to depend on anybody for anything. I have to say this, that one day you will be utterly alone; you will have hurt everyone that has ever cared about you. You'll realize that although you thought you could take on the whole world by yourself, that you can't, and no one will want to help you. I know, you're a fierce warrior and all that hate and anger feeds your strength and your fury. To let that go, would make you weak and vulnerable, or so you think. Realize that this is all you're going to have left inside. You'll be a bitter old woman talking about how fierce and ruthless you were in your younger days and find that no one cares except for other angry people that wish that they could vent in the same violent manner and without the consequences as you did. There are always consequences. You're losing yourself. Do you feel it? You must. You figure you'll die young in battle and won't have to deal with it all later. Surprise, I am dead. You don't just vanish. You'll be dealing with it all, and for you it will be torture. Your soul will feel the regret, sorrow, and loneliness, even if you choose to ignore it all your life. It will be a bitter and painful hell for you, Asdella. You know what, I think I've said enough. You need to wake up and take a good look at the world around you. I'm sorry, but if you truly want to suffer alone, so be it. I care about you, more than that, but it seems that this means nothing to you. Like I said, I'll be around. Good-bye, Asdella."

Asdella shifted her position on the log. Her mind was clear; he was gone. But what Narr had said had hurt her deeply. A tear rolled down her cheek to fall onto her bare knee making a clean spot in the dirty film covering her body. She wiped the tear away angrily.

"A tear? How often do I see one of those? What's wrong with me? Narr's not real. I don't want to be crazy anymore. I don't want people to call me that anymore. It's not like I care. Why should I? Others should be allowed to determine their own opinion about me before the 'crazy' label is suggested to them by someone. Why am I creating Narr's ghost? I don't want to lose my sanity. I know that it

<Zaylyn ><Quest For The Sword Of Anthrowst ><By Katrina Mandrake-Johnston >   <Ch 36> < 116 >

can't be real. Why can't I make it stop? Who am I really? I thought I knew, but now I feel as if I'm an empty shell even more so. I can't even be alone with my thoughts, because even my thoughts are tainted. Why can't I tell what's real anymore? Even if the things my ghost says are true, so what? I can't change the way things are, not now. I can't change the past. I can't just forget about things as if they never happened. I can't start fresh. I can never regain my old self... But what if somehow I could? My innocence, my sanity... Shut up. I don't want to think anymore. My own mind won't leave me in peace."

Another tear ran down her cheek, which she wiped away in disgust.

"Get a grip, you miserable wimp! What? Are you going to start crying like a little baby now? Boo hoo, things aren't perfect, my life is horrible," she mocked herself, *"So what! That's the way things are! I do miss Narr, but as a ghost, he's just not the same anymore."*

<World of Zaylyn ><Quest For The Sword Of Anthrowst ><By Katrina Mandrake-Johnston ><Ch 37>

CHAPTER 37 =   DENDROX AND WEENA

It was late afternoon when Weena arrived back at camp. She had gotten lost for several hours trying to retrace her steps. The others were roasting some sort of animal over the fire and it was the smell that had eventually helped her find the way. She was getting hungry. She normally didn't eat very much meat, but hunger ruled over preference.

"Weena!" Nodwel scolded, "You were told not to go far from the camp. Vordin, Dendrox, and Candra have been out looking for you for hours!"

"I got lost," she said sheepishly, "I didn't mean to."

"Didn't you hear us calling you?" Dendrox asked, "We all eventually gave up and came back here hoping you would show up on your own."

It was obvious that they all had been very worried for her. *"Funny, they didn't make such a fuss over Asdella,"* Weena thought to herself, *"She's been missing all day. Do they really see me as being so incredibly weak? I guess I am compared to them."* "What's that cooking?" she asked.

Candra answered, "Squirrels, it was all we could find when we were out looking for you. Broke another arrow too. I'm usually more cautious than that. We better hope that the majority of our troubles are already over as I'm down to only two arrows now."

"There is no way I'm going to eat a squirrel," she said in disgust. She happened to be very fond of squirrels and the thought of devouring one made her sick to her stomach. Also, without their fur, they resembled large rats which didn't help her appetite much either.

"You have to eat," Candra told her, "It's a long trek to Vackiindmire, and we're probably leaving early in the morning tomorrow. You'll need your strength."

"There's plenty of vegetation. I'm sure I can find something," Weena said, but she was doubtful.

Dendrox asked, "Do you even know anything about plants? Which ones are edible? Which ones contain deadly poison?"

"Well no," she admitted, feeling foolish.

"I'll come with you then," he offered.

Weena smiled as Dendrox led her away from the camp and into the trees. He was nervous about being alone with her, and he could tell that she was too, but she seemed pleased.

Squatting down, he said nervously, "Oh look here. Now this won't taste very good, but it is edible. Come on, help me pull up the roots."

She knelt beside him and begun pulling at the little plant. Weena raised her hand up to brush her hair away from her face, and in doing so, smudged a little bit of dirt onto her cheek. Dendrox looked at her with a warm smile. "You have a smudge," he said.

"Where?" she asked.

"Right here," he told her and gently wiped the dirt from her cheek with his thumb. Her skin was so soft and smooth, and he let his hand linger there. She wore a pleasant expression, and her eyes were wide with an excited spark which seemed to invite him in. *"Would she let me kiss those rosy lips I wonder,"* he thought with a smile.

<Zaylyn ><Quest For The Sword Of Anthrowst ><By Katrina Mandrake-Johnston >   <Ch 37> < 117 >

Weena's mind warned, "*The way he's looking at me gives me shivers, but in a good way. If I try to kiss him and he pulls away, I'll look like such a fool. I wouldn't be able to look at him ever again without feeling like he's laughing at me.*"

"*Will she slap me if I just go for it? Oh come on, do it or you'll never know,*" he told himself, "*Any humiliation would be worth it. Just look at her; how can you resist?*"

"*I think he's going to kiss me! Oh please! I can't believe this is going to happen! He really does like me,*" Weena thought excitedly.

Dendrox scolded himself, "*This 'just do it' stuff isn't supposed to take so long, now is it? If you wait too long, the moment will pass and who knows if you'll get a second chance.*" And then he kissed her, pulling her close against him.

"*Oh wow, I can't believe this is happening. I have tingles all over my body,*" Weena said to herself enjoying the moment and eagerly pushing herself closer.

"*Oh, I want her so bad! I never imagined that she had such passion,*" he thought kissing her again and again, "*Damn these clothes, why can't they just melt away or something. I wonder if she has anything on under that robe?*" He turned away from her lips, kissing his way down the curve of her neck relishing the little excited breaths she made. He let his hand roam over the curves of her leg, over her hip and waist, up to her soft breast. Weena let her fingertips run along his side and down his back.

"*Things are moving too fast,*" her mind warned, "*But I think I kind of want them to. What happens if I give in to him? What then? Sure, every inch of my body is aching to be invaded by him, but then what? Does it continue, or is it over? Will he stop pursuing me once he has taken all of me? Am I just a prize? Another number on his list of women he's gotten? Does he realize that I wouldn't act this way with just anyone? Or does he even care? If he gets what he wants, where will that leave me? How can I please him enough to make him want to stay? I'm inadequate. I don't know what I'm doing. What if I'm just a big joke to him? He'll brag about what happened and laugh at how horrible I was. Even if his intentions are good, what then? If I give myself to him fully so fast, I'll feel dirty, not being able to control my instincts. I'm supposed to be a lady. This is supposed to be a wonderful romantic and passionate experience. I'm scared. We've kissed. We've touched. I need to save the rest for later, draw it out, feel out the situation now that we know there's something here. I need to find out if it's purely a physical thing that he feels or not, and if that's what I feel for him. I don't want to be used like that and have my feelings tossed aside after he's done. I have to stop this, even though my body is crying out for more. My mind says no.*" Then she began to get scared, "*What if he doesn't stop when I ask him to? It's obvious he's not intending to. If I stop things, will he take it the wrong way and think I'm not interested in him anymore? I don't want him to lose interest in me, but I want him to like me for who I am. Unless I try to stop this, I'll never know for sure if it's me he truly likes, or if it's just a passing physical attraction.*" Dendrox inched up her robes to touch the skin of her calf and began slowly caressing his way up along her leg. "*Oh it's going to be very hard to stop. Very, very hard. I can most likely stop myself, but what if he doesn't stop?*" she thought getting extremely frightened now, "*What if he doesn't care whether or not I want to experience everything right away with him? He could take me, and I wouldn't be able to do anything to stop him, except say no and hope he listens and obeys. He's so strong. What if I make him angry? I don't know what he's capable of. We're all alone here. No one could hear me call for help. And like an idiot, I was actually excited about getting so far away from the others, hoping something like this would happen.*" "Please don't," she whispered, as he began to caress her bare thigh under her robes.

"What do you mean? I thought you wanted this. Did I do something wrong?" he asked, a worried and disappointed look in his eyes.

"I do want this, and you did nothing wrong, it's just too soon," she told him gently pushing him away.

"Oh…" he said. She could see the frustration in his eyes. He continued, "Well we don't have to go as far as that. We could do other things. It's not as if I was expecting anything, if that's what you're getting at. I don't want you to feel you need to do anything you don't want to."

Weena was still afraid of what he might do, and what 'other things' might lead into. Also, whether

<Zaylyn ><Quest For The Sword Of Anthrowst ><By Katrina Mandrake-Johnston >   <Ch 37> < 118 >
or not resistance was a possibility for both of them, if things went further. Besides, to Weena, his little speech sounded a little bit too rehearsed for her liking. She said, "No, I think we should get back to the others. We've been gone for quite awhile. They might start to worry."

They got up and walked back to camp in silence, with both of them feeling very awkward.

"Back so soon?" Candra said with a glint in her eye.

Vordin stated, "Asdella's been gone so long. Do you think she's okay?"

Nodwel told him, "Just leave her alone. She'll come to us when she's ready. It'll be dark in a few hours. I'm sure she'll be back before then."

"Maybe she's in trouble," Vordin added, "I'm going to go find her."

"Don't go far, and be careful," Nodwel told him.

"I'll be careful," Vordin assured him.

"You did realize, I was warning to be wary of Asdella, right?" Nodwel asked.

"Oh," he said, not realizing before that Asdella herself might prove to be a threat, "Well, I'm still going to go check on her."

Vordin went off in the direction he thought Asdella might have gone.

After fumbling about in the forest for quite some time, he eventually found her sitting quietly on a fallen log starring absentmindedly at the ground in front of her. He continued to approach her position and made quite a lot of noise doing so.

Startled, she jumped up and turned to him snarling with her sword raised menacingly and making such a grimace that it distorted her pretty face. "Oh, it's you," she said when she recognized him, "Come on and have a seat."

He did not sit, and instead said, "Are you wanting to head back to camp? I can show you the way." He was unsure of exactly how to get back to the camp and was hoping she would return with him and help him find his way back.

"Yeah, sure. You the only one brave enough to come find me, eh?" she said walking toward him.

"Ah, yeah," he said sheepishly.

She asked him, "So they scrounge up some food? I'm starved."

"Yeah, Nodwel's holding on to some nuts and berries for you, and when I left they were roasting some squirrels. You missed out on the rabbits," Vordin told her.

"Okay, great, which way to the campsite?" she asked him expectantly.

"This way, I think," he said apologetically.

"You have no clue, do you? Don't worry about it, I'll find it. Follow me," she said with a smile which put him at ease.

The two of them then made their way back to the others.

<World of Zaylyn ><Quest For The Sword Of Anthrowst ><By Katrina Mandrake-Johnston ><Ch 38>

CHAPTER 38 = WEENA AND CANDRA

When Vordin had left to find Asdella, Candra announced shortly after, "I'm going to scout around the surrounding area before it gets dark. Anyone want to come with? Weena?"

"I will," said Weena. She still felt awkward around Dendrox and kept avoiding eye contact with him.

Candra said, "Alright," with a quirk to her smile. She was hoping Weena would go with her.

They walked in silence through the forest and Candra returned Weena's yellow sash. Weena re-tied and straightened it about her waist.

Weena was trying to decide on something to say, wanting to make a good impression and wanting to be accepted by Candra. Weena thought to herself, *"Candra's slender form, my chubbiness; even in personality we're opposites. Her with her courage and strong will, and me with my weak crybaby attitude. We have nothing in common. Actually, I have nothing in common with Dendrox either, except for a physical attraction that was made clear by both of us earlier. What am I doing? I can't fit in with*

<Zaylyn ><Quest For The Sword Of Anthrowst ><By Katrina Mandrake-Johnston >   <Ch 38> < 119 >

these people and I never will. Except for maybe Vordin and even he's braver than I am. Yarin's gone from our little vulnerable group, so there's just me and Vordin left in the expendable category. And Vordin's more useful than me by far, so that means I'll probably be next to perish. Maybe I should have done more with Dendrox. I could be dead by tonight. That could have been my one and only chance. Oh would you stop being so paranoid and just think of something to say to her, anything will do as long as you don't sound like a fool, which is going to be a definite. But what happens if you go this whole scouting trip without saying anything? This is obviously a test, her wanting to talk one on one to find out what kind of person I am, to see if I'm worthy of her company and probably Dendrox's too. Why else would she want such a useless person to come on a scouting mission? I'm sure she could persuade Dendrox away from me, if she really wanted to, without much problem."

"That's an interesting ring," Candra commented as she stopped to rest a moment.

"It was my mother's," she told her as she held it up so Candra could take a better look at it.

"Yes, that's very nice. It would fetch quite a fair price. It looks valuable," Candra added looking eagerly at the ring.

This immediately made Weena very nervous, and she moved her ringed hand back to her side where she was able to hide it from view within the folds of her robes. Weena hoped that Candra might have been just joking around, but by the elf's serious face, she realized the true nature of a thief.

She hoped that she was simply being overly paranoid and was reading too much into Candra's words and expression. Weena nervously said, "Oh I could never sell it. It means too much to me," then she added, "But that's not what you meant, is it? You wouldn't take it, would you? I know you and Dendrox are thieves, but we're friends, aren't we?"

Candra started walking again and wore a smirk at the corner of her mouth. Weena reluctantly followed her. "For one," the thief told her, "I can't tell you how to be a good judge of character. Whether you should trust someone is completely up to you. As for thieves, there are no boundaries. The sentimental value of an object, whether it be of a friend or not, has no sway with a thief. If it's worth a fair amount of gold, I suggest you keep it well hidden and not display it so clearly for all to see."

Weena quickly removed the ring and placed it in her pouch once more.

The two women walked side-by-side in silence for awhile until Candra asked Weena, "How do you like my ring?" and she held her hand up for the human to see.

"Isn't that…" Weena started, and then felt inside her pouch for her mother's ring. It was gone. "That's mine!" Weena blurted out.

"Says you," the thief said with a grin.

"How did you…" Weena began, but was interrupted by the elf.

"A thief never explains its secrets." Candra waited just long enough for Weena's face to fall with the realization that her ring, which meant so much to her, was gone and could do nothing about it. "I wasn't going to keep it. I was just trying to prove a point. Have we learnt something?" Candra asked handing Weena her ring back.

"Yes," Weena answered relieved.

"Now watch my eyes," Candra told her.

"What? Why?" she asked puzzled.

"Just do it, and hide the ring at the appropriate moment," said the thief.

"What, I'm supposed to hide it with you looking straight at me?" Weena asked astonished.

"That's why I told you to watch my eyes. If I look the other way for a second or two, that's your chance to hide it," she explained.

"What? I can't possibly do it that fast," the wizard told her.

"You have to, because next time I won't give it back," Candra said seriously.

Weena realized that she wasn't kidding. She clutched the ring tightly in her palm and watched Candra's eyes. Her eyes sparkled like the greenest of emeralds and they darted around their surroundings, always watchful. The eyes also fell very often to the ring held tightly in her hand. *"Too*

<Zaylyn ><Quest For The Sword Of Anthrowst ><By Katrina Mandrake-Johnston >   <Ch 38> < 120 >

bad I couldn't just do some sort of spell and fool Candra completely," Weena thought feeling hopeless. A bird chirped. The eyes darted to where the sound had come from. *"I guess that's why thieves have such luck in crowds, since everyone's attention is usually somewhere else. If I fail, I lose my mother's ring forever. I have to do this,"* she told herself. She watched the eyes. *"Where am I going to put it so she doesn't see?"* she asked herself desperately.

"Hey what's that!" Weena shouted pointing off into the trees hoping to fool Candra into looking. Candra's eyes didn't stray as Weena had expected, and the elf gave her a mocking smile. "Okay, of course that's not going to work," Weena admitted.

"Obviously," she chuckled, "You could push me and use the commotion to get a chance to hide it, but that would just make me angry. That would not be very safe for you to do that," Candra said with a sly smile.

A squirrel scampered down a tree and rustled the leaves of the bushes beneath. Candra's eyes darted toward the sound and Weena tucked the ring into her yellow sash.

When Weena looked up again to check Candra's eyes, they were looking straight at her again. *"Was I fast enough?"* Weena immediately thought, *"I guess I won't find out until later."*

Candra and Weena continued their walk through the forest, getting farther and farther away from the others and the campsite.

After awhile Candra said to her, "One thing you should keep in mind, is that objects just get moved, not lost. A good trick is to sell something, get some gold for it, and then take back what you've sold. That's for master thieves. I haven't been able to accomplish that one yet. If your ring is taken, you always have the chance of trying to steal it back. Won't that be an interesting task for you?"

"I guess so," was Weena's reply, a little confused about what exactly Candra expected from her.

They continued in silence. Weena knew that at any time Candra could snatch her ring with ease, and she probably would never feel it. Perhaps she already had. *"I'll get it back. If she wants me to try to steal it back, so be it. I can play her game. I'll just have to be patient and wait for the right time and place."* Weena felt the icy buildup of frustration in her gut. *"I have to be calm. I can't give in to my anger, or I'll never get my ring back if she ends up taking it again."*

They stopped to rest once more, and Weena sat down upon a large boulder while Candra leaned against the bark of a large cedar tree. "You ready?" Candra asked with a smirk.

"Sure, I guess so. Back to camp then?" Weena said standing up and turning to head back the way they came.

"Not exactly," Candra said as she took an arrow from her quiver and turned to Weena.

"What are you doing?" she asked her, the growing fear showing in her voice.

Candra pulled the arrow back in her bow and asked calmly, "You know a Shield spell and a Heal spell, don't you?

"Well yes, but what are you doing?" she asked very frightened.

Candra said plainly, "Use your Shield spell to block my arrow. If you don't, you'll have to use your Heal spell to heal yourself. Or don't, and bleed to death, in which case I go back alone."

"You're not really going to shoot an arrow at me, are you?" she repeated, backing slowly away from her.

"They'll believe anything I tell them regarding your fate. Death by one of the Killnarin, or perhaps by some other terrible misfortune. I'd think of something. You'd be forgotten," Candra said coldly, "So fight back."

Weena's voice trembled with emotion, "After all we've been through? You're just going to kill me?!" Her mind raced, *"It can't be because I kissed Dendrox, can it? She's crazy!"*

Candra told her, "I'm not trying to kill you, but I'd rather see you die here than ripped apart by some creature because you can't protect yourself. You said you needed practice. Here it is."

"Not like this!" she practically screamed at her.

"I'm losing patience, Weena," she warned.

"She's seriously going to kill me! What do I do? What can I do?!" Weena asked herself and then

<Zaylyn ><Quest For The Sword Of Anthrowst ><By Katrina Mandrake-Johnston >   <Ch 38> < 121 >

said, "Well at least give me some warning before you fire!"

"Real life doesn't work that way. Do you think an enemy would give you a warning before an attack? An enemy will seek out any and every weakness in your defense," and Candra loosed the arrow.

Everything seemed to move in slow motion, as Weena watched in utter fear as the arrow left the bow and came at her. Like a reflex, the words flashed through her mind, and a multi-colored film surrounded her as before. She watched the arrow stop in mid air and fall harmlessly to the ground. The shield, having absorbed the force of the arrow, vanished. Everything all happened in what seemed less than a second. Weena stared at Candra's face in disbelief.

"I knew you could do it," Candra said as she took out another arrow.

Weena thought about fleeing but knew she would be any easy target for the elf and to run would be completely useless. Her only hope was to spark some sort of compassion within her. *"Surely Candra could not seriously mean to kill me. Can she truly despise me so deeply?! I saved her life! Twice, if you count the wound and poisoning as two. No, it's three times! She was to be held responsible for the wounded spider. Can this actually be some insane idea of hers to get me to practice my spells?!"*

The corner of Candra's mouth turned up in a malicious and contemptuous sneer. With slender and nimble fingers, she pulled back the arrow in the bow.

"My spell! I can't use it twice in a row!" Weena yelled at her, trying desperately to reason with her somehow.

"I know," Candra said calmly, "An enemy won't care. In fact, they'll count on it."

"No don't!" Weena screamed at her.

The elf loosed the second arrow and hit Weena in the shoulder, throwing her back in shock and pain as it struck her. She was now on the ground. Blood began to flow heavily from her wound. Weena stared in horror and amazement at the thin shaft of wood protruding from her, and she could feel it within her body. Her shoulder felt like it was on fire.

Candra stood over her, staring down coldly.

Weena tried to use her Heal spell and it failed miserably. The pain and the shock of what Candra had done, was almost unbearable.

"She can't just leave me here to die! The others will come to rescue me," her mind said to her. Then she realized that Candra was right. They would believe anything Candra told them. She would become yet another casualty added to the long list. There would be no questions asked. They would have to concentrate on their own survival. There would be no one coming to rescue her. If she were going to survive, she had to do it on her own. This was what Candra wanted her to realize in such a frightful way. This was her test to see if she were going to be a survivor or weigh the group down, endangering others. Weena realized that if she didn't fight back, she truly was going to be left alone to bleed to death. Candra wasn't going to have a second thought about doing it either.

Weena bit back the pain, and tried to ignore the fact that the loss of blood had already started to make her lightheaded. She mouthed the words of the spell, willing them to work with all of her body and soul, and felt the arrow slowly being pushed out of her shoulder as the flesh mended itself.

She felt the arrow drop to the ground and the pain subsided. When she looked up at Candra again, the elf had her hand outstretched toward her. "You need some help up?" she offered.

Weena felt like punching her right in the jaw with all her might, but she was far too weak and afraid to do so. Weena accepted Candra's hand and the thief helped the wizard to her feet.

"I knew you could do it," she said picking up the arrows and replacing them back into her quiver, "I really didn't want to have to leave you there. Plus, having to explain things to Dendrox. You do understand why I did it, right? No hard feelings?"

Weena glared at her, but did understand what Candra meant for her to learn from all of this. *"People you call friends can turn on you, so never let your guard down. Rely on yourself and not on others to save you. Don't give in to fear, use it to fuel the desire to survive. Turn anger and frustration into determination. But what I have truly learnt here most of all is, that jealousy can cloud someone's*

<Zaylyn ><Quest For The Sword Of Anthrowst ><By Katrina Mandrake-Johnston >   <Ch 38> < 122 >

mind to the point of insanity. I'm not trying to steal her friend away from her or somehow take her place. Surely she cannot believe this to be true. Maybe she is not even aware of it, but it would explain why she is so determined to teach me the ways of a thief, to hold me close for fear of losing Dendrox. She's willing to kill me, even after everything we've been through. Can I ever trust her again? Will she let me perish instead of coming to my rescue when she is able?" Weena hesitated but finally replied, "Yes, no hard feelings."

Candra suggested, "You better do something about that blood. You'll attract predators right to you. Rub some dirt on it. That should work well enough. It will look like you fell. The others wouldn't understand what I was trying to teach you," and then she warned, "You say anything stupid, no amount of luck or magic will save you. I'm very fast and a deadly shot. Are we clear on this?"

"Yes," she answered, her voice trembling slightly, "I fell. I won't say anything."

Weena began to rub handfuls of soil onto the blood soaked areas of her robes, and when she had finished to Candra's satisfaction, the elf smiled and said, "Let's get back to camp then."

Weena felt the sash for her mother's ring and discovered it to be missing. *"How dare she threaten me! I'm not going to say anything. I'm not a complete wimp. Besides, I've got to try to find a way of getting my mother's ring back. She thinks she's so clever. Wants me to try to steal it back? I'll find a way. I don't know how, but I'll figure something out. I just have to be patient about it,"* thought Weena.

They both started walking back to the camp.

<World of Zaylyn ><Quest For The Sword Of Anthrowst ><By Katrina Mandrake-Johnston ><Ch 39>

CHAPTER 39 =   DENDROX AND CANDRA'S WATCH

It was dark by the time Candra and Weena returned. The warm glow of the campfire was a comfort to all in the growing blackness of the forest. No one seemed to notice that Weena had apparently fell.

Candra and Dendrox offered to take first watch, and it didn't take the others very long to fall asleep with all of them being extremely exhausted.

Candra was seated on a rock while she absentmindedly poked at the fire with a stick, and Dendrox sat leaning up against a tree. He put his hands behind his head as he stretched out, decided to prop his feet up on a small nearby rock, and let out a sigh. "Hey, Candra?" Dendrox said looking very relaxed.

"Yeah," she replied still poking at the logs in the fire and watching the little sparks fly about.

"I thought I was the one that always fidgets with stuff. There something bothering you?" he asked her.

"No, not really. Just all that's been happening I guess," she answered.

They sat in silence for awhile, listening to the crackling fire as the others slept.

"Candra, you do know, that if you keep fiddling with the fire, you'll eventually make it go out," he warned.

"Yeah, I know. I've said the same thing to you a million times," she told him.

"That's why I said it," he said with a smile.

She stopped attacking the fire with the stick and turned to him. He could tell she had a lot on her mind and that she wanted to talk to him about something that was difficult for her to bring up. She finally said, "You know, I see more of your mother in you than of your father. I see a lot of your parents passed down into you."

"Why all of a sudden all about my parents?" he asked with a puzzled expression, "What's wrong?"

"I was just thinking, that's all. When was the last time we passed by Cranok anyway, to see how they were doing?" she asked.

"I don't know, a year maybe two. Or no, I think it might be three now, but why?" he asked. He had been expecting her to maybe say something about Weena. *"I highly doubt it, but maybe they had a long talk together on their walk and actually get along okay."*

"Well you know how my parents are gone, and I know I've sort of shut down since then. You know, a little standoffish now and then, sometimes a little too often. I was just thinking…" she trailed

<Zaylyn ><Quest For The Sword Of Anthrowst ><By Katrina Mandrake-Johnston >   <Ch 39> < 123 >
off.

"You miss them, don't you?" he said. *"She hasn't mentioned her own parents since we were kids, not since after retrieving her mother's necklace and visiting their graves that one time. It isn't something she talks about."* He added, "You actually miss my parents, don't you?" *"She never really cared for my parents, or at least that's what we all thought. She would hardly talk to them or spend very much time around them. They did adopt her into the family, treated her and even loved her as a daughter. She has always been so cold around them though. She would show respect, of course, but was always so distant. I was the only one she would really open up to."*

"Well, yeah, of course I miss them," she said finally and there was the beginnings of a tear in her eye.

"Wow, you've never admitted to that much feeling before," he said jokingly.

"Oh shut up," she said with a smile.

"So you actually care about them? But you always acted and treated them like they were more of an inconvenience, although a necessity," he said wanting to get everything said while she was willing to talk about it, "That you tolerated them because they happened to be my parents, and because they were providing for you. You would show them a small amount of respect and appreciation, but not much. 'Little Miss Independent' could do everything on her own, not needing anyone. Sometimes I even felt like you didn't want me around either." He knew that at any other time, she would forcefully change the subject, refusing to speak to him at all about anything to do with his parents. *"She wants to be completely free, living day to day, moment to moment, adventure to adventure. The thought of being tied down with thoughts of family, of being part of one, caring and worrying about others, having others worrying and caring about what might happen to her… Maybe that's the core of it. Knowing that they would disapprove of the thieving. That if she got in trouble or injured, they would be worried about her. Could it be that she has associated my parents along with the guilt of how we make our living, and has just pushed it all away? That would explain now maybe, but when we were kids? I guess she just felt strange being part of a family after losing hers. Feeling like she didn't belong, even though we made every effort to welcome her in. I mean, sure she's an elf and we're a family of humans, but the only real difference is the ears. We're all the same and she knows that. My parents didn't feel obligated to take her in. They didn't feel like she was invading their family and that she was an inconvenience they had to put up with. Although she sure acted as if this were so, despite all the effort they made to include her. Half the time I felt like she was getting all the attention. I used to feel so jealous of her sometimes and angry too, because all the attention was just being wasted on her when they could have been spending time with me, and I would have appreciated it. I don't know what her problem is. I mean, sure, I had my rebellious moments, but what she did was just not normal or fair. They didn't know what they were doing wrong, wanting to connect with her somehow but always getting an icy shoulder in return."*

Candra told him, "Yes, I know, I know. What I'm trying to say is that I know that now. I'm admitting that, and that I was wrong to be so cold. I am sorry, and I really do miss them. We should go see them soon, even if it means going out of our way to see them. Maybe even bring them a gift or something. Something that we didn't steal. It would feel funny if it was."

Dendrox was a little shocked by her. "Wow, is all I can say. They would just love to hear all this coming out of you."

"Yeah, well just keep it to yourself. No one needs to know that I might be going a bit soft," she said with a smile.

"I guess looking at Asdella and the way she is, it gets you thinking, doesn't it?" Dendrox added.

"Yeah, I know. I don't want to turn out like that, shutting everyone out with such bitterness," she said, and then she got a fearful look in her eye saying, "Hey…"

"Yeah?" he asked.

She asked in a worried voice, "You don't think that these creatures have made it all the way to Cranok, do you? And that your parents… well… you know?"

The thought of the creatures attacking Cranok, their home village, and doing what they did to

<Zaylyn ><Quest For The Sword Of Anthrowst ><By Katrina Mandrake-Johnston >   <Ch 39> < 124 >

Nilnont and Dexcsin, made him shudder. Visions of his kind parents screaming, running for their lives, hiding and desperately hoping the horrid beasts would pass them by. He came to a new realization of what Vordin must have gone through. Finding his parents slain, knowing what happened, and knowing that the creatures enjoyed every moment of it... And poor Yarin, so scared, but brave, so very brave. The talk about his parents seemed frivolous after the thought that the creatures may have gotten to them and that they could be dead. He said, "Yeah, I've been thinking about that too. Let's not, okay? We'll just have to stop them before any of that happens."

"Okay," and then Candra changed the subject by saying, "So, you and Weena, huh?"

Dendrox tried to keep a straight face but ended up blushing, "What about us?"

"Come on, I see the way you look at her. Anything happen when you two went on that so-called walk?" she said with a sly smile.

"Hey, come on, that stuff is supposed to be private," he grinned. He knew she would try to weasel every bit of information out of him and it would be fun keeping it from her for as long as he could.

"You know there's no such thing as that around me. Since when have we ever kept secrets from each other? Including the personal private stuff. What, you're just going to let this little piece of information boil up inside you until you burst? You know you want to tell somebody," she said with her mischievous smile.

"Oh, come on, Candra," he whined, "What if they're awake? What if she's awake?"

"Everybody is asleep," she told him, knowing that he was playing around with her. She was having fun with it too.

"You sure?" he asked.

"Yes, of course. You know me, I can just tell. What kind of thief would I be, if I can't tell whether someone's really asleep or just pretending?" she said with a smile.

"Okay fine," he said.

"Oh and don't forget, I can tell if you're lying, so no exaggerations," she added.

"Yeah, well just remember, that I happen to be better at the whole lie detecting thing. Remember the time when..." he pretended to start.

She made a little frustrated growl and said, "Quit trying to sidetrack the topic, you. I'm all ears."

"Yeah I know, you're an elf, remember?" he said trying to stifle a laugh.

"Hey," she said with a smile, "Just spill it already."

"Okay, we kissed," he admitted blushing slightly.

"And?" she pried.

"That's it... Well... I touched her thigh briefly but that's it," he told her.

"Naked?" Candra said, her sly smile gleaming.

"No," he chuckled. He knew how much fun she was having with her interrogation and at how uncomfortable it was making him, especially where Weena was asleep only a few feet away. Dendrox continued, "Just over her clothes. Well, her thigh was bare."

"So that's all? Yeah right," Candra said.

"I swear," he said trying to look as innocent as possible.

"Really?" she asked, "That's not at all like you."

He said, partially hoping that Weena was awake to hear, "Well, I don't know, she's different somehow. She's special; I actually care about her."

Candra told him, "Oh I didn't mean anything like that. I can tell, you know, the difference between just a physical interest and the other type. I just thought more would happen, especially with the way you two have been eyeing each other."

"It can't be that obvious, and anyway, I don't think things are going to continue any further," he said.

"What do you mean?" she asked.

He answered, "It was as if one minute she wanted me and couldn't keep her hands off me, and then she just stopped cold. I don't understand. Did I do something wrong?"

"Couldn't keep her hands off, eh? You forgot to mention that part," Candra said with a sly smirk.

<Zaylyn ><Quest For The Sword Of Anthrowst ><By Katrina Mandrake-Johnston >   <Ch 39> < 125 >

"No, that was nothing. Come on, Candra, I'm being serious," he said hoping she could clarify things for him. "It was as if she was scared to touch me, or just didn't want to. I don't know what to think," he said honestly.

Candra felt very awkward talking about this and continued to joke around. "Hey, you know what?"

"What?" he said plainly.

"Maybe you're just a bad kisser," she laughed.

"Oh gee, thanks," he said sarcastically and smiled at her.

"Well, it is a turn off when someone is trying to swallow your whole face or drown you in slobber," she told him matter-of-factly.

"Hey, that can go both ways, you know," he laughed.

"She definitely has an interest in you. You probably can't see it, but it's clear to me. So you think it might be the kissing then?" she asked with a mischievous look.

He replied, "I don't know. I've never tried to kiss myself, now have I? Besides, it's not as if anybody's going to be honest enough to tell me any different."

"Well, okay, kiss me then," she said plainly.

"What?!" he said shocked that she had suggested this.

"Yeah, I'll give you the truth. I might even be a bit insulting," she said grinning.

"Really?" he said doubting her, "You're serious? So what, you like me too all of a sudden?" Dendrox thought to himself, *"Could that be why she's been acting so strangely? Could Candra have been interested in me all this time and not said anything? No, that's silly. Unless she just realized it, now that I like Weena. Candra jealous; …that's a scary thought. I wonder what went on during their walk?"*

"Well of course I like you, but just not in the romantic way. The kiss is not going to mean anything. Well, unless you secretly have an interest in me or something like that. You don't, do you? You would have said something, right?" she asked him. He couldn't tell for sure, but he thought there might have been a slight hint of hopefulness in her voice.

"What should I say?" he asked himself, *"I mean, sure, I've thought about it. We'd be perfect together, probably. I never thought that she might have had feelings that way. She always made it clear that she didn't, but now I don't know what to think. If I say the wrong thing, I could really screw things up here."* "I don't know, I feel the same way you do, I guess," was his reply, "So you really want to do this?"

"I'll be honest. Now where else are you going to get that?" she said.

"Okay, so just do it, and then you'll tell me what you think?" he asked.

"Yes, exactly," she said moving over to where he was sitting.

She sat close beside him as she had done earlier when she had been preparing the rabbits. It was different now, however, and for the first time he felt uncomfortable around her. "Okay," he said and found himself hesitating.

"Well?" Candra said.

"Just give me a minute," he told her.

"Oh, somebody's shy," she teased with an overly large grin and a bit of a giggle.

"Hey, come on. Don't bother me about it," said Dendrox.

"Okay," she said, making it obvious that she was trying to hold back her smile and put on a serious face.

"You know, it's like you are two separate people," he commented, "One person around me and then someone totally different around everyone else."

"Yeah, I know. It's 'cause I can trust you. I can be myself around you," she said simply, "Quit trying to distract the situation. It's just me."

"Okay fine," he said, "You ready?"

"Am I ready?" she laughed, "I've been ready for awhile. I'm waiting for this shy little boy to get up enough nerve to do it. I'm surprised now that you were able to pull yourself together enough to kiss

<Zaylyn ><Quest For The Sword Of Anthrowst ><By Katrina Mandrake-Johnston >   <Ch 39> < 126 >
Weena."

"Well it's not like I've gotten complaints before," he said stalling, "I've kissed a fair number of women."

"But you're afraid to kiss me?" she challenged.

"I'm not afraid," he said defensively, "All this has just gotten me a bit paranoid. I've never really cared before whether or not a woman had feelings in return."

"Okay, so Weena's special and you want to find out whether your kissing turned her off or not, so you've got to kiss me or you'll never know. Oh, and by the way, being afraid and being paranoid are basically the same thing. So, are you going to do it, or not?" she dared him getting impatient.

"Yes," he told her, but again hesitated.

"Well?" Candra said expectantly.

"I'm going to," he assured her.

"It has to be an actual kiss or it won't serve its purpose," Candra reminded him.

"Okay," he said, this time looking into her beautiful emerald green eyes. This was the first time he was able to bring himself to do so, since she came to sit next to him for the awaited kiss.

"Oh, this is ridiculous. Come here," and she pulled him close and gave him a quick kiss to his lips.

"There. Is the tension gone now?" she whispered, "Now show me how you kiss."

She was very close to him now, looking into his eyes in a way he had never seen before. Drawn to her as if it always had meant to be so, his lips met hers. She had the scent of pine needles and honeysuckle about her.

Her kisses were soft and moist. They were long passionate kisses. He couldn't describe the love he felt for her. Weena didn't mean anything to him at this moment; she was but a passing interest compared to Candra. Dendrox pulled her closer to him in a warm embrace. No other woman was worth his attention, not if he could have Candra.

He had thought about it, imagined what it would be like to kiss her, and now he knew. It felt good to hold her close. They were meant to be together, but somehow it just didn't feel right. He couldn't exactly tell what it was. *"I love her more than anything, but could the kiss be just a result of us thinking this to be the next logical step? Could it be that the kiss happened simply because we thought it to be the right thing to do and not led by our hearts to do so as we had first thought? Is our love for each other more like that one has for a family member... No, it is much more than that, but not exactly to the point of romance... Well, could it be? Perhaps..."*

"Well?" he finally asked her, pretending that the kiss was merely an experiment as they had suggested it was to be. He wondered if she really did have feelings for him. It felt like she did. He wondered if she too had imagined it and thought about it before. If by some chance it had started out as some jealous move against Weena, it hadn't ended as such.

"That... that was pretty good," she said, stumbling over her words.

Her face was flushed and she wore a smile that was almost bashful. As she was, there at that moment, her beauty accentuated by the firelight, that smile, that magical look in her eye... He would forever remember her at that moment; the moment at which their love was expressed. He could see the love and affection she felt for him reflected in her, but he knew that he would probably never see that passionate spark in her again. He knew his realization to be true.

"You're pretty good yourself too," he admitted, not knowing what else to say in such an awkward moment of silence.

"Ah, thanks," she said, trying to hide the fact that she was blushing.

"So no hidden feelings or anything, right?" he questioned, truly wanting to know.

"Okay, yes, it felt good, and yes, I care for you more than anyone I know, but it just felt strange somehow," she admitted, "At first it was what I thought I wanted, but then... I don't know."

"Okay, that's a relief. Same here," he told her.

"So the problem is definitely not the kissing," Candra said pretending that the kiss had been completely meaningless to them, "You know what? It's probably just her."

Dendrox asked, "What do you mean?"

<Zaylyn ><Quest For The Sword Of Anthrowst ><By Katrina Mandrake-Johnston >   <Ch 39> < 127 >

"She's probably just shy and insecure. She'll get over it," she explained, "Just give her time. She'll come around."

"You think?" he asked and was answered with a nod.

"Yeah, I like her," Candra commented, "I just hope I didn't scare her too badly. When we took that walk to scout the area, well, I wanted to see how well she could handle herself when it came to a life or death situation. She's not as terrible as she thinks she is. If she learns a couple more spells, she'll be fine. I just don't want her to end up defenseless and dead, you know?"

"So what exactly went on with you two?" he asked imagining the worst.

"Never mind," was her answer, knowing he would pry.

Dendrox instantly knew that Candra had done something awful. "What did you do?" he said in a scolding tone, "You did something, didn't you?"

She winced as she told him, "I kind of shot an arrow at her."

"What?!" he exclaimed in disbelief, looking to Weena and her mud-covered robes with worry.

"Hey, I was all mixed up. I didn't know what I wanted. I was sick of her being a wimp. I wanted to see what she was really capable of and I had to scare her to find out," Candra said, getting defensive.

"So you shot an arrow at her?! What if you missed and hit her? You could have killed her by accident," and then seeing the shameful look beginning on Candra's face, hinted with an underlying maliciousness, and by the way the corner of her mouth was turned up revealing to him that she had done something rather nasty, and knowing what she was capable of, he knew to ask, "Candra, you didn't hurt her, did you?" The tone of his words showed that he already knew the answer.

"Okay, I'll tell you everything," she said and now almost looked pleased with herself, "Okay, I stole her ring, but I was teaching her a lesson with that, still am. Then, I shot an arrow at her and she blocked it with that Shield spell she has. Then I shot another arrow at her, and she had to use her Heal spell to get it out of her shoulder. But she's fine now. I kind of told her I was going to leave her there to bleed to death too. But I'm okay with her now. I got out my frustration with her and I think she's better for it too. I know I am. I actually kind of like her now."

"You just had to almost kill her first," he said with a chuckle. He was finding it hard to believe that Candra had actually resorted to such extreme methods and was even willing to kill Weena just because she found her annoying at times and unable to defend herself as Candra thought she ought to.

"Yeah, I'm really sorry," she told him, but he knew that the apology wasn't really sincere. Candra added, "It's just that she's always whine, whine, whine. And then, 'I can't do this, I can't do that', all the time. It was driving me nuts! She has the skills. She's just acting like a spoiled little baby, too afraid to even try. I didn't want to have her blubbering all over us when there's danger, not when she's perfectly capable of defending herself. Okay there, I've said it to you. She's proven that she can handle herself in a crisis and hopefully she'll have learnt something by it. And if she doesn't go back to being completely spineless, I think I can actually get along with her. I like her; she has spirit."

"So if things escalate with her and me, you'd be fine with it? You wouldn't be mean to her or anything?" Dendrox asked Candra knowing that she could be vicious at times.

"No, I'm actually willing to let her into our little group. Teach her the skills of the trade," she told him.

"You're going to try to teach her some thieving skills? The kind of things that we do?" he asked in disbelief, "Don't you think maybe you're trying a little too hard to accept her now? All you have to do is be nice to her."

"What, you don't think I can do it? Imagine the possibilities when you add a bit of magic into the mix," she explained.

He thought to himself, *"Candra's talking about adding a third member into our little group? It's probably going to get us killed and all because I like some girl. She's talking as if this is going to last forever with Weena. Candra's trying way too hard to make this work for me. Weena's not a thief. It's not in her nature. She can't change to suit our life style and she shouldn't have to change just to fit in with us. Or the other way around. I can't see myself settling down, giving up the pursuit of riches and adventure, and saying good-bye to all the excitement. I don't know, if Weena wants to learn to be a*

<Zaylyn ><Quest For The Sword Of Anthrowst ><By Katrina Mandrake-Johnston >   <Ch 39> < 128 >

thief, fine. She can pretend and Candra can play out her little fantasy. The first sign of real danger though, reality must take over, no matter how cold it is." "All I'm saying is it's going to be difficult. In fact extremely difficult," Dendrox said to her, "What are you going to start out with first?"

"I already have. I've started with a little pickpocket trial. She has to try to get her mother's ring back from me," Candra grinned.

"We'll see," he chuckled, "You're going to have your hands full, you know?"

"Yeah, but it'll be fun. I can hardly wait to see what she does. You should have seen her. She was furious. She's going to be coming after me and that ring with all she's got."

He thought to himself, "*Kind of like whoever those damn scissors belong to.*"

"I'm going to catch some rest," Candra announced standing up and heading over to where she had put her belongings.

"Sure," he said, "I'm going to stay up for a bit longer."

Candra wrapped herself up tightly in her blanket and went to sleep. Dendrox watched the flames of the fire dance as they reached for the stars in the night sky.

<World of Zaylyn ><Quest For The Sword Of Anthrowst ><By Katrina Mandrake-Johnston ><Ch 40>

CHAPTER 40 = NODWEL AND ASDELLA'S WATCH

"Nodwel," Dendrox whispered. The dwarf stirred slightly, but did not wake. "Hey, Nodwel, wake up," he said shaking him gently, "Wake up, it's your watch. I've got to get some sleep too."

Nodwel opened his eyes and jolted into sitting position. "What is it? Is there danger?" he asked urgently.

"No, no, relax," Dendrox told him, "It's just time for your watch. Candra's already asleep, and I've been fighting to keep my eyes open for awhile now. All has been quiet, but you better wake up Asdella too, just to be safe. I'm a little nervous of waking her actually. I thought about it, but then visions of her stabbing that sword of hers through my gut keeps coming to mind. I really think it would be safer if you got her up for the watch."

"Oh, what? Ah, yeah, sure," Nodwel said still trying to fully wake up, despite the first jolt of adrenalin.

"You sure you're awake?" he asked, knowing of his own habit of falling back to sleep right away after being woken to take watch.

"Yeah, I'm fine," the dwarf said standing up and heading over to a rock by the fire, "Get some sleep. There's no telling what we may have to deal with tomorrow. Everyone will need their rest."

Dendrox found what looked to be a somewhat comfortable spot to sleep, stretching himself out with his head resting on his arm. "*This is supposed to be the most comfortable spot? We better get to an inn soon. I mean, sure, I'm pretty much used to it by now, but I'm really starting to get sick of sleeping outside with rocks and twigs digging into my side and creepy crawly bugs swarming all over me,*" he muttered to himself. He looked over with mixed emotions to where Weena was sleeping. Finally, he got up, draped his blanket over her, and then quickly returned to his chosen spot once more.

"You going to wake up Asdella?" he reminded Nodwel, as it was obvious the dwarf had forgotten or was also nervous of waking the warrior woman and trying to avoid it.

Nodwel said, "Yeah," and headed over to where she was sleeping. Dendrox was already sound asleep by the time Nodwel reached her.

"Asdella?" Nodwel called, trying not to wake the others. "Asdella?" he repeated when he saw she hadn't woken. He thought about nudging her slightly, but then decided against it, being wary of what her reaction might be as Dendrox had been. "Asdella?" he said a little louder, "Wake up, it's me Nodwel. You're supposed to take the watch with me."

Her eyes opened and she sat up, giving him a withering stare. Then she stood, staring out into the forest for several moments, her eyes heavy with sleep, before finally stumbling sleepily over to the boulders by the fire, dragging her sword along behind her.

"*Okay, she's awake. Whether that's a good thing or not, I'm not sure,*" he chuckled to himself. He joined her by the fire and they sat in silence for quite a long while.

<Zaylyn ><Quest For The Sword Of Anthrowst ><By Katrina Mandrake-Johnston >   <Ch 40> < 129 >

Nodwel was the one to finally say something. "You know, Asdella," he said, "I thought Borin was dead. I was trying to accept that he was gone, like the others. And then, there he was, alive and well. And now, I have to go through the pain of losing my friend all over again."

Asdella asked, "What are you trying to say? It's the same for me."

He let out a big sigh and told her, "I'm just glad that you're still here, that's all. Running, trying to make it to Vackiindmire in time, trying to find someone to help us, well, I thought it was hopeless, after seeing Dimwar and Nimdor taken down so easily. I thought I had lost you too."

"You did, or would have if that amulet hadn't been around and if Candra and Dendrox hadn't come across me when they did," she said, "The fact of it is, that I didn't really care whether I lived or died. Whatever fate was coming for me, I was prepared to accept it. And yet, I found myself fighting to live, and for what reason I don't know, as none came to mind, but I was fighting just the same. Whatever that means, I don't know, but maybe at that last moment, when my final fate had already been decided, I was fighting to live just so if you did return, there would be someone around to find. So you wouldn't feel as if you failed, and so you wouldn't have to suffer through all of it alone."

This was the most compassionate thing he had ever heard her say. He had no idea that she in fact held their friendship more dear than what he had imagined. Past the hard warrior exterior, there was more to her than he had realized. He was beginning to see a little of what Narr had seen in her. *"You get her to talk enough, her inner self starts to peek out here and there through the tough outer wall she puts up. She isn't really as harsh as she makes herself out to be and maybe not as insane as she gets everyone to believe."*

He didn't really know what to say, so he ended up saying, "I can take the watch alone, if you want to get some rest."

"Thanks," she replied, and she lay down where she was on the hard rocky ground by the fire, stretched out on her back with a hand resting across her stomach, and she closed her eyes.

Nodwel chuckled to himself as she had the hilt of her sword clutched tightly in her right hand as always. *"Even in sleep, she's ready for battle..."* and then as a second realization thought, *"I guess, no matter what the situation, she never really feels safe. It must be hard for her, whatever the reason."*

<World of Zaylyn ><Quest For The Sword Of Anthrowst ><By Katrina Mandrake-Johnston ><Ch 41>

CHAPTER 41 = THE MIND LINK

Nodwel tossed the last piece of firewood into the fire. It sent sparks flying up into the sky. Above, he could see the stars through the treetops, and he was looking up at them when out of the corner of his eye he thought he saw something move. He quickly and silently took up his axe and scanned the darkness.

Finally, he decided that it must have been his imagination, being so tired and all. He looked back to his fellow companions and was surprised to see Lorenta leaning over Vordin.

"How did you... What are you doing?" he asked.

"Sorry Nodwel, being a spider I tend to move silently. I didn't mean to startle you. I just wanted to talk to Vordin," she answered and the dwarf nodded. "Vordin?" she whispered as she lay a hand gently on his cheek, "Vordin?"

He woke and exclaimed with surprise, "Lorenta?"

"I've finally learnt how to fully communicate with the other spiders. I can actually do it," she whispered with pride.

"Well, that's great," Vordin told her.

"They wanted me to ask you what is being planned. Is anything to be done about the creatures? And, what about this wizard behind them? They are accepting the loss of their home of course and that they will have to find a new one eventually. They are mourning their dead, but they refuse to sit idly by any longer. The spiders want to help in anyway they can. They have suggested that they monitor the activity of the Killnarin. They have this other ability where they can create a mind link with another, which allows them to communicate over long distances. The spider who has been decided as their new leader has created such a link with me and will relay any information they gather. I would like to try to

<Zaylyn ><Quest For The Sword Of Anthrowst ><By Katrina Mandrake-Johnston >   <Ch 41> < 130 >
create a link to you, Vordin, in case anything happens," she explained, "in case we get separated."

"Ah, yeah, sure, I guess. It won't hurt, will it?" he asked nervously.

"I don't know. It didn't hurt me when the leader made his link to me," Lorenta told him, "This will be my first time doing this of course, so I don't know what will happen. You do think that it's a good idea to do so, don't you?

"Sure. What do I do?" asked Vordin, "I'm nothing like a spider. Doesn't that matter?"

"No, I asked him. It will be all right," she said as she placed her hands to his forehead, "Just relax."

Green flames started to erupt from her body as she concentrated. Vordin looked up to the sky wondering if it were dawn, but it was not, and Lorenta did not change form.

Nodwel shot them a wary glance saying, "Everything all right over there?"

"Yes," Lorenta answered a little annoyed that he had broken her concentration.

"Vordin?" Nodwel asked.

"Yes, everything's fine," Vordin hoped, still nervous about Lorenta's ability.

"If I could just interrupt for a second," said Nodwel, "Lorenta, you didn't see anything out of the ordinary? Not any of the spiders are out there roaming about?"

"No, I didn't. I'm sorry, but I really need to concentrate," she explained.

A heavy weight began to push into Vordin's head from her hands, yet it was not her hands that were doing the pushing. It was a horrible feeling, and Vordin felt as if his mind were being squished into the bottom of his throat, as if another were trying to take its place.

He began to panic and almost cried out, but Lorenta whispered, "Shh, don't fight me. I'm not trying to hurt you. Relax and let me in."

Vordin got a horrible thought that maybe this was not Lorenta and that this was yet another trick by the Killnarin which he was so foolishly falling for. "Wait," he said, and the sound of his voice made him wince and it sounded so very far away.

"What's wrong?" she asked, stopping and taking her hands away from his forehead.

"I felt like I was slipping away. Like something was taking me over," he said looking at her suspiciously.

"Oh, perhaps I was doing it wrong then. It is possible to take over someone's mind for a short time, if the invading mind is strong enough. The others told me that occasionally they would do this with the villagers if they needed to listen for information or to gain food if they were short on supply," she explained.

Shocked, he asked, "You mean they would sometimes eat the villagers?"

"What? No, they would gain control over a villager and use him to deposit livestock and other food items down the well," she said giving him a disappointed look, "After all they've proven themselves to be, you still can think something like that?"

"I… Sorry," said Vordin.

"So, do you want me to try again?" she asked him, "I'll try to be less forceful this time, but for it to work, you have to accept me into your mind. Then I'm supposed to leave a bit of my mind in yours to maintain the connection. You will see this when you close your eyes as a little spot of red. If you want to contact me, concentrate on it, opening it up and enlarging it until it fills your mind, and I will answer. That is, if I do it right. Most importantly, if you resist me and try to reject my mind, it won't work. So, you really want me to do this?"

"I don't know. It doesn't sound very safe," he answered, but her eyes seemed to beg him with such a desperateness that he said, "but alright."

She replaced her hands to his forehead and the green flames once more began to whip about her. Vordin felt the push from her mind into his. It was slightly less forceful, but still felt invasive and made him start to panic. He fought the urge and let himself open up to her. He felt so vulnerable. He could feel her in his mind like a heavy stone inside his skull. Then he felt a sharp pain, as if a needle had been punched into his brain. She removed her hands and the weight subsided except for a spot about the size of a pebble.

<Zaylyn ><Quest For The Sword Of Anthrowst ><By Katrina Mandrake-Johnston >   <Ch 41> < 131 >

Lorenta announced, "It is done." Vordin rubbed at his forehead. "Are you okay?" she asked.

"I think so," Vordin told her.

"What are you two doing over there?" Nodwel asked with curiosity.

"Lorenta has learnt to communicate with the spiders, and she's trying to use the same method to communicate with me," Vordin answered.

"Oh, well that's good. We're out of firewood," he informed them, "Should I get some more?"

"Sure, I'll keep a look out," Vordin said.

"So is there a plan for what to do next?" Lorenta asked Vordin.

"We're planning to go to Vackiindmire to find out about that sword," he told her, "Am I supposed to have this horrible headache?"

"Oh, that's normal. I had one too when the leader made his link to me. It will go away in a few minutes," she assured him, "So you're going to find out about the sword at Vackiindmire? That's a good idea. Maybe the spiders will be able to find out something about the wizard. I doubt they'll be able to find out his location, but their efforts will help us out greatly. At least they'll be able to tell us where the Killnarin might be headed next. We could at least maybe warn some of the people before they strike. That is, if they even believe us."

"Do you really think we can make some sort of difference?" Vordin asked her.

"I've seen the way you've all been acting. You all think that coming to Dexcsin was a big failure. That since Yarin died, that no one was saved. We saved the lives of the remaining spiders. We helped save twenty-six lives! I hate how you all see them as unimportant," she said sadly. "Anyway," she continued, "they will try to monitor the Killnarin's activity. I shouldn't have to add, that this will be done at great risk to their lives. They will report anything they find to me. I'm coming with you all to Vackiindmire. They said that they will contact me every few days or so regardless, and sooner if there is anything of importance to report."

Nodwel, who had been listening in on their conversation, said, "That's great. Knowing where the main group of these creatures are will aid us more than anything. Also," he said deciding to wait until later to gather more wood, "if we do decide to look for the sword, we'll have less of a chance of running into them."

"What do you mean 'if '," Lorenta asked him, "We're useless against the wizard without the sword."

"It's good that you have faith in us, but we are but a few people. The truth is, if we do succeed in gaining the sword and finding out where this Dranngore is, there may not be anyone left to save. The Killnarin can destroy entire villages in but a single night," Nodwel explained.

"But we have to try," said Vordin.

"Yes, I agree. We will try," said the dwarf.

"It's not quite sunrise," Lorenta told them, "Perhaps we should start for Vackiindmire now. They only seem to come out at night anyway. This way we'll hopefully make it to town before sunset the next day. I really don't want to stay here any longer. I don't feel safe."

"You think we should leave now? It's still dark," Nodwel told her.

"Please, wake everyone up," Lorenta pleaded.

Nodwel finally gave in to her and bellowed, "Everyone up! Wake up! We're leaving."

<World of Zaylyn ><Quest For The Sword Of Anthrowst ><By Katrina Mandrake-Johnston ><Ch 42>

CHAPTER 42 =   EARLY DEPARTURE

Everyone awoke.

"What did you say?" Dendrox asked, "We're leaving now? While it's still dark? What's the matter?"

"It doesn't feel safe here," Nodwel replied.

"Yes, please, let's leave right away," Lorenta said.

Asdella said angrily, "So there's no danger? You just decided to wake everyone up for no reason?"

<Zaylyn ><Quest For The Sword Of Anthrowst ><By Katrina Mandrake-Johnston >   <Ch 42> < 132 >

Nodwel stated, "Lorenta can communicate with the spiders now. She will be coming with us and the spiders will remain in the forest to observe the Killnarin's activity as best they can. She's been having a bad feeling, and it's probably right. We should leave, and this way we'll make it to Vackiindmire before sunset tomorrow."

"Fine," Asdella snapped, clearly annoyed.

"It just doesn't make any sense," Dendrox said starting to pack up their blankets, "We'll have to travel back toward Dexcsin to reach Vackiindmire. I don't know exactly how long it will take us to reach town, but I don't want to be passing by the village in the dark."

Candra asked, "So what about breakfast? It's still too dark to see. Why don't we wait a bit longer until first light? Don't you think it would be dangerous to go through the forest by just the light of the lanterns? We could end up going around in circles, and if those creatures are out there…"

"Yeah, I agree with Candra," Dendrox said.

"I could use more sleep," Asdella grumbled.

"I'd like to wait until there's enough light to see by too. If you think it's safe enough," Weena added.

Vordin suggested, "Why don't we get everything ready to go first, and then see how things are."

"There's not much to get ready," Candra explained to him, "We basically are right now. Just our weapons, backpacks, lanterns, and pouches. Everything's ready for travel as soon as we are. All we have left to do is put out the fire. A couple full bladders from the guys should do the trick."

Weena commented, "Oh, that's disgusting!"

Candra told her, "Hey, it's the fastest way and it's not like there's a stream or anything to collect water from. And, that would be foolish carting water back and forth in the dark!"

"Can't we just let it burn out on its own? It doesn't look like it will last for much longer anyway," Weena suggested.

Candra laughed cruelly, "Yeah, if you want the whole forest to go up in flames. It only takes one little spark in the right place. I don't want to get roasted alive in a forest fire thanks."

"No, don't say that!" Weena shouted at her, "I'll put the fire out myself if I have to then, alright?" She was so upset, she was practically in tears.

Dendrox spoke up, "We just need to smother it. Just kick a bit of dirt onto it until it's out. Weena, there's no need to worry about it. We know what to do."

Asdella sneered, "What's her problem? So she didn't know how to put out a fire properly. What's the big deal? She has to cry about it?"

Nodwel thought he saw something move within the trees again. *"Maybe it wasn't Lorenta I saw earlier, like I thought. Could it be one of the spiders, I wonder? Lorenta may be right about it not being safe here anymore,"* he said to himself nervously, *"It's best not to panic. We should remain calm. If it is one of the beasts, our heightened emotions will give it the perfect opportunity to use one of its damn spells. I'm probably the one with the best night vision. I can't allow myself to get distracted; not like I did with Yarin. I want to see it and kill the damn thing before anyone gets hurt."*

Weena heard Dendrox say to her, *"What? You think that I like you? You're disgustingly pathetic! Get away from me! I don't want you anywhere near me! You were an awful mistake! If I knew you'd be begging and groveling after me, I never would have kissed you. Go away! I don't want to even look at you! Stop bothering me! Go away!"*

"How could you say such things, Dendrox!" Weena wailed, and then sobbing miserably, ran off into the woods.

"I didn't say anything; not a single word to her," Dendrox exclaimed, "Where's she going? She could get hurt."

"What's wrong with her?" Candra asked in confusion.

Nodwel alerted them all, keeping a watchful eye to the trees, "This doesn't feel at all right. I feel as if we're being watched."

Vordin said with worry, "We should go after Weena."

"No one's leaving!" Asdella yelled at them, "You think it's funny?! I know you talk behind my

<Zaylyn ><Quest For The Sword Of Anthrowst ><By Katrina Mandrake-Johnston >   <Ch 42> < 133 >
back!"

Dendrox said wearing a confused expression, "What?!"

"Stop it! Stop it, all of you! Stop laughing at me!" she screamed.

"No one's laughing at you! What the hell are you talking about?!" Candra blurted out.

"Something's not right here," Nodwel said lifting his axe, as his eyes searched the trees with his heightened night vision. *It must be one of them. I have to find it while it's off guard, while it fools with our minds. It's our only chance! I have to find it!"*

"Oh yeah?" Asdella said through clenched teeth, "You feel like dying a little? Just keep it up then!"

"What's wrong with her?" Vordin asked anxiously.

"That's done it!" Asdella said taking up her sword into a threatening position, "Who's going to be the first to die? Stop laughing! Stop it! I'm serious! I'll do it! I'll kill you all!"

"She really means to attack us?!" Vordin exclaimed in fear, "Someone do something!"

"It must be the Killnarin," Nodwel told them all, "I doubt she can hear us. She must be trapped in whatever illusion they're creating. Same with Weena. I can't see where the beast is! I thought I saw something moving around in the trees earlier, but now I can't see a damn thing!"

Asdella screamed at them in rage and yelled, "Stop it now!" She swung her sword at Dendrox, but missed him. Dendrox backed away from her as quickly as he could. She snarled at them all and after several threatening gestures finally decided, "None of you are worth the effort."

She then stormed off to the far edge of the campsite, crossed her arms in front of her chest, and sitting on a boulder there, stared off into the forest.

"Asdella?" Vordin asked timidly. She turned and glared at him, but said nothing in return.

Weena was stumbling blindly through the woods with tears streaming down her face.

Suddenly, a dark figure stepped out right in front of her from the shadows to block her path. He was dressed all in black. A hooded cloak hung about his shoulders, the features of his face hidden in shadow. A short sword in a black scabbard hung from his belt.

Weena, extremely startled, gasped and said hurriedly, "Who… Who are you?!" Something about him sent chills down her spine.

"I am The Black Shadow," he answered, speaking in a calm, soothing voice, "but that's not important now."

"The… The Black Shadow…" she managed to utter as she slowly started to back away from him.

"I'm not going to hurt you," he told her, "The creatures, the Killnarin, they are using hallucinogenic spells to frighten you. By nature, they will try to divide your group, make you panic, make you doubt yourselves and your abilities. You are running into a trap. There is only one Killnarin threatening your group at this time. It made its way up the well and has discovered the campsite. It has led you astray, distracted the others, and is now coming to claim its victim... you. Do you understand how they like to attack? They aren't following orders now. Now they are playing with their prey simply for pleasure. The attack on the spider lair, that was organized. That was Dranngore's doing. Same with Dexcsin and Vordin's village, Nilnont. Listen to me carefully, all of you have to learn how to detect when you are under the influence of their spells. It's only an extremely slight variance from reality, but it can be detected. Heightened uncontrollable bursts of anger and unnatural conversations and expressions can be signs. Their hallucinogenic spells are not strong enough to make you see or hear anything more than this, and only the ones with stronger magic ability can make you hear conversations that aren't real. A Killnarin is very difficult to kill and when there are more than one of them, they are stronger and even harder to kill, almost impossible. They draw strength from each other. Do you see what I am telling you? Do things make better sense to you now? You have to help hold the group together and make it to Vackiindmire. It will be safer there. They need the dark to regenerate and to draw their strength. That's why they only came out at night before, now that they have captured the home of the giant spiders, they will be able to draw strength from the darkness there. This means they will be able to venture out during the day and be stronger for longer when they do so. They are

<Zaylyn ><Quest For The Sword Of Anthrowst ><By Katrina Mandrake-Johnston >   <Ch 42> < 134 >

weaker during the day, but in numbers that won't matter and they are driven by a mad man who doesn't care whether a few of his creatures are sacrificed in his plans. Even though you have tried to cover it up, it is not wise to be covered in blood as you are…" Weena noted the unnerving pause he had made here. "The scent will draw predators straight to you."

Weena felt a strange tingling sensation all over her body, and then she noticed the ball of grime forming before her being drawn from her body and clothing. She stared in amazement at her robes which were incredibly clean now, and where Candra's arrow had torn into the cloth, it was completely mended as if it had never happened. She caught the scent of wild flowers, as if she had been cleansed by a fragrant soap.

"The scent of blood will no longer give away your location," he told her, "but it will not stop the beast for long. I have removed the blood from the elf's blanket just now in the same manner."

"How could you possibly do…" Weena began and then instead started to ask, "How did you know about…"

"Remember what I've told you. Have you understood?" he asked her quickly, and there was a hint of desperateness to his voice, "The Killnarin is drawing near." She stared blankly at him, not knowing what to do or if she should say anything further. "Go!" he commanded, "or I shall take your life before the creature does! It will, if you remain here. This is not an idle threat!"

Weena turned and started to stumble through the woods in what she hoped was the direction of the camp as quickly as she could, fear pushing her forward. She searched frantically into the darkness of the forest as she ran for any sign of the Killnarin.

She finally reached the others, gasping for air and with a horrified expression on her face. She told the others what had happened and of what The Black Shadow had said to her.

Asdella blurted out, "This Black Shadow doesn't scare me. I've heard the rumors. If it came down to it, I could beat him."

Nodwel scolded her, "Don't be so damn arrogant. You still have that death wish? The all or nothing attitude? If even a few of the things I've heard are even remotely true, you wouldn't last a single second. In fact, he'd most likely just laugh and walk away. There's a Killnarin out here somewhere. Focus on what's important!"

Asdella just said to him, "You forget, old man, that I see things as a threat only if they present themselves as one. It's either react or don't. It's as plain as that for everything. I don't waste my time worrying about problems that haven't arrived yet." The dwarf just nodded at the warrior woman not wanting to get into an argument with her about anything. "Okay," Asdella said to him, "I take that back. About The Black Shadow, I shouldn't have said that. I know damn well what that horrible being is capable of. Whatever he is, I know well to stay clear of him at all costs. You know me, it's a rare day that I back away from a fight. So believe me when I say this."

Nodwel apologized, "Hey, I'm sorry. It's just, some of the things I've heard, well, it's like something out of a nightmare. I didn't want you just running off and…"

Asdella interrupted, "So are we heading to Vackiindmire or not? I don't want to stick around here. I've been pestered enough by those damn Killnarin creatures. I don't feel like running into any more of them."

<World of Zaylyn ><Quest For The Sword Of Anthrowst ><By Katrina Mandrake-Johnston ><Ch 43>

CHAPTER 43 = LEAVING FOR VACKIINDMIRE

"Please, let's leave," Lorenta pleaded.

"The Black Shadow, he said there was a Killnarin out here! He said it was hunting us down, that it came through the well, that it tried to divide us, that it was coming for me because I was separated and alone! It must be on its way back to us! It's going to kill us all! We couldn't stop that one when it killed Yarin! What makes you think we can survive this one?" Weena said to them all in a panic.

"The other spiders, do you think they could be in danger? What should I say to them? What should I do?" Lorenta asked anxiously.

Dendrox told them, "We should head out toward Vackiindmire as quickly as we can."

<Zaylyn ><Quest For The Sword Of Anthrowst ><By Katrina Mandrake-Johnston >   <Ch 43> < 135 >

"What about the spiders?! They can't escape to the town! The people there will kill them! You saw what happened to the ones back at Dexcsin! They were just trying to save the villagers and were killed for it. They won't believe us if we tell them they mean no harm," Lorenta explained.

"The Killnarin could be anywhere. The Black Shadow said that it would be safer in Vackiindmire," said Weena nervously looking about her into the darkness of the forest.

"For us maybe," Lorenta said, her anger rising, "and only for me because I look human. I'll have to hide there during the day as it is. I shouldn't have to hide! If they weren't so quick to judge, everything would be fine! I shouldn't have to hide within my human form, hiding my true self as if I am some sort of monster! I'm not an evil being and neither are these spiders. It's not fair! They can't hide themselves as I can! What are they to do? We can't just abandon them! We just finished saving them!"

A terrifying howl filled the forest.

"It's drawing closer!" Vordin exclaimed, his words showing the terror he felt.

"Was anyone able to tell which direction it was coming from?" Candra asked, her voice taking on a commanding tone as she scanned the darkness around them with a stern face.

"No," Nodwel answered with a worried expression, "I really think we should leave though. We'll have to take our chances and hope we don't end up running toward the thing."

"What about the spiders? Could it be that it was never about saving them? That they just happened to escape with us and that it didn't matter one way or another whether they got out alive or not?" Lorenta said with tears starting in her eyes.

Vordin said, "I'm sure no one thinks that," although he wasn't sure if this were entirely true, but he hated to see her upset.

"So what makes all of you so eager to trust The Black Shadow?" Asdella asked them flatly, "Do you even realize that he is ten times worse than any Killnarin? I'm not about to believe that the creatures are weaker when alone. Even if it is true, it's well into the night which means the creature's strength has increased within the darkness. But that is according to The Black Shadow. And another thing, about this wizard Dranngore who is supposed to be behind these creatures, how do we know any of that is true? It was The Black Shadow that gave Vordin the information, wasn't it? Oh and a fairy, but I doubt that matters. Besides, I'm sure he is able to manipulate our minds far easier than any Killnarin. The images of the fairy queen could have just been planted in Vordin's mind. This could all be some twisted game. Directing us down some pre-chosen path, watching us suffer and die. I'm sure he was thinking about killing Weena out there, whether all that is true or not. Why a creature like that would want to help us, I don't know. He's certainly powerful enough just to kill Dranngore with a single thought from across an entire ocean if he wanted to, or so I've heard. Why bother with us? So Weena, what was he like? I bet he was thinking about ripping your throat out, wondering if anyone would notice or care if you were missing. Thinking about letting the Killnarin take the blame. How sure are we that it was even the Killnarin that did the bulk of the damage at the two villages? They may have just interfered with The Black Shadow's enjoyment. You have no idea what he's capable of, do you? You think just because The Black Shadow hasn't killed any of us yet, that we should just blindly do what he says and believe what he tells us?"

Everyone was silent. Not any of them had heard Asdella make such a large meaningful speech before and were a little shocked by it.

After several moments of silence, Nodwel asked them all, "So what do we do?"

The Killnarin made another shrieking howl. It was very close now.

"I don't want to die," Vordin whispered, trembling with fear. His eyes darted frantically around him, expecting the creature to leap at him from out of the darkness.

"Get your weapons ready," Nodwel commanded, trying to be strong and give the others courage, "It shouldn't be long now."

The beast began to howl again, and to the group's amazement, its howl turned into a frightened squealing. Then they heard a tremendous thud and felt the vibration through the ground, as something large and heavy fell to the forest floor with an incredible force. The terrified squealing had stopped and

<Zaylyn ><Quest For The Sword Of Anthrowst ><By Katrina Mandrake-Johnston >   <Ch 43> < 136 >
all was silent.

No one spoke. They just stared blankly into the darkness around them and then at each other.

"We don't have to worry about the Killnarin anymore," Vordin whispered finally.

Trying to accept what had just happened, Weena whispered, "The Black Shadow; it must have been. The Killnarin was actually frightened of him and was killed in a matter of seconds. It must be true."

Asdella said forcefully, "It was frightened for good reason. I say we get the hell out of here now. Just because he took out the threat of the Killnarin, doesn't mean we're safe."

"Which way do we go?" Candra asked, "Which way is Vackiindmire?"

"Let's head south, get out of the trees, and then head east across the plains until we see signs of the town," Dendrox suggested, "That way we'll be out in the open, but at least we'll be able to see what's coming."

"And the spiders, they will be safe? Now that the Killnarin is dead?" Lorenta asked them.

Asdella said getting frustrated, "Looks that way, let's go."

"We have to put out the fire," Weena said urgently. The fire she was responsible for starting at her school as a child constantly haunted her. The thought of causing yet another devastating fire was unbearable.

"We'll have to do all this in a hurry," Candra said, "Weena, grab your lantern and light it. You still have your flame box, right?"

Weena nodded and thought, "*You don't have to ask, Candra. You were in my pouch and know exactly what I have. Thanks to you, the flame box is the only thing I have left now. Well, and the few coins I had managed to save. I thought for sure she would have taken them as well.*"

"Alright then, the girls will head out first, while you three put out the fire," Candra decided.

"We're splitting up?" Weena asked the elf as she lit her lantern and shone it into her face, "Do you really think that's wise?"

She told her, trying to block the light with her hand, "They'll just have to catch up to us when they're done. Hopefully we won't run into trouble before then. And stop shining that light into my eyes!"

"Oh, sorry Candra," Weena apologized lowering the lantern, but found that she did not at all feel sorry she had done it after all Candra had put her through. In fact, it was probably Candra's fault the Killnarin chose her as its victim. She was made vulnerable through her weak emotional state which Candra was mostly responsible for, not to mention the smell of blood that had been on her clothing because of her.

"It is best to split up. Two targets means for a better chance of survival for at least one group," Asdella stated as she headed into the trees.

The women hurried through the forest by lantern light, and Weena had enough courage to ask Asdella, "How is it that you know so much about The Black Shadow?"

"I've heard enough about him to know he's one to be feared," she answered.

"So you don't know for certain if anything you've heard is actually true then," said Weena.

Asdella shot her an angry glare but said nothing.

The others arrived soon after and all seven of them met up on the southwestern edge of the forest. The mountain range could be seen to the west, and to the south beyond the grassy plains, were enormous cliffs rising up into the sky. Beyond these cliffs was the sea.

"Vackiindmire should be situated just south of the forest. If we travel far enough east, we should come across it," Dendrox told them, trusting his memory of the map he had seen of Dee'ellkka Valley.

"Do you think we'll be safe enough here? I've had pine needles wedged inside my sandals for such a long time and I'd really like to get them out," Weena said trying to shake out the debris, "You made sure that the fire was completely out?"

"Yes," Nodwel told her and then looking nervously to the nearby trees said, "Sure, we can take a minute, I guess."

"Looks like it's almost dawn, Lorenta. Did you want to get yourself into the safety of the

<Zaylyn ><Quest For The Sword Of Anthrowst ><By Katrina Mandrake-Johnston >   <Ch 43> < 137 >
backpack?" Vordin asked her.

"Sure, it will be easier for me to travel that way," she agreed, "I remember, Rasindell, he sometimes would take me along with him to gather food and herbs from the forest, and when I was a small child, on rare occasions to a town or village for supplies. I would ride along in that same backpack, with its magically created compartment to keep me safe from harm during the journey. To think that I actually wanted to go on an adventure of my own... Perhaps I should have just stayed at the hut and lived out the rest of my days alone and unaware of all the cruelty in this world," she said sadly, beginning to lose hope.

Vordin couldn't think of any comforting words for her. He opened up the backpack for her and watched the green flames arise. In a matter of seconds, her human body had melted down into a small pool of black shimmering liquid and then had reformed into her true spider form. Once Lorenta had climbed inside the compartment, Vordin swung it carefully onto his back.

"Is everyone ready?" Nodwel questioned, still keeping a watchful eye toward the tree line.

The group then embarked on their trek toward Vackiindmire once more, as the early morning light began to take over the night sky.

***

The Black Shadow looked over at the broken heap of flesh that had once been the fearsome Killnarin threatening the group. "*So easily, I bring death,*" he thought to himself, "*I don't want to be seen as an evil thing. They are safe for now, now that I have killed this beast. The fact that I seem to care what happens to this group of people, shows that I am not all evil, doesn't it? Perhaps I can fight my evil urges. Perhaps I can fight back the hunger and restrain myself from killing my victims. I've failed so often in the past when I have tried this, however, resulting in mass uncontrolled slaughter when the hunger took me over completely. Maybe now it will be different. I feel some sort of connection to these people. Maybe I can learn from them somehow. Perhaps what I lack is a better understanding. Sure, everyone seems to fear and hate me, and it's for good reason, but does it always have to be so? If I can suppress my powers enough, perhaps I can learn to understand things from their point of view better. Reading their minds isn't the same. I need to live as they do and try to hide the monster that is at my core. Am I fool to think it possible? Do I dare put lives at risk trying to interact with others?*"

A searing pain began to grow in his gut, causing him to double over and almost collapse to the ground. "*My hunger grows... I must feed. I must get far away from them, for fear of attacking them despite my efforts.*"

The pain subsided. He was losing control over himself. The next time the pain came it would be much stronger and he would not be able to hold himself back. Many would die horrible and very violent deaths. The pain that often came, it was as if his evil nature would physically fight against him every time he resisted, trying to force him to lose control, trying to make him give in, trying to free itself and unleash tremendous pain and suffering onto the world.

With his heightened senses he could feel the warmth of their bodies. He could hear them. They were close by and their fear had excited him. "*No, I must not! I have to get away from them before it's too late!*" he screamed at himself, but felt the evil part of himself argue. That part of him wanted to sink his fangs into their soft flesh and drain their blood and their warmth away. That part of him wanted to hear them scream and attempt to flee in terror. That part of him wanted to kill.

"*No, I have to fight it!*" he told himself, but the hunger only intensified and his eyes flashed red beneath his black hooded cloak. "No!" he screamed aloud, "No!" and finally he was able to push himself away from the others and soar into the night sky.

Dawn was approaching, but that didn't matter to him. He simply preferred the night over the day. He felt a serenity within the cool darkness of night, feeling hidden away from everything else in some way.

As he flew over the forest, he discovered the camp of three men. The camp was in the middle of the forest, a slight distance from the main road leading from Vackiindmire to the town of Shirkint.

<Zaylyn ><Quest For The Sword Of Anthrowst ><By Katrina Mandrake-Johnston >   <Ch 43> < 138 >
The Black Shadow fell silently from the sky upon the three unsuspecting bandits and fed eagerly. There would be three more corpses for their leader to puzzle over in the morning.

<World of Zaylyn ><Quest For The Sword Of Anthrowst ><By Katrina Mandrake-Johnston ><Ch 44>

CHAPTER 44 = TO VACKIINDMIRE

They all walked at a steady pace toward where they thought Vackiindmire would be, keeping the forest line in sight. Occasionally, a small animal would scamper through the grass startling them slightly, but all was peaceful. There were no signs of the Killnarin or of any other danger. For most of the day, they had been walking through knee high vegetation and a couple of times they found themselves wading through waist high grasses.

"Looks like we're closer to Dexcsin. Look here, how the grass and plants are shorter and the ground looks well trampled in places," Dendrox pointed out, "They probably used to bring their livestock out here to graze. I saw several different kinds of grain ready to be harvested back there as well. If I'm right, we might find some vegetables or perhaps a couple of fruit trees near here. I wouldn't want to get too close to the village of course, but if we stick to the outskirts like this, we might be able to find some food. If there is anything left, it would be a shame for it to go to waste."

Nodwel told them, "If we come across any, fine, but I don't want to stop. We're too close to the village and the Killnarin. More may come up out of the well. I want to keep moving and make it to Vackiindmire before nightfall."

Candra complained, "This is ridiculous. Do you even realize how much effort it's taking us to get to Vackiindmire?"

Dendrox said to her, "Well, of course, look at all that's happened."

"That's not what I mean," she explained, "We came down through the mountains and traveled all that way just to almost reach Vackiindmire. The town was just a little farther south from where we were at the crossroads, and then we traveled all the way to Dexcsin taking us almost all the way back to the mountains. Then, traveling through the spider lair tunnels, took us even closer to the mountains and even farther away from Vackiindmire. Now we happen to be a little farther south, but we still have to travel all the way back east to Vackiindmire again. We've been zigzagging our way back and forth ever since we entered this damn valley. Do you think we'll actually get there this time, or are we going to almost get there and then end up going all the way back to the mountains again? Because, I'm getting really frustrated with all of this."

Dendrox exclaimed, "Hey, calm down. I don't see any reason why we shouldn't get there. We're out of the forest now. We just have to travel across the plains until we reach Vackiindmire. We're so far south now, that we'll travel right past Dexcsin and probably not even know it."

"I don't want to go anywhere near that village," Vordin added.

Weena reminded them, "The Black Shadow had said that the Killnarin near our camp had climbed up out of the well there."

Asdella muttered, "Yeah, so what?" and then she said to them all, "I think we should get all the information out in the open. Every one of us should explain everything that has happened to him or her and see if we have something that will help us that we didn't realize. Besides, it will pass the time as we walk."

Nodwel thought to himself, "*That sure sounds like something Narr would say. A good idea though.*" He suggested, "Okay, I guess Vordin should start."

Vordin told how the beasts destroyed Nilnont and burned everything to the ground. He told how he had hidden and then made his way to Rasindell's hut.

Nodwel commented, "Rasindell, remember how I said before that name sounded familiar? I'm sure I've heard it before, but I just can't remember where."

Vordin told how he encountered the fairy queen and what she had said to him. He then told how he met Lorenta and how The Black Shadow rescued him from the scouting Killnarin. Vordin spoke of how he was kept in a mountainous prison, then taken into Dee'ellkka Valley, shown the slain Killnarin, and taken to the crossroads where they encountered the man with the medallion. Vordin also mentioned

<Zaylyn ><Quest For The Sword Of Anthrowst ><By Katrina Mandrake-Johnston >   <Ch 44> < 139 >

how The Black Shadow had told him of the potion given to Rasindell which enabled Lorenta's creation. He explained that Lorenta had hidden herself inside the magic compartment of the backpack when he had been at Rasindell's hut and remained hidden until emerging at the crossroads and encountered the man with the medallion. Vordin spoke of how the man had attacked her and that she had defended herself not realizing just how deadly she could be. He told how she hid again in the backpack, afraid of what the others might think of her, and that she had traveled with them to Dexcsin hidden in the backpack. He said that she must have emerged from the backpack when they were in the building beside the well and discovered the spider that had come up from it and then met the rest of them face to face for the first time.

Candra and Dendrox both told how they had discovered Nilnont destroyed, traveled through the mountains, and encountered the invisible wizard, later finding him dead. They spoke of how the Killnarin had played its mind games with them and how they finally defeated it. They told how Weena had come to save Candra and had traveled with them to meet Vordin.

Weena told how she had wanted to travel to the larger towns in Dee'ellkka Valley in hope of learning more magic, as she had heard Dee'ellkka Valley was the best place to go. She had traveled alone and had hoped to find an escort over the mountains at Nilnont, even though she hardly had any money at all. She told how she had seen that Nilnont had been destroyed, and being frightened, avoided the village and went directly up the mountain trail. She spoke of how she had been traveling through the forest and discovered the man slain at the side of the road and that she had therefore decided to continue traveling by the light of her lantern in the dark. Then she told that she had healed Candra's wound and then later found her to be poisoned. Weena explained that she had cured her and then they all traveled to the road junction where they met Vordin. She also retold what she had suspected about the man with the medallion and about the wizard's guild and their evil deeds. She then explained that they had to bury the man and his medallion to ensure that no one else would suffer from it, and that shortly after this, they had met Nodwel at the second junction where the road to Dexcsin met the main road.

Nodwel told them how he and his group had passed by Nilnont on their journey into Dee'ellkka Valley and it had been intact and full of life. He explained that they did not stop at Nilnont, but instead had headed up the mountain trail and had camped in the mountains that night. Then he told how they had made their way down into the valley and partially into the forest before making their camp there the next night. He explained that the following morning, the wizard who had recently joined their group, went off into the forest and didn't return. Nodwel told how his group eventually went looking for him and had traveled into the forest.

Asdella commented, "As you remember, dwarf, I was completely against looking for the fool."

Nodwel continued, telling that there had been no sign of the wizard and that they had finally ended up at Dexcsin. He told that the village leader had invited them for dinner and how the Killnarin first attacked the village. He told how Dimwar had been the first to rush out to defend the villagers and had been decapitated. He spoke of how they had to pull Asdella back from running into battle, as she was going berserk with such a furious rage that it would have gotten her killed. Asdella sneered at him. Nodwel explained that they had tried to get all the villagers into one location where they would be easier to defend and how Nimdor had been slain. He also told how the decision to send him for help was made, and that he had managed to escape Dexcsin, but his leg was injured by a Killnarin in the attempt. He spoke of how he had tried to run despite his injury and had hurried all night and half the day, as best as he could, to finally end up meeting the others at the road junction.

Asdella was the last to speak, and she retold how Nodwel had left to find help. She explained that come morning one of the villagers had tried to flee and that's when they discovered that the Killnarin were merely lying in wait and would not allow anyone to escape the village. She told how they had all remained in the building being cautious about leaving and giving away their location after Nimdor had gone to so much effort to keep their location somewhat hidden from them. They had spent the day tending to the wounded and trying to give them hope as best as they could. Asdella went on to say that come nightfall, the Killnarin eventually were able to discover their location and began to tear down the

<Zaylyn ><Quest For The Sword Of Anthrowst ><By Katrina Mandrake-Johnston >   <Ch 44> < 140 >

walls of the building. She explained that they had separated, running in different directions and each taking as many villagers with them as they could. She mentioned again that she had taken Nimdor's amulet and that Borin had obviously snatched up the Camouflage amulet and Blast potion off of him. She told how the villagers in her care were all eventually killed despite her efforts except for a young girl and that she had given the amulet to this girl in hope that it would help her to survive. Asdella then told how the Killnarin was intent on slaying her and the girl as well as it had done with the others and how she then had engaged in a fierce battle with it. She explained that she defeated the Killnarin but at great cost. Asdella said that she would have died if Candra and Dendrox had not discovered her and found and used the amulet to revive her.

Nodwel asked, "Why didn't Nimdor use the amulet? There was time, we could have saved him."

Asdella shook her head sadly and said, "I guess he never told you. You never were very interested in the workings of magic, eh? I remember how excited he was when he first got it. The amulet he had wouldn't have worked. His ribs were crushed. The amulet would have only healed his flesh, not his bone. He would have died either way."

"Oh," the dwarf said sadly, and then he went on to tell them how he had discovered Narr's body and Yarin hidden in the cabinet. Nodwel also mentioned how he had been slightly wary of Yarin, as he had been a twin and how he thought perhaps a creature had somehow copied the dead boy's appearance to fool and spy on them. "I, of course, had dismissed the suspicion shortly after," he told them, "I just thought that I better mention that. The Killnarin create distrust and paranoia in us even when they are not around. They like to divide us, to pick us off one by one, to turn us against each other, to create fear and hatred in us where there shouldn't be," and then, after a deep sigh, suggested, "Why don't we take a much needed rest?"

Everyone stopped walking and started looking around for somewhere to sit and rest their legs.

Weena mentioned, "The Black Shadow said basically the same thing. That they would try to divide us and that we should stand together against them. That way we would have a better chance of surviving."

Before anyone could seat themselves, Asdella snarled at them, "Black Shadow this! Black Shadow that! You don't get it, do you?! He's evil! We have no idea of what his true intentions are, and you still blindly trust him?!"

"So what happened when you left us back at Dexcsin? You know, before we went into the well?" Weena asked her coldly. She was getting annoyed with Asdella's attitude and her constant insensitivity toward everyone.

Nodwel was curious as well, as she had been acting out of character now and then ever since she had gone to see Narr, but he was still wary about saying anything.

Asdella shot her an icy glare and wore a bitter look on her face. "What do you think I did?" she snapped cruelly, "I heard that Narr was dead, and I went to see for myself."

"So you thought Nodwel lied to you? Why would he lie about something like that?" Weena interrogated.

Asdella glared at her again and snarled, "No, that's just what I did, alright? Now drop it."

"No," Weena said sternly, "Why did you go? You knew that the Killnarin were coming. What were you doing? Going to tell them of our location? I think it's very suspicious that they would just leave you out in the open still alive for Candra and Dendrox to find, when they were so intent on making sure that everyone was dead. It seems like a perfect opportunity to plant a spy. Yarin would have been too obvious, maybe so obvious that we would dismiss the idea all together and overlook the possibility that you in fact are the spy. They make it look like we saved you, so we let our guard down even further. Nodwel even thinks that you've been acting strangely, don't you Nodwel?" She didn't give him time to say anything in his defense. She accused, "That's how they were able to find us so easily every time, isn't it? Is that why you went off into the forest after we escaped the spiders' lair? To report to them?"

"I," Asdella said through clenched teeth, "am not a spy!"

Vordin suggested, "There must be a Killnarin around, trying to manipulate us again."

<Zaylyn ><Quest For The Sword Of Anthrowst ><By Katrina Mandrake-Johnston >   <Ch 44> < 141 >

"No!" Weena said angrily, "I'm just really fed up with all her insanity! I want answers! I'm tired of all this! I don't care if she's so insane that she might attack us if we say the wrong thing or ask the wrong questions."

"I am not insane!!" Asdella screamed raising her sword to Weena. Weena jumped back defensively, a little shocked at Asdella's outburst, even though she had provoked it.

"So why are you so defensive about telling us why you had to leave like that?" Weena dared to ask.

"*Just admit it,*" Narr's voice said in Asdella's head, "*You're in love with me, or were. It's true isn't it? It was that important to you that you say your final farewells to me, that you would risk encountering a whole swarm of Killnarin to do so. Admit it. It will end all these suspicions. Just tell them.*"

"Shut up!" Asdella screamed. Weena thought this was directed at her, even though it was meant for Narr's ghost.

Asdella would never tell them about his voice inside her head. This would confirm to them that she was truly insane. Asdella gave Weena a fierce look and her words were full of malice, each word spoken slowly for emphasis. "I'll gut you," Asdella threatened Weena with her sword, "If you ever say anything like that again or ask me again about wanting to pay my respects to a fallen comrade, I will kill you. Do you understand? I will slice you open and mash your insides into the dirt. Do you understand?"

Weena frightened and shocked, looked at her with a pale face and nodded.

"Maybe we should all just continue on our way," Nodwel told them.

The group began walking again with Asdella leading the way in a fierce stride.

Nodwel whispered to Weena, "She's serious about that. I wouldn't push her too far, if I were you. If she were a spy in disguise, I think she would have disposed of us long ago."

"Yeah, I think you're right," Weena admitted.

<World of Zaylyn ><Quest For The Sword Of Anthrowst ><By Katrina Mandrake-Johnston ><Ch 45>

CHAPTER 45 =   THE APPLE TREE

They continued to walk, even though everyone was greatly in need of a rest and most of all water.

"I'm so thirsty. My mouth feels like a desert," Weena complained, lagging behind.

"Hey, isn't that an apple tree?" Vordin said, being the first one to spot it, "That big one over there?"

Dendrox squinted and, with his hand shielding his eyes from the noonday sun, exclaimed, "Yeah, I think it is."

Everyone headed over to the great tree. Plump red apples hung from its branches.

"I can climb up easily enough," Vordin told them, "I could throw them down to you." Everyone eyed the delicious looking apples as Vordin removed the backpack and climbed up the trunk into the sturdy branches of the apple tree.

"Hey, Vordin," Candra called, "See if you can get me that really big one over there."

"Which one?" he asked, "This one?"

"No, the one just next to that one and over a bit," she told him.

"Candra," Dendrox scolded, "It doesn't matter. You're going to make him fall." She just ignored him. "Vordin," Dendrox called, "Just throw down as many as you can, okay?"

Vordin nodded and began to pass down several apples at a time. Weena immediately bit into a large juicy one and ate greedily. Vordin soon joined them after collecting as many apples as he could.

"We should probably take some of these with us," Nodwel commented sitting on the shaded grass and taking a large bite from an apple.

Soon all of their hunger and thirst were satisfied, but none of the apples remained.

"I should probably get some more," Vordin suggested, "to take with us, like Nodwel said."

"I think we've been here long enough," Asdella told them, "Dexcsin is not far, which means the Killnarin are not far, and I want to get to the damn town as quickly as possible."

<Zaylyn ><Quest For The Sword Of Anthrowst ><By Katrina Mandrake-Johnston >   <Ch 45> < 142 >

"It won't take long," Vordin told her.

"No, we leave now," she ordered holding up a small cloth doll not much larger than her hand. She had found and retrieved it from around the base of the tree. Its yellow stringy hair made of wool was frayed at the ends, and the hair had been collected and a small white ribbon had been carefully tied around it. The once deep blue color of the tiny dress it wore had faded with age. The doll was well used with a few stains and it had obviously been mended numerous times. "Look!" Asdella said wearing a foul expression as she shook the doll at them, "We are too damn close to the damn village! We are leaving, right now!" she commanded. Her eyes seemed exceptionally cold and bitter as she tossed the doll aside and started walking toward Vackiindmire again.

"We better catch up to her," Nodwel told them and stood.

Asdella was already a fair distance ahead of them by the time the others ran after her.

Weena, however, hesitated and picked up the doll from where it lay. Weena, remembering all the small children she had seen brutally slain at Dexcsin, wondered if this doll belonged to one of them. She imagined the owner of the doll laughing and playing happily here in her favorite spot under the large apple tree and feeling safe in its shadow.

How Asdella could just throw the object of a child's love away like that, was almost incomprehensible to her. *"This doll is probably all that remains of this child,"* Weena thought to herself, *"and Asdella just tosses it away, as if it were totally meaningless!"*

Weena propped the doll up against the base of the tree in sitting position. Its black button eyes stared up at her. Weena stared back imagining how the child must have cared so much for this little doll.

"Weena?" Vordin called, "You coming? The others are getting pretty far ahead trying to keep up with Asdella."

"Yes, I'm coming," she called back.

She looked back to the doll. It seemed to look sadly up at her, wanting to be remembered and being all alone now that its child was gone. Weena was about to leave, but she knew that if she did, the doll would just be a bit of cloth and string to the next person who came across it.

This was a child's love, not just a doll. Weena quickly picked it up and put it into her cloth pouch. She then hurried after the others.

"So what's with Asdella?" Weena whispered to Vordin.

"I don't know. She started to act strangely after she found out The Black Shadow was around. Could it be that she's truly afraid of him? I didn't think she was even capable of fear," he whispered back to her as they walked.

"We both encountered him. He made it clear that he wanted to help us. I don't think we have anything to fear from him. He saved us from the Killnarin, didn't he?" she said quietly.

"And me before, as well," he whispered, "He protected me from one of the beasts before taking me over the mountains to meet all of you. Remember?"

"I don't know. It's like she'd rather be surrounded by hundreds of Killnarin than be anywhere near The Black Shadow. You heard how she was talking back there," Weena whispered.

Asdella slowed her pace and let the others get ahead of her until she was walking beside Weena and Vordin. "You know, I can hear you. Sound travels in the open like this," Asdella explained to them. She was calmer now and there was a hint of sadness in her eyes. She sighed and said to them, "I have to tell you that, yes, I am afraid of The Black Shadow. I am utterly terrified of him. I pretend not to be, but I am, and it's because I've seen what he's capable of. Don't be so swift to call him friend."

"Why? What did you see?" Weena asked her.

"Just get to Vackiindmire," was her answer, and she sped ahead of them.

"But…" Weena began.

Vordin told her, "I don't think she's going to talk about it. This is Asdella, remember? Plus, did you see the look in her eye when you asked her? It must have been something terrible."

<Zaylyn ><Quest For The Sword Of Anthrowst ><By Katrina Mandrake-Johnston >   <Ch 46> < 143 >

CHAPTER 46 =   VACKIINDMIRE

The vision of the walled town of Vackiindmire was a welcome sight. It was just about sunset and wouldn't take them very long to reach the safety within its walls. As they neared, they could see that the large gates were wide open and seemed to be inviting the weary travelers in. The great rocky cliffs towered over the town to the south and the group could see the road leading from the forest as it sloped downward to eventually end at the town's gates.

"This valley must have some sort of magic on it," Dendrox commented as they walked, "It's enclosed on three sides by enormous rock formations and yet there is no shadow cast from them on the valley below."

"That's what you're thinking about?" said Candra, "All my brain is saying is 'warm bed', 'hot meal', 'hot bath', and 'hurry up because we're almost there'. I'm not thinking about anything else but that."

"So do you think there will be anything there about this sword we're supposed to find?" Vordin asked them all.

"You really are planning to go on that insane quest?" Candra scoffed, "What, if by some miracle, you actually find this sword? You're then planning to find an illusive wizard and then kill him with this magic sword, eh? Are you forgetting that this wizard also commands a huge army of Killnarin? It's a fool's errand. If anything, if we manage to obtain the sword, the wizard will just have to take it off our mangled corpses and then possess the one thing that could have stopped him and his army."

"Then I guess we're not allowed to fail in our quest then. We have to succeed in destroying the wizard," he told her.

"Yeah, okay. Count me out," she said with an insulting look.

Vordin was becoming frustrated, "If not us, then who?"

"I don't know, an enormous army?" she said with contempt, "Even then, they probably wouldn't stand a chance. All the wizard has to do is conjure up more of the beasts to replenish his numbers, right?"

"That's why we have to defeat him. Defeat him, and the Killnarin go back to wherever they came from," he explained.

"Wake up to the reality of it! If you think I'm just going to throw my life away…" Candra barked angrily at him, "There's nothing we can do!" Then she added, "Besides, you're not even sure if that will happen. Also, what's to prove that the Killnarin will go away once the wizard is dead? They've made it clear that they are enjoying the slaughter far too much to just simply go back where they came from."

"Well, why else would we be sent on such a quest?" Vordin asked the elf.

"I don't know, for sport? A bit of fun? To have a good and hearty laugh at what fools we are and how easily we get killed?" she laughed coldly, "Look at the source! A tiny fairy queen whose people are legendary for their pranks and mischief? Very few have ever seen this race of fairy and all who claim to have encountered them always have a story of disaster to go along with it. And don't forget about The Black Shadow! I'm nervous even to say his name! He is possibly the most feared and powerful creature or being or whatever he is, ever! They say he hears and knows everything, and can sneak up on you before you even know he's there, I don't know, like an evil shadow or something. One thing I do know, is that when there's an unusual death in a town or village, everyone is smart enough not to say anything about it, and those that do are usually next."

"So what's his concern then with all this?" Vordin asked her.

"I don't know!" she said giving him an annoyed look, "Maybe he's mad that all his potential victims are getting killed off by the Killnarin before he has a chance to get to them."

"Maybe you shouldn't be talking about all this," Nodwel warned them, "He could be anywhere, right?"

It was just after sunset by the time they finally arrived at Vackiindmire and stepped through its gates.

<Zaylyn ><Quest For The Sword Of Anthrowst ><By Katrina Mandrake-Johnston >   <Ch 46> < 144 >

"I can't believe we're actually here, Dendrox!" Candra exclaimed, "There's the inn. That building to the right there."

"The Twisted Eye," Dendrox read on the wooden sign hung over the door. It squeaked every time the breeze hit it, making the quiet eeriness of the empty street even more unnerving.

"Let's go in," Candra said eagerly.

"That's a weird name, not very appealing," Weena commented.

"Does it really matter?" Asdella said to her.

Nodwel asked, "Do we even have enough money between all of us?"

"Who cares, we can worry about that later. Right now, I just want to see another person alive," Candra told them with an excited tone to her voice, "Come on, Dendrox, let's go in."

"It's so quiet. Should it be?" Vordin questioned nervously, "You don't suppose the creatures have attacked here as well, do you? Could it be that not anywhere is safe anymore? It's so very quiet. I don't see anyone about. It's eerie, don't you think?"

Just then, the door to 'The Twisted Eye' burst open and two men staggered out. They were clearly drunk and as happy as could be. They were laughing and stumbling about. The glow of the room inside could be seen through the door. As the entrance had been built on a slight slant, the weight of the heavy oak door slowly began to pull itself closed behind them.

The entire group breathed a sigh of relief as they were all fearing the worst. After seeing such horrible sights, these two men were a welcome sight. One of the men noticed the travelers and cheered for no apparent reason. He was a portly man with shaggy blonde hair and a large bushy mustache. He had a round face, rosy cheeks, and small bright blue eyes that had heavy laugh lines at the corners. The man wore a beige shirt with a navy waistcoat, the buttons of which strained over his belly to remain fastened. The front of his matching navy jacket hung at his sides and was far too small for his size. The wide leather belt he wore, which had a large metal buckle, he had tightened over the waistline of his dark brown pants, and as was common among most town and village folk, he wore a pair of brown leather shoes.

The other man, with the narrow face and black hair, slurred in an overly happy tone, "Oh would ya look... dare be sem real purdy ladies!" This man appeared to be just the opposite of his friend. He wore a grey long-sleeved shirt, a dark green vest, and dark brown pants, but was slender with brown eyes, a thin black mustache, and had a short beard at his chin.

The portly man, who had first noticed them, nudged his friend saying, "Watch, dis be how a gentlemen do it." Then he slurred, "Welcome to Vackiindmire, ladies!" and took an overzealous bow that almost landed himself on the ground.

"Okay, okay," said the black haired man, clasping the other's shoulder in an effort to balance himself, "Quit yer showin' off. Let's go."

They both turned and headed down the empty street, leaning on each other as they stumbled. They began to sing some sort of drinking song for which they had forgotten the words and had obviously made up themselves. The group all chuckled as they listened to the two men singing their song.

"He drinks up all the ale, and..." then they fumbled over several undeterminable words before continuing loudly, "his brother's girl! Then he takes me bottle and..." they trailed off again before breaking into a bout of laughter and singing loudly, "and it be so old it made his hair curl!"

"At least they're happy," Weena commented with a pleasant smile.

"Come on," Candra called to them impatiently, already at the door.

<World of Zaylyn ><Quest For The Sword Of Anthrowst ><By Katrina Mandrake-Johnston ><Ch 47>

CHAPTER 47 = THE TWISTED EYE TAVERN

Inside, the atmosphere was cheerful and inviting. A warm fire burned brightly in the hearth situated in the right wall. Three large tables were along this wall: one close to the entrance, one on the other side of the fireplace, and one next to that and closest to the doorway leading to the guest rooms beyond. Numerous lanterns were hung on the walls lighting the room in a comforting glow.

At the table closest to the entrance, was seated a man in a dark blue hooded cloak. He had the

<Zaylyn ><Quest For The Sword Of Anthrowst ><By Katrina Mandrake-Johnston >   <Ch 47> < 145 >
hood drawn up about his face and cupped his mug of ale with both his hands. He paid them no notice upon their entry. The other two large tables were empty.

To the left of the entrance, a long bench ran the length of the wall under a large mottled window. Four smaller tables were situated in front of the bench with accompanying wooden chairs.

This large room of the tavern was quite beautiful with both dark and light colored wood used in appealing ways. The tables and chairs, although they looked well used, still maintained some of their former beauty and were clearly very well made.

The room was designed in the shape of an 'L', with the length of the room running along the front window and ending at the large double door leading to the kitchen. Next to the kitchen door and opposite the last smaller table was a large wooden desk with beautifully carved markings. Behind the desk were a few shelves with various bottles and mugs with two large kegs beneath on the floor. At the other end of the room, beside the doorway leading to the guest rooms, there was a small square stage.

Behind the desk stood a cheerful man with a round face and black curly hair. He was an average-sized man wearing a grey long-sleeved woolen shirt with a dark green vest over it and a pair of dark brown pants. He was checking over a supply list when he noticed the group enter. He put the list down, smiled, and waved a greeting to them.

At one of the smaller tables, the one closest to the kitchen, a woman and an older man were seated, engaged in a pleasant conversation and enjoying a dish of small seasoned potatoes. The man was obviously her father by the resemblance.

"We should speak with the innkeeper, maybe we can get some drinks or a bit of food with our combined money," Nodwel suggested.

"Maybe I can get something for my glowing rock," added in Vordin hopefully.

They all headed over to the desk to greet the innkeeper.

"Gee, looks like you lot have been through quite an ordeal. We have rooms available, our cook does wonders with roast lamb, and if you'd like hot baths, that can be arranged as well," the innkeeper said with a wide smile.

"How much would this cost?" Nodwel asked, a concerned expression growing on his face.

"Well, about five gold pieces for a room, two for a bath, and three for both food and drink. We like to keep our prices cheap. We get enough business to not have to be greedy," he laughed.

"First time I've heard of that," Nodwel chuckled.

"Yeah, that is pretty cheap," Candra commented.

"It keeps our patrons happy. We're the only town for quite a ways in both directions. Plus, we don't have all the extras that the town of Shirkint does, but we do a fine job. Oh, we have a special show planned for tonight: an excellent juggler. I'm sure you'll enjoy it, if you decide to stay for it."

"What kind of extras does Shirkint have?" Weena asked him, hoping her curiosity would not result in him taking offense.

The innkeeper beckoned them all closer and he lowered his voice to a whisper, "It's on account of The Black Shadow, I reckon. Ain't no one powerful enough to do the sort of things they have, but him. Instead of an outhouse, they have pots that when you do your business into them, it flames it up or disintegrates it or something. Anyways, the pot is empty when you're done. We acquired one from Shirkint for the inn here. It's convenient, yes, but I'm not entirely sure if it was very wise to do so. You know, on account of The Black Shadow and all. Oh and in Shirkint, you pull a lever on a wall or perhaps it's on the side of the bathing basin, anyway, it magically fills with water. Warm, hot, cold, whatever to your liking. Then when you're done bathing, you pull another lever, I suppose, and the water will just magically disappear. Then the town's shops all have a special protection against thieves. When you enter the shop, you are unable to discern what any of the objects are. So it's impossible to steal anything because the spell is only broken when the item is paid for. So you just ask the shopkeeper for what you want. They have everything you can think of too, or at least it seems that way. Oh and if you're the sort that takes a liking to whores, they have them there too. And with them, no matter what you do, you can't get 'em pregnant or receive any sort of nasty sickness in return, not even a common cold. Sorry, if that information offended any of you ladies. I didn't mean to be insulting or

<Zaylyn ><Quest For The Sword Of Anthrowst ><By Katrina Mandrake-Johnston >   <Ch 47> < 146 >

to suggest that any of you explore that matter further or anything. Now, I may seem like I'm talking highly of this town, and true, it is great in some aspects. They hold competitions, have a visiting storyteller, and I believe they have a thieves guild there although they are very secretive about that and I've only heard vague rumors about the guild's existence. Oh and speaking of thieves, it's supposed to be a thief's greatest challenge, that town, and not because of those spells and all. No one can get past that. I'm speaking of their law, that if a home is robbed of valuables, it's their own fault for not protecting it well enough. So all the homes are trapped with horrible deadly traps and mind-bending puzzles and such. Here, I'm getting off topic. You see this is the town that The Black Shadow frequents, and he is said to be seen now and then at The Old Scabbard Inn there." The innkeeper paused and then said in a sorrowful tone, "So many people have gone missing from that town, some even wound up dead clear in plain view and everyone just looks the other way. It makes me sick. Sure they grieve for their lost ones, but no one tries to do anything for fear of losing their own life or worse. And believe me, there's always worse things than death. They just accept their luxuries and watch helplessly as friends and acquaintances slowly disappear, always living in fear that they will be next, that they may say the wrong thing and anger him, as he is always listening, said to even knowing your very thoughts. I've probably said too much already." He looked nervously around and then continued, "It's just that my good friend Yorif went to Shirkint three days ago and still hasn't returned. I know that there are bandits within the forest as of late, who have been ambushing people along the road between here and there, but I doubt they would have bothered with him. I wouldn't be surprised if he had crossed paths with that monster The Black Shadow. There is a carriage that travels between the two towns. It may be faster and safer to travel that way if you are planning to head up to Shirkint, but if you can conduct your business here in Vackiindmire, I suggest you do so and stay clear of that town, especially when the bandits have become so bold in their attacks. Listen to me, I've been rambling on and on, when you clearly want to rest."

"Sounds like somebody else I know," Candra whispered and gave Weena a slight nudge as she teased.

The wizard returned a glare, but was glad Candra was in such a joyful mood. "What's his interest then with the other town?" Weena inquired.

"Don't know. Don't think anyone does," and then the innkeeper asked, "So what can I get for you? A drink perhaps? Oh, and it's getting pretty late, you may want to get your rooms now before they get snatched up. Perhaps a hot bath for each of you first? You still have time before the show starts, I think. So what'll it be?"

"He must think we stink pretty bad, and I wouldn't doubt it," Candra whispered to Dendrox with a bit of a giggle. She was thrilled at finally being in a town and among familiar things. Here, being a thief, she knew how to survive.

Nodwel told him, "Drinks, food, baths, and beds for all of us would be great as we've been through more than you could believe, but unfortunately all we have is this." He placed the few coins that the group had pooled together on the desk.

The innkeeper looked down at the coins with a frown and said, "Oh, I see."

Nodwel turned to his companions and said, "Well food is the most important thing, I suppose we'll get as much food as that will give us and then everyone can have a share."

Dendrox rolled his eyes and said to the dwarf, "I think I may have dropped my money pouch, I'll just go and have a look for it."

Nodwel gave him a stern look. "It would be too much trouble," he said emphasizing the word 'trouble' to get his point across, as he knew well that Dendrox meant to pick a few pockets. Sure it was for the good of the group, but it was still wrong and if he got caught, they would have an encounter they really could do without.

"I have this. Will this help at all?" Vordin asked offering the glowing rock he had made, placing it on the desk beside the coins.

The innkeeper looked all of them over for several moments before saying, "Okay, I'll tell you what I'll do. I'm taking a loss here, but I hate to turn you away. Because of the increased attacks by the

<Zaylyn ><Quest For The Sword Of Anthrowst ><By Katrina Mandrake-Johnston >   <Ch 47> < 147 >

bandits, I'm going to need extra protection for the horses of my customers out in the stable. A few of you stand guard for me during the night and I'll provide you with four rooms, a bath for each of you if you'd like, a hearty meal and one drink for each. If you manage to find out what happened to my good friend Yorif in your future travels and are able to send me a message, please do. As you can see, I'm taking a huge loss here, but I'd like to help you." The innkeeper pocketed the few coins and handed the glowing rock back to Vordin. "You keep this, it must be pretty special," he said with a smile.

Nodwel told the innkeeper, "Thank-you. You are a very kind soul, and we shall not forget this."

Asdella said to the innkeeper, "We are eternally grateful. I'll take first guard for the horses. I won't need any help so I'll take the little one with me, okay Vordin?"

"I guess so," he replied, not knowing what to think. Vordin thought that she would think of him as merely getting in her way. Why she would pick him to come along with her, he had no clue. Perhaps she thought he knew something about caring for horses, which he didn't really. Maybe it was because he had been the only one that had shown concern and gone to find her back when they had been in the forest.

"I'll take that bath right away and make it hot, my muscles are getting stiff. Tell someone to get me out when the food is ready," she forcefully told the man at the desk.

"Sure thing, miss," he replied.

"I guess I'll get washed up too then, if it's not too much trouble to have a bath poured right away," Vordin said timidly.

"Sure, it's no trouble," he told him, "So drinks then while you wait for your meals?"

"Yes, please, thank-you," said Weena.

The innkeeper rang a small bell, which made a soft tinkle. A boy in his late teens entered from the kitchen. He wore a pair of brown pants, a plain white shirt with short sleeves, and a white apron tied around his waist. His brownish-blonde hair hung just long enough to obscure his ears. His eyes were bright blue, and he kept a lowered gaze as he said, "Yes, sir?"

"Six lamb dinners are needed, and could you prepare two hot baths for these two and show them to the bathing rooms?" the innkeeper asked him.

"Yes sir," the boy answered and returned to the kitchen.

Nodwel spoke up saying, "We would be happy with a simple stew. There's no need for such an elaborate meal." Candra gave him a nasty jab with her elbow trying to shut the dwarf up that he simply ignored.

"Oh nonsense. Your stay here will be one to remember," and then the innkeeper told Asdella and Vordin, "It should only take him a short while to prepare the baths once the meals are prepared." He clasped his hands together and with a friendly smile asked, "Alright, so for drinks, what can I get you while you wait? Ale for everyone?"

"Just water," Asdella told him. Nodwel was surprised, as she normally was a heavy drinker.

"Me too," said Vordin, "I don't think ale would sit too well with me."

The group sat at the middle large table beside the hearth. The innkeeper quickly brought them their drinks and everyone gave their thanks as they accepted them.

"I have to thank you again for all that you've done for us," Nodwel told him.

"Don't worry about it. Just don't spread it around; I'm not planning to make a habit of it," he said with a smile before returning to his desk.

"I can't believe we're actually here, in Vackiindmire, in an inn, about to eat a delicious meal," Candra said draining her mug, "and a hot relaxing bath, and a soft comfortable bed to sleep in finally. I've been dreaming about this for days."

"I feel bad for the innkeeper though. He's being so kind and we have no way to repay him really," Weena commented.

"Hey, don't worry so much and just enjoy it," Candra told her.

A skinny man in a colorful costume of red, blue, and green stripes with a matching cap entered the room through the doorway, obviously coming from one of the guest rooms. He carried a medium-sized leather bag and was clearly the juggler the innkeeper had spoken of. The man had bright green eyes, a

<Zaylyn ><Quest For The Sword Of Anthrowst ><By Katrina Mandrake-Johnston >   <Ch 47> < 148 >
long nose, and a great smile of pearly white teeth.

The man stepped up onto the small stage and announced, "I am Beebarr The Juggling Wonder, and I have an incredible show set out for you this evening. I hope you enjoy."

The man took from the bag five different colored balls, which he juggled several different ways to the audience's delight, followed by a dangerous feat done with a collection of throwing knives. Finally, he lit three torches from out of his bag and juggled them as the climax and end of his show. Beebarr the juggler then took a low bow, packed up his bag, and left the tavern.

Their meals soon came, and they all ate hungrily, not leaving a single morsel behind.

The boy eventually came back from preparing the baths. Asdella and Vordin were led toward the back rooms and then down the hallway to the right. The room they entered, at the end of the hall, was a fair sized room with two tubs. A curtain hung from the ceiling on a rod and could be drawn across the room to give privacy between the two baths.

<World of Zaylyn ><Quest For The Sword Of Anthrowst ><By Katrina Mandrake-Johnston ><Ch 48>

CHAPTER 48 = NARTEN

The boy said to both Asdella and Vordin, "Well, this is the bathing room. It's not very glamorous, but I've made sure the water is hot enough and that you have clean towels and washcloths. The soap doesn't have a fancy fragrance, but it gets the job done. Is there anything else I can get for you at all?"

"Thank-you," Vordin said to him, "I'll take the bath at the far end, I guess, unless you'd like that one, Asdella?"

"No, go ahead. Doesn't matter to me," she said inspecting the room.

There were two small tables, one on either size of the curtain and against the wall. On each table, three large candles were situated as well as a bar of soap and a neatly folded towel and washcloth. A small wooden stool was placed below each table. The room was without windows, and the walls, which were made of a dark richly-colored wood, had been affected by the constant moisture here. Beside the door was a wooden bucket with steaming hot water in it.

Vordin went over to his chosen bath and placed his backpack, with Lorenta within, safely in the corner and then pulled the curtain across to divide the room.

"Okay then, enjoy," the boy said clearly without enthusiasm and was about to leave to resume his choirs once more when Asdella asked him a question.

"So what's your name?" she asked with a slight smile.

"Narten," he answered plainly.

Asdella, who was looking into the inviting bath water, started undoing her halter-top. Knowing that it was inappropriate to linger any further, Narten started toward the door trying to avert his eyes.

She said to him, "Hold on a minute."

"I'm not really supposed to stay in the room," he explained as he nervously rubbed a hand through his short hair and kept his gaze fixated on the door.

"That's okay, I don't mind," she told him tossing her halter-top into the corner followed by her shorts. She slipped into the tub and by this time Narten's face was visibly flushed.

"Maybe I should…" he stammered.

He knew he shouldn't look at the shapely naked woman behind him, as it would be inappropriate, but he desperately wanted to. Narten nervously fidgeted with the side of his apron, and he felt uncomfortably hot under his thin white shirt.

"I just want you to run hot water over my shoulder," she explained with almost a giggle.

He didn't really know what to say or do. He was in disbelief that such a beautiful woman would ask him, of all people, to do such a thing. "Are you sure you really want me to? I could get in trouble," he told her.

"I'm injured. I don't know if it was during battle or from the fall I took, but it really hurts," she explained, "If you could just put the hot water on it and maybe tell me if it looks bad or not?"

"Well, okay," Narten decided despite his nervousness. "Did you want to cover up or something?" he asked not wanting to offend her by catching a much desired glimpse of her exposed form beneath the

<Zaylyn ><Quest For The Sword Of Anthrowst ><By Katrina Mandrake-Johnston >   <Ch 48> < 149 >
clear water.

"It doesn't really matter to me. Am I really so repulsive?" she asked with a mischievous smile.

"Oh, no, no," he assured her, "I didn't mean anything like that," and then hesitating he asked tentatively, "So you don't mind if I happen to see…"

"Please just take a look at my shoulder for me. It's the left one," Asdella said getting impatient.

"Alright," said Narten picking up the bucket of hot water, taking a washcloth from the table, and pulling the little stool up behind her at the edge of the tub. The whole time he had been too shy to steal a glance in Asdella's direction.

He placed the cloth in the bucket and squeezed the hot water over her neck and shoulder. "That's ah, not too hot or anything?" he said nervously as he gazed longingly at her form before him.

She sighed, "No, it feels great. But my shoulder still hurts like hell."

He leaned over and grabbed the soap from the table, as she definitely needed it. Narten dipped the cloth once again into the bucket, created a lather with the soap, and gently began to wash the grime from her neck.

"Thanks. Does it look like there's bruising?" she asked in a pleasant whisper.

"Ah, I don't know. Does this hurt?" he questioned and placed his hand on the side of her neck and let his fingers slide down and over the skin of her shoulder. He wasn't really interested in what her answer was; he was relishing the feel of her skin.

Vordin, already soaking in his own bath, tried not to pay attention to the conversation and to what was going on, but it was hard not to.

She winced saying, "Oh, right there. Can you feel anything?"

"It doesn't feel too bad, but then I really don't know anything about all this. Maybe I should get someone else to take a look at it later," he suggested realizing that she probably really needed proper care and sitting here selfishly enjoying himself wasn't the right thing to do.

"No, it's fine. I'd like you to do it," she told him, "Just does anything feel out of place?"

"Wouldn't you be in a lot more pain if something was?" Narten asked with concern.

"I am in a lot of pain," she said through gritted teeth and then said in a gentler tone almost as an apology, "Put more heat on it please?"

He dipped the cloth in the bucket and squeezed hot water over her neck and shoulder again.

"You know, I think I might have something that will help," he told her, "It'll just take me a little while to get it."

"Is it lots and lots of whiskey?" she chuckled.

"Ah, no," he smiled. "A healing ointment made from both magical and herbal plants. My grandmother was a bit of a healer," he explained, "Unfortunately, I never took the time to learn much myself about it. But if you'd like to try the ointment, it's no trouble."

"Alright," she accepted.

He went quickly out of the room but not before taking a lingering glance at her naked form beneath the water. After he had closed the door behind him, Asdella sunk down into the water trying to immerse her neck and shoulder in the warm bath. As the tub was deep, she was able to submerge her head without too much pain to her injury, and then using her right arm, she scrubbed at her short reddish-blonde hair in an awkward attempt to wash it. She finally gave up and relaxed down into the bath again, keeping the injured area in the warmth. Her dark brown eyes grew heavy and she allowed them to close as she enjoyed the heat.

She heard Narten say, "Hello, I'm back." It seemed as if only seconds had passed since he had departed, but she then realized that she must have dozed off. She didn't know if it had been from the pain or a combination of exhaustion and warmth from the water.

"Hi," she said meekly.

"Okay, now I'm supposed to rub this in," he explained as he scooped a creamy white paste out of a jar and smeared it over her neck and shoulder.

"It's icy cold," she commented as his fingers slid back and forth over her skin.

<Zaylyn ><Quest For The Sword Of Anthrowst ><By Katrina Mandrake-Johnston >   <Ch 48> < 150 >

"Yeah, sorry. Does it feel any better?" asked Narten.

She thought a moment and then said, "I can't tell."

"It probably takes a while before it starts to work," he suggested.

"Okay, thanks. If there's any way I can repay you for your kindness…" she began.

"Maybe…" Narten began and let his hand slowly slip from her shoulder down to touch her bare breast, "Maybe I…" he began again.

"Just make it quick," she snapped viciously at him.

He was a little taken aback, but continued, "Maybe I could get a kiss?" he asked softly.

"No," she said sharply again, "I want you to leave, now."

"But I thought…" he said removing his hand immediately.

"Leave now," she ordered.

"I didn't mean anything by it, I just thought that…" he stammered, horribly upset and feeling incredibly guilty. He got up, walked over to the door, and looked at her with his kind blue eyes searching her face for some kind of explanation.

"I said," she said angrily, "I want you to leave now!!"

Just before he exited the room, he turned to her and said, "If you think that's why I wanted to help you, you're wrong. I'm sorry, I didn't mean to offend you." He looked away and took hold of the door handle saying, "Please don't say anything to the innkeeper. I really need this job."

The door closed behind him with a gentle click.

Narr's voice inside her head began, "*What the hell was that all about?!*"

"Don't. Just please don't," she whispered, and the ghost left her alone.

She closed her eyes again and sat there in silence beneath the water.

<World of Zaylyn ><Quest For The Sword Of Anthrowst ><By Katrina Mandrake-Johnston ><Ch 49>

CHAPTER 49 =   THE STABLE

Vordin had finished his bath and dressed quite some time ago, but found himself now awkwardly waiting for Asdella to finish hers and call out for him.

"Vordin? We should be out to watch those horses. You ready?" she asked coldly.

"Yes," he replied carefully cradling the backpack in his arms.

Asdella yanked back the curtain and ushered him out of the room, down the hall, and into the main room.

Narten was nowhere in sight. The innkeeper waved a greeting and told them, "Horses are located at the side of the building. You'll have to go out the front door here. Oh and thank-you by the way. Shouldn't be too much trouble. There's plenty of hay and water. The horses we get around here are pretty much used to the routine, shouldn't be a problem for ya."

"Thanks," the warrior woman grumbled and ushered Vordin out of the inn.

"Here we go," Vordin told her, "It's just around the corner here."

The tiny and narrow stable appeared to have been built as an after thought, with the side wall being shared with the tavern and the other being the thick outer wall of the town. The stalls were lined up along the shared wall of the tavern and there was a small area near the entrance in which hay had been heaped into several disarrayed piles against the wall. Also in this area were a couple of large rain barrels filled with water, a couple of wooden crates, a medium-sized pitch fork, a well-used shovel, and various pieces of equipment that Vordin was unfamiliar with.

Only two of the stalls were occupied. There was a tired looking grey mare and a younger horse with a chestnut brown coat. Vordin went over to the younger horse and gave him a friendly pat on the nose.

Asdella looked at the stalls and horses with a scowl. She then sat down on a pile of hay with her back against the wall of the tavern.

"Hey, I think this one likes me," Vordin smiled.

"Yeah, lucky you," she said bitterly.

Vordin reluctantly came and sat opposite Asdella on a small wooden crate.

<Zaylyn ><Quest For The Sword Of Anthrowst ><By Katrina Mandrake-Johnston >   <Ch 49> < 151 >

Asdella stabbed her sword into the hay beside her and then tried to get herself into a comfortable position.

"Why didn't you tell anyone you had been hurt?" he finally had the courage to ask.

"It wouldn't have mattered. If I need to, I will fight again. It's nothing," she told him.

"That's not the point," he tried to explain.

Asdella jumped for her sword yelling, "What the hell is that?!"

Vordin was almost scared out of his wits by this, but then noticed the green glow coming from inside his backpack beside him.

"Oh, hey, Asdella, calm down, relax, it's just Lorenta. Remember? I guess she's decided to transform tonight after all. You'll spook the horses yelling like that. Put your sword down," Vordin coaxed.

"Sorry," she said returning the sword to the hay beside her and wincing at the pain the effort had caused her.

"Is it me or is your injury getting worse?" Vordin asked with a concerned look on his face.

Lorenta now stood before them in her human form. "Asdella, maybe you should try not to force use of the area," Lorenta suggested, "It needs time to heal, even for magical ointments to do their task. I am going to explore this town. I've often wondered what Vackiindmire would be like. Rasindell brought me here once when I was little, but I wasn't allowed to leave the backpack." Lorenta then ran off down the street in excitement before either of them could say anything.

"Do you think she'll be okay?" Vordin asked, "She took this long even to show herself. She's clearly nervous here, perhaps even afraid. You heard what she said back in the forest and how she feared for the other spiders. Do you think she'll be safe all alone out there and at night?"

"Don't know, don't care," she said rubbing at her shoulder and moving it around.

"I guess she'll be all right," Vordin told himself. He shook his head and said, "She's right you know, just give it time to heal."

"Fine," Asdella submitted and then rolled her eyes.

"Why don't you get some sleep," he suggested to her, "I'm sure that will help, and you definitely need it."

With a glowering look, she snapped, "And what is that supposed to mean? I'm every bit as capable…"

Vordin interrupted her quickly, "We all need sleep. Don't you agree?"

"Then you sleep. I'll keep watch," she told him sharply.

Vordin decided it was useless to say anything more about her wound. "When I sleep, it's usually only nightmares that fill my dreams, so you go ahead," he told her.

"It's that way for all of us, but sure, okay," Asdella finally said, and closing her eyes, fell fast asleep.

<World of Zaylyn ><Quest For The Sword Of Anthrowst ><By Katrina Mandrake-Johnston ><Ch 50>

CHAPTER 50 = THE SCISSORS

The others had finally decided it was time to retire to the four rooms the innkeeper had provided for them.

There were two rooms opposite each other at the very end of the hall. Weena took the only room on the left, and Dendrox chose the end room on the right opposite Weena's. The rest of the guest rooms were along the right wall. Next to Dendrox's room, was the room Candra had taken for herself and beside hers was Nodwel's.

Before entering her room, Candra announced to Dendrox, "I'll be taking my bath in the morning," and then asked, "You doing the same?"

Dendrox, standing with his door ajar and about to enter, answered, "Yeah, I'll see you in the morning. I'll be sleeping in late though. At least I'm hoping to. Nightmares… might keep me up. I'm sure everyone will have plenty after all we've seen. I sure did past couple nights."

"I know what you mean," she said with a weak smile, "Good-night."

<Zaylyn ><Quest For The Sword Of Anthrowst ><By Katrina Mandrake-Johnston >   <Ch 50> < 152 >

"Sleep well everyone," said Nodwel rubbing his stubby fingers through his matted and tangled hair as he entered his room next to Candra's.

"Good-night," Weena called, already in her room and half way closing the door behind her.

Dendrox entered, closed his door, and looked around the room. Against the far wall in the right hand corner of the room, there was a wardrobe, and on the right wall, an oil lamp hung from a hook, its light illuminating the room with a flickering light.

Close to the door, against the left wall, was the bed. It was a simple mattress stuffed with straw with a couple of linen sheets and a thick grey blanket draped over it. A single large goose down pillow lay propped at the head of the bed.

Near the foot of the bed was a window made of thick glass. The bottom half slid up to open and was locked by a simple latch. Dendrox made a mental note of this as he usually did. He always liked to keep in mind possible escape routes, no matter what the situation, and also liked to be aware of accessible entry points for the future if the need came.

The room was adequate enough and would be a welcome comfort. Dendrox sat on the bed and for the first time truly realized how exhausted he really was. Ever since the wizard had stolen his pouch, Dendrox had been wanting to take a look inside it, suspecting that the scissors were still in his possession. He removed his pouch, opened it, and searched around in the lining until he found them.

As Dendrox held the scissors, the gold and silver on the ivory shimmered in the light. "*What is so special about this damn thing?*" he asked himself, "*I mean, sure, it should be worth a fair price, but to go to all that trouble and the extreme expense of hiring mercenaries to retrieve it? They even went as far as to send a wizard after us. To think what kind of spells he could have used on us… I'm glad he only chose to use the Invisible ones. I don't know what we would have done if he sent out a ball of fire at us or a lightening bolt or something like that. Perhaps the Invisible spells were all he knew or maybe he had a magic item of some sort that allowed him to become invisible for a short time. We should have searched the body more thoroughly. Something that could turn us invisible could be very valuable. Not against the Killnarin as that wizard had made obvious with his death, but as for doing a little thieving now and then, it could be very handy. Candra would have found anything like that though, I guess. So I guess he must have had several Invisible spells all jumbled up inside his head to be able to cast consecutive spells like that. Weena said that the spells need time to recharge themselves, so it has to be something like that. It's not very important, but I should ask her about it. It doesn't make any sense, even if the scissors were of some sentimental value, it still wouldn't be worth all the effort they've gone to. Hey, maybe the scissors are magical or something. I wonder what they do? They certainly can't really cut anything very well, being made of ivory, can they? Weena might know, being a wizard and all. I'll ask her. Plus, it'll give me something to talk with her about. Hopefully, it will give me a chance to smooth over some of the awkwardness that occurred after that kiss.*"

Dendrox quietly left his room and knocked softly on the door opposite his. Weena answered the door and gave him a shy smile.

"Hi, um, I have something to ask you about," he whispered.

She asked, "What is it?"

He replied, "It's about a pair of scissors. I think they might be magical. I'd like it if you came to take a look."

A little surprised, Weena said, "Sure, I guess. A pair of scissors? That's unusual."

He whispered, "Hey, shh, keep it down. I don't want Candra to hear. She thinks I got rid of them, and I thought I did… It's a long story. Why don't you just come to my room and I'll explain things a little better."

"*What is he really up to?*" Weena thought, "*Does he think I'm fool enough to fall for such a silly plan? I'm not sure I like where this is going. I mean, people do tend to form a special kind of bond when they go through a traumatic experience together. Is that what this is? Am I even really attracted to him or is it just some kind of false attachment? He can't be good for me, that's for sure. I mean, he's a thief. He robs people. I guess I'll never know, if I don't go. Now that the danger is over, I'll be able to tell. I'll be able to make the right choices, won't I? I'll look like such an idiot, going into his room to see about a pair of magic scissors. He could have come up with a better excuse to persuade me over there than that."*

Weena closed her door behind her.

"I didn't wake you, did I?" Dendrox asked her, realizing that he may have woken her.

"Oh no," she said following him across the hall and into his room, "Every time I close my eyes, all I see are images of the villagers we found at Dexcsin, and of Yarin, and that man Borin and what he did to save us."

"With me," he said closing the door and sitting down on the bed beside his open pouch, "I see the shiny black skin of the creatures, their huge teeth oozing that foul yellow slime, their black staring eyes, their claws... And Yarin, I liked the little guy. I think he liked me too. Remember how I stayed with him back at the village? When we were in the building by the well? Remember? With all the commotion when the first spider came out of the well, and with Lorenta?"

"Yes, I remember," Weena told him, feeling his sorrow.

"I really thought we would all get out of it together," he told her, "That we would all survive together. I made myself believe it then, for him. And then he was gone."

"Do you think the others are able to get any sleep?" asked Weena, not wanting to talk about what had happened.

"I hope so. Everyone needs a good night's rest," he commented.

He retrieved the scissors from his pouch and handed them to Weena. "These are them," Dendrox told her.

"Oh, I don't believe it! There really is a pair of scissors. What are the odds of that? So it wasn't just a ploy to get me into bed?" she thought a little shocked and confused, *"I hope that doesn't mean he's given up on me though. Maybe he's not so bad after all. I mean, he doesn't really act like a thief should. Well, or how I imagine a thief to act. I mean, he hasn't stolen anything since I've known him. He's had plenty of opportunity, hasn't he? Maybe he has and I haven't realized it. Candra still has my mother's ring, damn it."* "So what's the story on this then?" she asked him.

"Yeah, well as long as you don't tell Candra. I just had to tell someone that I still had them. I don't really know what to do," said Dendrox, "I told Candra I got rid of them and I really thought I did. Perhaps I was under a spell to make me forget. I only realized that I still had them when I found out that wizard was looking for them, the one the beast got."

"You mean the one I saw along the side of the road? The one that had been with Nodwel and Asdella's group?" she questioned.

"Yes, he had turned himself invisible and found our camp. He snatched my pouch right from under our noses and took off with it only to run into a Killnarin. He was after the scissors. Is it possible to have more than one of the same spell? Would that account for there not being a wait for the spell to recharge?"

"Yes, it would, or a magic item with several magic charges in it," she explained.

"Yeah, I had hidden the scissors in the lining of my pouch and forgotten about them. Candra and I have had bounty hunters after us, now and then, ever since we stole that horrible thing. It's been pretty quiet for awhile and maybe that's why I had forgotten about them."

Weena said, "There's a bounty on you two? I can't even imagine... People hired to kill the two of you? I would go insane with paranoia. I mean, it could be anyone really, couldn't it? I think I remember Nodwel saying that the wizard had muttered something about a pair of scissors. So the guy wasn't sputtering nonsense. There really is a pair of scissors. Who would go to all that trouble over a pair of scissors? It's elegant and pretty, but it's strictly just ornamental, right?"

"That's what makes me think that maybe it's magical or something. It must be something really important and special to go to all this trouble to get them back," he told her.

"Or they just have a lot of money and time on their hands. The scissors probably have sentimental value; a family heirloom perhaps?" she commented, "I can't tell if this is a magical item or not, if that's what you're asking. I have no clue whatsoever. Sorry."

<Zaylyn ><Quest For The Sword Of Anthrowst ><By Katrina Mandrake-Johnston >   <Ch 50> < 154 >

"I really don't know what to do," he said honestly, "I feel like throwing the retched thing away, but I doubt it will stop me and Candra from being hunted down. I don't know if these bounty hunters somehow have a locater spell or something on the scissors or somehow on us. If there is such a thing, I don't know. How do you tell? I thought maybe you would know."

Weena was pleased that he had come to her with his problem and that he and confided in her. *"This is something that Candra doesn't know. This is a secret shared by just the two of us. Oh you silly girl!"* she scolded herself, *"This is serious! Look at the poor guy, he's frightened out of his wits about this!"*

Then a solution to his problem came to her. It was so simple it almost made her laugh out loud. But then she realized that of course this solution obviously must have occurred to him and there was probably some reason why it wouldn't work and that she would sound like a complete fool to suggest such a thing. She said it anyway, as he was staring at her intensely, expecting some sort of answer. "Why don't you just return the scissors to the owner? Then the bounty will be called off and everyone would be happy," she told him.

Dendrox got a puzzled and astonished look on his face, as he pondered this. "Okay, I feel like an idiot now. Why didn't I think of that?" He paused a moment considering how to go about this and then said, "Wouldn't it be kind of suspicious, just one day the scissors showing up on their doorstep? It's obvious they want us dead, as well as the return of the damn thing. I don't think it would be enough. And besides, they moved from their place. I have no idea where they might be. We happened to pass by there once, and they definitely don't live there anymore. Don't know what they look like either. Asking around trying to find their new location would leave a trail right to us."

Weena suggested, "Okay, well, what if I returned the scissors and said something like, 'I discovered a couple of thieves slain by the road side. I checked their belongings to find out who they were and found the scissors and am returning them to the rightful owner'. Of course, there's the matter of finding out where they live, but that way they'll think that the two of you are dead."

Dendrox shook his head, "I know you're trying to help, but no one would believe that."

"Why not? If we just find out where their new house is..." she began.

He explained, "For one thing, anyone dead along a road side would have pretty much all their belongings picked clean, especially something this valuable."

She offered, "Well, I could say one of the beasts got you."

He chuckled, "Yeah right, would you believe me if I told you about these creatures, not knowing what you do now?"

"Okay, that's true," she admitted.

"And as for some other wild creature," Dendrox continued to explain, "you don't live very long as a thief, if you don't know how to handle yourself. They'd see right through your story anyway, if they had any experience. They would detect your lies through the way you handle yourself, and wonder how you came to know the scissors were stolen in the first place. You definitely don't look the part of a bounty hunter looking for a hire. I just thought maybe you could help me to understand the magical aspect of this all, like how they are tracking us or what exactly these scissors do."

"No, I'm sorry," she apologized, "I wish I could help, I really do. But it looks like I might end up making things worse for you if I try to get involved."

"As far as I know, they don't know who we are or what we look like," Dendrox told her, "so it must mean that the location of the scissors is being tracked, right? That makes sense, doesn't it?"

Weena didn't want to add to his anxiety, but she wanted to help him in any way she could. She said, "Actually, I think it might be possible to locate you as well, like the last person to possess them, or the last person to touch them. Or no, because they wouldn't know if you kept them, you could have sold them to someone. The person holding them? No, because that would be the same as just locating the scissors."

"What are you doing?" he asked her, slightly puzzled.

"Just give me a minute. I'm trying to figure out if it's possible to track you with magic and not just the scissors," Weena explained to him, "Okay, if they try to track the one who stole them, it would be

<Zaylyn ><Quest For The Sword Of Anthrowst ><By Katrina Mandrake-Johnston >   <Ch 50> < 155 >

too broad of a thing, so no. It would need to be more specific, more precise... Oh, oh, I know, I know!" With these last words, she almost did a little excited dance as if she had the winning answer to a contest question. Dendrox just smiled affectionately at this. She announced her answer, "Okay, the first person to touch the scissors after the owners."

She had a triumphant grin on her face. He smiled back at her. She was so intent on helping him. He wondered if she realized the gravity of his situation and that helping him or even to try would mean she would be putting her life at risk as well. They already had the threat of the Killnarin to deal with.

He suddenly felt like the biggest fool of all. *"Why did I even mention all this to her?"* he asked himself, *"Even to know puts her in grave danger. I should have just talked to Candra about it. So what if she gets mad? I've dealt with her temper before. I was so determined to find something in common with Weena and to have something to talk about. How is she supposed to understand the life of a thief? She'd probably end up getting us all killed trying to fit in. She even said something like that herself. Besides, a thief is always on the run, having to leave town on a moment's notice. It's thrills and adventure and plenty of danger. It's no place for someone like her. She'd want to study her magic, walk in the open, and all that... not sneaking about through back alleys. Oh and she would protest profusely every time something slips into our possession out of someone else's pocket, getting us caught for sure. And then as Candra always says, 'end up squirming on the wrong end of someone's sword'. Maybe it's best if Candra and I just take off. It'll be best for all of us that way. With the Killnarin to worry about, they don't need this added to their plate."* "Weena, I..." he began to say to her. *"Oh yeah, break her heart in two,"* he scolded himself, *"You told yourself this one was special... and she is. Don't be an idiot. You have to take off, fine, but that doesn't mean you should have to watch the innocence in her eyes turn to pain. She thinks the world of you and you know it, and this is knowing that you're a thief and an outlaw. Maybe she finds that exciting, but the more time she spends with us, she'll soon realize the reality of it."* "I just..." he started to tell her. *"You're just going to make things harder for yourself,"* his mind warned him, *"Remember, this is for her own safety more so than yours. So there, the decision's final. Early tomorrow morning, before the rest are up, Candra and I will take our leave and the others will be better for it. This means this is the last time you'll see Weena. Hell, who knows, I could be dead in the next couple of days. It looks like the bounty hunters are getting more and more efficient at finding us. We've had one too many close calls already. Not to mention those damn Killnarin. Hell, I'm surprised any of us survived this far dealing with those beasts. So this is definitely your last chance to be with her."*

He pulled her close and kissed her passionately and felt her arms wrap around him in a warm embrace. He did not want to think of leaving, he did not want to think of the scissors and the bounty hunters, and he did not want to think of the Killnarin and the insane wizard behind them. He did not want to think of all the death and companions lost.

Weena was warm and soft, and her skin and hair had the faint and inviting scent of wild flowers. There was desire in her kisses and it was desire for him. No fake names or titles were needed, no pretend personalities and backgrounds. It didn't matter how much gold was in his pouch. She wanted him; Dendrox. It was him; Dendrox, the thief. Why? He didn't care. He was lost in the moment and willingly let all his worries melt away wanting the moment to last forever as he held her close.

<World of Zaylyn ><Quest For The Sword Of Anthrowst ><By Katrina Mandrake-Johnston ><Ch 51>

CHAPTER 51 =   THE BOUNTY HUNTERS

There was a commotion out in the front room of the inn. They thought nothing of it at first, lost in each other's eyes and soft kisses, until they heard someone announce in a deep bellowing voice that he and his heavily armed friends were looking for a couple of thieves that had long overstayed their welcome among the living.

"Could he mean you and Candra?" Weena asked with a worried look.

"Not now, why right now!" his mind complained. "Sounds like it. I have to get to Candra," he said urgently.

"Search the rooms!" the deep voice loudly commanded.

"*Damn it, no time! I've got to get out of here,*" he told himself, "*I'll have to meet up with her later.*" He ran over to the window and tried to open it. "It's jammed! If I break it, they'll hear, and if they have horses, I'm dead meat on foot. What do I do?" he said frantically, his eyes darting madly around the room, "I can't hide, they have that locater thing they do."

Weena stood there looking as if she were about to say something but her mind was coming up blank. He could see she was starting to panic as well. He wondered what might happen to her, if she would be named as his partner in crime or that they might not even care if she was one of the accused or not. "*It would be less hassle just to slaughter anyone in the way. No one would have the nerve or be foolish enough to protest their actions either, lest they meet the same fate,*" thought Dendrox.

Nodwel's voice could be heard bellowing in a heated argument with the men.

Dendrox thought, "*At least I have a few minutes before they reach my room. Would I be able to fight my way out? Against trained assassins? Yeah right, play the dying hero protecting his lady to his last breath. Sounds like a nice way to die, but I'd rather not. There has to be some way. Damn it, and what about Candra? Did she make it to safety? Should I break the window? At least I might have a slim chance of escape. Of course, if they have half a brain, they'll be expecting this and have men positioned outside waiting for the two thieves to attempt their escape. If that locater is on the scissors, I could plant them on some drunk and maybe escape that way, but there's no time, and I do have a conscience to deal with. There has to be somewhere for me to hide. The floorboards maybe? No time, and they'd notice, and probably no room. Bed's out too. Maybe the walls? The ceiling? No, no, no! Damn it, I'm trapped! What's Candra doing?*"

He grabbed Weena by the shoulders and whispered frantically, "Weena, what can I do? I'm trapped! They'll most likely kill you as well! Do you realize this?! Think, damn it! I'm all out of ideas! What about magic?! Is there anything you can do?!"

Her face was pale and fear-stricken. Panic filled her eyes. "Magic... magic," she mumbled, "They're using some sort of magic to find you, right? So maybe we can block it somehow, so they can't detect you."

"But what about Candra? And if they search the room and find the scissors, we're dead!" he emphasized.

"My Shield spell might be able to block the locater magic, if the spell they are using is a weak one, which I doubt, but I will try. And this is all provided that my spell works for me, it might not," Weena told him.

"Okay, fine, get started," he said, quickly taking a dagger from his belt and prying up a section of the floor.

"What are you doing?" she asked puzzled.

"Just start the spell, there's no time to try anything else. They're on their way to this room now," he whispered, slipping the scissors out of his pouch and down into the alcove in the floor. He jammed the floorboard back into place with the heel of his boot just as Weena finished casting her Shield spell around him. Weena breathed a sigh of relief when she saw that the bubble-like film was not present when cast on another. The spell had worked. She was sure of it. As long as the shield was not being used to absorb a physical attack or that of another spell, it would hold for a short while at least.

Seconds after the spell was in place, the door to the room was kicked in and four large burly men entered.

One wore an eye patch over his right eye and had a scimitar at his belt. A brown leather jerkin was over this man's chest. His muscular arms displayed a great number of colorful serpent-like tattoos. He had black greasy hair and had a satisfied grin on his face.

Another was bald and wore a brown bushy mustache under his bulbous nose. As he grinned a wicked smile, Weena could see that one of his front teeth had been replaced by a gold one. This man had a heavy looking spiked mace in his right hand.

The third had a whip strapped to his belt and five large daggers at his waist. The daggers were easily double the size of Dendrox's largest one. He had short dirty-blonde hair, and to Weena, appeared to have his eyes set a little too far apart reminding her of a funny looking lizard she had once seen.

<Zaylyn ><Quest For The Sword Of Anthrowst ><By Katrina Mandrake-Johnston >   <Ch 51> < 157 >

The men stood aside, as a fourth stepped forward. He seemed to be their leader. He was taller than the other men and almost twice as wide. A huge war hammer, which he held in his right hand, was balanced on his shoulder by a large, visibly muscular arm. He wore a small black vest over his wide bare chest on which many tiny scars could be seen. It made Weena think that perhaps he had been a blacksmith at one time. She also decided that he must have gotten in a lot of battles to receive such a display as well. He was bald, and had dark green eyes which gazed over the two of them suspiciously.

"Well, what do we have here?" the leader bellowed through a mouthful of misshapen and rotting teeth.

Dendrox was about to make some sly remark, but Weena spoke up surprisingly. "Thank goodness you're here! We heard a commotion out there but thought nothing of it until this filthy little man burst out of that wardrobe there and leapt out the window. I think he was planning to rob us, slit our throats in the night! Good thing you came looking for him and scared him off, or we would have been goners for sure."

Weena's face became flushed as the men looked her over. "*Oh no, Weena, they're going to see right through you. You should have let me handle this,*" Dendrox thought nervously to her, wishing she could hear him.

"Please excuse me, I just realized that he must have been here the whole time, and when I was getting undressed, he must have been watching me. The dirty little pervert! Who knows what he might have done to me, if you hadn't shown up to rescue us," Weena explained, realizing that her body language must be giving her away and trying to justify it.

"*Good save, Weena, I guess,*" Dendrox thought nervously, "*Maybe I underestimated you a little. You're a terrible liar, but you probably saved it there, I hope.*"

The man with the eye patch and the serpent tattoos took a couple of steps toward the window and viciously criticized, "So this thief, he just jumps out and takes a leap out da window, eh? This window that's shut?"

"*Oh no, I have to say something! But what?*" Dendrox's mind panicked.

"Well obviously it was open when he jumped out," she said, trying to sound offended, but her fear was starting to show.

"*I could say that we closed it after him, thinking he might come back to take us hostage,*" he suggested to himself, "*Yeah, right, and me with my daggers all along my belt here.*"

But Weena continued, "I was so frightened," she said trying to justify her body language to her story, hoping to keep from giving herself away, "I'll never forget his words. He said that if we told anyone that he had been here, that he would come back and kill us, and he pointed a huge dagger at us, and looked at us with an insane look in his eyes, and then he shut the window behind him. I guess to make it look like he didn't escape that way."

Dendrox's mind said, "*Weena slow down, don't panic. Not so much information, it makes it more like a story, fabricated, definitely not natural, which means dead, dead, dead. There's no way we can make it out alive.*"

"Oh and the dagger he had, it was at least the length of my forearm, easy," she added.

"*Weena, please stop, no more,*" he pleaded.

The man with the bushy mustache and spiked mace went to the window and tried to open it, finding it stuck. The others were eyeing Dendrox suspiciously.

"Window's stuck, how he manage that?" the man said with a smug look on his face, the flickering light glinting off his gold tooth. The man with the tattoos gave his companion a nod at this and let out a faint snort.

"*We're dead, so dead,*" Dendrox told himself, "*They're mocking her. Doesn't she realize this?*"

"That's simple. I thought you would have been intelligent enough to realize," she answered.

"*Oh yeah, make them angry, insult them, that will convince them to let us live,*" he thought hopelessly with great sarcasm. He let out a sheepish smile trying to appear as apologetic as possible for Weena's curtness.

"Oh? Please, enlighten us," the leader growled, displaying that his temper was shorter than the

<Zaylyn ><Quest For The Sword Of Anthrowst ><By Katrina Mandrake-Johnston >   <Ch 51> < 158 >
hair on a rat's tail.

"Magic of course," Weena said plainly, "He sealed the window with some sort of magic so you couldn't follow him as quickly. I'm a magic user myself, that's how I recognized the spell."

Dendrox let out a frustrated mental sigh, "*Oh great, if this Shield spell is working, they know now to check for one.*"

"The spells don't last very long, so I'm assuming he had planned to delay you for just a few moments," she said as she gave Dendrox a nervous glance.

"*I guess this means the Shield spell isn't going to last very much longer,*" he thought to himself.

"So, your man here. He's armed. He didn't try to stop the thief?" the leader questioned displaying his grotesquely misshapen teeth once again.

Weena quickly fabricated, "He's so brave. He was going to try to stop him, but I was so frightened and when I saw that huge knife the thief had, I grabbed on to my sweetheart and held him back. But now that you're here, you can catch him, right? He did say he was going to come back if we told anyone."

"Oh, we'll catch him," he said with a chuckle, readjusting his grip on his massive hammer, "Don't worry about that." He gave Dendrox a knowing look and then said, "Let's go boys."

The blonde man with the wide-set eyes was the last to depart, running his fingers along the leather of his whip as he looked them both up and down as an unspoken threat. "Pleasant evening then," he grinned at them and then headed down the hall after the others.

Weena quickly closed the door behind them, having to adjust it several times to get it into place as it had been damaged by the entrance of the men. Dendrox was about to say something, but Weena quickly put her finger to her lips motioning him not to say a word.

She came over and hugged him tightly whispering in his ear, "They are listening."

"We have to escape now," he replied.

She told him. "No, that's what they're waiting for."

"They saw through you," Dendrox explained to her.

"I know, but we're not dead. They're not completely sure. That's why we can't leave. If we leave, they'll know for sure," she whispered.

"I have to check on Candra. What if they did something horrible to her?!" he whispered with a worried look.

"No, that's too suspicious," Weena decided, "You're not thinking clearly. They'll be watching our every move. You contact her, they'll know you two are the ones they're looking for. I don't seem like a thief to them, you're safer with me right now."

"So you're staying here tonight? You're not going back to your own room?" he asked, thinking about the possibilities.

"I can't, it would be suspicious," she said with a cunning smile, "You don't mind do you?"

Dendrox answered her with a kiss. "Do you think they know where 'the item' is?" he whispered.

"Probably, but not exactly where. We're safe for now. If the locater is on it, I say we leave it here and then try to leave tomorrow. They don't seem the sort to give up easily," Weena commented.

He asked, "And if it's on me?"

"Let's worry about that in the morning," she said with a passionate kiss.

Dendrox quietly said, "Shh, listen."

"I don't hear anything…" Weena began and then she heard it too, "No, wait, a faint tapping sound, right?"

They rushed over to the wall, and Dendrox put his ear against it.

"Is it Candra?" Weena whispered.

"Shh, it's a special code we made up for emergencies. Let me concentrate, we haven't used it in years. I don't really remember too well how to decipher it. I need to concentrate."

Weena remained silent, as Dendrox listened for several minutes, and then watched as Dendrox returned a set of taps, scratches, and knocks. This continued back and forth for quite awhile.

"Okay," he whispered, "So basically what she said was, that she's okay. We're going to pretend

<Zaylyn ><Quest For The Sword Of Anthrowst ><By Katrina Mandrake-Johnston >   <Ch 51> < 159 >

we don't know each other, as you suggested, and wait to see how things are in the morning. And I'm in big trouble from her about 'the item'. And she heard everything and says that you did a pretty good job dealing with the bounty hunters, all you need is practice. Not in so many words, but that's basically what she meant."

Weena smiled at him, staring intensely into his eyes for a few moments before taking him by the hand and leading him over to the bed.

"We should get some sleep," she whispered pulling back the sheets and sitting down on the bed.

Dendrox also seated himself and removed his boots, as well as his belt of daggers. Weena, who was blushing, slipped her feet out of her sandals and tucked herself under the blanket. Dendrox followed.

He gazed longingly into her eyes and then his lips met hers. Each kiss led to another and another. Each touch led to yet another and another, and soon they were in a romantic embrace, despite all that had happened.

<World of Zaylyn ><Quest For The Sword Of Anthrowst ><By Katrina Mandrake-Johnston ><Ch 52>

CHAPTER 52 =   DENDROX'S SCAR

Weena and Dendrox lay awake in the room unable to fall asleep. They lay beside each other in the small bed staring into each other's eyes, listening to the creaks of nearby floorboards and the muffled conversation of people enjoying themselves in the main room of the inn. There was no further indication that they were in any immediate danger from the bounty hunters and the rest of the night would probably be uneventful. Still, they both were wary of falling asleep.

Dendrox shook his head in disapproval and at the same time the corner of his mouth turned up in slight amusement. He said to her, "I can't believe she stole your mother's ring. She's gone, I take it?"

"Yes, she died when I was very young, but I still remember her very well," she replied.

Dendrox explained, "You see, when Candra was a girl, her father was murdered right in their very home by a couple of thugs and they stole her mother's necklace. It was the only thing they had left of hers and it was also their only item of value. She came to live with my family. We practiced our weapons until we were old enough to leave home and go after the thugs, as Candra desperately wanted revenge. Ironically, that's how we became thieves ourselves. We had to adopt the trade, mingle with the right people, and show our worth in order to eventually find them. They actually still had the necklace too. I guess they felt guilty or something, or more likely they had kept it as some gruesome trophy of what they had done."

Even though Weena suspected what the answer might be, she still asked, "Did she kill them?"

"Yes," he told her, "I don't really want to talk about that. It's a part of Candra I'd rather forget is there."

"I see," Weena said knowingly.

There was an awkward moment of silence between them; Dendrox lost in thought.

"I guess she's trying to create a thief out of you in sort of the same way she was made one, by stealing your mother's ring," he finally said, "To see if you have what it takes."

Weena displayed a cunning smile as she told him, "Oh, I'll get my ring back. I just don't know how yet."

"Candra's pretty sneaky and it sounds like she's taking these little trials of hers pretty seriously," he commented with a smirk.

"I don't know," Weena said, still trying to absorb the fact that Candra had killed two people and maybe more that she didn't know about. It made their little walk back in the forest even more frightening, as she knew for certain that Candra would have gone through with her threat to kill her. "One thing I know is, I'll never kill anyone," Weena decided about herself, "I just couldn't do it, even if it was in self-defense." The back of her mind whispered to her, "*Yeah, I didn't murder my classmates and brother. It was more of an accident, right? It's not as if I stared down at them with hatred in my eyes and painfully ended their lives as they begged for mercy.*" She ignored this little voice that kept trying to remind her of that horrible incident. That guilty little voice that would never leave her alone,

<Zaylyn ><Quest For The Sword Of Anthrowst ><By Katrina Mandrake-Johnston >   <Ch 52> < 160 >
that was always trying to destroy her illusion of innocence.

"Candra and I are thieves," he admitted, "but we never want to end up like those thugs that attacked her and her father. Being a thief means a lot of running, fast-talking, and…" he hesitated slightly, "sometimes you may have to kill in self-defense."

A chill ran down Weena's back as she asked, "Have you ever?" It was hard enough for her to imagine Candra taking her revenge. To imagine Dendrox in such a manner, frightened her.

Dendrox pulled back the blanket slightly to show the large scar across his torso and explained, "This is what made me realize that I had better learn." He tucked the blanket around Weena's exposed shoulder affectionately and continued, "Candra might not have been taken, I might not have been almost killed, and I might have been able to save her."

Weena, who was always very curious about everything, asked eagerly, "What happened?"

"Hey, you better not say anything to Candra about all this," he said, getting defensive, "If she found out that I told you about her past or of what I'm about to tell you, she'd kill me." Weena's eyes widened. He chuckled, "Not for real. It was merely a figure of speech."

"Oh," she said a little embarrassed and then assured him, "I won't say anything, I promise."

Dendrox continued, "Anyway, there was a fight in this tavern. I think it was called The Wyvern's Tail. These guys grabbed Candra to sell her to one of those whore caravans. It's slavery in the worst way. Two had their hands full holding Candra. I could have killed the third, the one with the sword. I would have been quick enough to do it too, and maybe even had a chance to kill or at least wound the two holding Candra. I could have at least distracted them long enough for her to maybe get free. Because I was unwilling to kill that bastard with the sword, I was almost killed myself. I was lucky to have survived it. Candra was taken, and I was helpless to save her. The one with the sword decided to give me this scar before following after the others with Candra. It was just by chance that she was freed by one of the whores who had escaped them on her own. To think that Candra could have been violated like that, makes my blood boil."

Weena decided it was wise not to bring up anymore unpleasant memories. Killing Killnarin was one thing, but to talk about killing people in such a way, even in self-defense, made her feel extremely uncomfortable around him. She hoped he did not seriously feel this way and that it was just the anger and frustration from the memory speaking. She told him, "We should really try to get some sleep. We'll need our wits about us tomorrow."

"Yeah," he agreed, although it was obvious that his thoughts were elsewhere. He caressed her shoulder and kissed her softly before turning over onto his back to try to sleep.

When Dendrox finally drifted off into a much-needed sleep that night, in his dream, he began to relive that awful event. His thoughts still lingered on the memory after the conversation with Weena.

It was quite a few years ago, back when he and Candra were still learning their skills as thieves, and just before he had acquired his scar. He and Candra were sitting around a small wooden table in a dark smoky tavern. They had just acquired a pouch with a fair amount of money in it from the belt of an unsuspecting traveler. Candra had distracted him, while Dendrox had skillfully removed the pouch by slicing through the cord with one of his daggers.

They were about to celebrate by ordering a large mug of ale each, when three men entered the tavern and their eyes scanned across the faces of the patrons. Dendrox and Candra had tried to avoid being identified, as they recognized one of the men as the one they had robbed. The thieves both knew that they were about to get into a very bad situation when they heard the man say to his companions, "That's them."

The men headed over to the table, as Candra and Dendrox desperately tried to come up with a plan.

The one man, the one they had robbed, laughed coldly and said to them, "I believe you have something that belongs to me."

"What do you mean?" Candra asked a little too innocently.

"Do you take me for a fool?" he chuckled.

<Zaylyn ><Quest For The Sword Of Anthrowst ><By Katrina Mandrake-Johnston >   <Ch 52> < 161 >

One of the man's companions had been eyeing Candra from the moment they had entered. He suggested, "We could sell her. She's pretty enough."

"Alright, grab her," said the man.

His two companions grabbed Candra by the arms, one on either side, and dragged her away from the table. Candra looked nervously to Dendrox, as she tried to force her way free of the strong grip each of them had on her. The other patrons looked on, but made no move to help the two of them.

Dendrox got up from his chair, trying his best to look somewhat threatening.

The man looked him up and down with contempt and chuckled. "Sit back down little man. What are you going to do?" he dared.

"Take your stupid pouch back. All the money's still there," Dendrox hissed, retrieving the pouch from the inside fold of his vest.

To Dendrox's dismay, the man simply laughed at him and his two companions joined him in his mirth to the point where Dendrox and Candra both began to think that maybe they had missed something. The man finally said, "Nice try, but this way we make a profit. You forced us to come after you, so we's gonna need a little something extra for all that trouble, now don't we?"

The other man holding Candra, who had remained silent until now, said, "Let's go, she's squirming about."

With a malicious grin the man quickly unsheathed his long sword. Dendrox looked nervously about, not knowing what to do, hoping someone would come to their aid. The man suddenly and viciously slashed his sword across Dendrox's stomach. Luckily, he had managed to move back slightly and save himself from being disemboweled, but the tip of the man's sword cut deeply into his flesh.

Dendrox doubled over in pain and shock, his eyes showing his fear and desperation as he looked into Candra's horrified face. Her green eyes welled with emotion and her thin-lipped mouth twisted in a hateful grimace toward their assailants.

The blood from his wound seeped through his fingers as he instinctively tried to hold the wound closed. The man sneered at him as Dendrox looked in disbelief at his blood-covered hands and the thick sticky pool forming below him. The man wiped his sword clean on the sleeve of Dendrox's shirt as a final insult, while the thief stood there dumbfounded and in complete shock.

"Dendrox! No!" Candra wailed and she desperately tried to wrestle herself free.

"Help me hold the bitch," one of the men holding her told the other.

His vision started to blur and his legs felt weak beneath him. He grabbed onto the back of his chair with one hand, the other still clutching at his wound. The sounds around him seemed to fade far away as if he were underwater, and he felt as if he were sinking into the floor.

He was vaguely aware of the men walking away from him and of Candra screaming.

"Dendrox!" she screamed and her voice echoed in his mind until there was only blackness…

<World of Zaylyn ><Quest For The Sword Of Anthrowst ><By Katrina Mandrake-Johnston ><Ch 53>

CHAPTER 53 =   DANGER IN THE WOODS

His heart was pounding hard in his chest. The Black Shadow had been running for quite a long while, somehow trying to escape himself. The blackness of the night enveloped him now as he sat in the forest clearing, his black cloak draped around him as he rested, his legs crossed beneath him. The hood of his cloak was drawn up about his face as always.

He had thought to himself once that it was almost funny how the village and town folk had become wary of anyone wearing a hooded cloak with the hood drawn up. It had become unspoken knowledge that if someone had their hood drawn up, that this meant they wanted to be left completely alone. He knew that this had arisen out of the incredible fear they have for him. Not many had the courage to wear a black cloak, and if they did, they definitely did not raise the hood. He thought surely a few would use this to their advantage, perhaps scare some folks out of their loot. No one ever dared. Could they think that he would take offense and inflict horrible death upon anyone who dared to resemble his likeness? He did not care. In fact he wished others would, making it easier for him to move about

<Zaylyn ><Quest For The Sword Of Anthrowst ><By Katrina Mandrake-Johnston >　　　<Ch 53>　< 162 >
undetected. Maybe that was the whole point of it all.

Surrounded by dark looming cedar trees, the cool air chilled and numbed his body. He was alone and it was silent except for an occasional breeze now and then rustling the treetops.

Still sitting, he put his head back and looked up to the black sky. He watched the stars and the treetops dancing in the wind beneath them. He took a deep breath and relaxed slightly. The ground under him was cold and wet. The smells of earth and trees filled the air. The taste of blood still lingered on his lips and tongue. He felt somewhat safe now that he was here alone in the silence. Being alone meant that there wasn't anyone around for him to worry about harming.

"And what will happen if I succeed at sparing lives? What if they remember? What if they know who I am and what a horrible monster I truly am?" his mind asked, *"I will be greatly feared even more so than I already am. No, it's best forgotten. There's no use in worrying about it, because I'll just end up worrying about the same thing again tomorrow night. I don't want to think about it. All is best forgotten."*

Indescribable sensations flowed through him, numbing his body and mind. He licked the precious remaining droplets of the thick, dark crimson liquid, savoring its taste… and at the same time was disgusted with the savage beast within him. He knew the hunger would slowly begin to rise within him yet again to tear at his soul. He tried to enjoy the short amount of time and peace he had while the hunger was so briefly satisfied. He closed his eyes and let his mind wander.

"I have to admit that the hunt for victims is sometimes thrilling," he said to himself, his evil nature showing through, a wicked grin starting at the corner of his mouth exposing the tip of a fang.

Opening his eyes once more, he inhaled another deep breath, this time letting out a deep melancholy sigh which broke the silence for a moment. The wind then whistled through the trees making an eerie sound. He closed his eyes again.

The Black Shadow finally rose from the ground where he had been sitting and decided to walk. Folding his arms over his chest to keep warm, he walked briskly through the dark forest. He climbed over logs and pushed branches aside. Unseen animals scurried around in the bushes as he continued.

***

"I'm dead serious. That be exactly what I saw," one of the bandits on watch duty said to the other.

"Yeah, alright," the other laughed.

"I'm tellin' ya the truth," the bandit said to the other who clearly wasn't believing a word he had said.

"I admit, it was odd to be seeing a set of clothes neatly folded with a pair of shoes placed beside 'em and just there in the middle of the forest beside a tree. But that's all I be saying, it was a little odd and that's all," said the second bandit warming his hands over the tiny campfire.

The first continued, "But you never saw!"

"See what? What'd you see in your drunken haze, eh?" he asked with a laugh and then pulled a small bottle from out of his vest pocket.

"Hey, you remember what he said 'bout drinking on watch duty! If he catches us again…" the first warned.

"Oh relax," said the second bandit, "Besides, you sound like you be needin' a good shot of whiskey, maybe two."

"Alright, fine," he said taking the bottle, uncorking it, and taking two large gulps of the strong liquid.

"Hey, slow down there, pal, save some for me," the other chuckled taking back the small bottle and taking a swig.

"Listen, so you just need to believe me on this. I tell ya, so I go back towards where we saw them clothes. I was just heading in that direction and I thought I sees somethin'. Somethin' like a wolf, I think, out of the corner of my eye. So I gets nervous and I sort of stay a little bit out of sight," the first bandit explained.

"Wow, this is pretty exciting," the second said mockingly and took another swig from the bottle.

He was ignored and the first bandit continued, "Anyways, I still can't believe what I saw myself,

<Zaylyn ><Quest For The Sword Of Anthrowst ><By Katrina Mandrake-Johnston >   <Ch 53> < 163 >

but I swear it be real. This wolf, he comes into the clearing where the clothes be laid. He has an unusual intelligence behind the eyes, ya know, as if he wasn't really a wolf at all. He be lookin' all around, almost a bit nervous I think. I thought he was goin' ta find me, but I sat very still. Then right before my eyes, the wolf's body, it starts twistin' and flopping about. And as the beast was all thrashin' about, it be slowly changing from wolf into a man."

"Yeah, really? How much of a fool do ya take me for?" the other snorted.

"No, I swear, honest! He changed right before my eyes! The man, he then puts on the clothing as if nothin' happened. He looked like a common merchant! Then he just walks off into the woods," the first bandit told the other, his eyes wide.

"So, I take it this be why you were holdin' back then at the last raid? You were frightened the merchant was going to turn into some sort of ferocious monster wolf and be protectin' his goods? What a load of crap," he laughed and then said handing him the bottle once more, "Here, ya want some more of this?"

***

The Black Shadow thought he detected footsteps and movement behind him, but when he turned around, no one was there. If he wanted to, he could have used a little more of his power to become completely aware of his surroundings, but he had put a damper on his abilities in hope that with a less heightened awareness he would be unable to detect any people within the area. The awareness of unsuspecting prey would just fuel his hunger, and he was trying to suppress it and keep it under control.

"I feel like I am being stalked by someone or something. It is almost the same techniques I sometimes use to hunt down my own victims, having fun with their fears. Could it be a Killnarin? No, they seem to know to be wary of me. Could it be that someone is so foolishly and willingly walking into the arms of death? Perhaps it is nothing. I am not used to relying on just my outer senses and having them diminished so. I must maintain this state for my own good though and for that of others, no matter how much the curiosity nags at me," he told himself.

He continued a short way through the trees where a majority of pine trees grew and visibility became a little more difficult. Then he stopped suddenly. He heard the distinct snap of a twig. *"Someone is following me,"* he exclaimed in disbelief.

The Black Shadow continued to walk, not wanting whomever was following him to know that he had been discovered. He was actually beginning to enjoy this. He walked quickly ahead and then hid himself in the bushes and the darkness. Then he waited, listened, and watched.

He heard the person approaching, the leaves rustling and twigs snapping. The person was moving more slowly and carefully, but it was too late as The Black Shadow was already aware of him.

"Soon I will be able to see whoever this is, and then perhaps be able to enter his mind to discover who he is and his intentions," he thought to himself and then scolded, *"No, what's the point of learning to rely on the simple senses and abilities as do ordinary people, if you're just going to revert back to using them whenever it's convenient? No mind powers."*

The man stopped and The Black Shadow could see him now from within the shadows of the forest. His pants were torn almost to shreds. The man's body was splattered with mud, and his short blonde hair was tangled. He looked nervously around.

The Black Shadow looked into the man's eyes trying to detect what he might be thinking without just quickly taking a look inside his mind.

"Perhaps the curiosity will overpower the evil urges inside me," he thought hopefully, although horribly frightening scenarios were already forming in the back of his evil mind. This man would not be safe for long. A little bit of curiosity would not stop his evil self and The Black Shadow knew this too well. *"He is clearly lost and confused. I can see that now in his eyes. But why?"* he asked himself, *"Could it be that he was not following me at all, but had taken an unlucky turn which led him along my path? If so, what caused him to be in this state? What was he running from? Perhaps he is not the only one out here."*

The Black Shadow watched his every move. He watched the man breathe and the blood pulse through his body, exciting his hunger. The sound of The Black Shadow's heartbeat and breathing got gradually louder and soon started to almost pound in his ears as the craving for blood grew and grew. The Black Shadow started to breathe in low rasping breaths, sucking the air in through his teeth as he desperately tried to maintain control over himself.

***

"The night before last, the three on watch duty," the first bandit said taking a swig from the bottle, "they were all found dead."

"Yeah, what of it? That's what happens when you go against the leader's orders. They probably tried to make some quick coin off someone traveling through the night, underestimated his abilities and got themselves killed," the other suggested with an uncaring chuckle and accepted the bottle back from him.

"What if it isn't that simple?" he said.

"Oh, gee, you think this wolf beast you imagined is responsible for that too, don't you?" the other laughed.

"No, actually I don't," the first said very seriously and tried to convince the other, "I think there is somethin' far worse out there. I think you know of who and what I mean."

"So what are you sayin'?" he asked with a mocking smile.

"I'm sayin'," the first told him snatching the bottle out of his hand, "Maybe we shouldn't be drinkin' anymore of this t'night. Who knows what could be lurkin' about in the night? And most frightening, in the blackest of shadows, if ya get what I mean."

"Well, the bottle's empty, and so's yer brain. You paranoid fool. Just relax, would ya?" chuckled the other.

***

Unable to resist any longer, with a great agility, he crept silently through the bushes, watching and listening like an animal stalking its prey. The Black Shadow had made his way silently around his intended victim until he was standing behind him.

In one swift movement he grabbed the man with one arm around his torso and sunk his fanged teeth deeply into the soft exposed flesh of his neck. The warm, thick liquid started to flow slowly over his lips.

"*Turning the natural pain of my bite into pleasure in the mind is the least I can do for my victims,*" he commented to himself and then as an after thought said, "*Of course it can work the other way as well, intensifying the pain to incredible levels for a deserving individual.*"

The man struggled a moment, as he bit deeper into him. Then the man surrendered himself to the pleasure and to The Black Shadow, as his blood began to gush from his neck.

"*Shut up,*" he yelled at himself, "*Just do what you must. Just try not to kill him.*"

The man, weakening, sunk slowly in his arms to the ground as The Black Shadow bent over him and drank heavily.

He withdrew, the hunger still burning fiercely within him, and desperately hoped that it wasn't too late to save the man. The Black Shadow willed the wound to heal and it quickly did until it was completely flawless.

The Black Shadow's fangs ached to be embedded once more in the soft flesh. He wiped his darkened, wet lips against the back of his gloved hand.

The man looked up at The Black Shadow, his eyes showing his fear and helplessness, his breathing shallow, as he lay there weak and afraid.

The hunger burned, pulsating within him. He bent down toward his exposed neck once more, almost without realizing what he was doing, but then he saw the look of horror on the man's face and he was able to stop himself again.

"*He looks so innocent, and he knows that his life is in my hands,*" he thought to himself.

The man stared at The Black Shadow's face beneath the hood. It was shrouded in shadow to the point where his features couldn't quite be seen clearly no matter which way he turned. Even if he allowed someone to see his face, which wasn't very often, he would make sure their mind could not remember it.

<Zaylyn ><Quest For The Sword Of Anthrowst ><By Katrina Mandrake-Johnston >   <Ch 53> < 165 >

After a few moments, the man was able to muster enough strength and courage to say in a weak and trembling voice full of confusion and fear, "What's going to happen to me?"

"Nothing," whispered The Black Shadow, "Go back to your life and enjoy it while you still can."

The man staggered up to his feet, still very weak, and started to make his way through the forest as fast as he could, having to hold onto trees for support every couple of steps.

The Black Shadow remained kneeling on the ground, fighting desperately with the urge to follow… to leap upon the helpless man and drain the last bit of life out of him.

Before the man was completely out of sight, he stopped and turned to look at the dark figure in the small forest clearing.

"Go, it will cost you your life if you linger here!" The Black Shadow growled at him.

The Black Shadow watched as the man continued until he was out of sight. He could smell his scent, hear him moving across the ground, and sense the warmth of his body. The man was still in danger from his hunger. He tried desperately to diminish his senses to that of an ordinary person in hope that in this way he may not be able to detect the man he had freed from death.

It was quiet now. Darkness surrounded The Black Shadow in complete silence. The man was safe now, at least from him. Something had been watching, lurking just out of sight. Whatever it was, it was furious that The Black Shadow had interfered with its prey.

<World of Zaylyn ><Quest For The Sword Of Anthrowst ><By Katrina Mandrake-Johnston ><Ch 54>

CHAPTER 54 = ASDELLA'S PAST

Asdella was now in a deep sleep upon the pile of hay. Vordin rested silently taking great care not to wake her. A dream filled her mind…

Asdella was in a forest glade. The sunlight filtered down through the treetops. The occasional bird chirped its song. It was a peaceful atmosphere; no sign of danger.

She of course was on guard, suspicious of every sound she heard, expecting the worst no matter how appealing this place was. Although after a few moments, she did allow herself to relax slightly.

She was uncertain of where she was. Asdella suspected that she must be experiencing a dream. It felt somehow different though, as if it weren't entirely coming from her own subconscious, but that of another. She did not want to move from the glade. She did not want to move from where she stood. She wanted this strange dream to end. It made her feel uneasy.

She heard a noise. It was footsteps coming toward her through the forest. She could hear the rustle of leaves as whomever it was approaching brushed past them. She instinctively raised her sword and then it slowly faded away until she was grasping at nothing but air.

Narr emerged from the forest, pushing away a leafy tree branch as he ducked his head under it. He was as she had remembered him. He gave her one of his sly smiles.

Narr's blue eyes met Asdella's, but she returned no emotion at seeing him there before her. He stepped into the sunlight, making his wavy blonde hair shimmer for a moment, before he decided to lean up against the trunk of a large oak tree. He crossed his arms in front of his chest in a relaxed position and looked at her expectantly.

As usual, he wore plain dark brown pants and his leather jerkin with a white long-sleeved shirt under it. At his waist hung his short sword in its scabbard. It was what he usually wore, and he looked the same as when she had last seen him alive, only he was exceptionally clean, especially his clothing. It was this that struck her as being especially odd. His shirt was extremely white and his pants were a deep rich brown, as if they had been worn for the first time. The leather of his jerkin looked comfortably broken in, but was very clean which also seemed unusual. As an adventurer who often got into trouble, his clothing was always well-worn and clearly showed it, especially the leather jerkin he wore almost every day.

Narr, however, still had that unique exuberance about him that she remembered. Narr rubbed at the stubble that was beginning to show at his chin and then said, "You're not even going to say 'hello', are you?"

<Zaylyn ><Quest For The Sword Of Anthrowst ><By Katrina Mandrake-Johnston >   <Ch 54> < 166 >

"Was I supposed to?" she replied rudely.

"Ah, come on," he grinned, "I find out this great trick and you don't even say hello? You're mad at me, aren't you?"

"Annoyed is more the word. What is the meaning of all this?" she said curtly, "You nag me all day, and now you've decided to invade my dreams as well?"

Narr let out a frustrated sigh. "I already apologized for that. And I also left you alone just like you wanted, for quite a long time," he told her and then announced, "Anyway, I've solved that problem. My thoughts won't be tumbling into your head all at once anymore."

"How so?" she asked impatiently.

"Wow, just relax," he said to her, "You're so tense and uptight. We have plenty of time and there's nothing to worry about here. Come on, why don't we sit down and talk? There's no harm in that, is there?"

He motioned with his hand to a wooden bench at the side of the clearing. Asdella was sure that it hadn't been there a second ago. Reluctantly, she finally submitted and sat down. The bench was surprisingly comfortable. Narr sat beside her, stretching his legs out in front of him and slouching down into the seat with his arm resting on the back of the bench and the other on the armrest. "So, pretty nice here, isn't it?" he commented.

Asdella, who sat rigidly upon the bench, said, "Just tell me what you want and then leave me alone."

"Cold as ever I see. It's not like you have anywhere to go. You might as well enjoy yourself," he explained.

"Is this my dream or yours? Things don't feel right here," she said looking about the forest.

"It's sort of a shared dream I think. A place created by both our minds," Narr told her, "Oh, and about our little problem? Well, you see, here, where our two minds meet, I can be more of the old me."

"And that's good how?" Asdella asked with the beginnings of a smile.

"Hey, that wasn't very nice," he gave her a mischievous look, "It means that all my thoughts won't get dumped on you anymore. I can center myself here and speak to you as if I were here in person. You know what I mean, don't you?"

"I guess," she answered.

"What I'm trying to say is, that I'm slowly gaining more control over myself, learning my abilities and boundaries," said Narr.

"So now what?" she asked looking him in the eyes, "What happens now?"

He was lost for words for a few seconds, as he stared longingly back into her dark brown eyes. Then he said, "Well, I don't know. Are you still mad at me? Because I can't really tell."

"I'm not angry with you," Asdella told him.

"Will you talk to me then?" he coaxed, "I feel as if I know nothing about you, and I want to know everything. You must know how I feel about you."

Asdella decided, "You know, I am angry after all at you, and it's not because you annoyed me."

"What did I do then? What else could there possibly be?" Narr questioned with surprise.

Asdella stared deeply into his eyes and for several moments couldn't bring herself to say anything. She was breaking down. She wanted to tell him many things, to finally be able to confide in someone, to let someone in past her hard outer shell she had hidden herself beneath.

"You died," she said, her words cracking with emotion.

"Oh," was all Narr could say. It looked as if Asdella was finally on the verge of opening up to him, which was something he never thought possible. He could see that tears were welling up in her eyes. He said, "So you're angry with me because I died? You do know that I didn't do it on purpose, right? It sort of just happened. It wasn't something I had planned on doing, you know? Will it help if I say I'm sorry?" He hoped that his words might cheer her up and take the weight off the subject, but she remained looking into his eyes with a hurt behind them that he wished he could just wipe away for her. "I did die trying to save some of the villagers. That was pretty heroic of me, wasn't it? To tell the truth, I always kind of imagined myself dying like a coward in some drunken brawl," he chuckled.

<Zaylyn ><Quest For The Sword Of Anthrowst ><By Katrina Mandrake-Johnston >   <Ch 54> < 167 >

"You did save someone, a boy named Yarin. As long as he lived, your death had meaning. Now that Yarin's dead, you died in vain," said Asdella.

"That's not true," said Narr, "I tried, and that's what matters."

"Fine," she said looking away, "So you wanted to talk. Let's talk. What do you want to know?"

"How did you come to be the Asdella I know today? You know what I mean. The warrior, the furious rage, where does it all come from? You've obviously had schooling like the rest of us. Most that call themselves barbarians can hardly string a sentence together. Although mostly the ones I'm thinking of happened to be half Garc, but you know what I'm asking. Something must have happened. I'm just curious as to what. If you don't want to talk about it, fine, I'll understand. I mean, I'm not going to ask about that bath boy incident. I mean, Narten, Narr, maybe you just got confused for a minute," he said trying to make a joke out of it and then fell silent at the fierce look he received.

She stared at the ground as she started to tell her story. "Asdella the warrior, the cold and bitter monster you joke about, the insane rage and pain, wasn't always so. You know how a circus travels from place to place with exotic animals in cages for people to see and poke at? Well imagine the same thing, only the animals are young girls taken against their will. I was part of that injustice. I was different then, innocent and vulnerable. Many of the girls who resisted or couldn't take the severe beatings that occurred regularly, didn't survive long."

"I'm so sorry. Why didn't you say something before?" asked Narr.

She snapped at him defensively, "What good would that do? Go around telling everyone that I had been a victim once? To have people dump heaps of their pity on me? To have them utter dry meaningless words of comfort over and over, again and again? So I can blame every little thing on that abuse? So that can be my reason for all I do wrong, instead of taking responsibility for my own actions? It's part of me unfortunately now, and I have to deal with it and live with it and work hard to eventually overcome it. That's all Narten was, to see if I am able to feel any sort of emotion other than hatred." She paused and then said, "Even you. I feel anger, instead of sorrow, because you died."

"I think you're feeling more than just anger," he told her, "You just don't know how to describe it or how to express it, but that's alright. We can work through all of it together, and like you said, eventually overcome it, even if it takes us years. Don't be afraid to talk to me. I mean, it's not even as if you are telling someone, you're actually only talking within your own mind."

Asdella continued, "Like I said, many of the girls that resisted didn't survive very long. I always fought back no matter what, and my hatred grew and grew. I survived every beating and every rape. I had to be chained up constantly, and since I was a 'resister', I got all the ones that liked it. All the ones that enjoyed the fact that they were able to cause such suffering in me. My one reason for surviving was my hatred of that bastard who ran the whole thing. I dreamed of revenge every second, and every bruise and every lashing just fueled that rage and frustration. If I ever got free of those chains, I would have brought death upon him five thousand times over. He knew this, and it amused him to see me suffer so. Most of the other women decided just to accept their fate and be submissive. The ones that did resist usually gave in after a fair amount of beating. Or, they ended up dead, their broken bodies tossed away at the side of the road or dragged into the trees for the wild animals to feast upon. They were treated like they were nothing, just untrainable pieces of meat to be thrown out with the rest of the trash. He would save me for the most brutal of men and laugh at my agony. He would never 'sample the merchandise', as he called it, with me, which I was thankful for. After about a year of constant torture, I trained myself to focus my pain and rage into my plot for revenge, one that in the end worked. I slowly and carefully executed my plan of seduction, learning to say the right things, and all that. Anyway, after several months of convincing him that I was only fighting back because I wanted him, and that I was jealous of the other girls he 'sampled', and that I wanted him all to myself, and that I could please him better than any of the others, and that I had proven that I had the stamina, and so on..." A tear rolled down her cheek. She wiped it away and continued, "Anyway, I got him to start entertaining himself with me, but with chains still restraining me of course, he knew that I despised him still. I think he enjoyed that fact more than anything. I tried very hard every time, saying the right things and all that. Eventually, after several months of this disgusting torture and further degrading with

<Zaylyn ><Quest For The Sword Of Anthrowst ><By Katrina Mandrake-Johnston >   <Ch 54> < 168 >

this creature of a man that I loathed most in the entire world, he began to be less cautious of me and the chains started to be taken off occasionally. I did not spring at that first moment the chains were off. He would have expected that. Instead, I continued my falsehood, hoping he would begin to let his guard down even more, and I waited patiently for the perfect moment to strike. I continued with the deception for several more months, all the time making sure that he never got bored of me, which was far harder than simply stomaching the nausea every time that revolting monster of a man touched me. But eventually, over time, he began to let his guard down. Finally, I got my chance and there was no one to come to his rescue. As strong as he was, he wasn't able to pry my hands and fingers away from his throat as I choked the life from his putrid mass of a body. He couldn't die enough for me, and when it was over, I didn't really feel avenged. He had ruined me and everything I was, and I could never get that back. I freed the others and went on my way. I naturally became a fighter, as it was the new me and what I had become."

"I don't really know what to say," Narr admitted.

"Asdella?" Nodwel's voice echoed throughout the forest clearing.

"What was that? It sounded like Nodwel. I think you better wake up, Asdella. I'll be here if you need me…" Narr's voice trailed off as Asdella slowly opened her eyes.

<World of Zaylyn ><Quest For The Sword Of Anthrowst ><By Katrina Mandrake-Johnston ><Ch 55>

CHAPTER 55 = AWKWARD BREAKFAST

Asdella awoke. She saw that she was still in the stable next to The Twisted Eye Tavern. Vordin had fallen asleep while sitting awkwardly on the wooden box.

"Asdella, Vordin, wake up, the both of you," Nodwel said hurriedly.

"It's morning already? I thought someone was going to relieve us," Vordin said rubbing his eyes.

Asdella asked, "Is there something wrong, or you just fall asleep for too long?"

Vordin asked as he stood up and started to stretch, "What is it? There is something wrong, isn't there? Oh no, did someone steal the horses? I didn't mean to fall asleep…"

"No, no," Nodwel told him, "We have a bit of trouble. I don't know for sure, but I suspect our two friends are in a bit more trouble than we know. A group of bounty hunters entered the tavern last night looking for two thieves. I have a feeling that Dendrox and Candra were the ones they were looking for. Did you see anything last night?"

"No, we must have fallen asleep by then," Vordin told him and then commented meekly, "Some guard duty, eh?"

Nodwel said, "I'm sure the innkeeper has to deal with this sort of stuff a lot. He didn't look too upset by the whole ordeal and neither did anyone else in the tavern. Anyway, I was able to get a message from Candra."

"So it really does look like Candra and Dendrox are the ones they were looking for," commented Asdella.

Nodwel said to them, "Candra suggested, and I agree, that in case the bounty hunters are watching, which they probably are, it's best not to associate with them or Weena. She was caught in the middle of all this too. Gain all the information you can about the sword, the hunters, and anything else you might think useful. Then we'll spend another night at the tavern. I'm hoping I can get enough money for us all. I've already talked to several merchants about moving boxes of merchandise from their wagons to their market stalls for today. A few said they were willing to part with a bit of coin for the help. So we'll all meet back at the inn at sundown, feel out the situation, and decide what to do then."

Asdella questioned, "So where did Lorenta run off to?"

Vordin quickly checked the secret magical compartment in the backpack and found it to be empty. He said a little worried, "Don't know, she's not in the backpack. I thought she would have returned before dawn."

"You think someone squashed her?" Asdella asked calmly.

"Don't say that!" Vordin pleaded, imagining that it easily could be true.

<Zaylyn ><Quest For The Sword Of Anthrowst ><By Katrina Mandrake-Johnston >   <Ch 55> < 169 >

"Hey, I'm just being rational," she explained, "She'll probably turn up."

"Nodwel, do you know if anyone has seen Lorenta?" Vordin asked.

"No, sorry, I thought she was with you. I'm sure she's all right though," Nodwel told him.

"What about money?" Asdella asked him, "I doubt you'll be able to raise enough for all of us for tonight. You going to have the thieves get us some?"

"Hell no," Nodwel exclaimed, "They can't risk getting exposed. They're lucky to still be alive after last night. They have to be extremely careful. I'm hoping there may be a few odd jobs I can do around town to raise more. We'll at least have enough for rooms for tonight with the money I'll get for helping out those merchants I told you about. As for food and supplies, we'll have to see. It's probably a good idea for you two to stick around the tavern. Maybe you'll learn something about the hunters. If anything, you'll be there to overhear any messages our friends try to get to us. I'll see you two back at the tavern at sundown then, okay? Remember to stay clear of the others for all our safety." Nodwel left the two of them and quickly headed off down the street.

Asdella got up, retrieved her sword, and said, "Hey Vordin, how about getting a bit of breakfast? The innkeeper did say he was providing it, didn't he?"

Vordin, collecting his backpack and checking that his lantern and dagger were safely tucked inside, said, "I don't know. I don't think so, but we can go check."

The two of them entered the tavern. It was empty of customers at the moment and the innkeeper was behind the desk flipping idly through a book.

When they asked about maybe getting some breakfast and hinted that they hoped he could give it to them free of charge as he had done with the meals the night before, the innkeeper replied, "Greed never gets a person anywhere they really want to be. Listen, I'd like to, but I just can't do it. I can't give you free food again, you understand, don't you? I'm still trying to figure out how I'm going to make up the cost of what I've given you already."

"We understand. Thank-you, you've been very kind and very generous already," Vordin told him apologetically.

Narten, who had been listening from the kitchen doors, said, "I'll pay for their meals."

"What was that Narten?" the innkeeper asked a little shocked at his sudden offer.

He repeated, "I'll pay for their meals."

"Oh no, please, you shouldn't," said Vordin feeling even more ashamed for asking about breakfast.

Asdella grumbled, "I don't need your pity, Narten."

"No, I want to," Narten explained to them, "Please, let me do this for you."

The innkeeper shook his head slightly and asked, "I am to deduct the meals from your wage then? For these strangers? This is truly what you want to do?" The innkeeper was clearly trying to persuade the boy out of his decision and at least make sure that he had thought his decision completely through.

"Yes sir," Narten replied with pride, "I will go to prepare the meals now."

As soon as Narten had entered the kitchen and the innkeeper was sure that he was unable to overhear the conversation, he said to the two adventurers, "I am sad to say that he does not make a lot of money working here for me. If I could afford to pay him more, I would. What I am saying is, that for him to pay for your meals will mean he'll be tightening his own belt to do so. I just hope you two truly appreciate what he's doing for you."

Vordin felt even worse than he did before. "Yes, of course, but if he is making such a sacrifice to do so, he really shouldn't. We'll be fine, really."

The innkeeper shook his head and explained, "He's made up his mind. He's determined to do this, although I can't imagine why."

Asdella grabbed Vordin by the arm and dragged him away from the desk. Then she firmly said, "Let's go, Vordin."

"The food is being made for us already by now, we can't just leave," he told her in a hushed voice.

She whispered angrily at him through gritted teeth, "I don't need his pity. I don't want his kindness. I don't deserve it. I don't deserve any of it! Why does he insist so?"

Vordin awkwardly coaxed her over to a table and got her to sit down with him. He smiled at her

<Zaylyn ><Quest For The Sword Of Anthrowst ><By Katrina Mandrake-Johnston >   <Ch 55> < 170 >

and said, "I guess he's interested in you. It's not as if you're ugly to look at, you know. You're actually quite pretty."

"He's wasting his time. There can never be anything between us," she told Vordin.

"Well," Vordin said trying to think of something to say, "There is the age difference. He can't be very much older than I am. He looks about seventeen or so. It's probably just a silly crush."

"None of that matters," she said, her voice showing that there was a great hurt within her and that he did not understand at all what she was meaning. She looked into Vordin's eyes and he caught a glimpse of a well-hidden sorrow there. "I…" she started. Her voice had a weakness to it, and then she corrected herself forcing her words to be strong again, but Vordin could tell that she was pondering whether she were going to say anything at all. "I tested myself…" she continued, and now her words were angry, showing a great hatred toward herself, "to see if there was anything left inside this husk of a body. There is nothing. There is no feeling left inside me. There is no desire. To be adored by another, means nothing now. Everything has been stomped out and crushed into dust. There is no excitement at another's touch. I couldn't care less about another's kindness toward me. A smile from a handsome face does not bring me joy. I am full of hate and rage and that is all. I tried to feel something else. I should have at least felt something. Narten's innocence and his unconditional kindness to me, the way he looks at me… I'm incapable of any gentle emotion, and I feel guilty that I can't return any sort of kind feeling toward him. No, you know, I don't think I even feel guilty about it. I don't think I even care. I should care, shouldn't I? I want to care. I want to care so badly, about anything. I'm like an empty shell, and all that has been left inside is a hollow aching pain that makes my fury burn like the hottest fire to the point where I just want to choke and smash the life out of everything around me. That can't really be healthy, can it? Do you think I'm crazy, Vordin?"

"Ah, only sometimes," he said truthfully, "Maybe you just haven't found the right person yet. Feelings for others usually have to develop, don't they? Just because you think you should have feelings in a particular situation, doesn't necessarily mean that they're going to appear. Even if you deceive yourself into thinking so. Do you see what I'm trying to say?"

"Well," Asdella admitted, "I think maybe I could have felt something for this one man."

"Well, there, that's who you should pursue then. There's no sense in being alone, if there's someone who makes you happy in your life," he told her.

"Yeah," she said despondently, "He's dead now."

"Oh," Vordin said, "I'm sorry. I didn't know."

"It was Narr," she said plainly, "I never had the chance to tell him how I felt. Well, I had plenty of chances. I just never took any of them. I don't think I even realized it myself until it was too late."

"I'm so sorry," Vordin said knowing how she must feel, as there were many things he would have said to his parents if he had one more chance to do so.

"I'm… ah… haunted by his ghost now," she told him, and seeing the odd look forming on Vordin's face, quickly said, "I wasn't going to say anything at all because all of you think I'm crazy, but I feel more comfortable talking to you for some reason." She paused in thought and then said simply, "Perhaps it's because you are the easiest to kill." Vordin was more nervous and wary of her than usual now, his earlier thoughts that she perhaps wasn't as crazy as he had first thought quickly disappeared. "So, I hear his voice inside my head all the time. Most of the time, I can't get him to shut up. At times, I think he takes over my personality, makes me do things I normally wouldn't do," Asdella explained to Vordin.

"Really?" he commented nervously.

"I think I've gotten him to leave me alone for awhile though," she said and then narrowing her eyes questioned suspiciously, "Why are you looking at me like that? You look frightened."

"I… ah… Oh look," Vordin breathed with relief, "Here comes Narten with our meals."

<World of Zaylyn ><Quest For The Sword Of Anthrowst ><By Katrina Mandrake-Johnston ><Ch 56>

CHAPTER 56 = EXPLORING VACKIINDMIRE

Dendrox and Weena, who both had intended to wake with the early morning light, instead woke up late the next morning.

"I didn't mean to fall asleep for so long. Candra may have already tried to contact us," Dendrox said quickly dressing and adjusting his belt of daggers into a comfortable position.

"I thought," Weena said still half asleep, "I thought we weren't supposed to contact any of the group. You know, in case they're still looking for you two."

"Yes, I know. It puts us all in danger if we appear to be more than just a couple of tourists visiting the inn," he said, "But it's driving me insane not knowing what is happening. If only I could get a message to her, maybe find out something."

"Dendrox, this is silly," Weena said now fully dressed and tying her yellow sash about her waist. *"Why is my little pouch so full?"* she asked herself as it had distracted her attention, *"Oh, I picked up that doll. Why? I don't know. It just felt right at the time, I guess."*

"What's silly?" he asked her impatiently.

"You don't need to contact Candra," she explained, "and besides, you did that secret code tapping you two did to get a message through. You and I can go about getting the information and supplies we need just fine." *"Gee, you'd think he's never gone or done anything on his own,"* Weena commented to herself, *"Maybe he's so used to Candra bossing him around that he doesn't know anything else, not trusting himself to make his own decisions."*

"Maybe..." he began.

"Now he's going to make some excuse like 'maybe we should wait here until we hear something from Candra'. Candra, Candra, Candra! This is ridiculous!" she told herself, very annoyed. "Come on," she said taking him firmly by the hand and thinking to herself, *"If I have to act like Candra to get anything done around here, then so be it. I guess it helps that I'm not much of a morning person too, otherwise, I'd have a hard time being so stern."* Weena told him, "I think a magic shop or a library or something like that would be our best bet for finding some sort of reference to this sword we're looking for. Sound like a good place to start?"

"Yes, but Candra may have already checked..." he began to say.

"Well then we'll have double the information, maybe we'll find out something she didn't or vice versa," she explained. Seeing that he was still very reluctant, she added, "Maybe she has left a message with one of the clerks, or at least we can ask if anyone fitting her description passed by there. Oh, and most importantly, if anyone has been asking around about you two, maybe learn something about these bounty hunters and gain a bit of an advantage."

This surprised him a little and he submitted saying, "Sure, that sounds good to me. Remember, if you see her or anyone else, it would be wise not to acknowledge them just to be on the safe side. We don't know how much these bounty hunters know already. Best to let the others come to us."

"Agreed. What about the scissors?" Weena questioned.

"Best to leave them here. If they find them, they're welcome to them. Maybe they'll leave us alone then," he grumbled.

Weena suggested, "We should retrieve them before we leave Vackiindmire though. If another thief takes them, you'll still be to blame. Like you said before, it's better to have them."

He let out an unenthusiastic sigh and said, "Sure, let's be on our way then. We can probably save some time by asking the innkeeper about what shops would be the best to check. But I have to say, that I don't really want to be roaming the streets, especially by myself."

"I'll be with you," Weena said.

He gave her a halfhearted and seemingly forced smile. She then realized what his words had meant. *"Being with me is just the same as being alone, is it?"* thought Weena, her feelings deeply hurt, *"How can he be so rude after... Well, yes, I guess it is true. I'm no match for Candra's abilities in battle or in knowledge of how thieves behave. I'd walk right into a trap and not even know it. But damn it, how else am I supposed to learn? I'm trying my best and I do have my magic, don't I? Well, that's not very useful, not to the extent that we need. I could be the most powerful member of the group, if I had the right spells and supplies. I have to learn some offensive spells and quickly, provided we have enough time. It could mean the difference between life and death."*

<Zaylyn ><Quest For The Sword Of Anthrowst ><By Katrina Mandrake-Johnston >   <Ch 56> < 172 >

"What are you thinking about? Are we going or not? I thought you were so eager to leave," he said curtly.

They headed out the door, down the hall, and into the main room of the tavern.

Dendrox scanned the faces of the patrons, noting that Asdella and Vordin were there, but made a point not to acknowledge them. Dendrox was made aware that they also knew now about the trouble they had last night, as they were doing the same. "No sign of the men from last night," he whispered to Weena.

"Not so," she informed him, "Ducked into the kitchen when he saw us enter. You must have been looking the other way. I barely caught a glimpse of his face, but I'm sure it was one of them. Probably going to spy on us, see if we slip up. Good thing magic shops and bookstores aren't the usual thing for a thief to be interested in, am I right?"

"Yeah. And you're sure about…" he whispered.

"Yes, I'm pretty sure," she replied, "Better safe than sorry anyway, right?" Weena walked up to the desk saying, "Excuse me, innkeeper?"

"Oh yes, miss? Something I can help you with? Oh, you're one of the ones from last night. I take it the incident wasn't about you and your friends, was it?"

"Oh, of course not," said the wizard calmly and inquired, "I was just wondering if there were a magic shop or perhaps a bookstore or maybe a library of some sort? I'd like to do some research on old legends, mysterious artifacts, and the like. Would you happen to know where I might find something like that or perhaps of who to talk to?"

"Well, Shirkint for sure," he replied right away, "but as I advised before, not wise to travel that way with bandits and The Black… well, you know who. But for Vackiindmire… There's a bookstore at the end of the street just across from this tavern. I think there might be a magic shop around in that area of town as well, but the entrance I believe is over by the market place. It's at the end of the street just before the marketplace. You'll see a bakery and that's the street where you would turn down to find it. I've never been there myself, but I'm pretty sure that's where it is. Oh, you know, if you really get desperate in your search, you might even want to try the marketplace. That'd be on that same side of town, but just all the way south to the far edge. You can't miss it, especially if you are able to get to the magic shop all right. The marketplace is just a jumble of stalls various merchants rent to sell their wares."

"Thank-you, you've been most helpful," she politely said and then turned to Dendrox and asked, "Shall we head out then?" Weena giggled to herself, "*I'm kind of enjoying this take-charge attitude I'm using, although it definitely isn't me and I feel guilty about acting this way.*"

The morning sun shone brightly as Weena and Dendrox began to walk side-by-side along the cobblestone street.

"We shouldn't appear to be in too much of a rush. We are supposed to be sight seeing," Weena whispered to him, slowing her pace to a very slow stroll, "Besides, we might as well enjoy ourselves a bit, especially after all we've been through."

They were slowly passing by the town entrance and could see the street opposite the tavern, the one they were supposed to head straight along in order to reach the bookstore as instructed by the innkeeper. The street edged along the northern outer wall of Vackiindmire, passing by several shops until ending at the far eastern wall.

Dendrox walked over to the side of the nearest building and sat down on a little wooden bench that was there. From here they had a clear view of The Twisted Eye Tavern and its stable, the town entrance, and down the dead end street leading to the bookshop. The main street leading south and into the rest of the town was obscured from sight.

"Come and sit with me for awhile," he said to her, motioning her over to him.

When she had seated herself beside him, he explained, "I don't really want to rush off in search of information either. Like you said, we should enjoy ourselves for awhile. We can worry about all that later. Besides, it's amazing how much information is available to you just by listening to the

<Zaylyn ><Quest For The Sword Of Anthrowst ><By Katrina Mandrake-Johnston >   <Ch 56> < 173 >
conversation of others. We might get lucky and hear something about the bounty hunters and if there has been any sort of trouble we should know about."

"Okay," she said, eager to learn.

There weren't many people in this area of town, but the few that did pass by them nodded a friendly 'hello' to the two travelers.

"I need to pick up some more daggers," Dendrox commented, "I lost three fighting the beasts in the tunnels. Those were some of my best daggers, damn it, and half of what I started out with. But, I guess I shouldn't complain as they helped to save our lives. Candra was down to having only three arrows left. She had eight at the beginning of all this. I doubt we'll have much of a chance if we run into any more trouble. No, she only has two left. She broke one getting us the meat back at the camp."

"We should be wary then of the place where she'd find arrows, if we're not to be seen with her," Weena advised, "We shouldn't even be talking about her, should we? Am I right?"

"Yes, it's a good idea," he breathed with a heavy sigh, clearly not enjoying the situation.

A carriage, drawn by two tired but sturdy looking horses, stopped just outside the town gates. Both the horses were dark grey. They were small, but strong, and were no more than four feet high to their backs, as was common in Zaylyn. The carriage was painted deep burgundy-brown and was faded with age. The carriage driver got down from his seat near the top of the carriage and gave both of the horses a loving pat on the nose.

He was an average-sized man and looked as if he could handle himself in a fight well enough. He had greyish-green eyes and a thin narrow nose, under which was a large bushy mustache. He had a cleft chin and on his left side he had a deep scar along his jaw line. His shoulder length hair, tied back in a ponytail, had once been dark brown but now was streaked grey by age. Weena thought he might be just slightly older than Nodwel.

There was a dark blue scarf around his neck and he wore a black long-sleeved shirt, over which was a brown leather jerkin. His billowy, light brown pants were tucked into the tops of his high black leather boots.

There were two small windows on either side of the carriage. Both were open to the air, and on the side closest to the road was the door. They could see a passenger within the carriage, and opening the door wide, he got out.

He was a short man of five feet and was human. He had short black hair and a heart-shaped face ending in a small pointed chin. His large dark blue eyes looked about his destination and he seemed relieved to have arrived. He wore a light blue tunic and loose fitting pants of a dark blue color. A small burlap bag was tucked under his arm.

"Enjoy the ride?" the carriage diver asked with a smile.

"Actually, it was a little frightening traveling through the forest at night as we did," the man admitted.

"Dookarnim, is it?" the driver inquired.

"Yes. Thank-you for giving me a safe passage. I've heard many frightening tales," said Dookarnim.

"Well, if you ever need to travel through the forest again by carriage, be sure to ask for me by name then," he told him with a happy chuckle.

"It was Vexcindor, wasn't it?" he asked.

"That's me," he answered, "So where you headed? Me, I'm going straight to The Twisted Eye to get some much-needed rest. I just have to wait until the other carriage driver arrives to relieve me, and so he can feed and water the horses. It will either be Koosenor or Mantoez. I'm not sure who. You ever travel with either of them? There's only the three of us now."

Dookarnim said to him, "I'm just after a book on rare plants. My wife and I own a shop at the town of Shirkint with all manner of vegetation. It's a fair distance from Leekkar where we live, but Shirkint is definitely where all the business is. Anyway, it's urgent that I get this information and Vackiindmire is supposed to have a great shop with a wide selection of books, old and new alike. I am not very familiar with Vackiindmire. This is the first time being here since I was a small boy and same

<Zaylyn ><Quest For The Sword Of Anthrowst ><By Katrina Mandrake-Johnston >   <Ch 56> < 174 >

for taking the carriage. Is the bookshop very far from here? Oh and may I ask why there are only three drivers now? It seems odd to have so few, with so many passengers back and forth."

Vexcindor shook his head sadly, "I shouldn't have said anything. Let me just say that you had good reason to be frightened during our journey. There are things out there, which your wildest imagination couldn't dream up. The bandits, as of late, are nothing compared to some of the horrors I've seen. Very few are brave enough to travel through the forest anymore. It's not very often that we get many passengers going to and from Vackiindmire. Most of the passengers we pick up are north of the forest, traveling from village to village or to Shirkint. In fact, I believe there are only two people, at least that I know of, who dare to travel back and forth between the towns on a daily basis on their own. I give them each a ride once in awhile, when they want to leave their horses at home. Colex works at the Old Scabbard Inn at Shirkint. Beanvit, I think his name is, works at the animal shop. You know, where they sell exotic animals and steeds and what not. He was telling me about all the wonders they have there, and he said they are always getting new creatures in stock. Anyways, they both live in Vackiindmire and travel to work through that damn forest. If I were one of them, I'd introduce myself to the other real quick and travel together through there, as to not have to go alone. There's a better chance of survival that way."

"Of survival?!" the man asked shocked that he had taken such a risk in coming to Vackiindmire and had not known it.

"Yeah," Vexcindor said simply, "Anyway, the bookstore is just down this street here. It's a dead end street and it's the last shop. You can't miss it."

"Ah, thank-you. I'll try to return during the day then. Thanks for the warning," he said heading down the street and passing by Weena and Dendrox who had been listening in on the conversation from the bench.

A man came out of the inn, and Vexcindor exclaimed with a grin upon seeing him, "Mantoez! It's about time you got here. I'm exhausted and so are the horses."

Mantoez clearly wasn't human. He stood just under four feet tall and had pink eyes. "He must be one of the fairy folk," Weena commented in a whisper to Dendrox, "There are all different sorts, so many that everyone has just categorized them all into one big group."

This small man had short and curly red hair, a round cheerful face, and a small round nose. He had on a pair of plain brown pants and his shirt was dark blue with a yellow vest over it. "Sorry. You have any trouble during the night?" asked Mantoez with a concerned look.

"Nothing unusual, if that's what you mean," he gave him a knowing look.

"Okay, well that's good news," he commented detaching the horses from the carriage and leading them toward the stable.

"I'm heading to the inn. Take care out there," Vexcindor said with a wave and entered The Twisted Eye Tavern.

Weena and Dendrox decided they had better be on their way and continued down the street after Dookarnim.

"I think we had better travel during the day as well, like the carriage driver told that man. Perhaps we can get enough money somehow to buy all of us passage in one of the carriages," said Weena.

Dendrox told her, "It looks to me as if there is only the one carriage with three drivers each taking turns. I agree though. They would know better than us what dangers are out there, and that is besides the Killnarin."

They could see Dookarnim racing ahead to the end of the street where the bookstore was located.

"Hey, a cobbler," Dendrox pointed out as they passed the open door. There was a wooden sign overhead with a picture of a shoe and a tiny hammer painted on it. They could hear the cobbler going about his work within and they caught the faint scent of leather as they passed by. "Candra really needs a new pair of boots. She was complaining about the ones she has on, all the way over the mountains into this valley," Dendrox commented.

"Is that why she has been a little cruel now and then, because her boots have been hurting her feet?" Weena asked trying not to sound too offensive, but she meant what she had said.

<Zaylyn ><Quest For The Sword Of Anthrowst ><By Katrina Mandrake-Johnston >   <Ch 56> < 175 >

"Unfortunately, no," Dendrox chuckled and gave her a smile, "She's pretty much like that all the time."

"Great," she said sarcastically.

As they were passing by the window of a clothing shop, Weena exclaimed, "Oh, would you look at that dress!"

"It's nice," Dendrox said, clearly not very interested.

"It's so beautiful. The amount of work that must have gone into something like that! The intricate patterns, and…" she trailed off seeing that Dendrox didn't really care. Weena decided, "Maybe we should just hurry on to the bookstore. It's probably going to take a long while to find what we're looking for. A lot of people are counting on us."

The two of them approached the end of the street and the shop with a large wooden sign hanging over the door displaying a picture of an open book. They entered the shop and a little bell tinkled to announce their entrance.

<World of Zaylyn ><Quest For The Sword Of Anthrowst ><By Katrina Mandrake-Johnston ><Ch 57>

CHAPTER 57 =   THE BOOKSTORE

They found the place to be dimly lit by lanterns and that the whole shop had a musty smell to it. There were rows and rows of shelves and each long shelf had books packed very tightly along them. Many of the books, for which there was no more room for on the shelves, were neatly stacked in piles on the tables, the back counter, and even the floor.

There were three long tables placed end to end running down the center of the shop, and one rickety looking wooden chair positioned neatly at each. There was only a tiny area at each table that was free of books, and the books were stacked so high that you would feel as if you were in a miniature fort if you were to sit at one of the tables.

On each side of the tables, were three rows of long shelves that ran the length of the shop. Between the shelves there were books stacked neatly in a row down the length of the aisle. The smallest stack of books was piled as high as Weena's waist, while many towered high above her head.

The back counter, which they could barely see, was all the way at the very back of the shop. This also had stacks and stacks of books piled very high on it and also along the side of the counter all the way to the back wall.

"Well it looks as if it's all very organized, I guess, just incredibly crowded," Weena commented.

"What? Is someone there?" they heard an old man call out.

"Yes, we have a few questions," she called out blindly.

"Well come down to the counter, child, where I can see you," the old man's voice said in a quick snappy tone, "Just please, I beg of you, do not knock over any of the books. Everything is precisely organized, and most importantly, perfectly balanced. I will not be meeting my end under a landslide of books, you hear?"

They carefully began to make their way to the end of the shop.

"Didn't that man come in here? The one from the carriage? If he's in here, I don't see him anywhere," said the thief, as he skillfully maneuvered between the books and shelves.

As she inched along, Weena tried to hold her robes as closely to her as possible, being worried they would get caught and bring everything down upon them.

When they reached the counter, she called out again, "Hello?"

"There's no need to shout. Was there something I can help you with?" the voice said.

"Where are you?" she questioned with curiosity.

"I'm here at the counter, you silly girl," said the voice from behind the wall of books on top of the counter.

Weena tired to peer through the stacks of books, which completely obscured and obstructed whomever was behind the counter. Finally, she found a tiny space between the piles and was able to see a tiny white-haired man with a long, neatly combed beard and a little red cap on his bald head. He was dressed in white robes with a dark blue sash tied tightly at his waist.

<Zaylyn ><Quest For The Sword Of Anthrowst ><By Katrina Mandrake-Johnston >   <Ch 57> < 176 >

"Oh, there you are," she exclaimed almost laughing at how ridiculously overstocked this place was.

"I've found the book on tracking I was looking for, Karnez," a man's voice called out from somewhere at the front of the shop, "Thank-you. Maybe I'll be better for detecting ambushes, and animal attacks, and hopefully other things after reading this through."

"Good-day to you, Koosenor, and you're welcome," Karnez called out from behind the wall of books. They heard the tinkle of the bell, which meant that the carriage driver had left the shop. "That Koosenor is one of my best customers. He has such a yearning for knowledge," Karnez commented.

"We're trying to find out some information about a sword. We thought there may be a legend or something about it," Dendrox told the shopkeeper.

"Oh, a legendary sword? That does sound interesting, doesn't it?" he exclaimed a little too overzealous. Dookarnim emerged from out of the rows of books and shelves to approach the counter. "Oh, but it will have to wait just one minute," the shopkeeper told Weena and Dendrox.

"I think I've found it," Dookarnim told Karnez, "How much do I owe you?"

"Well let me see." The little man crawled out through a small space, just large enough for him to fit through, and escaped his tiny enclosure. Dookarnim handed him the book. "Oh, what's this? A book on rare plants, eh? I see you have marked off the pages with Silbreen and Dilkane. Now what would you be wanting to know about those for, eh?" Karnez asked raising an eyebrow as he looked up at the man.

"Would you just tell me how much I owe you? I don't have time for you to be nosey. I assure you, my intentions are noble. I really would like to get home as quickly as I can, for more reasons than one," he said with urgency in his voice.

"Alright, that will be two gold pieces, sir. When you are finished with the book, we will purchase it back from you for one gold piece," Karnez explained.

"Very well," said Dookarnim as he rummaged inside the burlap sack he had with him.

Dendrox heard the jingle of coins within the sack and he got a certain gleam in his eye that only Candra would have noticed if she had been there. Dendrox waited until the exchange was just about to take place and then positioned his boot in the right spot to execute his plan.

Dookarnim stepped forward, money in hand, and with his sack balanced loosely on his arm as he outstretched his hand to accept the book. Dookarnim tripped over Dendrox's boot, practically falling on top of Karnez. His sack fell to the floor spilling some of its contents.

"Oh, my goodness! I'm so sorry, I must have stumbled," he apologized to Karnez who appeared to be quite shaken by the experience.

"Here, let me help you," Dendrox offered, "You must have tripped over my boot. It's so terribly crowded in here, it forces one to stand so close to another. Anyway, let me help," he said bending down and helping Dookarnim to pick up the spilled contents of the sack, "It's the least I can do."

"Here, I'll help too," Weena offered.

"No, it's quite all right, we have it," Dendrox told her. Dendrox palmed one of the gold coins off the floor, but that was all he was able to manage.

"Thank-you," Dookarnim said to Dendrox for the help, "I really must be going now."

Karnez handed him the book and bid him good-bye. Once he had left, the tiny man turned to Weena and Dendrox and said, "Now you were saying something about a sword?"

"Yes," Weena told him, "The Sword of Anthrowst. Do you know if there is a book about it? Or perhaps, if you have heard any bit of information about it?"

Karnez looked at them both suspiciously, "I have heard of it. I'm probably one of the few that have. I have a book here with a bit about the legend. I'll get it for you." The little man disappeared amongst the shelves and books.

"Well this is good news, isn't it? At least we don't have to search for the book ourselves. That's what I was dreading," commented Weena.

"I don't know. I don't like the way he was looking at us," he told her.

"It will be fine. He was suspicious of the other man as well. I suspect he is so overprotective of

<Zaylyn ><Quest For The Sword Of Anthrowst ><By Katrina Mandrake-Johnston >   <Ch 57> < 177 >

his books that it pains him to let them out of his possession. I mean look at this, he's practically made himself a little house out of books at this counter," she explained. Weena then lowered her voice, "How are we to pay for this though? Do you think he will let us take a look at the book without buying it?"

"Don't worry about it. I think I've figured a way to get us what we want," he assured her.

"You're not planning to steal the book, are you?" she whispered.

"No, but I managed to swipe a coin," he whispered back to her, "Just let me handle this."

Karnez returned with a small book with a leather cover that had been dyed green. "It will be two gold pieces to purchase, and we will buy the book back from you for one gold piece when you are finished," he explained holding the book out to them.

"What if we just quickly look up the information we need here?" Dendrox suggested, "Wouldn't that be the equivalent of one gold coin for the use of the book?"

"I suppose, but the book may not leave the premises. I will be watching you very carefully," Karnez said eyeing both of them with a stern expression.

Dendrox deposited the coin into the man's tiny hand, and then taking the book from him, passed it to Weena.

Weena took the book over to the nearest table and sat down. She opened the book and began to read within the tiny area of table that was clear. Weena found herself actually enjoying the little enclosure the books made for her. Dendrox watched patiently over her shoulder as she read.

"I hope you two are not thinking of retrieving the sword. Only an utter fool would wish that kind of doom upon the world," Karnez commented.

Weena continued to read by the dim light of the lanterns for quite some time.

She whispered to Dendrox finally, "Well it is an actual sword. I thought that maybe there was a chance it wasn't a sword at all and that it was just a name. You know how they sometimes do that?"

"Yeah, yeah, like the Wings of Aramist or the Gem of Irigite," Dendrox said, getting impatient, "What does it say about the damn sword?"

"I've never heard of those," Weena said hoping to learn more and ease her curiosity.

Dendrox let out a sigh, but indulged her by saying, "The Wings of Aramist is a suit of armour supposedly so light it allows the wearer to move with great speed. The Gem of Irigite isn't a gem at all. It's a large polished seashell that, when the sunlight hits it, shows the location of the cave entrance leading to the massive treasure trove. I used to love that story as a child. I can't believe you never heard it. But, what about this sword?"

"Yes, sorry," said Weena and then she went on to explain, "This sword, if used to kill a wizard, will undo all the magic he or she has ever conjured. No wonder this sword was broken into pieces. Three, to be exact. The extent of the damage this could do, it's incredible. If what this says is true, and for example, if it was used on me, and remember that I have not cast very many spells at all in my life, this is what would happen," she paused thinking back, "Candra's wound would open up and she would become poisoned once more, the wound of the spider I healed would reopen, and the wound in me from the second arrow Candra fired at me would also open up. Well I guess the wound in me wouldn't matter because I'd be dead anyway if I were killed by the sword of Anthrowst. The Shield spell I used twice, once to save Asdella and myself from the blast in the tunnels and the second time to block Candra's arrow, in those it wouldn't have any effect if the spell was to be reversed as that would be turning back time and altering physical events. Same with the Shield spell cast back at the tavern. I hadn't realized just how many spells I've cast. I guess I have had more success than what I give myself credit for. Pure luck is more behind my spells than anything really. I would never be as foolish to think that I could rely on my spell casting abilities. I'd get us all killed for sure. But, anyway, about the sword, what I'm saying is that with the Shield spells, Asdella and I wouldn't suddenly be engulfed in flames and an arrow wouldn't just appear to punch into me. Do you see?"

Dendrox said, "Yes, it only undoes things the magic has caused to happen. Which means all the damage the Killnarin did and all the deaths they've caused will not be reversed, only the spell that summoned them here. They would be drawn back to wherever they came from and we would have

<Zaylyn ><Quest For The Sword Of Anthrowst ><By Katrina Mandrake-Johnston >   <Ch 57> < 178 >

stopped them from doing any further damage."

"Yes, exactly," said Weena. *"Well, I see now that he not only knew about Candra taking my mother's ring, but also about her shooting a couple of arrows at me."*

"And this is only if the sword even exists and only if what this book says has any truth to it," Dendrox reminded her.

"Well, yes. But anyway, you can see what kind of damage this sword could do if it fell into the wrong hands," and then she added, "And here's another thing to consider, how do we know that this wizard, Dranngore, hasn't done some good with his spells throughout his life? If everything reverses, we may be doing more harm than good. And still, what if a spell which was intended for evil actually made it possible for things to be better in the end?"

"Does it say anything of where the pieces of the sword might be?" he asked her.

"No, it doesn't," Weena told him with disappointment.

"So all we've really learnt is that an impossible sword to find has now become even more difficult because the damn thing has been broken into pieces and no doubt scattered all over the damn place. Forget it. It's all completely useless. I'm done with all of this. I'll be at the tavern," Dendrox said despondently and quickly left the shop leaving Weena sitting alone at the table.

"Dendrox, wait!" she called after him, but he was already out the door.

"I take it, you're done with the book then?" Karnez asked the young wizard.

"Yes, and thank-you," she said politely, and then she began to slowly and carefully make her way down the aisle to the exit.

Dendrox was already at the tavern door, when she emerged from the bookstore.

"Wait! Please!" she called out, but he didn't seem to hear her.

Weena finally caught up with him inside the inn. The carriage driver, Vexcindor, was seated at one of the smaller tables eating a hearty meal. Asdella and Vordin were sitting at one of the tables as well, but they purposely avoided eye contact, still being wary of the bounty hunters.

"We still have the rooms until nightfall, right? I'm going to get some sleep," he told her.

"Why did you run off like that?" she asked, feeling hurt by his actions.

"I didn't want to have to listen to some big speech on why we shouldn't give up and bla, bla, bla. It's just hopeless or at least that's how it seems. I'm just tired, that's all," he admitted, "It's been so much already with everything, and now we find out the sword has been broken into three separate pieces. That means we will have to go on three perilous quests instead of one just to get the sword! And then there is the matter of getting the pieces back together again. I just want all this to end and for everyone to be okay. I need to get a bit more sleep, hopefully clear my mind."

"Alright. I'm going to get some rest as well then, in my own room," she told him.

Dendrox retired to his room, but Weena stopped to speak with the innkeeper.

Vordin whispered to Asdella, "Three pieces? That can't be good. At least some of us have so far found out something about the sword."

Asdella suggested, "Maybe we should get some sleep too. This time in a real bed. Candra and Nodwel's rooms are still free, we might as well use them. It doesn't seem right to come all this way and not even get a chance to sleep in a proper bed."

"I agree. I'm still extremely exhausted," Vordin told her.

They too retired to the two remaining rooms the innkeeper had provided for them.

<World of Zaylyn ><Quest For The Sword Of Anthrowst ><By Katrina Mandrake-Johnston ><Ch 58>

CHAPTER 58 = FURTHER EXPLORATION OF VACKIINDMIRE

"Excuse me? I was just wondering where everyone was," Weena said to the innkeeper.

"I don't quite get what you mean, dear," he replied.

"Outside, there weren't many people out on the street. Is there some event that we haven't heard

<Zaylyn ><Quest For The Sword Of Anthrowst ><By Katrina Mandrake-Johnston >   <Ch 58> < 179 >
of?" she inquired.

"Oh, I see. You aren't from within Dee'ellkka Valley, are you? The towns and villages are quite tiny within the valley compared to the towns and villages of other lands," he explained and then he motioned her a little closer as he said, "Plus, it doesn't help the population much to have so many people go missing and with all the unusual deaths and all. It pains me to realize just how accustomed we have become to all of it."

Weena commented, "Oh, that's awful."

"Yeah, I believe the population here in Vackiindmire is anywhere from a hundred and fifty to two hundred at any given time. There's only about forty houses here, most of our number comes from visitors. A lot of merchants come here to our marketplace and end up staying for several months at a time before moving on to another location. The villages north of here have most likely anywhere from seventy-five to a hundred people each."

"Really? I had no idea," said Weena.

"I bet you haven't really had time to explore Vackiindmire as of yet. It's actually quite small compared to something you're probably used to," said the innkeeper. "The marketplace takes up a fair amount of space, but after that, there is just a small cluster of shops on the east side of town. On the west side, there is this inn of course and its stable, then farther south are a few houses, then a blacksmith's, and farther south still, are more houses along the south wall. If you travel all the way west, behind the tavern, you'll find the rest and majority of the houses all along the length of the west wall."

"I hadn't realized Vackiindmire was so small. I guess I wasn't really paying much attention to how big the town was when we traveled here," said Weena.

He told her, "Actually, miss, Vackiindmire is the largest in the valley by size. I believe Shirkint may have a larger population though, could be two hundred and fifty to three hundred people there. I can never tell, as that place is always swarming with adventurers and the like. At times, I'm sure there must be near four hundred or more, especially during the competitions they hold."

"Well Dexcsin was a tiny little place, only a cluster of a few buildings really, but I had no knowledge about the other places in the valley," she explained, "It's good to know. All I had heard was that this was the best place to learn spells, Shirkint in-particular."

"Yes, I've heard Shirkint is the best place also. The magic energy is supposed to be more concentrated there or something like that. I don't really know very much about spells, but I've heard it's far easier to learn them there, and supposedly taking less time. But you've been to Dexcsin, have you? That's the smallest village in the valley. I've been there a couple times. It's a really peaceful place. Hardly anyone bothers to travel there; it being so far out of the way. Not many people there either, fifty maybe sixty is all. They do have some wonderful festivals though. Were you lucky enough to see one of their dances?" he asked.

"Ah, no," she said as the memory of the village gave her a chill. She didn't have the heart to tell him what had happened there, plus he probably wouldn't have believed her.

"Now that's a sight to remember," the innkeeper commented, "During one of these festivals, there is such a variety of food with dancing and music all outside by firelight. Merchants from other villages and towns sometimes set up their tables in the main hall displaying their exotic wares. Some of the younger women dress in colorful flowing costumes and perform a dance involving different colored sashes. The coordinated dance gives the viewers a wonderful and vividly colorful show of beauty and youth, and the feeling that they are beholding something rare and magical. It's as if a rainbow falls in love with a lightening bolt and they have a wild and passionate dance together, which is what the story behind the dance portrays. It's a shame you missed it."

"I should probably get some rest. Thank-you very much, you've been most helpful and very kind," said Weena and retired to her room in the back of the inn.

Candra, who had been wandering the streets of Vackiindmire for most of the morning, ended up at the blacksmith's. She had struck up a conversation with the blacksmith about different types of

<Zaylyn ><Quest For The Sword Of Anthrowst ><By Katrina Mandrake-Johnston >   <Ch 58> < 180 >

weapons and the damage they are capable of, in hope that she might gain some knowledge of how to battle the Killnarin with less difficulty. Her efforts were futile, but she was enjoying herself. She was examining the various weapons and asking the friendly blacksmith many questions about his work.

The blacksmith was a dwarf and had a wide barrel-like chest. His muscular bare arms and his face were marked with soot and he was covered in a gleam of sweat from the heat of the forge. He wore a thick leather apron down the front of his body, and his leather boots came all the way up to his knees. The dwarf was bald except for a thin fringe of light brown hair around the edges with a closely cropped beard and a thick mustache.

Unlike the traditional workshop of a blacksmith, the building was enclosed on all four sides by thick stone walls and only the roof was open to the air. She assumed that there had to have been a good reason for the design, but dared not ask. The door opened and sent a cool breeze into the shop, which Candra welcomed. She had not minded the heat from before, as the blacksmith worked at his craft, and it had not been uncomfortable for her to have stayed there as long as she had already.

An older man, a human, perhaps a little over the age of fifty, entered the shop. He scratched at his squarish jaw saying, "Pretty warm in here, ain't it?" He was a little shorter than Dendrox with a thick upper body and his head was completely bald except for a pair of bushy black eyebrows. A small leather sack was slung over his shoulder. Candra just nodded a polite 'hello' and then continued to inspect a finely made short sword. "Gornam? That blade I ask for ready?" the man asked the blacksmith.

"Garnash, you best be comin' back later today. That multi-bladed dagger has proved to be a bit more troublesome than I had first thought. As you can see, I'm still working on it. Feel free to wait if you'd like, but I know how you mind the heat of the forge so."

"You know me well, friend. So later today then? Late afternoon perhaps?" he asked Gornam.

"Yes, I'm certain that I will have it for you by then. How's the butcher shop of yours up at Torrnell?" the blacksmith asked Garnash as he began to hammer the piece of metal at the anvil again.

"Oh, well enough. We're still having a bit of trouble with the raids from the trolls, but we do our best despite them. There's a dragon now as well. Snatches up a couple of sheep now and then, but it hasn't put too much of a damper on my business," he explained, "If anything, I think the beast may be the reason the trolls have eased up on their attacks."

"Don't know how you can be so calm 'bout all that," and then Gornam questioned, "Your younger brother, Gulair, he's doing all right in his job at The Old Scabbard Inn? Don't know, some of the stories I hear about Shirkint make me pretty nervous if you ask me. I hear The Black Shadow frequents that very inn. Gives me the shivers to think your brother is in the same room as that... that..."

"Whoa, hush now. You know you shouldn't speak of such things," he said in a frantic tone, "I'll be back later this afternoon. Take care Gornam and remember to watch what you say." Garnash left the blacksmith's, closing the door behind him.

Candra now had a curious interest in the multi-bladed dagger that the blacksmith was making. She thought of Dendrox and how he would marvel over such a weapon. She considered an attempt to steal it when it was finally finished, but she knew such a thing would draw unwanted attention and she needed to be careful for both their sakes in case the bounty hunters were still about.

<World of Zaylyn ><Quest For The Sword Of Anthrowst ><By Katrina Mandrake-Johnston ><Ch 59>

CHAPTER 59 =   DENDROX'S NIGHTMARE

Dendrox had the dream again...

He found himself alone in the dark of night, the moon and stars shining brightly in a cloudless sky. He could see the tombstones around him and he let out an angry curse, as he knew this dream all too well.

An eerie unnatural mist began to roll along the ground. The fear inside him began to rise, as he knew what would come next and that there wasn't any chance of escape or anywhere to escape to.

He could smell the damp musty smell of the soil, and the cool crisp air chilled his skin. It all

<Zaylyn ><Quest For The Sword Of Anthrowst ><By Katrina Mandrake-Johnston >   <Ch 59> < 181 >
seemed so real and every time he had this dream, he could never bring himself to overcome his fear and realize that this was only a dream and nothing more. Except for the sound of his heartbeat quickening and his breathing becoming more rapid with fear, there was only silence.

Then he heard a horrible haunting wail from somewhere nearby. There was the faint but distinct sound of crumbling dirt, as a skeletal hand worked its way up from its grave to the surface.

He could see now that there were more rising out of the soil from all around him, escaping their graves, and shambling out of their tombs toward him. Weapons, in the hands of the slain, were being made ready once again as the corpses pulled themselves into life and action in their battered and broken armour.

Dendrox frantically looked all around in a panic for somewhere to run to, as the moaning and wailing horde of bone and rotting flesh began to close in on him.

It was now too late for they were upon him. Bony fingers pulled him to the ground, tearing at his clothes and clawing into his skin. Rusty weapons were thrust into his gut again and again, as the undead creatures stared with blank, lifeless eyes. Dendrox was screaming in sheer terror and was still screaming when he violently awoke.

He was thankful no one was around, as he was embarrassed and knew that this was just the type of thing Candra would love to ridicule him about. It was one of her ways of dealing with weakness in others where she thought there shouldn't be. This is why he hadn't told her about his frightful reoccurring dream. For him, it was not something that he could just laugh about or simply overcome for fear of being teased about it.

There was a knock at his door and the sound of Weena's voice calling his name. "Dendrox? You all right? Dendrox?"

When he came to the door and opened it, she suggested that they go to the magic shop the innkeeper had spoken of, in hope of discovering more information about the sword. He had fallen asleep fully dressed, so he simply nodded and followed her into the main room of the inn. He still felt as if the odds were stacked impossibly high against them for finding the pieces of the Sword of Anthrowst, but he didn't want to give up all hope just yet.

Weena could see that the innkeeper, who normally was at his desk, was absent and that Narten had taken his place instead. No one else was in the tavern at that moment as far as they could tell.

Narten was wearing the same clothes he had the night before and still had the apron tied about his waist. Weena wondered if he had gotten a break at all from his work since then. His hair had been neatly combed away from his handsome face and his bright blue eyes kept looking expectantly around to the point where Weena got the impression that perhaps he was waiting or hoping for someone to show.

Before Weena or Dendrox could say anything, Narten announced, "Innkeeper is asleep. I watch the place for him so he can get some rest. Otherwise, he runs the whole tavern by himself, night and day. If it's something urgent, I can wake him. It isn't, is it?"

"Oh no," Weena answered, "We just need directions to the magic shop is all."

"Sorry," Narten apologized, "I always get nervous when he puts me in charge of things like this. Just go south down the main street from the town gates, then turn left when you come to the bakery, go all the way to the end of the street, and that's where it will be. It's right across from the marketplace."

"Thanks, it shouldn't be too hard to find then," said Dendrox leaving the inn with Weena.

<World of Zaylyn ><Quest For The Sword Of Anthrowst ><By Katrina Mandrake-Johnston ><Ch 60>

CHAPTER 60 =   THE THIEVES

It was late afternoon by the time they left the tavern, and Weena and Dendrox walked side-by-side down the well kept main street of Vackiindmire. They passed by the bench on the far end just outside the cobbler's shop where they had been sitting earlier that day, but this time they continued farther into town down along the main road. On this side of the shop, there were two small windows and both of them had their little blue curtains drawn.

<Zaylyn ><Quest For The Sword Of Anthrowst ><By Katrina Mandrake-Johnston >   <Ch 60> < 182 >

A teenaged couple holding hands, their faces beaming with large smiles, walked past Weena and Dendrox. *"Isn't this what we should have? Dendrox won't hold my hand or even hardly look at me,"* Weena said to herself with disappointment, *"I don't know what to think anymore."*

Farther ahead they could see a white door with pink trim, which was the door to the teashop. As they passed the shop, they could smell a splendid combination of teas coming from within. A pregnant woman, who had been waddling very slowly down the street rubbing and trying to support her enormous belly with her hand, entered the teashop.

Next to the teashop was the butcher shop, and a father and his tiny son exited. The little boy was holding his father's hand and wearing a large happy smile. The father, who was looking affectionately at his child, carried a big package of meat for their dinner. The little boy waved at Dendrox and Weena as they passed by.

Next to the butcher was the bakery and the scent of freshly baked bread filled the air as they approached. A mother and her young daughter were coming out of the bakery. The daughter had a large bag of rolls in her tiny arms. The mother smiled at how independent her daughter was trying to be and looked prepared to rescue their purchase in case it was too much for her. Weena giggled as the bag was almost as big as the girl and her little eyes were trying to peer over the top to see where she was going.

On the other side of the street, opposite the butcher shop was an alley in-between the tavern and a small row of houses. Up ahead they could see two boys running around in the street with wooden swords pretending to be on some grand adventure. Their mother called out from one of the houses telling them that it was time for their dinner.

Dendrox noticed the two rough-looking men whispering back and forth over by the entrance to the alley.

"Bad news, those two," Dendrox whispered to her, "We should stay clear. We can't afford to draw attention to ourselves with all that has been going on."

"Hey you!" the younger of the two called out. He wore a simple long-sleeved white shirt, reddish-brown pants, and a pair of black leather boots. He was a fairly handsome man except that there was something unnerving and definitely unfriendly about his dark brown eyes. "Yeah, you!" he said to Weena and Dendrox, "Come here a minute, we have something to show you!" The younger man, who had short black hair and a thin mustache, now started to casually stroll over to them, while the older man kept eagerly waving them over to him.

"Damn it! Listen, don't do anything stupid," Dendrox whispered to Weena, "Do what they say. I don't want to give those bounty hunters a reason to get involved if they're about. If this gets serious, don't worry; I can handle them. Just don't panic if there is a need for blood."

Weena gave him a frightened nod. She wasn't sure which frightened her more, the two men or the fact that Dendrox was prepared to fight them to the death if trouble started between them.

The older man had a stupid grin on his face, not realizing that Dendrox knew exactly what they were intending. He had blonde hair and a short-cropped beard. Under his light brown eyes was a large crooked nose, obviously having been broken several times in the past.

The man with the thin black mustache came up to them and firmly ushered them over toward the alley and then a little way into it, all the time saying, "You won't believe what we found! You just have to see this! It won't take but a minute."

"Not very original are you? This actually works for you two? A pair of pathetic amateur fools is what you are, and if either of you try anything, you'll be a couple of dead ones," Dendrox thought to himself in anger.

A dagger tip pressed up against the small of Dendrox's back once they were away from the street and far from curious eyes, just as Dendrox had expected.

"Alright girly, hand it over," said the older man. Under his black jacket which fell open at his sides, this man wore a blue tunic over his fair sized belly. Weena wondered if he had a weapon concealed within the folds of his clothing. She suspected maybe a knife at his side, hidden from view under his jacket, as she caught the glint of metal every now and then. She knew Dendrox was being

<Zaylyn ><Quest For The Sword Of Anthrowst ><By Katrina Mandrake-Johnston >   <Ch 60> < 183 >
threatened with a dagger by the other man.

"Hand over what? I don't know what you mean," said Weena.

The man let out an impatient sigh, resting his hand at his side near the edge of his jacket where Weena was sure now that he also had to be carrying a weapon. As he stared into her wide and frightened blue eyes, his gaze was cold and threatening and he said to her, "Don't make us resort to violence, honey. That fat pouch hangin' 'round your pretty little hips there. It's ours now. Hand it over." At first she hesitated, but then remembering that Candra had taken her mother's ring and that it no longer was in the pouch, she handed it over to them. The ring was safe in the elf's possession as far as Weena hoped. She was thankful, as she would have lost her most precious possession to these thieves now if Candra hadn't taken it. "Thank-you kindly," he said with a smirk as he accepted it.

The younger one, still holding the dagger to Dendrox, said, "Now get lost if ya know what's good for ya, and don't try anything neither."

"Alright, we don't want any trouble here. We'll go peacefully," Dendrox said. He wanted to punch the smug look off the older man's ugly face. He had a feeling that it was he who had instigated this little plan of theirs. Dendrox was afraid for Weena and didn't want to aggravate the situation any further.

Weena and Dendrox left the alley, and Dendrox muttered, "We're skipping the damn magic shop. Let's just go back to the inn." He took her by the arm and started leading her quickly back in the direction of the tavern door.

"I definitely agree. That was really frightening. Good thing there wasn't anything of value in there," she commented.

Dendrox looked furious that this had happened and that he couldn't really do anything about it. He wasn't being very gentle leading her back to the inn as he was. It made her feel as though she were a misbehaving child being dragged back to safety and to be scolded.

"Well let's just hope they're not the type that decide we somehow did that on purpose and come after us. Some blame and even attack the victim for not having anything of value when they have gone to all the trouble of robbing them. I've met people who are that insane before," he told her pulling her quickly along and opening the door.

Weena and Dendrox entered the inn, and upon seeing Nodwel, came to seat themselves at the large table next to him closest to the fireplace. They were still wary of the bounty hunters and didn't want to take any chances.

<World of Zaylyn ><Quest For The Sword Of Anthrowst ><By Katrina Mandrake-Johnston ><Ch 61>

CHAPTER 61 =   FATE OF THE THIEVES

Lurking in the shadows, hidden from sight, The Black Shadow had watched as the two thieves had taken Weena's pouch. He had watched as Dendrox and Weena headed quickly back to The Twisted Eye Tavern trying to maintain a low profile. He watched until his insatiable hunger could be restrained no longer.

His eager dark form crawled along the side of the building like a spider, his black cloak moving like liquid about him until it was hard to determine if he even still had a humanoid form. His eyes began to glow a deep red as the hunger burned inside him.

He leapt across the street with incredible speed and landed like a great black cat with grace and silence. The two men were below in the alley. He could sense their presence and the hunger intensified.

Instead of rushing in for the kill like the beast inside him desperately wanted, he held himself back. He crept into the shadows near the back of the alley where the rooftop met the high wall of one of the houses. There he sat trying to fight his evil nature and the need to feed. The row of houses, their side walls connecting, ran the length to the north wall of the town. The backs of these houses formed a wall of sorts continuing the alley north along the back of the inn where most of the windows to the rooms were. Dendrox's room had its window facing the alley, but it was situated just before the alley turned to the right and around the corner of the tavern.

<Zaylyn ><Quest For The Sword Of Anthrowst ><By Katrina Mandrake-Johnston >   <Ch 61> < 184 >

"Am I no better than Dranngore? He does not care about who he hurts in his ludicrous plan for power and revenge. I care, don't I? At least a small part of me does and doesn't want to hurt anyone anymore.

"I do care. I think about all the people I hurt when I take a life. I have to admit that the larger evil part of me gets excited at the thought of this, but it's the good part, no matter how small, that has to be the one that matters. I don't want to be a monster anymore. I don't want to be known as the creature in the dark that takes friends and family members away.

"I could simply kill Dranngore and end all of this he's causing, even send the Killnarin back to where they belong. But I don't want to get involved like that. If I kill the wizard, in doing so, I'm giving in to my evil nature no matter if the outcome is for good. I don't want to intentionally kill anyone, no matter what the reason. I may not be able to get control over myself again before I've killed several others after Dranngore is slain.

"Sending the Killnarin back would mean I'd be using more of my powers than I've been allowing myself. The hold over myself and my evil nature is so fragile as it is, sending them back would probably weaken that hold. I'm afraid of what might happen. Being so close to those creatures and knowing their evil, may fuel my own enough to lose control of it. Then I'd be no better than one of those beasts. I'd be much worse and do far more harm than any of them for sure. I can't allow that.

"I have the most power in all of Zaylyn. I can do pretty much anything and everything I wish with ease. I have all the power in this whole damn world, and all I really want is what they all take for granted.

"I can make people do what I want, feel and believe what I want them to, but in doing that, I can't fool myself. Love and friendship can never be real when I know it to be fake. I suffer in this loneliness I am forced to endure. Must it always be so? No matter how hard I fight the evil inside me?

"I could fool people into thinking I am one of them, but that just angers me, knowing that if they knew who I really was, that they would despise me and that any kindness they would have shown me would immediately become lost and meaningless. Although, maybe I should try to interact with people once again. I feel that perhaps I could be around this group without the risk of casualties.

"What, am I trying to fool myself? With me, there is always an incredible risk of death. No one is safe around me.

"But I have to try, don't I? Otherwise, why go to all this trouble to fight and go against my evil nature in the first place? There has to be some sort of reward for me, however small, otherwise I will find myself slipping, relaxing my hold over the evil and find myself starting to think 'What's the use in trying?'. It's so hard to control myself and there has to be something to fight for, as it would otherwise be hopeless.

"When the urges start to take over, my reasons for sparing lives, for holding back even though it will mean the urges will become stronger, my reasoning simply seems to dwindle away until it loses all its importance and until only the need to feed remains. I cannot bring myself to stop before I drain them completely. The hunger is always stronger than the few good intensions I may have had beforehand. And then, the evil is forever pushing at me to do far worse, whether the hunger is still in need of being satisfied or not. Every time I try to fight it, the hunger and my evil urges become more and more intense, and with it, a greater chance of me losing control altogether. If that ever happened, the evil monster within me would slaughter hundreds just for the fun of it, and I wouldn't be able to stop myself, no matter how hard I tried. I'd be no better than one of the Killnarin, only far deadlier and far more cruel and malicious.

"Is that a risk I am willing to take? I am constantly fighting a battle within myself; that massive amount of evil against my few good intensions. Do I want to take the chance that the evil will finally and completely consume me? Is it worth it to endanger the lives of many in the effort to save a few?

"I need something that will scream out to me, to make me stop myself, to make me fight no matter how strong the need to feed is, even if it means the hunger and the urges will become stronger. The chance for friendship is strong enough, isn't it? Enough to maintain a firm hold over the hunger? The chance for love? I don't want to be alone anymore. Perhaps I am being selfish to think I can have *more.*

"If I can prove to myself that I can be among others without being afraid of what I might do to them, that is definitely worth it. So many people fear me and I know it's for good reason, but I, in fact, am the one who fears myself the most, for I truly know what I am able to do… and of all the things I find myself wanting to do.

"I was able to stop myself from killing my last victim, the man in the forest. That's a start in the right direction, isn't it? But I fear, in doing so, that it has made it harder for me to hold the evil back. It burns within me, so greatly intensifying the hunger, furious that I have dared refuse its will."

He could hear the two thieves below.

"Nice fat pouch, eh?" the older man said to the other.

The younger man tucked the dagger into a tiny scabbard hidden inside the top of his boot and he said to the other, "Well, whatcha waiting for? Open it up."

The blonde portly man opened the pouch and took out the contents. "What's this?!" he exclaimed, looking at the doll Weena had picked up earlier.

"Eh?" the younger asked with curiosity.

"There's just this doll inside it, and a flame box!" he told him.

"A doll? Are you sure there's nothin' else in there?" he asked, "Gold, maybe a couple gems, a bit of jewelry, anything?"

"I'm telling you, no," the older man replied firmly.

"It must be cursed," the man with the black mustache told him, his dark brown eyes growing wide with fear.

"What are you talking about?" the other laughed.

"She was a sorceress or somethin', right? And look, how this doll looks sort of like her? Yellow hair and blue dress or robes or whatever, just like hers? She's out for revenge now, she is. Waiting for us to turn our backs," he suggested looking all around for any sign of danger.

The blonde man with the short beard tossed the doll, flame box, and empty pouch to the ground as he ridiculed the other saying, "Don't be such a damn fool."

The black haired man got a strange confused look on his face, and then he said starting to panic, "Hey, all of a sudden I can't move!"

"Quit playin' around," the other scolded, "The damn thing's not cursed."

"Well somethin's goin' on that's not right," he snapped back at him, annoyed that he wasn't taking him seriously.

The older man was getting frustrated with him. "Listen," he said to him, clearly irritated, "I'm serious, quit playing around. I'm not puttin' up with one of your idiotic pranks!"

"No, it's the truth!" he said honestly, "I can't move!"

The blonde man just stood there glaring at him for a few seconds, and then the younger man said with fear, "What was that?!"

"What now?" asked the other with a sigh.

"I thought I saw somethin'…" he told him, his eyes straining to see into the darkness at the back of the alley.

"Quit fooling around, I mean it!" the older thief warned.

A worried and terrified look crossed his face as he said hurriedly, "Hey! There it is again! There's somethin' crawling down the wall! Down at the back of the alley!"

"I told you, quit playing around!" he warned again, now becoming extremely angry with his companion's apparent foolishness.

The other man was very frightened now and still could not move from the spot where he stood. "It's somethin' awful, I just know it!" he whined.

"Look, there's nothing there," the older man tried to tell him, staring into the darkness at the back of the alley.

Then he saw two blood red eyes start to glow in the blackness like two orbs of fire come into view. Then The Black Shadow leapt from the shadows at the astonished man, while the other tried desperately

<Zaylyn ><Quest For The Sword Of Anthrowst ><By Katrina Mandrake-Johnston >   <Ch 61> < 186 >

to run but found that he still was unable to move as before and that something magical must be holding him there.

The Black Shadow viciously bit deep into the throat of the older man. The younger man cried out in terror, but found that not only was he unable to move, that now his voice had no sound.

The Black Shadow drank heavily. He was going to kill this man, if he continued. Most of him wanted to, but a little part of him was screaming out at him to stop. This little part of him was so very faint in his mind, but he knew it was there, and he desperately wanted himself to listen to it. But so many times before, it had been drowned out by the excited pounding of his heartbeat, the incredible hunger, and the viciousness inside him. He feared that this would happen once again and that he would end up killing this man despite his efforts. It was so hard to think clearly, his dark and savage instincts taking over in a warm flood into his mind.

"*Don't kill him. Don't kill…*" the little voice called out from his mind.

But he wasn't stopping. He was trying so hard to pull himself away, but found he couldn't, no matter how hard he tried. He was a slave to the hunger and his evil nature, and it was too much for him to fight. He had gone too long without feeding fully. He had held his evil desires back too long for them to be subdued any longer.

"*No!*" he screamed at himself, feeling the man's body becoming limp as he began to pass out from the loss of blood. "*It's not too late, if you stop right now! It will take him a long time to recover, but it's not too late!*" he told himself.

When he finally dropped the man's body to the ground, he was dead. The evil inside him had won yet again, as it always did in the end.

The Black Shadow's entire body burned with the pleasure of the kill, while his evil nature sent a cold chill throughout him as he started to imagine all the terrible things he was wanting to do. He stared at the remaining man from beneath his black hooded cloak. He let out a low and malicious growl, which sent shivers down the frightened man's spine.

He wanted to tear this helpless man to pieces. He wanted to hear him scream in terror, which would also bring him more victims when others came to this man's aid. He wanted him to run, providing him with a chase that would open up all sorts of possibilities for inflicting terror upon the entire town. He had felt this man's fear growing as he had helplessly watched his friend being fed upon. The fear he had caused this man excited The Black Shadow greatly. An evil grin began to spread across his blood-stained lips.

However, the hunger was the strongest need in him at the moment, not the desire to create chaos and terror. The Black Shadow approached the man from behind and firmly grasped his shoulder. With a vicious snarl, he then grabbed the man by his short black hair with his other hand, yanking his head back to expose the flesh of his neck. His fangs eagerly bit in deeply, making the man cry out in fear and pain. He made sure that everyone else in the surrounding area was deaf to the man's cries, as he did not want to be interrupted.

He drank slowly this time and increased the pain the man felt, enjoying his suffering. The man was screaming, and uselessly and desperately trying to struggle free.

The Black Shadow then noticed the doll lying on the ground. It had become soiled lying there in the dirt within the alley, and its black button eyes seemed to be looking right at him, as if sadly watching him destroy all he had fought for.

"*What am I doing?! No, I have to stop! I already killed his friend! I have to stop! I can't let myself become nothing more than an evil monster! The horrible thoughts going through my head, I can't lose myself to the point where I decide to act on them. And of the others? What will I do to them? Weena, Dendrox, Nodwel… they are so close and in danger… as is everyone else in the town. The increased suffering I'm causing this man, prolonging his death, it's just not right. No, I can't simply not prolong his death. I have to stop myself from killing him, not simply make it a quick and painless death. I can't allow myself to kill this man!*"

The Black Shadow released him and pushed him away, sending him backwards to land on the ground. The frightened man instinctively put his hand up to his neck in an effort to try to stop the

<Zaylyn ><Quest For The Sword Of Anthrowst ><By Katrina Mandrake-Johnston >   <Ch 61> < 187 >

bleeding, even though he knew he would surely bleed to death in a very short time. The Black Shadow caused the wound beneath the man's fingers to heal, and the man felt at where the wound had closed in amazement, finally taking his hand away and all the time staring in disbelief at the mysterious black figure in front of him.

The Black Shadow wanted to dive at him again, the blood still warm in his throat. He felt his mind starting to cloud over as he began to lose control again.

"Please," the man sobbed, "I promise. I won't steal ever again. Please, I'll do anything you want!"

Again, a low deep growl rumbled within him, his eyes flashing red. His fangs were eager to pierce warm flesh again. "*No*," his mind told him, as he tried to control himself. The evil grin that had spread across his lips, faded away, his mind saying, "*I must do what I must, and that is feed, but the evil inside me will not get the satisfaction of another kill!*"

"That guy I knifed a month ago? I didn't really mean it. I'm sorry. I won't do anything like that again. Please, I beg you! …Wait! You're The Black Shadow, aren't you?!" the man said, his voice trembling and his fear rising even more, "What the hell are you?! Oh no, please no! You can't be him!! I'll do anything! I swear!! Just don't!! Please! Let me go! I won't tell anyone what I saw, I swear!! You don't have to kill me!" he begged.

"*I will not be the monster anymore. I'm no better than a Killnarin then. I don't want to be hated like that*," he said to himself sadly. There was a horrible pain in his gut forcing him to almost lose control again. "*Damn it! I still need to feed!*" he thought in anger and frustration, wondering if he would be able to stop himself a second time.

"Why won't you say anything?!" the man wailed. He grabbed the man by his shirt and lifted him up from the ground with incredible strength. "No…" he screamed as The Black Shadow bit once more into the man.

This time he took the pain of his bite away. The man had suffered enough.

He was able to stop this time, leaving the man alive, but barely, and unconscious. The Black Shadow collected Weena's belongings and simply walked through the wall of the tavern as if it were air.

Making himself invisible, he walked through the large kitchen where Narten was preparing several dinners, and then he passed through yet another wall to enter Weena's room. Realizing that there was no real reason for her to return here except for her lantern, he entered Dendrox's room and laid the items on the bed, as he knew about the problems they were having with the scissors.

The Black Shadow would have killed again and perhaps others within the town had the doll not been there to help him to get himself back under control. He would not allow himself to become a monster.

He had wondered if his interest in Dranngore and the wizard's actions were motivated because he and the Killnarin were simply threatening his food supply. The Black Shadow had heard Candra suggest the same thing on their way to Vackiindmire. He always made it a point to avoid harming children if he could help it. He had often wondered if the reason could have been that it was simply to ensure that his food supply would not be depleted.

He knew this now; that it was not so. He had returned the doll to Weena as sort of an unspoken thank-you.

"*So many children, so many families, the Killnarin will not be allowed to kill anymore. I will help this group on their quest if I can, although I am unsure of how much longer I can hold myself back. I fear I may be putting them in danger, the more I try to help and the longer I stay around them.*

"*Why is it that I am so fascinated with this group? Could it be that, in each of them, I see a little of myself, some similarity now and then? Some aspect in each of their personalities and the way they think, that reminds me a bit of myself? Perhaps I did have more to do with them coming together than I realize. If I did, I was unaware of it.*

"*Perhaps it goes all the way back to Rasindell. I did feel for him when he lost his love and I protected him from the Killnarin. I even provided him with a daughter of sorts, so he wouldn't have to be completely alone, even though he had chosen to be after her death. And then, for Vordin, I do the same. I saved him from a Killnarin and placed him and Lorenta under the care of the two thieves and Weena. I even delayed their travel just so, in order for them all to meet.*

"I will continue to watch them as I have been doing and help when I feel I am able to safely do so. I guess it makes me happy to watch them; it makes me feel as if in some way I am one of them somehow. They are the closest thing I have to calling friends, and Lorenta in a bizarre way is my child as I did have a hand in her creation.

"No, you stupid fool! You have no friends or family and that is how it must be! Do not start to create an illusion in your mind that they are in some way, or they will be the first ones you turn on if you lose control! You know that! And from experience, damn it! There is a reason why you gave up on friends… why you gave up on love. There are no families that would take you in as one of their own."

He could hear Nodwel, Dendrox, and Weena in the main room of the tavern, and The Black Shadow decided to leave, but kept part of his mind aware and focused on the group as always.

CHAPTER 62 =   REUNITED

After some time, the dwarf got up and went to the desk. "Thank-you so very much for your hospitality. I didn't catch your name though," Nodwel said to the innkeeper.

"Declort," he replied with a smile.

"And your friend's name was…" he added trying to remember.

"Oh yes, it is Yorif. Please send me word, if you find him." He hesitated a moment. "Even if the news is unfavorable," Declort told him.

"I will," the dwarf assured him and then whispered, "I see that not many of my companions arrived back here yet. Any word on any of them?"

Declort replied, "If you're worried about the bounty hunters, I believe they left town sometime around mid day. I don't think you'll have to worry about them. Most hired thugs, as such, don't have much patience unless it's bought with a high price. If the price on your two friends wasn't worth the time and effort, most likely they headed off in search of a less evasive bounty with a higher price on his or her head."

"I hope you are right, but somehow I highly doubt they would have just given up," Nodwel commented.

"You'd be surprised then at how lazy some are. There are definitely many who are precise and meticulous when it comes to bounty hunting, but that bunch did not seem the type," Declort told him.

"I hope you're right. I'll just sit and wait for the others then. Would it be too much trouble to get a mug of ale? I made far more than I had hoped helping out the merchants at the marketplace. I should have enough to pay for a couple of rooms for tonight as well," he told him.

"Well, that's great," the innkeeper said with a cheerful smile, "I'll get you that ale right away."

"You're sure about not seeing my friends though?" Nodwel asked, still dreadfully worried about their welfare.

"I'm the only one running the inn. Narten watches the front when I do manage to catch a bit of sleep. He would have woken me if there had been some sort of problem," Declort explained, "I'm sure they are just fine. The warrior woman and the young man were in here early this morning for breakfast. Sorry I don't remember their names."

"No, I saw them just before that. I'm sure they are all okay, like you said," said the dwarf placing payment for the ale on the desktop. The innkeeper gave him a friendly nod. "Thank-you once again," Nodwel said with a smile and then seated himself once again at the large table by the tavern entrance. A few moments later, Declort presented him with a frothy mug of ale and then went back to his duties.

Nodwel leaned over to the next table and said to Weena and Dendrox, "Looks to be that the hunters left town, as strange as that sounds. There's been no sign of them for quite awhile."

"Well that's a relief," Weena commented moving over to Nodwel's table to join him, as did Dendrox.

<Zaylyn ><Quest For The Sword Of Anthrowst ><By Katrina Mandrake-Johnston >   <Ch 62> < 189 >

"Have you seen any of the others?" Dendrox asked, eager to hear about Candra.

"No, nothing so far," Nodwel answered, "I have seven gold coins left for tonight. So, unless the others come up with anything, it's enough for one room and a bit of food to split between all of us."

The three of them sat chatting about the day's events for some time before Weena suggested, "We should get the item out of the room now, don't you think?"

"Yeah, alright," Dendrox agreed, "We'll be right back, Nodwel. We left a few things back in the rooms." Nodwel gave them a nod as they headed down the hall.

When Weena and Dendrox entered his room, they immediately noticed the stolen items neatly laid out on the bed. Weena asked in confusion, "Dendrox, did you go after the thieves?"

He replied, "No, when did I have the chance? I've been with you the whole time."

"Then who?" Weena asked, still very confused, wondering what could have happened, "Did the thieves return it somehow?"

"Please," he laughed, "not very likely. But I have no clue either. Something odd is going on here. We should check to see if the scissors are still here. I want you to leave the room, very slowly and very carefully. I'll remain and check the room for any traps that may have been laid."

Weena simply nodded and followed his instruction. Dendrox departed the room shortly after and handed Weena her pouch with the flame box and doll within. "There was nothing strange," he told her. He placed his backpack on the floor containing his empty water skin and the two blankets he and Candra had brought with them. He then tied his small leather pouch around his waist, positioning it at the small of his back, and told her, "Everything's back where it belongs." Next he swung the backpack over his shoulder and said to Weena, "Well, I guess we better get back to Nodwel then."

"I left my lantern back in my room. I should get it?" she asked.

"Might as well. We don't know if we're going to have enough money between us all to rent the rooms for the night. Besides, we might get different rooms assigned to us. Hell, depending on how much we have, we may end up all in one room, if the innkeeper will allow such a thing," he told her with a miserable look on his face.

"Okay, I'll just be a moment," she told him and then, after an unnerving thought, added, "You don't suppose someone has been in my room, do you?"

"I could check," said Dendrox, but he didn't look at all pleased with the suggestion. He followed her to her room and took a few moments to gaze about the room standing from the doorway. "Looks all right," he decided, "Get your lantern, but make it quick."

Weena had hoped that he would have taken this opportunity to steal a kiss from her now that they were alone once more. He did no such thing. He just waited impatiently for her to retrieve the lantern and then headed down the hall quickly with Weena following after him.

Weena and Dendrox returned to the main room of the tavern and sat at Nodwel's table once again. It was then that Candra entered through the door followed by Asdella and Vordin.

"They've left," Candra told them all, talking about the bounty hunters, "Doesn't look like we'll have to worry about them. Overheard one of them saying that they'd lined up something far better."

Weena wondered, *"Could it be that they backed off because I said that I was a magic user? I know that most people tend to be nervous, not really knowing what is to be expected, but could it really have deterred the bounty hunters as far as to leave? Being so wary of what I might be able to do, that they deemed the bounty on the thieves not worth the trouble? It's a little hard to believe. Did they really imagine that I could be so powerful? I suppose it could be true."*

Vordin told them, "Asdella and I, we had a quick look around after getting some sleep, but we didn't come up with much. We ran into Candra on our way back here."

Nodwel told them that he had managed to get some money for the night, and Dendrox and Weena told them what they had learnt about the sword.

Some time later, Lorenta entered the tavern. The man she had entered with had his arm draped over her shoulder. They were talking back and forth, smiling and laughing. Lorenta didn't even seem to notice that the others were sitting at the large table together. If she had noticed, she showed no sign

<Zaylyn ><Quest For The Sword Of Anthrowst ><By Katrina Mandrake-Johnston >   <Ch 62> < 190 >
that she had.

The man she was with sat down at the middle large table, beside the table with Lorenta's companions and next to the fireplace. Lorenta went to the desk to speak with the innkeeper.

The man's black long-sleeved shirt had a tan colored vest over it and he straightened this slightly before smoothing his black greasy hair with his hand. He gave Lorenta a large toothy grin and spread himself out over the bench, his legs spread out beneath the table and his arms resting outstretched on the back of the wooden bench on either side. He wore an incredibly smug look on his round clean-shaven face and there was something deceitful about his expression. His dark brown eyes watched Lorenta a little too closely as she spoke to the innkeeper.

Someone in the inn whispered loudly, "Oh no, not this arrogant bastard again. There goes my whole evening."

"Poor girl," another whispered, "Maybe someone should warn her about that creep, although I doubt it will do any good."

"What is she doing? Who is this guy?" Vordin whispered, as he leaned forward so only his friends could hear him.

The innkeeper gave Lorenta a handful of gold coins. She turned with an excited look on her face as she smiled and nodded to the man.

He clapped loudly and bellowed across the room to her, "Alright! Great news!"

The other patrons were obviously annoyed, as he was acting as if he owned the entire place and everyone in it, intruding on their privacy with his uncouth behavior. He kept looking at everyone with just a hint of a smile on his thin lips, as if he were challenging everyone around him. Most of the people just ignored him, while a few returned him cross looks.

Declort, the innkeeper, set up a chair on the small stage and announced, "I didn't have anything planned for tonight, but this young lady here has agreed to tell a couple of stories for your enjoyment. Now, this is her first try at storytelling, so go easy on her."

This man, who had come in with Lorenta, had obviously been here before. Everyone appeared to be hoping this man would be quiet and keep to himself for the duration of the storytelling.

Lorenta sat down upon the chair, her face clearly blushing, and she looked nervously around at all the people staring expectantly back at her. The man clapped a little too loudly again in the quiet tavern, making sure everyone was painfully aware of his presence.

<World of Zaylyn ><Quest For The Sword Of Anthrowst ><By Katrina Mandrake-Johnston ><Ch 63>

CHAPTER 63 =   LORENTA THE STORYTELLER: THE FARM

"Once long ago, there was a man," Lorenta began keeping her voice strong despite her nervousness, "He was a good man with a kind heart and had a kind and loving wife.

"This man was a farmer, but luck had not smiled on this unfortunate couple for their tiny piece of land only contained dry and barely useable soil. Still, he worked very hard at that piece of land. Each time, he would plant the seeds that contained all their hopes of survival into that hostile ground, water them as best he could, and beg them to grow.

"This went on year after year. But they struggled on together in the face of their misfortune, always hoping for better days in the future. Come market day, they would take what few shriveled vegetables they had managed to produce in hopes that someone would buy them, providing them with the money they desperately needed to be able to keep their land. As it was, the poor farmer and his wife had to go hungry several days at a time just to be able to have something to bring to the market.

"All day, they would wait patiently, trying not to lose hope as the potential customers passed them by, sometimes letting out a surprised laugh at how miserable their produce looked, but most of the time they gave a disgusted look at the shriveled vegetables neatly laid out and moved on. The farmer and his wife tried not to look at the plump delicious vegetables and the healthy well-fed people that had brought them, as it was too much for the couple to bear.

"Thankfully, at the end of each market day, out of pity, a few people would offer them a few coins for their produce merely to give to their horses as a treat for the ride home. It wasn't much, but at least it

<Zaylyn ><Quest For The Sword Of Anthrowst ><By Katrina Mandrake-Johnston >   <Ch 63> < 191 >
was enough for them to keep their farm.

"One night after coming home from a most depressing and disheartening market day, the farmer came out to the field after his wife had gone to bed. The farmer looked bitterly at his miserable excuse for a farm and then collapsed to the ground weeping heavily. It was the first time in a long time that he had let their misfortune get to him and he wept, lying distraught for several hours on the hard dry dirt in the dark.

"Then he saw something very odd and something he had never noticed before. There in the hard-packed soil was what looked to be a long blue and wispy tuft of grass. He reached out and gave the plant a tug, but it held fast.

" 'Could it be that this odd plant is what has been causing all of our problems?' he wondered, and he also hoped this was so, as then everything could be solved so easily just by removing it.

"He got up, and kneeling on either side of the little blue plant, gave it another tug.

" 'I've never heard of a plant like this,' he told himself, 'It must be magical and here to forever curse my land. All I have to do is pull it out.'

"This time he yanked with all of his remaining strength and he fell backwards as it came free of the dirt. When the farmer looked at his hand, he was amazed and shocked to see that it was not a plant at all that he had pulled from the ground. It was a tiny man that he held by the long wispy locks of blue hair that were on top of his small head.

"The tiny man let out a deep bellowing laugh, which surprised the farmer even more, and he dropped the tiny figure.

" 'Why do you weep?' the tiny blue-haired creature asked.

" 'Just look all around,' answered the farmer, 'Nothing fit to eat or sell grows here. My wife is nothing but skin and bones. Why she stays with me is beyond me. I am so weak myself, that I can barely even work this field anymore and I'm failing to see the use in it. I'd have better luck trying to grow crops in a field made up entirely of dust and salt.'

" 'Is that what you wish?' bellowed the little man.

" 'What?! No, of course not," exclaimed the farmer.

" 'Would you rather have a field of rich dark soil perfect for growing grand vegetables of exquisite flavor?' the tiny man asked.

" 'Well of course. I'd be happy with less, just as long as my wife and I don't slowly starve to death,' the farmer grumbled getting even more upset and annoyed by this being's questioning.

" 'Would you give your first born son to gain this?' the strange little man asked.

" 'What are you talking about?! I doubt we will even live much longer, and to bring a child into this kind of life would be murder, especially where we can't even feed ourselves,' the farmer explained with tears in his eyes, as he and his wife would have liked to have children but clearly wouldn't be able to provide for them.

" 'Is your answer yes?' the tiny man asked, looking up at him with black beady little eyes.

"The farmer now despised this little man for all he was doing was bringing more tears to his eyes and heartbreak at his situation, making him feel worse and worse for failing to provide a better life for himself and his wife.

" 'I don't know, sure. Will you leave me be now?' he said hastily with annoyance, 'All you are doing is making me feel worse!'

" 'I will leave, but I shall one day return,' bellowed the man, and he vanished.

"The farmer, too tired to return to the house, fell asleep right there in the middle of the field thinking to himself that he surely had finally gone mad with hunger and that he had started to hallucinate.

"He awoke the next morning and was so astonished to feel dark moist and loose soil at his fingertips that he believed he was still dreaming. His wife, upon seeing this, ran out to him rejoicing. Neither of them dared question what had happened, as they feared doing so would somehow end their miracle.

"Years past. Each market day, they would bring such grand vegetables that everyone would come to them first and everything would be sold in a manner of minutes. Their farm grew such an abundance that half the time they didn't really know what to do with so much extra food.

<Zaylyn ><Quest For The Sword Of Anthrowst ><By Katrina Mandrake-Johnston >   <Ch 63> < 192 >

"The farmer and his wife ate well, and eventually after several years of good fortune, gave birth to a son. The farmer was wary that perhaps the little blue-haired man had not been a dream, but they had many years of harmony and his wife gave birth to two more sons.

"When his children were old enough to help him work the land, he showed them what to do in great detail. His eldest son was incredibly lazy and did not pay attention to his father's instructions and had no intention of doing any of the work at all. The father told them that he and their mother were going to town and that when they returned he would inspect their work. He divided the land into three parts assigning one part to each son and then left for town.

"The two younger sons started on their chores right away, while the oldest son sat relaxing under an apple tree. When his brothers spoke to him about this, he told them that he would give them part of his allowance if they would do his part of the work. They agreed and finished their lazy brother's work first before continuing with their own.

"When the father and mother returned, he was disappointed to see that his two younger sons had not yet completed their work. He praised his eldest for doing such a fine job, not knowing what had occurred.

"Come nightfall the farmer was admiring the work of his sons when he heard a bellowing laugh. There was the tiny little man with the wispy blue hair. 'I have returned. Give me your eldest son.'

"The farmer didn't know what to do. He begged, 'Can't we make some sort of deal? I can't lose one of my sons!'

" 'Alright, I am feeling generous,' said the little man.

" 'If your sons can work the land to my satisfaction in a specific amount of time, you shall keep all of your children. Should one of them fail, they will be mine.'

"The farmer agreed, as it was his best chance at saving his oldest son, but he feared for his two younger children as he thought they worked so slowly. The next day the little man called forth the farmer, who in turn called forth his three sons. He explained to them the story of their farm and the deal he had made with the strange little man. The two younger brothers looked nervously at their older sibling for they knew he would fail. The sons were sent out to do their task.

" 'Brothers, help me. I do not know what to do,' the eldest said.

" 'To help you would mean our own doom. We cannot help you. Watch what we do and try to follow, for you are dear to us and we do not wish you a horrible fate.'

"The allotted time passed and the little man inspected the land. 'Fine work. Fine work. Wait! What do you call this?!' he exclaimed with a wicked grin.

" 'Son!' the father said in disbelief, 'Just yesterday you were finished first and with beautiful work. What happened?'

" 'I am sorry father. I did nothing that day, while I paid my brothers to do my work,' explained the son with great shame.

"The little man chuckled, 'And now you will forever make up for your laziness.'

"The eldest son was transformed into a tiny bee, and the mysterious little man vanished. Every day, the brothers would see a bee which looked slightly different than the others, working harder than ever pollinating the flowers of the farm and forever knowing the punishment for his laziness."

Lorenta looked sheepishly around hoping for approval and was pleased to hear everyone give their applause. The man she had entered with, of course, was making a point to clap the loudest and watching to see if Lorenta had noticed this.

"Tell us another one!" he called out, "That was great! See, I told you that you could do it! Come on! Lorenta, tell us another!"

A spider crawled across the stage in front of Lorenta.

"*This used to be me,*" she thought to herself looking at the spider crawling innocently across the smooth wooden boards of the stage, "*Funny, it's so hard for me to believe. This is not me anymore. I am no longer the same as this spider here. This is not what I am anymore. I can't even remember what it was like to be this. I don't even know who I am. One thing I do know is that it feels right to be*

<Zaylyn ><Quest For The Sword Of Anthrowst ><By Katrina Mandrake-Johnston >   <Ch 63> < 193 >

accepted as a human. This is what I want, but that would mean I would have to hide my true self, which is something I wouldn't be able to stand. This man I met last night seems to accept me, seeing more in me than the others. The others, even Vordin, they don't really see me as part of their group. I bet they've already discussed any information they've collected and have made their plans of what to do next in our quest without me as usual. I shall have to discover things for myself second hand, as it seems I always shall have to."

Declort told her, "Go ahead. Tell another, if you have one. You're doing very well. You're a natural at this."

"I shall tell another, if you wish," Lorenta said blushing.

<World of Zaylyn ><Quest For The Sword Of Anthrowst ><By Katrina Mandrake-Johnston ><Ch 64>

CHAPTER 64 =   LORENTA THE STORYTELLER: THE CLOSET

"The old woman reluctantly put up a notice advertising her house for sale," Lorenta began, this time having more confidence in herself, "When a young man showed interest in the home, the woman seemed very pleased, as she wished to live with her son and his family in her old age. The man was amazed at the low price the old woman was asking for the large and beautiful house.

"The man told the woman that he would purchase the house from her, and this is when the old woman pulled him close and whispered, 'Then I must tell you the secret of this house.'

" 'What is this you speak of? What secret could there possibly be?' the man asked with curiosity.

" 'You must swear that you will be very careful if you decide to use its power. I have been so wary of selling this place because of it. Follow me,' the old woman said leading him up several flights of stairs.

"So the man followed the old woman to the attic. There was a closet door here, and this is where the old woman stopped.

" 'What is it that you're talking about?' the man exclaimed, 'I see nothing here.'

"The old woman put a bony finger to her lips. 'Watch,' she said as she knocked once, twice, three times upon the closet door.

"Then she slowly turned the rusty doorknob and opened the door. To his amazement, he saw a wondrous and amazing world through the doorway. He could do nothing but stare in astonishment.

" 'You may go through, and the passageway will lie open to you until you return here to this house. None of the beings within can come into our world, and although you will be able to interact with the wondrous beings within, none can do you harm. You must remember to knock only three times to activate the magic of the doorway. Promise me, that you will knock only three times and never four. Please, I must have your most sincere promise.'

" 'Alright,' he agreed.

"So the man bought the house and the old woman went to live with her son and his family. The man could hardly wait to explore the magical world.

"He however was wary of doing so alone. He told his best friend about the closet door within the attic, and he of course didn't believe him until he came and saw for himself.

" 'Shall we go in?' he asked his friend.

" 'I don't know, are you sure we'll be safe?' his friend asked, extremely nervous.

"The man answered, 'The old woman who sold me the place said we would be, and she seemed to know what she was talking about.'

"His friend was still not convinced and he said, 'But are you sure it will be safe for both of us? Maybe it only works for the one who knocked.'

" 'Well, we'll never know unless we try,' the man told him, 'Besides, we can stay close to the doorway in case there is any trouble.'

"So the two men entered through the doorway and found themselves in a wondrous and amazing world. Here everything shimmered in a strange light. Large colorful crystals had sprouted from the ground like trees. The ground itself was as smooth and white as an eggshell. A small stream was nearby, but it was not water that flowed in it. It was filled with a white cream-like substance.

"Overhead in a light purple sky, an immense serpent-like dragon beat its wings. They edged toward

<Zaylyn ><Quest For The Sword Of Anthrowst ><By Katrina Mandrake-Johnston >   <Ch 64> < 194 >

the doorway, but the dragon seemed to ignore them. Landing beside the white milky stream, it dipped its snake-like neck beneath the surface and a few seconds later rose with an odd creature between its teeth. This creature had a round scaly body with eight spider-like legs and three eyestalks on the top of its body. The creature screamed a shrill cry as the dragon devoured it. The dragon then continued its flight into the sky.

"The two men looked at each other in astonishment and quickly decided to leave.

"The next day, they went through the portal again. This time the scenery was a little bit different. They realized that they were in a different location within this strange world. Here there were blue fuzzy plants surrounding a pool of black water. Many strange colorful bugs chirped and buzzed around the plants.

" 'Wow, would you take a look at that!' his friend exclaimed.

"There, sitting around the pool was a huge green insect which half resembled a large grasshopper. It had no wings and instead of two large legs used for jumping, all six of its legs were large. What was most odd about this creature, was that its size was that of a full-grown cat.

" 'There are more of them, look!' the man said to his friend.

" 'We haven't seen you two before. Where is the old woman?' the insect asked the two men.

" 'It just talked!' both the men exclaimed together.

"The man finally told the bug, 'She sold me the house and went to live with her son.'

" 'Oh, I see,' said the large green insect, 'I do hope that she reminded you to only knock three times and never four. You wouldn't want to be responsible for unleashing that kind of evil into your world.'

" 'What do you mean?' he asked, 'What will happen if I knock four times?'

"The insect told him, 'Return tomorrow and I shall tell you more. You must always keep your visits short.'

" 'But we just arrived!' he told the bug, wanting to find out as much information as possible about what would happen if he knocked four times and what evil it was speaking of.

" 'There are two of you,' the bug explained, 'so it's more draining on the magic of the portal. You should leave now and return tomorrow.'

" 'Alright,' agreed the man, and he and his friend left, returning to the house.

"The next day, the man met his friend and asked him if he wanted to enter the world again.

"His friend replied, 'Maybe you should go by yourself and find out all the information you can. It sounds more dangerous than what it's worth.'

"So the man went home and went up to the attic.

"Knock. 'One,' he counted. Knock. 'Two,' he said.

"Then a voice called out to him from outside. It was his friend. 'Maybe I should come with you after all,' said his friend.

" 'Alright,' the man shouted back, 'Thanks. Let me just activate the portal so I don't lose count. Come on up. The door's open.'

"The man returned to the closet door. Knock. 'Two,' said the man. Knock. 'Three,' he said.

"He opened the door and was astonished to see himself looking into a mirror. No, it wasn't a mirror, because a wicked grin spread across the lips of his reflection.

"Before he could do anything at all, his double had stepped across the threshold and pushed the man into the closet and closed the door after him.

"The man found himself in a black void where the only thing visible was the transparent doorway back into his house. From this side, the door was invisible. He could see that his duplicate had a vicious looking dagger behind his back. His friend entered the attic.

"The man pounded furiously upon the door trying to warn his friend, but he remained unheard no matter what he did.

" 'So are we going in then,' his friend asked.

" 'No,' the imposter replied, 'You were right. It's just too dangerous, especially when we don't know very much information about the other world. We wouldn't want to accidentally unleash a terrible evil, now would we?'

<Zaylyn ><Quest For The Sword Of Anthrowst ><By Katrina Mandrake-Johnston >   <Ch 64> < 195 >

" 'Well no. What are you going to do?' asked the man's friend, totally unaware of the danger.

" 'I don't know, board it up perhaps?' the evil thing suggested, eagerly fidgeting with the dagger behind his back.

" 'Well, I have wood and nails at my place. Let's do this right away then,' said his friend turning around to head downstairs.

" 'Yes, let's,' the evil being said, as he grinned a viciously wicked smile at the trapped man within the closet. Then he followed his friend out of the room with the dagger in his hand, ready to strike.

" 'No!' the man screamed pounding on the door.

"A few minutes later, the evil being returned, its hands and the dagger drenched in blood. He opened the closet door without knocking upon the door at all. He tossed the dagger into the closet. The man tried to escape but found he couldn't. The evil creature then dragged his dead friend into the closet.

" 'What have I done!' the man wailed, 'It's all my fault! I must have knocked four times by accident.'

"The evil being, laughing, set the house on fire.

"The creature said to the man, 'There will be no one to let you out now, and I shall be free to terrorize this world. Thank-you for letting me take over your life. No one will know the difference, until it is too late that is, like your foolish friend here.'

"The house burned to the ground with the man watching the doorway slowly vanish before his eyes until he was in complete darkness within the void."

Once again, Lorenta received applause. She stood up and took a slight bow to announce that she had finished her storytelling, and then came to sit with the man, not her companions.

"Oh, that was excellent," the man said to her, putting his arm around her.

"Thank-you," replied Lorenta looking up at him.

"Both of your stories didn't have very happy endings like I had expected. Why was that?" he asked, lustfully eyeing her body.

"Life rarely has happy endings, at least as far as I've seen. Why should it be any different in the stories I tell? Besides, it's not as if they are real. There is no one to protest," she said to him.

"You obviously haven't been looking in the right places then. There are plenty of happy endings as well as beginnings and middles. It's just that most people tend to dwell on the bad parts instead of the good, sometimes so much that they themselves become unaware and unable to see the good in their lives," the man told her.

"Yes, that is true," Lorenta agreed, "I shouldn't have said that."

"Isn't it a good turn of events that we happened to meet? Don't be shy. Why don't you sit a little closer?" he coaxed caressing her shoulder.

"Perhaps," Lorenta said, unsure of herself.

Asdella had a foul grimace on her face, as she watched the man and Lorenta speaking to each other.

<World of Zaylyn ><Quest For The Sword Of Anthrowst ><By Katrina Mandrake-Johnston ><Ch 65>

CHAPTER 65 = ASDELLA'S RAGE

Asdella got up from the table, her sword in hand, and came to stand before the table Lorenta and the man were at.

"Asdella, what are you doing?" Weena whispered to her.

"Best to not get involved, whatever she's up to," Nodwel explained to the group, "She's been known to start fights. Nothing to worry about, usually just a few heated words. I have no idea why she is so upset. He is annoying, yes, but Lorenta can make her own decisions. I'm sure Lorenta will be joining us before it's time to leave this place."

"If you're looking for a whore to brutalize, you're looking in the wrong place. Preying on innocents now I see?" she said with a vicious sneer and looking at the man in disgust.

"You call that normal?" Candra whispered.

"No. What's the matter with her?!" Nodwel exclaimed, "You know, it's probably best just to

<Zaylyn ><Quest For The Sword Of Anthrowst ><By Katrina Mandrake-Johnston >   <Ch 65> < 196 >
leave it be."

"How dare you insult and embarrass my lady friend here by making such accusations about me. I'm sure she would not associate with me, if such terrible things were true," he said to Asdella.

"You just met her. Shut up you filthy cur," she snarled back at him between clenched teeth.

"You don't know that for sure," he said glaring at her in a degrading manner from beneath his brow, "It just so happens that this is true. I did only meet her last night, and she asked that I join her again tonight for her attempt at storytelling. Which, I might add, is very good for a beginner. We spoke throughout that entire night, and she is a very interesting and talented girl. Now leave us be, you monster of a woman."

Asdella did not falter in her stance and said in a firm voice, "There is only one talent you are interested in."

The man removed his arm from around Lorenta, trying his best to sound completely shocked by her accusation, saying, "You are implying… You must have me confused with someone else." Asdella just stood there with a bitter look on her face. He shook a finger at her and said viciously, "How dare you! You horrible person!" Then he let out a cruel laugh as he added, "The way you are dressed would suggest that this is your line of work. Being a whore? You accused me of looking for one, didn't you? What the sword is for, I can only imagine. I obviously can see that you don't even know how to care for one. Look how it's all banged up. You don't even have a scabbard for it, do you? Anyway, as I was saying, if you think that this fine woman here beside me is that type of person and interfering with your section of town, you are so wrong. Now leave and take your uncouth behavior with you. How dare you suggest such a thing about her or myself?! I've never been so insulted in all my life!"

Asdella remained standing where she was, unwavering, her lips pressed firmly together as she continued to stare the man directly in the eyes. She seemed to remain strong in this man's onslaught of hurtful words, but her sword arm had begun to tremble with emotion.

Seeing that his act of innocence wasn't going to deter her and that he would probably have to give up on Lorenta to deal with her, he said with contempt and changing his tone to have a malicious edge to it, "Get lost. Can't you see I'm busy?" He knew well who she was. He had recognized her when he had entered and wondered if she had recognized him. He had hoped that she had, as he knew it would pain her to remember. "Hey, you look real familiar," he said with a wicked grin, "I know where I've seen you before." He smiled at the tension and the frightened look building beneath her angry face, "Didn't you used to belong to old-what's-his-face?"

He loved how his words cut her like a knife. She could do nothing about it either, which pleased him even more. The hurt he had caused her when he was pretending to be an innocent was wonderful; suggesting that she was a whore when he knew well she had been forced to behave as one and that he in fact had abused her physically and mentally several times. To everyone in the tavern, he was the one being harassed by this hateful woman. He felt like laughing out loud at her, but instead just expressed it in a mocking grin. He wondered, "Hey, whatever happened to him?"

"I got revenge," she snarled, as she suddenly thrust her sword deep into the man's belly and then yanked her sword upward until it caught on his ribcage. With an insane look in her eye, she grinned a large insane and satisfied smile at his horrified expression. She pulled her bloodied sword out of his gut and then thrust it into his throat.

Everyone in the tavern stared in horror and shock at what had just happened. Lorenta had been splattered with the man's blood. His body slumped slightly forward but remained on the bench as his blood spilled down onto the floor beneath the table.

No one dared approach Asdella, as she stood there with a wild look in her brown eyes, holding her sword up as it dripped with blood, as if she were daring for someone to challenge her actions of revenge.

"What are you doing?!" Lorenta exclaimed, "He liked me. He was nice to me. Why did you kill him?"

"He deserved it," Asdella answered plainly.

"How? He didn't do anything," she questioned, but lacked the emotion one would normally have in the severity of such a situation. She appeared merely curious.

"Yes he did. You have no idea. He would have hurt you," Asdella tried to explain.

Many of the people were trying to cautiously edge their way toward the exit. Others tried to get to the back rooms in an attempt to hide, while a few remained seated but drew their weapons in case they were forced to use them. None of them had the gall to say a single word, not even Nodwel, Dendrox, Candra, Weena, or Vordin, who all felt that they somewhat knew Asdella and had a rough idea of what to expect from her.

Lorenta continued, "He wasn't being violent, and if he started to act as such, I could have protected myself. Remember the man with the medallion? You heard about what happened with him on the way to this town."

Asdella said through gritted teeth, "You can't protect yourself from that kind of hurt."

Vordin finally got the nerve to say something, wanting to know what had driven her to murder this man, "He knew you before? What did he mean when he said you used to belong to someone?"

Asdella shot him an icy glare saying, "He hurt a lot of women I used to know, and I was one of them."

"Maybe he had changed, you don't know that," Lorenta added, "He appeared to be a different man than what you remember, didn't he? He didn't make any unwanted advances toward me or any sign of being a violent man."

"I don't really care, now do I?" Asdella said in a bitter voice, but it showed signs of cracking. She was extremely upset and was desperately trying to hide it.

Lorenta began to cry, and Asdella headed out the door into the night.

<World of Zaylyn ><Quest For The Sword Of Anthrowst ><By Katrina Mandrake-Johnston ><Ch 66>

CHAPTER 66 = DRANNGORE'S PLAN

The innkeeper said to the group in a stern voice, "I suggest you leave, before the fate of your friend affects you as well. Murder is not something to be taken lightly. I doubt she'll make it very far without having to face the consequences. That woman is clearly insane. I want you to know that I am not judging you as a result of her actions. I wish you well and hope you will find some trace of what happened to my friend Yorif and can get word to me about it. There should be a carriage leaving soon. You should depart before the authority arrives and I pray you escape before any of his companions find out what has happened here. I shall try to keep as much information as I can from them and I'm sure I can sway the other witnesses to do the same with promises of ale and what not, at least until the authorities can handle the matter properly."

"Thank-you," said the dwarf, feeling that he should have been able to stop her, especially where he was the one who had known her the longest.

"Just go, and quickly," Declort said.

The carriage was situated just outside the town gates. The two dark grey horses were hitched and looked well rested. Vexcindor, the carriage driver, was standing nonchalant beside the carriage. He was leaning up against its side calmly twirling his fingertips around the side of his dark brown full and bushy mustache. Vexcindor had a relaxed expression upon his face as his greyish-green eyes searched the blackened sky above, but Candra thought she detected a hint of nervousness in his eyes. He then adjusted the snug fit of his dark blue scarf about his neck, never taking his gaze from the sky and the dark clouds drifting high above.

Nodwel asked, "Excuse me sir, how much is it to buy passage to Shirkint?"

Vexcindor gave the dwarf and his companions a large friendly grin as he said, "You nearly startled me there for a moment. Welcome, welcome. I was beginning to think that the flow of customers had finally slowed to a full stop, at least coming out of Vackiindmire that is." He clapped his large hands together continuing, "Well, let me start with names. I always like to do introductions before a journey. No need to feel defensive either. Whether you give me real names or fake ones, it makes no difference to me. It just makes the journey a bit more pleasant knowing what to call each other is all. I don't take

<Zaylyn ><Quest For The Sword Of Anthrowst ><By Katrina Mandrake-Johnston >   <Ch 66> < 198 >

to anyone questioning me about my passengers either, past or present so no need to worry there. By the expressions on your faces, I would assume you're in a bit or trouble. No business of mine though. The name's Vexcindor. And yours?"

Nodwel told him quickly, "I'm Nodwel, this here is Vordin, Weena, Lorenta, Dendrox, and Candra. We're expecting a friend of ours shortly, a woman named Asdella."

Candra shot Dendrox a glance to mean that perhaps Nodwel shouldn't have been so hasty to give up their proper names as he did. Dendrox waved it away, and Candra tried to dismiss her worries.

"Well, I'm pleased to meet you all," said the carriage driver, "So there will be seven of you traveling tonight then? Might be a tight squeeze. There are two benches within the carriage, rather nice too, with soft cushions and the whole bit. Each bench will seat maybe three on each side in quite a snug fit. If you squeeze the smaller passengers together, you might be able to fit four. Well, I'll let you figure things out for yourselves."

"We may not have enough to buy passage, as we are a little short on money," Nodwel explained and then asked again, "How much will this cost us?"

"Oh yes, sorry, I guess we should take care of the business side right away then. It is ten gold coins for the voyage. It matters not the number of passengers, it is just a little more difficult for the horses to pull a heavier weight. As such is the case, especially with seven of you, I ask that you give me time to slip the horses a bit of a treat before they make the journey. It's not much, but I'm sure they'll appreciate it."

"Oh yes, of course," Nodwel told him, "We have to wait for our friend as it is. As for payment, I have seven coins left from all the odd jobs I did at the marketplace, but that is all."

"I made three with the storytelling, so we have enough," Lorenta spoke up, "I don't think we should wait around for her though, after all she's done."

"I'm sorry, but I can't just leave her here," the dwarf told them all, "For one, doing so might result in more violence directed on innocent people because of her anger. Besides, I can't just abandon her, no matter what has happened. I know she would not do so, if the situation was reversed for any one of us."

"It would never be the reverse!" Weena exclaimed.

"That doesn't matter," he snapped, clearly upset about the entire situation.

Vexcindor entered the stable to retrieve a special treat to pamper the horses with.

When the carriage driver was out of sight, Weena said, her words filled with emotion, "She can't just go around killing people!"

"I know!" Nodwel told her, "But we can't do anything about it, at least not right now. You know what she would say, if you said that to her? She would say something like, 'Oh yeah, I just did'. It wouldn't do a bit of good. Would it make things right, if she were killed in return for her actions?"

"Well no," Weena admitted, but then added, "Unless it's the only way to stop her from doing something like that again."

"I think we should just be on our way," Nodwel said, "Besides, if we are to continue in our quest for this sword, we will need her, and you all know this. We can't afford to make this an issue, all of Zaylyn…"

Lorenta winced in pain, holding her head.

"What's wrong?" Vordin asked with great concern.

"I think… the spider leader… is trying to… contact…" she managed to get out before she went into some sort of trance.

"Lorenta?" Vordin questioned, "Are you all right?"

She simply stood motionless, her body rigid, and her eyes blank and staring.

In her mind, Lorenta could see things clearly through the giant spider leader's eyes. She was experiencing his memory of recent events, as if they were taking place right before her eyes.

Lorenta could see a young girl in her early teens standing within a forest clearing. She estimated that she might be thirteen maybe fourteen years of age. The girl was dressed in a tattered grey dress tied

<Zaylyn ><Quest For The Sword Of Anthrowst ><By Katrina Mandrake-Johnston >   <Ch 66> < 199 >

with a piece of cord at the waist. Her feet were bare and blistered, obviously from a long trek over the countryside. Her hair was a lovely deep reddish color and her skin was a pale creamy white. Her blue eyes were vacant and staring.

The giant spider had recognized this at once as a Possession spell being used, similar to their own abilities. Lorenta was amazed that she was aware of the thoughts the spider had had within this memory as well.

It had to be Dranngore; Lorenta was sure of it. The girl, in a strong commanding voice which didn't seem her own, addressed the Killnarin that had crowded around her upon her arrival.

"Do not go above ground from now on. Stay below in the tunnels and practice your spells. I want to have the wizard's guild worried. Any spies within the two villages and any along the way would have been killed. They won't have a clue as to what's going on. I will have my revenge, but first all of you need to prepare and practice those spells. They won't be as easy to defeat as weakling villagers. All of you are here now to hear my instruction? Let me see," Dranngore said, using the girl's body as his own. He appeared to be counting the number of his evil creatures. "Some of you are missing," he announced in an angry tone, "Where are they?!"

Deep guttural noises were made by one of the Killnarin.

"They were killed?" Dranngore asked in a surprised voice, "How is this possible? I see that two of you are wounded, but no matter as they should be able to regenerate in time. Tell me what has happened here."

The same Killnarin replied with more guttural noises.

"Resistance in the tunnels? Giant spiders, eh? Clearly they were no match for you with your magical resistance and your poison resistance, which would include their venom. The most they could do, would be to weaken you slightly, not enough to kill one of you," he said.

The beast made more noises.

Dranngore laughed, "A few measly adventurers trying to survive my unstoppable army? They are of no consequence. No one would believe what they say. But if you come across them again, finish them off. "

The girl stood silent for a few moments. The spider had thought that Dranngore must have been considering his plan, from the satisfied look on the girl's face.

"Only I would be so bold as to attempt such a glorious revenge," Dranngore announced, "They will regret the day they denied me my seat within the guild. Now get below and practice, damn it! I will not have my plan fail! You'll have plenty of time to go off on your own now and then later, when we make our next move. But that won't be for several days, perhaps as long as a week. I want them all to worry themselves sick wondering what is happening. 'Who could possibly be so powerful to do all this?' they will say to themselves. And then, won't they be surprised when they see that I, Dranngore, have commanded an army of Killnarin! They said it was impossible, that the risks were too great. But I have done it, and they will perish miserably for laughing at me. Anyway, go, go! You had plenty of fun at the two villages and apparently in the tunnels as well, so now it's practice, practice. Good-bye."

The vacant look in her eyes faded. Dranngore had left the girl's body.

"What? Where am I? How did I get here?" she said very disorientated and confused. "What… what are these strange creatures?" the girl said frantically in fear.

The Killnarin, that had been speaking to Dranngore, bit the girl in half with a sudden twist of its powerful jaws.

The giant spider leader ended the connection, having shown her his memory. Before he left her mind, he warned her to be careful and that he would contact her again if they came to learn anything new.

Lorenta relayed all she had seen and heard to the others.

Dendrox, a little relieved, commented, "Well at least we know for certain now that none of the other villages have been attacked in any of the other areas."

Candra said to him, "Yes, Cranok is safe at least for the moment and so are your parents. It seems

<Zaylyn ><Quest For The Sword Of Anthrowst ><By Katrina Mandrake-Johnston >   <Ch 66> < 200 >
that their goal is here in Dee'ellkka Valley now."

Lorenta, rubbing at her temples, advised Vordin not to attempt the mind link they had established unless in a dire emergency.

Vexcindor returned with a wooden bucket filled with a wide variety of treats. Vordin wondered where he had found such an assortment, as he hadn't noticed such things the night before during his watch within the stable.

"Oh please, feel free to sit within the carriage. There's no need to wait outside. Might as well be comfortable while you wait for that friend of yours," the carriage driver added as he presented the bucket to the two horses and let them each grab a large mouthful.

They all agreed and entered the carriage after Nodwel and Lorenta had paid him the fare. It was in fact quite comfortable and elegant inside, not what they had expected at all. Vordin hung his magical lantern on a small hook improving visibility within the seating compartment. The women and Vordin managed to all seat themselves on the back bench while Dendrox and Nodwel sat on the other, leaving enough room for Asdella if she ever decided to show herself again.

"I wouldn't be surprised if the Killnarin started to use their fire magic, when and if we next meet them," Vordin said to them all, "They used fire magic at the attack of Nilnont, don't forget that. We should be prepared for such an attack, just in case. We're becoming more resistant to their spells and starting to recognize their mind games. They are likely to resort to more damaging methods."

"Well said," Nodwel commented, "At least we know now, that there is some sort of insane plan and motive behind this horrible man. He cares for nothing other than himself. He doesn't even realize that the other wizards probably made that comment about the Killnarin because they were aware that the creatures kill and destroy everything in their path. Simply letting them do this, is not controlling them. They do seem to show some sort of loyalty to him, probably for summoning them into this world from wherever they came from, but I doubt that he could stop them if he wanted to. A stream can be directed along a certain path easily enough, but when you try to stop it however, it merely decides to simply flow around whatever is trying to block it, forming an ever growing pool and spreading outward over everything."

"Okay, we get the picture," Dendrox told him, "We are all doomed unless we kill Dranngore with the sword and reverse all his spells including the damn Killnarin."

Weena added, "Well, if we are to find out anything more about the sword, it will definitely be at Shirkint. I'm actually a little excited about going there."

Asdella knocked at the side of the carriage saying, "You didn't think I'd let you all leave without me, did you?"

Asdella climbed inside to sit farthest from the door on the bench beside Nodwel. Everyone sat in silence as Vexcindor gave the command and the carriage began its journey. Asdella stared out of the window with her arms crossed defensively in front of her chest with her murder weapon, which she had cleaned, beside her.

****

NEXT = <u>WORLD OF ZAYLYN</u> = BOOK # 2

(Quest For The Sword of Anthrowst = Part 2)

Quest For The Sword Fragments And The Hunt For Dranngore

****

<u>About the author ::</u>

I have been writing stories all my life starting as young as seven years old, with this book being my first book published at the age of twenty-seven. I've always been a big fan of fantasy, sci-fi, adventure, and horror, enjoying movies, comics, books, and video games with good story backgrounds. Writing has always been my passion. Being a big fan of 'choose your own adventure' books and 'fighting fantasy' game books at a young age, most of my early writing followed this similar style, creating stories with endless possibilities to be explored in whatever mystical world I had imagined.

One of my first attempts in writing a straightforward story, stemming away from the multi-choice and dice rolling adventurers I usually wrote, was at the age of eleven. This story is actually what inspired the idea for the first book in the World of Zaylyn series. The first three chapters are taken from this story, being modified to fit the rest of the book. Not much was changed actually, just elaborated on. So I encourage all the young writers out there to write if the ideas are there, because years later those dreams and adventurers can be relived and re-imagined and perhaps one day shared with others.

As a young writer, I found that I was bursting with ideas, always writing beginnings of stories, scenes and situations, or even just character personalities and backgrounds. But my problem was that I had a hard time finishing a story as another better and more exciting one would come into my mind and I would begin on this instead, always planning to get back to the others. So I found that I had an enormous collection of story bits and ideas. I was looking through them and found that most had to do with the world I had created in my mind over the years to explore as I try to fall asleep each night.

Originally, in my mid to late teens, I had attempted to create a game based on my dream world. Over a course of three years, I complied a large number of characters and backgrounds, quests, places, mystical and magical objects, spells, riddles, puzzles, houses and families, and much more, even daily routines and work schedules of the minor characters the others would be interacting with. Basically, it became so complicated and elaborate, and more and more life like, that, in my late teens, I decided to write a series of books about the world I had created instead. I began, but found that I was still having the problem of starting, getting stuck, and wanting to move on to other later events that were fresh and exciting in my mind.

So, at twenty-two, after the birth of my first child, I was looking over my growing collection of story bits, both from when I was younger and from my teens and those meant for the game I had designed, and saw that I could incorporate many of them into several stories about the same world. I began to write, not start to finish, but in many, many pieces, jumping around from scene to scene and piecing the bits together like a giant puzzle into their proper order and chapters. Many times, I found myself writing twenty to forty chapters all at once. So, my advise is, if you discover that you have writer's block and still have ideas, move on to later sections and come back when you have a better idea of how things are to flow together.

After five long years, the first book in the series was ready for others to enjoy, with the second book following close behind.
****

<u>Special Thanks ::</u>

**   Thanks to those who modeled for my cover.
**   Extra thanks to my two main editors, my husband and mother, for their extensive time and effort.
**   Thanks to my father for the support and encouragement in my writing.
**   Special thanks to my mother for the encouragement, support, and readings at all stages.
**   Extra special thanks to my children for their patience, enthusiasm, and encouragement with my writing.
**   Special thanks to my grandmother, who inspired me to write as a child with her own storytelling and for the encouragement, enthusiasm, and support in my writing.
***   Thank-you to all that have shown an interest in my writing over the years and to those that have inspired me to continue with my ideas and writing.
****

Quest For The Sword Fragments
And The Hunt For Dranngore

World of Zaylyn

By Katrina Mandrake-Johnston

#2

Quest For The Sword Of Anthrowst
By Katrina Mandrake-Johnston
World of Zaylyn

Enter the World of Zaylyn. This is a world filled with strange creatures, magic, and mystery. This is the continued story, in the quest for the Sword of Anthrowst.

Evil, malicious creatures called Killnarin have entered this world to do the bidding of an insane wizard named Dranngore. Can this horrible man control these beasts as he believes?

Vordin has been told that the evil wizard had to be slain by the Sword of Anthrowst in order to send the creatures back to where they came from.

Lorenta, the mysterious being who is spider by day and human at night, has taken on this quest with him. The two thieves, an elf named Candra and Dendrox her human companion, have also joined Vordin in this quest, as has the amateur wizard Weena, Nodwel the axe-weilding dwarf, and the berserk warrior woman Asdella.

Discovering that the sword had been broken into three pieces and hidden away in three separate locations, the group continues on what seems like a hopeless quest. Through the help of the giant spiders, a message was relayed to Lorenta that Dranngore is seeking revenge on the wizard's guild for denying him membership and that it would be several days before the Killnarin made their next move.

After Asdella brutally takes revenge on a man from her past, the group must flee Vaekiindmire and have decided to make their way to the town of Shirkint. They desperately hope that they will be able to discover more information about the sword there.

Vexcindor, the carriage driver, is to take them through the forest to Shirkint, but will they run into trouble? They were warned about the increasing raids by the bandits within the forest.

Are the rumors true about a thieves guild being located at Shirkint?

It seems that The Black Shadow has been guiding them along from the beginning. Does he have some sinister plan for the group?

He eventually asks them to perform a task for him, but what are his true motives for helping them as he has?

Will he eventually turn on them as Asdella fears? Does Asdella know more about The Black Shadow than she is letting on?

His hold over the hunger is quickly diminishing the more he resists. Will he be able to keep himself from killing? Will The Black Shadow be able to stop himself from attacking and feeding from one of the group?

The World of Zaylyn is an elaborate mystical place and I hope you enjoy exploring it through this and many more books.

Enter the World of Zaylyn website at:
< www.webspawner.com/users/worldofzaylyn >

View updates on upcoming books with the option to pre-order.

TRAFFORD

Welcome to the World of Zaylyn by Katrina Mandrake-Johnston.
****
THE WORLD OF ZAYLYN SERIES
****
BOOK #1 = = > Quest For The Sword Of Anthrowst (Part 1 of 2)
BOOK #2 = = > Quest For The Sword Fragments And The Hunt For Dranngore (Part 2 of 2)

See website for order information and special features.
****

(World of Zaylyn website = http:// www.webspawner.com/users/worldofzaylyn)

****

<Zaylyn ><Quest For The Sword Fragments And The Hunt For Dranngore><By Katrina Mandrake-Johnston >   <Ch 1> < 1 >

CHAPTER 1 = THE BLACK SHADOW

"*I have watched them, followed them, even helped them in their journey to save this world and rid it of the wizard Dranngore and the army of Killnarin he has summoned. Dranngore is a foolish and small-minded man, thinking he is able to control such evil and malicious beasts. He is so blinded by his desire for vengeance that he refuses to realize the true horror he has unleashed. Zaylyn, our world, will be utterly destroyed if these creatures are allowed to roam free. I don't think he even cares what his plan for revenge will bring, as long as it is carried out to the end.*

"*He's willing to risk our entire world and everything in it, simply because he was denied membership within the wizard's guild. The guild enslaves unsuspecting wizards, stealing their magic and then forcing them to steal that of others, eventually even draining their very life away. And all the while, this evil guild absorbs the magic power and life force to share between its members. Thank goodness that many are wise to their evil ways now, but they still remain strong in their deeds.*

"*I could easily kill Dranngore and even destroy the wizard's guild, but then I would be giving into my own evil nature, even if it was done for the greater good. My hold over myself is far too weak to willingly let myself kill. To think about the horror and death I could cause if I ever lost control, makes me shudder.*

"*Vordin… the Killnarin slaughtered his entire village. Nilnont was the first to be attacked, the creatures burning it to the ground with their spells. Was I wrong to save the boy as I did? To come between the creature and its prey? I saved Rasindell as well from a Killnarin long ago, and in turn, it was Rasindell's stories about the event that helped to save Vordin at his village. I was unsure about why I had mentioned a hollow tree to Rasindell and that to be within one could save him from a Killnarin. Now that I am aware of how Vordin survived them, I see why I had given Rasindell that information.*

"*Sometimes I am completely unaware of the things I am responsible for causing and the reasons behind them. As with Candra and Dendrox, I delayed their journey in order for them to meet up with Weena and eventually Vordin. I physically took Vordin away from a scouting Killnarin that would have surely killed him and hid him away in a rocky alcove within the mountains. The creature came over the mountains and into Dee'ellkka Valley beyond, where it hunted and battled the two thieves. Candra and Dendrox would have been slain by the beast if they hadn't managed to see through its deceptions. They survived and even managed to kill the creature. Luckily, they had been delayed long enough in their journey along the road for Weena to find them and she was able to heal the elf. Candra, as well as being wounded, was also magically poisoned by the creature. Weena was able to cure this as well, saving her life.*

"*Lorenta, neither spider nor human, in a way I am responsible for her creation. It was I that gave Rasindell the potion. Could it have been more than to ease the loneliness Rasindell felt in his old age after his beloved had been slain by the Killnarin? Perhaps, but if so, I am unaware.*

"*Everyone in the group Nodwel and Asdella were traveling with were slain battling the Killnarin along with the entire village of Dexcsin. I knew of this, and yet I did nothing to stop it. Should I have?*

<Zaylyn ><Quest For The Sword Fragments And The Hunt For Dranngore><By Katrina Mandrake-Johnston >   <Ch 1> < 2 >

"In the spiders' lair, Yarin was killed by one of the beasts. He was just a child and had been the only survivor of Dexcsin. Why is it that I rescued Vordin, but did nothing when it came to that boy's demise?

"Narr's ghost, Nodwel and Asdella's slain companion, am I responsible for Asdella being able to communicate with him? It was he that alerted her to Borin's location in the tunnels within the spiders' lair. If it weren't for him, the group would have become hopelessly lost within those tunnels and would have been easy prey for the Killnarin.

"Borin sacrificed himself to save the others. Is that the reason why I finally stepped in and killed the Killnarin that later threatened their camp? I did alter time, turning night into day within the tunnels during their escape to give them an edge in their favor. I even spoke to Weena about detecting the creatures' spells and about how the Killnarin draw their strength from darkness and from each other.

"Asdella... I am worried about what she might cause to happen to the group. If they are to complete their quest for the sword, she can't go around killing whomever she likes. Instead of dealing with the hurt and emotions of the past, she would rather hack and slash everything to pieces, letting the hate and rage control her every move.

"Perhaps guiding them on this quest has been a mistake. The fairy queen told Vordin of the sword. She has taken an interest in this. I fear that the more I try to get involved, the more I put them in danger.

"I am their greatest threat, not the Killnarin. Asdella seems to realize this.

"Because she killed that man, they are now fleeing the town of Vackiindmire and are on their way to Shirkint by carriage. It's probably for the best. I'm sure that at the town of Shirkint, they'll have a better chance at finding what they are looking for. I see that it is Vexcindor taking them through the night. He still wears that ridiculous scarf about his neck as if it will somehow deter an attack from me. I let him be. If I do attack the carriage, feeding from the passengers within usually satisfies my hunger enough to leave the driver alone, although I am responsible for a few of the disappearances. I admit that I've taken a bit of a liking to Vexcindor. It's something about him; perhaps his courage and determination to continue during the night despite the dangers.

"It will be best if I stay away from them for awhile. I don't think I can fully trust myself around them, at least not right away. After I came so near to losing control in the alley, with the two thieves that robbed Weena and Dendrox, I fear I may turn on the group and not even realize what I have done. After I have become so attached to this particular group of people, I can't allow myself to destroy them."

<World of Zaylyn ><Quest For The Sword Fragments And The Hunt For Dranngore><By Katrina Mandrake-Johnston ><Ch 2>

CHAPTER 2 = THE MEAL

By this time, everyone in The Twisted Eye Tavern had left. Declort, the innkeeper, stood behind his desk not knowing what to do. The dead man was still at the large middle table beside the fireplace, his body slouched slightly forward upon the bench, his head hung low, the front of his clothing drenched in a sea of blood, a thick sticky pool beneath the table… Declort on occasion had to deal with disputes in his tavern, some even ending bloody, but never a murder.

Narten was left unaware of what had taken place, as he had been working in the kitchen the whole time. Declort did not want to tell him about what had happened, as he knew that the boy had shown fondness of the warrior woman and her companions, even purchasing meals out of his own pocket to please them.

A thought also crossed his mind that perhaps the friends of this dead man, upon finding him here, might decide to take their anger out on him and Narten, as they were the only ones left in the tavern.

The tavern door suddenly burst open and a gust of wind blew into the room. A figure, dressed all in black, stepped forward into the inn, a hooded cloak obscuring his face in shadows. An icy chill running down his body, Declort instinctively ducked down behind his desk.

The innkeeper heard the heavy door close with a dull thud. As The Black Shadow surveyed the room, Declort could hear his slow and deliberate footsteps as he walked over the wooden floorboards

<Zaylyn ><Quest For The Sword Fragments And The Hunt For Dranngore><By Katrina Mandrake-Johnston >   <Ch 2> < 3 >
nearing his position.

"*It can't be him!*" Declort said to himself in disbelief, "*Could it be he is here for revenge against me? What was it I said? I know I spoke of him earlier when that group first arrived. I accused him of harming my friend Yorif, didn't I? Please, I so hope Narten doesn't come out of the kitchen. I wouldn't know what I'd do! Black Shadow or no, if anything bad happened to that boy! Wait! The Black Shadow can hear a man's thoughts even from far away; surely he can hear mine being so close! Can he be reasoned with? Maybe this is just a silly rumor. Please, just leave us be!*"

The Black Shadow stepped up to the desk and peered over the edge at the innkeeper who was cowering near the floor.

"Good evening innkeeper," The Black Shadow said in a calm melodious tone, "Please, get up. There is no need to be frightened." Declort, the fear emitting off him in great waves, slowly stood, and trembling, stared wide-eyed at the being before him. "I sense another here… a boy. I saw him earlier in the kitchen. He is still there… I can smell his scent. I wish to have a meal," said The Black Shadow, relishing in the fear he was creating through his choice of words, even though he had planned not to do so on his arrival. Simply his presence there was creating enough as it was.

Declort managed to raise up enough courage to ask, "You don't mean to ah… devour the boy, do you? I mean surely…" He looked into the shadowed face with pleading eyes.

The Black Shadow hesitated just long enough to drive further terror into the heart of the innkeeper. He had thought of it, quite often actually. A smile crept across his lips. "No, of course not," said The Black Shadow, but in such a way that Declort greatly doubted his sincerity.

"*Perhaps I am the intended victim after all then?*" the innkeeper's mind feared.

"Could you have him prepare a meal? Nothing fancy, just a bit of lamb with a few vegetables. I can pay you handsomely for it," he said pouring several coins onto the desk from a small black pouch. He had retrieved the pouch from his waist, but Declort could have sworn that it had not been there a moment ago.

Usually the sight of gold would make someone lower their guard slightly, their greed for gold taking over as the priority. Declort, however, had had plenty of experience with thieves and con men. If anything, the gold made him increase his wariness, wondering even more so of what his true intentions were. The Black Shadow had not intended to do either with the gold.

"So… you wish to have a simple meal?" the innkeeper asked suspiciously, "And that is all?"

"Yes," was the reply.

"*Perhaps this isn't The Black Shadow after all. Has someone foolishly donned the appearance of that monster? But in order to do what? He's offering to pay for the meal,*" he thought confused. "It will take awhile to prepare," he explained.

"I'm in no hurry," The Black Shadow told him, and he walked over to the large table nearest the tavern door.

To Declort's surprise, the dead man at the next table burst into flames until only ash remained, leaving everything else unscorched by the event. The Black Shadow sat calmly at the table, the fingertips of his gloved hands folded comfortably in front of him, as if nothing had happened. The innkeeper realized that it must have been the workings of this powerful being and decided to not say a single word on the matter.

"*It is him,*" he thought with fear, "*Why would he dispose of the body? Was it merely a show of power? Why would he bother? Has he done something? Why has no one come to investigate the murder? What is he doing here?!*"

The innkeeper was dreadfully afraid that Narten may have already been killed by this being, and that his placing a meal order was part of some demented joke for him to find him slain. It frightened him that The Black Shadow had mentioned being in the kitchen earlier without him knowing, and so close to this kind boy. Declort went over to the kitchen doors and looked within. He was relieved to find him well. The innkeeper quickly placed The Black Shadow's order, not mentioning whom it was for.

Declort remained at the kitchen doors waiting for the meal to be made, watching the figure in

<Zaylyn ><Quest For The Sword Fragments And The Hunt For Dranngore><By Katrina Mandrake-Johnston >   <Ch 2> < 4 >

black calmly seated at the table. He did not want Narten to come into the other room, especially when he was unsure of The Black Shadow's intentions. When Narten handed him the plate, Declort gave him a few extra tasks to ensure that he would have to remain there.

"Here you are," he said placing the food before him and setting a fork and a dull knife beside it.

"Thank-you," The Black Shadow said with a slight nod.

The innkeeper returned to stand behind his desk, and he watched the dark figure intensely. When The Black Shadow removed his gloves, Declort half expected to see vicious claws beneath. But to the innkeeper's surprise, the hands were normal; his youthful skin a pale creamy color. The gloves, however, as he removed them, seemed to melt back up into the rest of his clothing. He ate his meal as any normal person would, slowly and in silence.

Declort got the courage to make a comment, hoping that he would not take offense, "I, ah… hadn't expected you to, ah… eat regular meals like the rest of us."

"I don't have to, but once in awhile I like to enjoy one," he explained taking another mouthful of potato off his fork.

When the meal was finished, The Black Shadow got up to leave.

"I'm sorry," Declort dared to say, "but I simply must know. A friend of mine, Yorif, he disappeared several days ago…"

"I know what you want to ask. No, I did not have anything to do with his disappearance. I have sworn off the use of my stronger powers, but I will do this one thing for you. Give me a moment and I shall tell you what occurred," he explained.

Declort nodded, as The Black Shadow seemed to stare off into space for a few moments.

"Your friend, Yorif, he was traveling to Shirkint through the forest," he told him, "The bandits, they decided to harass him. You have their leader to thank for this. Their leader wishes his identity a secret, but he is the one-armed man of their group. He was attacked by a dragon, or more accurately provoked an attack in his attempts to hunt and slay the grand beast. The dragon had him pinned to the rock floor of the cavern, resulting in terrible scars along his chest from the dragon's claws. The dragon bit the hand of his right arm, severing it from his body at the elbow. This man managed to grab his weapon and thrust it into the dragon's heart. It was a lucky blow on his part and even luckier still that the dragon let loose a flame which burned the horribly bleeding flesh of his severed arm and therefore saving him from bleeding to death as he surely would have. He had a small crossbow fashioned onto what remained of his right arm and is able to fire it with deadly accuracy. He also had it enchanted, at great cost, and it now is able to fire an unlimited supply of bolts. This evil man is the one behind the activity of the bandits. Yorif begged for his life, explaining that he was but a simple merchant. The leader is the one who slew your friend. I am sorry to have to tell you this. I thank you for the meal and this conversation. It has been awhile since I last had the chance to speak with someone in such a manner." The Black Shadow opened the door, but then hesitated which made Declort take a step back in worry. His head was lowered, his gloved hand on the door. "None are to go to Dexcsin," he breathed uneasily.

"What? But why?" Declort asked.

"None…" he repeated, appearing to almost be in pain, "None are to go to Dexcsin. Everyone there is dead, and anyone who goes there shall follow. Make certain no one travels there."

"Yes, I will," the innkeeper assured him. "But why? What has happened? Everyone is dead? How can that possibly…" he trailed off, his suspicions arising.

"I was not the one that caused it," The Black Shadow said wincing in pain and then staggered out the door with a fierce snarling growl.

Declort pulled the heavy door closed behind him in terror.

Narten came out from the kitchen saying, "I've finished what you've asked," and then he exclaimed, "What has happened here? Where did everyone go? The place is completely empty. Weren't there a lot of people here just not that long ago, and I thought I heard something about a storyteller?" Declort was lost for words. Narten gave him a confused look, as he had only seen the

<Zaylyn ><Quest For The Sword Fragments And The Hunt For Dranngore><By Katrina Mandrake-Johnston >   <Ch 2> < 5 >
innkeeper look this way after a terrible fright. The boy asked, "Did the warrior woman return? I had hoped to see her before she left town."

Declort was unsure what to say after all that had happened. He finally said to Narten, "Nothing happened here. Nothing at all. Just go back to the kitchen. I'll, ah… It's best to just go back to the kitchen. I'll help you with the dishes, if there's some to be done."

Narten obeyed, but greatly wondered what could have taken place and why Declort was so afraid to tell him anything about it.

<World of Zaylyn ><Quest For The Sword Fragments And The Hunt For Dranngore><By Katrina Mandrake-Johnston ><Ch 3>

CHAPTER 3 = THE CARRIAGE RIDE

***

After a long time of silence, watching the dark forest from out of the carriage window, Asdella finally said, "I suppose you want to know in detail who that man was."

Asdella told them about her past, as she had done with Narr within her mind the night before.

Weena told her, "I'm sorry that happened to you, but that doesn't give you the right to just go around killing anyone and everyone that was ever involved in that. Like Lorenta said, that was a long time ago, what if he was a changed man? I'm sure we've all done things we're not proud of, but that doesn't mean we should be judged for it all of our lives. What if he spent his whole life trying to make up for that one mistake?" and then her mind inquired, "*And who exactly are you talking about here, Weena?*"

"No one can make up for that!" Asdella snapped angrily, "There's no way to atone for those kinds of evils!"

Candra told Asdella, "I was kidnapped by a bunch of men once. They took me to a place that was like what you spoke of."

"Yeah, I remember," commented Dendrox, "And I have the scar to remind me."

"It was you, wasn't it?" Candra asked her, "Before anything happened to me, I was rescued by one of the women there who had escaped and came to free everyone. It was you, wasn't it?"

"Could have been. I don't remember," she said staring sadly out the window again.

"So what do you have against The Black Shadow?" Vordin asked, still curious from their conversation earlier just before they had arrived at Vackiindmire.

"You won't leave anything be, will you?!" Asdella said angrily at him, "You want to know? Fine."

Asdella told of how it was a few months after she had been captured. The Black Shadow had dropped out of the sky and began to brutally slaughter the men who had been violating the women. She explained that it had been a gruesome sight, but she hadn't cared as they were getting what they deserved. Asdella had thought that she and the other women were being rescued by The Black Shadow. She had thought that this was their chance for freedom, but then he began to turn on the women as well, his eyes as red as the blood he was spilling. Then he had simply flown away, leaving everyone dead except for three of the men and five of the women.

Vexcindor called out to them, "If it's getting a little chilly in there, there are curtains you can drape across the windows. There's a place on the bottom to clasp it to the carriage wall to keep the wind out. A large one is rolled up near the ceiling for the side with the door."

It was apparent that Lorenta was intending to remain in human form for the duration of their journey this night. Lorenta, who was sitting near the window opposite Asdella, decided to pull and attach the curtain across the small opening. Asdella did the same.

Candra, who was sitting rigidly beside Lorenta, had her bow awkwardly positioned in front of her. Weena had her hands folded in her lap, her arms tightly tucked in, as she tried to give Candra as much room as she could on the cramped seat of the carriage. Next to Weena was Vordin, and he was sitting by the large window that made up the upper half of the carriage on the side with the door.

Vordin was feeling chilled by the night air and he asked Dendrox, who was sitting opposite him

<Zaylyn ><Quest For The Sword Fragments And The Hunt For Dranngore><By Katrina Mandrake-Johnston >   <Ch 3> < 6 >

next to Nodwel, "Dendrox, did you want to put the curtain down?"

"No," he firmly answered. He was sitting with his elbow resting on the window's edge with his hand positioned just under his jaw. He was searching the trees with his eyes.

"*What's wrong with Dendrox? He appears to have gotten so distant as of late,*" Weena thought to herself, "*I mean with the news about the sword, the trouble with the bounty hunters, and the thieves who robbed us; it's understandable, isn't it? What if it's more than that? What if it's me? What if he's just not interested in me anymore now that things have gotten a little more serious? Was that night just to add a bit of comfort to a terrible and dangerous situation? Maybe I'm just trying to read too much into it. Well, at least I hope I am anyway.*"

Lorenta found herself falling asleep. The motion of the carriage was surprisingly soothing, as the road was well made compared to most other dirt roads and the wheels ran somewhat smoothly over it.

She had the dream again…

She found herself in the village once more. The villagers viciously screamed their hateful words. This time she was not an observer though. Lorenta found herself within the burning building, the flames eagerly consuming the wood of the walls around her. In her arms, wrapped in an old blanket, was the child. The grotesque baby gargled a sickening noise at her.

Lorenta did not know what to do. So many emotions were boiling up inside her; she didn't know which one to give voice to. She despised the horrid villagers outside. She felt helpless and angry and scared.

Lorenta looked down at the child in confusion. It disgusted her. Part of her wanted to hurl the hideous thing into the flames and escape the burning building disguised as a human. Part of her wanted to somehow save the child. The back of her mind kept saying, "*And then what? Doom the poor thing to a life of hiding? Knowing that everywhere this creature turns he will be hated, no matter what he's done, just because he exists?*"

The flames were engulfing the building more rapidly now than before. She could hear the villagers cheering and encouraging the fire to burn faster.

Lorenta continued to look at the child, and bit-by-bit, it slowly began to not appear so horrible as she had first thought. The baby remained the same, but now he didn't seem as awful as before.

"*This is what I am, isn't it?*" she whispered to the baby, "*I foolishly try to see myself as still being a spider, that my human form is just a disguise my spider self puts on to hide from the hatred of the humans. This is not so, is it? I am not completely human, but I have a human's desires and emotions. Part of me is human, and I need to accept that. I can't keep telling myself that the human side of me is just a shell; that it's not actually a part of who I am. So what am I then? I'm not a just spider, that's for sure. I stopped being that a long time ago, as soon as I was created. I'm not a true human either; at least I don't think I am. Could it be now, that I am in fact a human who pretends at being a spider? That is how it feels sometimes. This is what I am, this child here. Neither fully human or fully spider, but somehow both all mixed together. This is who I am and I need to accept it.*"

It was getting hard to breathe now, as the room had been filling with smoke. Her eyes began to sting and the baby sputtered out a cough. "And the father of this child?" she asked aloud, "Did he flee in terror at the sight of his offspring?"

"*Am I to become like the dragon in the story Rasindell told me as a child? Am I to spawn a race of spider people? Who would accept them? They would be hunted down for sport or made slaves to be beaten by their masters. The human-dragons were accepted into society. Of course that is only in places where race diversity is common. I doubt this child would be accepted, look at how the giant spiders were treated.*"

The smoke and flames threatened the life of her and the child. They would be dead in a matter of seconds. "I will not let the villagers win!" she yelled, "I will not let them destroy us, just because they are so ignorant!"

Lorenta, with the child, crawled along the ground trying desperately to breathe below the thick deadly smoke so close above them. There was an opening in the wall, which Lorenta was certain hadn't

<Zaylyn ><Quest For The Sword Fragments And The Hunt For Dranngore><By Katrina Mandrake-Johnston >   <Ch 3> < 7 >
been there before.

They both made it out of the building and then her dream shifted, and she was in a forest clearing. The baby was gone, but she knew that the child had simply been a representation of herself and nothing more. At least, that was something she wanted herself to believe.

It was dark in this forest and there was an eerie silence.

"The Black Shadow was supposed to have given Rasindell the potion that created me. Does this mean I am an evil being?" she asked herself, speaking into the night, "Does it mean that my existence is part of some evil plan set in motion so long ago? I am being silly. I am not evil. I try to do good deeds. I do not have evil intentions. I am not a selfish person; I put others before myself. I did kill that man though. Was I to let him kill Vordin and myself? Would that have been the right thing to do? Maybe there was another way; maybe I didn't need to kill him. I didn't even do it intentionally. I just reacted. I didn't even know I could do something like that. Besides, Weena said that he would have killed many others if he had survived. He would have killed others, probably Weena, providing an evil wizard with more magical power and spells. But the man I killed was an innocent victim. It wasn't his fault that he had been cursed like that. There was no choice, we couldn't have saved him. I did a good thing, didn't I?"

A dip in the road jarred her from her slumber.

<World of Zaylyn ><Quest For The Sword Fragments And The Hunt For Dranngore><By Katrina Mandrake-Johnston ><Ch 4>

CHAPTER 4 = AMBUSH

Dendrox alerted the group, "There in the large oak, Candra!"

Candra skillfully eased down off her seat to crouch in the bottom of the carriage. She took an arrow from her quiver and with it in her bow, carefully took aim toward the oak tree, all in a matter of seconds and without questioning. Everyone else was confused as to what they were doing and what exactly Candra was aiming at, but they all suspected and prepared for danger.

"I see him," Candra told Dendrox, but before she could loose her arrow, the horses whinnied in pain, Vexcindor cursed loudly, and the carriage lurched forward as the horses broke into a mad gallop. Candra fell backwards, her arrow biting into the wood of the roof, as the carriage shook violently.

"Hold on! We have some trouble!" Vexcindor called to the passengers.

"What is it? What did you see?" Weena asked the thieves, fearing the worst.

"The bandits we heard about. We just encountered them. Be prepared," Dendrox instructed her calmly.

"Well at least," Vordin said trying to hold on as the carriage rocked back and forth, "it's not a Killnarin!"

"Keep your arms in, lad, unless you want to lose one of them," Nodwel warned him.

"Damn it!" yelled the carriage driver as he desperately tried to regain control of the horses, "Log! Log!"

The horses jumped over the log, which the bandits had placed across the road as part of their ambush. Just as the bandits had intended, the wheels of the carriage hit the log at great speed, sending the compartment crashing to the ground on its side. Vexcindor, seeing what was about to happen, jumped forward onto the back of one of the horses saving himself from being thrown to his death. Upon impact, the horses broke free of the carriage, and luckily after awhile, Vexcindor was able to get them settled down despite the fact that each had an arrow embedded in their flank.

Meanwhile, as Vexcindor was dealing with the horses, within the carriage, the passengers had been thrown against each other in the fall and were desperately trying to get out before the bandits closed in to attack.

"Get your stubby fingers out of my face, dwarf! Ow, damn it! You weigh a ton! Get off me!" Asdella barked angrily.

The large window with the carriage door was exposed to the air in their advantage.

"Is everyone okay?" Nodwel asked, "Watch out for my axe!"

<Zaylyn ><Quest For The Sword Fragments And The Hunt For Dranngore><By Katrina Mandrake-Johnston >   <Ch 4> < 8 >

"And my sword, you great oaf!" yelled Asdella, "Get out! You're crushing me!"

Weena had been thrown into the center of the carriage and had broken Candra's fall with her body. Vordin had landed on both Lorenta and Candra. Nodwel who had managed to somewhat brace himself in the fall with his arm against the side wall of the carriage, tried to keep his near three-hundred pounds of dense body mass from crushing Asdella beneath him. Luckily, he had managed to stay clear of her sword during the crash. Dendrox had managed to hold on to the side as the carriage fell and was able to keep himself from slipping down onto the blade of Nodwel's exposed battle-axe.

Dendrox was the first to escape through the window and he helped Vordin through. Candra was next to pull herself free of the carriage, but not before retrieving a burlap bag from out from behind one of the cushions of the bench as Weena grunted and groaned with each ill-placed limb by Candra.

Candra opened the bag, handed numerous daggers to Dendrox from it, and next took out several arrows, placed them into her quiver, and tossed the bag away. Dendrox gave her a surprised look but said nothing.

"Your turn dwarf, get the hell off me!" commanded Asdella angrily.

"I can't! I'm positioned just so. If I move I'll slice myself on your damn sword or you'll get a few broken bones as I'll have to step all over you to be able to get out. They have scabbards for a reason," he said through gritted teeth as the strain of supporting his awkward position was getting to him.

"You'll have to get out of there pretty quick," Dendrox told them all, as he scanned the trees.

Vordin commented, "We're lucky to have escaped with only a few bruises."

"We'll be lucky to get out of this alive, fool! You have no idea how serious this is!" Candra snapped at him, "Shut up and watch the trees! We need every advantage!"

Lorenta told Nodwel, "Don't worry, I can get you out."

She climbed out of the carriage and then standing over the large window, reached down and grabbed the heavy dwarf by the arm with her good hand. Next she simply lifted him out with incredible strength. Everyone stared at her in amazement.

"How the hell..." Dendrox began.

"Well, well, well," a low masculine voice rang out.

"Damn it!" cursed Candra, "I shouldn't have let myself get distracted. I know better than that!"

"Oh, that's just too bad," the voice mocked.

<World of Zaylyn ><Quest For The Sword Fragments And The Hunt For Dranngore><By Katrina Mandrake-Johnston ><Ch 5>

CHAPTER 5 = ATTACK OF THE BANDITS

Candra raised her bow. "No," said the voice sternly, "I wouldn't do that if I were you. Our number is great, and I guarantee that at least one arrow or crossbow bolt is already aimed at the heart of each and every one of you."

Candra looked around and saw that this was true. It seemed as if the bandits had appeared out of nowhere. Asdella was next to come out of the fallen carriage.

Candra shouted, "Show yourself coward!"

"Oh, aren't you a feisty one," the voice laughed.

Weena whispered, "I'm stuck, I can't get out."

Vordin helped to pull her out and her robes were torn slightly in the process as they had become caught on one of the curtain clasps. Weena had received a large scrape from this same clasp during the fall and it had begun to bleed.

The bandits came forward out of the forest and Candra counted thirty-two in all. They carried an assortment of weapons and Candra could see that it would be suicide to try to fight their way out of this situation. The bounty hunters from Vackiindmire were among them. She could see that whomever had spoken had been telling the truth about the arrows and crossbows being aimed at them all.

"Well, this is all of you then?" said the one who had addressed them before as he stepped forward with his arms extended as if he were about to greet them to a grand event.

He was a large man wearing a small black open vest. His muscular chest was horribly scarred by thick slashes. Candra got the impression that he was displaying his scars almost like some sort of

<Zaylyn ><Quest For The Sword Fragments And The Hunt For Dranngore><By Katrina Mandrake-Johnston >   <Ch 5> < 9 >

trophy, although she couldn't imagine why. What was most interesting about this man was that the greater half of his right forearm was missing and that a small crossbow had been attached and specially fitted into place probably by magic as the flesh and wood appeared to be melded together as one. His arm was now aimed directly at her. He obviously found her to be of the most threat and was probably right, considering her accuracy with a bow. Candra suspected that he was the leader of these bandits.

Weena and Vordin slowly edged around the carriage in hope that if things got violent that perhaps they could take cover behind it.

Vexcindor was trying to sooth the injured horses and then suddenly both of the animals collapsed to the ground. "What have you done!" the carriage driver screamed at the bandits.

"Calm down, the arrows used on the animals were enchanted with Sleep spells. Can't have our new horses running off on us, now can we?" the leader chuckled. The cruel and unmerciful man looked over his captives with a disgusted look. "Nexzath! Where are you!" he called out angrily, "The ugly one who always wears that damn hood. Where is he?!"

"I am here," Nexzath answered meekly, coming to stand beside the leader. Over a simple dark greenish-brown long-sleeved shirt, a light brown hooded cloak, which had been cut off at mid waist, obscured his face. Other than this, he wore plain light brown pants, matching gloves, and a pair of dark brown boots.

"This here is supposed to be the carriage containing three wealthy merchants transporting their goods? Three wealthy merchants with several highly trained bodyguards?" asked the leader, clearly furious with this man.

"Hey, it don't matter as there be a bounty on them two here," one of the bounty hunters spoke up, the one with the eye patch and the scimitar.

The one with the whip and daggers added with a laugh, "All 'bout a pair of magical scissors it was."

"Yeah, a couple of dwarves out of Shirkint hired us for the job, but it proved more trouble than it was worth. Looks like we'll be able to collect after all," said the large bald man with the huge hammer, formerly the leader of this bounty hunter group.

"You new recruits know nothing about proper respect. Speaking whenever you wish, trying to dominate the situation? You will learn your place," the leader of the bandits sneered viciously and fired a crossbow bolt from his arm into each of the four bounty hunters, killing them, even the bald mustached one with the gold tooth and spiked mace who had remained silent.

"That is what I was told, I swear!" Nexzath told the leader, fearing for his life.

"And you are sure it was this carriage?" he snapped, his temper showing as he glowered down at him.

"Yes, please, this is the only one traveling at night. This is the one! From what I was told, we would have needed all our number to take them down. I would not lie to you! Please, you must believe me!" Nexzath pleaded.

Asdella could stand it no longer, sword in hand, she charged screaming a fierce battle cry at the nearest bandit.

"Asdella, no!" Nodwel shouted at her, but it was too late.

The bandit, in reaction to her attack, simply raised his crossbow and fired a bolt at her. The leader laughed at her recklessness. The bolt punched its way into her shoulder, the force and pain making her stagger back. Blood began to trickle from the wound. Weena and Vordin cowered behind the overturned carriage. Asdella's scream of pain quickly turned to one of rage, as she continued to lunge forward and impaled him on her sword.

***

Narr now had a better understanding of where the warrior in Asdella came from, as with time, he was becoming more and more aware of the world and the inner workings of the people around him.

Narr thought from within Asdella's mind, "*Asdella, with her raw unbridled fury, fueled by every vile touch, every violent violation, every bruise, every beating, all the helpless unheard cries for help, all the cruel and malicious laughs... For her lost self. The one that they had taken away from her.*

<Zaylyn ><Quest For The Sword Fragments And The Hunt For Dranngore><By Katrina Mandrake-Johnston >   <Ch 5> < 10 >

"The self that still had her innocence, the one that would have had no trouble falling in love, the self that didn't have such hatred burning inside her... the one that didn't know what it was like to choke the life out of a man with her bare hands and to be so insane with malice to be strong enough to do so... and had no regret in doing so, and enjoyed the desperate shocked expression on the face of that monster of a man... and wished she could have tortured the life out of him slowly and painfully over several years as he had done to her.

"She hated what she had become. Whenever she fought and killed, it was like she was getting a little more of that vengeance, even if it was so very wrong. Her body was no longer hers. She had lost it a long time ago. She had taken it back, but it would never truly be her own ever again.

"And now, now she still uses it merely as a tool in battle and nothing more. She still doesn't care whether she lives or dies. Life holds no joy for her anymore, then and now, except for battle and the deaths of those that intend to harm her.

"Do I really want to give up on her though? I thought things were going so well, that she was opening up to me and that I was finally able to truly understand her. But after she murdered the man back in the tavern... I hadn't expected her to go as far as that... Here it's self-defense, but I doubt that makes any difference to her, and I doubt she will back down once that excuse has passed."

***

Candra and Dendrox immediately began to take out the bandits armed with missile weapons. Candra suffered an arrow to the thigh and Dendrox a bolt to the stomach, but they kept on in their attack.

The leader did not attack right away as Candra figured he would, it was as if he were waiting for someone to dare an attack on him. He simply stood there with a smug look on his face, his crossbow arm held out, his other hand on the trigger ready to fire. He had clearly shown that his crossbow could magically fire repeatedly without reloading. It was for this reason, Candra and Dendrox avoided him but were wary of what he might do.

Nodwel swung his axe, dispatching several of the inexperienced bandits wielding swords and other similar weapons.

Asdella's sword was stuck fast within the body of the first bandit. She was now without her weapon but that didn't seem to bother her in the slightest. She merely attacked one of the bandits barehanded, punching and clawing, biting and kicking, and doing so with a bolt lodged painfully in the meat of her shoulder. It was a miracle she wasn't killed. Finally, she managed to wrench the sword out of her opponent's hand. It was a much shorter blade than her own sword, but that didn't matter in the least. After dispatching her opponent, she eagerly searched the battlefield for yet another, having no qualms about continuing her massacre.

Meanwhile, Lorenta had decided to change into her spider form. Her body had appeared to liquefy as she stood there in the middle of the road as the battle raged around her. One of the bandits, fearful of what strange magic was taking place, fired an arrow at her, but before it could find its mark, engulfed in the green flames, Lorenta's body collapsed down into a black inky puddle.

"The girl! She be a witch! She disappeared!" the bandit shouted in terror to no one in-particular, before one of Candra's arrows punched deep into his chest.

From the liquid-like mass, which appeared no more than a shadow in the darkness, Lorenta changed into her spider form. She easily crept across the battlefield undetected, moving among the fallen and staying hidden within the shadows. Slowly and meticulously, Lorenta moved toward the bandit leader.

When Lorenta was positioned behind him, she could hear him chuckling to himself and saying, "Look how they are slaughtered. Pathetic fools the lot of them. These are the idiots that think they deserve to serve under me? I think I'll let them die a little longer before taking out this scraggly bunch of adventurers myself."

Lorenta crawled quickly up the back of the leader, and before he could react, she had changed into her human form, pushed her arm against his neck with her great strength, and as her spider fangs emerged, she bit into his shoulder sending deadly venom into his body. Lorenta then simply released

<Zaylyn ><Quest For The Sword Fragments And The Hunt For Dranngore><By Katrina Mandrake-Johnston >   <Ch 5> < 11 >
him.

The leader spun around to face her, but the color of his skin had already turned to a sickly grey. He tried to raise his crossbow, but he instead collapsed to the ground. He stared up at her in terror and disbelief as her fangs retracted back into her face and she regained her human appearance once more. Lorenta stood calmly over him as he convulsed for a few seconds before his death.

One of the bandits, intent on slaying Weena and Vordin, approached them as they cowered in fear behind the carriage. Asdella, seeing this, bolted toward their attacker slicing his head clean off his body with an incredible force. Weena screamed in terror.

"It's him!" one of the bandits shouted.

The Black Shadow, sitting upon a pitch-black mare, was a little way up the road. Nexzath, who had stayed out of the battle by the edge of the forest called out, "It was him! He was the one who set this up!"

The Black Shadow dismounted and slowly approached the battle that had come to a halt upon his presence. Asdella, blood-splattered, motioned her companions over to the overturned carriage.

Asdella said to them all, when they had joined her behind the carriage, "Whatever you do, don't draw attention to yourself."

Vexcindor, who had also come to crouch behind the carriage, nodded in agreement.

The Black Shadow bolted forward with great speed after the closest bandit, his form almost a blur. The man had tried to run, but it was useless, The Black Shadow soon had him in his grasp and he bit deeply into him, feeding until the bandit became lifeless.

One of the bandits, her hands trembling, picked up a crossbow and bolt from one of the fallen and fired at him. The Black Shadow laughed maliciously, his eyes beginning to glow red beneath his hood. The bolt she had fired struck him in the chest but merely fell to the ground as if it had hit solid stone. The attack didn't seem to faze him at all.

Another bandit attacked The Black Shadow wielding a short sword. He welcomed the attack, his control over himself fading more and more. The Black Shadow slapped the blade aside and threw the man clear across the road and into a tree, with such strength and speed that the man's spine wrapped around the trunk with an awful crunching sound.

The remaining bandits stood motionless, not knowing what to do.

Vexcindor said bitterly, "Many a passenger has been taken from my carriage by this foul creature. He'll not have any more!" He took a blowpipe from his waistband.

Another bandit was slaughtered by The Black Shadow, having his arm torn from his body with blood bathing the ground in great spurts.

"Could… could it be that I've misjudged the reasons behind his attacks?" Vexcindor questioned hesitating, "Maybe his attacks in the past were not on innocent people as I had believed."

"No, he'll kill us all regardless," Asdella replied.

"You don't know that!" Vordin said to her, "How can you say this after all he's done to help us?"

"I've seen this before," the warrior woman whispered as her answer, "If he goes into a killing frenzy, that is all that will matter. No amount of running, no amount of fighting, no powerful spells, nothing will be able to stop him, and certainly not that little blowpipe, carriage driver. You really think that will have any effect on him?"

"Well, no. But this time I wasn't just going to stand by for fear of my own life while others lose theirs. I was at least going to try this time," he said with desperation in his eyes.

The remaining bandits had begun to flee in terror. The Black Shadow fed on them eagerly and only three of the eleven managed to escape with their lives into the forest.

Nexzath cowered at the edge of the road next to a tree trunk. The Black Shadow's gaze fell on him, and as his black boots stepped nimbly among the dead, he slowly moved toward him. Nexzath could do nothing but tremble in fear as the dark figure calmly approached.

"Don't say a word," Asdella whispered.

The glowing red eyes of The Black Shadow darted in the direction of her voice, a low growl emitting from his throat. Although after a moment, he returned his attention to Nexzath.

<Zaylyn ><Quest For The Sword Fragments And The Hunt For Dranngore><By Katrina Mandrake-Johnston >   <Ch 5> < 12 >

"Wait! Please!" begged Nexzath, his forked tongue flicking out from beneath his hood like that of a snake.

<World of Zaylyn ><Quest For The Sword Fragments And The Hunt For Dranngore><By Katrina Mandrake-Johnston ><Ch 6>

CHAPTER 6 = NEXZATH

His mind opened up to him. The Black Shadow saw a memory of Nexzath's mother. She was a small child, no more than five years old. He was instantly curious of how this came to be. The Black Shadow pried further.

"One day, I was playing here," she said speaking of the field by the far edge of her village near an old abandoned hut, "and I found a strange bottle with a black goo inside. The bottle had a crack in it, and when I picked it up, the goo got all over my hands, and it went right inside my skin!" she told him showing Nexzath her hand.

"What happened, Mummy?" asked the young Nexzath.

She continued to tell him the story of how he came to be, "I started to feel really sick and my belly started to really, really hurt. It was so scary! Mummy and Daddy told me I was never to play there, and I was going to get in so much trouble! My belly started to grow like something was inside it, and it was so very fast. An old witch was supposed to live in that old hut a very long time ago. I went inside there to hide, and I thought my belly was going to explode, and then a baby crawled out of it, and I got to be a mummy. You had big orange eyes, and a scrunched nose, and a big funny tongue like a snake, and soft yellowy scales. And then I heard my mummy calling me, so I tucked you up in an old blanket and went home for dinner. I snuck some food into a little bag and some of my dolly clothes, and I came back when I came to play after dinner. I mushed it up, and you ate it all. You were bigger too than before. When I had to go home for bedtime, I wrapped you all up, and I was worried all night. When I came back, you were even bigger, and you could talk. You called me mummy, and we played all day. And every day, I would come to play, and you are bigger every day. Soon you're going to be as big as me!"

She gave him a hug and young Nexzath snuggled up to her.

The Black Shadow searched beyond Nexzath's memories wanting to discover more about this strange event.

There had in fact been an old woman living in the old hut who had been dabbling into darker magic and had been quite powerful. It was when she started preying on the nearby village to acquire subjects for her experiments that the villagers turned on her. They hired someone to rescue their village from the threat that was the witch. This man they had hired is the girl's father.

The Black Shadow searched even further to discover that the substance within the bottle the girl found actually created a duplicate of the girl, but with some very unique and extraordinary differences. It had used the makeup of the girl's body as the basis for Nexzath's creation; she was in fact his mother.

The Black Shadow went back into Nexzath's memories. The next memory he saw was of Nexzath and his mother playing in the field by the old hut. He had grown to be around the same age of his mother and his rapid growth had slowed to normal. She had not heard her mother and father calling her, and when they came to find her, they discovered the strange child.

"Get away from that monster!" they shouted in panic.

"He's not a monster! He's my baby, and I'm his mummy. He's good!" said the little girl.

"We told you never to play here! It's dangerous! Now get away from that creature!" they told her.

Nexzath didn't know what they were screaming about, his mind trying to make sense of things, "*Do they think I am the monster? Why don't they want my mummy to play with me? I love her. Why are they trying to take her away from me?*"

Her father stepped forward saying, "I said to get away, Vina!"

"Please, Vina, listen to your father!" her mother pleaded.

"No!" she shouted fiercely at her father, "I told you that he is good!"

<Zaylyn ><Quest For The Sword Fragments And The Hunt For Dranngore><By Katrina Mandrake-Johnston >   <Ch 6> < 13 >

Her father came and took her firmly by the arm.

"Mummy?" said Nexzath, afraid and unclear of what was happening. The girl's mother looked on with a horrible expression of anguish, fear, and worry.

"Come on! Let's go!" her father commanded.

"Mummy? Where are you going?" Nexzath asked starting to cry, his round orange eyes looking sadly at her as large tears rolled down the yellowy scales of his short snout, "Don't leave!"

"Stay away you foul thing! I'll not have her life ruined by some devilish magic!" her father snarled in anger at him and pushed him viciously to the ground.

Nexzath cried out in pain and fear as he fell to the ground hard. He looked up at them and wiped away the tears with his clawed hand, his forked snake-like tongue exposing itself to the air as it often did when he was confused or curious, and especially when he was nervous and frightened.

"Daddy, no!" Vina cried, tears rolling down her cheeks, "He's good, Daddy! He's my baby! Don't hurt him!"

She was finally dragged away from him and the old hut, while she sobbed and tried to wriggle free from her father's grip.

"Mummy! No, wait! Don't leave me! Mummy, come back! Come back!" Nexzath shouted after them, but to no use. He finally retreated into the old hut for shelter, as it was growing dark with the approaching night.

The Black Shadow switched his focus onto the girl and her family. Her parents brought her to their home and locked her in her room hoping that she would eventually calm down.

"Acklore, I cannot take this any longer," the girl's mother explained to him, "When we were married, you agreed to leave the reckless life of an adventurer. You agreed that having a family was more important than all the dangers and risks of your old life. You agreed that once you had a family that to continue that way would be insane, that you would never wish those kinds of dangers on your family."

Acklore replied, with concern in his voice, "Dear, what are you saying? I have done exactly this. My life is here with you and Vina; I want nothing more than this."

"The witch, the one you were supposed to handle, her belongings, her hut on the outskirts of the village, the one you were supposed to be watching over just in case there was some slight chance that some of her evil magic survived… This is our daughter!" his wife sobbed.

"Everything will be taken care of. Yamith overheard our little squabble on our way into the village. You know how nosy he can be. He'll have the whole village in an uproar. Nothing will be left of that hut, or that creature, magical dangers or no. Now that the safety of the children is at risk."

She stared in astonishment at him, "You don't get it, do you? That place should have been destroyed a long time ago, burned. Even the ground dug up, everything to get rid of any trace of that horrible woman. The risk should have been taken then, not now! Not after our daughter is lost to us! This is all your fault! You always speak about all your grand adventures, all those narrow escapes. But when it really matters, when there is a potential danger so close to your family, you do nothing about it! Holding on to it like some damn relic of your past. Are you afraid someone might forget what you did for this village? That if the witch's hut was properly destroyed, that you would fade away and become an ordinary man, that your status as an adventurer would disappear, that no one would remember your name or tell stories about you anymore?"

"Dear, how can you say such things?" he said, trying to coax her into calming herself.

"I can't believe I didn't realize any of this before," his wife shook her head sadly, "You were hoping something like this would happen, weren't you? That you would have to become the hero again and take care of some magical occurrence that had survived all this time. You just didn't expect it to be our daughter that would be the victim. How could you?!"

"No, how can you think that?" he exclaimed, "Besides, Vina is all right."

"All right?!" she shouted at him, "All right?! She will never be all right! Never, not ever! That damn thing is connected to her! It has tricked her into thinking that she is its mother! She will always

<Zaylyn ><Quest For The Sword Fragments And The Hunt For Dranngore><By Katrina Mandrake-Johnston >   <Ch 6> < 14 >

believe that, damn it!" She went to the door and flung it open.

"Stop! Where are you going?!" Acklore said, rushing over to her.

"I... I'm leaving you," she replied with tears streaming down her face, "I'm sorry, but it will be better this way."

"What?! But surely things cannot be as serious as you think. You're just upset. You just need to give it time," he pleaded with her.

"No. I have to leave. I must. I keep on thinking about what next horror will arise out of your past to tear our family apart. I can't bring myself to live through that. I don't have the courage to face those kinds of dangers," she tried to explain, "I cannot prepare Vina for that kind of life, and I would in fact hinder her from developing the skills she needs to survive. You must raise her on your own. I'm sorry, I do love you both so very much, but this is best. I was wrong to think you could escape the dangers of your past and settle down into such a life as I wanted. I am sorry."

"Wait. Please wait," Acklore said taking her by the arm, "What are you saying! Please, let's talk about this. I know things haven't been too great lately, but you can't just leave! What about Vina? What am I to tell her? Will you be visiting her in the future? Surely you cannot simply abandon your own daughter because of this!"

"Do you think I want to?!" she screamed into his face, "Didn't you see?! That creature is like some horrible duplicate of our daughter. You forget that I've lived here long before you came. I was not blind to the activities of the witch. I've seen the same things happen to others. They are connected! This is the only explanation of how that creature could learn to speak within such a short time. Its mind is linked with hers. Whatever she knows and learns, so does it. Did you ever think what might happen if that connection is severed? It was the witch's way of ensuring her creations would thrive. We fought back only to discover that in doing so, we were also inflicting harm on our own friends and family that had fallen victim to her. We sent for you to destroy the witch, while the ones connected to her monsters bravely and selflessly sacrificed their lives to finally rid... I can't help her! I can't keep her safe! If I get in the way... Vina needs to learn everything she can from you. I will just cause for time to be wasted. She's a mother teaching her child without physically doing so or even being aware of it. You teach her what she needs to know. You teach her, to ensure the survival of that beast and therefore hers. Please..." she said looking into his eyes with overwhelming emotion, "do not try to find me," and with that she closed the door behind her.

Nexzath shivered and wrapped his blanket tightly around his shoulders. He saw a glow coming from outside the hut from across the field. He peered through a crack in the wood and saw that many villagers carrying torches and weapons were making their way toward him. He was so incredibly frightened as he realized they were coming to hunt him down. His mother had warned him about something like this, and why he should never follow her into the village.

He crawled through a hole in the back wall of the hut and ran into the nearby forest. He hid there, sleeping and shivering during the nights, and eating insects and berries, a few of which made his stomach upset.

After several days, the villagers eventually stopped looking for him, assuming that he was either dead or had fled the area. His mother, however, had not given up on him, and she soon came to find him.

"You have to leave," she told him, "It's not safe for you here anymore."

"But Mummy, I don't understand. What did I do? Why do they hate me? I want to stay with you," he told her, tears once again starting in his eyes and he hugged her tightly.

"But they will hurt you if they find you. You can't stay here any longer. I can't hide you. Daddy always finds out when I try to hide something and he will know," she explained trying to act as grownup as she could.

"Please don't make me go, Mummy. I'm scared," he said holding onto her and sobbing into her shoulder, "Where am I to go? It's so scary out here all alone, and I got so hungry I ate some things that made me sick. Don't make me go, Mummy, please!"

<Zaylyn ><Quest For The Sword Fragments And The Hunt For Dranngore><By Katrina Mandrake-Johnston >   <Ch 6> < 15 >

"No, it's too dangerous. You're supposed to listen to me, okay?" she said speaking how she thought a parent should, "I've brought you some things. Here look."

She opened up the backpack she had brought with her and pulled out some clothes and a big hooded cloak to hide his face that she had stolen from her father's closet. She had cut the cloak in half so it would fit his small form. She also showed him that she had filled the backpack with plenty of food.

"Mummy, you could come with me," Nexzath suggested.

"I... I can't," she told him, "I want to, but Daddy's all alone now. He would get sad if I left too. He would find us; we wouldn't be able to hide."

"But..." he began.

She was crying heavily now, and she told him, "You have to go! You have to go so you will be safe!"

"Okay," he finally said, but they both cried for a long time before he left on his own into the forest.

The Black Shadow saw other memories of the cruelty Nexzath was shown over the years every time he would come to a town or village looking for food. Rocks would be thrown, hurtful names would be called, and he had to survive on what scraps of garbage he could find, especially during the winter.

Finally the memories showed him that Nexzath had recently joined the bandits a few days ago in hope that they might accept him.

"Come with me," The Black Shadow said to him, "We shall speak further at Shirkint. I will not harm you."

Nexzath looked up at the figure before him in fear and did not know what to expect. The red glow of his eyes had subsided to nothingness as he stared down at him, the features of his face hidden in shadow beneath his black hood.

The Black Shadow extended a hand toward Nexzath in a gesture to help him to his feet. Nexzath was shocked by this and was reluctant to do anything at all, but finally he accepted his hand.

"Come," The Black Shadow told him and led him to where his horse awaited his return.

With Nexzath on the back of the horse behind The Black Shadow, they sped off in the direction of Shirkint together.

<World of Zaylyn ><Quest For The Sword Fragments And The Hunt For Dranngore><By Katrina Mandrake-Johnston ><Ch 7>

CHAPTER 7 =   AFTER THE BATTLE

Vexcindor, who had gone over to the side with the horses after the battle, announced, "The horses are comin' 'round. I'll be taking them back to Vackiindmire. I wish you luck. You have a long journey ahead, as we have only come a short distance into the forest."

The carriage driver led the injured horses back south along the road, all the while whispering comforting words to the two animals.

"You killed all those people!" Weena blurted out at Asdella, "First the man at the inn and now here!"

"And I guess the fact that I saved your life has nothing to do with any of this, does it?" Asdella snarled, "I didn't have to. I could have easily let the both of you die. Most people would be grateful when someone saves them from a violent death."

"I'm grateful," Vordin spoke up.

Weena said, "But you enjoy it! All the killing! Those were people. Does that mean nothing to you?!"

Asdella retorted, "Stupid girl. They were trying to kill all of us. It's self-defense. I do what I must."

"No, you don't!" Weena glared at her.

"You know everything, do you? You think you are so perfect and that everyone should think and

<Zaylyn ><Quest For The Sword Fragments And The Hunt For Dranngore><By Katrina Mandrake-Johnston >   <Ch 7> < 16 >

be like you? Is that how it is?" Asdella snapped at her, absolutely furious, "Guess what! No, I don't care if I kill a few miserable bastards! No, I'm not going to feel badly about it, and especially not when they are the ones trying to kill me first! And no, I definitely don't give a damn one way or another if some feebleminded wimp of a girl approves of it or not!"

"I'm grateful," Vordin added again, trying to make certain that he was not included in the argument.

"Weena?" Dendrox said weakly, easing himself to the ground, his hands red with blood as he held his side where the bolt had struck him. "Weena?" he called again, clearly in great pain, "I could really use one of your healing spells."

Candra hobbled painfully over to him, the arrow still protruding from her thigh, and carefully eased her leg down to sit beside him with both her legs outstretched before her. A look of great concern was on her face. "What's with you and getting struck in the gut? One scar not enough?" she said forcing a laugh, but she was almost in tears, which was a rare thing for this strong-willed elf.

Weena rushed over to them both, purposely ignoring the fact that Asdella's wounded shoulder was in need of care, and she hoped that Asdella had noticed this. "Are you all right, Candra?" Weena asked looking at the arrow.

"Damn it! Never mind me! Help Dendrox!" Candra told her.

"But if I use the spell, I won't be able to use it again for quite awhile. It needs to recharge itself in a way," Weena explained.

Frustrated, distraught, and in pain, Candra picked up a fair sized rock from the ground and threw it at her. "Shut up! Help him! Use your damn spell and save him!" Candra screamed at her. Tears were streaming down her face now and the incredible fear she felt was fully showing.

Dendrox weakly took Candra's hand, hating that she was seeing him like this yet again.

Weena obeyed, and kneeling beside him, performed the spell. Once Dendrox's condition had stabilized and the crossbow bolt had been pushed free of his body, Candra relaxed slightly. Weena half expected an apology from Candra and at least some sort of praise for her spell working correctly, but she received nothing.

"Nodwel," the elf called to the dwarf, "Could you find me a bit of cloth and a belt? I'm going to need something to stop the bleeding when I pull this arrow out."

"I'll be pulling that arrow out," Nodwel explained to her, "I have a bit of experience with this sort of thing. You just deal with the pain, I'll handle the rest."

Candra nodded.

Asdella seated herself on top of the fallen carriage and proceeded to pry the bolt out of her shoulder with her fingers, trying to ignore the excruciating pain she was causing herself. The more she poked about in the wound, the more blood oozed out, which made it all the more difficult to locate the bolt. Every time she tried to grasp it, her fingers would slip. The pain was almost unbearable. Tears were streaming down her face and every now and then she would stifle a cry of pain into a whimper. She would have refused any help, had it been offered her.

"I'll take watch," Lorenta offered, "I think it would be wise to wait here, at least until daylight."

The group went about tending to their injuries and rested as best as they could where they were.

After several hours, Weena asked Candra, "Do you want healing? I can try the use of my spell again now."

Candra glared at her and then said, "Alright... But don't you ever hesitate like that ever again! Not when it's Dendrox. Do you hear me?!"

Weena simply nodded, afraid to say anything in reply, and began her spell casting.

When the spell had finished working its magic, Candra rubbed at the sore and itchy spot where the arrow had wounded her and where the flesh had roughly mended itself. She asked the group, "So why do you think The Black Shadow saved us? Or did he? He appeared to have his own agenda with the bandits."

"He's probably saving us for later," Asdella said with a grimace, "to kill for himself." Asdella had bandaged her shoulder with a strip of cloth torn from one of the bandits' clothing.

<Zaylyn ><Quest For The Sword Fragments And The Hunt For Dranngore><By Katrina Mandrake-Johnston > <Ch 7> < 17 >

"How are you doing, Asdella? You all right?" Vordin asked her.

"I'm okay," she replied, but she seemed distant. He wasn't sure whether it was because of The Black Shadow, or what Weena had said to her, or the incident back at The Twisted Eye Tavern. Whatever it was she was thinking about, perhaps something he had no clue of, it was hurting her.

"You sure?" he asked.

"Yeah," she answered, her voice cracking slightly with emotion as she stared absentmindedly into the forest around them.

<World of Zaylyn ><Quest For The Sword Fragments And The Hunt For Dranngore><By Katrina Mandrake-Johnston ><Ch 8>

CHAPTER 8 = THE BOX

Lorenta watched over them throughout the night as they all tried to rest and sleep behind the carriage. This was the only place where the horrors of the battle could not be seen. After Lorenta's transformation into a spider with dawn, she made her way into the safety of the backpack and its magical compartment Rasindell had designed especially for her.

Candra was the first to wake later that morning not being able to sleep very well at all or even lie still for very long. She searched about the surroundings as best as she could for any signs of danger, as Lorenta had returned to her spider form. Lorenta should have woken one of them to take over the watch before her transformation, but perhaps she thought she could continue the job even though she had reverted back to a spider. Candra watched as the front spider legs of Lorenta's body disappeared into the backpack with the rest of her. She had kept watch until Candra awoke, but how did she think she was going to alert any of them to danger if there had been some? The surviving bandits may have decided to come back, although it was unlikely with what The Black Shadow had done to the others.

Candra's leg was still giving her pain when she walked, despite the fact that Weena's spell had healed most of the damage. She looked over the arrows, salvaging what she could of them, and also collecting some of the daggers. Then Candra came to sit on top of the overturned carriage to rest and wait for the others to arise.

The others woke soon after, and Dendrox, who had regained some of his strength from Weena's spell and the much-needed rest, decided to search through the belongings of the fallen bandits.

Nodwel was trying to coax Asdella into letting him check her wound. Weena also was doing the same, offering to heal it, as she had rethought her motives for refusing. Letting her suffer needlessly wasn't the right thing to do, no matter how heated the argument between them had become. Vordin added in a few words, hoping to convince Asdella to submit, but he doubted she would ever give in. It was as if she thought she deserved to suffer.

"Vordin," Dendrox called to him, "Here, take these would ya?" Dendrox tossed over several water skins and a sack he had filled with the food he had collected out of the various backpacks and pouches of the fallen.

Vordin brought one of the water skins over to Asdella. Lorenta, with her transformation during the battle, had thus been able to discard the man's blood from her clothing and body that had gotten on her from back at the tavern. Asdella, however, still wore his blood, that of the bandits she had slain, as well as her own from the wound in her shoulder.

"Here Asdella," Vordin said holding out the water skin to her, "I thought you might want to wash up a bit."

"Yeah? What for?" she rudely replied.

"Here lad," Nodwel said taking the water skin from him, "It's a fine suggestion." After the dwarf had washed, he handed it over to Asdella saying firmly, "You look awful. Wash up, Asdella. You can't go around looking like that."

"Fine," she snapped at him, and then snatched the water skin out of his hand and poured the contents out over her head, "There, you happy now?"

"Asdella," Weena tried again, "I really wish you would let me try my spell. Come on, I might be able to do some good here. I helped Dendrox and Candra, didn't I? At least let me try."

"I don't need your pity," she barked at her. She wiped the water from her face, her fingertips

<Zaylyn ><Quest For The Sword Fragments And The Hunt For Dranngore><By Katrina Mandrake-Johnston >   <Ch 8> < 18 >
following the trail of freckles running across her cheekbones and nose.

Dendrox, after his search, came to sit beside Candra holding a small box in his hands. "Not much on them of use. I did find this though, but I'm having a little trouble getting it open," he told her, pulling on the lid and inspecting the seams, "So I can't help but wonder about where and how you happened to come up with a bag full of arrows and daggers just when we were in need of them."

Candra explained hurriedly in a whisper, "I went back to the blacksmith's. He was concentrating really intensely on this multi-bladed dagger, and I couldn't pass up the opportunity. I grabbed some arrows and daggers. I didn't want us to be caught off guard and weaponless. We were so ill prepared coming into this damn valley; I didn't want that to happen again. I heard that the bounty hunters had left, but of course, I wasn't going to take any chances so I stashed the bag within the carriage in case we had to get away quickly. That's when I discovered an empty hidden compartment behind the cushions, so it worked out perfectly. I was thinking we might have to leave in a hurry, with or without the others, and because I didn't want Weena to say anything when she saw what I had done. It was best for her not to know, and I didn't want any nosy townsfolk overhearing."

"Yeah, okay, okay," he chuckled, "I'm glad you did is all. Don't start feeling guilty about it. We'd be dead otherwise."

"It's just that Weena's always…" she continued before Dendrox cut her off.

Dendrox exclaimed with delight, "Oh, I think I've got it! If I pull on both the top and the bottom… Look, Candra. And I slide it this way and…" The lid of the box popped open like the lid of a jack-in-the-box.

"So what's inside?" Candra asked peering into the blackness within the tiny box.

"Don't know. There's something. I think…" he began.

A greenish-blue blur of something leapt from the box out toward Dendrox's face making him drop the box and jump in astonishment. Whatever it was, bounced like an enormous flea all about them growing slightly larger until it finally stopped, balancing itself on the wheel beside them.

It was a small creature, standing only a foot and a half tall, with tiny fingers and toes, and small beady eyes that looked over the two of them with an excited and eager look of delight. Its small mouth had sharp pin-like teeth, and it had pointed ears that extended from the sides of its head, as well as a tiny little tail.

<World of Zaylyn ><Quest For The Sword Fragments And The Hunt For Dranngore><By Katrina Mandrake-Johnston ><Ch 9>

CHAPTER 9 = THE IMP

"Ha ha, hee hee! I am free! I am free!" it said in a high-pitched little voice and with an overzealous grin.

"What is it?" Candra whispered to Dendrox in amazement.

"An imp I be," he replied jumping up and down in excitement, "And I've been set free! Allow me to express my glee!"

The others came over to the carriage, their attention immediately drawn to this strange little being.

"What is that?" Weena asked with curiosity, staring in amazement at the imp who was grinning at them all immensely.

"Says it's an imp," Candra told them.

"An imp?" Vordin exclaimed in astonishment, "I thought they only existed in stories."

Nodwel added, "Apparently not, it seems."

The imp announced suddenly, as he started to bounce up and down again as before, "Be woman or man…help you I can… I can lend a helping hand…by telling about this land," and then he bounced all about the group singing, "Ha ha, hee hee! You can't catch me!" He disappeared into the forest briefly and the group could hear him calling loudly, "Ha ha, hee hee! You can't find me! I bounce from tree to tree!" Then he leapt out and bounded over to Candra. He scuffed his little foot back and forth over the dirt as he stared up at her.

"It's sort of cute in a way," Asdella said with a grunt.

The imp looked up at Candra innocently, his beady little eyes looking the elf over, a curious and

<Zaylyn ><Quest For The Sword Fragments And The Hunt For Dranngore><By Katrina Mandrake-Johnston >   <Ch 9> < 19 >
definitely mischievous expression on his tiny childlike face. As if a wonderful idea had just crossed his mind, the imp started to sing with glee, "A harp with one string…what music does it bring?… It won't take long…I'll play you a song," and as he bounced up, he reached out his little hand toward Candra's bow.

Candra snarled angrily, pulling the bow away and saying, "No one touches my bow! I'll kill the little pest!"

"Immortal I be…me dead, you shall never see," the imp giggled, delighted at Candra's reaction. He made a tremendous leap toward Nodwel, and as he descended, the imp grabbed onto to his beard making him grunt in pain. "Wee! Without a care…I swing from hair…to get a glare…and angry stare."

Candra saw this as a perfect opportunity and she dashed forward trying to grab the imp.

He shrieked and jumped to Dendrox's shoulder at the last second saying, "Angry elf, can no one hold her?…I jump quick to this man's shoulder." But by his mischievous grin, it was obvious that the imp was having great fun.

"Recites silly rhymes and plays annoying pranks, I think I know why it was locked up in that box," Nodwel said rubbing at his chin.

Asdella asked impatiently, "Doesn't this thing say anything useful?"

The imp giggled and said, "To perform this task…all to do is ask."

Nodwel suggested, "We should probably head out. We have a long way ahead of us and not much time if we are to find the pieces of the sword before the Killnarin strike again. What was it that Lorenta found out? A week, perhaps less, before they move onto the next part of Dranngore's plan for revenge, whatever that may be. All we really know is he seeks vengeance on the wizard's guild. Who knows what other horrors he is willing to let happen before he achieves his goal."

Weena announced, "I can't seem to find my lantern. I had it when we left Vackiindmire. It's probably somewhere in the carriage."

"Then leave it, Vordin has his," Candra told her.

"Well, okay," she replied hesitantly.

They quickly collected their belongings, dividing up the food and water between them, and traveled north along the road, leaving the awful sight of the battle behind them. The imp skipped gleefully along beside them, encircling them, as he continued his torments.

The imp decided that Vordin, on occasion, would have handfuls of dirt thrown into his face, and the little pest found it to be absolutely hilarious when a couple of worms were added to this.

For Dendrox, he continuously would give him a nasty jab in the back with his little finger and then bounce away before anyone could grab hold of him as he always managed to do.

He pulled on the elfin tips of Candra's ears so often that it appeared she would explode with fury.

With Weena, he would land on top of her head and quickly tangle her hair into all sorts of odd-looking shapes and then let it fall down into her face.

The imp continued to pull on Nodwel's beard every once in awhile, and he would sometimes grab leaves and twigs from the forest to decorate it.

For Asdella, he would occasionally grab two fistfuls of leaves and bounce over her head to shower her with them.

Asdella would just wipe them away with a smile. She was far too interested in the reactions the little imp was getting out of the others to be annoyed by what he was doing to her. Perhaps it was because he reminded her of Narr in this way; how he used to test the patience of their group so often in their journeys. Only with Narr it was to a far lesser degree than the imp.

In-between the individual torments, the imp would leap from shoulder to shoulder among the group, and occasionally jump up to meet someone at their eye level to merely grin wildly in their face.

"Well at least the little pest is staying quiet," Candra said taking yet another angry swat at him. Of course, he swiftly escaped her as always.

He said to her laughing, "It's hard to rhyme all of the time. Ha ha, hee hee! You can't catch me!"

"Listen you little pest!" Dendrox snapped at him, "If you're not going to leave us alone, do

<Zaylyn ><Quest For The Sword Fragments And The Hunt For Dranngore><By Katrina Mandrake-Johnston > <Ch 9> < 20 >
something useful then!"

"Ah, I see you ask...I will perform this task," and the imp bounded up ahead of the group to face them so that they would have to observe him as they walked.

<World of Zaylyn><Quest For The Sword Fragments And The Hunt For Dranngore><By Katrina Mandrake-Johnston><Ch 10>

CHAPTER 10 = RETURN OF THE FAIRIES AND WISDOM FROM THE IMP

Unknown to them, the tiny fairy queen and several of her most loyal subjects had made a journey of their own into Dee'ellkka Valley. In curiosity, the queen and her advisor had come to observe the group more closely from the trees, wondering how they were faring in their quest.

"Oh, is he not the most wondrous being you have ever seen?" the fairy queen whispered to her most trusted advisor and friend.

"Yes, my queen," she replied, the blue light emitting from her tiny body glowing brighter with excitement.

The little imp cleared his tiny throat and began to recite an odd poem to the tired group. "Love, you are an ugly thing...you cause hate, pain, and sorrow...."

The fairy queen giggled as she explained to her advisor, "Ah, I see he is starting with love, many messy emotions here to play with. Let's listen carefully and see what he does with this."

"Love you are a beautiful thing...you cause joy, pleasure, and happiness..." the imp continued, "People spend all their lives looking for you...some don't know when they've found you..."

"Oh did you see the reaction in Candra and Dendrox?" the fairy queen giggled in delight and explained, "She's the elf and he's the other thief. Oh and in the wizard, Weena, he stirred up quite a few mixed emotions within her. Oh I do hope they continue to take his words seriously. His magical power lies heavy in this I see. Do you see how he is able to affect them so without them really even being aware of it? Quite a special and unique power he holds."

"Some don't know what to do with you...some know your evil ways and don't want you...some know your warm kindness and don't care about your faults," said the imp.

"Oh yes, see how he plucks at their emotions like a harp? This will be a very interesting show indeed, my queen," her advisor added.

"Wonderful, wonderful! Asdella, the warrior woman, read deeply into that one. Did you know she has the ghost of a friend haunting her, one that is in love with her? She ignored him in life, refusing his love because she felt she didn't deserve it. Oh and wait, and even the spider creature Lorenta found some meaning in the imp's words. Poor thing, sees her spider form as some sort of curse and is all confused about how to..."

The imp then broke into a giggle and bounded about the group once more. The fairy queen had ended her conversation in mid sentence, as she was so eager to hear what the imp would do next that she had forgotten what she was talking about.

Soon he returned to bounce before the group and he said to them, "Ah now I see...something here, among we...listen carefully...and you may see...of about whom this may be...could be one, could be two, three, or more...this is something you should not ignore."

"Ah, but will they realize?" the fairy queen wondered, "Can he affect them so, as he hopes? If he succeeds, it shall be such a marvelous prank."

"Yes, my queen, a complete masterpiece of mischief it will be," she agreed.

He cleared his little throat again and began another odd little poem. "I gave you all the love I've got... all my love from deep inside...you loved me or so I thought...now you push me aside..."

"Oh, he is marvelous beyond what I had first thought!" the fairy queen admired, "Even Narr, the ghost I spoke of, has been addressed. Oh, and Weena, he has opened up an incredible wound in her about what is occurring between Dendrox and herself. She fears he may have lost interest in her. I think Candra may have even felt this as well, being selfishly jealous of the attention Weena is getting from him."

"Yes, I agree, my queen, the imp is most impressive," she beamed, "Yes, quite fascinating."

The imp went on to say, "Why did you have to make me cry...you could have at least said

<Zaylyn ><Quest For The Sword Fragments And The Hunt For Dranngore><By Katrina Mandrake-Johnston > <Ch 10> < 21 >

good-bye… now I'm alone, oh me, oh my…all I do is sob, weep, and sigh…there is betrayal in your eye… I tried so hard, I tried a lot…but I only found heartbreak and pain…maybe I don't deserve the love I've sought…my love and kindness: they're to blame."

The two fairies giggled at the sorrowful look in Weena's eyes caused by the imp's words and the magical impact they held over her emotions.

The imp then rubbed at his chin, as if he were contemplating something, as he continued to bounce up and down before them as they walked. "I see more…a heart gone sore…could be…maybe…is there more here I see?" He cleared his throat once again and said, "As he tosses you away…into the bitter wind astray…don't let your heart forever close…like a broken and withered rose."

"Oh, dear queen, I even felt the reaction in them with that one," her advisor commented, "Am I right to say that all the women felt a connection within his words here, even the spider woman?"

"Definitely. I don't think I've ever been so infatuated with…" the fairy queen began to say, and then letting out a girlish squeal of embarrassment, whispered, "Oh, I think he saw us! And here I am acting so unlike a proper queen of fairies. It is just that all of the suitors within my realm are so unfit, so dull, nothing like him. Can you blame me for being so fascinated with him? Is that so wrong?"

"Oh no, my queen, I quite agree," her advisor giggled, "It gives me tingles of delight to think that such a wondrous being might accept the position as our king."

The queen's lavender light turned bright pink with embarrassment at her dear friend's suggestion. "Do you really think the others would accept such a thing? I have to admit, I shall enjoy pondering the possibility and the marvelous pranks we could concoct together."

"Our days would be filled with constant excitement, I assure you," she smiled.

"No, shh, I think he is listening," the queen whispered, dulling her light and ducking behind a tree.

"Oh, please, let us follow them farther, I want to see what happens next, my queen," she begged, watching anxiously as the group continued to travel farther up the road.

The fairy queen nodded, and giggling, the two fairies sped on ahead to meet the pace of the group once more.

Vordin spoke up, as he saw that the imp was surely going to cause problems within the group with his rhymes, stirring up emotions now and causing conflicts where they might have been ignored before. The imp seemed to possess knowledge beyond the norm, and as Vordin was quite skilled at riddle solving, he had quite a few good ideas about whom the imp was speaking of, and that each of his poems was meant to strike a cord within several members of the group at once. "Maybe we can find some treasure along the way," Vordin commented. It was a foolish thing to say, but he could think of nothing else.

To his surprise and relief, the imp began to spew forth yet another poem and this time having to do with Vordin's suggestion. He cleared his throat, as if to signify that another poem was about to begin, and he glanced over into the trees hoping to continue to make such an impression within the fairies. "It came, the lightening flashed outside the door…the shadow of a dark figure was there…the sound of its boots echoed on the floor… everyone stared, no one spoke, no one would dare… Its face was hidden by a dark hood…there were all sorts of creatures here…in silence, in the room, the figure stood…the creatures stared and nervously sipped their beer… Its black robes rustled as it turned…the bartender, fat and ugly, looked concerned… 'what do you want?' he asked in an odd tone…it pulled back its hood to show a face of bone… Everyone gasped as it turned to the room…it spoke in a rattled voice 'this is your doom'…it took from its robes a small chest…it was jeweled and had a small crest… The chest opened… A dark figure rode into the night…far into the distance and far from sight."

"What's that supposed to mean?" Candra said letting out an irritated sigh.

"Greed causes doom…all around the room," the imp explained.

Candra said angrily, "Can't we just shove him down a hole and leave him there? I can't stand this little pest!" Candra said angrily.

"Candra, calm down. Don't listen to him," Dendrox told her.

"If only he'd let me catch him," Candra said with a sinister smile.

"You can't catch me…and immortal I be…," the imp giggled once again, and then clearing his

<Zaylyn ><Quest For The Sword Fragments And The Hunt For Dranngore><By Katrina Mandrake-Johnston > <Ch 10> < 22 >

throat, went on to say, "You are so beautiful…misty and colorful…magical and mystical… In the sun, you beam… in the mist you shine… Fairies and elves…dance and play…under your light… Your colors are vivid…and full of life…you are quick and lively…cunning and mischievous…you flash your colors…and hint of treasures at your end…but let no one get near…and when we lose interest…you are quick and disappear."

"I believe, he is merely showing off now, my queen," commented her advisor.

The fairy queen replied, "Oh, that is of no matter. I quite liked it. You see, he is more than just a prankster. I would graciously accept his love should he consider mine."

Candra snapped, "I happen to be an elf, and you won't find me dancing under a rainbow. You, however, might do a funny dance after I shoot you with an arrow from my bow. That's about it though."

"You figured out his riddle," Vordin commented, with a slight hope that he might be able to ease some of the tension between her and the imp.

Dendrox chuckled, "Did you realize, Candra, that you started to speak in rhyme just now? It must be true what they say about all of them deep down being related somehow." Candra gave him a nasty jab in the arm. "Hey, I was just teasing. Why are you taking all of this so harshly? He's just a little annoying. You're treating it like an attack!"

The imp took this opportunity to sing out, "Your love is like a darkened arrow…stuck deep into my heart…nothing could remove this love…which makes my soul fly like a dove…please don't tear out this arrow…I'd be a bone without its marrow…and if you do, with a painful cry…alone and hollow, I'd surely die."

"Oh my, that was meant for Dendrox, although the entire meaning, probably having to do with Candra, I haven't yet figured out," the fairy queen commented.

"I believe you may have been admiring the imp a little too intensely, my queen, if you pardon me saying so," she told her, "You near missed the tree back there. I wouldn't want you to injure yourself."

"Did I really?" the queen laughed.

"Does he ever shut up?!" Candra yelled.

"Don't read so much into what he says. It's probably just all nonsense anyway," Dendrox told her.

"It's hard to rhyme, all of the time," the imp giggled.

"So far you haven't been finding it too hard," Candra grumbled, "Do you think he's lying about being immortal and all? Because I really want to find out."

Asdella added, "Think about it, if he wasn't, someone would have done him in a long time ago."

<World of Zaylyn><Quest For The Sword Fragments And The Hunt For Dranngore><By Katrina Mandrake-Johnston><Ch 11>

CHAPTER 11 = THE IMP, ASDELLA, AND NARR

"Immortal I be…me dead, you shall never see," he sang again. "Ha ha, hee hee…one, two, three… I buzz around like a bumblebee," he said scooping up a little handful of pebbles. "And sting you in the knee!… One, two, three!" he said whipping three pebbles out with incredible speed and accuracy, hitting the left knee of Vordin, Candra, and Weena.

"Ow! That stung!" Weena exclaimed, rubbing at her knee.

"Hee, hee, hee… Four, five, six!" he said whipping out three more pebbles, this time hitting Dendrox, Nodwel, and Asdella. "I play tricks!" the imp giggled with delight.

"I am definitely going to crush that little annoying pest, if I ever get a hold of him!" Nodwel said gritting his teeth with frustration, "He's really starting to get on my nerves. There's only so much I can put up with, and he's crossing the line."

"You can't catch me…hee, hee, hee," the imp sang out to them again.

Nodwel tried to calm himself, deciding that it was best to ignore the imp or at least try to, and he said to them all, "Once we get to town, I say we stop by the local tavern first thing. I think we all need a few drinks after all we've been through or at least a good rest."

The imp now gleefully sung out a limerick, "There once was a goblin named Slugs…whose friend left while he drained all the mugs…and when he came back…the gold he did lack…now they're dead,

<Zaylyn ><Quest For The Sword Fragments And The Hunt For Dranngore><By Katrina Mandrake-Johnston > <Ch 11> < 23 >
and full of fat bugs."

Nodwel added with annoyance, "Okay, yes, we will need some gold first."

The imp decided to jump around Asdella now. Perhaps it was because his earlier torments hadn't really bothered her as much as he would have liked. He closely encircled her as he recited his poem, and no matter how fast she walked, she couldn't get away from him or get him to stop.

"What's wrong with my mind?…help me, just be kind…help me, I am blind…help me, I can't see… help me, to be free… What's wrong in my head?…I'd be better if I were dead…I want to hide in bed… nothing more can be said… I have an imaginary friend…who will stay with me 'till the end…he will always care for me… Knowing me, not what others see…when the world around seems so blurry…with just me and him, I don't worry… Do you wonder what others think?…getting embarrassed and turning pink?… He's the one you can really trust…and do I detect a hint of lust?… With him you can truly talk…seeming alone in a silent walk… What is it, I don't know?…what is it, I must show?…what is it, I must be?…Who is this person, me?… I feel like dirt…underneath my shirt…won't someone flirt with me?…someone who will like me…for personality?…how do I know they won't treat…me like I'm a piece of meat?… Is everyone just using me?…maybe I don't want to know really… I don't deserve this pain…it's making me insane…I must calm my brain…help me, I don't want to cry…help me, I'm wanting to die…Why should I take the blame?… I'm burning up in flame… I don't deserve this pain…What is it, I am insane?…What is it? No where to turn…In this pain, I burn… What's wrong in my head?…Nothing more can be said…Would I be better, if I were dead?"

"I can't take this anymore!" Asdella finally screamed out at the top of her lungs.

Like a cork wedged into a steam vent, the stopper holding back her inner emotions had finally been pushed free by the building pressure. Asdella stood there dumbfounded, confused and upset, a blank expression on her face with just a hint of bewilderment showing. A realization started to form in her mind that they all knew far too much about her… things that were meant to stay private, buried, and never spoken of. She had not fully realized all that she had said, until the imp blurted out his poem.

Asdella turned and ran off into the trees. This was the reason why she hated lengthy conversations.

"Well I guess we're stopping here for awhile, perhaps even the night," Nodwel told them all, "It seems to be farther than we had hoped, anyhow."

Asdella grumbled to herself bitterly, "*People always have to pry into other people's lives, trying to force out any little bit of information they can to be later used against them. It's all meant to be simply polite conversation, but people are always trying to find out any and every little secret they can, and the more private the better. Then once they know, you have to be so very careful not to do anything to offend the person because of that secret they have captured and stolen, or they will tell others until you have no peace at all and you always have to live in fear because of this. Even if you despise the person, you need to go out of your way to keep yourself on their good side because of that secret. If they ever become the slightest bit annoyed, that's the first thing they would use against you. It's all because they want to hold some sort of power over you. They need to be able to manipulate you to their every will, constantly dangling the fact that they are keeping that secret and can reveal it at anytime. The only way to truly end that problem is to get rid of it!*"

"*Asdella! How can you think such a thing?!*" Narr exclaimed in shock, fearing that she may in fact be unreachable, "*Is that how you truly feel? You would rather kill to stay alone? To have friends means that you can confide in them. The minute you open up to someone, you immediately become defensive and think of how they can hurt you by what you've told them? You can't shut everyone out like that!*"

Asdella snarled with frustration, and as she continued to run farther and farther into the woods, she shouted at him, "If it's none of their business, they should just stay away! What goes on in my mind is mine alone. I don't need to share it with anyone!"

"*Is that why you despise me so intensely, now that I am able to speak to you like this? You feel I've invaded your safe little place you retreat to within your mind while shutting everything outside it*

<Zaylyn ><Quest For The Sword Fragments And The Hunt For Dranngore><By Katrina Mandrake-Johnston > <Ch 11> < 24 >

out?" he asked, the hurt showing in his voice.

Asdella stopped running. She was far away from the others, but there was no escaping Narr. "And how do you think I survived what they did to me?" she said, her voice trembling with emotion, "You just don't get it, do you? I would be dead like the other girls, if I hadn't learnt to shut the outside world out. I couldn't physically escape, so all I could do was retreat away from the pain within my mind and block everything out," and then, as the long held back tears began to flow, she continued, "How dare you lecture me! What did you think I would be? Of course I'm going to be antisocial and defensive, you idiot! I choose to be alone. Alone, I can avoid the hurt. My mind is the only part of me left that is safe for me."

"*Is it?*" Narr said plainly.

"No, I guess not. Maybe it was stupid to fight as I did. If I had died like the other girls who resisted, at least I would have retained a bit of myself. Instead, I let them kill me from the inside out. Now I am but an empty shell. A hollow corpse filled with hatred and sorrow. Only the rage remains."

"*You're wrong,*" Narr told her, "*You're not seeing the full meaning behind what the imp said. He's annoying, but not an evil being. He is trying to help at the same time he is causing chaos.*"

"And you know all this, because you have this higher enlightenment now, I suppose?" she snubbed him.

"*Well yes,*" he stated, "*I guess I am more aware of how things are now.*"

"Yeah, you always did think you were better than everyone else, didn't you?" she muttered.

"*Come on, Asdella, you're intelligent! You don't really think you need to believe things can't be changed, that your life can be nothing but damned?*" he tried to reason with her.

"There's no going back," she sobbed, "Even you have changed so much, you don't even seem like Narr anymore. You don't even really talk the same as you used to when you were alive."

"*And so you again choose to ignore what needs to be addressed. Answer me truthfully, Asdella, do you seriously want to live your life this way, facing every problem with anger and rage instead of reason?*" he said to her.

"Even after I murdered that son-of-a-bitch in the tavern, you really believe I can change?" she questioned, "For me, it was self-defense back there in Vackiindmire. It just took longer for it to be applied is all. I wasn't able to fight back years ago, so what he deserved in return merely became delayed."

"*That's revenge, Asdella, not self-defense,*" Narr tried to explain.

"Is it? I fail to see the difference," she snapped with such incredible hatred toward Narr and what he had dared to say to her, that it made him cower from her mind slightly, "How does a factor of time make such a difference? How does time make it all right for what he did? How does any amount of time cancel out my right to fight back? I suppose you're going to say that with time I should have forgiven him for what he did, aren't you? You wouldn't dare even suggest such a thing, if you had been in my place."

"*But Asdella…*" Narr began.

"What?!" she snapped at him again with disgust.

"*I'm not saying it's right, but killing him in return wasn't the right thing to do either,*" Narr tried desperately to explain.

"And who makes up these idiotic rules? That time makes a difference? That this thing is right, and this thing is wrong? You're starting to sound like Weena, forcing your opinion on everyone else," Asdella said to him.

"*Damn it, Asdella!*" he shouted at her, "*It's not just me! If you had a conscience, you'd know that! Deep down, I think you do, and it's tearing you up inside.*"

"And?" she said plainly.

Narr let out a breathy mental sigh as he tried to collect himself, "*Listen, Asdella, self-defense is something you do only when there is a dire need for it. Only if it means your very life is at stake, and sometimes not even then. Revenge is motivated by hatred, not self-preservation. If you try so hard to make them mean the same thing in your mind, then you are saying that what the evil wizard,*"

<Zaylyn ><Quest For The Sword Fragments And The Hunt For Dranngore><By Katrina Mandrake-Johnston > <Ch 11> < 25 >
Dranngore, is doing with the Killnarin is all right."

"Now you're pushing things. Why would I say that? Run out of things to justify your reasoning, did you?" Asdella laughed cruelly.

"*No, damn it!*" Narr yelled, "*In your reasoning, because his character was attacked and his reputation ruined by the wizard's guild or whatever he believes, that it is okay for him to take his revenge as you have labeled self-defense and revenge as the same thing. Do you see what I am saying?*"

"Those are two very different situations," she answered.

"*Not really. In his mind, what they did to him is just as bad, if not worse, than what happened to you,*" he told her.

"Narr," she said, her voice hinted with sorrow, "You don't really think that I would go as far as he has done, do you? That if I had an army of Killnarin at my disposal, that I would do what he is doing to get my revenge on everyone that ever hurt me?"

"*But what you don't realize, Asdella,*" he said with disappointment, "*Is that you already have hurt people on a much greater level in taking revenge as you did. Strangers aside, do you realize that you have also hurt everyone around you? People that you call your friends? Nodwel, the others, me, but most of all you? Was it worth all that? Did killing him give you any bit of peace?*"

She did not answer him, but instead went on to say, "I was an innocent once. One of the top students in my classes in the school I attended. I had a cousin once too. She was intelligent, as you say I am. That didn't help her any, did it? No amount of reasoning could save her. All the pleading and begging for me to come to my senses that you have been doing is useless, just as my words had been for her. I have been touched by evil, if you want to call it that, and there is no going back. Do you really think that I will be able to deal with people? It is so easy to hate. Do you really think it possible for me to hold my fury back while some arrogant fool is barking off about something in my face? No, not when I know how easy it is to spill the life out of a man with the twist of my blade. Not when I have no remorse in doing so," she tried to explain to him.

"*Your cousin? Why is that so important? Why did you bring her up? There was such a surge of... I don't know, emotion, I guess you would call it, when you mentioned her. What are you not telling me?*" Narr asked Asdella with fear and confusion. He did not want to believe that she had simply embraced being a heartless killer and found nothing wrong with it.

"Oh, don't try to tell me that you haven't pried into my memories. That would be the first one you'd try to get your nosey little fingers around," she said cruelly, despising that he was able to invade her mind. She had been cautious earlier when Narr first came to her in his spirit form that perhaps he might be able to take over her mind completely, but now she didn't care one way or another. She already suspected that he held a great influence over her thoughts and actions, which was impossible for her to escape.

"*No, I told you, I haven't explored your mind like that. Okay, once in awhile I catch a glimpse of something now and then, but that can't be helped. Sometimes, a thought or emotion will surge forward that happens to be connected in some way to a past feeling or memory. And yes, I admit I've been learning a lot through this method, but I promise, I have not searched through your mind as you believe I can. I would never violate your trust like that, Asdella. Please believe that. I'm not even able to do such a thing to that extent, or at least not yet, if ever,*" he tried desperately to convince her, "*Asdella, I've never felt anything so foreboding as what I felt when you spoke of your cousin. You must tell me, please!*"

"Yeah, wouldn't you like to know," she said defensively, "I'm not telling you a damn thing. You can't access a piece of my mind, so that's the bit you want most of all. You think this is somehow the key to save my soul, don't you? That this will unlock and solve all the problems that you've been trying to fix in me?"

"*Asdella...*" Narr began.

"No! I would not tell you, ever! Not even if my life depended on it! Actually, my life probably does depend on me not saying a single word about it. I doubt you would even be allowed to see it, if

<Zaylyn ><Quest For The Sword Fragments And The Hunt For Dranngore><By Katrina Mandrake-Johnston > <Ch 11> < 26 >

you could look into my memories. Leave me alone! You have enough information already to figure out why you shouldn't be asking anyway," she told him forcefully with a sinister smile, knowing that she held the upper hand in this. She no longer felt afraid of his spirit within her mind.

She was the one in control, his curiosity being his weakness. She could manipulate him how she pleased, dangling her secret he so desperately wanted just out of his reach. She had the power now, and she knew that he would probably never be able to access it no matter how hard he tried.

"*What are you talking about?!*" Narr asked her with confusion, "*What do I already know?*"

"You never wondered how I seemed to know a little more about The Black Shadow than the others? You didn't see with your enlightened awareness the way the carriage driver looked at me? It was so brief, I don't think anyone else noticed, but it was there. He seemed to know a bit more than one should as well, didn't you think?"

Narr interrupted, "*You mean with the battle against the bandits?*"

Asdella said, "Think about it. Out of everyone here, I seem to know the most about The Black Shadow's behavior. The suggestion to split our party for a better chance of survival during our camp after the spiders' lair when The Black Shadow was about, for one. Well no, that's not a very good example. With the bandits, how I knew about the feeding frenzy I spoke of and how not to draw his attention. Now that I talk about it, I suppose it isn't as obvious as I had thought, although I know it helped to ensure a better chance of survival when we were dealing with him. I'm pretty sure I let a few things slip on the way to Vackiindmire. Damn Weena, wouldn't stop prodding where she should have just let things lie. And Vordin, he had wondered how I seemed to hold a bit more knowledge about him than I should. What I can't get around, is why he let me keep those memories... Narr," she then commanded, "I want you to get out of my mind, and right now. I am to be left alone for awhile. You may return later if you wish, but I am to be alone now. Do you understand?"

Narr agreed, not knowing what else to do. He thought he was finally getting to know the real Asdella better after all this time, but now he found himself even further away from her than ever.

Asdella's mind was now clear and she was alone with her own thoughts. She removed the makeshift bandage she had applied and felt at the swollen flesh around the wound in her shoulder. It was the same one that Narten had tried to heal with the ointment back at The Twisted Eye Tavern. It throbbed with pain and she doubted she would be able to endure it much longer. She was thankful it hadn't been a more serious injury. If it had been, she wouldn't have lasted through the night like she did. Asdella sat up against the trunk of a tree, biting her lip with the pain as she bumped her shoulder against the bark. Exhausted, she closed her eyes, enjoying the calmness of the forest around her.

<World of Zaylyn><Quest For The Sword Fragments And The Hunt For Dranngore><By Katrina Mandrake-Johnston><Ch 12>

CHAPTER 12 = ASDELLA'S COUSIN

Asdella began to remember her cousin... images and events she had not thought about for so long, most of which were hard to accept as even being real.

Asdella had been on her way home from school when her cousin approached her from out of the trees. It had been quite awhile since she had last seen her, and Asdella had wondered what the occasion was. She remembered what her cousin had said to her that afternoon as they sat there at the side of the road by the forest's edge.

"Asdella, a marvelous thing has happened. I've met someone," Ezmeara told her, her face flushed with excitement and joy, "Oh, it's amazing! All the wondrous things he's shown me. Oh, I wish I could tell you. I just have to share it with someone. I doubt you'd even believe some of the things. Oh, and when I'm with him, standing beside him, the incredible feeling I get inside. I really do think I'm in love this time. Asdella, he's only kissed me once, but the passion and desire in it, oh, I felt like I was on fire, it was amazing. I'm so incredibly afraid when I'm near him, but I wouldn't have it any other way. I don't think I could ever let him go, even if I wanted to, and I don't."

"What do you mean afraid?" Asdella asked with worry, "Why would you be afraid of someone you feel so strongly for? He hasn't ever hurt you, has he?"

<Zaylyn ><Quest For The Sword Fragments And The Hunt For Dranngore><By Katrina Mandrake-Johnston > <Ch 12> < 27 >

"Oh no, no he hasn't. But he could, very easily," she said to Asdella with fear in her eyes as she considered the possibility.

"Ezzy, damn it, just tell me what's going on. You're scaring me," Asdella said taking her by the shoulders and staring her directly in the eyes.

"It would never come to that. He loves me. He needs me. That is strong enough for him to overcome the hunger," she tried to explain, but the tear that escaped her eye betrayed her.

"No, you listen. I need you to tell me everything. It will just be between you and me, okay, no one else. It will be all right, don't you worry," Asdella tried to coax.

"Okay," she submitted, "but you must promise not to say a word to anyone. If anyone knew, there are those that would harm me in order to hurt him."

"What have you gotten yourself into?" Asdella exclaimed, "His hunger? Your fear of him? You have to tell me. Of course I promise, but if you're in danger..."

"Understand that I really do love him," and then she said hurriedly, "He's The Black Shadow, but he's changed, he really is trying his best to be a man and not a monster."

"Is this some sort of cruel joke?" Asdella asked her in disbelief.

Ezmeara shook her head, and a moment of silence passed between them. Then her cousin went on to explain how they would often talk for hours at a time, and how he had confided in her, telling her several of his well kept secrets and fears, and assuring her that he truly wants to fight his evil nature and do good with his powers. She told Asdella about the control his hunger had over him and the severity of it if he ever lost control and let the hunger consume him. She explained that the evil inside him was constantly and desperately trying to get out, trying to make him do horrendous things, and that the true extent of his power reached far beyond all that was comprehensible. She told Asdella all she knew, but even Ezmeara did not know of all that The Black Shadow was. It was, however, enough to be aware of the danger and know where it stemmed from. She told Asdella how he took her flying with him and how they had watched the sunrise together above the treetops, and about so many other amazing things he had shown her and told her about.

"Asdella, I'll be fine. I know to keep my distance when I should. I know not to do anything to arouse his hunger. Getting as close as to have that kiss I told you about was taking a risk I know. But I feel so safe the few times he's dared to hold me in his arms, even though I know I should be fearing for my life. It doesn't seem to matter. Perhaps it is, in fact, the underlying danger that makes our flirtations so exciting."

"Listen to what your saying, Ezzy! You would risk your very life for a little affection? You're not thinking clearly!" Asdella tried to reason with her, "Has he tricked you somehow? Altered your perception of things? How can you stand by him, knowing of all the lives he's taken, all the lives he will take in the future?"

"He needs me, Asdella. I can't let him face this alone. If there is even a slim chance that I might be able to help him come away from his evil ways, to give him something to fight for, to praise him when he succeeds even a little in the right direction, to show him that he indeed is making a difference and that it's not going unnoticed and that it is important."

"And if it costs you your life?" Asdella asked her with concern, "Is that worth it?"

"I am hoping that love can overcome the danger, but of course I've considered what would happen," she explained, "Dear cousin, this is why I have come to you today. Each night, I have watched that hold, over the hunger and the evil, deteriorate further and further. He is becoming more and more aggressive. So far these past few days he has managed to hold himself back from killing his victims when he feeds."

"Listen to yourself! You speak as if this is normal! Have you not heard the rumors? Know you nothing of the horrors he is held responsible for? How can you say this so calmly?" Asdella asked her, shocked and afraid for her.

"Asdella," said her cousin, pulling her closer, "I need you to hear me out. So far he is resisting, but I can see that his efforts are waning. It's not for lack of trying, please believe me. The more he resists his evil nature, the more fiercely it drives him." She hugged Asdella tightly saying, "I'm so

<Zaylyn ><Quest For The Sword Fragments And The Hunt For Dranngore><By Katrina Mandrake-Johnston > <Ch 12> < 28 >

afraid. The next time he feeds, I doubt he will be able to stop himself from killing, and if he avoids feeding for too long, he'll feed uncontrollably and all our efforts will be lost. I can't let him revert back, accepting the evil inside him and letting it take him over. I can't let that happen. I know there has to be hope. The small part of him that is fighting for good, the part of him I love, cannot be allowed to be lost. I can't let that part of him be drowned out by the evil inside him, not when I know the pain he feels because of this cursed life he must lead. By being with him, I have helped save several lives that would have been otherwise lost. I have helped him to resist the full extent of his hunger, even if his hold is now dwindling. The days he resisted mattered. He will remember this, I know he will. And… and he will remember me."

"What?! What are you saying?!" Asdella looked to Ezmeara in confusion, watching the tears run down her face.

"I have to go, Asdella," she told her wiping away her tears, "I am to meet him soon."

"No, Ezzy, wait," Asdella said, watching her cousin head off into the woods.

Asdella's mind was full of fearful questions. *"Would he know she had told? Would he be angry with her? If I follow after her, will I come face to face with The Black Shadow himself? Would he attack me, if I race after her? Would the fact that I am her cousin mean anything to him, if the hunger takes him over like she says? And if his ability to resist the kill has dwindled, so when he does feed, if he did attack, would he be able to stop? If the hunger pushes him so intensely to feed, stronger than before, is she in danger? She seemed to think so. She loves him so blindly that…"*

Asdella raced off into the woods after her cousin, her shoes crunching over the forest debris.

"No… No, she couldn't be. She believes that the next time he feeds, he will kill. There's no escaping this. She's not going to let him kill an innocent. Damn it, she's going to sacrifice herself instead and hope he can regain control afterwards. She's going to hope it doesn't happen, hope it doesn't go as far as her death, hope that it will only come to him feeding slightly from her and the shock of what he was doing would bring him back to his senses in time to save her."

Her long skirt caught on a bush, and as she yanked it free, she called out her name.

"I know she's thinking that, and I know damn well that she believes this to fail, that she will lose her life in this. Why didn't she just tell me what she was planning! I can't let her do this! If she believes so strongly that she can somehow save lives this way... No, I can't let her risk her life any further. I have to stop her somehow."

Soon she came to a clearing, and as she stood there trying to catch her breath, she beheld an awful sight. A figure dressed all in black with a hooded cloak drawn up about his face, who could be none other than The Black Shadow, was standing over her cousin. Ezmeara lay unmoving on the forest floor.

He looked up to Asdella, being aware of her presence all too well. There was only silence between them. Tears were streaming down Asdella's face.

"How could he?!" she screamed within her mind, *"This is what he does to someone he says he loves? This is what he does with her trust?! Am I to be next? She didn't deserve this! She believed in you, damn it! This is how you repay her? This is how you repay her love? Why didn't you go find someone that deserved to die. Not her! Not her!! All she ever did was think of others before herself! Even a horrible monster like you! She didn't deserve this!"*

Asdella's light blue skirt ruffled around her in the breeze below the white loose-fitting blouse she wore. She could not bring herself to say a single word, but her mind said with hatred, *"Why couldn't you have waited?! I would have taken her place. She was a better person than I am! How could you do this! I hate you! You should be the one to die, not her! If you're so powerful, then destroy yourself, and then no one else would have to suffer your evil! If you're going to kill me too, then get on with it, you demon! Was it fun stringing her along? Playing your little games? Tossing her emotions around? Did you enjoy the look on her face when you betrayed her?! Did you see the love she held for you as a foolish weakness? She was probably the only person who ever could possibly have any feeling other than fear and hatred for you. You horrible monster! How could you do this to her?!"*

The Black Shadow fell to his knees beside her cousin. An invisible force passed over Asdella, his emotions seeping into her mind in his anguish.

<Zaylyn ><Quest For The Sword Fragments And The Hunt For Dranngore><By Katrina Mandrake-Johnston > <Ch 12> < 29 >

She could see within her mind that he had realized what he had done. The tears were streaming down his face as well, but his remained hidden in shadow beneath his hood. He had been aware of Asdella's thoughts, and her words had struck him like a thousand knives.

He stroked Ezmeara's cheek as she lay still before him. He wanted so desperately to breathe the life back into her. He wanted to hear her voice, to see her smile, to feel her soft touch… He didn't want to be alone, not after he had finally found her.

Asdella watched, despising him completely. She couldn't care less about how he felt. He had murdered her cousin and all she felt for him was hate, not even fear.

The Black Shadow was sobbing heavily now, and Asdella could see that perhaps there was something there other than the awe-inspiring creature everyone else saw. The ground began to shake and tremble with his heartbreak and sorrow. The trees around them started twisting and contorting in waves of pain, hopelessness, and frustration. Several large rocks exploded with the anger he felt, and Asdella knew from what her cousin had told her that he was still maintaining a great control over his powers despite this.

He finally stood, stared at Asdella for a few moments, as if he wanted to say something to her but knew that there wasn't anything he possibly could. After the surroundings had calmed and he had regained his control, he ran off a little way into the forest before taking to the air.

<World of Zaylyn><Quest For The Sword Fragments And The Hunt For Dranngore><By Katrina Mandrake-Johnston><Ch 13>

CHAPTER 13 = NARR'S RETURN

Asdella awoke, disorientated at first and not sure of where she was or what had happened, not really realizing until a few moments later that she must have dozed off. *"Oh, now I remember, that damn imp and his stupid rhyming."*

She felt at her shoulder. It was completely healed. *"The Black Shadow; it must have been. No one else could have done it. It means he's lurking about somewhere like I thought, spying on us, watching our every move, reading into our minds. But why would he go to the trouble of healing me? What does he want from us?"*

An invisible force slammed into her, settling into her mind, and sending an icy shiver throughout her body. Narr had returned.

"I have a poem of my own. It's a terrible one, but here it goes," Narr said to her from within her head, *"It can't be as bad as the imp's, can it? I had to do something while I was gone, didn't I? You'll listen?"*

"Sure," she allowed.

"Please don't cry, I am here…beside you, close and near…I see you here, as you weep… If only you could see me…as you beg, want, and plea…please don't cry, and get some sleep… I am here! Can't you see?…in your dreams, here and real…touch my hand so you can feel… I know that you miss me…my spirit sits beside you…holding you close to me… Remember and don't forget…that I am here beside you…and always in love with you."

Asdella grunted and shrugged her shoulders in response, as if his words had not meant much to her at all.

"I made you blush," he told her in a cheerful tone, *"It was an awful poem, I know, but at least it served its purpose. Was it as bad as the imp's?"*

"No, nothing can be worse than that. Well then, I have one for you too then. Get out of my head for a moment so I can think of the wording," she told him and after some time she announced, "Okay, here it goes," she cleared her throat, imitating the imp, and began, "Every single heartbeat, and every breath…is filled with sorrow that my love has brought…I can't bare my memories of your death…you are always part of my every thought… My heart breaks in the night…my dreams are shattered by the light…you seemed to be the only one who cared…you're gone, I'm alone, and I admit, scared… I imagine you here beside me…I can say things that I couldn't before…if you were here, how different things could be…now my eyes are red and my head is sore… Your voice grows faint and your image

<Zaylyn ><Quest For The Sword Fragments And The Hunt For Dranngore><By Katrina Mandrake-Johnston > <Ch 13> < 30 >
grows dull…someone please remove this pain from my skull."

"*This is obviously not what I wanted to do to you,*" Narr said sadly, "*I hoped with it being later in the day and all, that we could have a bit of a fresh start after the morning went so poorly, as emotions were stretched a little thin. I hoped things might be better. I don't think you realize how hard it is for me being like this. I thought I might be able to make you happy or at least save a bit of the friendship we had when I was alive. If you need time to deal with all this, fine. You'll be a very old woman when that happens, and knowing your attitude, you definitely won't make it there. You're never going to deal with anything are you? No, wait, I didn't come here to argue. I came to try to make amends. Just know that I am here to help, if you are willing to accept it.*"

"Narr?" Asdella questioned, but she received no reply. He was there; she could feel his presence around her, but her words had finally forced him away. He had given up on her. This was what she had wanted, but now that she had it, she began to question it.

"*Narr, is he even real? I treat him as such, but is he in fact just an insane delusion? A weak attempt to fill some kind of void?*" she thought to herself, "*He's gone, at least for now. And yet, I now find myself missing him, like some part of me is missing. Could it be that I am able to see more than one should because of the glimpse I received into the mind of The Black Shadow? Or perhaps part of me did die back at Dexcsin. The amulet revived me, but… Is it possible there is more to this than I realize? Narr is real, he must be, and he has become a part of me in a way. Maybe I shouldn't have tried to fight it. But how can anyone want to stand by me after all I've done? How can he say he's in love with me? There is nothing left in me to love. No, it's best this way.*"

<World of Zaylyn><Quest For The Sword Fragments And The Hunt For Dranngore><By Katrina Mandrake-Johnston><Ch 14>

CHAPTER 14 =   THE IMP, THE BLACK SHADOW, AND VORDIN

It was nearing dark by the time Asdella headed back toward the road. Nodwel was the first to see her emerge from out of the trees. "Asdella! Over here!" he called out to her. "We've already made the camp without you as usual," he added, annoyed at her tendency to storm off on her own anytime she pleased. "*You know, one of these days you're going to go off all in a huff and find that we haven't waited around for you to mosey on back,*" he muttered under his breath.

They had moved just slightly into the forest away from the road, as they had done on their way to Dexcsin and again at Nodwel's suggestion. Trying to conceal themselves from sight would have been pointless anyway because of the imp. He had continued to loudly make himself a complete nuisance in every possible way he was able.

Candra pulled off her boots, as she sat by the fire they had built.

Dendrox said to her, "You have to get new boots. This is getting ridiculous, Candra. We'll just have to get some money together and buy you a pair."

"I'd rather just steal a pair," she grumbled, rubbing at her aching feet.

"Then you'll get ones that don't fit properly," he replied.

The imp threw a handful of pebbles at Candra as he giggled uncontrollably.

Candra scowled and tried desperately to ignore him saying, "I should have just gotten a better pair off one of the bandits."

Weena exclaimed, "That's disgusting! How can you even think of wearing the foul sweaty boots off the dead?"

"It's not like they're going to need them," Candra snapped back. "*She always has to say something, doesn't she? No one's opinion matters other than hers,*" the elf complained within her mind, "*The judgmental little…*"

"Yeah but…," Weena began and then decided, "You know what? I'm just going to say that, I would be way too repulsed to be able to do that, and if you're okay with it, fine. And I don't want to know if that's where you got the pair you have now, so don't tell me."

"Okay," Candra said breaking into a smile. She had been pleasantly surprised by what Weena had said. Candra added, "I've considered going bare foot anyways just so I can throw these boots at that damn imp. But I'd lose them for sure and then be even more angry at the pest than I already am."

<Zaylyn ><Quest For The Sword Fragments And The Hunt For Dranngore><By Katrina Mandrake-Johnston > <Ch 14> < 31 >

"Hee hee hee…Look at me…Look at me!" the imp sung out over and over again as he skipped around the campfire.

"He doesn't ever shut up!" Candra exclaimed, "He's driving me crazy! There has to be some way to strangle the life out of the little creature. Maybe he's just saying that he can't be killed so we don't try."

Dendrox remarked, "Do you really want to spend all your time trying to catch the imp? He's not going to let you catch him."

"Yeah I know," she admitted, "But he's so annoying!"

"Immortal I be…" the imp sang out laughing as he continued to dance around the fire.

"He's utterly useless," Dendrox commented, "There has to be a way to get rid of him."

The imp called out, "Be woman or man…help you I can…I can lend a helping hand…by telling about this land…to perform this task…all to do is ask."

Suddenly, the imp skidded to a stop and stared out into the forest.

"I don't believe it. He stopped," Candra said in disbelief.

"That's what has me worried," Nodwel said to her, "What possibly could have made him stop and be silent like that?"

The imp ran frantically along the ground, back to cower within the middle of the group beside the fire. He started to hop up and down wildly, shouting out a poem with a frightened expression on his tiny face. "He came walking slowly up the road…getting as close as you wouldn't allow…clad fully in black, like this cool clear night…unnoticed, he does creep away from sight… The air is still, and night falls to silence… musty earth and fresh trees are its fragrance…the moon's big and bright, and the sky is clear…cool winds whispering things no one can hear… He says not a word as he travels on…knowing that we too shall move on with dawn."

Looking frantically around, the little imp now tried desperately to hide within Candra's boot, shrinking in size to do so.

Vordin wondered, "If he is immortal like he says, what possibly could frighten him like that? He's invulnerable, or at least he's acting as if he is."

"Like I said. That's why I'm worried," Nodwel told him.

Everything seemed especially quiet now that the imp had ceased his chattering. The fire crackled. The treetops swayed in the wind.

"What do you think is out there?" Weena whispered, "I can't make sense of what the imp had said, and it probably doesn't have any meaning, but I'm extremely frightened."

The imp popped his little head out of Candra's boot to say, "Stale air fills the old barren shack…he sees dark shadows around the small room…he seems to be waiting and expecting his doom…two eyes glow red in its attack…dark and stained with blood is the floor…it must leave and stay out of sight…silently, it crept to the door…black sky, full moon, sweet, cool, reviving night…away, out the door and off into flight."

"This is creepy," Weena commented, "What does he know? What is out there?"

"Shh. Be quiet!" Dendrox snapped at her.

The imp answered Weena by telling yet another one of his poems. "Cool, gentle winds…not harsh and icy…but soft and cool…gentle, soft winds…drift through the night… Bright, glowing moon…not dark and faint…but white and bright…glowing, white moon…there in the night… Distant, vivid stars…not plain and dull…but mysterious and distant…vivid, mysterious stars…there in the night… Black, vacant night…not light and blue…but dark and black…vacant, dark night…you are my serenity… Silent, calm night…not loud and stressful…but peaceful and silent…calm, peaceful night…you are my serenity."

"Damn it, you little pest!" Candra said grabbing her boot and shaking it viciously, "Get out of my boot and tell us what is out there! And don't you dare waste our time by telling us about everything but what we want to know like you just did, you little smart ass!"

The imp called out, "Your heart is blacker than night!…Lonely, I feel its chill bite!"

"What is that supposed to mean?" Weena wondered.

<Zaylyn ><Quest For The Sword Fragments And The Hunt For Dranngore><By Katrina Mandrake-Johnston > <Ch 14> < 32 >

"Why you little," Candra muttered reaching into her boot in an attempt to grab him. She immediately pulled out her hand, exclaiming, "Ow! The little pest bit me!"

"Just ignore him then," Dendrox suggested.

She let the boot drop to the ground and grinned at the little grunt the imp made on impact. He poked his head out once more and looked nervously to the trees.

Asdella knew whom it was that was lurking about, but she did not say anything to the others. They already knew, as he was the only explanation for how her shoulder was miraculously healed. There was no need for her to state the obvious.

"Maybe we can get him back in that box we found him in," Vordin suggested.

The imp squealed and shouted, "No, no, no!...I don't want to go!... In the box...that locks!... No, no, no!...I will never go!"

Vordin smiled as a clever idea had just come to mind. He took the glowing pebble he had made out of his backpack. It still shone as brightly as it had done when he had first poured the few drops of the lantern's magical flask out onto it.

"Oh!" the imp said, his beady little eyes growing wide with curiosity, "What is it, that glow?... Yes, yes, I must know!"

Vordin whispered to Dendrox, "Give me the box."

Dendrox handed it over, and Vordin dropped the rock into it.

"No, no, no!" the imp shouted in dismay, "Not in the box...that locks!... That thing with a glow...what is it?...I must know!...Let me near it!... Take it out!...Let it shine about!... Not in the box...that locks!"

Vordin merely smiled and placed the box down beside him. The imp hopped out of the boot, looking anxiously at the box as he paced back and forth on the ground.

Finally, he jumped in the box.

"Ooohhh... It is a rock!...But how does it glow?...I still must know!...But I must jump, before the lock!"

Vordin slammed the lid down, sealing the imp inside just in time. Not one more word was heard from the imp. "What shall we do with it?" Vordin inquired.

"Just leave it here over in those bushes, no one will find it there. Here let me do it," Nodwel said grabbing up the box in his large hand, and then, with the greater strength of his upper dwarven torso, he tossed it as hard as he could up over the treetops and into the forest.

As they all tried to get some sleep, Nodwel muttered to himself, "*Damn it, Asdella, you wasted us almost a full day's travel. We would have been in town long ago had you not taken off as you do. You don't even care that lives are at stake, do you? If there is any chance of us succeeding, time is a very important factor here.*"

Nodwel said to them all, "You know, I've been thinking about The Black Shadow. Do you really think he could he have done all of it? What happened with Vordin, then looping the road for the thieves to meet up with Weena, the potion to create Lorenta? Could it all be some sort of elaborate plan?"

"Rasindell's story, the one which had mentioned hiding in a hollow tree, a mysterious man in black was supposed to have told this to Rasindell in his younger adventuring days," Vordin reminded them.

Dendrox told them, "I'm just glad that when that looping started that we didn't decide to travel through the forest trying to find Dexcsin. We would have ended up at Dexcsin the same night the Killnarin first attacked."

Vordin mentioned, "If The Black Shadow hadn't hidden me away in the alcove in the mountains, that Killnarin, which he rescued me from, would have found me as it came over the mountains. It was the same one which attacked Candra and Dendrox."

"So he wanted us to kill the Killnarin?" Candra wondered.

Asdella added in, "Or to be killed by it, who's to say?"

Weena got a cold shiver as she realized, "To think that that thing was lurking about in the dark when I was traveling all alone..."

"Which one, the Killnarin or The Black Shadow?" Asdella muttered.

<Zaylyn ><Quest For The Sword Fragments And The Hunt For Dranngore><By Katrina Mandrake-Johnston > <Ch 14> < 33 >

The Black Shadow chuckled to himself from within the forest. *"Being around them is far more enjoyable than merely being aware of them from a different location. If I am to swear off the use of my powers, stop using them, and for example, actually take the time to read a book instead of just absorbing the knowledge within, I might be able to start living more of a normal life. If I am able to suppress my hunger enough to do so, to be around others without posing a threat, perhaps I might even be able to join their party, speak with them directly as one of them. With Nexzath's help, it could very well be possible. Now I am wishing beyond what I know to be true. I am glad he has decided to accept my friendship, despite the dangers he is all too aware of. I am beyond grateful of the friendship he has dared to show me so far. I fear that this may end as it has in the past, but with him it is somehow slightly different, perhaps because of his peculiar background, but the hunger is not as intense around him. I don't think I would turn on him as readily as I would anyone else, when the hunger starts to take over my reasoning. I am to meet him soon at The Old Scabbard Inn. I shouldn't linger here too much longer. Besides, they are almost out of the forest now. Oh, and what's this I detect? The fairy queen has freed the imp? That should be interesting."*

"Asdella, your wound, it's healed," Dendrox noticed aloud, having been wary of saying anything until now.

"I suppose it is," she replied bluntly. Everyone had a pretty good idea of what must have taken place, and none of them dared question the matter further.

The Black Shadow took to the air and flew across the grassy plains toward Shirkint. The moonlight shimmered off the water to his right. From above he could see the village of Leekkar and the flickering lights from the torches they light to guide in the fishing boats at night and to ward off predators. The village of Torrnell lay farther up to his left near the mountains, and he thought about stopping there to feed as the hunger was growing fast within him, but he decided against it. He continued on to Shirkint in hope that with Nexzath there, that he could somehow help him resist making a kill during his feedings.

<World of Zaylyn><Quest For The Sword Fragments And The Hunt For Dranngore><By Katrina Mandrake-Johnston><Ch 15>

CHAPTER 15 =   THE THIEVES REMINISCE

At daylight, the group once again began their journey toward the town of Shirkint.

"Looks like we're coming out of the forest now. It's starting to thin out and I believe there are wide-open fields beyond the forest to the north," Nodwel commented.

"Weena?" said Vordin, "When you were telling us about the guild of wizards, the one responsible for enslaving others to steal magic for them, did you mean to refer to it as you did, the wizard's guild?"

"What do you mean?" she questioned.

"Well, as in being one wizard, and not wizards' guild, belonging to many," he explained, "Is that what you meant?"

"Oh, well I don't know," she admitted, "That's always how I've heard it. It's probably just a case of poor grammar. To say it properly is a mouthful, wizards' guild."

Vordin, clearly disappointed, said, "Oh, I see. I was hoping that it might be a clue."

Nodwel added in, "It very well could be. It's good to keep an open mind and not dismiss things before you have reason to. I agree with Weena, but it is something we can look into if we have time."

"Hey Dendrox, I don't know what made me think of it, but do you remember that time at that bakery? It was a long time ago now, but you remember, don't you? With the little gingerbread men?" said Candra. The sunlight filtering through the branches of the last few trees that flanked the road seemed to accentuate the pleasant smile she displayed to him.

"Vaguely," Dendrox answered, "Figured we wouldn't make it out in time or something."

Candra added, "If I hadn't knocked over that pitcher of cream, you would have been spotted for sure. Remember that? 'Oh, Mittens! How could you?!' She must have scolded that poor cat for at least ten minutes. What was that all about anyhow? Wasn't it a stupid dare to steal the first gingerbread cookie?"

Dendrox chuckled saying, "Oh, yeah, I remember now. It was to prop them up on the table so it

<Zaylyn ><Quest For The Sword Fragments And The Hunt For Dranngore><By Katrina Mandrake-Johnston > <Ch 15> < 34 >

looked as if the cookies were coming to life off the pan and trying to escape. Remember? You had a bunch of silly pranks you wanted to pull. You were determined to have that poor woman convinced her goods were bewitched and out to get her."

"It was fun, wasn't it?" commented Candra with a grin.

Weena had noticed that she again had been excluded from the conversation entirely. Candra had been bringing up a lot of old stories from their past the day before while they had waited for Asdella to return, and Weena now suspected that she might have been doing this on purpose just so she could dominate all conversation between her and Dendrox. *"No, that's ridiculous,"* Weena told herself, *"She knows I'm not trying to come between their friendship or anything like that. It would be nice to be included once in awhile though."*

"So where did you hide?" Weena asked Dendrox, increasing her pace to match theirs and carefully watching Candra's reaction to her attempt to join them.

"Oh," Dendrox said avoiding eye contact with her, "In a flour bin."

Weena got an awful feeling inside and slowed her pace. It was obvious they didn't want her to intrude. *"Was it because I hesitated with my spell? Candra was so angry about that. I guess he is too. But it's not my fault! Everyone was wounded. Candra had a damn arrow sticking out of her leg! There was blood everywhere! Asdella with her shoulder! Nodwel even had a few cuts.*

"Oh, I did waste a lot of time arguing with Asdella, didn't I? I didn't even realize that they needed my help until Dendrox called out for me. Could... could he have died? If my spell hadn't worked, would he be dead now? I never realized the severity of his wound. How could I?! I don't have any experience with this sort of thing. I've never been caught in the middle of a battle before! Then with the Killnarin, and now against other people... I was just wanting to further my study into magic, not get involved with something like this. And what The Black Shadow did to the bandits, those men and women... Oh, it was awful. It doesn't even seem real!

"Hey, I healed him and Candra both. Why should they hold a grudge?! I did extremely well, I think. So what if I hesitated? It won't happen again," she said to herself defensively, *"But what if it had mattered? What if because I was arguing with Asdella, Dendrox had died? What if he had died before I could have even tried using my spell? Yarin had died because we were all arguing with each other, but that had been because of the Killnarin's spell.*

"If Candra hadn't been able to tell me otherwise, I probably would have healed her wound first. Hers had looked the worst, with the arrow protruding... and because, thanks to her, I know what it feels like to have been shot with one. If I had used my spell on anyone but Dendrox, he could have lost his life in the time it would have taken to recharge the spell and it would have been my fault."

"So Candra," Dendrox asked, "Did we ever end up fooling with the cookies?"

"You know, I remember having all the details worked out in my mind, but I'm not sure if we actually went through with it or not," she admitted with a grin.

"What about that time we got into that one house?" Dendrox smiled proudly, "That one was my idea and quite a clever one I might add."

"Which house?" Candra asked him.

"Remember? I was standing on the roof while you slipped in through that hole. And then the rope and the bell, with the chimney?" he reminded her.

"Oh yes, that was amazing!" Candra exclaimed.

Weena wanted to ask about it, but decided against it. Vordin, however, had become curious and he inquired further into this.

"You wouldn't believe this, Vordin, but we looted this one house for an incredible amount. We lived well for almost a whole year off what we got from there and it was all because of my idea," Dendrox explained to him cheerfully.

"I see Vordin isn't getting the same treatment I did," Weena muttered to herself, *"If it's because Dendrox has lost interest in me, he should just say so. I don't deserve to be treated like this by either of them. Not after I've done so much to help them. But I guess that's what they do. Take, take, take."*

Dendrox continued, "So anyway, this place was fortified with everything you can think of. There

<Zaylyn ><Quest For The Sword Fragments And The Hunt For Dranngore><By Katrina Mandrake-Johnston > <Ch 15> < 35 >

was no way of getting in it seemed. Candra, however, notices this little hole in the fence and squeezes through."

"Yeah, I picked the lock on the door. It was quite easy actually, even back then. Dendrox here is better at pockets than he is locks. I've been trying to teach him, and he has a steady hand, but he just doesn't seem to have any luck with it," the elf explained to Vordin.

"I climb my way up to the roof somehow, and we only had a limited time for some reason," Dendrox went on to say.

"The owner only left his house on rare occasions, and when he did, it was only briefly. Dendrox was up on the roof as a lookout, with a little bell he had tied onto a rope that he had fitted down the chimney. He was to pull on the rope as a warning to get the hell out of there as fast as I could," said Candra, "And if I remember correctly, you were a little slow on your part, nearly getting us caught."

"I wasn't sure if it was him or not at first," Dendrox said in his defense.

"Well at least you're sticking to the same excuse," she chuckled, "I still say you dozed off."

"So what happened then?" Vordin asked them, pleased that they had included him in their conversation.

"You really think you should be tellin' the lad all this?" Nodwel added in, "You don't want to be putting the wrong kind of ideas in his head."

"Oh, it's fine," Candra told the dwarf. "So anyway, Vordin," she continued, "I start tying things onto the rope, Dendrox rings the alarm, and I scramble out of there and through the hole in the fence. Meanwhile, Dendrox is pulling up the loot through the chimney and bagging it. He throws me the bag and gets down from the roof just as the owner arrives home. It was great fun."

"You know, Candra, now that I think about it, we didn't have to do it that way," Dendrox told her.

"Yeah, I know, but we were younger, and the more elaborate the plan, the better we thought it was. I'm amazed we pulled most of them off," she said with a smile, "We had a lot of luck on our side back then."

"They are doing this on purpose, the bastards," Weena said bitterly, a lump forming in her throat.

Weena spoke up saying, "And what of the owner? What happened to him? What happened to him when he discovered all his hard earned valuables had been stolen?"

Candra laughed, "Who cares? You're missing the point."

Weena blurted out, "No, you are!"

"Weena," said Dendrox, "This is what we do. If you don't like it, then just don't say anything. You do realize that probably the only way we are going to get any money for what we're going to need at Shirkint is if Candra and I use our skills at this, right? I hope you know enough not to cause a scene."

"How dare he talk down to me?! What, he just tosses me aside now? That night in the tavern was just a selfish act, wasn't it?" Weena fumed, *"How can treat me like that?!"*

"Hey, Dendrox," said Candra, "Remember that one merchant? He had no concept of simple mathematics. It was absolutely pathetic. We had him convinced that... oh, well, we ended up getting the goods for a fourth the price. He was so confused, it was hard to keep a straight face."

Weena told her, trying to keep the anger out of her voice, "Oh, that's mean. You took advantage of that poor man?"

Candra replied, "So? If he was too lazy to go to school, that's his own fault."

Weena was getting fed up with the elf's arrogance. "What if he was unable to go for some reason?"

Candra answered, "So? That's not our problem. Schooling is offered all over the place and for free, and with all the books and people willing to teach new things to others, I hardly feel for him. Perhaps if enough people take advantage of him as we did, he'll learn his lesson and start learning a few things. I know we've had the upper hand many times because we finished our schooling."

Dendrox realized that Candra was getting out of hand, and he said to her, "Candra, if you remember, I was the one who convinced you to stay, finish school, and continue to practice with our weapons. You wanted to run off right then and there."

She shot him an angry glare. "I was young and under a lot of... I would have come to my senses

<Zaylyn ><Quest For The Sword Fragments And The Hunt For Dranngore><By Katrina Mandrake-Johnston > <Ch 15> < 36 >

eventually," she told him and then thought, "*Not before I was dead. How dare he bring that up! He must not have meant to. He has enough sense not to remind me of what happened to my father and what I eventually did to his killers.*"

"I was thinking about finishing school," Vordin commented with a heavy heart, trying to sound strong, and determined to show hope toward his future despite his true feelings, "That is, after things settle down. I know that many are satisfied with what education they achieve at a much younger age, but I had hoped to continue with my schooling for a few more years if I could. I'll have to find a way to provide for myself first somehow, a place to live, and things like that. I probably won't be able to go to an actual schoolhouse, but I'll be able to learn from books in my spare time, I suppose."

Nodwel thought to himself, "*That's right, now that his family and village are gone, he has nowhere to go if we survive all this. He had said that everyone he ever knew was gone now. I hope that's not entirely true. Something will turn up. We won't leave the boy with nowhere to go and no one to turn to. I just sincerely hope that everyone survives this and he is not left alone because the rest of us are no more. I am unsure now whether or not the two thieves would be as sympathetic to him as the rest of us would. Even Asdella has taken a liking to him in her own strange way. She would protect him; make sure he's all right. Lorenta and Vordin would be lost without each other. They need each other more than they realize, I think.*"

To Weena's surprise, Dendrox came to walk beside her and asked, "So, how are you dealing with what happened back with the bandits?"

"Ah, what…" Weena mumbled not knowing what to say and thought, "*Perhaps I have been overreacting and reading too much into things again.*"

"You just are looking a little overwhelmed. Don't let Candra get to you. She's hasn't had it easy, and with me needing your spell so urgently back there, well…" he trailed off.

"Dendrox," Candra called to him as she shielded her eyes from the sun with her hand, "I think I see a road up ahead leading off east. We keep heading straight, right?"

Instead, Nodwel answered her, "Yes, all the way north to Shirkint."

But then Dendrox's eyes went wide and he raced up to meet Candra. "Candra! You have the best distance vision. Can you make out what that is? Way off in the distance, what is that?" he said pointing off to the west toward the mountains.

Candra stared off in that direction for a few moments before announcing, "It's a dragon."

Dendrox exclaimed in amazement, "What?! A real dragon? Are you sure?"

"Yes, and besides, I overheard someone talking about a dragon back at the blacksmith's at Vackiindmire. The village of Torrnell must be off in that direction. They apparently have been having trouble with trolls as well."

"I've heard the rumors about dragons and trolls in the mountains, but I never thought any of them to be true," Vordin told them. He could only see a hovering blur on the horizon and marveled at how sharp Candra's eyes must be being an elf. "We should do something," he suggested.

Candra snapped, "And what would you have us do, Vordin? March in and save the whole entire village of Torrnell from the creature's attacks? It's the dragon, or Dranngore. You choose, because I doubt we'll live long enough to do both, if we succeed at all. They'll all be killed by the Killnarin anyhow, if we don't do something about Dranngore and fast. Never mind the dragon or the trolls for that matter. At least they'll have a chance of surviving those at least for awhile. If the Killnarin attack, they'll have no hope."

"Hey, you hear that? There's a carriage coming up behind us," Asdella announced.

<World of Zaylyn><Quest For The Sword Fragments And The Hunt For Dranngore><By Katrina Mandrake-Johnston><Ch 16>

CHAPTER 16 = TO SHIRKINT

"Hello there!" called the carriage driver pulling the carriage up beside them, "You the ones Vexcindor spoke of? Looks that way. As you can see the horses are all healed up and feelin' great. Wonders those healing potions are. So anyway, hop in. You paid for passage to the town of Shirkint, didn't ya?" This middle-aged man wore tan colored pants and a tunic with high-topped brown leather

<Zaylyn ><Quest For The Sword Fragments And The Hunt For Dranngore><By Katrina Mandrake-Johnston > <Ch 16> < 37 >

boots. His short tawny blonde hair was ruffled by the breeze, and he had a round smiling face. His eyes were such a vibrant green that it made Candra suspect that perhaps he was not fully human, although he appeared as such.

"Well thank-you," Nodwel told him, "We definitely weren't expecting this."

"The name's Koosenor. So Vexcindor told me what happened and sent me up with the horses after they were all healed up. I know a few things about fixin' carriages and the like. But I have to ask, what exactly happened back there? I came across the carriage, but everything seemed so clean, not a drop of blood, not a stray weapon, or anything. Vexcindor spoke as if there had been a horrendous battle with blood and bodies littering the road, with a log in the middle of the road used as part of their ambush. When I got there, there was absolutely nothing. No log, no bodies, no blood, no sign of a battle whatsoever, just the overturned carriage. And what was most strange about that, was that it wasn't damaged at all. All I had to do was right it and rig up the horses to it. It was so incredibly eerie, like something unnatural had occurred there, and I found myself talkin' to the horses to take off the edge. I can see why Vexcindor often does. Treats those horses better than most people he does at times. I'm sure those horses must have saved his life on more than one occasion. They have a special bond with him, that's for sure. Do you know, he told me he jumped onto the back of one of them when the carriage hit the log to keep himself from bein' thrown? I'm finding that hard to believe. Had he been anyone else, I'm sure he would have been thrown from the horse to his death, especially with the poor creature bein' wounded as it was."

"Well, The Black Shadow was involved, and about the battle area, perhaps it was he that…" Vordin started to suggest.

"Say no more," Koosenor cut him off, a worried look in his eye.

Weena said to him, "I think we might have been in the bookstore at the same time as you. You got a book on tracking?"

"Oh yes, that was me," Koosenor replied, "Funny place there, eh? Yeah, I thought readin' up on that sort of thing might help. On one of my runs, this huge wolf-like creature bounded across the road spooking the horses somethin' terrible, as well as myself for that matter. I thought I might be able to maybe determine the age of tracks and what not, givin' me a bit of an edge, but I doubt it's goin' ta help."

Nodwel introduced everyone as he had done with Vexcindor, and they all seated themselves within the carriage.

"Look at this!" Candra commented, "The carriage was never this clean or in such perfect shape. It must have been The Black Shadow. It's the only explanation. I don't know, it makes me nervous knowing that we are doing exactly what he wants us to."

"I know what you mean," said Dendrox, "It really does look like he has some sort of plan for us."

"I don't see any harm in it," Weena stated, "Where's the harm in getting a ride the rest of the way? I don't want to walk, that's for sure, and Koosenor seems to think it's all right."

"I agree," Asdella told them all, gazing out the open window as the carriage began to roll over the dirt road in the direction of Shirkint.

As the horses hurried along the road, Koosenor called out from his seat near the top of the carriage, "You see this side road comin' up? Leads to Leekkar; the village on the edge of Seedelle Bay. There's a tavern there called The Red Claw. It's run by two ladies. I don't know how they do it. That place gets a lot of pirates and the like comin' in from the ships, or so I've heard. Can get pretty rough in there at times. Rest of the village is a nice enough place to live, bein' on the water and all."

"Oh! I can't believe we were so stupid!" Candra blurted out suddenly, "With being wounded and then that damn imp distracting us to the point where we couldn't even think straight…"

"What do you mean?" asked Dendrox.

"We left behind the magical crossbow the leader had!" she explained.

"It was somehow grafted right onto his arm! How were we to take it?" Weena snapped at her, "Hack it off and then carry around a weapon that has a piece of his decaying flesh attached to it?"

<Zaylyn ><Quest For The Sword Fragments And The Hunt For Dranngore><By Katrina Mandrake-Johnston > <Ch 16> < 38 >

"Hell yes, if it means we can kill a Killnarin with it!" the elf snapped back at her, "It could rapidly fire without reloading it. Didn't you see? A new bolt would just appear in place; all you had to do was pull the trigger. Imagine the advantage we would have over the beasts, over anyone who stood against us for that matter."

"The Black Shadow destroyed it along with everything else it seems," Asdella commented absently.

"Well, maybe that's why, so no one would have the power the bandit leader did," Vordin added in, "Look at what he was doing. People were getting killed in the raids and everyone was afraid to go through the forest because of them."

"I'm sure The Black Shadow gave them reason enough to fear going through the forest, the bandits just added to it," Asdella told them, "The bandits were probably interfering, driving away his victims, to the point where he was irritated enough to set up that attack. Remember that one with the hood said it was The Black Shadow that had arranged it all, bringing all their number into it?"

When they neared the second side road, leading west toward the mountains, Koosenor called out to them, "This road here leads off to Torrnell. A lot of folks live in the villages and come in to work at Shirkint, Torrnell more so than Leekkar though. It's nice there, a lot more laid back than at Shirkint. I can see why a lot of people choose to live there. Right now, I'd advise against goin' there as I've heard they've been havin' a bit of trouble from out of the mountains."

Vordin leaned out the window, looking out toward the village for any sign of the dragon but it appeared to have retreated back into the mountains.

"This huge wolf-like beast the carriage driver spoke of, what do you think that could be? Could that be another form of The Black Shadow, or something we haven't even heard of?" Weena wondered.

Nodwel furrowed his brow. "We're out of the woods, so unless we have to go back in, let's not worry about it."

"Could it be he saw one of the Killnarin? I mean, they are unlike anything I've ever seen. He might have mistaken it, especially if it sped across the road," said Dendrox.

Candra added, "No, I doubt it would have let him live. It must be something else."

"It's not The Black Shadow," Asdella informed them, "He can't change form, not like that."

"You don't know that!" Weena snapped at her, "It could very well be him. Just because you think he can't, doesn't make it so. No one really knows what he can do."

"I know, because my cousin knew," Asdella snarled at her with tears wetting her cheeks, "She loved him once, the fool, and he couldn't stop himself from destroying her. And you, you're so eager to trust him, all of you are. Do you really think you're safe around him when he couldn't save the one he said he loved from the evil inside him?" She pushed past them and opened the carriage door.

"Asdella!" said Nodwel, "What are you doing?!"

Koosenor brought the carriage quickly to a halt wondering what was taking place.

"I'm walking the rest of the way!" she barked at the dwarf and jumped out.

"You sure you want to walk it?" Koosenor asked her, "It's not much farther."

"Yes!" she said angrily.

"If you say so," he replied, and the carriage traveled on without her.

Soon Koosenor called out, "We're almost there now. Do you see the little side road up ahead, the one just before the town? That leads to the water's edge and there's a little dock there. An odd fellow resides there as well. I've never been, but I've heard stories."

Shortly after, the horses slowed to a stop outside the town entrance. A high wall surrounded the town, the same as at Vackiindmire. Koosenor jumped down from his seat and opened the door for the passengers. "Welcome to Shirkint," he said with a cheerful grin.

"Thank-you," Nodwel said to him, as he exited the carriage followed by his companions.

"You would be wise not to wander about at night," the carriage driver warned them.

"Why is that?" asked Weena.

"I'd rather not say," was his answer.

<Zaylyn ><Quest For The Sword Fragments And The Hunt For Dranngore><By Katrina Mandrake-Johnston > <Ch 16> < 39 >

Vordin whispered to her, "The Black Shadow probably."

"The Old Scabbard Inn is by the town entrance," Koosenor informed them, "Oh and have you heard about the dagger and sword competitions?"

"I heard a little about them from the innkeeper at Vackiindmire," said Weena.

"Well they will be held at the town square which is at the far northeastern edge of town. If you're looking to get in a little practice beforehand, they allow for dagger throwin' and archery there. If I remember correctly, I think the dagger throwin' competition is bein' held tomorrow and will continue on these next two days and then the sword fightin' one after that for three. Usually around this time people offer training for daggers and swords," Koosenor went on to say, "If you're lookin' for a job or for information about special events, be sure to check out the message board by the town entrance. Ah, what else should I tell you? There's a magic shop near the south wall. Oh, if you're lookin' to buy a horse, ask at the animal shop at the southeastern edge of town. I've heard rumor that in this town if a thief is skilled enough to solve the puzzles and traps that the residents have placed to protect their valuables, that the thief is welcomed to it. I'm not sure how much truth there is to that though. Just the same, be on your guard for pickpockets and such, as the authorities may be powerless to do anything if this is true. Take care then. I'll be headin' back toward Vackiindmire as soon as the horses are ready and I've picked up any passengers."

"Thank-you once again for everything," Nodwel said as he glanced anxiously back south hoping to catch a glimpse of Asdella.

Koosenor smiled and assured him, "If I see your warrior friend, I'll direct her toward the inn, tell her what I told you. Asdella was it?"

The dwarf gave him a friendly nod. "I'm afraid we can't afford to wait for her. We've been greatly delayed already."

"No worries," Koosenor told him, "If you can't find what you're lookin' for at Shirkint, you'll most definitely find someone who knows where to find it."

<World of Zaylyn><Quest For The Sword Fragments And The Hunt For Dranngore><By Katrina Mandrake-Johnston><Ch 17>

CHAPTER 17 = SHIRKINT

The entrance to Shirkint was at the southwestern corner of the stone wall surrounding the town and was merely a parting of the wall. Just outside, to the left of the road where Koosenor was tending to the horses, a large and ancient oak tree stood, its thick strong branches stretching upwards to the sky.

"At Vackiindmire, I noticed that there seemed to be only the one entrance into the walled town," commented Nodwel. "I'm assuming it's the same here. Why exactly is that?" he asked Koosenor, "It doesn't seem very wise to not have means of escape if danger presents itself at the town gates."

"Yeah," added in Dendrox, "I would have at least expected to see some sort of guard stationed at the entrance here, if only to keep track of who comes and goes. The town gates were unmanned at Vackiindmire as well. Shirkint doesn't seem to have anything in means of defense either. No guards, not even a gate; it's wide open."

Koosenor appeared slightly embarrassed, perhaps a bit ashamed, as he clearly held the valley in high regard and especially so to have remained here despite the dangers. "Yes, well, you see," Koosenor said to them, "most of the danger resides within the towns. We don't have to worry much about what might be tryin' to get in, not nowadays anyhow," he replied with a forced laugh, "But that's not the point really. You see 'round here, anyone willing to patrol the streets to help ensure the safety of the residents, well, they are welcome to the job and are paid well for it too. We call 'em simply 'town protectors', but ain't no one brave enough to go 'round at night like that much now, and the ones that do, well, I'd rather not talk about it."

"So if the town were attacked, invaded by a group of creatures or raided by pirates being not far from the sea, what would happen?" Candra asked him.

Koosenor's face fell even further and he answered, "I suppose, the town's people would defend themselves as best as they could. There's not much: a few strong magic users, warriors, and the like. I have to say though, that most from afar tend to avoid Dee'ellkka Valley on account of The Black

<Zaylyn ><Quest For The Sword Fragments And The Hunt For Dranngore><By Katrina Mandrake-Johnston > <Ch 17> < 40 >

Shadow bein' here most of the time," he cleared his throat nervously, "I really should be tendin' to my work. I don't want to be found talkin' ill of him. You'll be able to find lodging at the Old Scabbard, if it's not already full up. It's the only place in town, but there's usually a room or two free come nightfall. Although, many a time I've seen people wait out the night below in the tavern over a drink. It beats bein' out and about in the dark any day, I say. Good luck to you then," and with that he returned his attention to the horses with a concerned look upon his face.

Through the entrance, they could see the inn. The chill autumn breezes made the wooden sign swing back and forth on its rusted hinges above the thick wooden door. The words painted in red on the sign were faded and almost illegible, but they could make out the words 'The Old Scabbard Inn'. The building was two stories high and the three windows facing them on the second level all had their shutters shut tight. On the bottom, beside the door, a large window could be seen, but it was covered in so much filth that it was impossible to see within.

As the group entered the town, Vordin noticed that the ground was paved with well-trodden cobblestones. To the left of them, an equipment shop lay, tucked into the southeastern corner of the town wall. A straw mat in front of the door had the word 'Welcome' woven into it.

"Well there's that message board Koosenor was talking about," Nodwel pointed out. It was a wooden board nailed into the stone wall in front of the equipment shop.

They came to stand before the message board, and Vordin peeked through the window of the shop that was beside the door, but the light coming from inside was too dim to see by.

The street continued north past the equipment shop, past a stable, then up into a residential area with tall two-story houses, and then beyond what he could see. The stable was across the street, opposite the west wall of the inn, and seemed to be mainly for the use of the inn's customers.

Looking to the right, Vordin could see another street running east along the south wall which continued past the inn and, beside it, the magic shop. After several junctions, the street eventually came to a building with an attached fence that appeared to enclose a large area right up to the far eastern wall of the town. It looked as if this last place dealt in horses and other similar animals, and perhaps even a few exotic ones.

It appeared that the majority of the town lay to the north rather than to the east. Vordin could see all sorts of people hurrying along the streets of the town, entering shops, carrying goods, arguing and bartering, and women walking hand-in-hand with their children going about their errands.

Nodwel read aloud what he read upon the board. "Stable boy needed, ask at The Old Scabbard Inn…taken. Bodyguard needed, ask Daslimb, house number fourteen. Cleaner needed, ask at animal shop…taken. Assassin needed, ask Gornim, house number eight. Not very subtle about it is he? Bouncer needed, ask at The Old Scabbard Inn. Apprentice needed, ask Norick, blacksmith…taken. Apprentice needed, ask Ascinoir, magic shop…taken. Town protectors needed, ask at equipment shop. So far there doesn't look like much that'll help us in way of money unless any of us wants to become an assassin, a bodyguard, a bouncer for a bunch of armed drunks, or patrolling around town in the dark which Koosenor warned us against. Ah, let's see, help needed, village of Torrnell, being attacked by trolls, big rewards, ask at equipment shop."

"See, I told you. It pays to eavesdrop when you can. You find out all sorts of useful things," Candra beamed.

"Yeah, well that's not an option," Nodwel added and continued to read from the board, "Gatherers needed, herb shop."

Weena commented, "That seems like an easy way to make money and safe as well. But it seems like it would take a lot of time to collect herbs and especially not knowing very much about plants."

"I do," said Dendrox.

"Collecting herbs," Candra scoffed, "Probably deadly poisonous ones all around the ones they want. Probably turn your blood to jelly just like that dead wizard we found, the one who was turning invisible, or the herbs will be at the very top of some remote mountaintop, or, even better, some horrible creature guarding the stupid little weeds."

"Gee, you're so optimistic," Dendrox chuckled.

"Actually, Candra, it's only a magical Poison spell that would have that effect. A plant would have a natural poison," Weena told her.

Candra glared at her and said, "You're missing the point. Besides, it would be too much effort. We're going to need supplies fast."

"Well you can't steal them. This town has some sort of magic spell on the shops so you won't even know what you're taking. You have to pay for it to have the spell lifted," Weena explained in defiance, "Remember what the innkeeper at Vackiindmire told us? They have some sort of incredibly strong Confusion spell on everything, as impossible as that sounds. He said that The Black Shadow probably has something to do with it, remember?"

Candra snapped, "Well I guess we're going to need to get the money fast instead, now won't we? You can go digging around in the dirt after herbs if you want, but I'd rather do things the easy way."

Nodwel cleared his throat, trying to intervene without getting involved in the argument. He realized that they might have to rely on the two thieves here in order to gain an advantage over the Killnarin. It was wrong, but so many lives were at stake here, and that was more important. "Valuables wanted, jewelry stall, marketplace," Nodwel read, "A little oddly worded, but basically willing to buy and sell I suppose," he commented looking to Candra and Dendrox.

"That's convenient, eh? Well at least there's somewhere we can pawn off anything we acquire quickly enough. I don't really like having to pay for things with suspicious looking objects and then haggling over how much the object is worth, and then if they question where we got it from... it's all too much hassle. Gold coins are so much more convenient," Candra explained with a smirk.

"Dagger throwing competition, big prizes, town square. What did Koosenor say, tomorrow that's being held?" the dwarf questioned.

"Hey, there's some easy money right there. I bet you can beat anyone that shows up for it. You are quite good you know," Candra grinned at him.

"We'll see. I'll have to think about it," Dendrox replied.

"We may not have that long before Dranngore makes his move," said Nodwel, "but all we can do is try, and if it takes us that long to get the money for supplies, so be it. Gaining information on the whereabouts of the sword fragments I doubt will be very easy to find, and questing for them even harder. The odds are against us incredibly."

"Hey, if there was an archery competition, I'd enter," she told Dendrox trying to convince him into it.

"I just don't like being judged, that's all. It meddles with my confidence," he explained with a smile.

Candra grunted saying, "Fine. You come through when it's important, that's all that matters. I really do think you'd win though."

"Come on, Candra, you know the real reason. If I did win or even came close, everyone would know about my abilities when I'd rather have it to our advantage if you know what I mean," he explained.

"Yes, yes, I know," she breathed, "Plus the fact that we would be advertising that we had prize money just waiting to be stolen away or killed for. It's just I'm trying to please everyone in the group and it's clouding my judgment. I say we just do things our way, the two of us."

"Here's something interesting," Nodwel commented, "Stolen, ivory and gold scissors, reward if returned, house number two." He thought to himself, "*Yeah I can see what kind of trouble you two can get into on your own. I'm just hoping they stay with us in this quest. We need them. They seem to run from danger when they can. I hope they realize that if they decide to run, that the Killnarin threat will eventually find them, as they will spread throughout our entire world. That should be the lesson learnt by this trouble with the bounty hunters they've been having. If they run, we'll have no chance. If they stay, we might have a slim one.*"

Weena was about to say something to Dendrox with the mention of the scissors, but Candra was already giving him a fierce look. It was obvious that Candra wanted their torment about the scissors to end and Weena wondered if she were considering killing the owners as a means to that end. At least

<Zaylyn ><Quest For The Sword Fragments And The Hunt For Dranngore><By Katrina Mandrake-Johnston > <Ch 17> < 42 >
they knew where to find them now. The bounty hunters had said that a couple of dwarves had hired them out. She sincerely hoped that such a horrible thought hadn't entered the mind of either thief, as she knew they were getting desperate.

Nodwel read out, "Crew needed for sea voyage, ask at seaport. Exotic animals wanted, animal shop. Adventurers needed for dangerous journey, ask Acklore, house number ten."

Dendrox stated, "Well, that is not an option. I've had enough danger for ten life times already with these damn Killnarin. I'm not about to go looking for it, not now. Well, okay, maybe if there is a big chest of treasure to make it worth my while."

Candra laughed, "You have a comment about everything today, don't you?"

"And your point is?" he replied with a smile.

Asdella came through the entrance and joined up with the group at the board near the shop.

"Hey Asdella, Koosenor said there's a sword fighting competition being held after the dagger throwing one, big prizes, you going to enter?" Vordin asked her.

Nodwel turned to Vordin, and making sure Asdella couldn't see, mouthed the word 'No'.

"I don't know. I'll have to think about it," Asdella answered.

Nodwel continued, "Carriage drivers needed, ask Balin, equipment shop. Revenge wanted, assassins needed to destroy The Black Shadow, very secretive, ask at Old Scabbard Inn…this person was found slain, please ignore the previous message."

Everyone fell silent for several moments.

"That's some sort of joke, isn't it?" Weena said uneasily.

"Or a warning, most likely," Dendrox added.

"Unless someone was so desperate and distraught after having everything taken away from them by that monster that they dared to take a stand against him," stated Asdella.

Several more moments of silence passed between the group.

Nodwel eventually cleared his throat to break the awkward silence and went on to say, "Oh look here. Horse riding lessons, animal shop. That might come in handy. Anyone here know how to ride a horse?"

Vordin's backpack began to glow with a greenish light and he quickly removed it. Lorenta was emerging into her human form.

"The sun has only just begun its decent. I didn't know you could change so soon," Vordin said with surprise.

"Usually, I wait until the sun has completely set as the dark helps to conceal my change, but this is Shirkint. Remember all the things Rasindell told us about it in his stories? I'm not going to miss one second of this," she told him, "Besides, you're going to need my help. I am part of the group, am I not?"

"Of course. Why would you say that?" said Vordin.

"Yes, I've been reading the board aloud mainly for your sake," the dwarf told her and continued to read, "Prove your worth, Crystal Mountain, ask at equipment shop."

"I wonder what that's about?" Vordin commented.

"Hey, look at this. Help needed, again at the village of Torrnell," said Nodwel, "being attacked by dragon, big rewards, ask at equipment shop. It looks like that's exactly what you saw out there, Candra. Ah, there's a few more here. Prove your worth, Cinder Top Mountain, Rindle the riddling hermit, ask at equipment shop."

Vordin told them all excitedly, "I used to love solving riddles and puzzles and am pretty good at it too. I'd like to find out about that. Of course we have more urgent things to worry about and climbing to the top of a mountain doesn't sound like much fun, but it wouldn't hurt to ask though, just to ease my curiosity?"

Nodwel read on, "Help needed, father dying of strange illness, ask at The Twisted Eye Tavern in the town of Vackiindmire. Rasindell the storyteller, at stage, town square."

Lorenta and Vordin both looked at each other in silence with a shocked expression on both of their faces.

<Zaylyn ><Quest For The Sword Fragments And The Hunt For Dranngore><By Katrina Mandrake-Johnston > <Ch 17> < 43 >

"That can't be right," said Lorenta, her eyes wide as she read the board for herself.

"Hey, that's where!" Nodwel exclaimed, "Remember how I said that the name sounded familiar? Rasindell was the name of this skeletal figure, wears a long grey hooded robe, and supposedly travels from place to place telling stories and legends. It's said you can ask him about almost anything, and if there is a story to tell about it, he'll know it. At least I think that's how it works. If you ask me, it's pretty eerie. Gave me the shivers. I saw him once years ago in my travels, wasn't here in Dee'ellkka Valley though. Looks like Shirkint is where he is most of the time now."

Candra added, "We could ask him then about the sword. Might be the first good source of information we'll get about it."

Lorenta said urgently to Vordin, "I need to see him. If there is anything left of my father still there, I want to know."

Vordin assured her, "Yes, of course. I'll come with you. But we should wait for the proper time, find out what we can beforehand."

Lorenta nodded in agreement. She knew well that the chance of Rasindell continuing his storytelling at the stage after dark was very slim and that she most likely would be trapped in spider form and unable to speak with him when they did get the opportunity to meet with him. Vordin had been kind in not stating the obvious, as he suspected the frustration she must be feeling after traveling all this way and actually finding him but still forced to have all her questions concerning her father remain unanswered. She could never say what she wanted through a third party, instructing them the night before in order to relay her messages to him. And then was she to wait until the next day just to make a reply?

"I'm heading off to the inn," Asdella announced, "I'll see about getting us some information if I can, find out how much a room for the night will be for us. Follow if you wish."

When she was out of earshot, Nodwel took Vordin aside saying, "You don't want to be suggesting she get into a sword fighting competition. She's not one for following rules as you can see; meaning whomever she competes against will end up dead. I'd like to remain in this town without worrying about her being hunted down for murder here as well."

"Yes, I wasn't thinking when I said that. I'm sorry," Vordin said meekly.

A message started to form below the rest on the bottom of the message board, the ink appearing to seep forward out of the very wood to create the words.

"Oh wow! Would you look at that!" Weena exclaimed, "I've never seen or even heard of anything like this before. It's amazing! It says, dagger-throwing lessons, outside by the entrance to Shirkint, ask for Vendor, staying at The Old Scabbard Inn during the dagger throwing competition."

<World of Zaylyn><Quest For The Sword Fragments And The Hunt For Dranngore><By Katrina Mandrake-Johnston><Ch 18>

CHAPTER 18 = THE OLD SCABBARD INN

Asdella heaved open the sturdy oak door to the inn, and as her eyes adjusted to the dim candlelight within, the sour smell of ale, sweat, and wood smoke, assaulted her nostrils. Normally, a half-clothed warrior woman brandishing a bare bladed sword would draw the attention of everyone in the room. Here this was not the case; the patrons barely seemed to notice her entry.

To the right was a counter which ran half the length of the room facing the tables along the opposite wall. Behind it, a bald, fat, and greasy-looking man was wiping a mug with a filthy cloth. His grimy sleeveless shirt, that once upon a time had been white, was stretched unsuccessfully over his sagging belly and a stain-splattered apron hung below it over a dirty pair of dark brown pants.

Unlike The Twisted Eye Tavern, with its richly colored wood and comforting fire within the hearth, the walls here were made of grey stone and the room had a cold and gloomy feel to it. A large empty rectangular table with eight chairs was positioned in the corner beside the door of the inn under the large mottled window. Between the counter and this table was a plain wooden door. The window was clouded over by years of grime making it almost impossible to see whether it were day or night outside except for the faint glow that escaped through in places. Asdella wondered if perhaps this had been done intentionally once long ago, as she doubted so much filth could collect there on its own to

<Zaylyn ><Quest For The Sword Fragments And The Hunt For Dranngore><By Katrina Mandrake-Johnston > <Ch 18> < 44 >
create such an effect simply by neglecting to clean it.

Along the left wall were three square tables with a separate bench for each set against the wall and wooden chairs around the remaining table edges. In the very far left corner of the room was yet another table, but this one was round with the high-backed bench wrapping around the corner providing the only seating for this table. In-between this table and the far end of the counter, in the center of the far wall of the inn, was an arched doorway that led to a staircase and the guestrooms on the upper floor.

Asdella could hear the usual din of laughter and conversation one would normally find in a tavern, peppered with the occasional argument, the clink of mugs against the blackened wooden tabletops, and the odd rude remark directed at the two young serving girls. These girls busied themselves delivering mugs of ale, wiping down the tables, and then running in and out of the door in the right wall with armloads of linen for the upstairs.

The others entered the inn a few moments after Asdella.

"So, you want to talk to the barkeep, or should I?" Asdella asked Nodwel.

"I'll do it; I might as well. Why don't you find a table with the others?" he suggested eyeing the other patrons scattered about the room.

He was glad she had decided against confronting the barkeep, as he had been nervous of what problems might have arisen if she had confronted him, as Asdella, when speaking to others, tended to welcome conflicts instead of avoiding them. Nodwel had been surprised by this, as she often was eager to make her presence well known, especially in a tavern, making sure everyone was aware that she could handle herself in a fight and was one not to be threatened with. Many times they had to pull her out of a drunken brawl that she had provoked. Her and Narr were the ones that usually got out of hand; Asdella's short temper and Narr's mouth. It pained the dwarf to be reminded of those days and the times he had spent with his old companions.

Now only he and Asdella remained. Nimdor, the wise old elf who they all admired and looked up to... Dimwar, the skilled fighter whose sense of honor topped all and his strong belief in his duty to those in need... He was the first one out there to protect the villagers from the Killnarin back at Dexcsin. Narr wasn't very good with a sword, but he had a way with words. Usually he would tease and irritate the group, but he could often con his way out of a situation. And although sometimes he made things worse than they were, he had a good heart. He didn't have a chance against the Killnarin. "*He should have been the one to go for help; not me,*" Nodwel thought regretfully. Borin, he was more at home in the wilderness than anyone Nodwel knew, having a certain connection with nature that the dwarf couldn't quite explain. "*He was a good man, damn it, he shouldn't have sacrificed himself like that in the spider tunnels. There must have been some other way. He was going to give his life to block the Killnarin from following the remaining spiders long before we arrived. He seemed to have the same connection with them that Lorenta did, trusting them to enter his mind when none of us were. I can't believe they're all gone now. It all seems like ages ago, but it was only a week ago now that we were all in Dexcsin eating dinner together at the home of the village leader. Bren, Kreasa, and their two sons, they're gone too. And Yarin, the poor kid didn't stand a chance, and instead of protecting him, it seems we just made things worse.*"

The first two tables closest to the door along the left wall were occupied. At the first table sat two men: a dwarf and an elf. Both were middle-aged and were discussing different types of weapons and the best places to acquire them.

Then at the other table was a younger group of men: two humans and an elf, and they were all extremely drunk and involved in a game of cards. One of the humans had smooth long black hair half way down his back with light brown skin. The other human was fair-skinned, blonde, and had his shoulder-length hair tied back in a tight ponytail. The elf wore his mousy-brown hair short, which accentuated his pointed ears.

Leaning up against the wall over by the third table was an odd creature. He was humanoid in stature but his hands ended in claws not fingers. His skin was a dark rich brown, but in places, there were patches of fine scales. He had no hair of any kind, and as he glanced in the group's direction, they could see that he had bright red eyes. This human-dragon, a Dragonite, was speaking with a centaur

<Zaylyn ><Quest For The Sword Fragments And The Hunt For Dranngore><By Katrina Mandrake-Johnston > <Ch 18> < 45 >

who stood beside him. The horse half of the centaur was a chestnut brown, and the human torso that extended up from the front of the horse's body wore a grey short-sleeved shirt. The centaur's hooves clicked against the wooden floorboards of the room as he shifted his weight and idly pawed the floor while he talked and took several swallows from his mug of ale.

Nodwel walked up to the counter while the others sat at the larger table by the blackened window. The bartender glanced over at him in disgust and then continued to wipe at the mug with his greasy rag. Nodwel was extremely thankful Asdella had not been the one to approach this man. He was certain it would have ended very badly.

Nodwel cleared his throat, but the man continued to ignore him. "I was wondering how much a room for the night is," he asked him.

"You got money?" he replied rudely, refusing to give Nodwel his full attention as he idly wiped at the mug.

"Yes, of course," Nodwel lied, "I'll just have to discuss it with my companions first."

The bartender snickered, exposing a few of his rotting teeth to the dwarf. "A room be ten gold and you gotta be out by dusk tomorrow," he told him, breathing his foul breath into his face.

Trying to ignore the rancid order hovering about this man, Nodwel inquired, "Do you know of any work available in town? Anything short term, enough to make some fast coin for supplies we'll be needing?"

He laughed and said, "There's always work here. You need a job, eh?"

"We're planning a journey within the next day or two, if possible," Nodwel explained to him.

"I'll be needing a new stable boy. One of your friends over there be up to that? You just have to tend to the horses people bring to you and make sure no one steals 'em," he told the dwarf with an unfriendly grin.

"Oh," said Nodwel, "On the message board over by the town entrance, I thought it said that the job at the stable was taken."

One of the serving girls, clearly with her hands full, interrupted them saying, "Ondaff, I need three more mugs of ale. Could you…"

"You know where it is, so get it!" he snarled at her.

"But…" she began and then decided against arguing the matter and went about getting the ale herself from one of the large kegs behind the counter.

"The job at the stable, it is taken," explained Ondaff, "but I thought you were lookin' for somethin' short term."

"I don't quite understand," said Nodwel confused.

"That one always is. The job'll be free by morning, or by the next few nights maybe," he chuckled.

"What are you saying?" Nodwel asked starting to realize what he was implying.

"I doubt you'll be going on any journeys if one of you takes the job," he laughed.

Nodwel turned and headed over to the table to meet the others. He was a little shocked at how the man could find amusement in such a thing.

Rolling his eyes, Nodwel whispered to them, "Did you hear all that? I guess it's true about not staying out at night around here. How he can joke about it…" he trailed off in disbelief, "Well, anyway, it's ten gold for a room, or so he says. I think I'd like to sit around for awhile, see what he charges others before we commit to anything though."

At the nearest table where the dwarf and elf were seated, the group was able to overhear the dwarf say to the elf, "So you really think it's safe to stay the night here? I've heard things, you know. I mean, I'm eager to watch the competitions and all, but not that eager, if you know what I mean."

The elf replied, "Well, I for one would rather know where The Black Shadow is than be out and vulnerable. Besides, there's never been any unusual deaths in here or so I've heard. He supposedly likes this inn and sometimes even rents a room, paying handsomely for it too, or so the barkeep says. You'll be safe unless you do something stupid. Just relax, I'll buy you another drink." The elf then waved one of the girls over and ordered two more mugs of ale.

<Zaylyn ><Quest For The Sword Fragments And The Hunt For Dranngore><By Katrina Mandrake-Johnston > <Ch 18> < 46 >

"I'll stay here if the rest of you want to go about town quickly before it gets too dark," Asdella told them, "I doubt I'd be of any use otherwise. Besides, I might hear something that could help us."

"No, I think we all better stay put for the time being," suggested Nodwel, "We all deserve a rest. There'll be plenty of time in the morning."

<World of Zaylyn><Quest For The Sword Fragments And The Hunt For Dranngore><By Katrina Mandrake-Johnston><Ch 19>

CHAPTER 19 = NEXZATH'S MESSAGE

The door to the inn swung open and in stepped a hooded figure dressed in browns. The group recognized him as being Nexzath from the bandit raid. He came over to their table.

"The Black Shadow, he requires you to perform a task for him," Nexzath told them, "Will you meet with him?"

Asdella snarled, "I will do no such thing for that monster!"

"We should at least hear what The Black Shadow has to say," Vordin suggested, "We owe him that much after all he's done for us."

At this Nexzath pulled out the eighth remaining seat at the table, farthest from the door, and sat down.

"After all The Black Shadow has done for us? And if we are just being strung along as his puppets, bending to his every will and command, half the time not even realizing it?" asked Nodwel, "He makes us think we owe him favors and gets us to perform the next step of whatever evil plan he has," and then he added, speaking to Nexzath, "And you, the same applies to you. You should listen well to what I've just said."

"No, I agree," said Dendrox, "We shouldn't refuse to hear what The Black Shadow has to say. I, for one, do not wish to have him angry with us. I suspect he won't have any qualms about disposing all of us whether we are part of some plan or not."

"Fine, so we go. We see what type of task he wishes us to perform and then we'll discuss it," Candra stated, "I don't want to make any hasty decisions. I'm assuming he has something to give us in return for doing this task for him. I wonder what it will be."

"So you will meet him?" Nexzath asked, his voice trembling slightly, "This is good. You will be meeting him here at The Old Scabbard Inn. Sit at the far table in the corner," Nexzath instructed them, "It's the one there with the circular table and high bench that wraps around along the wall." He pointed to the table with his gloved hand. "Do not worry, it will be empty as The Black Shadow is the only one who sits there, no one else dares to do so. Just sit and await The Black Shadow's arrival. It will be later into the night, within the next few hours. He will know when you are ready to meet with him, or so he has told me." He reached into the folds of his clothing and retrieved a small black drawstring bag. "He wished you to have this," Nexzath told them placing it on the table.

Candra snatched up the little bag and opened it, her eyes growing wide as she beheld the contents and a smile crept across her lips.

"Is it what I think it is?" Dendrox asked her. She nodded with a grin. "We should hand it over to Nodwel then."

"What?" she said with astonishment, holding the bag closer.

"He's sort of our unspoken leader in this quest, is he not? And besides, it may not be wise to accept such handouts, especially from The Black Shadow."

Nexzath assured them, "He thought you might be reluctant at first to accept the gold. It is yours whether or not you agree to perform the task or even to meet with him this night."

"There, you see?" Candra said clutching the bag tightly, "We can take it. Let's go get what we need, starting with a room for the night along with plenty of food and drink," and then she whispered excitedly to Dendrox, "There's plenty in here for that and a whole lot more."

"Divided between the whole group?" Weena inquired, obviously challenging Candra's honesty.

The elf glared at her and said, "Sure, of course," but not in a way that put Weena's suspicions at ease.

"What do you think, Nodwel, should we accept it?" Dendrox asked the dwarf. He could see that

<Zaylyn ><Quest For The Sword Fragments And The Hunt For Dranngore><By Katrina Mandrake-Johnston > <Ch 19> < 47 >

Nodwel clearly didn't want to be responsible for such a decision, but Dendrox knew that he was the best one to make it.

"Okay," Nodwel finally said, "We'll use what we need of it, but only to fill our bellies and to have shelter for the night here. We find out what The Black Shadow has to say and decide what to do from there with the money."

Vordin noticed that several people in the inn gave their table nervous glances every time they mentioned The Black Shadow. A few had looked their way when Nexzath had mentioned the gold, and he could see why the two thieves had tried to avoid saying what was in the bag.

"And what about all the supplies we need? We're going to need food to take with us, weapons, magic items if we can afford them, all sorts of traveling equipment, and we might even need to bribe someone into giving us the information we need," said Vordin thinking back to Rasindell's adventure stories.

"We can get our own money if we need to, and if problems arise, even pay back what we use out of that bag," Dendrox told them, "Best to be safe."

Candra reluctantly passed the bag down to Nodwel at the other end of the table. Nexzath got up to leave.

Asdella said rudely, "So you have befriended that monster? I suppose you are one as well, hiding beneath that hood? I see he has clouded your face in shadows as he does for his own."

Nexzath walked over to the door of the inn and opened it, but just before he exited, he turned to her and said, "I wouldn't be so quick to say that. I was there at the battle. I saw two so-called monsters that night. The Black Shadow, I admit, was one, but I was not the other."

The door shut behind him. Knowing well that he was implying that Asdella had been the other, Nodwel quickly said, "Well, I'm going to get us some food. Anyone like anything in-particular?"

The dwarf waved over one of the serving girls to their table, as Asdella's emotions boiled under the surface. After everyone had ordered, Nodwel paid for the meals and rented the rooms for the night.

<World of Zaylyn><Quest For The Sword Fragments And The Hunt For Dranngore><By Katrina Mandrake-Johnston><Ch 20>

CHAPTER 20 = KREASA

The group enjoyed themselves, sipping frothy mugs of ale and talking of past adventures, avoiding the subject of their present situation. Later, everyone was presented with a delicious and hearty meal.

Lorenta noticed that it appeared that the two serving girls were the ones that did all the work for the inn. She suspected they had also prepared the meals. She was thankful that the revolting barkeep had not been the one to touch their food or handle their drinks, but she found it unfair to the two girls who clearly did not receive the respect they deserved.

Halfway through their meals, the door was pushed open. It was completely dark outside, as the last few rays of sunlight had disappeared beneath the horizon. A woman entered the inn with fear in her eyes and pulling her two young children in after her. They looked awful, as if they had gone through some terrible ordeal. The woman appeared to be on the verge of collapsing to the floor, and Nodwel quickly got up from the table to come to her aid.

"Are you all right?" he said leading the sickly looking woman to the table and offering her his chair. Her two boys followed and the youngest snatched a potato off Nodwel's plate and stuffed as much of it as he could into his mouth.

"Oh no, I'm sorry," the woman apologized, and then, looking into the dwarf's face for a few moments, exclaimed, "Nodwel? That's your name, isn't it? No, yes it is, I recognize the woman there. Back at Dexcsin, do you remember? My name's Kreasa, we invited you to dinner at our home just before the attack."

"Yes, yes, of course," Nodwel said realizing. She was the wife of the village leader back at Dexcsin and these were their children. *"How is it that they managed to survive? It's a miracle!"* he thought to himself, *"They've been out in the wilderness for a week now! I can't imagine what they must have gone through, and the two small boys traveling all that way."* Nodwel called over one of the girls. "Food and water, and a room for the night for them, and quickly please."

<Zaylyn ><Quest For The Sword Fragments And The Hunt For Dranngore><By Katrina Mandrake-Johnston > <Ch 20> < 48 >

She nodded, seeing the terrible shape the three of them were in, and accepted the payment that Nodwel handed out to her from the bag.

"Oh I couldn't ask you to…" Kreasa began.

"No, you get your children fed and off to bed. Don't you be concerned with anything else," Nodwel told her.

The serving girl suggested, "I could show 'em to the room now if you wish ma'am, and bring 'em their supper. Might be better there than in 'ere with this lot."

"Oh yes, thank-you," she answered weakly and watched her children led away up the stairs to the top floor.

Nodwel pulled up the empty chair to the other end of the table to sit beside Kreasa, and so he could finish his meal. The other serving girl quickly presented Kreasa with a large plate of meat and vegetables. As she ate, it was clear that she had been ravenous, probably giving most of any food they had been able to find in their journey to her children. The others finished their meals, waiting for the appropriate time to hear her story.

Nodwel eventually asked her, "Do you feel well enough to tell us what happened? How you came to arrive here?"

Kreasa nodded, the anguish reflected in her pale and tired face. "Our family and village has been terrorized now and then by a monstrous wolf-like creature," she told them and then begged, "Please, just hear me out. I know it sounds unbelievable."

"It's okay, please go on," Nodwel said to her trying to put her at ease as best as he could, and he was surprised to hear her speak of something other than the Killnarin.

"At first it was only the livestock this beast killed, but then our eldest son was brutally slain by this creature and it did far worse... far worse than it did to any of the animals. After that, it was peaceful for awhile until we realized that the horrid beast was stalking us, watching our every move. How can anything be so evil?" Tears were welling in her eyes, but she continued, "When those other creatures attacked, the black six-legged horrors, we immediately assumed it was the wolf beast. We fled the village, hoping to draw it away from the others, as it was us that it was after. We made it to the tree line before realizing it was these other creatures. Bren, my husband, he would have returned to help defend Dexcsin, but the wolf creature was there. It was there, I tell you, and it was searching for us! We had no choice but to run. I… I couldn't watch that evil thing…" she stammered, "my other children… I… not again…" she sobbed, "Not after what it did to…"

Nodwel tried to comfort her, putting his broad hand upon her shoulder. "Shh, it's all right," he whispered softly, "I understand."

Kreasa told them, "My husband, he's not a coward. I know it looks that way, the village leader fleeing when it needed him the most. We both ran with our children through the forest for I don't know how long, and we were hopelessly lost and traveling so very slow. It was so demanding on the children, you see. I'm not sure how many days had passed, three maybe four. We hoped to make it all the way to Shirkint, as that was the only place we felt would be safe from such a terrible monster. The creature…" she said with fear, "it caught up with us somehow. Bren, he led it astray while I escaped with the children…" She cupped her hands to her face weeping, "He's not here… He said he would meet us here… It got him; I just know it did…" After a few minutes she was able to compose herself enough to say, "I'm sorry. I… Thank-you. Thank-you for all your help. At Dexcsin… how many were killed? Who is handling things? The festival should proceed despite the tragedy. They will need the preparation to keep their minds off what has happened. I needed that when my first son was taken from me. Oh, without us there, I just know they'll try to cancel it."

Nodwel winced slightly, as it pained him to be the one to tell her. None of the others could muster the courage to do so. "Kreasa… I don't know how to tell you this… but there is no one there."

Kreasa asked, "But why, where did they go? To Vackiindmire? Who's in charge then? Surely they cannot simply abandon the village? We can rebuild. The land, the traditions, all that has been passed down through the generations. How can they simply turn their backs on that?"

Nodwel, his heart breaking for her, tried to explain. "No," he said, putting a gentle hand to her

<Zaylyn ><Quest For The Sword Fragments And The Hunt For Dranngore><By Katrina Mandrake-Johnston > <Ch 20> < 49 >

shoulder, "There is no one left. Everyone is dead, sweet lass." She kept shaking her head, not able to accept what Nodwel was telling her. The dwarf attempted to lighten the situation by saying, "You and your two boys were able to survive though, so there may be others. I'm not saying to give up all hope," but he suspected that it wouldn't have any effect on her.

"Everyone?" she said staring at Nodwel in disbelief, "No. How… how can that be? It isn't possible. How can that be?!"

Nodwel asked, "A boy named Yarin. Do you know him?"

Kreasa answered, "Ah, yes, yes, the twin boys. Oh, what was the mother's name? Lost her husband years back during the winter."

"Yes, okay, we found him alive hiding in a large wooden cabinet at the general store," he told her, "He… he's not with us now, however. Those damn beasts are to blame. What I am saying… I don't know why I'm telling you this; I just thought you should know, I guess. He was a fine lad, a brave boy."

"I see what you're saying, Nodwel. It is possible that others survived. Isn't that right then?" she asked with hope, "The boy, Yarin, he was able to. We were able to; it is possible."

"Could be," Nodwel told her, but the doubt lay heavily in his heart. "I want you to take this," he told her pressing the bag of gold into her hand.

"No, I couldn't," she protested.

Asdella warned, "Do you think this wise?"

"I have to tell you that The Black Shadow was the one who gave us the gold. I don't care what he has planned for us. You and your sons need this. I want you to take it," he told Kreasa.

"The Black Shadow? I will take this," she said to him, "Our festivals, he often would come to watch them, lurking in the shadows about our village. He would never come out into the open, but I always would get an odd feeling every now and then. I can't describe it, but I would just know. The mysterious deaths you hear about? I know it must be him. Our village, however, he would spare, or at least that was what I believed. The wolf-beast had been kept at bay many times because of him since the death of my eldest son. I liked to think that our village was protected somehow because our festivals had sparked some sort of compassion within The Black Shadow."

"*What you believed is true,*" thought The Black Shadow, as he listened in to their conversation from the roof of the inn, aware of everything that was happening down on the first floor of the building.

"I suppose I was wrong," said Kreasa, "A woman went missing from our village the night before the attack by the six-legged creatures. I should have seen it for the dark omen that it was. She was the sister of the lead dancer in the festivals, a beautiful girl, gorgeous long black hair. If he had been protecting us, her disappearance was clearly a sign that he had forsaken us. I will gladly take this money. I am beginning to think that The Black Shadow was the one that sent the six-legged creatures into our village. Perhaps the wolf-like creature was him all along, and if this is true, why does he torture us so? What can he possibly gain by it?"

"*Am I to be blamed for the evil deeds of another now?*" The Black Shadow thought sadly, gazing up to the moon and stars above him, "*It was I that lured the woman out of Dexcsin, and I know now that it was Kreasa's husband, Bren, that I encountered in the woods. I did not slay him. I fed, but I left him alive. It was that foul werewolf that took his life. He wouldn't have lived whether I had fed or not. The woman, however, I couldn't stop myself. I tried, I really did. How can you consider that I could be responsible for sending the Killnarin into Dexcsin? If I could have stopped them without the risk of unleashing my own evil onto the world, I would have. I would have destroyed the werewolf long ago as well, if I could have, but with that, there would be no going back for me. The world of Zaylyn would fall prey to the full extent of the evil within me. But I'm afraid, Kreasa, that in your attempt to escape the creature that has been hunting your family, that you have come directly into his lair, so to speak, as Shirkint is where he resides in his human form.*"

"Please, will you promise me that you will not send anyone to Dexcsin, as they will surely be killed," Nodwel begged Kreasa, "There is a way to defeat them, and we are on this mission and mean to succeed in it. Please, promise. They cannot be beat through strength and skill alone. Promise me."

<Zaylyn ><Quest For The Sword Fragments And The Hunt For Dranngore><By Katrina Mandrake-Johnston > <Ch 20> < 50 >

"Yes, of course," Kreasa assured him, and then she tried to laugh saying, "No one believes me about it anyhow. I wouldn't be able to convince anyone even if I wanted to. Thank-you so much. I will use the remainder of this money to hire someone to destroy that evil wolf-like beast, as what is left of my family is doomed as long as that thing lives. I just hope I can get someone to believe my story, although I'm almost certain no one will, about the six-legged beasts or the wolf creature."

Nodwel put his hand to her shoulder once more, a grave look in his eye, and he said to her, "Listen, you will stay here at Shirkint? If we fail in our quest, at least there will be some protection for you and your children here, with the wall surrounding the town and with so many capable fighters and magic users here."

Kreasa replied, "Yes, of course."

"I must return to Dexcsin once we have succeeded," Nodwel told her, "as several of my friends, and including the boy, Yarin, have fallen to these foul creatures. When all this is over, I shall return here to find you, and we will then head to Dexcsin together. I need to lay their bodies to rest, and I insist on helping to do the same for the others. I wouldn't feel right allowing you to travel alone and to return to such a task. Promise me that you and your boys will wait for my return?" he said with a smile, but there was worry behind it.

"Yes, certainly," said Kreasa, "You are such a kind man, Nodwel. I don't know how to thank-you enough."

"Just stay safe is all," was his answer.

She gave a weak smile to the group and told them, "I should really be getting up to the room, get my sons into bed. I know I should relax at least a little now that we are here, but I don't think I'll ever be able to truly feel safe ever again."

"I'll walk with you up to the room, if that's all right?" Nodwel offered.

They both headed through the archway at the back to the rooms above.

Vordin thought to himself, "*Could it be possible that a few may have survived Nilnont? Seeing them here proves that it is possible, that all hope is not lost, doesn't it?*"

<World of Zaylyn><Quest For The Sword Fragments And The Hunt For Dranngore><By Katrina Mandrake-Johnston><Ch 21>

<u>CHAPTER 21 = THE WEDDING</u>

The door to the inn opened and in stepped a dwarf with a wild look in his eyes. His reddish hair and beard were twisted and tangled and decorated with ribbons, flowers, and leaves. He was covered in scrapes and bruises and his clothing was torn and soiled.

"Ha ha!" he rejoiced giddily, "I've escaped them! I've escaped!"

"Look at yourself, man," exclaimed the other dwarf at the first table, "What has happened to you?!"

He laughed hysterically. "I've escaped them! Damn wedding it was! I was to be the entertainment for the little devils! Ha ha, but I escaped!"

"What are you blabbering on about?" the elf at the same table asked the deranged dwarf.

"Tiny fairies they were, no bigger than a speck of dust and all aglow. They did this to me," he said with tears in his eyes tugging at his beard. "They pulled and twisted and tied and tortured me, they did. They thought it was great fun, playing a game of which one of the little monsters could make me holler the loudest. There was this little creature there too. I assume the groom to their queen. A horrible little thing it was. Long pointed ears, blue-green skin, sharp little teeth, and with a little tail. Damn right pest he was, almost as bad as the fairies. I escaped though. Who knows what would have become of me if I hadn't! I'll have to shave everything right down to the skin," he said in dismay looking at his hair and beard, "I'll never be the same!"

"I've heard my share of tall tales before in my time, but this tops them all," the other dwarf exclaimed, "Come on, join us, we'll buy you a drink or two."

"I'm tellin' ya, it's all true," he insisted and took them up on their offer.

Dendrox couldn't help but snicker.

"I guess we didn't hide that box well enough, eh?" Candra whispered with a chuckle, and then she

<Zaylyn ><Quest For The Sword Fragments And The Hunt For Dranngore> <By Katrina Mandrake-Johnston > <Ch 21> < 51 >

asked, "Should we move over to the other table? It's about time we found out what The Black Shadow wants with us, don't you think?"

"I suppose," said Asdella, "Nodwel will have to join us over there then, when he returns."

Vordin and Lorenta were the first ones to head over to the shadowed corner of the room where the table lay. They pulled up the three chairs from the empty table beside it and seated themselves on the bench waiting for the others to join them. They received looks of warning, a tense worry expressed in the eyes of the onlookers, as the two of them were sitting at the forbidden table. No one in the room dared to say anything on the matter and soon after returned to their drinks and conversation.

The rest of the group came to join them at the table, as did Nodwel upon his return from the upper floor. Asdella explained to him about the imp and the fairy queen, as Nodwel was eyeing the newly arrived dwarf in utter confusion. Nodwel couldn't help but laugh.

<World of Zaylyn><Quest For The Sword Fragments And The Hunt For Dranngore><By Katrina Mandrake-Johnston><Ch 22>

CHAPTER 22 = THE BLACK SHADOW'S REQUEST

The door to the tavern burst open with the rumble of thunder from outside. A dark figure was standing in the doorway. A heavy rain began to fall. His cloak flapped about him on the wind as a flash of lightening lit up the sky, the thunder rumbling shortly after. A hush fell over the room and the infamous Black Shadow took a slow menacing step forward into the candlelight.

The door closed behind him, an unseen force causing it to do so. The flames of the nearest candles flickered, almost being extinguished. Everyone stared as he tread across the wooden floor; the once cheerful mood of the lively tavern had completely ceased. His black leather boots made a hollow sound upon the floor as he stepped farther into the room, the incredible silence accentuating his every move.

The Black Shadow slowly gazed about the room from beneath his hood, his face hidden in shadow. The elf at the first table stared wide-eyed at him in fear and awe, following his every move, and so intensely, that upon this evil being's entry, he had dribbled some of his drink down onto himself and barely seemed to notice.

One of the serving girls backed up against the wall. The Black Shadow looked her over: her hair in a tight braid, her creamy brown skin, her chest heaving rapidly beneath her white blouse in fear... She shut her eyes, desperately wishing that he would turn his focus somewhere else.

The other serving girl, her blonde hair smoothed back into a bun, stood beside the second table with the two humans and the younger elf. She had been refilling their mugs with ale when he had entered. Now she just stared in fear, her hand trembling terribly as she held the pitcher.

Ondaff, the barkeep and owner of the inn, was wary as well, his nervousness clearly showing in his eyes despite his attempt to hide it.

"By now, I thought they would be used to my visits to the inn. Every time I get the same reaction," he sighed, *"Once upon a time there had been three girls here at the inn. I should have just stayed away. Why I thought things could be any different... She had been the only one that had the courage to speak to me upon my visits here. Every time anything good comes my way, it gets ripped from my grasp by my own doing! I can't take this much longer. It seems so hopeless and everything ends in pain, death, and sorrow."*

He went to the counter and said in his calm and soothing voice, "I'll be needing a room for tonight, same as the night before." From out of nowhere it seemed, he deposited a handful of coins onto the countertop. Ondaff nodded, too afraid to say a single word in reply. The Black Shadow slowly and firmly instructed, "When Nexzath returns, you are to provide him with the key to the room and whatever meal he asks for. You may keep whatever remains of the gold. Do you remember him from the night before?"

Ondaff nodded again and stammered, "Yes. He... he was here, earlier he was, talkin' to that lot over there."

The dark cloaked figure turned and approached the table in the corner. He leaned against the wall beside the archway leading to the upstairs and folded his arms over his chest. He stood there in silence, looking over the group for a few moments, as everyone in the rest of the room looked on expectantly.

The Black Shadow let out a frustrated growl and then turning to the room said threateningly, "There's nothing to fear here. I mean you no harm. Return to your drinks. Ondaff, a round of drinks for everyone as proof of my word."

Ondaff quickly waved the girls over, and as they went about delivering the drinks, everyone tried desperately to resume their earlier conversations and ignore The Black Shadow's presence as he wished.

"What is it you want of us?" Nodwel dared to ask him.

"Ever hear of the Gem of Enarr?" The Black Shadow asked them calmly.

Weena was about to answer, to tell him no, but as she stared at him, all she could think about was how she had seen him tearing into the bandits like some wild and vicious animal, and she fell silent.

"No," Asdella replied firmly, "What of it?"

"I want you to find it," he told them.

"Damn it! Get outta here you mangy cat!" Ondaff barked shooing an orange-haired cat out of the room and out the front door. "Hey, you find out where that cat keeps gettin' in yet?" he asked one of the girls.

"No," answered the blonde serving girl, taking a nervous glance in The Black Shadow's direction, and she tried to continue on as if he wasn't there. "There's been another complaint 'bout things goin' missin', Ondaff. You know it's us girls that get blamed for it."

"Well, it ain't me, you ungrateful wretch..." he started to say and then, noticing that The Black Shadow had turned to focus his gaze upon him, said nervously with sweat upon his brow, "Sorry, I didn't mean to shout at you so. You know, it's probably just rats or somethin'. Just find where they're gettin' in and board it up."

"So what is this Gem of Enarr, and where are we supposed to find it? And most importantly, why, what do you want with it?" Dendrox boldly asked.

"It's a large green gem. I've told you all you need to know. Return here when you have it," The Black Shadow instructed, and then he headed out the door into the night.

Candra blurted out, "Well that was a complete waste of our time! I'm going up to my room to bed."

"I got two rooms," Nodwel told her handing her a small iron key, "I figured the women in one and the rest of us in the other."

Candra opened the door to their room, and she, Weena, Asdella, and Lorenta all marveled at what lay beyond the threshold.

"This can't be right," said Candra in confusion, "There's no way that this can possibly be our room."

"Well I think it's great!" exclaimed Lorenta stepping into the room and spinning around in delight, "It's like a room out of some grand castle! I would have never guessed the rooms here could be so luxurious, at least not by what we saw coming in."

The rest of the women entered and inspected the room. It was at least four times larger than the rooms at The Twisted Eye Tavern in Vackiindmire. The walls and floor were such a rich dark brown that they were almost black. Laid out upon the floor were several plush carpets; each a medley of dark reds, blues, and greens. Thick velvety curtains that were a deep navy blue were draped across the window and its plain wooden shutters. In one corner of the room, on one side of the window near the door, was a large high-backed beige armchair. On the other side of the window, in the corner, a large blue-flowered vase was situated on the floor with a healthy-looking green fern-like plant within. Beside the plant and the large four-poster bed was a small table with a drawer set beneath the tabletop. Upon the bed were three plump pillows and a cushiony goose-down quilt was laid over the mattress. In the other half of the room, there was a large tub with faucets attached onto its side, and against the wall, there was a large oak table and another comfortable-looking armchair. In the far corner of this wall, there was a small area no more than a few feet across that had been separated from the rest of the room by two thin burgundy curtains hanging from the ceiling.

<Zaylyn ><Quest For The Sword Fragments And The Hunt For Dranngore><By Katrina Mandrake-Johnston > <Ch 22> < 53 >

"This must be The Black Shadow's room," said Asdella plainly, "We must have gotten it by mistake."

"Unless all the rooms are like this," commented Weena, "Look at this tub! You can see that there aren't any pipes attached to it, can't you? Remember what the innkeeper at Vackiindmire told us about the inn here at Shirkint?" She turned one of the faucets and said in disbelief as she watched the water start to pour into the basin, "The water's coming from out of nowhere! Look at this! Can you believe... This is amazing!" Weena placed her hand under the tap and exclaimed, "It's even warm!"

"It's The Black Shadow's doing. It's not right. I don't trust it," grumbled Asdella.

"I'm sure there's no harm in it," said Weena and turning off the water next yanked out the plug.

"I'm going to check with the others," Candra told them, "See what their room looks like."

"The water's vanishing into nothingness!" exclaimed Weena in amazement, "It should be pouring right out onto the floor, but it's just disappearing!"

Lorenta announced, "Looks like this here behind the curtain is the toilet. Probably works in the same manner as the tub."

"Did you notice the wicker basket under the table?" said Weena cheerfully as she headed over to it, "Would you look at these towels?! You have to feel how soft and thick they are," she told them unfolding one from out of the basket.

"Yeah," said Candra with a bit of a laugh, "I'll be right back then." The elf left the room.

"Do any of you mind if I try the bath?" asked Weena, "We could probably wash out our clothes as well. They'll most likely be dry by morning."

"If you wring them out properly, maybe. Go right ahead," said Asdella, "You three can take the bed. I'll be fine for the night in one of these chairs."

"Do you really think this might be The Black Shadow's room?" Lorenta asked them nervously.

"Well, you saw what the barkeep was like," Asdella told them, "I wouldn't doubt him sending us up here on purpose. A sacrifice of sorts, if that's what you want to call it, to ensure he keeps in good favor with The Black Shadow."

Candra came back into the room. "Their room is like this too; seems all of them are. I asked one of the girls as she was heading downstairs and she told me that The Black Shadow always stays in the same room when he does. His is a window room, like ours, one of three, but his is the one on the other end of the building. Apparently the center room between us with the window is empty right now. I don't know how much comfort there is in that. The others are just in the room next to ours and are settling in fine. I'm not sure which is worse. Does the window give us an option for escape if the need comes? Or does it act as an entry point for who knows what, even with us being on the second floor? But then again, being in a room without, as the others are, would just make me feel trapped."

"Listen, if you're worried about The Black Shadow," said Asdella, "It makes no difference where you are, or how he gets in. If he wants to, he will; it's as simple as that. There's no stopping it. I'm taking one of the chairs for the night, so I'll be the best guard there possibly can be against whatever decides to show itself."

"Yes, I suppose we had better enjoy this while it lasts. Get cleaned up and get a good night's rest," stated Candra.

<World of Zaylyn><Quest For The Sword Fragments And The Hunt For Dranngore><By Katrina Mandrake-Johnston><Ch 23>

CHAPTER 23 = FAILICK THE CENTAUR

Come morning, it was decided that Vordin, and Lorenta hidden within the backpack, would accompany Nodwel. Weena was to travel with the two thieves about town, and Asdella would be remaining at the tavern, listening in for any useful bit of information that might come up.

"So Vordin," Nodwel said as the two of them came out of the gloomy tavern and into the sunshine, "I thought we might head down to the end of the street to the place that deals in animals. It's probably unlikely, but I was hoping we could learn a thing or two about the Killnarin there."

Vordin agreed and they strolled down the busy street until they reached their destination. It was a large stone building that they entered, and they beheld a room that had numerous cages, large and small,

<Zaylyn ><Quest For The Sword Fragments And The Hunt For Dranngore><By Katrina Mandrake-Johnston > <Ch 23> < 54 >

lining the walls as well as in the center of the room forming two aisles. Vordin and Nodwel both stared in amazement at the creatures within the cages, for they could not identify any of them. A long counter was to the left of the door and an opening in the far right wall led to the fenced area outside.

"Oh, hello!" a centaur greeted them coming in from tending to the animals outside, "Anything I can help you with?" He came toward them, his tail swishing back and forth. "Ah, by your expressions, I see you are new to Shirkint," he chuckled, "With the animals, it's the spell you're seeing. It's hard to explain, but it is as if you're seeing things for the first time. My name's Failick by the way. So, ah, anything you looking for in-particular?"

"Information actually," said Nodwel, "A six-legged beast called a Killnarin; shiny black skin, dagger-like teeth and claws. Do you know anything about that?"

The centaur furrowed his brow in deep thought, finally asking, "Could it be related to a dragon, perhaps? There is such a thing as a wingless dragon, but six legs? Black scales you said?"

"No scales; they have smooth skin. Not so much reptilian but more similar to a newt or salamander," Nodwel informed him.

"Really? How large would you say this creature is? And you said 'they', there's more than one you've encountered then?" Failick asked.

Vordin added in, "They can rear up onto their back four legs too."

"I'd say about four to five feet high when they're on the ground and close to eight maybe nine feet high when they raise their front half to slash with their claws," the dwarf explained.

"So you've battled against these creatures then? I'm afraid I've never heard of such a creature," said the centaur, "I'm assuming you're looking for advice on how to deal with the beasts?"

"Yes, anything you can tell us would help us greatly," said Nodwel.

"Okay, now I've dealt with these land dragons. The wingless ones I spoke of? That would probably be the most similar creature to what you have described. With them, the trick is to get into the one position where they are unable to attack, which is between the shoulder blades. Now I've never brought down a land dragon myself obviously, but I've trained others to do so. If you can avoid the teeth and where the claws can reach up, you just have to worry about being thrown. Ambushing the creature from above is the best method, getting some sort of restraint around the creature's neck if you can. I'd advise against confronting such a creature as what you spoke of, if you can help it, or a land dragon for that matter. It's a sure way to get yourself killed," he warned them, "Where did you encounter such a beast? A 'Killnarin' you said it was called? Where did you learn the name?"

"They are magically summoned creatures. They destroyed my entire village, Nilnont, and then moved on to Dexcsin, killing everyone there as well," Vordin told him.

"What kind of prank is this?!" he snapped, a cross expression forming on his broad face, "Do you think I have time to waste on such nonsense?"

"No, it's true! Please believe us!" Vordin said, as tears began to form, "The villages are gone; they killed everyone! I only survived because I hid inside a hollow tree!"

"If it is true," he said, eyeing the two of them suspiciously, "I need to know everything you can tell me about them; every detail. What's this about a tree?" he asked, his voice strong and commanding, "Start with that."

Vordin tried to explain, "They can see the living force of everything, but you can fool them by hiding within something that already has a life force or once did. I'm not really sure how exactly it worked, but I'm alive because of it."

"Yes, another boy at Dexcsin was able to survive by hiding inside a large cabinet. It looked as if it had been carved out of one very large tree. I don't quite understand it either, but it is something we should find out the most about if it can indeed help to save lives," said Nodwel.

"They prefer the night but are not restricted to it," Vordin told him, "They draw their power from darkness and each other."

"Their eyes are black, completely solid," Nodwel added, "And poison, it has a lesser effect on them. Magic as well, remember what Lorenta told us?"

"They can cast spells; burned my village to the ground with fire and then fooled with our minds

<Zaylyn ><Quest For The Sword Fragments And The Hunt For Dranngore><By Katrina Mandrake-Johnston > <Ch 23> < 55 >
with all those other spells they were able to cast on us," Vordin explained, "How can anyone stop them? There are so many of them. They can even regenerate if not fully killed, and if their number is depleted, what's to stop the wizard from just summoning more of them?"

"You see, we've learnt of a sword that can send these creatures back to wherever they came from, but with it we must slay the wizard who summoned them. The sword, however, has been broken into three pieces and has been scattered to ensure that no one retrieves it. The Sword of Anthrowst, have you heard of it?"

The centaur shook his head gravely. "I see why you have been asking for advice on how to battle these beasts. It sounds like a hopeless quest, but I'd say you have a better chance at retrieving the sword than going against the creatures. I haven't heard anything about such a sword, but I do happen to have an interest in magical creatures. I think I may have read something about such a creature after all, now that I think of it. You two, however, seem to know much more than what I happened to read about. I doubt you'll find out much more. Let me see if I still have the book."

He rummaged about beneath the countertop and pulled out a large dusty tome. He carefully flipped through the ancient yellowed pages until he pointed out, "Yes, here it is, see, not much I'm afraid. It has a vague physical description... black with six legs. Mind altering spell-casting abilities such as Confuse, Hallucinate, and Hate. Yes, here it is, Killnarin they are called, just as you said. Evil creatures that thrive on chaos and suffering. Says that with the right magic, they can be summoned from out of another plane of existence using a strong emotional source of hate and maliciousness as a conduit between the worlds. And you say someone has conjured up an army of these things?" Both Nodwel and Vordin nodded. "There isn't anything about their vision or how to hide from them. I have a friend that may know more about these creatures or at least more about the magical aspect of it all. Ascinoir, he and his wife own the magic shop in town. I'll speak to him, maybe together we can come up with some sort of defense against the beasts," said Failick, "As for this sword, speak to the blacksmith. Quite a few magical blades have passed his way over the years. He might know something that could help you, especially when this sword is in three pieces."

"Thank-you so very much," Nodwel said to him with renewed hope, "We'll head over to the blacksmith's right away then."

"It's near here. When you leave, head up the street to the north and eventually you'll start to near the marketplace. When you see the market stalls, you'll want to turn to the right, and when you get to that street, it's the second building. It shouldn't be that hard to find. I truly wish you the best of luck."

***

<World of Zaylyn><Quest For The Sword Fragments And The Hunt For Dranngore><By Katrina Mandrake-Johnston><Ch 24>

CHAPTER 24 = ALOFT IN A TREE

When Candra and Dendrox left the inn, they headed out toward the parting of the town wall. Weena followed after them as had been agreed upon.

"Where are you going?" she called, quickening her pace to catch up to them, "You're not leaving Shirkint are you?"

"Oh, no, come on, we'll show you," Dendrox replied with a cheerful smile.

Weena was pleased to see that the acrimony they had been showing her had apparently subsided.

"You've agreed to come along with us in this. Are you still interested in learning a few things about what we do?" Candra asked her.

They were apparently giving her a second chance to make amends after what happened back with the battle. As she had done before, in her own twisted way, Candra was trying to include her again and once more trying to accept Weena into their company.

Weena was glad for this, as she didn't want things to end so horribly with Dendrox. She had not intentionally neglected the fact that he was seriously wounded. She did not want to be hated by Candra, not when the elf had tried so hard to befriend her because of the interest Dendrox had shown her. *"Hell, she even shot me with an arrow in an attempt to prove whether or not I was worthy of their company or whatever was going through her head at the time. I'm not going to let that all be for nothing!"* Weena

<Zaylyn ><Quest For The Sword Fragments And The Hunt For Dranngore><By Katrina Mandrake-Johnston > <Ch 24> < 56 >

decided, "*If they are going to give me a second chance, I'm going to take it.*"

"What do you think, Candra?" he asked looking up at the tree just outside the entrance, "Might be the fastest way."

"I guess. Whatever you think," she replied.

Dendrox climbed up the tree until he was seated comfortably among its branches. Candra followed soon after, helping Weena in her climb.

Weena, trying to balance herself, asked, "So why exactly are we up in a tree?"

"From here we can watch for which is the best place to explore," Dendrox explained to Weena.

"I don't understand," she said wanting to learn more.

"We're going to look around in the residential part of town. It's way over in the north side, but Candra, being an elf, can see that far from here. This way we don't have to hang around the place looking suspicious to all that pass by," Dendrox told her.

"I don't believe that. How can she possibly see that far?" Weena scoffed.

"No, she can. We can focus near and far; well she has a third sort of eagle eye focus point beyond that. She can narrow in on something from far away and is probably why she is so good with a bow."

"Yeah and my skill and all those years of practice have nothing to do with it, I suppose," she laughed, and then smiling said, "This is pushing it a little, Dendrox. At this distance, I can't really get a good look at things, but I can still probably find out what we need to know."

"So all elves can do that then? This superior distance vision?" asked Weena.

"No, not all. There are many different kinds of elves," explained Candra, "I just happen to have the height and the better vision is all. I'm sure there are plenty of stories about where all the races originally came from, before being integrated into towns and villages and mixing their traditions and blood with the other races. I think the type of elf I am, used to be cave dwellers at one time. Maybe that was what the spiders chose as their lair; an old elfin or dwarven ruin. We should ask Lorenta to ask the giant spiders for us, when all of this is over. Looks like we have a common interest. I used to listen to stories about things like that as a girl."

"Hey, come on, Candra. Do you see anything yet?" Dendrox said directing her back to the town.

"Just give me a minute, would ya?" she said holding onto a branch and peering out over the wall and out towards the houses to the north.

"*Could it be that she actually was trying to have a conversation with Weena? And with her talking about the stories her father used to tell her? I see she made a point of not saying who used to tell her the stories as to avoid any and all questions on that subject, but it was a major event for her to even mention anything along those lines. And to Weena? She barely even talks to me about anything having to do with her father. Candra's opening up a very tender area to her, in her attempt to befriend her further, and I hope it doesn't end badly as it very well could, for both of them. Candra's on her way to lining up an opportunity to be hurt, and Weena's going to get herself physically hurt or even killed,*" Dendrox thought to himself with worry, "*I should have never entrusted Weena with the knowledge of Candra's past and what happened with the two thugs that attacked her and her father. If Weena brings that up in an argument about us thieving, it's going to crush Candra, especially when she's trying her best to try to bond with her. And it will hurt her even more, knowing that I was the one who told her about it, thinking I betrayed her somehow.*"

"I can see a few, but we're in a really bad position for this. The houses are split into upper and lower floors. The houses on the top have a front door with a little porch that acts as an awning for the lower, and there is a winding metal staircase that leads from the upper porch down to the street. It's kind of a nice set up; conserves space and allows for extra housing within the town."

"So what is she looking for then?" Weena asked Dendrox.

"Well, we're going to be here for awhile, but I'd rather do it like this than take unnecessary risks, especially if what they say is true about the traps and all that. This way we'll have a rough time frame to work with. She reports what she sees, I create a mental picture, and we decide from there, although it's a little more complicated than that," he tried to explain.

"*Seems they still haven't lost the tendency to concoct elaborate plans for simple actions,*" Weena

<Zaylyn ><Quest For The Sword Fragments And The Hunt For Dranngore><By Katrina Mandrake-Johnston > <Ch 24> < 57 >

observed, "*We're in a tree, and for what purpose? This is ridiculous. The results might be worth it in the end to take all these extra precautions, at least in their minds, but this is totally unnecessary. If anything, being up in a tree is going to draw attention not deter it. Everyone will recognize us as the fools that were up in a damn tree. How is that supposed to help us blend in? This is a joke. They're not serious about this. They're just playing around with me, having a laugh at my expense, trying to make stealing seem like some elaborate art form, rather than the reality of just grabbing what you want from others and running the other way.*"

Candra told her, "Basically, we find out who lives where, and how long it looks like they're going to be gone, and whether or not anyone else is going to be home in the meantime."

"You're really serious about this? You can't just break into someone's home," said Weena.

Candra's voice regained some of the hardness that it had before, "Why not? Back in Vackiindmire, you heard the innkeeper at The Twisted Eye."

"Well, it's just wrong," Weena said timidly.

Candra smiled, trying to smooth things over with her. "That's what makes it so exciting! Come on, traps, puzzles, exquisite treasure, and there's bound to be amazing magical items hidden away." Candra hoped that the mention of magical items might spur Weena's interest, as she remembered Weena complaining about not having any when she felt she should.

Weena tried to explain, "We can't just steal what people have worked so hard to gain."

Candra, determined to persuade her, said, "Oh, we'll work hard too. It isn't easy, and we could even get killed if we get caught, or from one of these traps we were told about."

"You really think all that's true? That they just blame themselves if they get robbed? It's a little hard to believe," Dendrox commented

"One way to find out," Candra stated, "Pick a house and wait about to find out when the optimal time to strike will be."

Weena, shaking her head, said, "I can't let you two do this to innocent people."

Candra let out a frustrated grunt and said to Dendrox with a sigh, "I told you she'd be like this."

"Actually," Dendrox reminded her, his tone taking on an irritated edge, "I was the one that said it. You were the one that wanted to train her to be able to work with us."

"I was just saying that I was the one that said it, because I didn't think you'd want to hurt her feelings. So you don't care anymore?" the elf asked, truly wanting to know.

"That's the point," and then Dendrox said to Weena almost as if he were giving her a scolding, "Weena, we know what you think. We've heard all the lectures. Nothing you say is going to make a difference. This is what we do. We live life hard, fast, and always at someone else's expense. We live everyday like it's our last, because it very well may be. So we live as kings and queens when we have enough loot and opportunity, as we never know what the next day may bring."

Weena wasn't about to take this and she blurted out, "So you're going to horde up all this gold and jewels and treasure and do what with it?! How can you take pleasure from stealing from others? Do you realize that if you gain wealth, there will be a million thieves eager to steal from you just as you have done?"

"We'd have enough money to hire bodyguards if it ever came to that," Dendrox snapped back in retaliation, "Anyway, that's not the point. It's the thrill and the glory."

"So that's why you hear stories of pirates burying their treasure? So others can't steal it? They can't very well spend it really. At least not until people stop looking for whatever it was they stole. So what's the point? They end up dead in the meantime and their buried treasure gets sought after by others," Weena yelled at them.

Candra's eyes narrowed as the anger began to build. "What the hell are you blabbering on about? Do you even make sense to yourself? You don't even think about what comes tumbling out of your mouth, do you?" Candra hesitated for a moment and then hissed at her, "Dendrox is obviously fed up with you, and so am I. We are going, no matter what you have to say about it, and when we return to the inn, we're getting a big glorious room all to ourselves, fill our bellies with the finest food and drink, and live in luxury for the next couple days."

<Zaylyn ><Quest For The Sword Fragments And The Hunt For Dranngore><By Katrina Mandrake-Johnston > <Ch 24> < 58 >

Dendrox told her hoping to redirect her anger, "Actually that would kind of be a bad idea to start throwing money around like that so soon after."

Candra barked at him, "Not if the Killnarin are about to wipe everyone out of existence. I'd like to enjoy my last days."

Dendrox could see that Candra had grown quite fond of Weena and not just tolerating her as she would have everyone believe. Candra wouldn't have made such an effort to include her, and definitely not been so lenient had this not been true.

Dendrox questioned, "So you've given up on the sword then? If there is a chance we can succeed, we should at least try."

"I know, I'm just trying to make some sort of point to Weena," said Candra, her voice hinted with a sorrow that only Dendrox noticed, "You know, I just realized, what is the point in even bothering? Just get lost!" she told her, "I'm sick of trying to justify things with you! You're not my keeper or my conscience, so get lost! We've had enough!"

Weena was dumbfounded for several minutes, not knowing how to react, and then she begged, "Please, I'm sorry. It's just, I get carried away and I sometimes say things I shouldn't. I didn't mean it so harshly. Please don't let our friendship end this way. And Dendrox, I…"

To Dendrox's surprise, as Candra would have normally ignored or even slapped anyone else in such a situation, he saw that she was going to give her yet another chance. Candra sighed and said, "Okay, look at it this way. We need money and a lot of it. You think we should go after this sword and Dranngore after that, right? We get enough money, we could even hire a bunch of people to search and defeat this guy for us; someone actually willing to do it."

Weena told her, "They would get scared and run, or more likely, get themselves killed. Money can only drive a person so far."

Dendrox chuckled saying, "You obviously haven't seen how far some people go over money and how much they're willing to give up. Me, I'd rather give up the chance for ultimate riches, if it means I get to keep my life."

"Ah," Candra smiled at him, "You say that now, but I could tell you of several times when…"

Dendrox quickly interrupted and with a glare added, "Although, it doesn't mean I won't try my best to obtain it."

"We've seen what these beasts can do," Weena said, "It's up to us. I can't just sit by expecting someone else to risk their life in place of mine."

"Okay fine," Candra said, coming to her point, "That doesn't change that we need money. Probably more than we can get from a couple houses. But we'll hopefully get some magical items for you. This Dranngore's a wizard and a strong one by the sound of it. We'll need some strong magic on our side too. We'll need travel arrangements, food, equipment, weapons, armour, lodgings; everything we can get. All that takes lots of money and shiny trinkets."

Dendrox added, "Besides, we are trying to save all their lives. They should contribute, don't you think?"

To their surprise, Weena said, "Alright, I see your point. We are doing this in order to save them. I don't really approve, but I guess we have no choice. Let's do it then."

Dendrox suggested firmly, "Maybe you should just let us handle it." Dendrox thought, "*This is such a mistake trying to string her along. She's going to get us killed, or in the least, arrested. I've given up on her. I'm not going to risk my life idiotically because of her. All this nagging. We don't have to justify our lives or motives to her. But Candra's on her own mission with her, I guess. Maybe Candra feels that if she can convince Weena into all this, that it will somehow make all that we do all right within her own mind. I know she's haunted by guilt, but corrupting Weena isn't going to make things any better. After this quest for the sword, we should go our separate ways.*"

Weena tried to convince him, "There will probably be magical traps and puzzles as well. I might be able to help."

Candra told her, "This is going to be extremely dangerous. I don't want you to get hurt."

Weena said, "The people have to live in their homes too. It can't be all that dangerous."

<Zaylyn ><Quest For The Sword Fragments And The Hunt For Dranngore><By Katrina Mandrake-Johnston > <Ch 24> < 59 >
Dendrox chuckled, "Never underestimate the paranoid and wealthy. Be wary of anything and everything, and never let your guard down, ever."

***

<World of Zaylyn><Quest For The Sword Fragments And The Hunt For Dranngore><By Katrina Mandrake-Johnston><Ch 25>

CHAPTER 25 = THE BLACKSMITH

Nodwel and Vordin entered the hot and smoky building. The roof was open over the blacksmith's work area for added ventilation, but still they found it uncomfortable to be there. Enclosed within the stone walls, they could make out the forge, an anvil, and various forging tools, but in the area where Nodwel and Vordin stood just inside the door, they were unable to discern what any of the weapons were on the racks or on the shelves and countertops.

"Welcome!" greeted the blacksmith upon their entry, a large smile on his weathered face, "My name is Norick. What might I be able to help you with then?"

Vordin explained to him, "We were hoping that you could tell us a few things about a magical sword we're looking for. It has been broken into three pieces though. Is it even possible to restore a sword like that?"

"It'd be best to melt down the metal and forge a new blade out of it. Not a very good one, mind you. The balance wouldn't be there as one would quite like, especially as you be in such a hurry it seems by your expressions. But you see now, I be speakin' here about the blade itself. What y' really be askin' here is the enchantment on the sword, is it not?" Norick questioned, "You see the trick here is not within the metal blade of the sword, but in the magic. Even if I was successful in recreating the sword from the metal, the enchantment would be lost to you. Yes, and in your case, the enchantment along the blade has been broken twice. The sword be but a useless bit of metal without its enchantment. Three pieces you said the sword was in then? It might be possible to mend a sword that's been broken as you say. A lot of effort and patience, but it could well be possible to get the pieces back into the shape of the original blade, perhaps even a workable one. But this task is much more difficult than you realize, as I wouldn't be able to do anything in way of altering the makeup of the sword. The welding of the pieces, heatin' it and all, everything I would need to do to fit them together, it would destroy the spell completely. I would have to only be doin' just enough to basically hold the pieces back in place. And if the metal be enchanted against this kind of destruction and alteration, it would be impossible. I'm sad to say that you'd probably have better luck trying to mend a magical sword with tree sap than asking a blacksmith to attempt anything with it. You see even if it were possible to fit the sword back into its original form, the enchantment would never be fitted back the way it was, and definitely not in two places. Your best luck would be to have the sword enchanted again with whatever spell it once had, if you can, and be less hassle and expense to use a new sword instead of repairing the old one. But by the sounds of it, this is the only spell of its kind for all the trouble to be taken in breaking it. Appears that there ain't nothing that can be done to restore the sword."

Nodwel said to him, "Well thank-you for your time then. What about the Gem of Enarr? Ever heard of it?"

Norick shook his head.

"What of The Black Shadow? I bet he could mend the line of enchantment within the blade and even meld the pieces together as if they had never been broken," said Vordin.

"I'm sure he could," Norick said with a nervous laugh and fear in his eyes, "And what makes you think he would do such a thing? You just going to walk up to him and ask him nicely, are you? He a friend of yours, I suppose?"

"Well, yeah, sort of," Vordin answered, not really knowing what else to reply.

"No!" the blacksmith yelled at him and grabbed Vordin by the shoulders, looking fiercely into his eyes.

"Ow, you're hurting me," Vordin exclaimed.

Nodwel was about to say something, but Norick blurted out, "No! You listen and you listen good, you hear?! You stop thinkin' that sort of nonsense right now, boy! That creature ain't nobody's friend!

<Zaylyn ><Quest For The Sword Fragments And The Hunt For Dranngore><By Katrina Mandrake-Johnston > <Ch 25> < 60 >
Ignorance, innocence, whatever you want to call it, it's not going to save you!" Then he apologized, "I'm sorry. I didn't mean to hurt you, but you must listen and understand. Please. A few years back, a stable boy, new to Shirkint he was, heard the rumors about The Black Shadow, thought nothin' of them really, believed them to be stories without much credibility to them. Anyways, this here boy, Thorin I think his name was, he comes in here a few times, starts talkin' about how this stranger sometimes would stop by the stable to chat once in awhile. When he described him to me, I knew at once that this boy was in grave danger and that it was a miracle that he even remained alive to tell me this. I asked him what they spoke about, sittin' alone on the haystacks there in the stable, and the boy replied that they just spoke of everyday things and nothing special at all, but that the conversation helped to pass the time, and that they were becoming quite good friends, and that he looked forward to the visits in the lonely hours of the night. I explained to him that by the description he gave, that it could be none other than The Black Shadow. And he merely shrugged! Can you believe that?! A mere shrug at this! After that, he thought it was a grand thing. Thought he was something special, he did. Next couple days I saw him now and then out and about in the streets. I can still remember the look he had on his face the last couple days I saw him. The carefree and proud attitude he had shown before was gone and had been replaced by a nervousness, a fear, and a look of one who had gotten himself in way over his head in somethin' that one could only dream of comprehending. Do you know what happened to that boy? Do you?!" and Norick shook him violently with fear and desperation in his eyes. "All they found was a bloody mess upon the cobblestones!" the blacksmith shouted into his face, "Do you see?! There's no telling if The Black Shadow was the cause of it, but it didn't help being a so-called friend of that monster either. Do you see what I'm saying?! I won't let it happen like that! Not again! Not if I can help it! You listen, and you believe what the people say! Even if some of it isn't true, it's better to be overly cautious than dead. Do you understand, boy?"

"Yes, yes, I do," Vordin answered timidly, and he was released.

Nodwel didn't know what to say. The blacksmith was only trying to help, and Nodwel definitely wasn't going to say anything in The Black Shadow's defense.

"About your sword you be askin' about. I suggest you find some other means of going about it. Good intentions or no, The Black Shadow will lead to your doom," Norick warned them and bid them farewell.

***

<World of Zaylyn><Quest For The Sword Fragments And The Hunt For Dranngore><By Katrina Mandrake-Johnston><Ch 26>

CHAPTER 26 =   THE SEAMSTRESS

"Hey, looks like someone's on their way out of town," Candra grinned, "You two should go check out the place."

"What, me and her?" Dendrox asked in astonishment.

Candra replied, "Why not?"

"Well, I'd think it would be self-explanatory," he muttered.

"Come on, you at least have to give her a chance. I am," Candra tried to convince him.

"Fine," he submitted, "What are you going to do, keep watch from here then?"

"Sure, but we really should get out of the tree before he passes by and thinks we're absolutely insane for sitting up here like this," Candra added.

When they had reached the ground, Candra instructed Dendrox on how to find the house she had decided on. "He's leaving town," Candra said to Weena, "so it should give you two plenty of time, so don't panic. Dendrox will show you what to do. He'll look out for you, don't worry. You can learn a lot from him."

"How close is he?" asked Dendrox.

"He'll be heading this way any minute probably," answered Candra.

"Alright, Weena, shall we head out then?" said Dendrox, the corner of his mouth turning up in a mischievous smile.

Weena asked, "Aren't we going to wait to see what he looks like?"

<Zaylyn ><Quest For The Sword Fragments And The Hunt For Dranngore><By Katrina Mandrake-Johnston > <Ch 26> < 61 >

"Best not to," Dendrox told her, "Not where you're just starting out with this sort of stuff. There's a tendency to unintentionally stare or make frequent nervous glances toward the owner. We're going to avoid going through this with you, and this way, you can concentrate on learning other things with us. Okay?"

"Okay," said Weena, unsure of herself.

"Come on, you two better be off," Candra hurried them along and wished them good luck.

As Dendrox led Weena along the streets of the town toward their destination, Weena asked him, "So Candra really believes I can do this? She's being so trusting, well, compared to what I've begun to expect from her."

"I guess," Dendrox answered plainly, leading her toward the marketplace.

"So are you able to give me any advice before we do this?" Weena asked him.

Dendrox explained, "We studied the behavior of thieves in order to fit in, so we could eventually track down the thugs that attacked Candra and her father. Thieves tend to justify their actions by making some sort of excuse for themselves, like 'I've had such a run of bad luck that I deserve this', or 'this person here has all this and I've had to work so hard to gain what I have, and it's not fair', and things like, 'he doesn't even appreciate what he has, therefore he doesn't deserve it and I do', or even, 'I'm teaching him a lesson by it and therefore doing some good'. What I've discovered most is that people are most often stealing for someone else, for a family member or loved one in order to better their lives, and that is the reason they use behind their actions. With that one, the love outweighs any guilt that may accompany the theft. But where do you draw the line between what is acceptable and what's not? It's the reason behind the stealing, isn't it? Is it wrong for a man to steal food to feed his starving family? Is he supposed to simply let his loved ones die because stealing from someone who selfishly hoards more than his share is considered wrong? It is the same here. We either steal, or let everyone die because of the Killnarin. You know that we will never be able to defeat them with what we have and on empty stomachs. I don't know exactly what we will need on this quest and I don't think the others do either. But nothing comes for free; we will need money. Even the money from The Black Shadow is tainted. It most likely comes from his victims. Did you ever think about that? Do you think it all right to accept it knowing that?"

He thought to himself, *"We became corrupted. Now we know nothing else; I couldn't imagine a life anything but, not now. I learnt to act the part of a thief for Candra to be able to locate her father's murders. But what justification are we using now? That was ours in the past, but now? To be able to defeat the Killnarin, and that all our activity prior to this was just practice? Is that our excuse? It's not right to manipulate her into this, but for Candra, I've helped to pave the way for Weena. I'm sure she'll continue to make justifications until she has no problem with any of this. Weena's already agreed to rob a house with us. I just hope she doesn't end up in real danger because of us. I couldn't live with myself if that happened."*

"Oh, my word," exclaimed a short chubby faced woman from under a red and blue awning. Racks and racks of clothing, and all manner of cloth and color surrounded her. "Come here, please," the woman said to them waving them over. Puzzled, they obliged. "Oh dear, I did see correctly," she said taking hold of the bottom of Weena's robes, "You have a terrible rip in this gorgeous material. Will you let me mend this for you? It will take but a moment."

"We can't pay you for it, I'm afraid," Weena explained to her.

"Oh nonsense. I'm not about to let a beautiful young girl go wandering around with a tear like this. This is going to rip farther and fray. It's best I repair it now before these robes are ruined completely," she insisted taking out a needle and then several spools of thread trying to find a matching color. Dendrox sighed heavily, and he then began to pace idly back and forth, occasionally stopping to feel and fidget with a segment of cloth or ribbon. "You can see I'm struggling to keep up with the demand; carrying what pieces of clothing I can along with my fabrics and what not," the woman commented as she stitched.

"I don't quite know what you mean," said Weena.

<Zaylyn ><Quest For The Sword Fragments And The Hunt For Dranngore><By Katrina Mandrake-Johnston > <Ch 26> < 62 >

"Oh there's a pair of wonderful tailors in town, but they aren't able to set up shop for some reason. The old tailor has passed on you see. Rumor has it that these new tailors don't have any talent at all and rely completely on a pair of magical scissors to do their work for them. Supposedly, the clothing made with these scissors will have a perfect fit for whomever it's made for and made precisely to what the customer had envisioned. Pretty spectacular, I say, and they're desperate to get them back. They apparently were stolen some time ago, and before they eventually moved to Shirkint."

Weena glanced over to Dendrox at this. Dendrox just bit his lip and continued to examine a piece of blue silk.

The woman continued, "It's a shame as it would increase my business with my cloth and take a lot of the work load off of me. I'm better at mending rather than trying to pass myself off as a proper seamstress. Oh here, I've finished. What do you think?"

"I can hardly even tell where the tear had been," Weena complimented her.

The woman returned a cheerful smile and bid the two of them good day.

<World of Zaylyn><Quest For The Sword Fragments And The Hunt For Dranngore><By Katrina Mandrake-Johnston><Ch 27>

CHAPTER 27 =   THE BREAK IN

"Dendrox!" Weena whispered excitedly, "We found out what the scissors are for. They are magical just as we thought."

Dendrox said nothing, his face twisted in a bitter grimace. "What's wrong?" asked Weena, "I thought you'd be happy to finally find out about the scissors."

"All this trouble over a ridiculous pair of scissors!" he said with anger, "All they do is make clothes! They sent people after us, tried to kill us, all over a pair of scissors that magically makes clothes! Clothes!! They would rather have us hunted down than learn how to make a simple pair of pants for themselves. I can't believe this!!"

"Dendrox, please, calm yourself," Weena pleaded as he was making quite a scene with his outbursts.

She had never seen him this angry. He always seemed so reserved to her; never letting his emotions get too far out of hand. He always seemed to be thinking one step ahead in everything he did, and now he was blurting out to everyone they passed about the scissors and his connection to them.

"Calm down?!" he said bitterly, "You have no idea what we've been put through because of those damn things! Back at Vackiindmire, that was nothing compared to before! Don't pretend that you know all about it and are somehow part of this mess! I would never wish that upon someone!" He stopped, looking into her face and relaxed saying, "No, I'm sorry, Weena. I didn't mean to yell at you like that, and you're right. It's just after all me and Candra have been through, to find out that our lives are at risk because of a useless…" he breathed, "Just because some arrogant bastards have enough money to spread around trying to have their revenge over something so trivial that anyone else would have let lie long ago…"

"Well, it's apparently important enough to them," Weena told him.

"Enough to have us murdered because of it?!" he barked at her.

"I wasn't saying that!" she said in her defense, "I don't think anyone should be put to death over any stolen object!"

"Oh I'm sorry. I'm taking my anger out on you again. It's not you I'm angry with," Dendrox apologized, "Come on, we're almost to the house, and we shouldn't waste anymore time."

Soon they reached the place Candra had told Dendrox about. It was the bottom apartment. No one appeared to be there in the home above, nor in their chosen target. Dendrox casually looked over the surroundings, calculating a careful plan of action.

Weena could see the long flowerbeds of fluffy white and red blossoms around the base of the building. The winding metal staircase leading up to the top apartment had a leafy vine, with many large white cone-shaped flowers, which had twisted its way up the railing giving it an added beauty to it. Weena wondered who it was that had taken such great care in trimming and manipulating the plant to grow in such a manner and at which house they resided at.

<Zaylyn ><Quest For The Sword Fragments And The Hunt For Dranngore><By Katrina Mandrake-Johnston > <Ch 27> < 63 >

Dendrox asked firmly, "Can you pick a lock?" It was clear he would have rather had Candra here in this. Weena remembered Candra saying that she was the one who could pick locks with ease, where Dendrox had an easier time with pockets.

Weena told him, "There's a spell that can open locks and such, but it's one I haven't learnt."

"That doesn't help us here," he commented plainly, "Can you look for another way in then?"

She nervously edged her way around the house and discovered a window that was partially hidden from view to anyone casually passing by. Weena took up a fair sized rock, her cheeks burning. She had to show that she had the gall to do this. They were testing her. They needed the money. Everyone would fall prey to the Killnarin if they were unable to stop them. They needed to do this in order to quest for the sword.

"If Nodwel hadn't given the bag of gold to Kreasa, we wouldn't need to do this. Stopping the Killnarin should take priority over everything else. However, I would have done the same thing had I been in his place," she said to herself, *"Okay, here it goes."* Weena smashed the window with the rock, trying to make as little noise as she could in doing so.

Dendrox ran over, a look of shock and anger on his face. "What did you do?!" he whispered furiously.

"I found us a way in," she replied, trying to keep her voice strong and unwavering.

"Any idiot can do that!" he barked at her, "The trick is to leave things as they were, to give us a few days before they notice that anything has gone missing in the first place. They see this; they'll begin a search right away! Anything we get, we won't be able to sell! You idiot!"

He paced back and forth searching the street, trying to decide what to do. Weena's face burned as she held back her tears. "Come on. It's too late now. We might as well take a quick look around before someone comes to investigate the break. I mean fast!" he said sternly, "A minute, maybe two, no longer."

Ashamed, Weena asked meekly, "Okay, should I go in then?"

"Just don't cut yourself," he told her with concern, "Here, I'll help you up." His mind cursed saying, *"Damn it, she's going to get hurt! This was a stupid idea!"*

They had been mistaken in thinking the homes in this residential area were two-story buildings; there were in fact four. Each house had a upper and lower floor with eight foot high ceilings, where the ones in the shops and tavern were near twelve. Once inside, they could see that on the far back wall to the left, a staircase led up into a second level of this ground floor home. On the right, a doorway led to what looked to be the kitchen. A large wooden cabinet took up the remaining area of this wall between the kitchen and the stairs. A sturdy looking metal chain was wrapped around the handles of the cabinet doors.

"See that?" Dendrox said motioning over to the locked cabinet, "Means there's something worth taking there. Saves us some time."

"Seems odd then, don't you think? If they are supposed to go to all this trouble to protect their valuables, why advertise where they are by displaying it so visibly?" Weena said to him.

"Actually, that's a good point. The rules of logic might work against us depending on how clever this person is. See, if it were me, I'd do exactly that. I'd lure the thief right into a nice big trap behind those doors," he smiled at her, "But you'd be surprised how stupid most people are. Most people don't think things through, don't consider all the possibilities and prepare for them before they act. That's what defines the line between those that succeed and those that get caught when it comes to us thieves."

"So what are you saying then?" Weena asked. She couldn't decide whether or not he had just directed an insult towards her; his expression told her that he hadn't meant it as such, but she couldn't be sure.

"We take a look around, get a feel for this person, and then decide on whether we should waste all our time with the cabinet," he told her, "There's also the chance we may find a key."

"Couldn't we saw through the wood of the handles to get it open too? I mean, if that's a good idea?" Weena suggested timidly.

<Zaylyn ><Quest For The Sword Fragments And The Hunt For Dranngore><By Katrina Mandrake-Johnston > <Ch 27> < 64 >

"Only as a last and desperate resort. Remember, we don't want to make it look like anyone was in here, right?" Dendrox reminded her, "Why don't you have a look around while I check out these shelves over here by the tapestry, okay? It's kind of nice, eh?"

"Dendrox, what exactly should I be looking for?" she asked, as she walked over to an elegant looking table and chair over against the wall with the window.

"You won't know until you find it," he told her, "and never use names. You never know who might be listening in. It's very hard to learn how to fight the urge to respond to the sound of your name being called out, and I'm talking about a simple glance or even a twitch of your eye, and if it's used to identify you to the wrong people, it can be deadly. It's best not to use names at all, as even false names can work against you if the right people are after you. Tell me if you find anything."

"I had no idea," she replied.

The rich reddish-brown wood of the table had a glass-like finish, and a thin white candle in a shiny brass candleholder was placed precisely in the center. A small drawer was set beneath the tabletop, but Weena was afraid she might do something wrong if she attempted to open it.

A small round table was positioned in the middle of the room and nearer the front door. A beautiful vase rested here, once again exactly in the center of the table. The design upon the vase was made up of light and dark blues swirling together. Weena wondered if something like that might be considered valuable. If it were, it was something they couldn't afford to take, being such an awkward and breakable item, and then there was the even more difficult task of finding a buyer for it.

She crossed the room to get a closer look at the magnificent tapestry that occupied the wall almost in its entirety except for the long heavily cluttered shelves Dendrox was looking over. It was marvelous. It depicted a pack of wolves in a forest glade with a silver tower off in the distance. The detail put into this work of art was amazing.

Weena stepped back and bumped the small table on which the vase was displayed. She quickly tried to steady the table, but the vase toppled and rolled off the edge. Dendrox, who luckily had been watchful of Weena's actions, dashed forward and managed to catch it before it smashed.

"Get out!" he screamed at her between clenched teeth, "If this had broken, all chances of the owner thinking some kid accidentally broke the window would be gone. Why the hell Candra thought you could do this…" He tried to calm himself. It wasn't her fault. "Come on, back out the window before it's too late."

Candra raced through the streets toward the house. She went to the window, seeing the broken glass scattered about, and looked inside, a terrible fear building within her. Then to her relief, Candra heard her name called out from across the street and she hurried over.

"Hey what happened?" she asked and then went on to explain, "I got worried. I thought I better come to check on you two. With all the talk of traps and such, I began to think that perhaps you ran into some trouble or that someone had returned to the house without me knowing."

Dendrox said accusingly, "Weena decided to break the window, and then, once inside, she bumped into a table and nearly broke a vase. Luckily, I caught it before it hit the ground. There's no evidence that we were in there. Hopefully, the owner will just think a kid threw a rock or something."

"Well, she's learning. No need to be so hard on her," Candra said in Weena's defense.

"Candra, she can't do this!" he said angrily, "Not like we can. She doesn't even think what might happen before she does something! She's going to get us arrested or more likely killed. Do you think that's fair to her even? If she comes along with us, she's going to be in danger. She doesn't know how to survive, not like we can, and you know that."

Candra simply avoided giving him any kind of response to this and suggested, "Let's just head back to The Old Scabbard Inn and see what the others have done."

<World of Zaylyn><Quest For The Sword Fragments And The Hunt For Dranngore><By Katrina Mandrake-Johnston><Ch 28>

CHAPTER 28 = THE JEWELRY STALL

When the three of them returned to the inn, Nodwel and Vordin were already there and were

<Zaylyn ><Quest For The Sword Fragments And The Hunt For Dranngore><By Katrina Mandrake-Johnston > <Ch 28> < 65 >

sitting with Asdella at the larger table by the blackened window where they had sat the night before. Vordin and Nodwel explained to them what they had learnt that morning from Failick and Norick the blacksmith.

Dendrox told them that they had come up empty-handed. Weena wondered why he had not told Candra about what they had found out about the scissors. But then she suspected he was avoiding a similar outburst with her about them as he had had and it was for good reason.

Candra mentioned, "The dagger throwing competition begins today. I saw a crowd gathering up at the town square; so it should be starting soon."

"I'll come for other reasons, but I'm not going to enter," said Dendrox.

"You three would probably be the best ones to head out that way," Nodwel told them, "Let us know if you find out anything of importance. I want to find out more about who Dranngore is. Maybe we'll get lucky and run into someone who has heard of him. I want to be sure that using the sword on him won't end up being a horrible mistake. Asdella's been asking around about the wizard's guild. It apparently relocated and now no one really knows where it is. Oh and Vordin, she found out that the guild was started around two hundred years ago by a wizard who defeated an incredibly powerful dragon. He became known as the greatest wizard of that time and his guild became known as such, the wizard's guild. I remember you asking Weena about whether it was singular or plural. Did the man mention anything else, Asdella?"

"Just that back then the dragons were ruled by their dragon king or something like that. A battle was engaged between the king and his brother for some reason or another, and this wizard was supposed to have something to do with that battle's outcome. He claimed that he was the one who defeated the evil brother of the dragon king but not before the king was ensnared by an evil spell. The man who told me this heard the story from the storyteller, Rasindell," she explained, "I don't know how much truth there is to it. It's useless information, but at least I managed to learn something related to our quest."

"We should probably hurry if we're going to head up to the competition," commented Candra, getting up to leave.

"Could you maybe find out when Rasindell will be there?" Vordin asked them, "I'd like to go, but I should really wait in order for Lorenta to be able to go with me."

Candra gave him a slight nod and the three of them departed.

Once at the town square, the three of them could see that the competition was about to begin. Several hundred onlookers were standing around trying to see down into the lower area where the competition was being held. Target boards were lined up along one edge of the area. The contestants waved to the crowd as they received a few cheers here and there. Then they descended the short flight of steps to stand in their designated places. An announcement was made introducing each contestant and then the competition commenced.

"You going to work the crowd?" Candra whispered to Dendrox.

"Yeah, might as well, perfect opportunity. Be back in a bit," said Dendrox, and he disappeared off into the crowd.

"Where's he going?" Weena asked her.

"You'll figure it out," was Candra's answer, "A word of advice, in a crowd like this, where attention is diverted, it's best to keep your valuables well hidden." She chuckled, "And sometimes even that isn't enough. I'm not very good with my hands like that, but I can cause enough of a distraction for Dendrox to work his fingers into where they don't belong. I'm more of a locksmith myself. Together we can accomplish a lot. Anyway, we might as well watch the competition until he returns."

"Candra still has my mother's ring," Weena reminded herself bitterly, *"If she says he's better than her, he must be good as she was able to snatch my ring away twice without me knowing. Could this be the chance I've been waiting for? If only I knew where she has it stashed. She better still have it. If anything happens to it because of her… Okay, so let's think for a minute. She has those two pouches about her hips, but if what she says is true about crowds like this, she wouldn't have hidden the ring in*

<Zaylyn ><Quest For The Sword Fragments And The Hunt For Dranngore><By Katrina Mandrake-Johnston > <Ch 28> < 66 >

either of them. Although, Dendrox did hide the scissors in his pouch. Where else? She wouldn't have it in her boot with her constantly complaining about them. Besides, I would have seen when she took them off back at camp with the imp, wouldn't I?"

"Dendrox is way better than any of them down there," Candra boasted, "Did you see that one older man there with the blonde hair? He does this big elaborate show of taking aim, and even after all that, his accuracy was really poor. Well, compared to Dendrox. And on top of that, Dendrox can fire a blade out so fast you're not even sure where it came from. He has great aim, even at a distance as what they've been given. He could beat this bunch any day."

"She's in a good mood. I need to try, otherwise, she'll never give my ring back," Weena told herself firmly, *"If anything, I might be able to find out where she's hidden it and then try again later if I get a chance. Here it goes."*

She lurched forward as if someone had pushed her and fell against Candra. Attempting to regain her balance with Candra's help, Weena patted down the elf's clothing as much as she could without seeming overly suspicious. As far as she could tell, Candra hadn't suspected her motives, but she didn't discover where the ring was located either.

Dendrox, approaching from out of the crowd with a sly smile, said to them, "Well at least the whole day wasn't a waste of time."

"So he did steal. I tried my best at the house, even though what we were doing was wrong. Does he realize that? Does he even realize that he's hurting my feelings when he says things like that? I didn't foul things up on purpose. I really did try to follow his example. Does he think I did those things intentionally because I disapprove of them thieving?" thought Weena with frustration, *"I don't know why I'm going along with all this. I need to get my ring back, but on top of that, they both have a certain infectious charisma about them, and I am still foolishly attracted to Dendrox. I can't help but break into a goofy smile every time he looks at me. Is there something still between us? I wish he would say something about it. Deep down, I know that no matter what I decide on the matter beforehand, I'll end up melting like butter if he ever goes to kiss me again."* She blushed as she glanced over in Dendrox's direction. Her eyes fell longingly over the curves of his arms and his chest, remembering how good it had felt to be warmed by his gentle embrace, her fingertips relishing the touch of his skin, his lips moist against hers with passion... *"What happened to that? He's become so cold towards me, and I don't know why. I've been trying to do my best at everything I can. I can't stop being me! I'm not perfect! I make mistakes, but I try to correct them and learn from them. What else can I do?!"* She was terribly upset and incredibly angry. She hated this horrible feeling of rejection. Weena decided that she wasn't going to stand around feeling sorry for herself any longer. She didn't know what, but she was going to do something about it.

"Wasn't there a jewelry stall around here somewhere where we can pawn some of this stuff off?" Dendrox asked Candra.

"Yeah, I saw it a ways back. I'll go with you," she replied, and then said to Weena, "You should probably wait here in case there's trouble."

Candra was merely concerned for her safety and Weena knew this. However, all it did was reinforce her feeling that she was a member of their group who was completely useless and merely tagging along, getting in the way of the others. Once they had enough money to buy magic items, they wouldn't need her amateur spells.

"Weena?" said Candra with a smile, unsure of exactly why Weena was standing there with such a miserable expression on her face.

"Yeah, sure, I'll wait," Weena told her plainly.

The woman seated behind the tabletop of the jewelry stall waited for them to approach, the corner of her mouth turning up in a smile that suggested she somehow had been expecting them. She was an elf and had the same slight slant and brilliant green color to her eyes that Candra had. She was around the same height as Dendrox, however, with long blonde flowing locks of hair about her heart-shaped face. Over a loose fitting dark green long-sleeved shirt, she wore a light green vest with a pair of brown

<Zaylyn ><Quest For The Sword Fragments And The Hunt For Dranngore><By Katrina Mandrake-Johnston > <Ch 28> < 67 >

pants. The woman impatiently scuffed her black boot back and forth across the gravelly dirt of the unpaved marketplace. Both Candra and Dendrox noted that a small crossbow was propped up against the side of her chair. She lacked the slenderness to her face and body that are normally associated with elves, which suggested that perhaps she was only half.

"About time you show us your skills," the woman said oddly when they came to stand before her, "We've been keeping an eye on you two. Nice moves out there. Dendrox, is it?"

"Yes, but how did you..." he began, but she bluntly interrupted.

"I'd like to invite the two of you to a gathering of a few friends of mine," she told them, "There is someone who is particularly interested in meeting both of you. She said something about the Gem of Enarr. Will you join us?" The young woman at the stall looked them over, studying them, a large grin forming across her face that didn't quite meet her eyes in a friendly demeanor.

"You've heard of the gem?" Candra asked her excitedly.

"Oh yes, many times. It was the mention of the gem that brought your group to our attention. It had been hidden away, protected by deadly traps, and guarded by ferocious creatures, and so on, and so on, until it was stolen from its resting place," she explained.

"So it's hopeless then? Its location is unknown?" said Dendrox with disappointment.

"Not to me, as I know the thief who retrieved it," she explained with another grin, as if they were falling into some premeditated plan, "She's the one who is so eager to meet you."

"We'll meet with her. We'll come to this gathering you spoke of then," Candra replied, but she was wary of deception.

"Wonderful. It's a pleasure to meet you, Candra and Dendrox. My name is Sinva," said the woman, "You wanted to cash in a few items first, did you?"

Sinva made the transaction quickly, sliding the coins out towards Dendrox in exchange for what he had presented to her. She then closed up the stall in a matter of seconds, scooping the goods she had displayed there off the tabletop and into a burlap bag. Candra and Dendrox then began to follow her toward the northern residential area on the west side of town.

Candra hurried back to Weena and told her quickly, "We have a lead on the gem. You'll wait for us at the inn to return?"

Dendrox, annoyed with the delay, called out to Candra, "Come on! What are you doing? Let's go!"

"Well at least she told me what was going on," Weena thought, her feelings hurt once again, *"Dendrox was just going to take off leaving me with no clue as to what was happening whatsoever. I'm supposed to go around town with them today! Dendrox would rather just get rid of me!"*

Back at the inn, Weena discovered that only Vordin had remained there.

"Nodwel and Asdella took off to check on a few things together," Vordin told her as she pulled up a chair, "They took Lorenta along with them in the backpack. I hope that's going to be all right. So where's Candra and Dendrox?"

"Do you really want to sit here, Vordin?" she questioned with irritation, "because I don't. They stick us here because they figure we can't do anything right, that we can't contribute. I think we should just go and show them that they're wrong."

"Why, what do you want to do? The tavern here is the best place to find out information, or so Nodwel says," Vordin told her, "and so far, no one seems to mind us just sitting here."

"No, I have something better in mind," Weena explained.

<World of Zaylyn><Quest For The Sword Fragments And The Hunt For Dranngore><By Katrina Mandrake-Johnston><Ch 29>

CHAPTER 29 = A SECOND ATTEMPT

"So tell me again where we're headed?" Vordin asked Weena as she led him through the streets toward the house she and Dendrox had attempted to burgle.

"Candra and Dendrox selected a house where there was minimal risk at getting caught. Dendrox took me with him, and I apparently did everything wrong. Now they hate me and think I'm some

<Zaylyn ><Quest For The Sword Fragments And The Hunt For Dranngore><By Katrina Mandrake-Johnston > <Ch 29> < 68 >
bumbling idiot."

"Weena," Vordin tried to reason with her, "I doubt they think that about you. I mean you saved both their lives. They're your friends."

"Apparently, all of that means nothing to them. They only care about themselves. I'm going to rob that house on my own and show them that they are wrong about me," she said bitterly, "They think this is some sort of art form they have mastered or something."

"Weena," Vordin said nervously, "I don't think this is a very good idea. I don't want to become a criminal. We need money for weapons and supplies and magic items, but do you really think such a drastic step is necessary?"

"Yes!" she hissed, "I need you to watch my back. Do you want to end up like Yarin? I need to prove to them that I'm not expendable!"

"Weena, this is crazy! We should at least tell someone what we're doing, where we're going," he told her, as she grabbed his hand and pulled him along after her.

"What, so they can come to rescue us? Once again proving that we are useless, a burden to the rest of the group? No, we have to do this on our own."

"Alright," Vordin finally agreed, as he was afraid for her and of her attempting it alone.

"This is it over here," Weena directed him, "We can get in through the window. The man left town for the day so we should still have time to get something from inside."

Once again, Vordin asked her, "Weena, are you sure about this?"

With a nod she said, "I'll need you to boost me up through the window."

"Are you sure no one's home?" Vordin asked with worry.

Weena peeked in through the window and then answered, "Yes, give me a boost."

Vordin helped her through the broken window and then clambered in as well.

Once inside, Vordin whispered, "Let's hurry, okay? I don't feel right being here."

"Yes, I know, I don't think we should be doing this either, but I need to prove my point and maybe we'll get something that can help us in our quest for the sword."

"What should I do?" he asked nervously going over to the reddish-brown table with the candleholder.

"I don't know. Start looking around, I guess, but don't mess anything up too badly if you can help it," she instructed as she rummaged through the contents of the shelves by the tapestry.

She pawed over a small black box which was locked and sounded as if it contained a few coins, a tiny empty cloth pouch, a pair of brown leather gloves, three empty glass potion flasks, a small twisted stick that had been carved with swirl-like designs much like that on the vase, and another locked box that was of a blue color and sounded and felt as if there were two or more marble-like objects within.

"This is actually kind of fun going through all this stuff and looking for treasures," Weena admitted to herself.

"Weena?" Vordin whispered, "This drawer is locked. I wonder what is…" Vordin said trailing off.

She looked over and saw why Vordin had stopped in mid sentence.

<World of Zaylyn><Quest For The Sword Fragments And The Hunt For Dranngore><By Katrina Mandrake-Johnston><Ch 30>

CHAPTER 30 = THE WEREWOLF REVEALED

Standing in the middle of the room was a man. His arms were folded neatly across his chest over his loose fitting grey vest, and oddly, he didn't at all look surprised or shocked that there were two intruders in his home. In fact, he almost looked pleased.

"When did he get here?!" Weena gasped in shock and horror.

Vordin said to her as he stared white-faced at the man who had caught them, "I thought you were watching the door."

"I thought you were," she hissed at him, her face burning, and she felt the sting of tears.

The man just stood there looking at the two of them and then sniffed at the air focusing in on Weena.

<Zaylyn ><Quest For The Sword Fragments And The Hunt For Dranngore><By Katrina Mandrake-Johnston > <Ch 30> < 69 >

"*He just looked at me as if he recognized me,*" she exclaimed within her mind, "*Have I seen him somewhere before? He doesn't look familiar. Actually, it's silly, but it made me think of that wolf we saw at Dexcsin.*"

Weena, fumbling horribly over her words, made a feeble attempt to justify their actions to the man, explaining about the Killnarin, and how because of them, it had led to this desperate action. Vordin, too afraid to say anything, merely nodded in the appropriate places.

"I believe you," said the man.

"You do?" she exclaimed, shocked that anyone could believe a story as incredible as what she had just told.

"I was there at Dexcsin," he said plainly.

"What?! But how?!" Vordin had the nerve to ask, "Is this some sort of joke, because we were serious about everything we told you."

He chuckled and explained calmly, "You saw me there, but I looked a little different then. Here, let me show you."

His eyes turned from blue to yellow and his front teeth elongated into that of a canine.

"You, you were the wolf we saw!" Weena exclaimed accusingly.

"Who was the second wolf, the larger one that was pulling the girl away from you?" Vordin dared to ask.

"It doesn't really matter to you, now does it?" he sneered, "That pathetic mutt is dead now anyhow," he laughed coldly, "Were you hoping that he would come to your aid once again?"

"What do you mean?" asked Vordin.

"I tire of this petty conversation," he said, his voice taking on a malicious edge.

"You're Dranngore!" said Weena, "You're behind all of this!"

"Who?" the werewolf replied, "I have no idea what you're talking about, you irritating woman."

"Okay, maybe not," said Weena, looking nervously to Vordin, "But then why are you doing this?"

"Simple," he grinned wickedly, "Because I feel like it, and I can."

They watched in horror as the man began to transform. His ears receded and elongated. His nose started to change and darken, as his jaw lengthened and his skull narrowed taking on the shape of a snout. His fingers shortened and his nails grew into vicious looking claws. A grey fur erupted from every pore in his skin, as his body began to bend in inhuman places and change its shape entirely. A long tail grew from the base of his spine.

All Weena and Vordin could do was stare in amazement and fear at this incredible transformation taking place before them. A large grey wolf now stood before them, the clothes he had been wearing hanging loosely about him. He quickly wriggled free of them and then stood there, watching the two humans intensely as he let out a low growl.

Weena nervously glanced toward the window. "He didn't say anything about wanting to kill us, right?" she said anxiously, "We probably should have run away while he was changing form."

"Yes, that would have been a good idea," said Vordin back to her, "Unfortunately, now, it isn't going to help us too much."

She said hopefully, "Well, why would he want to kill us? Look, he's just standing there."

"Should we run?" Vordin whispered to her, "Do you think he can understand what we're saying when he's in this state?"

"We know his secret now," Weena stated fearfully, "I have a feeling he's not just trying to be friendly by showing us his ability. It is more that it doesn't matter if we know his secret, because he's going to kill us!"

"I don't know. Be quiet! Do you want to give him ideas?!" Vordin hissed at her.

"Oh, Vordin, that was him chewing on that dead girl's leg, remember? I don't want that to be me!" she whimpered, "Do something, please!"

"Shh, be quiet!" he repeated to her.

"Do you think he might be angry that we broke into his house earlier?" she asked.

"Hey, I wasn't part of that for good reason, and if he didn't know about it a minute ago, he does

<Zaylyn ><Quest For The Sword Fragments And The Hunt For Dranngore><By Katrina Mandrake-Johnston > <Ch 30> < 70 >

now. Why the hell did you bring that up for?!" Vordin snapped at her, nervously watching the wolf.

"Look at him! He can smell that someone was here earlier, and especially that I was," Weena almost wailed.

"Hey wait, don't they have that law here that thieves are allowed to get away with stealing if they are clever enough or something like that?" Vordin suddenly realized.

"Vordin, I don't think it counts if the owner catches you," and then she said with heavy sarcasm, "What do you think, Vordin? Were we clever enough?"

"Weena, we have to do something," he told her, "Maybe he's just waiting for us to leave. You know, because of the law about thieves. We didn't even steal anything. We should be able to leave, right? He's just trying to scare us."

"Does he look as if he is one to follow rules and the law?!" she asked him, "Remember what Kreasa said? That he killed her eldest son and probably her husband as well?! He's a murderer!"

"Hey, Candra and Dendrox were the ones who picked this place, weren't they? It was their idea. They're the ones responsible," Vordin commented angrily.

"Oh great, now he knows their names too," said Weena realizing that they had just betrayed the two thieves and Kreasa as well. *The only way we would know about her, is if she survived and came to Shirkint. Now he knows! After all her efforts to escape this monster, we've led him right to her!*" she thought with a heavy guilt.

The wolf took a couple steps toward them and growled.

"He hasn't killed us yet," Vordin said backing up toward the door, "Maybe he just wants us to leave."

Weena followed his example, edging nearer and nearer to the door and knowing that at any second the beast could spring at them and tear their throats out before they could unlock the door. They would never make it out the window in time; the door was their only option for escape.

The wolf snarled viciously at them but did not approach any farther, as they fumbled frantically with the lock. As soon as they got it open, the two of them ran out the door, slamming it closed behind them, and escaping across the street to what they hoped was a safe enough distance.

"Why do you think he didn't attack us? You know we should have run a long time ago. Instead, we stand there arguing like idiots! We are beyond all luck to be alive right now, you know that, don't you?" Vordin said to her.

"Hey, what was that?!" Weena exclaimed in terror, extending her arm.

"What?!" Vordin asked searching wildly in a panic with his eyes in the direction.

"I don't know. I thought I saw a shadowy shape dart past down that alley there," she told him.

"Wait a minute," said Vordin, a thought forming in his mind, "You think that maybe the only reason the werewolf didn't attack us was because he couldn't, that The Black Shadow was somehow holding him back from killing us?"

Weena wore a look of astonishment on her pale face as she pondered this. "Could be. He supposedly held back the Killnarin in order for me to make it safely back to the camp through the forest when we were outside the spiders' lair. Or at least that's what I believe happened. I'm sure the Killnarin would have found me otherwise. So is that what he is, a werewolf?"

"I guess so, from what I've heard in stories. Do you think he'll come after us?" Vordin asked with an anxious look toward the house, "Hunt us down in both human and wolf form? Waiting until there is nothing protecting us? What about Candra and Dendrox? He knows their names now and that they were in his house; that they invaded his territory."

"And Kreasa. How could I be so stupid?!" said Weena, the tears streaming down her cheeks, "Maybe Candra's right. I don't think before I say things, do I? Candra, Dendrox, Kreasa… Nodwel… Everyone. They'll know that it was us that told the creature. I don't know what's worse," Weena wailed.

"Let's not worry about that now," said Vordin, "We'll just have to be on our guard, that's all."

"I need to go to the magic shop. I've got to learn some offensive spells and quickly, for more reasons than one now. Shirkint is supposed to be the best place to learn magic."

<Zaylyn ><Quest For The Sword Fragments And The Hunt For Dranngore><By Katrina Mandrake-Johnston > <Ch 30> < 71 >

"Sure, good idea," Vordin told her, "How is it that he can change at will though? I thought werewolves only made their transformation during the full moon and at night. Isn't that how the stories go?"

"I don't know," she answered.

He decided, "I should ask Rasindell. Perhaps he will know of a legend or at least some sort of story, which may give us a clue. One thing I know for sure, is that we both have made a terrible enemy. The more information we have, the better chance we have of avoiding him. Lorenta wanted me to go with her to see Rasindell, but I'll have to go without her. I can't wait until nightfall. He may not even be there after dark."

"I don't want to go alone. Will you walk with me to the magic shop?" Weena begged.

"Sure," he told her.

On the way to the magic shop, Weena told him with great concern, "Be back at the inn before dark. I doubt he would be so bold as to come after us in daylight and in the open. Plus, so many people have warned us about roaming about after nightfall. I'll be right next door to the inn, so I should be fine. I'll make sure I stay around others. It should be safer that way. You do the same. Don't go anywhere alone, okay? Find out what you can, especially if there is a way to defeat such a creature, or at least of some way to protect us from it, and then get safely back."

***

<World of Zaylyn><Quest For The Sword Fragments And The Hunt For Dranngore><By Katrina Mandrake-Johnston><Ch 31>

CHAPTER 31 =   THE THIEVES GUILD

Sinva led Candra and Dendrox to a house at the very northwestern corner of the town wall.

"This is it," Sinva told them as she unlocked the door to the bottom house and entered.

Candra gave Dendrox a nervous look. It was dark within, and Candra was still wary of blindly trusting this woman in hope of finding the gem The Black Shadow spoke of.

"Come on," Sinva called out to them, "Everyone's downstairs. You were interested in finding the thieves guild, well, here it is. If you are going to refuse this invitation to meet with us, then say so now."

"And now that we know of its location?" Dendrox inquired.

"We have methods of disposing those that threaten us, and the two of you pose no threat," she grinned.

"We might as well risk it. We're dead eventually anyway if the Killnarin continue to gain power. The Black Shadow seems like our only hope of restoring the sword, and he's the one who wants this gem," said Candra.

"Whatever you decide, you know I'll follow," Dendrox added with the hint of a smile, but he eyed the darkness of the room with suspicion.

They stepped into the house. The door slammed behind them, and they heard and saw a panel slide open, a bright light coming from beyond. Sinva's dark silhouette stepped into the light.

"Follow me," she said with a gesture toward the opening, and Sinva descended out of sight.

Candra muttered, "I don't like this."

Dagger in hand, Dendrox hurried after her followed by Candra, her bow no longer slung over her shoulder and with an arrow between her fingers.

They descended into a white circular room. Seating was arranged roughly in the middle of this room and two others besides Sinva were there lounging about.

"Well at least they aren't completely naïve," said the male elf. He had short dark blonde hair with heavily tanned skin. His grey eyes thoroughly examined the two of them before breaking into a welcoming smile. "Welcome to our little den of thieves," he snickered, "The name's Etor. Looks like we have a similar interest. Nice blades, you any good with 'em?"

"I do all right," Dendrox replied warily.

Etor was a few years older than the two of them and was dressed in a brown shirt with a black vest and pants. The other was an odd-looking character. A white vest was over his broad and muscular

<Zaylyn ><Quest For The Sword Fragments And The Hunt For Dranngore><By Katrina Mandrake-Johnston > <Ch 31> < 72 >

chest, and he had a pale greenish tint to his skin. A tattoo of a dragon skull decorated the top of his bald head, and his eyes were a bright red. A short sword in a reddish-brown scabbard rested across his lap. Dendrox noticed that all three of them had a ring with the same design and was probably used to identify the guild's members.

"Hello," greeted the odd-looking man, "You look curious, so I'll save you the trouble. I'm half dwarf and half human-dragon. My name's Zindle. Etor over there is half Dragonite too, although you'd never know it by looking at him. He takes after his father."

"Yeah, never really knew my mother much," added Etor.

"There's no need for weapons here," Sinva told them firmly and offered them, "Please, have a seat."

Dendrox and Candra obliged with caution. They certainly seemed eager to welcome them into their group. Perhaps it was because they had shown themselves to be in good favor with The Black Shadow, as they had not done anything noteworthy within the town to prove themselves as exceptional thieves or even been in town long enough for rumor of a theft to come to the guild's attention if they had.

Zindle went on to say, "Etor here is pretty good with locks, his night vision helps him out a lot with that. Me, I'm good at disarming traps, far better than Etor, although he does have his moments. He usually has me double check things before he starts picking away at a mechanism though." Candra and Dendrox weren't about to offer up any information about what skills they possessed. "I've tried my hand at picking pockets," Zindle told them, "and I ain't too bad, but I think most of the time I get caught and they're just too frightened to say anything about it, with my eyes and skin color being as they are. I inherited a lot from my father's side, the lack of hair included, but I'm sure glad I didn't end up with his claws as well, or the scales. What about you Etor, you never did answer me about whether or not you be hiding some scales beneath them clothes."

"I'm surprised you haven't started bragging about your days as a pirate, Zindle," commented Etor, ignoring the question.

An orange-haired cat strolled across the room from behind one of the chairs.

Dendrox realized, "Hey, that's the same cat from the inn." It jumped up onto Dendrox's lap, nuzzling its nose into his hand affectionately.

"Rinna is our other member here. We haven't heard anything from the others. They either left the valley or are most likely dead or imprisoned. It looks like we're the only ones left now out of the guild. Anyway, Rinna is one of our best; she gives a whole new meaning to the term cat burglar."

The cat transformed into a woman right there on Dendrox's lap, putting her arm around his shoulder. As Rinna looked over Dendrox with the same curious and excited look to her pale green eyes a cat gets at play, Sinva explained, "Her mother's a feline-shape shifter. She inherited the talent. She can be as quiet as a kitten or as fierce as a tiger, and I mean that literally."

Candra could see that Dendrox was blushing, but did not at all seem uncomfortable with the situation of having a beautiful woman so close. A dark green vest tightly hugged a pair of voluptuous breasts beneath a low cut black shirt, and her close fitting black pants and boots showed off her shapely legs.

"So are you going to let them have the emerald, or what?" Sinva asked her.

"I'm thinking about it. He is a handsome one, isn't he?" she smiled, caressing Dendrox's cheek with her fingertips. She turned to Candra asking, "Is he yours?"

"Oh, no, he's a friend of mine," she answered plainly and then added, "We're not together if that's what you're asking." "*It's no concern of mine if she's interested in him,*" Candra told herself, "*It's not my place to interfere. I've already made a mess of things between him and Weena. We proved to each other that there could be no romance between us, so it's up to Dendrox about what he decides.*" Still Candra felt the uncomfortable sting of jealousy, but she couldn't determine whether it was for herself for whatever reason, or if it was for Weena's sake.

Rinna got up, her fiery red hair cascading about her in waves as she moved, and she strolled idly across the room saying, "You know, the gem, it's my claim to fame, well among the thieves here at

<Zaylyn ><Quest For The Sword Fragments And The Hunt For Dranngore><By Katrina Mandrake-Johnston > <Ch 31> < 73 >

least. I went to a lot of trouble to get it. There were ingenious traps in my way, terrible beasts to get past, not to mention…"

Sinva interrupted with a heavy sigh, saying, "Alright, alright, we've heard it a thousand times. Are you going to give it to them or not?"

"Well everyone here has seen it and knows that it was I who stole it from its resting place. I suppose I could lend it to you perhaps. You're telling the truth about The Black Shadow, aren't you? I'd be a fool to get involved with something like that. I don't want to be the one to stand in the way of his plans. Alright, come over here and I'll give it to you."

She reached into an inner fold of her vest and retrieved a well-concealed dark green gem about the size of a walnut and held it in her outstretched hand for Dendrox to take. Bewildered that she was giving them the gem without anything in return, he gave Candra an odd look and then decided to approach. Just before he was able to collect the item, Rinna's arm, along with the gem, seemed to melt into the rest of her body as her form changed shape and size. A large tiger now stood before him and let out a roar. Dendrox jumped back, truly astonished.

The tiger quickly changed back into the woman as she laughed, "Did you see his face?! Oh, I'm sorry," she said placing a hand on his shoulder, "I just couldn't resist. Here you go." She placed the gem into his hand. "Now you know not to forget about bringing it back to me, don't you?"

Candra stared in astonishment. "That's amazing! So your clothing and possessions change into your new form with you?" Candra tried to clarify, "I don't see how that can be possible unless the transformation is merely an illusion."

Dendrox added in, "We have a friend who can change from one form to another, but with her, it is clearly a physical transformation; one part of the first creature becoming a part of the second. I don't quite understand how it's possible, especially with multiple forms. So is it merely an illusion?" He tucked the gem into the inside fold of his vest, similar to what Rinna had done.

Sinva laughed, "Oh, now you've hit a nerve, she really doesn't like to talk about this."

"No, it's okay. And quit talking as if you know my every thought, as if you know me inside and out. It's not true, so stop it," she snapped at her, "Yes, normally a transformation more than just physically would be suspicious, and I'm surprised that you would be intelligent enough to state this as so. I think I'm starting to really like you two." She gave them a flirtatious smile.

"How is it that the weight can change from one form to the other?" Dendrox asked her, "It's the same way for our friend. I've always been curious about how that is possible."

"She doesn't know," Sinva chuckled, "She has no clue of how the change occurs."

"Fine, alright, I admit that I don't really know how it works, only that it does, and that it is in fact an actual transformation along with clothing and small belongings, and not an illusion of a transformation," Rinna told them, "Oh and I did try many times with different items of all different types and sizes, to see what I could absorb into my transformations. Small weapons such as daggers and small items of value are fine, but say a sword or a big chest of gold, no. One time I had my hands on a large ornamental plate of gold and silver with valuable-looking jewels all around the rim. I thought surely I'd be able to absorb it within my change and escape undetected as an innocent little alley cat. The damn thing clattered to the floor, and I got a heavy boot thrown at my head by the owner. Good thing I was quick enough to escape. I tend to revert back if unconscious, well, and when asleep or so Tekrox says. That's my little brother. So far he hasn't been able to make a change. I keep teasing him that one day he'll make a change right in front of the horses and scare them into bolting down the streets of the town in terror. He works over at the stable for The Old Scabbard Inn. We're both only half feline-shape shifter; our father's human."

Zindle asked her, "So your brother ever see anything over there? I hear that those that work at the stable often tend to go missing."

She replied, "He works during the day. Only a desperate fool would dare attempt the night shift. The owner of the inn, Ondaff, pays an incredible amount of gold to anyone brave enough to work the night and always seems to be able to fill the position. Another one went missing about two weeks ago. I remember the look of terror on my brother's face when he told me about it. I think he saw something

<Zaylyn ><Quest For The Sword Fragments And The Hunt For Dranngore><By Katrina Mandrake-Johnston > <Ch 31> < 74 >

awful, but he wouldn't say, and I don't have the heart to pry. Something terrible like that happened to a good friend of his a couple years back too. My father put up a notice on the message board just at the town entrance there. You may have seen it. It's about wanting a bodyguard to escort him and his merchandise back and forth to the villages. His name's Daslimb. Right now he's too afraid to go all the way to Vackiindmire. Bandits, monsters in the night, who knows what the reason. I keep telling him that I'd come along with him, but he insists that Mother and I should keep our abilities a secret and Tekrox as well if he ever develops any."

"How is Goreena anyhow?" asked Etor, "Is she enjoying the plant business, sitting around surrounded by catnip?"

"That was incredibly stupid," Sinva remarked.

"Sorry, bad attempt at a joke," he apologized.

Rinna glared at him saying, "Next time think before you make any sort of comment about my mother. So Dendrox," she turned to him with a grin, "You won't have any problems returning the gem to me then, right? If you can't find me at home, house number fourteen, or at the jewelry stall in the marketplace where I work for Sinva, you can always reach one of my family members, or someone here to get a hold of me. But be sure to return it to my hand only, and not to anyone else."

"What?" Etor said with a playful smirk, "You don't trust any of us enough to get it back to you?"

"Exactly," she said returning a sly little smile back to him.

"The bandits won't be a threat anymore," commented Dendrox, "Your father won't have them to worry about."

"What do you mean?" asked Etor.

"They're all dead, well, except for a few that escaped," Candra told them, "Their leader's dead too."

"We came across them on our way to Shirkint," added in Dendrox.

Their faces fell as the four of them stared at Candra and Dendrox in disbelief.

"There was near thirty of them! How…" Etor began and then stopped himself, "You're taking us for fools, aren't you?"

"*Well,*" Candra thought to herself, "*all of you are pretty loose with information in such an overly friendly manner that doesn't quite add up. I don't know if they think they are buttering us up into letting something slip or what? Perhaps they are merely seeing if we will let our guard down given the right situation. Or maybe it's because they're afraid that The Black Shadow might retaliate against them if they don't cooperate with us. But it has to be more than just that. They certainly seemed shocked when we told them about the bandits, but they seem to know more about us than they are letting on, even more so than what Rinna could have overheard as the cat. How is that possible?*"

"No, it's the truth. They weren't too much trouble for us. They attacked us and got what was coming to them. Apparently, we did everyone a favor by the sounds of it," said Dendrox.

"I see," said Sinva, "and the two of you did this alone?"

"Mostly," said Candra, being wary of what they said to the guild.

"And what of the crossbow?" asked Zindle.

"Lost," answered Candra.

"They weren't friends of yours by chance? It was they that attacked us, you understand," explained Dendrox.

"No, just the opposite at times," commented Sinva, "It's just a little hard to believe."

"Is it?" Dendrox asked with a clever smile.

<World of Zaylyn><Quest For The Sword Fragments And The Hunt For Dranngore><By Katrina Mandrake-Johnston><Ch 32>

CHAPTER 32 = THE GEM OF ENARR

"The gem, what exactly does it do? Why would The Black Shadow be so interested in it?" Candra asked Rinna.

"Don't know," she shrugged, "Enarr was a necromancer, or so the story goes. As far as the gem, I have no idea. So you think it might have magical powers or something?"

<Zaylyn ><Quest For The Sword Fragments And The Hunt For Dranngore><By Katrina Mandrake-Johnston > <Ch 32> < 75 >

"You aren't worried about handing the gem over to him?" Dendrox questioned, studying her.

"If The Black Shadow truly desires it, I'd rather have you two deliver it to him than have that creature collect it himself. Very few survive an encounter with that monster," Rinna told them with a concerned look.

Etor asked her, "And the, ah, 'thing', didn't tell you what the gem was for? That's odd, don't you think?"

"Well it's valuable money wise, but I doubt that is why The Black Shadow wants it, and I highly doubt that anyone would go to all the trouble to guard a single piece of treasure like that unless it had some further purpose," Rinna told him, "And for the gem to get past the 'thing' from detecting what it's all about, I'm becoming more and more curious. But like I said, not enough to come into harm's way because of it."

"What's this 'thing' you keep referring to?" Candra asked them.

"Yeah, well, you see, we can't risk telling you about it. It's the reason why our little guild has managed to remain so prosperous among other things. It's for members of the guild alone, and for any of us to reveal its secrets, is to be met with a penalty of death," Sinva explained to them.

Zindle warned, "I don't think it too wise for you two to be speaking in such a 'laxed fashion, Rinna and Etor, 'bout things you know you shouldn't. I don't think your intentions be to be making these two so curious that they decide to start snooping around. Am I right? It would be awful if you caused an accident to occur to them, and then I shudder to think what The Black Shadow might have to say about it afterwards."

Rinna nodded her understanding and went on to say, "Hey, maybe the gem has the power to raise the dead or something like that? It is the gem of a necromancer. Perhaps it was used to channel dark energy in some sort of ritual. Anyway, I'm certain that whatever power it contains, it won't be anything that The Black Shadow can't already obtain, and that makes me all the more curious why he wanted you two to collect it for him. What is it about you two that The Black Shadow finds so interesting?"

"I'm sure they don't have any idea," Zindle broke in again, "No need to scare 'em anymore then they already are, I'm sure."

"So Sinva, I was wondering, are you a full elf? You have similar features to myself but lack the height that is common with my type," Candra asked, mostly just to change the subject of conversation.

Etor was the one to answer. "Yeah, you're the only pure breeds here. Were all half and half of one thing or another. There are a lot of half-breeds here in this town. Balin, the old man who owns the equipment shop is the biggest example of interracial love. Great adventurer in his time too."

"Looks like a tall skinny dwarf to me with oddly colored eyes," Zindle added.

"His eyes are greeny-blue," Etor argued, "You're the one with a weird eye color."

"Well he is part human-dragon, isn't he? Like you and me?" asked Zindle.

"I think so. He's dwarf, elf, and Dragonite, I believe," said Etor.

"Well, he told me once," Sinva said to them, "that he has that creepy Possession ability. You know, where you can take over someone's mind or create a mental link with someone over a distance. He doesn't like to talk about it though, as it makes people nervous. Oh, I guess I shouldn't have said anything. But what I'm saying is that there must be maybe a bit of fairy folk or something in him, for him to inherit that ability and lucky too for it to be passed down like that, as usually the special abilities of a race are the first to go when blended with another race. Rinna here is lucky to have gained her mother's abilities. Her brother most likely will never develop them, as these special abilities are rarely passed down. I was lucky enough to inherit mine, although I'd rather keep my heritage a secret."

"She's a serpent-shape shifter. They're always a secretive bunch," Rinna betrayed her by saying.

"I should kill you for that," she said with a frustrated snarl and a glare.

"But you won't," Rinna grinned daringly, "Relax, we can easily dispose of them if they cause a threat to the guild. Me, I'd actually like them to join one day, if they can prove themselves worthy. We'll see when they return my gem."

"So is it really true about what we've heard? About this law about thieving?" Dendrox asked them.

<Zaylyn ><Quest For The Sword Fragments And The Hunt For Dranngore><By Katrina Mandrake-Johnston > <Ch 32> < 76 >

"Oh yeah," Etor chuckled, "If you don't get caught, that is. You attempt searching through any of the houses yet?"

"We were going to, but the opportunity got fouled for us. We had to abandon it," Dendrox explained.

Candra described the house to them.

"That big place?" Etor asked with surprise, "I know it. No one ever goes near that place. Ain't that right, Sinva? Ever since, ah, oh what was his name? That skinny fellow with the trembling hands, like he had too much sugar or something, remember?"

"How can I forget?" she said shifting her position uncomfortably.

"Yes, he tried getting into that place, trying to prove he was worthy of joining our little guild here if you can call it that," Zindle told them, "Anyway, the next morning she finds him outside her market stall. It was like he had been mauled by some wild beast, wasn't it? It was awful. Like a warning to the rest of us. Ain't nobody brave or stupid enough to go near that place since. I suppose it was a good thing you didn't linger."

***

<World of Zaylyn><Quest For The Sword Fragments And The Hunt For Dranngore><By Katrina Mandrake-Johnston><Ch 33>

CHAPTER 33 = THE MAGIC SHOP

Weena went into the magic shop; a little bell announcing her entrance. The walls had shelves from top to bottom and they were jumbled with all manner of items. The Confusion spell was present here as well, as within the other shops. The room was dimly lit by lantern light and the air had a mysterious odor to it. Weena thought it most resembled the mixed fragrance of roses and pepper. This front area of the shop was very narrow, the countertop only a few feet from the door. Behind the counter, at the far left of this back wall was a heavy mauve curtain drawn across a doorway.

"Candra was right in what she said. I hadn't really realized until she said it actually. Everyone will be relying on me most of all. Dranngore is a wizard and powerful enough to summon the Killnarin. Without magic on our side, we don't stand a chance. Blades and arrows are no match for the power of a wizard. Not one who knows what they're doing at least. I need to learn more magic. It probably won't help; a few weak little spells against a master wizard as he probably is. He'll definitely know more and have more skill than I do. How can we possibly battle him? Even if we get the sword, we'll never get close enough to use it. He won't let us. And now with this werewolf after us… Me and my big mouth and my stupid idea. Now he'll come after all of us."

"Oh, there you are, dear. I thought I heard someone come in," an elfin woman said coming to greet her from behind the curtain. Like Candra, she stood about six feet tall. She was around the same age as Nodwel but with long silvery white hair just below her shoulders, and she had eyes that were as blue as a cloudless sky.

"What's behind the curtain?" Weena asked her in curiosity.

"Oh, that's the library, my dear. The biggest collection of spell books is here in Shirkint, well, in this part of the world anyway. Are you a student of the magical arts?" asked the woman with a pleasant smile. She wore silky light blue robes, the same as Weena, but her slender frame gave the clothing an entirely different appearance. A dark blue sash was positioned about this woman's waist. To Weena, she had the look of a proper magic user and it made her painfully aware of how inept she felt. She felt like a fool standing there, as if she were merely playing at being a wizard, with her robes, which had become filthy and worn from the journey, draped over her chubby ungraceful form as if she thought this was all there was to it.

Weena nodded. "I'm interested in learning a new spell or two. Is it true that spells can be learnt quickly here?"

"It is true. Magical energy seems to be concentrated more so here than elsewhere, which allows for an increased ease for one to bring a new spell into themselves. You must realize that these things cannot be rushed though," the elf explained.

Weena's face grew hot. "Oh, no, I do," Weena tried a little too hard to assure her, "I know the

<Zaylyn ><Quest For The Sword Fragments And The Hunt For Dranngore><By Katrina Mandrake-Johnston > <Ch 33> < 77 >
patience and dedication needed to obtain a new spell."

"What spells do you have already?" the woman inquired.

"Shield, Cure, and Heal," she answered.

"My name is Voasta. I will show you into the library, but I suggest you look over the available spells before you begin, to make sure you have made the right decision. I'm assuming then that you already have a spell in mind?"

"Not anything specific," Weena replied, "What kind of fee is there for use of the spell books?"

"There is no payment needed for the use of the books, dear, but it will cost you in another way. Are you unaware of a spell book's nature? No, I believe you don't fully know, do you? Let me explain then," she said and paused in thought for a moment before saying, "Actually, I think the best way, would simply be to say, that the spell books that remain unread, slowly begin to fade away, becoming nothing more than blank pages within a book. The spells need to connect within a living person ever so often, even if it is merely for a wizard to refresh an existing spell within themselves. I remember how one boy became convinced that the spell books were somehow vampiric in nature, tricking him into feeding them his life force in promise of spells that would never come. I can understand how he came to this assumption, as to someone not fully trained in the magical arts, it very well might appear as such. Of course, this is not the case, but the study of magic is very taxing as I am sure you must already know. I shall leave you to tend to yourself, but please let me know if you wish to begin from one of our spell books. We have a small room that is strongly contained for the purpose of practicing a spell. You probably remember how the learning process occurs? Studying from the book for the allotted time, then practicing it over and over until it is time to return to the book, and repeating this again and again without sleep, food, or drink, and without pause, until the ability for the spell begins to form within you?"

Weena nodded and stated, "It usually takes quite a few days."

"Yes, that's right. Here the process may be a little more demanding than what you're used to, but the results will be powerful, I can assure you that," Voasta told her with just the hint of a smile.

***

<World of Zaylyn><Quest For The Sword Fragments And The Hunt For Dranngore><By Katrina Mandrake-Johnston><Ch 34>

CHAPTER 34 =   A LAW OF SHIRKINT

Vordin hurried along, following the familiar path he and Nodwel had taken earlier to reach the blacksmith's. The town square was beyond the marketplace. Rasindell was supposed to be there storytelling at the stage. He had seen the marketplace to the north when they had entered the blacksmith's, and he hoped he would be able to find his way all right. He made his way to the street where the blacksmith's lay and instead went east toward the shops and houses that ran the length of the east wall and alongside the stalls of the marketplace. Vordin hoped that eventually he would come to the town square following this street and not have a very hard time finding his way back to the familiar street the blacksmith's was on, and then from there being able to make his way back to the tavern. Vordin was so afraid that he would become lost within the town and not be able to make his way back before dark. He didn't want to be out alone, as with the night came danger.

He needed to talk to Rasindell desperately. *"But how much of the old Rasindell is there? Can it truly be him? And if it is, will he even be able to help me? Will he recognize who I am? If anyone knew anything about werewolves, it was him."*

Vordin traveled a fair distance along the street, and on the left side, there were now a few shops, houses, and other buildings, scattered on the outskirts of the market area. He still couldn't see anything that could be called the town square.

"It must be farther north," he told himself, *"Maybe I should ask over there at that fruit stand."* Vordin rounded the corner of a building, heading farther into the market area to speak to the friendly looking man who was the merchant there.

Then he heard the voice of the werewolf. Vordin's heart pounded with fear, adrenalin rushing through his body. There was a large rain barrel against the wall of the building he was near, and he

<Zaylyn ><Quest For The Sword Fragments And The Hunt For Dranngore><By Katrina Mandrake-Johnston > <Ch 34> < 78 >
ducked down behind it.

"*What do I do?!*" he panicked, "*He'll find me for sure now! What is he doing here?! Is he searching for us? How could he possibly know I would be headed this way?! Is he trying to prevent me from reaching Rasindell? What is he doing?*"

Vordin listened in, trying to hear over the din of the marketplace to what the werewolf was saying.

"So Acklore," said the werewolf, his voice having the same underlying threatening tone to it as before, "You're sort of the mayor of this town, are you not?"

"Well, I handle the special events within the town and things like that, yes, but I'd hardly call myself the mayor. I don't make up the laws or anything like that," he explained.

"But you do know about the laws, right?" the werewolf asked him.

"Well yes, I suppose. Was there something I could help you with then?" Acklore inquired, "I didn't catch your name."

"It's Hoatam. It's the rule about thieves I want to be clear on. For example, if I caught a couple of thieves in my home, could I kill them?"

"Murder?" Acklore exclaimed with a nervous laugh, "I highly doubt that is the proper way to handle things, but I understand you are upset about this. You shouldn't say such things even in anger; someone might think you mean it seriously. If you catch a thief in the act, you may hold them, if you are able, for the town protectors to collect and detain for punishment, which is usually just restriction from the town and posters put up warning others of the thief. However, in most cases, if a thief is caught, the items are simply returned and all is well, without getting the town protectors involved in it. Besides, not many are willing to take on that job anymore, as they have to be out at night, and well, I need not say anymore. In fact, those that prove themselves to be, let's say, undesirable and that tend to cause major disruptions within this town, they usually find themselves mysteriously going missing, if you know what I mean. As I said, it is not I that keeps Shirkint in good order. It is best not to cause a commotion about the theft. Shirkint gets a lot of people with loose morals coming in with these 'laxed laws we have here about thieving and the like. They usually take care of themselves; only a handful of their type leaving Shirkint out of the many that enter. The townsfolk are better off with how things work here, I say, and no one really complains if an object or two goes missing in return despite the measures they've taken to protect their belongings. As for the more violent crimes, folks with those types of ideas going through their heads, well, they don't seem to stay very long here either, if you know what I mean. There is a thieves guild of sorts, or so I've heard, but they have come to understand just how important it is to keep their actions in good favor with the real authorities around here."

"I assume you are speaking of The Black Shadow," he commented with contempt.

"Not a thing to be taken so lightly," stated Acklore, "So anyway, as I was saying, the rule is, if items are stolen and the thief gets away, the owner must leave it as such, at least for the duration that they are within this town."

"I see," said Hoatam, "So if I know who the thieves are, the most I can do is have them restricted from the town with the possible return or reimbursement for whatever was stolen."

"Yes, exactly. I don't really know how such a law got started. I believe it was meant to create a sanctuary here of sorts, I suppose."

"It's more like The Black Shadow is trying to lure in more deserving prey it seems to me," Hoatam laughed.

"Ah, well," Acklore stammered.

"You know it's true. Letting thieves run off into the night unopposed, undetained. Not to mention the whores doctored up to basically be bait for whoever is foolish enough to go after them. Yeah, I'd say it's a sanctuary of sorts for all those damn half-breeds that come here. No one is brave enough to say anything against them all here, are they? All the oddities are accepted here simply out of fear. And when these scoundrels stop coming, who do you think will be left, eh?" he laughed cruelly, "Anyone having an ill thought? The line between those that remain safe and those that are destined to be his prey will start to creep up until no one is safe anymore. Anyone with a brain can see that what is happening with The Black Shadow is short lived. Sure, he's been slowly growing more and more compassionate

<Zaylyn ><Quest For The Sword Fragments And The Hunt For Dranngore><By Katrina Mandrake-Johnston > <Ch 34> < 79 >

over the centauries or so it seems. But it's only been a little over ten years or so that the innocent have truly started to come into his favor, enough for it to almost be counted on, am I right? And past three years about, even more so?" he chuckled, "It won't be long now until he reverts back to being what he was. Ha, I see the hold he has over the people here and it makes me gag at how pathetic…"

"Was there anything of importance you wanted to discuss?" Acklore interrupted, his voice firm and having the hint of a threat behind it.

"Yes, what about this Rasindell character? Is it true that he has all the knowledge of Zaylyn within him and is able to recite its legends or whatever story is suitable to provide the information a listener is searching for?" Hoatam asked, his voice showing the irritation that he felt about this. He wanted his secret kept quiet, and he knew Rasindell could make it known, revealing the source of his power.

"Oh yes, Rasindell. Did you know he was quite a good friend of mine when we were younger? He was a lot older than me at the time, but we had some grand adventures, we did," Acklore reminisced, "I'm afraid my daughter, Vina, has that same adventurous spirit I once had in my youth."

"So if I want to take action against these thieves, I have to take it into my own hands, but outside of town," Hoatam stated.

"Well no," Acklore tried to reason with him, "If you have been wronged and can describe them, we can have them restricted from town, perhaps have your belongings returned. This is sufficient punishment for the crime, don't you think? Are you suggesting some sort of vengeance be taken? I hope you will come to your senses and that it is just the anger talking. I assure you that such nonsense will not be tolerated within the town of Shirkint. These rules are in place to ensure that nonviolent methods are used to deal with theft here. If you know the identity of the thieves, they are safe within these town walls. The only action you may take against them is to have them banned. Do you understand?" Acklore said, his voice now strong and unwavering.

"Yes completely," Hoatam answered, his voice having a sinister lilt to it.

"If he has us banned from town, he can do anything he wishes, but he's not going to have us banned. He knows that will take time and that we will be able to speak to Rasindell beforehand. He's going to come after us as the wolf," Vordin realized with fear, *"and as quickly as he can."*

"Do you smell that?" asked Hoatam.

"No, what?" asked Acklore.

"I think I'll walk around a bit, see if I can't find where it's coming from. It's making my mouth water," said the werewolf eagerly.

"Probably the fruit stand, or no, I smell it now, fresh cinnamon rolls I think it might be," commented Acklore.

The werewolf chuckled, "No, I don't think so."

Vordin held his breath, trying not to make a single sound. Could he actually smell him? Sense his fear?

He heard the two of them walk off farther west into the heart of the marketplace. Trembling, Vordin dashed from his hiding place behind the rain barrel and quickly entered one of the shops across the street along the east wall of the town.

***

<World of Zaylyn><Quest For The Sword Fragments And The Hunt For Dranngore><By Katrina Mandrake-Johnston><Ch 35>

CHAPTER 35 = RINNA'S TREASURE ROOM

Rinna asked Candra and Dendrox, "So, do you two think you'd ever consider joining our little guild here, if you were offered?"

"Well, what exactly would that mean?" Dendrox inquired suspiciously.

"You mean why would anyone want to join? What does it have to offer that you already can't obtain?" Rinna said with a grin.

"Well yes," said Candra. *"Why are they so eager to invite us into their little group here?"* Candra wondered to herself nervously, *"What are they trying to do? As far as they are concerned, we are complete strangers. They are so trusting it's ridiculous. Can they really believe themselves to be so*

<Zaylyn ><Quest For The Sword Fragments And The Hunt For Dranngore><By Katrina Mandrake-Johnston > <Ch 35> < 80 >

superior that we can't possibly be a threat to them? Is this all some sort of joke? They can't be serious. What is it they are after? We ask them for the gem, and they simply hand it over with nothing in return. No, actually, they were the ones that came to us, in a way, about the gem. As soon as Rinna in her cat form overheard The Black Shadow ask us to retrieve it for him. They all have been far too eager to befriend us, sickeningly so. Can that truly be the reason though? Are they so willing to disregard commonsense in order to please The Black Shadow? Can the people here really be so spineless? But then again, they have to live every day with The Black Shadow lurking about. Perhaps I shouldn't be so rash in my judgment. If it's a matter of survival, I can understand that. And it's not as if we are merely claiming to have a connection to The Black Shadow, as Rinna was there as the cat back at the inn when he was speaking to us."

"I can't tell you everything that the guild has to offer, but I can tell you this, and this is my favorite by the way, each member is granted access to a room to be used as their very own personal treasure trove. Mine is basically my home away from home. Here, why don't you come in with me and I'll show you about," she said holding her ringed hand up to the wall. The outline of a door began to glow with a brilliant blue light, and Rinna then stepped up and pushed open the wall segment revealing a long dark corridor. She gestured with a flourish of her hand for them to enter and awaited their next move.

"Maybe we should just head back to the others now that we have the gem," Candra suggested. *"A lot of people would like to take some sort of revenge against The Black Shadow,"* she thought to herself with worry, *"He wants the gem, and we are the ones to bring it to him. He may or may not be vulnerable, but I am definitely certain that we are here."*

"You might as well," commented Sinva, "I doubt she'll make the offer twice. She rarely lets anyone into her little sanctuary. We just use ours to store our valuables where no one can detect them, but with her, she treats hers like a second home. Her family doesn't know about her secret life as a thief, you see."

"Beware," Etor joked, "you are about to enter the fearsome lair of Rinna!"

"Oh shut up," said Rinna, "So you two comin' in or what?"

"Sure, why not," said Dendrox with a sly grin forming at the corner of his mouth.

"Oh no, I know that look. She definitely has a rather fetching charisma about her. But what about Weena?" Candra thought following them in.

Rinna led them down the corridor until they came to a small room. A magnificently ornate silver candelabra was positioned on the largest table lighting the room in a dim glow. All the tables along the walls were laden with glistening items of gold, gems, and valuable trinkets of all sorts.

There were plush cushions piled up in the corner, and this is where Candra decided to seat herself. Candra noticed that the large basket beside her contained fine silks and what looked to be several expensive looking gowns.

Instead of candles, small glowing orbs had been placed in the candelabra and also about the room. Dendrox assumed that they were similar to Vordin's magical lantern, but then realized that the light from the orbs appeared more like that of a flame and not the uniform glow that the lantern flask produced. Curious, he went to touch one and felt that it was emitting heat, as if a candle flame had been magically trapped within.

Rinna smiled at him saying, "Haven't you ever seen one of those before? Go ahead, if you want to pick it up. It's harmless. It grows cold as soon as it comes into contact with skin."

"Damn it, Dendrox. I hate it when you disregard possible danger for the sake of a pretty face. Don't you see the hidden motives behind their words? They're testing us; I just know they are. Watching our reactions," Candra thought nervously, *"Besides, you know I get edgy where magic is involved, you never know what to expect and you can't rely on instincts. I live my life by mine, and not being able to trust my own judgment…"*

As Dendrox examined one of the light orbs, Rinna warned him with a laugh, "Yeah, you just don't want to put it in your pocket. I found that one out the hard way. It's cool to skin, but without, the heat'll give quite a nasty burn, like putting a lit candle in your pocket."

Rinna then went about showing Dendrox several other pieces of treasure and telling the exciting

<Zaylyn ><Quest For The Sword Fragments And The Hunt For Dranngore><By Katrina Mandrake-Johnston > <Ch 35> < 81 >

story that was attached to each with a flirtatious glint in her eye. Dendrox was clearly interested in her and everything she had to say.

Candra thought, *"Dendrox is right, I don't want to be responsible for Weena getting hurt or even killed. This is not the kind of life for her. I realize now what I've been doing. I value her as a friend, but that doesn't mean she has to become like us to remain that way. I've never really felt strongly enough to call anyone but Dendrox friend. I guess I'm afraid that when this quest is over, that is if we succeed with everyone alive and well, that we'll all depart going our separate ways. I suppose that has been the underlying reason behind my actions. But it's more than that... The more I think about it, the more I suspect that it might be because a certain part of her, in a way, reminds me of my father. I know that must be the reason behind it. And then without realizing it, I've been trying to hold on to that, and so tightly for fear of losing it, that I've been strangling the very thing I want to keep. If we continue to try to manipulate her into becoming like us, we'll just be encouraging her to destroy the very qualities in her that we have come to admire. Dendrox is right. I was a fool to try to change her into something she's not. Dendrox is just afraid for her safety, and is so much so, that he is clearly willing to end their relationship over it. He still has feelings for her, and it pains me to see him become so cold toward her. Every time those feelings start to show, he bitterly suffocates them and it has been more often to persuade his own feelings away from her than the other way around. I hope that it's not too late for things to go back the way they were. Magic is her passion, and if I want to keep her as a friend, I should just let things be. Nothing says that we need to part paths. Before, I was counting on it, expecting only a brief acquaintance out of necessity. And now, I can't bear to think of us going our separate ways. I've changed. We all have, I think. Whether or not for the better, I can't really say. She could travel with us. It wouldn't be as safe for her to do so, but if she means to travel alone anyhow, it could be beneficial for her as well. And, we wouldn't have to worry about selling off any magical items we come across. She could sell them, which would be far less conspicuous for a wizard to do so, or she could even use them for whatever she wants to do with them. Could even be better this way. She could help us out on our part with Invisible spells or maybe use a spell to confuse a merchant and cause enough of a distraction that way for us to clean him out. No, again I am trying to get her involved where I know she shouldn't be. I'm being selfish; Dendrox is right. I have to think about her and not how her being with us could be to our benefit. Maybe he is right to just let her go."*

***

<World of Zaylyn><Quest For The Sword Fragments And The Hunt For Dranngore><By Katrina Mandrake-Johnston><Ch 36>

CHAPTER 36 = THE SPELL BOOKS

Weena pawed over the large book resting upon the lectern, trying to refresh her memory on how spells were presented within the spell books. An overwhelming feeling of frustration and desperation started to take her over as she tried to remember her lessons and make sense of what she was reading. That feeling quickly turned into panic, her face growing hot as her eyes roamed across the pages.

She idly flipped through a couple of pages as if she were looking for something in-particular in hope that it would ease the appearance of inadequacy that she felt was painfully obvious. She considered asking one of the others already studying magic there in the library, but she knew that she would probably be berated for making any sort of interruption. She didn't want to appear a complete fool in asking either; she would probably be asked to leave. Spell books weren't just handed out to people that had no understanding of how to read them or of what the spells would entail.

There were two young men and a woman huddled closely to their spell books in each of their individual cubicles. Dark circles surrounded their bloodshot eyes as they stared intensely at the pages before them. Their lips were visibly dry and cracked, their faces pale and sickly looking, their hands trembling as they followed along with their fingers across the clusters of incandescent symbols; this was what was in store for those that wished to learn magic. It seemed to drain the very life out of a person, the wizard continuing the process of studying and practicing without drink, food, or sleep, as was necessary, until the spell finally took form and rooted itself within that person.

"I know this, I've learnt spells before. I just need to relax and focus. But after such a terrible

fright with that damn werewolf, how is anyone supposed to concentrate?! I have to do this though. I've learnt these symbols. I know I am able to decipher them," she tried to reassure herself, *"I just need to start small and then it should all start to come back to me, I hope. Damn it, if I'm having trouble reading the damn index, how the hell am I supposed to work through an entire spell book?! No, I can't let myself get all flustered; that's not going to help anything at all."*

She ran her finger across the thick yellowy paper until she came to a symbol that looked familiar.

"Okay, this one means roughly… 'intelligence'. Now in context with spell casting, it means… Come on, Weena, you know this! The ability to cast forth the spell," she said to herself trying to remember, *"It was a set of four things… the ability to cast forth the spell... drawing one's energy into the spell… and bring together the entire spell in one's mind, and link it to its task.*

"Okay, now this symbol here means… 'strength', but in spell casting it means… willpower, concentration, and focus. It has to do with… maintaining the hold over the spell in one's mind, expanding it to another target, and extending the duration of a spell.

"Oh, and this one here means 'skill', which has to do with working the spell around its intended target, and manipulating or guiding the workings of that spell.

"See, I knew it was in there somewhere. I'm not a complete moron. Luckily, most of the spells have similar formats; I should be able to follow it easily enough, provided I remember the meanings of the symbols. So here is the list of all the different spells they have available for study. Each spell book contains only one spell and usually it takes days of study before its pages start to reveal their magic to a student, if at all, and not to mention the extensive time that must be spent practicing the spell in order for it to develop within. If I'm going to choose, I'm going to have to do it wisely.

"Okay, this here is 'Fireball'. It can be used on one person, animal, or object; so basically one target. As it usually takes a little more time and concentration, it most often is cast at a distance. The fireball cast forth will follow its target and will draw on both 'intelligence' and 'skill'. The higher levels take less out of a caster to perform and will be more effective obviously. This spell is one of the stronger Black magic spells, and even at the lowest level, it still does a fair amount of damage.

"Now it's starting to come back to me. This is the spell for 'Lightening'. It is pretty much the same as Fireball but can be cast as either a bolt of lightening or by touch. The spell takes twice the amount of 'intelligence' to perform however, and like the Fireball, takes 'skill' as well to work the spell around its target allowing for the bolt to follow it.

" 'Invisible', both a Black and White spell, turns the caster, an object, or person invisible. It also enables other items or persons currently under an Invisible spell to be seen when entering this state as well with this spell. It can be used on more than one target, using 'strength' to include every addition into the spell, and if an attempt fails, the whole spell will fail. Against the Killnarin, I might be able to turn someone invisible for a short while, but I don't have the inner strength and willpower to maintain something like that for the whole group. Look what happened when I tried to include Asdella within my Shield spell. I was unconscious for most of that day because of it, as the strain was just too great. Thank goodness it worked, but I can't take that chance with Killnarin about. Besides, this is what the wizard after the scissors was casting, and it didn't seem to help him out very much against the Killnarin that killed him.

" 'Harm' causes harm to an opponent, and takes 'strength' for use on more than one. It probably won't do anything but make a Killnarin angry and draw its full attention down onto me.

" 'Open', again both a Black and White spell, it unlocks and opens things like doors and the like, or closes and locks them. It takes 'intelligence' to cast and then also 'strength'. Perhaps it would be something good to learn, but it won't help with the Killnarin. Besides, I'm sure Candra can open any locks we come across.

" 'Blast', this will cause an energy burst to travel toward an opponent or object. There are two different degrees of this spell, but each would have to be learnt as if they were two different spells. The spell which deals with the increased amount of damage, takes 'intelligence', 'strength', and 'skill'.

"I don't think any of the more offensive spells are going to be very easy to learn at all. The size and complexity of most of these spells are so great that it would be very difficult for me to cast one, let

<Zaylyn ><Quest For The Sword Fragments And The Hunt For Dranngore><By Katrina Mandrake-Johnston > <Ch 36> < 83 >

alone maintain the spell long enough for it to have any effect or connect it to its intended target and direct its purpose. I have to keep looking. There has to be something that can help us. I can't just give up; I'm the only magic user in our group, and I doubt anyone else would willingly volunteer to go up against Dranngore.

" 'Freeze' causes something to freeze obviously, but for anything living, it only stops its movement for a short while, and for more than one, again 'strength' is needed or else all fails. I doubt that would help for very long, if at all.

" 'Burn' causes the intended target to burn and catch fire. At level two it can cause metal to melt, and at level three, can burn something to ash. But on something living, it gives a feeling of being burnt alive, with great pain, but inflicting no damage and lasts only a short while at level one. This looks like a pretty complex spell anyhow, I'd have no chance whatsoever with a spell like this.

" 'Hate' will cause a person or animal to hate or dislike someone or something to any degree. Using 'strength' for an increased number... and will take 'intelligence', 'strength', and 'skill' to perform. At level one, it will only last a short while but 'strength' can also be used to further maintain the spell for a longer duration. This must be what the Killnarin used on us in the spider tunnels when Yarin was killed.

" 'Choking fog' creates a fog around the caster that will harm anyone that is near the caster, including an ally. The spell seems to be less complex in order to cast, which is good, but the caster is unable to defend in the casting of this spell and therefore will suffer all damage inflicted by an opponent if attacked. The spell is fairly damaging, but at level one, it won't last very long. It's good, if I'm only concerned about my own life, but I'm not going to be responsible for harming the others no matter what the reason. I don't want to have to make the decision of who should be allowed to suffer for the benefit of the rest.

" 'Ice', that will create ice where cast. And then that's it for Black magic unfortunately. I might as well skim through the White, but I doubt any of them will be of much use.

" 'Cook' allows you to cook food items without a fire, but cannot be used on living people or animals.

" 'Purify', used on water and other liquids. It can eliminate poison from a drink, turn befouled or sea water into drinking water, turn a magic potion to water, and so on. That would be marvelous; Dranngore goes to drink or use a potion on us, and I turn it to water in his hands. But I need something that is guaranteed to help us.

" 'Heal' is also a Natural magic spell and one I already have. It seems that I am getting better at it the more I've been using it too," she thought to herself proudly for a moment before focusing her attention back to the book and to the next spell.

" 'Levitate'; both a Black and White spell. It only lasts a short time, same as with the Invisible spell, and takes 'intelligence', 'strength', and 'skill' to perform. I don't see how that would help. Besides, Vordin said the Killnarin are able to use fire magic and we don't need to give them a reason to resort to using that against us simply because we've put ourselves out of reach. We'll probably have a better chance of survival if they continue to see us as merely a few adventurers that have stumbled along their path. If we clearly present ourselves as a threat, and they learn that we are on a quest for the sword and mean to stop them, we are surely doomed. A full attack by even one or two, with destroying us as their only goal...

" 'Shield'," she read on, "which I have... at level one protecting from all physical damage and from other level one magic spells. Against Dranngore, my spell is useless. His higher level spells would pass right through my Shield spell, and I wouldn't be able to protect the others with it as well as myself, even if I did have a stronger level of spell, as I just don't have the inner strength to extend it that far.

" 'Cool' might be able to reduce the heat from a fire, I guess, allowing us to come close to a flame. But the spell wouldn't be able to diminish the fire's capability to burn. It's of no use. There has to be something that can aid us. White magic spells aren't going to be enough. Defending ourselves is not enough. We need aggressive spells, not ones that can only counteract what is thrown our way.

" 'Warm' is useless, well unless he tries to freeze us, but again that's merely counteracting his spell,

<Zaylyn ><Quest For The Sword Fragments And The Hunt For Dranngore><By Katrina Mandrake-Johnston > <Ch 36> < 84 >

only delaying our fate. With White magic, the idea is, to make the attacking wizard diminish the number of useable spells. As spells need time to recharge themselves in a way and casting draws on a wizard's mental strength and energy, the offending wizard will soon exhaust himself to the point of collapsing or until he no longer has any spells available to cast.

" *'Love'. That would not help... not in way of Dranngore and the Killnarin. Besides, knowing it was merely the result of a spell, would hurt far worse than what it is now. I know I should just let it go... but it still hurts... to be rejected... Why should I care what another thinks? I like who I am...*"

She forced her attention back to her task once more, irritated that, despite her efforts, she still was dwelling on what was happening between her and Dendrox.

" *'Confuse', also a Natural magic spell, and it makes a person or animal feel lost, unable to discern what is happening, unable to think clearly and reason, or unable to discern what certain objects are used for. It takes 'strength' for each additional person, so it seems that the Killnarin have exceptional strength when it comes to the willpower of casting and maintaining a spell. They seemed to have no trouble at all using this spell, and on several of us at a time. If one of them decides to cast a spell, we have little chance of wavering the creature's concentration and ability to hold that spell in place once it's cast. What The Black Shadow said is true. We need to learn to recognize when we are under the influence of a spell and fight its effects, as we have little hope of stopping the spell at its source.*

"Okay, Natural magic, and the last class of magic. 'Cure', which is also a White magic spell and one I already have. 'Poison'. This is what the Killnarin used against Candra. It can only be used on one person, animal, or plant, and the caster must touch the intended target to affect it.

" *'Camouflage' can be used on the caster, another person, an animal, or an object. The target, if looked upon, will not be noticed as the target will not register in the viewer's mind as being separate or standing out from common surroundings. Spell efficiency diminishes the more sparse or contrast the surroundings are. Yeah, so basically, you don't want to be using this spell out in the open where it is obvious where you are, or trying to blend a giant in with a room full of midgets. But in any other crowd or forested area, for example, it would work great. It would help Dendrox and Candra blend in with a crowd if someone was searching for them. With the spell, there wouldn't be a very good chance of them being spotted with the naked eye. It would at least give them enough time to get farther away in order to naturally blend in. There's no reason why I should aid them in stealing from others, but I could maybe mention it to them if they ever decide to get a few magic items to help them out in the future. I wouldn't want anything awful to happen to them because of what they do. I mean, I wouldn't want them to end up killed over a few material goods. I can kind of see how the law about thievery here might have gotten started; not really approving of theft, but against drastic measures being applied because of it. And with the reason behind the theft, and what was being taken, this way a man stealing food to feed his starving family won't be put to death or disfigured for doing so. But in our case, just ripped to shreds by a terrible and ferocious werewolf,*" she thought with a dry and nervous laugh, "*The Killnarin would see through a Camouflage spell anyway, as they slaughter anything alive it seems, just for their mere enjoyment. They were able to eventually see fairly quickly through the spell Borin placed with the amulet on the tunnel entrance back in the spiders' lair.*

" *'Sleep'. Possibly, but that would only allow us a short time to escape if it did work. The creatures have proven themselves to not be easily killed. Any attack would break the spell, and most likely, not even faze the beasts.*

" *'Speed'. If I were only concerned about my own escape, yes, but the others would perish and I would too as soon as the spell came to an end. It would be the same result if I cast it on one of the others.*

" *'Hallucination' allows you to choose what your target sees, but I don't think anything would be able to fool the Killnarin one way or the other, at least not for very long, nothing that would give a lasting effect. They apparently were able to cause mistrust between Candra and Dendrox before I first came to meet them, but they were able to overcome it, their friendship strong enough to not end in violence which the Killnarin most likely was hoping for. It was probably the reason why it decided to physically*

<Zaylyn ><Quest For The Sword Fragments And The Hunt For Dranngore><By Katrina Mandrake-Johnston > <Ch 36> < 85 >
confront them instead.

"'Speed pregnancy' *is clearly not of use. 'Breeding', again, not of any use. I don't think I'll need magical aid in having a child with an incompatible race. I'm sure this is the case with a few of the couples in this town I've seen though. It looks like an incredibly complex spell, and at only the highest level and with a lot of luck, can an offspring be achieved between the couple. And then, that appears to be all they have in way of spells.*"

Weena stood before the book in dismay, trying to make a decision. If she were going to take the time to learn a new spell, she needed to begin now as time was short, and the time and effort to learn a spell was extensive. She was counting on what was said about spells being learnt with greater ease here at Shirkint and therefore taking less time, even though it would mean for an increased strain on the wizard's body and mind.

"The only ones I think might be able to help us are Lightening and Fireball. These are both extremely large and complex spells, but these are the only ones that might prove to be of some use. If I'm going to try at all, it should be for one of these. I hate to admit it, but I would have better results with Fireball, even though the Lightening spell causes a little more damage to its target. The Lightening spell takes more effort to bring forth the spell. I don't think I would be able to block out everything happening around me to cast such a spell, and especially with the Killnarin attacking us and where everyone could be relying on me to come through for them. Fireball is a less complex spell, but only when compared to the Lightening spell which is rated as one of the more powerful Black magic spells. With the incident at the schoolhouse and the loss of my brother because of it. I have a lot of emotion to put forth into a spell of fire, and therefore, it will have to be my choice in order to help the others. If I'm able to bring forth and channel that emotion, that energy, and not overwhelm or distract myself from the spell casting, it could prove very powerful. What would my brother think of me?

"I'm responsible for my brother's death. If only I hadn't run. If I didn't hide, he would have never run into the burning building looking for me. It was hopeless; no one could have escaped the flames. But he had tried, for me. If only I had come forward, he would still be alive. What would my brother think of me? Learning a spell, a Black magic spell, one that gives me the power to release a flaming inferno from my very fingertips. A spell that, for it to work, needs to find in the caster a heightened desire to burn and cause pain. A part of me wanted that fire at the schoolhouse, but not to hurt anyone with it, not like what happened. I'm not a malicious person at heart, I know I'm not. I might be able to cast this spell against a Killnarin, but against Dranngore? Consciously causing him excruciating pain, scorching his flesh with my desire to kill, to watch him writhe in agony, to hear him screaming and still continue to add strength and hatred into that spell? I don't think I could bring myself to do that to a Killnarin either, even with Yarin's death, not even after all they've done. But I have no other choice than to learn the spell; I can't survive stumbling weakly through all our hardships.

"Why can't The Black Shadow just destroy the Killnarin and stop Dranngore? Why does he insist on having us do it? I don't think I have it in me. I hope that I am not capable of such destruction, but if I needed to protect the others? ...I would never be the same after that. There would be a darkness haunting me, a realization of a capable evil existing in me. Dendrox tried to tell me a little about that, and the effect it had on Candra when she avenged her father's death. If we do recover the sword, who will be the one that will be given the deed of killing Dranngore with it?"

***

<World of Zaylyn><Quest For The Sword Fragments And The Hunt For Dranngore><By Katrina Mandrake-Johnston><Ch 37>

CHAPTER 37 = RINNA

"You seem to have quite a lot of magic items here. How is it that you know what you're looking for?" Candra asked Rinna, "How can you discern a magic item from the rest of a person's junk?"

"I know exactly what you mean," she told her, "And if you go around asking for a potion or something to be identified, you are clearly labeling yourself as a thief. I can't disclose any information about that until you become a full member of the guild and that is up to the others. You two have my vote so far. We have magical means of monitoring certain situations as well as gaining information on

<Zaylyn ><Quest For The Sword Fragments And The Hunt For Dranngore><By Katrina Mandrake-Johnston > <Ch 37> < 86 >

certain items, but that's all I'm allowed to say. We can't tell a magic item beforehand, but you can train your eye to recognize items that are most commonly magical, such as amulets and rings which are usually worth taking anyway, and stuff like flasks of colored liquids, funny-shaped sticks, and the like."

And then she went on to tell Dendrox about several magic items she had acquired.

"*So I guess it's officially over between him and Weena. He's clearly given up on her despite his feelings,*" Candra observed, "*I remember wanting that once, but it's just not fair.*"

Rinna called Candra over to examine a magical piece that she thought to be the most remarkable out of all the ones she had collected. "*Is she trying to tempt our hand?*" wondered Candra, "*Does she really believe there is some sort of honor among thieves? We're not part of their little guild. I don't care how eager she is to 'befriend' Dendrox. It doesn't explain her blindly trusting us to such a degree, or why any of the others are. The thieves here are either all fools or there is some other motive behind their actions.*"

When Candra returned to the pile of cushions, she idly scooped a couple of jewels off the table and slipped them down beneath the lip of her boot as she sat.

"Whatcha doing?" Rinna asked her plainly as she looked her over, her eyes narrowing slightly.

"Oh, no," Dendrox said coming to her defense, "She's always fiddling with her boots. They've been bothering her since before we came to the valley. I keep telling her to get new ones, but she can be real stubborn at times."

"*He's so infatuated with her, he didn't even noticed what I did, did he?*" thought Candra, "*And luckily for me, I don't think she noticed either. At least I don't think she did.*"

Candra chuckled, "Yeah, if you ever hear of magical 'Boots of Comfort' or 'Boots of Never Blister', let me know, would ya?"

"You know, there's a real good cobbler in town. He can work leather like butter. Why don't you go down there and pick up a new pair? Here," she said tossing her a small bag of coin, "That should take care of it. My gift to you."

"*Yeah, I get it, and leave you two alone for awhile. Well at least I get a new pair of boots out of it,*" thought Candra. "Thanks. So I can meet you two back here then?" Candra asked.

"Sinva or one of the others will let you back into the circular room there. They usually end up chatting for hours at a time," she explained.

"*So I'm to leave Dendrox trapped in here then? And he's the one holding on to the Gem of Enarr,*" Candra thought nervously to herself and then decided, "*Well, he can take care of himself, I suppose. I can't really do anything about it.*" "I'll see you later then," Candra said to Dendrox with a nod as she left.

***

"*I suppose I too have to give up on Weena,*" Candra decided, "*and stop trying to include her in a life of thievery. She doesn't calculate her actions like she should before she acts. I can't expect her to learn how to defend herself when she needs to. She has no confidence when it comes to her spells. We can't rely on her to come through when it really counts. No, I need to do this, if anything, for my own peace of mind.*"

With the tinkle of a bell, the door to the magic shop opened, and Candra entered. Voasta was behind the counter.

Candra asked her, "What can I get for this?"

Voasta examined the ring that Candra was holding out to her. It was Weena's ring. "Oh yes, this will do very nicely," she replied taking the ring from Candra, "Is there anything in-particular you were looking for then?"

She took quite awhile but she finally made her decision, and Voasta then bid her good day.

<World of Zaylyn><Quest For The Sword Fragments And The Hunt For Dranngore><By Katrina Mandrake-Johnston><Ch 38>

CHAPTER 38 =   A SPELL OF FIRE

Once Candra had departed on her quest for a comfortable pair of boots from the cobbler, Voasta headed into the back behind the soundproof curtain.

<Zaylyn ><Quest For The Sword Fragments And The Hunt For Dranngore><By Katrina Mandrake-Johnston > <Ch 38> < 87 >

She gently and gracefully adjusted the richly-colored curtain back into place with a slender hand, and then turning to Weena, Voasta asked her with a warm and pleasant smile, "How are you coming along then?"

Completely unaware that Candra had been in the building speaking with Voasta, Weena replied, "I think I'd like to learn something a little more defensive than my Shield spell. Perhaps Fireball."

"Oh, I see," said Voasta tucking a loose piece of silvery hair behind her elfin ear, a great look of concern seeming to haunt her brilliant blue eyes as she studied Weena. The worry showed in her voice as well as she went on to say, "A defensive spell you've called it? You do know that this is a Black magic spell you are interested in? Black magic isn't necessarily a bad thing, but as most of the spells tend to be offensive and dangerous, with the ability to do harm to others, it is seen as such. If you are able to gain this ability, be careful of how you use it as people may begin to perceive you in a different light. Many tend to be wary of magic users for fear of what they are capable of, as our strength comes from within and cannot be measured by outside appearances."

"Yes, I have noticed this in others. I intend to use this new spell only as a last option for defense," she assured her, afraid that she might be refused access to the spell books.

The elf explained solemnly, "The library is available to all, regardless of character. We do not judge the motives behind why a person wishes to learn. We do, however, have ways of dealing with those that pose a threat to others here in Shirkint with the use of their magic."

"And what's that? Have you ever heard of a Killnarin? Would this method work against them, restricting their powers?" Weena asked hopefully.

Voasta gave her a confused look and said, "Funny you should mention that, as Failick is meeting with my husband, Ascinoir, at this very minute about just this very matter. Apparently, someone came into his shop asking about these same creatures and made a ludicrous claim that an entire army was making its way across the valley. If true, we don't have much hope, and no, the containment orbs would never be able to hold a Killnarin."

"I see," said Weena, "Then we cannot fail in our quest. The Sword of Anthrowst, have you heard of it?"

"I have," she answered, "I think I know what you are about to ask. The spell that is enchanted along that blade can never be duplicated. The only existing spell is the one that the sword contains. It was broken for good reason, and I doubt it could ever be mended, at least not by the likes of any of us. It is impossible, I'm afraid. Our world could suffer horribly if misused, and this is why it was hidden away. Even if what was said about these Killnarin is indeed true, and a wizard is the one who is behind them, and the sword is somehow found and restored, solving the problem through this method may be horribly wrong and instead do more damage than it does good."

"I understand," said Weena.

"Now about the spell you are interested in. The magics here are concentrated, so you learn quickly and the ability will be stronger than what you are used to, which means it will take a lot of time and patience trying to master control over it once you have it," Voasta explained, "Few, however, have the courage to go through with it to the end."

"Why? What do you mean?" Weena questioned.

She explained, "Some say they see things during their lessons. Things that they couldn't explain. Some become too frightened to continue."

"Oh, yes, I've heard this too. I'm aware of the mental endurance needed in learning and the tricks that extreme fatigue can play on the mind," Weena explained.

"Are you prepared to begin?" Voasta questioned, looking her over decisively.

"Yes. Yes, I am," said Weena.

Voasta asked plainly, once again raising her eyebrow, "You really do believe that Killnarin are about? A whole army of the creatures?" Weena nodded. "You realize that Killnarin, if one did venture across into Zaylyn, that their heightened resistance to magic would…" she sighed heavily, "If you believe those creatures are here and that you need to fulfill this quest for the Sword of Anthrowst to stop them, that this cannot be your sole motivation for learning this spell. You said that you've been

<Zaylyn ><Quest For The Sword Fragments And The Hunt For Dranngore><By Katrina Mandrake-Johnston > <Ch 38> < 88 >
studying spells under the White magic class… Such a drastic decision to switch to Black and trying to obtain such a powerful spell… When you choose to bring a certain type of magic into yourself, it cannot be for a single purpose. In fact, it cannot be for any purpose whatsoever. Do you see what I am trying to explain?" She didn't give Weena enough time to give any sort of answer. "A spell, a class of magic, is to become part of who you are, to become rooted deep within yourself. I'm not questioning the reason behind the learning of the spell, just of whether you are making the right choice. Perhaps you should instead seriously consider a magical item? A staff or wand charged with the desired spell? It is quite a decision in choosing to risk altering the very core of your being in attempting to obtain such an ability, and in such an obvious contrast from White to Black, it would be quite the risk. If you are determined, which I can plainly see that you are, perhaps Natural magic would be a better course of action. Natural magic is sort of a medium of the two."

Weena bit her lip. She felt like a child, but she was aware of the dire consequences. She knew that people would begin to see her differently; respecting her wishes out of fear of her magic abilities. She could no longer believe in herself that her intentions were completely innocent, as to possess such a spell would mean otherwise. *"To have such power, there is a very real risk of becoming corrupt as it happens quite often in the pursuit of the darker magics,"* she thought nervously, quite aware of how alluring the incredible power could be, *"It certainly would be easy to bend others to my every will, simply by the threat of using my magic against them. Dendrox, for example, would think twice before turning a cold shoulder to me. But then, would carrying on knowing this be any better?"*

She knew well of the changes she would have to go through and that frightened her most of all; that she would be allowing a darkness to grow and thrive within her. She was all too aware of what she was willing to undertake with this and the sacrifices she would be making to do so.

"I am fully aware," Weena told her forcefully, "I understand all that… I'm not making a hasty decision."

"Alright, very well, I shall get you the book. Wait here," Voasta instructed.

***

<World of Zaylyn><Quest For The Sword Fragments And The Hunt For Dranngore><By Katrina Mandrake-Johnston><Ch 39>

CHAPTER 39 =   THE CHASE

The shop Vordin had taken refuge in, was that of a candle-maker. Much too fearful of venturing outside, he ended up spending several hours there, roaming about pretending to inspect the different colored and fragranced candles, and then watching the candle-maker at work as she continuously dipped the candles over and over into the hot wax.

It was getting dark. Vordin poked his head out the door of the shop. It didn't look as if the werewolf had waited about.

"That's what this creature is, isn't it? This man?" thought Vordin, *"A werewolf, like out of the stories? Only this one is real! How can it be a real werewolf?! They are just in made-up stories. They're not real! Not like that!"*

Vordin wondered if perhaps the man hadn't detected him earlier as he had thought. It didn't matter, as he needed to get back to the inn, and Vordin could wait no longer.

He stepped out and could see people hurrying off the streets with the fading light and bolting their doors and windows.

Vordin heard someone say to another, "Quickly, you don't want to be out in the open when night falls, for reasons you know well."

As Vordin headed down the street, he heard the howl of a wolf. Someone near him cursed and said, "We have enough to fear already, and now wolves are wandering our streets as well!"

Vordin hurried as quickly as he could in the direction of the inn, but he was a fair distance from it. An eerie quiet began to fall around him, broken only by the jilting sound of doors closing and locking. To him, the sound of his footsteps became an awful sound, as he knew they were giving away his location with every step. He ran down the empty street, his eyes darting all around him as his fear grew. It was clear that no one would offer him aid. Besides, it would only mean that they would probably be

<Zaylyn ><Quest For The Sword Fragments And The Hunt For Dranngore><By Katrina Mandrake-Johnston > <Ch 39> < 89 >

killed as well in their attempt to protect him. He felt like such a fool.

"I should have stayed hidden within the shop. I should have never ventured outside, especially with the fading light. But would that have even mattered? I suspect he would have hunted us down no matter where we were hiding, simply by following our scent. I doubt we would have found safety even at the inn. And now the creature knows about Kreasa and her children; that they are here in Shirkint. It would have been simply a matter of time before he found all of us, including them. I hope Weena is safe."

Another wolf howl resounded throughout the street. This howl, although distinctly the howl of a wolf, sounded unnatural like that of some terrible monster, not at all like the first one he had heard. Perhaps it was the night that had added to this further transformation. Vordin could hear the skitter of claws against the cobblestones, as the creature drew quickly nearer. The beast was now behind him, chasing him down. There wasn't any hope of making it all the way to The Old Scabbard Inn now.

Vordin ran and ran. He had no clue of what direction he should run in or where he could escape to, and he suspected he would meet his doom by running foolishly down a dead end street. There was no way he would be able to outrun the wolf, and he could hear it gaining on him.

Vordin took a quick glance over his shoulder and could see that it was nearer than he had hoped. He could see its fierce yellow eyes and its snarling jaw of vicious teeth. It didn't look exactly like a wolf anymore. Its head was larger. Its eyes, nose, mouth, and teeth were all disproportionate to the size of its head, even with it being a larger size now. Its paws were at least five times larger and had enormous claws that could have easily been mistaken for daggers. Its massive muscular body was at least twice the size of a full-grown man and was covered in a coarse blackish-grey fur.

It was seconds away from tearing through his flesh. Vordin was almost unaware of the frightened scream that had started to come from him, as he tried to run faster despite the fact that it was useless to do so. He would not just give in to this horrible fate. He would at least fight for survival to the gruesome end.

Then to his amazement, he heard a whelp from behind him. Vordin stopped and turned around in astonishment. This ferocious beast was now whimpering and pulling himself over to the side of the street, nursing a severely broken leg. Vordin watched as the beast slowly changed. Its size began to shrink, its fur gradually changed to a soft grey, its features became normal, and soon the beast's appearance had returned to that of a large wolf. It was the same one Vordin had seen in the village of Dexcsin and at the house he and Weena had broken into.

Vordin looked around for some sort of explanation, but saw nothing. The wolf lay whining from the pain by the wall of a nearby building. Vordin wondered what else the people in this town were so afraid of and of what they knew to roam the streets at night. He wondered if the attack on the wolf were mere coincidence. He feared that perhaps he had not been saved and could easily be the next target of whatever was out there.

"Could The Black Shadow be the one that did this?" Vordin asked himself, *"Once again saving my life? Could it be that The Black Shadow is who these people are so afraid of and why they run and hide at night? I find it hard to believe all the things he is supposed to be, when he has helped us in such great ways and so often now. Can he really be as evil as everyone says? If so, then what purpose does he have for us?"*

He decided that he had better get back to the inn as quickly as possible, and as he ran, he thought he caught a glimpse of a shadowy shape following him now and then, but finally decided it was just his fear playing tricks him.

<World of Zaylyn><Quest For The Sword Fragments And The Hunt For Dranngore><By Katrina Mandrake-Johnston><Ch 40>

CHAPTER 40 = VORDIN'S RETURN

Shaken, Vordin stumbled into the tavern. He had hoped to see the reassuring face of one or more of his companions after his frightful brush with death, but none of his friends were there. He looked around the room, still in shock and disbelief that he had lived and arrived here safely. His breath was coming out in great trembling heaves. His legs felt weak and he had to steady himself against the cold

<Zaylyn ><Quest For The Sword Fragments And The Hunt For Dranngore><By Katrina Mandrake-Johnston > <Ch 40> < 90 >
stone of the wall.

Closest to the door and Vordin, at the first of the smaller tables along the wall, sat three green-skinned creatures. One of them was a very large and muscular humanoid with a low brow and wide yellow tusk-like protruding teeth. He was easily eight feet in height, his arms like great dark green tree trunks.

Vordin decided that this creature must be a Garc. He had heard a bit about them from Rasindell, but they had been just something out of a story, and now that he was looking at a real Garc in the flesh, he couldn't help but stare in amazement and fascination.

Garcs were supposed to have very low intelligence, but had enough to co-exist with the other races when they wanted to. They were known for their short tempers and almost always dealt with their problems with brute strength.

The other two creatures were small and wiry, standing only three maybe four feet tall Vordin estimated. Their faces were long and narrow, almost like that of a dog or wolf, with sharp and jagged triangular-shaped teeth, and their pointed ears were set near the top of their heads. *"These two must be goblins,"* he thought. Their small deep-set eyes looked Vordin over, and sinister smirks formed across their thin black lips.

The Garc was dressed in what looked to be a deerskin loincloth and the goblins both wore brown suede. One of the goblins cupped his long skinny fingers around his mug and then swallowed a large mouthful of ale from it. He was now eyeing Vordin suspiciously, as he had been staring at them for some time now, although unintentionally. Vordin was merely fascinated by them.

The Garc slammed his empty mug against the table, making Vordin jump in astonishment. The Garc then gave him a threatening glare and demanded, "You buy Briff drink."

"Was he talking to me?!" thought Vordin. He nervously shook his head. *"I don't want any trouble with these creatures! I barely escaped from the werewolf with my life. I didn't mean to stare!"*

"Y' bett'r do what he says, if y' know what's good for ya," one of the goblins said excitedly, "Best t' keep 'im happy. Hey, Snog, ain't that right?"

Snog laughed and warned, "Yeah. Y' bett'r listen to m' pal Snick over 'ere. Briff can git real mean."

The Garc's grotesquely long black toenails scrapped along the wooden floor as he stood up from his chair to tower over him. He snarled threateningly, "Buy drink now!"

The door opened and in stepped the formidable Black Shadow, his cloak billowing about him on a gust of chill night air from outside. As he strode across the room toward his favorite table in the shadowed corner of the tavern, Briff was forced back down into his chair by an unseen force.

Briff looked around in surprise, unsure of what had just happened. He didn't want to sit back down. It was some sort of attack. He slammed his fist down onto the tabletop in anger. "Briff crush him!" he growled.

"No, no, no!" Snick said waving his hand into the Garc's grimacing face with fear, "Don't y' know who that is?!"

He growled, "Briff strong! Me crush!"

Snog added in trying to help, "Sit back down. Come on, just do it."

Snick whispered, "That's The Black Shadow! Yer lucky ya even gits a warnin' as y' did. He'll kill ya, if y' make 'im mad! Just poof and dead! Just like y' got pushed."

"Him kill Briff?" he asked, the confusion showing in his dark yellow eyes, "But me big."

"Nope, doesn't matt'r," Snog explained with a nervous chuckle, "Squash like a bug."

Briff thought about this for almost a whole minute, his large brow twitching as he considered what to do and the reasons behind them that didn't quite make sense in his train of logic. "Me sit," Briff finally decided to the relief of the two goblins.

Vordin didn't know what else to do, so he hurried over to The Black Shadow at the circular table in the corner. "Did the others come by?" he asked nervously, his voice trembling.

"It's not the wolf you need to be wary of. It's the man behind the wolf. That is where the real danger lies," he said to him.

"It was you then? You stopped the beast?" Vordin asked him.

"Please, sit. It is clear that you are still quite shaken by the whole ordeal," The Black Shadow said to him gesturing with a gloved hand to the empty place on the bench beside him.

Vordin hesitated, his instincts were screaming no, even though his mind was considering it and trying to convince himself that there was nothing to fear. Finally, he was able to force himself to sit upon the bench.

Vordin had the courage to say, "It's just that they were supposed to meet back here. It's after dark, and well, they're not here. They were going to try to get some money to rent a room for the night."

"Will he be angry that we no longer have the money he gave us? Does he have something to do with the others not being here?" Vordin thought nervously.

The Black Shadow folded his hands in front of him upon the table. "I do not mean to cause such fear in you, and I am glad you chose to sit beside me now despite everything you've seen, but you should trust your instincts with me no matter how much you think otherwise. I cannot always control the motives behind my actions. I am an evil being and am feared for good reason. I cannot change this. But I cannot let the people of Zaylyn suffer the evil of the Killnarin as well as my own. The quest for the sword is a means to remove this second evil from our world, as they were never meant to exist here. I am the greater evil, but I am doing my best to hold back what I can of it. Do not rely on my help. I shall try to offer it when I can and when I believe that it is safe for me to do so. You don't realize the risks I have taken to aid you as I have. I don't want to be the one to cause any of you harm," he paused in thought, and then continued, "The werewolf has caused me a great pain once before. I could not let him have the satisfaction again."

Vordin commented, "Norick the blacksmith told me something that…"

"I know. The werewolf, you see, he knows that I protected the two of you back at the house and then you again in the street. This second rescue has confirmed that you are now to be his intended target. He will continue to hunt you until he succeeds in killing you or," The Black Shadow stopped, the emotion beginning to show in his voice, "or cause me to remain around you, or even to simply have my attention focused in your direction in order to protect you from him. In doing that, however, it would ensure your death by my own hands when the hunger or the evil slips out of my control even slightly. I'm my own enemy in this. Hoatam would be ecstatic in that triumph. You see, he believes he is able to control me, bend me to his will, using my desire to resist my evil against me by either threatening or killing those I find the slightest interest in. He knows I struggle against the hunger and the evil inside me, that I am trying to resist, that I am trying to… I'm sure he would love to drive me back to my evil, cause me to lose all hope, destroy everything I hold dear beyond what I have already caused myself to destroy. He would love to be responsible for the carnage that would follow the full release of my malevolent nature, even if it means causing me to take revenge against him to do so. I can't risk killing the werewolf, for fear of unleashing my evil, for fear of becoming the monster that is at my core and nothing more than that. He knows this and believes he holds power over me in this, that he is untouchable, and in a way he's right. Plus he is not really a werewolf in the traditional sense, not what you have come to know from Rasindell's stories at least. I can't take the time to explain it to you, but he holds an innocent being captive and has thus obtained his power. I can't intentionally kill Dranngore for you either, and I can't risk being so closely connected to the Killnarin and their malicious ways in order to send them back. Remember the advice of the blacksmith. I can't protect you. The more I stay near, the greater chance of it being me you need protection from. He said that, good intentions or not, that I would ultimately lead to your doom, and I'm afraid that what he says may very well be true in the end." He rubbed at the muscles on the back of his neck. To Vordin, he had seemed to gradually take on the mannerisms of a normal person instead of the awe-inspiring powerful being that he was. He sighed and then said, "I suppose I should get you a place to sleep for the night."

The Black Shadow got up from the table and paid for a room at the counter.

He waved Vordin over to the staircase saying, "Come on."

Vordin reluctantly followed him up the stairs to the second floor and then to the room. The Black Shadow slipped the key into the lock, twisted it, and then opened the door as Vordin watched.

<Zaylyn ><Quest For The Sword Fragments And The Hunt For Dranngore><By Katrina Mandrake-Johnston > <Ch 40> < 92 >

"Here's the key then," he told him, holding it out to him. At Vordin's hesitation, he added on a lighter note, "Come on, I'm not going to bite." Vordin backed away, staring wide-eyed into the shadowed face beneath the hood. "Sorry, it was a bad attempt at a joke. Go on, it's all right. You need to get some sleep after all you've been through. It's safe."

Vordin took the small iron key from his outstretched hand. He couldn't exactly describe it, but it was as if a certain menacing aspect of The Black Shadow had diminished. Vordin could easily visualize that there could be just a regular person under the cloak and not the horrid monster he had seen tearing into the bandits, and he no longer felt as if he were in the presence of such an immensely powerful being as he was.

Vordin entered the room and sat down upon the cushiony mattress of the bed. He hadn't realized just how incredibly exhausted he really was.

"Goodnight, Vordin, and, for what it's worth, thank-you for being a friend," he told him before shutting the door and heading back down the stairs to the tavern below.

Vordin curled up beneath the thick soft blankets, and as his mind tried to make sense of all that had happened that day, he fell fast asleep.

<World of Zaylyn><Quest For The Sword Fragments And The Hunt For Dranngore><By Katrina Mandrake-Johnston><Ch 41>

CHAPTER 41 = LORENTA'S QUESTIONS

The Black Shadow sat at the table, alone with his thoughts. Nexzath was out on his own somewhere. He greatly enjoyed his company, but it wasn't right to subject him to the feedings each night. The Black Shadow couldn't allow himself to begin to rely on Nexzath to help him regain control over the hunger. He had to maintain the control on his own. With Nexzath there, if he started to slip, he might be able to stop a feeding from becoming a kill, but at the same time Nexzath would be risking his own life to do so. He would be standing between the vicious beast inside and what it desired most and be preventing that monster from obtaining it. It wasn't right to ask him to endanger his life like that, not when he was already risking so much just by being a friend to him. Allowing that friendship and connection to him grow and build, at the same time fuels the evil's desire to rip apart every aspect of it.

Lorenta entered the inn, and she walked boldly up to his table. She stared directly into his face and said with strength, "I must know. Rasindell raised me, but ultimately, I am truly your daughter, am I not? You were the one who gave him the potion that spurred my birth from the spider. I have to know. Am I evil? Am I meant for some awful purpose? Please, you must tell me!" Tears were beginning in her eyes now.

"Do not say that you are a daughter of mine," he told her. "*If she went around believing that, or worse, telling others that, she would surely get herself killed.*" The part of his being that was female, lingering at the back of his mind, wanted to come forward to embrace Lorenta as any mother would, the emotion swelling within her. "*No, I am afraid,*" he admitted to himself, "*I can't allow myself to believe in such a connection. If the evil inside me ever escaped...*" He told her, "Lorenta, you are not evil. Rasindell is your father, not I. You must understand that you were not meant for any evil purpose. You exist because of Rasindell's desire to one day have and love a child of his own, to end his loneliness that he had immersed himself in. I merely provided a means to do so, leaving it to his own curiosity for its beginning."

"But you understand what I am meant for. The half life I am to live," she said to him, "The children I have, if even possible, what is to happen to them? Are they to become like the human-dragons of this world?"

He sighed heavily, saying, "I do not know. I can't give you the answers you desire. You must decide your own fate, not I."

He could feel the female self wanting to push her way forward, not caring if she emerged in front of everyone giving away a well hidden secret about The Black Shadow's being. The two halves of The Black Shadow; one male, one female... both the same person but with different personalities. The Black Shadow often tried to see this as being similar to a brother and sister sharing the same mind. But

<Zaylyn ><Quest For The Sword Fragments And The Hunt For Dranngore><By Katrina Mandrake-Johnston > <Ch 41> < 93 >

it was really only an attempt to ease his loneliness; trying to pretend that there was another like him, trying to convince himself that there was indeed another but only one of them could emerge at any one time. In reality, there was only one, but it pleased him to make the division in his mind. He thought differently, had different desires and feelings than his female self, and therefore it was easy for him to imagine himself as two people instead of one. He could feel her personality, her self, in the back of his mind… as she could feel his, when she came forward as the dominant half. The male half tended to be a bit more aggressive, the hunger harder to hold back, but his female self had not dealt with the death of her beloved stable boy. After Ezmeara, for the female half to also lose a love, it was too much to bear and so she retreated into the mind of her male self to avoid the full grunt of the sorrow. She chose to remain where her thoughts and feelings had to be filtered through the mind of the male and where they had to be viewed secondhand instead of being forced to embrace them. He knew that she would have to emerge eventually, but not yet, not now.

Lorenta said with passion, "No, you will give me the answers I need. You are responsible. You gave me this life. How is anyone supposed to see the real me, when I have to scurry away at dawn like some sort of monster?"

Ezmeara had not known about this other half. Thorin, the stable boy his female self had later fallen for, had been told almost everything. This female half of The Black Shadow's being had often thought about what it would be like to have a child. She knew she would never be able to birth one, as the risk was too great that even a small portion of the power be passed down into the offspring, not to mention the dreaded thought that the hunger may also be inherited. She knew that she would never be able to raise a child; the risk was too great to be so near. Still, she had thought about it, and the desire to hold another in a motherly embrace caused a great sorrow in her, knowing she could not for so many reasons. She could not bear to think of the hatred brought upon that child because of its connection to The Black Shadow and all the horrors he was responsible for.

The memory of returning to the stable here in Shirkint still remained vivid. *"Had it been wrong for my female self to seek love as she had done? To tell him of the powers she held and everything else about The Black Shadow? The pain of his loss is too great even to say his name. She loved him, but in turn, he had become a very dear friend to my male half as well."*

The stable had been empty. The female self had feared that it might end as horribly as it had with Ezmeara. She believed that, because of this, Thorin had finally left her, fearing for his life and knowing the risk of them continuing to meet.

But he had not left her. She had let her guard down and the werewolf had discovered them speaking together within the stable. He was the one who had killed her love. The Black Shadow, as a whole, desperately wanted revenge, but couldn't lose himself in doing so and not when that malicious monster continued to hold an innocent creature captive.

"Answer me!" Lorenta demanded, "So what am I to do?"

He placed his gloved hand upon her shoulder, but felt the fear rise inside her. He told her, "If you wish to see the day with human eyes, so be it. It is my final gift to you. Do not question the reason." Then, The Black Shadow vanished before her eyes.

Her body tingled slightly, and in astonishment, she realized that he must have altered her very makeup in the middle of their conversation, and so easily, that it frightened her greatly.

<World of Zaylyn><Quest For The Sword Fragments And The Hunt For Dranngore><By Katrina Mandrake-Johnston><Ch 42>

CHAPTER 42 =   THE FEMALE BLACK SHADOW ARISES

On the west side of The Old Scabbard Inn beside the street leading past the equipment shop and out of town, the second floor of the building jutted out a few feet and was supported by large and sturdy posts of wood. Beneath were a few empty crates and barrels scattered about. It was here, in the shadows near the wall, that The Black Shadow reappeared and then transformed.

He made the transformation from his male self into the female form of The Black Shadow in a single deep breath, inhaling as one, exhaling as the other. Although it took mere seconds to complete, it was a very complex occurrence.

<Zaylyn ><Quest For The Sword Fragments And The Hunt For Dranngore><By Katrina Mandrake-Johnston > <Ch 42> < 94 >

The Black Shadow's entire body tingled as the new and different flesh arose out of the other. He shrunk in stature as the body and skeletal frame took on its new form, the male characteristics changing from male to female, the flesh turning from one into the other, the hair becoming long cascading waves of glistening black as the female body took on her desired appearance.

The clothing on her form shifted, flowing along her body like liquid until settling into the desired shape. On her body, under the hooded cloak, was now a silky skirt which was split on either side up to mid thigh exposing the smooth creamy skin of her shapely legs. A tight long-sleeved top hugged her round and ample breasts in a v-shaped neckline.

The transformation was over, ending the breath with new lungs, and seeing the surroundings with different eyes as if looking upon and sensing everything anew, even though the being had not moved from its place. She ran her tongue along the front of her teeth, feeling the moisture in the air upon her lips. She breathed in the cool crisp air of the night, delighting in how good it felt on her skin.

She looked across the street to the stable. The lantern, hung near the entrance, was swinging gently in the cool breeze. The archway was illuminated by its light in a welcoming glow, but it pained her to look. As the male, The Black Shadow had returned quite often to the stable to feed during the night, despite the loss of his friend. But for her, he had been much more than a friend. She had loved him dearly, and she could not bare to be here now in person.

Eventually she would have to face that sorrow, but she could not do so now. She returned control of The Black Shadow's being back over the male, and once transformed, he reentered The Old Scabbard Inn.

***

<World of Zaylyn><Quest For The Sword Fragments And The Hunt For Dranngore><By Katrina Mandrake-Johnston><Ch 43>

CHAPTER 43= WEENA'S STUDY OF THE FIREBALL SPELL

Weena, cradling the spell book in her arms, carefully brought the ancient tome to an empty chair. She lay the book down on the table in the little enclosure and quietly pulled the chair up to seat herself before it. The library was actually quite beautiful; the walls were mahogany, the tables of oak, the chairs and the dividers to create privacy for each individual were made of redwood, and the floor was made of long polished slats of cedar that were fitted together and ran the length of the room. It gave the library a calming and soothing atmosphere which Weena was thankful for. She was still a bit hesitant of what lay before her. The ceiling, she noticed as she stalled, was made of a richly dark colored wood. She made herself push her worries aside, as she knew they would interfere with her study. She tried to strip everything clear from her mind that didn't pertain to the grueling task before her.

Weena opened the spell book, once again marveling at how the symbols within such a book shone with a mystical light. She had forgotten just how dazzling looking upon a spell book directly could be. It took her a few moments before she could bring herself to begin deciphering the symbols within their clusters upon the page.

The symbols upon each page appeared as if they had a life of their own. As she looked upon and read each symbol, drawing out or shortening the sounds in the name for each, as she stretched the syllables out and along the curves, loops, angles, and lines… some of the symbols began to glow brighter, while others dulled in their shimmering light, and others miraculously began to move about the page shifting position ever so gently as if they were floating upon a pool of water. Weena knew that, ever so gradually, a few of these symbols would make their way to the last page to form the makeup of the desired Fireball spell. It would be a spell that was being uniquely created to co-exist within her body and mind from what the spell book was able to read from her as she studied the pages before her. Once Weena came to reach the final page of the spell book, the symbols would be arranged in various complex and intertwining clusters. In order for her to decipher the symbols and their meanings into a workable spell, she would have to make sense of their connections.

<Zaylyn ><Quest For The Sword Fragments And The Hunt For Dranngore><By Katrina Mandrake-Johnston > <Ch 43> < 95 >

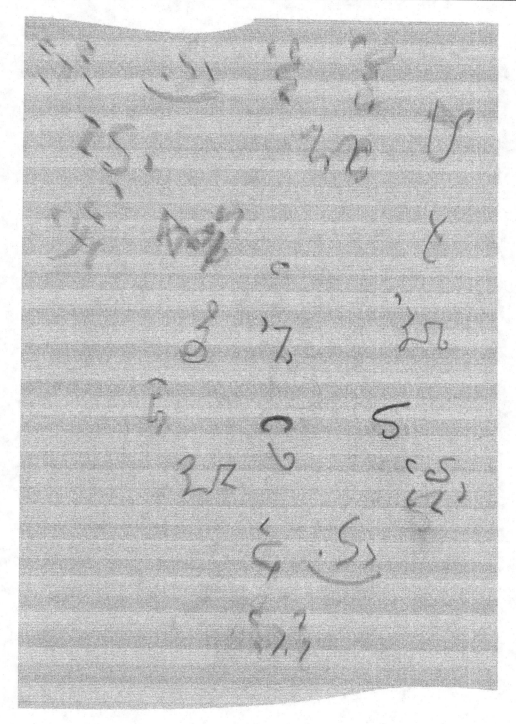

<Zaylyn ><Quest For The Sword Fragments And The Hunt For Dranngore><By Katrina Mandrake-Johnston > <Ch 43> < 96 >

<Zaylyn ><Quest For The Sword Fragments And The Hunt For Dranngore><By Katrina Mandrake-Johnston > <Ch 43>< 97 >

Diy = inside self / spirit

Lure-va = self

Miy = outside self / body / personality

Me-ca-tore = intelligence

Creat-tah = skill

Creat-tore = strength

Doanda = peaceful

Bin-drost = hate

Blicka = small amount

Sam-blor = large amount

Dan-dost = heat

Brur-down = come / being called / follow

Dae-mond = don't want

Zool-va = will care for / protect

Do-la = you

Cac-coon = collected / focused

Coke-ca = open / push out

Black-ca-ist = shock / strike / affect aggressive

Drat-tone = hurt

Kai-na = want

* *

Weena's Fireball Spell:

Lure-va * bin-drost * dae-mond * zool-va * do-la *

Lure-va * bin-drost * sam-blor * dan-dost * brur-down * do-la *

Lure-va * miy * me-ca-tore *

Lure-va * miy * creat-tah *

Lure-va * miy * creat-tah * bin-drost * sam-blor * dan-dost *

cac-coon * coke-ca * black-ca-ist * do-la * miy *

Lure-va * kai-na * drat-tone * do-la * miy *

<Zaylyn ><Quest For The Sword Fragments And The Hunt For Dranngore><By Katrina Mandrake-Johnston > <Ch 43> < 98 >

Amazingly, once she got started, she was able to read through more swiftly than she thought. Weena soon reached the last page.

"Now that I am able to read the symbols, remembering what they mean, all I have to do is memorize the whole thing and hope that their meanings within the clusters begins to make sense enough to form a magical connection within myself." She sighed heavily, and then, realizing she may have disturbed the others, turned back to the book.

She flipped back to the first page again. After a few hours, she believed she had it committed to memory well enough and got up from her chair to move onto the practice room Voasta had mentioned. She received quite a few glares at this from the others.

"I suppose I did complete the first reading rather quickly. It should have taken me longer, and especially with such an advanced spell, but I did everything I was supposed to. It just seemed to come to me. With my other spells, for each one, it took me near a day straight to get through the first reading. I actually found this fire spell to be quite easy to learn. These poor wretches look like they've been here for days. I wonder what stage they're at? Well it's not my fault I've learnt faster than they have. I wish they would stop looking at me like that."

Weena proceeded to walk down to the end of the narrow room where she could see a doorway in which the air visibly shimmered with some sort of magical power. She warily put a hand out over the threshold, feeling that the air within the doorway was icy cold and vibrating with a strong magical energy.

"This is definitely some sort of barrier and apparently strong enough to withstand whatever spell is to be cast within. If the Killnarin attack Shirkint, perhaps some of the people could escape here and be protected from their spells," Weena thought with hope, but then asked herself, *"And when their spells fail, what's to stop them from just prancing in and physically slaughtering everyone who has willingly trapped themselves in here?"*

It was a surprisingly large room that she entered through the doorway, and it was completely bare. The outside structure of the magic shop could not have possibly allowed for such an area. Weena just had to accept it as being so and attempted to cast her spell.

The memorized words with their symbols flashed through her mind. She closed her eyes and tried to put as much feeling as she could into the casting of it, as she silently mouthed the spell. Weena held out her hands, her fingers spread and her palms facing outward, and then she waited. She waited, and as she was about to turn back and begin the second reading, as spells rarely got any sort of reaction on the first practice casting, she found that her fingers had begun to tingle.

Weena stared in disbelief at her hands. *"Something happened! Something actually happened! But should I be so ecstatic over this success? What does that say about me? A Black magic spell being acquired so naturally and of fire? I have to do this though. If I get a tingle in my fingers now, I wonder what my second trial at casting will bring?"*

Weena exited the room, returning to the library. She sat back before her book and began reading through the symbols once more. This time she found it harder to focus, and the clusters seemed to swim about on the page. Her concentration began to falter as a weakness began to cloud her mind. It was far more draining on her than any of her other spells had been, and she knew the more she proceeded, the more strenuous it would become.

Placing a hand on either side of the spell book, she brought the first cluster into focus with an odd feeling inside her gut and mind. The spell was beginning to take root within her. Each symbol within its cluster began to invoke a heightened awareness to its form and the relationship within the thought pattern the cluster was creating in her mind. It was working. Weena was absorbing the spell into herself, the spell weaving itself into her being. With four more readings and five more attempts at casting, the process would be complete and the spell would be hers, unless she collapsed beforehand or the spell refused to take hold any further.

<Zaylyn ><Quest For The Sword Fragments And The Hunt For Dranngore><By Katrina Mandrake-Johnston > <Ch 44> < 99 >

CHAPTER 44 =   GLIMPSE OF THE UNKNOWN

Out of the corner of her eye, Weena thought she saw something. She tried to ignore it, as she needed to concentrate, and she couldn't allow anything to distract her focus from the page.

"It's probably one of the others, most likely the woman by the looks of things. I wouldn't be surprised if they were jealous of how well I'm doing and decided to make it more difficult for me by causing a distraction on their way to the casting room," she thought with irritation.

Weena tried to focus, but it was just too difficult to maintain with all of them now moving about in her peripheral vision. Weena turned, ready to give them the nastiest look she could muster, and that's when she saw it.

A solid black humanoid form, without any features whatsoever, was in the library with them. It was as if she were staring at a portion of the night sky that had been molded like a piece of clay into a humanoid shape. Its slim form was hunched over, its back long and arched forward like some sort of predator sneaking up onto its prey. Its thin arms were also long and disproportionate to its body and it held them out in front of its form like a praying mantis, its elongated spidery fingers slowly testing the air in front of it. It was staring right at her. Even though it didn't have a face, she could feel it looking at her.

Weena could see that there also was an identical being in the room, but this one was completely white, and as brilliantly white as if staring into the sun without the blinding glow of its light. This creature was staring intensely at her as well with its eyeless face.

Another black being was over by one of the men. It took a glance toward the man's spell book, and then turned its attention to Weena as well.

The three beings began moving towards her. They didn't come forward directly but seemed to be

almost sidestepping, as they each kept one side of their hip turned to her at all times. They had quick jerky movements, but at the same time maintained such a fluid and graceful motion that it appeared almost as if every other second they became invisible but happening far too quickly to determine. It therefore resulted in the appearance of the jerky movements similar to the flip book drawings Weena's brother had often made for her, making the figures he had drawn appear to move before her eyes. The humanoids crept closer and closer, appearing almost curious in their movements and constantly staring at her with their expressionless faces. The fear was rising quickly in her.

"What are these things? Can it be that my assumptions were right? Are these the shapes sometimes glimpsed out of the corner of the eye when learning new spells? How... how can I be looking right at them? They're creatures, not shadows, not a trick the mind plays on itself with fatigue like everyone says. What do they want with me?"

Another black being appeared, crawling through the ceiling as if the ceiling weren't even there. It began to climb down the wall like some incredibly large lizard and all the while its gaze was fixated on Weena.

A second white being climbed up through the floor to approach Weena who was trembling in her chair. The others studying in the library seemed oblivious to them; she was sure of it.

As another black creature passed through the wall to join the approaching mob, Weena's thoughts

<Zaylyn ><Quest For The Sword Fragments And The Hunt For Dranngore><By Katrina Mandrake-Johnston ><Ch 44> < 100 >

went back to the story Lorenta had told back at The Twisted Eye Tavern. In the story, the evil being within the closet had escaped and taken the place of the man. It had adopted the man's appearance and trapped him within the prison of the closet while the evil creature took over the man's life. The worst thing about it was that no one had known, and the creature killed the man's friend in this deception.

The closest black being reached out with its long fingers toward Weena. She started screaming in terror, falling backwards in her chair.

As she scrambled to her feet from the floor, one of the men asked the other, "What's wrong with her?"

"Don't you see them?!" Weena shrieked frantically, racing between the beings toward the curtain, fearful of letting them touch her.

"See what?!" the woman snapped looking up from her book, her concentration lost, "There's nothing here but us!"

Weena whipped back the curtain and almost leapt into the other room.

Voasta came rushing to her side as soon as she saw the horrified look upon Weena's face. "What's wrong?! What's the matter?!"

"Creatures… black and white things… reaching for me… trying to get me," Weena gasped, with tears streaming down her cheeks.

"Dear, it's only your mind playing tricks on you, because of the strain and endurance it takes to learn new magic," Voasta told her, trying to calm her, "You just think you see shadows at the corner of your eyes. They're not real. There aren't any creatures in there, dear. It's a normal thing, you don't have to be so afraid."

"No, I'm looking right at them! They're coming for me! I have to get away!" Weena shouted at her.

A black being's head passed through the curtain which spurred Weena to run out of the shop and slam the door shut behind her in terror.

"She's completely mad!" Voasta exclaimed, "If I had known, I would have never sent her back there with the books." The group of beings, more arising by the minute, passed right by Voasta as they followed Weena. "She appeared normal when she entered," Voasta said to herself, "I guess you can never tell by appearances alone."

It was dark. Night had come quite some time ago. Vordin had probably told the others that she had gone to the magic shop to study magic. The others most likely had already turned in for the night. It would only be a short distance for her to run to the inn.

She started to run. Weena could see that the beings were lurking around the buildings to her right, watching her. More of the creatures were coming forth to creep towards her, passing right through the walls of the shops, rising out of the ground, and even passing through the thick wall on her left that surrounded the town.

She burst through the door of the tavern, looking frantically around the room. Her gaze fell on The Black Shadow sitting at the corner table. His head was lowered, his hands folded before him upon the tabletop, as if he were deep in thought.

"The Black Shadow. He's probably the only one who can help me. No one else seems to see them. No one can protect me from them. He's helped us before. It's my only chance," she reasoned.

With a frantic look of desperation in her eyes, she came toward him saying, "Black Shadow, I need to speak with you!"

The people around her within the room were shocked by her reckless action, and she could hear several of them gasp and question her sanity in their whispers to each other. Then, an unseen force knocked her hard to the ground.

Bringing herself up on her hands and knees, stunned and unsure of what had just happened, Weena watched as The Black Shadow got up, walked past her, and headed out the door with his cloak billowing about him as he moved.

"Wait, no," she called out, coming to her senses and getting up off the floor.

<Zaylyn ><Quest For The Sword Fragments And The Hunt For Dranngore><By Katrina Mandrake-Johnston ><Ch 44> < 101 >

The creatures were in the tavern now, climbing up through the floor, and through the walls. She let out a panicked cry, tears welling in her eyes once more as she looked around the room. *"It's hopeless! No one will help me! There's nowhere I can run! Nowhere I can hide!"* she screamed within her mind.

One of the beings placed its hand on a man's shoulder. The man simply continued sipping at his mug of ale, completely unaware that the creature was touching him. Nothing seemed to happen to the man, but then Weena realized that the being was merely trying to peer its way around the man to gaze upon her.

"Look out!" she shrieked pointing to the creature behind him, "It's right there! Don't you see it?! It's right there! There are creatures all around us!"

The man was oblivious to what was happening. He merely rolled his eyes and tried to ignore her.

"It is true! I'm the only one who can see them! They aren't even interested in anyone else. All they want is me! They know I can see them. Maybe that's the reason. I'm doomed. Will one of them take my place? What is to happen to me?!"

"No!" she screamed at them, as they began to close in on her, "You won't take me! I won't let you! Stay back! Keep away from me! Leave me alone!"

"Yeah, alright lady," one man snickered, "We won't let them get you," he told her mockingly, and then added with real concern in his eyes, "Just don't go confronting The Black Shadow like that again. I mean, you are real lucky he didn't just…" he paused shaking his head, "Take your problems elsewhere if you know what's good for ya." There was a hint of fear in his eyes, feeling he may have put his own life at stake simply for speaking about The Black Shadow as he had done.

As Weena slowly backed away from the approaching beings, another man whispered, his voice on edge, "That's the last thing we need; some crazed moron running around endangering us all with that dark beast."

"I know," someone else whispered back to him, "To go to The Black Shadow like that! I don't care what her damn problem is. To endanger the rest of us like that! To think what could have happened here makes me shudder! The selfish bitch! She angers him enough to kill her, and then guess what happens to the rest of us, eh? We have enough to worry about without her provoking things further."

Weena escaped the inn back into the night, the darkness broken only by the faint light from a few candles and lanterns within the homes and buildings.

"Is there nowhere I can turn?!" she asked herself in dismay, *"The others are probably waiting for me in the rooms just above, but they can't help me! They would have expected me to be in the magic shop all night anyway, continuing with learning the spell as there can be no interruptions for sleep. They have no reason to come looking for me! I have to find The Black Shadow. I have to convince him to help me! No one else can! Why did he push me aside?! I know I didn't trip. How could he just ignore me like that, when I so desperately need his help?!"*

The beings were coming through the door of the inn behind her. Weena bolted down the street to the right, away from the magic shop, away from the door to the inn, and fleeing in the direction of the town entrance and the equipment shop. She could see that the shop was locked up tightly for the night, but she could also see the glow of a candle through the grime-covered window.

"No one will help me! No one wants to! Everyone is too afraid to do anything!" she thought with panic, *"But I can't leave the town!"*

Looking behind her, Weena could see their number had increased incredibly and that they were all creeping slowly after her. She could also see many of them lurking about ahead of her as well. To the right, the street continued north following the town wall up into the rest of the town. The light from a lantern shone like a beacon in that direction. It was at the entrance to the stable. She remembered how the innkeeper had joked cruelly about the people going missing from there so often during the night, but the light felt safer than the dark. There was nowhere else to go. It was either there, or continue up the street drawing nearer and nearer to where the home of the werewolf lay.

<Zaylyn ><Quest For The Sword Fragments And The Hunt For Dranngore><By Katrina Mandrake-Johnston ><Ch 45> < 102 >

CHAPTER 45 =   WEENA AND THE BLACK SHADOW

As Weena rounded the corner, she could see that The Black Shadow was walking briskly down along the side of the inn, disappearing into the dark. Relieved that he hadn't taken flight, Weena ran after him.

"Wait, please, I need to speak with you," she called out.

He stopped, and she caught up to him.

The Black Shadow spun around, and grabbing her by the shoulders, slammed her hard up against the wall of the building letting out a vicious snarl and leaving her breathless and dazed for a few moments.

Terrified, Weena stared into the shadowed face beneath the hood, unable to determine his appearance.

Finally, she had enough valor to say, "Please, I see these creatures. I can still see them; they're here right now. Although now they do seem to be keeping their distance, but they've been following me. I tried to learn a new spell, and that's when they came and have been coming towards me ever since. I'm afraid of what might happen if they get me. You can see them, can't you? You can make them go away, can't you?"

"Yes," he hissed, "But there is a reason why the rabbit does not ask the wolf or the fox to help it remove burrs from its fur." He let out a low growl.

"I... I..." Weena stammered in fear, "I didn't know what to do. I... I didn't know who to turn to." She was beginning to panic.

"So you turn to the one person that can do ten times worse to you than any of them?" he snarled.

"But you won't, right? We can trust you. You've helped us before," she tried to remind him, fearing for her life.

"I can't promise anything. You should learn to stay away, they do," he said speaking of the mysterious beings she saw.

He moved a little closer to her and whispered in her ear. "I don't want to hurt you." His breath was cool on her cheek and neck.

"Then don't, please don't," Weena begged, a tear rolling down her cheek.

"I'll try," he told her, "It's just so very hard to resist."

He breathed in deeply, relishing the smell of her skin. His eyes flashed red for a moment, and Weena could see his pearly white fangs so close to her throat.

"Please don't hurt me," she whispered almost beginning to weep, "Please, I need your help."

The beings were looking on, most of them were black now, eagerly looking on wanting harm to come to her. A few were of a greyish color, but they remained farther back than any of them. The very few white beings seemed to motion sympathetic gestures but nothing more.

The Black Shadow explained, "They are around all the time. They weave the magic around and within us. White magic, Black magic, and Natural magic. Do you understand? Why they have taken such an interest in you, I don't know. They usually remain unseen, a few people only catching a glimpse of them now and then out of the corner of their eye when they are close to magic, altering their perception in an attempt to learn a new magic spell, to bring a new type of magic into themselves. Please tell me you understand, as I can't remain here with you for much longer without something terrible happening."

"Yes... sort of," she replied. He was so very close, whispering in her ear.

"They have probably taken an interest in you because of the Killnarin," he went on to explain, "Killnarin are magically summoned creatures. And these creatures you see are sort of the guardians of all the magic in the world. Their intentions depend on whether or not they want the Killnarin destroyed. Or it may be about the sword. That sword will undo all the magic a wizard has ever done when slain by it. They can't be happy about that, or perhaps they will be, if Dranngore is interfering with them as well. Their intentions may or not be hostile. I can cloud your vision to them, but I can't make them go away. I don't want to interfere with the way things are."

The creatures vanished.

<Zaylyn ><Quest For The Sword Fragments And The Hunt For Dranngore><By Katrina Mandrake-Johnston ><Ch 45> < 103 >

"They're gone," she told him, "Thank-you." She was still so very afraid.

"I'm sorry," he whispered, drawing closer to her.

The fear was unbearable. "For what?" she choked out.

"I can't stop myself. I'm trying to resist," he said softly, his cheek resting on hers. His skin was cool, soft, and smooth.

"Don't," she begged.

"Please forgive me," he whispered as he slipped down to her neck. She could feel his cool soft lips move gently along her skin, but he had not yet bitten her.

"No, don't. Please stop," she begged with desperation and dread.

He groaned, pulling her tightly to him, and then she felt his fangs pierce her skin and bite deeply into her flesh.

It burned hot with pain, and she cried out which made The Black Shadow grip her more firmly. The pain then oddly turned into a cool pleasant sensation which wasn't at all natural and must have been his doing.

She could feel her blood slowly leaving her with every heartbeat as The Black Shadow drank. The pleasure was intensifying throughout her body to the point where she didn't want him to stop. But she knew she was dieing and that soon it would be too late.

"Stop," she cried out, but she could only manage a quiet whimper.

"Stop," she begged, trying to push him away. But he held her tightly, and she was becoming too weak to resist.

"Stop," she begged again. She began to feel dizzy, the world around her seeming to spin about, and her vision began to blur. Her knees felt weak beneath her and she felt as if she were falling.

Then to her surprise, The Black Shadow withdrew from her. Weena tried to steady herself against the wall.

"I'm sorry," he said between heavy breaths, "I'm healing the wound. You'll live. You'll be okay."

Then his eyes burned bright red, and she could see his fangs wet with her blood. A low growl rumbled in his throat as he began to dive in toward her again.

Weena let out a weak and frightened whimper, unable to do anything to stop him.

He stopped himself before he bit into her again and pushed her away from him, knocking her to the ground.

He then leapt into the air to land on the roof of one of the houses across the street, and then continued along the rooftops until he was out of sight.

Weena lay slumped up against the wall of the inn in the dark. She felt dizzy and she couldn't think clearly, her mind feeling hazy. Finally, she passed out, completely vulnerable to anything around her, sprawled out on the cobblestone street beneath.

***

<World of Zaylyn><Quest For The Sword Fragments And The Hunt For Dranngore><By Katrina Mandrake-Johnston><Ch 46>

<u>CHAPTER 46 = WEENA'S ABSENCE</u>

As Dendrox tossed and turned in his sleep, his thoughts drifted back to several years ago. In hope that he and Candra could further their contacts and gain additional knowledge into the workings of the darker side of society, they had become involved with a particular group that was continuously immersing their lives in crime. The group had been mainly thrill seekers, always embarking after elaborate and rare treasures when they had the means to. Perhaps meeting Rinna, with her similar lust for adventure, had caused these memories to stir within him. His thoughts began to focus in on the time when one of their number had lost his life in pursuit of this one particular treasure. Dendrox had been the one to deliver the news of the death to his friend's wife. He began to relive that heartbreaking moment...

Dendrox knocked upon the door of the small cottage. The door was answered by a woman. Her

<Zaylyn ><Quest For The Sword Fragments And The Hunt For Dranngore><By Katrina Mandrake-Johnston ><Ch 46> < 104 >

face fell at the sight of him, already suspecting what she was about to be told.

"He… he went back for it," Dendrox told her, "We told him not to, but he insisted. If only he… He managed to toss it out to us, before he, ah… He wanted me to give this to you," he said unwrapping a golden statue of an owl near the size of a large potato, "He was right to entrust it to me. The rest of them turned on him like vultures after it happened. If it weren't for me, everything he owned would have been snatched up by their unfeeling, greedy hands."

"I see," she said, but there was no indication that his actions in securing her husband's belongings had brought her any bit of relief. She sighed heavily and said, "I kept telling him that we were happy. He kept insisting that he wanted the best for us and our children. But we were happy all along, he just couldn't seem to see that. I kept telling him that we didn't need all kinds of riches and special treatment; that we had enough to eat and we were content with what we had."

"He never mentioned he had children," Dendrox commented, not knowing what else to say.

"He was always out, off on some scheme to make us rich, to solve all the apparent problems we were supposed to be having. It was all on their behalf, our children, or so he always would say. All they really wanted was their father, not what he could buy them or anything like that. All they wanted was his time, it was all I wanted, but he just couldn't see that, no matter how hard we tried. He just couldn't realize," she explained to Dendrox and taking the statue from him went on to say, "This, I suppose, was to somehow make up for all that in his mind, but it doesn't. He was dead to us long before this day, I am sad to say. It was only a matter of time."

Dendrox's thoughts shifted, and he began to have the dream again…

He found himself alone in the dark of night, the moon and stars shining brightly in a cloudless sky. He could see the tombstones all around him and he let out an angry curse, as he knew this dream all too well.

An eerie unnatural mist began to roll along the ground. The fear inside him began to rise, as he knew what would come next and that there wasn't any chance of escape or anywhere to escape to.

He could smell the damp musty smell of the soil, and the cool crisp air chilled his skin. *It all seemed so real and every time he had this dream, he could never bring himself to overcome his fear and realize that this was only a dream and nothing more.* Except for the sound of his heartbeat quickening and his breathing becoming more rapid with fear, there was only silence.

Then he heard a horrible haunting wail from somewhere nearby. There was the faint but distinct sound of crumbling dirt, as a skeletal hand worked its way up from its grave to the surface.

He could see now that there were more rising out of the soil from all around him, escaping their graves, and shambling out of their tombs toward him. Weapons, in the hands of the slain, were being made ready once again as the corpses pulled themselves into life and action in their battered and broken armour.

Dendrox frantically looked all around in a panic for somewhere to run to, as the moaning and wailing horde of bone and rotting flesh began to close in on him.

Then there was something new in his dream.

Weena was here. She was here in the graveyard. They were after her as well. He couldn't protect her! He couldn't save her! She was calling out to him. They were attacking her! He was helpless to do anything!

"Fight back, Weena! Save yourself!" he shouted at her.

"Dendrox! Save me! Help me!" she wailed.

"Run! Run, damn it! Do something! Don't just stand there!" he yelled at her in frustration.

"Dendrox! I'm frightened! Save me!" she called out to him as the undead horrors swarmed her.

"No! No!" he cried out, knocking a skeleton aside, "No! Weena!" He wrenched his arm free from the grasp of one of them, trying to reach her, but there was just too many of them. They held him back.

It was too late to save her. It was too late to save himself, as always within his dream, for they were upon him now. Bony fingers pulled him to the ground, tearing his clothes and clawing into his

<Zaylyn ><Quest For The Sword Fragments And The Hunt For Dranngore ><By Katrina Mandrake-Johnston ><Ch 46> < 105 >

skin. Rusty weapons were thrust into his gut again and again, as they stared with blank lifeless eyes. Dendrox was screaming, but this time, the anger, frustration, and helplessness he felt when it came to Weena was at the root of his fear.

He violently awoke. Candra and Vordin were also awake. "I'm going out to look for her," Dendrox announced to them, straightening his belt of daggers.

"Nodwel, Asdella, Lorenta; they are all searching for her," Candra reminded him, trying to reason with him, "You need to stay here. If she is anywhere to be found, they'll be able to do it. Besides, most likely she'll show up here back at the inn. There's no need for you to risk your life as well with whatever is supposed to be out there. Not on her account. I told her to remain at the inn while we were gone. It's her own fault."

"But…" Dendrox began, and then sat back down upon the bed. Candra was worried about her too, but was clearly more fearful of losing him.

"Nodwel has better night vision than any of us," Vordin commented, "and Lorenta has a heightened awareness of her surroundings. Remember in the tunnels? She was able to detect the other spiders before any of us were, feeling the vibrations of their movements or something like that. And then with Asdella along with them, I'm sure they can handle any danger they come across out there." Vordin then asked himself with worry, "*And if they run into the werewolf? What then?*"

Candra came to sit beside him saying, "She went to the magic shop. We know that much for sure. They said she left in a hurry, as if she had been afraid of something."

"That was hours ago though, she could be anywhere," Dendrox added, "And what about what they said here at the inn? That some nut came in talking about some sort of creatures? It could have been her. Maybe she learnt something about the Killnarin and was trying to warn them."

"Why wouldn't she come up and talk to us then?" asked Candra.

"*The werewolf got her, I just know he did,*" Vordin thought with dread, "*That would explain why she didn't come upstairs. Doing that would have led him right to the rest of us, and Kreasa and her children as well. Maybe if I had been more reluctant to go along with her, she would have reconsidered going back to the house in the first place. We should have stayed together. We should have never separated. When he couldn't get at me, he must have turned on Weena. And now the others are out there with that beast. I suppose it's best for the three of us to remain here. Candra and Dendrox don't know it, but he knows their names now. And then Kreasa and her children, what about them? They are totally unaware that the creature is so close and aware of their location. He probably knows our scent. Me, Weena, Dendrox, Candra; everyone that was at the house, and he already is definitely able to track Kreasa and what's left of her family. At least I know what the man looks like and his name. It was Hoatam or something like that. I hope that is enough to help us.*"

"It's almost morning. We should try to get some sleep while we can. We'll probably have better luck in the daylight," the elf said with a halfhearted smile.

"Go ahead then. I can't bring myself to sleep anymore," Dendrox muttered.

"But you only dozed off for a few moments. You should at least rest," Candra coaxed.

"Take your own advice, Candra. You too, Vordin. I'm staying up in case she returns," he insisted, "I'll be fine. Hopefully the others will return with news."

<World of Zaylyn><Quest For The Sword Fragments And The Hunt For Dranngore><By Katrina Mandrake-Johnston><Ch 47>

CHAPTER 47 = THE EQUIPMENT SHOP

Weena wearily opened her eyes, sunlight spilling onto her face from an open window. Despite the light coming in from outside, the room was dark, and out of the corner of her eye, she could see the glow of a candle flame. Many shelves along the walls were filled with all sorts of items, but she couldn't make out what any of the objects were. This frightened her at first until she realized that it must be the result of the Confusion spell cast on the shops in Shirkint. In the far right corner was a counter, with a glass top and front side, in which there were large peculiar looking weapons displayed.

She felt groggy, as if she had been drugged. She was lying flat on a hard wooden surface of some

<Zaylyn ><Quest For The Sword Fragments And The Hunt For Dranngore><By Katrina Mandrake-Johnston ><Ch 47> < 106 >

sort. It was a bench. She lifted her head to get a better look at her surroundings. A wave of nausea hit her hard with the motion, and she rested her head back down.

"*Where am I?*" she thought, and then said aloud remembering, "The Black Shadow… He attacked me."

"If I were you," a man's voice said from the shadows, "I wouldn't be complaining like that about being attacked, I'd be rejoicing about still being alive."

"Who's there?" Weena asked searching with her eyes in the direction of the voice.

"I'd say you're damn lucky," said the man coming to her side, "You're at the equipment shop, and my name is Balin."

He was an older man, standing a tall six and a half feet. Over a pair of brown pants and shirt, he had on a grey robe that was tied loosely by an orange sash. Having such a broad face and bushy beard, he looked a lot like a dwarf. His skin was heavily tanned to a creamy golden brown and perhaps was his natural color. He was balding and only a fringe of chalky white hair remained around his ears and neck. His eyebrows were like large fuzzy white caterpillars, and they shadowed his kind eyes, as he looked down at her with concern.

"Your friends are here," he went on to tell her, "They've been worried. I found you out in the street. Saw what looked to be a body from out my window. Your friends contacted me this morning as soon as they saw the message I left at the board. I'm amazed you were able to recuperate. The others should be back any minute; they just stepped outside to get some fresh air."

Asdella entered the shop and called out, "She's alive and awake," which brought the others in behind her.

Candra was the first of them to speak to her. "What the hell happened?!" the elf shouted at her, "I told you to stay at the damn inn until we got back! It was safer for you to be there. What the hell were you thinking wandering about all by yourself in the dark?!"

"Well, I probably should have left when he told me to," said Weena, "But I needed answers."

"Who?" Dendrox interrogated coldly.

"The Black Shadow," she told them.

"Let's just forget about all this and go," Nodwel suggested nervously.

Lorenta came to her side, placing a hand ever so gently upon her forehead. "How do you feel?" she asked with concern, "Do you feel all right? You're so chilled and so very pale."

"I feel weak, kind of dizzy," Weena replied, and then realizing, asked, "How are you able to appear like this during the day?"

"The Black Shadow," she answered.

"So what happened?!" Dendrox asked Weena crossly.

"He, ah," Weena said remembering the incredible sensation it had been, "He bit me. He must have healed the wound somehow after he released me."

"Why would he bother with doing that?" wondered Balin, "He wanted you to live? That doesn't sound at all like The Black Shadow. All that fall prey to him are slain."

"Is that really what happened?" Vordin asked her, "After all he's done for us, guiding us in this quest, and he just decides to attack you? He made sure I returned to the tavern in one piece and gave Lorenta full control over her ability to change form. Why would he attack you? Understand that it's just hard to believe."

"*The werewolf… Vordin must have been attacked on his way back. It doesn't look like he told the others though,*" she thought to herself, "*I wonder if he was able to find out anything.*"

"Well, I don't think he meant to," Weena tried to explain.

"You know he's dangerous," Dendrox scolded, "Why would you go looking for trouble? You should be dead right now because of what you did. You better realize how lucky you were."

"*And alone, unconscious, with that werewolf after us… I do know,*" she said to herself solemnly.

Weena expected Asdella to make some sort of remark, as this is what she had been warning her about for days. Instead, Asdella merely said, "Glad you're still with us. Come on, we might as well be off then."

<Zaylyn ><Quest For The Sword Fragments And The Hunt For Dranngore><By Katrina Mandrake-Johnston ><Ch 48> < 107 >

CHAPTER 48 = SCISSORS OF IVORY AND GOLD

Back at the tavern, Dendrox told her, "Stay here and rest. We have some things to tend to."

"We have the Gem of Enarr," Candra told her excitedly, "Dendrox is right, Weena. You need to recuperate. We can handle everything on our own."

"In other words, I'm being rejected," Weena thought bitterly, *"They're basically saying that I'm useless, and they're using the attack as an excuse to get me off their backs. None of them even believe that I was attacked in the first place. They probably think I made it all up to get attention or something like that. Besides, I feel better now, just a bit faint now and then."*

The group left The Old Scabbard Inn, telling her that they would be back around noon to relay anything they discovered. Lorenta had looked so incredibly pleased with her new ability to travel as a human in daylight, that Weena couldn't help but smile.

Weena left the inn shortly after them and searched through the messages on the board until she found what she was looking for. She had noticed that Dendrox had been traveling light this morning, leaving his backpack and pouch behind in the room.

"Stolen, ivory and gold scissors, house number two," she said decisively.

Weena knocked at the door of the bottom house, and a woman, a dwarf, with a round and cheerful face answered it.

"I heard someone talking about a pair of scissors like what you described on the message board. I could easily retrieve them for you. Is there a reward? And do I need to dispose of the one who is in possession of them, as I think that may cause problems where they could otherwise be avoided," Weena said to her in an icy tone.

The woman was astonished at what Weena had just said to her. "Ah, yes, well you certainly know how to go about things it seems. My name is Dooka. Doomair and myself would be much obliged if you could succeed. And your name is?"

"That's not important, now is it?" Weena said coldly.

"Oh, I see," she said, the friendly smile fading from Dooka's face, "Yes, retrieve the scissors and we shall deliver the reward. So far we have lost a fortune because of that theft. You shall be handsomely paid for the return of them, for it will allow for our business to resume once more."

Weena returned to the inn and hurried upstairs. She tried the door that the barkeep had told her that the men of her group had taken as their own. He had also mentioned that it had been The Black Shadow that had paid for it. Weena found it to be locked.

One of the serving girls exited a room a little farther down the hall with an armful of linen. The girl locked the door behind her, and Weena witnessed her placing the key into the pocket of her apron.

"Hello," Weena said pleasantly as she walked towards her.

"Mornin' miss. You the one made the scene last night? If you don't mind me sayin', you look mighty pale," the girl said nervously with a hint of fear, "Are… are you not feelin' well?" she asked shifting the linen onto one arm so she could tuck a loose piece of blonde hair back behind her ear.

"I've felt better, but I'm all right," Weena answered, and then appearing as an act of clumsiness, bumped the girl's arm knocking the linen to the floor. "Oh, I'm so terribly sorry," said Weena, fumbling around with the linen in an attempt to gather it for her.

The girl knelt, a cross look on her tired face, and began collecting the sheets as well.

Weena carefully and quickly knocked the key out of the wide pocket of the apron and maneuvered it down the sleeve of her robes as she released the last bundle into the girl's arms.

"I suggest you be gettin' some rest," she told Weena before descending the stairs into the main room of the tavern below.

Weena unlocked the door to the room and snatched up Dendrox's pouch. She felt around inside and it appeared to be completely empty, but the scissors were still there carefully hidden within the lining. If she hadn't been looking for them, she most likely wouldn't have discovered them. The

<Zaylyn ><Quest For The Sword Fragments And The Hunt For Dranngore><By Katrina Mandrake-Johnston ><Ch 48> < 108 >

scissors weren't very large, fitting easily into the palm of her hand. She concealed them in the folds of her sash as best as she could, and then left the room, relocking the door behind her. Weena tossed the key onto the floor in the general area where the linen had fallen, and then hurried downstairs on her way back to the house.

When she arrived, Weena knocked firmly at the door. It was Dooka that answered the door as before.

"Oh, is something the matter? Have you decided against searching for them?" the dwarf asked a little confused to see her return to her doorstep so soon.

"Do you have the reward?" Weena asked her.

Dooka eyed her suspiciously saying, "We are able to get it, if the scissors are returned to us," and then her voice took on an angry tone as she asked, "Are you trying to discover whether or not we have it here? I tell you, we do not take kindly to thieves, no matter what the damn laws are here!"

"I have the scissors," Weena told her plainly, "I just want to be sure that you are able to hold up on your part of the deal."

"You have them?!" she asked in astonishment, "But how could you possibly, and so quickly? No… no, never mind. Let's see them." Weena, keeping the scissors in her possession, allowed the woman to take a quick glance at the scissors. "That's them!" Dooka said gleefully, "I will fetch your reward."

Weena was left at the doorstep wondering whether or not she were to be presented with a proper reward or by some sort of attack. *"Perhaps the woman has decided that I am the original thief or has realized that I must be somehow connected to the thieves that stole them. What if they send out spies to discover who I have contact with, leading them straight to Dendrox and Candra. Maybe I shouldn't have returned here so quickly. Don't be paranoid, Weena. This will work,"* she told herself, *"And besides, if it doesn't, it's their own fault anyhow… for everything."*

Dooka returned holding a small bag.

"It doesn't look like much," Weena commented, trying to maintain the more aggressive persona she had adopted for this risky attempt.

"Oh, it's not gold, dear; it's jewels," she explained, "They're worth quite a lot, I assure you."

Weena hoped that she wasn't getting cheated after all her efforts, but she accepted the bag and examined the contents. It actually was better this way, as the jewels would be easier to conceal than a large bag of gold.

"Thanks," said Weena, and she headed back to The Old Scabbard Inn.

Once back in her own room at the inn, Weena transferred the jewels into her pouch, removing the doll to do so. She ended up placing the doll just under the leaves of the large bushy potted plant that was in the corner of the room. "It's no apple tree, but hopefully you'll end up at a good home. I unfortunately need the room in my pouch now," she whispered to it before coming to sit upon the edge of the large comfortable bed.

"I did it, didn't I?" she realized in disbelief, *"I'm not as useless as they think I am. I just saved them from ever having to worry about any more bounty hunters. Hey, I guess I was actually sort of a bounty hunter for a short while there, wasn't I? You know, this is ridiculous. I don't need to come pleading for some sort of approval from them. I'm going to wait. Then when they discover the scissors missing, I can see if I receive any real praise before they know that it was me. That will shock them. I can keep this money long enough for that. Besides, Dendrox stole a bunch of money pick pocketing the crowd at the dagger competition. I didn't see him offering up any money toward the group. If we need some, I'll provide, but not until I see whether or not Dendrox is going to offer any up first. And, I also want to find out if these jewels are actually worth something. If I get an opportunity to boast, I don't want them to be able to belittle my triumph by telling me they're fake."*

***

CHAPTER 49 =   WITHIN THE STREETS OF SHIRKINT

The female Black Shadow arose again. It had been awhile since either form had ventured out during the daylight. She let her face be seen, as to have it remain hidden in shadow would have caused unwanted suspicions as to her true identity.

She strolled idly down a street that was bustling with life.

She passed by two people, strangers to each other, having a ridiculous argument over something insanely trivial over by one of the market stalls.

"*The ignorant fool,*" The Black Shadow thought in disgust about one of them, "*Someone in the past made this loathsome man feel inferior, so now he's trying to boost his ego by creating an argument where there clearly isn't one. And it's just about anything that comes to mind. He refuses to hear what the other has to say, even when it's in agreement! The arrogant lowlife, trying to triumph over the other in his invented quarrel and raise his self-esteem by intimidating the other to back down. It's incredibly pathetic really, and it is sad that his display of ignorance and his refusal to listen to logic will bother the other for days, even though the other was not at fault for anything and is clearly a victim of harassment by this egotistical imbecile. It's sickening to watch them sometimes. Do I really want to bring myself down to this level of existence, to be able to interact with the humans and other people of Zaylyn? Degrading my behavior, pretending I don't see through their petty thoughts and actions? And for what? To be berated by fools like this man here, and simply tolerate it? It's hard to see the appeal. What was I thinking before? So blindly striving for this? Is this what I really want? To act this way myself in order to fit in with their masses? Constantly feigning ignorance? Playing along with their little games the people put themselves through? Does this fascination I have simply exist because it is the one thing I cannot have? I can never truly be as one among them. And so, this is what I find myself wanting?*"

Two men were whispering in the shadow of a building. Their conversation was about some secret they thought to be of utmost importance.

"Shh, someone comes this way," one of them said to the other as she passed by.

The other nodded.

"Would you look at her!" the first exclaimed in a whisper, "I wonder who she be, eh? Never seen her 'bout, and I reckon I'd be remembering if I did."

"Such a pretty lass wearin' a hooded cloak like that 'round these parts," the other commented, "Someone should warn her 'bout 'you-know-who', don't you think?"

"Naw, better it be a stranger suffer his wrath than one of us from Shirkint. Just let it be," said the first, "Pity though."

"Yeah, a real shame it is," the other agreed truthfully.

A woman came to stand before her.

"Dear child," she said to The Black Shadow, "do you know not about the vicious beast that plagues our valley, this town in-particular, that abomination which lurks our very streets?"

She just stared plainly back into the woman's face which was twisted with fear and concern with an underlying anguish that had been taking its toll on her clearly for some time.

"The Black Shadow!" the woman almost shouted at her, as if the name alone was self explanatory. When she didn't respond with any sort of visible reaction she added, "Near everyone has been touched in some way or another here by that foul monster. He constantly preys on us. No one is safe. You are dressed in his image. He sees and hears everything, even your very thoughts if he wishes. Wearing that black cloak as you are with the hood drawn up about you is a clear mockery of that creature. He'll strike you down where you stand. Do you not know of him?"

"I know of him," The Black Shadow answered plainly.

"Do you have some sort of death wish, child? Believe me, if so, you do not want to meet your end by his hands," the woman told her.

"If The Black Shadow is all knowing as you say, then would it be so wise to speak ill of him as

<Zaylyn ><Quest For The Sword Fragments And The Hunt For Dranngore><By Katrina Mandrake-Johnston ><Ch 49> < 110 >

you do?" she asked the woman, curious as to what she would reply and also because she was starting to feel very irritated by her hurtful words despite any truth they held.

"I do not care what that beast thinks. Come!" the woman called out angrily to the sky, "Let him take me!" and then she explained to her bitterly, "He has already taken everything from me. He murdered my son… the love of my life. I have nothing left."

She wanted to pry into this woman's mind, the evil wanting to exploit everything possible that might be found within, in order to cause further wickedness and pain for this woman, especially after she had just outright challenged her. But that was the evil inside that wanted this, and it would not have its way. This poor woman knew nothing of true suffering, not the kind The Black Shadow could so easily inflict if he truly wished to do so. *"For those that believe they have nothing, in reality, there is always something more, something else that can bring them further anguish. But then to become this, to torture my victims physically and mentally to such an extent, I would be no better than that horrid monster Hoatam, using the power now begot to him as a werewolf to do further evil. I will not allow myself to be like him,"* The Black Shadow told herself, and she fought the temptation to enter the tormented mind of this woman.

"I shall remove the cloak if it pleases you," she told her coldly.

"Oh bless you, child," she smiled clasping The Black Shadow's gloved hand in hers, "I could not bear to have another suffer as I have, not when I could do something about it."

Then, the woman departed into the congestion of the marketplace.

She already felt exposed, having her face visible to all that looked upon her. A certain sense of security was felt when beneath the hood. Without it, The Black Shadow, in a way, felt vulnerable. Hidden within the cloak, the hood, and the shadowed face, it was as if the person inside weren't part of the monster that was The Black Shadow. It was easier if they couldn't see. He didn't want them to see him. He didn't want to be known for being the horrible creature that he was, but they did need to fear him.

They needed the element of mystery, of having his appearance being unknown to add to that fear. The fear is the only thing that might help them to remain safe. The Black Shadow could so easily discard the cloak and move undetected among them causing all sorts of horrors and mistrust between them. He could not bring himself to do that, no matter how hard the evil pushed him. They needed to know that the black hooded cloak meant danger. They needed to know that they could carry on in their lives and be able to recognize when he was near. *"They need to know that The Black Shadow is not secretly among them. And I realize now that if I walk around pretending to be one of them, and if I am unable to maintain a firm hold over my control, I will be destroying what little peace of mind they have."*

Her emotions boiled within her. The hatred… the incredible frustration… the sadness… the desperation… the anger… until she finally screamed inside her mind, *"I don't want to be that horrid evil thing anymore! I don't want to be alone! I want to feel love! I want to walk among others without fear, and without my own fear of what I might do!"* and she lowered the hood. *"But in pretending that I am not The Black Shadow, I am removing their only recognition of the danger they are in when they are near me. Is that fair to them? But the real question is, do I even care anymore?"* she thought bitterly, *"I could so easily take what I want, anyone I want, and there would be no stopping me. I had allowed my thoughts to become so stale, so indecisive, pathetic and weak. I had lost my zeal for life, the thrill of the hunt. Why should I hold back when it's clear I have no choice in the matter anyhow? Why do I try so hard to resist, and then ponder and berate myself over each individual feeding when I know it will eventually result in myself breaking down. The more I fight it, the harder the fall."*

A handsome young man passed her by, nodding a friendly smile towards her. She could smell the scent of his flesh, the rhythmic pounding of his heart… He was too close. He had no idea that he could cause himself to be in such terrible danger just by simply passing by a pretty woman on the street as he thought he was. Shadow sped on ahead, afraid of what she might do and trying to suppress the rising hunger that he had enticed without even knowing it.

<Zaylyn ><Quest For The Sword Fragments And The Hunt For Dranngore><By Katrina Mandrake-Johnston ><Ch 49> < 111 >

"I did so enjoy annihilating the bandits. They had proven to be such a nuisance as of late. No, the real thing is, that I am glad that it was with them that I lost control and not somewhere like here in Shirkint… It is awful that I began to lose control like that after trying so hard not to kill. I resisted the kill with two of my victims, the thief in the alley at Vackiindmire and Bren, Kreasa's husband, in the wood. And then as a result of that I ended up later viciously taking the lives of eleven bandits. I guess if it had to have happened, it was better that it was the bandits that it happened to. The frightening thing is that the whole time it was the group that I wanted to slaughter most of all, even after becoming so fond of them. It was wise to have not slain the leader myself, or lucky I should say that it didn't come to that. It would have ended very badly, if things had gone that way. Killing with such a purpose other than to merely feed and clearly enjoying it so… Ending the life of the bandit leader would have excited the evil just enough to have risen to the point where it could wriggle out of my weak hold, and then, at that point, no one could have survived my thirst for blood, and I know there could be no telling if I would ever be able to regain control or even want to at that state. My evil desires would reign over all other thoughts. Am I never to have any sort of peace? Am I to destroy everything in my wake until there is nothing left at all?"

She neared the blacksmith's. She could hear the repetitive clang of his hammer against metal, and then after a few moments, there came the sputtering hiss of the metal being cooled. Norick the blacksmith had installed a roof made of metal slats that he could pull down over the open top of the building and attach within. The blacksmith at Vackiindmire had adopted this same design. Norick had done this to protect his shop from thieves, but the main reason behind it was because he believed it could somehow help to stop The Black Shadow from entering. He would lock up and race home every night before dusk. She remembered one time on her way to meet Thorin at the stable, that she had alighted on the metal roof of the blacksmith's, and walked along it, delighting at how terrified Norick had been below.

"I detest what I have become known as. I hate what I am forced to become when the hunger beckons. I loathe The Black Shadow more than anyone. I don't want to be him anymore. The Black Shadow is the monster that preys on others, not me. That creature is what feeds on the people here, not me. It's not who I am, and it's not who I want to be. From now on I am just Shadow. It is what Ezmeara called me, and alone in the stable, it is what Thorin had called me. That is who I am, not that horrible beast that everyone fears. My male self, he could never… would never hurt Ezmeara, not intentionally. He loved her, so much. And even though she never met my side of our being, I considered her the best friend I could ever wish for, just as the male felt the same about my beloved Thorin. It was the foul evil thing that is The Black Shadow that killed Ezmeara, not me… not the real me…" She wept openly, leaning up against the wall of the blacksmith's. *"But it was me… Just as my male and female sides are one, so is the evil an undeniable part. I can't escape. I can never escape. I can never be just Shadow. I will always be that evil creature, no matter how hard I try to separate myself from it. I even attacked Weena. What does that tell me?"*

<World of Zaylyn><Quest For The Sword Fragments And The Hunt For Dranngore><By Katrina Mandrake-Johnston ><Ch 50>

CHAPTER 50 = THE CONFRONTATION

As Shadow wandered along the street back south, she could hear the animals in the southeast corner of town. That was a place she had not been for quite some time. It was run by a kindhearted centaur named Failick. *"Who better to be in care of them than one who is half animal himself? I wonder if the horses even know he is their caretaker. They probably consider him to be one of them. It's from him that acquired my black mare. I let her run freely now, as I could never properly care for her. I remember the one time I brought her to the stable here at Shirkint. That had been a happy time. She had taken a liking to Thorin right away, and come morning, we had to try almost everything to coax her out of her stall to leave. I thought revisiting her, riding her again as I did, would ease the insatiable hunger that was building inside me because I had not killed my last two victims, but it did not work and I still came to slaughter the bandits. I guess I had known I was about to lose my control, otherwise, I would have never set up the ambush by telling Nexzath about who was supposed to be*

<Zaylyn ><Quest For The Sword Fragments And The Hunt For Dranngore><By Katrina Mandrake-Johnston ><Ch 50> < 112 >

riding in that carriage that night. Actually, it would have been the truth had Asdella not caused the need to flee the town. And because I let Weena live, what is to become of that? I will surely kill whomever my next victim is when the need to feed comes. Knowing that, I should perhaps make a decision of who it will be and stay near that person until the hunger takes hold. But then that would technically be murder, wouldn't it? One more thing to grate at my conscious. But that's what I'm trying so desperately to avoid. To wait around, knowing that I'm intending to kill that person, waiting, letting the evil desires build and build. I would lose myself in it. That is the very reason why I am refusing to kill Hoatam, the same reason I will not kill Dranngore, and why I was so frightened that I might end up killing the bandit leader that night."

As Shadow rounded the corner, heading down the street now to eventually pass by the magic shop and then to The Old Scabbard Inn, she noticed the woman that had come to warn her about donning the appearance of The Black Shadow. *"How very ironic,"* she thought to herself with a chuckle, *"I wonder what she would have done if she had known that she was in fact speaking to The Black Shadow the whole time?"*

Her curiosity brought forward an idea. Shadow ducked down behind a building into the shadows, and allowed the cloak, gloves, and boots, to take shape of the male and flow off her form like a liquid-like mass to reform on the ground before her. From out of her own clothing, as she could alter the quantity at will, she expelled enough cloth to take form of the male's.

"Okay, so up you go, and let's see what happens," she said poking at the pile of clothing with a bare foot. She made the pile rise up and take shape, as if The Black Shadow was standing before her. It had no face, but as his face was always hidden in shadow, it would make no difference.

She seated herself so she had a clear view of the street and sent her puppet out to walk toward the woman. *"Would she run in terror? Or stand up to the cause of her sorrow? It is cruel, yes, but I really don't care anymore. Besides, she should have her chance to confront him. It's what she's been wanting. It might do her some good after all,"* Shadow said to herself with a smile, *"And for me to go out there myself wouldn't be wise. It would probably mean her doom."*

The woman turned around to see The Black Shadow standing behind her. A grimace formed on the woman's face, the fury building within her. *"No fear whatsoever, it looks like this is going to be interesting,"* Shadow laughed and then stopped herself realizing that this was not something she should be ridiculing.

"So now even the day is no longer safe from your evil?!" the woman snarled with hatred.

One of the townsfolk who had backed away to the edge of the street with everyone else upon the appearance of The Black Shadow, bravely came forward to pull the woman away from him. She wrenched her arm out of his grasp, and the man turned back to the crowd which was gathering around the woman and the dark figure. No one else had the courage to approach, but everyone was curious as to what would happen. This woman clearly was willing to confront The Black Shadow when no one else was brave enough to stand up to him.

"Are we merely cattle to be slaughtered?!" the woman screamed at the figure.

Shadow spoke forth out of the puppet in her male voice. "To me that's exactly what you are. You are my prey. It is from you that I feed," he said truthfully in his relaxed and melodious tone, which only added to the woman's frustration and hopelessness that such a thing could be said directly to her so matter-of-factly, so calmly and without emotion, "I am trying to see beyond that, taking only the milk and not the meat, so to speak. I do not regard you in the same manner that you tend to regard the animals under your care. No, you are not merely cattle to me. The question is, how do you regard yourself when you take a calf away from its mother."

A contemptuous sneer crept across Shadow's lips. Apparently she did not have as firm a grip over the evil as her male self had achieved. Too long had she been locked away in the mind of her other self, and now all her repressed emotions were surfacing. The woman and her family had a cattle farm, and this had spurred such emotion in the woman, that an evil grin spread across Shadow's face, her fangs elongating to normality and destroying the deception that she had created for her masquerade as a human.

<Zaylyn ><Quest For The Sword Fragments And The Hunt For Dranngore><By Katrina Mandrake-Johnston ><Ch 50> < 113 >

"How dare you try to compare such a thing?!" the woman screamed, to The Black Shadow's delight.

"If its any condolence, I feel for your pain," he answered plainly, and Shadow smiled.

"How can you say such a thing?! You took everything away from me! You're a horrible monster! A demon with no end to the suffering you cause! Die! Die you evil despicable creature!!" the woman screamed, lunging forward and viciously clawing and tearing at The Black Shadow's form in a desperate act of vengeance.

Shadow, coming to her senses, realized, "No, I deserve this. She deserves her revenge."

She let every blow, every lashing, transfer through the puppet to herself, as if she were actually inside the clothing. This woman deserved to have some sort of vengeance, as little as it was. It would not bring back her son, but perhaps it would give her a little peace to attack The Black Shadow in such a way. Shadow felt the pain of her words and of the injuries the woman inflicted on her.

It had been a long time since she allowed someone to physically harm her, and she was thankful that she had separated herself from the confrontation to reduce the chance of retaliation.

Then the ground trembled beneath them. One man shouted at the woman, "You fool! What have you done?!"

Between Shadow's tears she could see that the form of The Black Shadow had collapsed to the ground, now merely a pile of cloth. "What's happening?" she wondered, unaware herself of what was taking place.

The woman fell to the ground writhing in pain.

"What?! No! I didn't want to defend myself! Stop! Stop it!" Shadow shouted at herself.

All the people in the crowd that had gathered suddenly dropped to scream and twitch on the ground in horrendous pain as well. "No!" Shadow screamed at herself, "What am I doing?! I didn't want this! Why can't I stop it?! I'm losing control! Stop it! Stop! Why can't I stop it?!"

She ran out into the street, tears streaming down her face. "I have to help them! They'll die! But what can I do?! I'm the one who's doing this to them!" she cried in desperation, as she stared down at all the people in horror.

"No stop!" she shouted at herself, but it was too late. Everyone in the street was dead.

The clothing that had been her puppet flowed back onto her body. Shadow, keeping the hood lowered, wandered aimlessly down the street passing the magic shop and eventually walking past the Old Scabbard Inn.

"Why do I do things like that?" she asked herself, "How am I supposed to live like this? I can't even make my own decisions. I can't even control my own actions. That didn't even have to do with the hunger. That was the evil inside me coming forward, and it frightens me to know that what happened was just a glimpse of what I am capable of. I thought I had a strong enough hold over it. I guess I was wrong."

<World of Zaylyn><Quest For The Sword Fragments And The Hunt For Dranngore><By Katrina Mandrake-Johnston><Ch 51>

CHAPTER 51 = THE STABLE

Shadow could have merely flown away or magically transported herself to some other location, but she found that she was subconsciously heading toward the stable. Now she stood at the entrance, her hood drawn up about her face, her head lowered, as she wondered what she could possibly gain by being here.

Tekrox was the one working the stable during the day and had been for a few years now. He was Rinna's younger brother by two years, but had not developed the ability to transform into a feline shape as his mother and sister could. He had become a good friend of Thorin's, and their shifts at the stable had often overlapped for about an hour or so each day.

Tekrox, curious as to what she was doing there, said, "Ah, hello. Is there something…"

"No," she told him, "I knew someone here. I was just…"

"I understand," he interrupted, "Another person was taken from here during the night a few weeks back."

<Zaylyn ><Quest For The Sword Fragments And The Hunt For Dranngore><By Katrina Mandrake-Johnston ><Ch 51> < 114 >

A new wave of guilt passed over her, forcing her to look away. "Yes, I know," said Shadow.

Tekrox left her to her thoughts and went farther back into the stable near where the hay was kept. He sat upon an overturned crate and began to cut up an apple into smaller pieces to later treat the horses with.

"After Ezmeara, I thought I would never find any sort of happiness ever again. Then when I found Thorin, it felt like all hope was not lost, that with him I could bring myself to experience love once again. I had enough trouble as it was trying to keep myself from destroying what we had, to keep from harming Thorin as I had Ezmeara. I was succeeding too, and then Hoatam tore him away from me. I was so concerned with my own problems that I never even considered that someone else would claim his life. It's not fair. No, maybe it is fair. I am painfully aware of the vicious irony of it all. I am responsible for causing such sorrow in so many others, that it's only fair I be made to suffer the same. Perhaps it's better this way. If things had been allowed to continue as they were, most likely I would have turned on him as my male half had done with Ezmeara. I don't know if I could deal with being responsible for his death as well. I have the power to bring him back to life, Ezmeara too, but doing so would take the use of more power than I can safely use while trying to maintain control over the evil. They wouldn't want me to become that, to lose the person they had cared for. The evil would rule over my every move. I would not be able to regain my conscience. I cannot be so selfish either. Why should I regain those who have been lost to me while everyone I have hurt is forced to remain grieving."

She went to touch the nose of one of the horses. It would have pleased her to have it nuzzle against the palm of her hand, but the horse gave a frightened whiney as it tried to back away from her in its stall.

Shadow was now wary of drawing any nearer to Tekrox. *"Will I hurt him as well? I don't even know myself anymore. I recognize a few of the same horses from when I used to visit here regularly, but even they now fear me."*

"Out of everyone," she said to Tekrox, needing the conversation as she felt so very alone, "I'd have to say that he was the one who had the greatest positive impact on my life. He saved me from myself, so to speak, when I was at my most self-destructive and weakest point." *"And the consequences of losing myself in continuing down that path would have meant the people of Zaylyn would have eventually felt the full extent of my evil,"* she admitted to herself uneasily. "I just didn't care anymore, not about who I hurt," she went on to tell him, "I did not care about anyone, including myself. Others to me then were merely puppets, and I would pull their little strings to see how they would react. I would laugh at their pain and sorrow, loathe and envy them in their joy. He changed all that. He reminded me of what it was to feel again, that there was more to life than what is given to you. That living is what you make of it. That there will always be something to be pessimistic about and the trick to happiness is that there is always something positive as well, even if it is just that a disheartening event makes it possible for a favorable one to take place later on. Even if the bad simply allows for a better understanding of one's self or the world around them, it ends up being beneficial in a way. He told me a story once, a fairytale really, about a man who went through countless hardships, all of which led to him finally becoming stranded on a small island. This, however, is where he ended up being happiest of all, falling in love with one of the natives and starting a family. If it weren't for all the terrible things that happened, he would have never found his happiness."

"So you've come here to pay your respects?" Tekrox commented, a unnerving suspicion growing in the back of his mind.

"Yes, in a way, I suppose I have," said Shadow, "I think I just needed to be here, to fully remember him and what he taught me, the feelings he stirred in me. Sorry, I didn't mean to carry on so." As she looked at him, she was able to detect a certain wariness that had arisen in him that had clearly not been there before. "You know, don't you?" she asked him.

"I know now who it is you are talking about, yes," he said nervously, "It's Thorin." She could see and sense the incredible fear this realization had brought him.

"And so you know. You know more than you'd like, I suppose," she said to him. He took a step backwards, panic in his eyes. "You were a friend of Thorin's," she said, and he nodded. "It wasn't me.

<Zaylyn ><Quest For The Sword Fragments And The Hunt For Dranngore><By Katrina Mandrake-Johnston ><Ch 51> < 115 >
I was not the one who…" she tried to tell him. She could see that anything she might say wouldn't really make much of a difference in how he felt. "Don't worry, I'm not intending to do you harm. In knowing this, I guess it makes no difference now whether or not you take the nightshift. Might as well, it pays better," she said with a halfhearted smile.

<World of Zaylyn><Quest For The Sword Fragments And The Hunt For Dranngore><By Katrina Mandrake-Johnston><Ch 52>

CHAPTER 52 =   THE HILT OF ANTHROWST'S SWORD

Sensing that everyone in the group was seated at the circular table in the corner of the tavern and awaiting word from The Black Shadow, she walked the short distance back to the inn. Shadow could see that the activity in the street was now back to normal. The bodies were gone. No one seemed to be aware of what had occurred.

"I must have disposed of the evidence and not known it. Now all that's left of those poor people is dust," she thought with remorse.

Drawing everyone's attention elsewhere by simply willing them to look in the other direction, Shadow absorbed her cloak and gloves into her clothing. She then opened the door and stepped into the dark and gloomy tavern.

"I can't live like this," she thought as she inspected the room and the people within.

It had been far too long since she had last entered this place as a woman. Ondaff was just as repulsive as ever. She had made it a priority not to speak to the revolting innkeeper unless in male form, as to avoid the foul man's leering eyes. She also noted that Ondaff and the serving girls had remained on past their shift during the night.

Shadow wondered, *"Perhaps there is some reason why Gulair is not here minding the inn. Or no, I think it might even be late enough into the day for Deckbar to be due for his shift. I wonder if Colex will be coming in from Vackiindmire to work the afternoon as he usually does. Ondaff, no doubt, plans to work these girls all day as well just to ease his curiosity about what The Black Shadow wants with this group of people, doesn't he? I've come to know them as an element of the night. They shouldn't be here during the day; it seems so out of place. But then again, here I am, a known creature of the night, out and about in the daylight. I shouldn't be here. But I can't keep living in fear of my actions, constantly hiding in order to avoid confrontations. I should allow myself to interact with others. I've been depriving myself of the very life I wish to have. And yet, I find myself afraid of being so near to others here. And with what I just did to those people on the street without consciously acting upon it, I'm even more fearful that I might cause something similar to happen here as well. But I can't go hide away, wallowing in self pity, only coming out to feed as if that is all these people are to me. I don't want to go back to that. I've tried so hard to get this far."*

Shadow nervously and meticulously walked into the room, coming slowly nearer to the empty table near the circular one the group was at. She could feel the presence of everyone she passed, feeling the warmth of their bodies, hearing the sound of their heartbeats, catching glimpses into their thoughts. With her hold so weak, she feared she would turn on some unsuspecting wretch and feed uncontrollably, disregarding that her appearance was not hidden beneath her cloak, and not stop until everyone was slain. All it would take was for one of them to catch her interest a little more than the others, drawing her focus down upon them. The evil would push against her will to keep it subdued, and the hunger would intensify until it was unbearable, even giving her increasing waves of excruciating pain within her gut the more she tried to resist, as if it were trying to shake her hold loose, which it always managed to do.

Shadow made it across the room and sat down at the table on the bench-like seat against the wall. She was aware that the group was hoping that by sitting at this corner table that The Black Shadow would show, now that they had the Gem of Enarr.

"This is pointless," Candra breathed heavily, "He obviously only comes out at night."

"There's nothing else we can do," Nodwel told her, "We've been all over this town, talking to pretty much anyone that might be able to help us. All we can do is wait to see what he wants with this gem. This woman you got it from said that Enarr was a necromancer? That can't be good."

<Zaylyn ><Quest For The Sword Fragments And The Hunt For Dranngore><By Katrina Mandrake-Johnston ><Ch 52> < 116 >

Vordin gave Shadow a shy glance, wondering why such an attractive woman had come to sit in the tavern by herself and refuse the offer made to take her order by the serving girl.

"He's supposed to know everything that goes on, right? So he'll just somehow know we're waiting to speak to him?" Dendrox asked with doubt.

"Apparently, yes," answered Nodwel.

"So what spell were you trying to learn, Weena?" asked Lorenta.

"Fireball," she answered.

Asdella grunted saying, "Useless. Nimdor, and with him being an experienced wizard, he cast a fireball right into the face of one of those foul Killnarin. It didn't even faze the creature. The beast just decided to crush him under its foot as if he were nothing. We can forget trying to use magic against the Killnarin, that's for sure."

"It makes sense though," commented Lorenta, "If Dranngore means to take revenge on a guild full of powerful wizards, the Killnarin are a perfect weapon with their resilience to magic."

"Do you think he will come? What if The Black Shadow has given up on us because of what happened to Weena?" Vordin added in.

Asdella said to them, "If he's allowing himself to become more of a monster than a man, we should be thankful that we're on our own in this then. Otherwise, I'm sure Weena won't be his last victim out of our little group, and we wouldn't live very long once he gets started."

"You mean he'll start turning on us as well?" Vordin asked nervously.

"Well sure. Why not? He has obviously lost interest in the quest. It's us he's drawn his attention to now."

"I'm sure that's not true," said Weena.

Twisting her face into a scowl, Asdella snapped viciously at her, "Haven't learnt a damn thing, have you?!"

"No, it's not true," thought Shadow, *"I am here, so close to them now, and I feel no indication that they are in danger. Well, no immediate danger. I can do this. I can be near and control myself. I've been so afraid to try, but if I don't, I'll never know. What would be the point of all I have been striving for, if I never give myself the chance."*

Shadow got up to leave, and as she headed toward the door, she overheard one man sitting at a table ask his companions, "Has anyone seen my brother? He was supposed to meet us here. I'm starting to wonder what could be keeping him."

"Yeah, really?" another man said, passing by them and carrying a frothy mug of ale in each hand as the girls had been too busy to serve them directly to the table, " 'cause now that I think of it, my friend is running kind of late too. He should have been here by now. You don't think somethin' could have happened, do you? You know, somethin' unnatural like?"

"During the day?" the first man asked, a worried look coming over his face as he pondered the possibility.

Shadow exited the inn, trying to ignore the awful feeling of guilt. They would soon get their answer in a few moments anyway. Outside, as she had done before, she averted the eyes of all the people passing by in the street as she changed into the male Black Shadow. His face concealed in darkness beneath the hooded cloak, he pushed open the door with a gloved hand.

Everyone in the tavern stared upon his entry, astonished and also fearful that he had come to walk the streets of Shirkint during the day. He did not want to hear the thoughts of the two men who had lost someone because of what happened out in the street. He would encounter so many others affected by what he had done, and it wouldn't matter that he had tried to stop it from happening. It was his fault. Everything was his fault in some way or another.

Weena commented as he approached their table, "I suppose he doesn't only come out at night."

Candra placed her hand on top of Weena's. Weena had been confused as to why Candra would do such a thing, but then she realized it had been to steady her trembling hand. Weena hadn't even been aware of how much it was affecting her in seeing him again so soon after last night's encounter.

"You going to be okay with this?" Candra whispered with concern in her eyes.

<Zaylyn ><Quest For The Sword Fragments And The Hunt For Dranngore><By Katrina Mandrake-Johnston ><Ch 52> < 117 >

Weena nodded, appreciating the sympathy where she had believed none could be found when it came to the elf.

As The Black Shadow stood before them, Dendrox announced, "We have the gem."

"Then I shall tell you that you will need to find Anthrowst's grave," The Black Shadow explained, "That is where you shall find the hilt of the sword."

"So Anthrowst was a person, someone who forged the sword?" Nodwel tried to clarify, but The Black Shadow was already leaving and clearly ignoring the question.

"After all that, he doesn't even want the gem?!" Candra said in disbelief once the door had shut behind him, "I suppose it was some sort of test. Knowing there's a grave out there somewhere doesn't help us much though. We have no clue as to how to find it. We know the hilt is there or so he tells us, but he could have been more specific. How are we to…"

"I bet Rasindell would know," interrupted Lorenta, "As you can see, The Black Shadow granted me the ability to become human during the day as well. I could go with Vordin to the stage at the town square and hopefully find out what we need to know. He should be there now; from high noon to just before dusk he's supposed to be there."

Nodwel added warily, "I don't like where this is going. It's far too obvious that he's stringing us along in this."

Vordin suggested, "Perhaps he just wants Dranngore and the Killnarin stopped."

Asdella said to them all, "Or did you ever think that perhaps Dranngore is the only thing preventing The Black Shadow from taking over control of those beasts himself? He can't do it directly, so he gets us to do it for him."

"But the sword will undo all the magic Dranngore has cast, including summoning the Killnarin. It will send them back to where they came from," explained Weena.

"And if the Killnarin are not the reason behind his motives?" asked Asdella, "Did you ever consider that? The threat of the Killnarin could just be masking whatever spell he really wants to be undone."

"She has a really good point there," commented Nodwel, "I think we better make looking further into Dranngore's background our priority, find out some of the things he's done in his lifetime before we act. The Killnarin might be the least of our problems depending on this wizard's past. As of now, we know absolutely nothing about him other than a name and his hatred toward the wizard's guild. And we haven't been able to come up with anything but that; no one seems to know anything about Dranngore or even much about the wizard's guild."

"We'll see Rasindell then," said Vordin, "and try to learn as much as we can."

"Hey, listen," said Nodwel, "You two knew him when he was alive, but he's not really a man anymore. Just don't be expecting…" Nodwel sighed not knowing how he could possibly prepare them for what they were about to discover. "You will see for yourselves, I suppose."

**

<World of Zaylyn><Quest For The Sword Fragments And The Hunt For Dranngore><By Katrina Mandrake-Johnston><Ch 53>

CHAPTER 53 = LORENTA AND VORDIN

Vordin and Lorenta left the inn on their way to the town square.

"What do you think we'll find?" Vordin asked her, "Do you think there will be anything left of the man we knew? He might not even recognize us. It may be harder for us to see him like this than we realize. We shouldn't get our hopes up. We can't expect him to…"

"Vordin," she interrupted him, her thoughts clearly somewhere else, "I need to know something. Kiss me."

Completely shocked, Vordin stared at her in disbelief. "What?" he managed to say in confusion, suspecting that perhaps he had heard her wrong.

"A simple little kiss, Vordin. It doesn't have to mean anything. I just need to know something," she explained, stopping him in the middle of the street.

"Well, okay," he told her, "sure," and he boldly drew nearer to do so.

<Zaylyn ><Quest For The Sword Fragments And The Hunt For Dranngore><By Katrina Mandrake-Johnston ><Ch 53> < 118 >

Just before he met her lips, however, the memory of seeing the spider fangs erupting from her cheeks flashed into his mind, and then of their first meeting back at Rasindell's hut when she had been crawling all over his face as the spider.

"No," he said, his voice wavering, "No, I can't," and he took a step back away from her.

"So you see only the spider and not the human part of me," she concluded, "It's what I thought." She looked away, as the sorrow grew within her.

"Well, no, maybe with time. I didn't mean…," Vordin tried to apologize.

"No, it's alright," she attempted to assure him, "I understand. It's what I thought. I just wanted to know for certain. It's what everyone sees, I suppose, even Rasindell to a degree. There's no need to apologize."

Vordin wanted to say something, but he was lost for words. *"What can I possibly say. I can't lie to her; that would make everything even worse. I hate to see her feel this way, and it's not all true. I don't only see the spider, but it's hard to ignore that part completely too. Otherwise, I would have kissed her. I still want to. I was shocked that she had asked me to, and maybe with time I might be able to forget about the spider part of her. Somehow separate the two in my mind. But it had just been a test, and I had failed her terribly in it."*

"We should probably get going," she told him plainly and forced a smile.

Vordin could still see the hurt behind her eyes. "This is the way I went with Nodwel," he told her, "We went up this street here after talking to the centaur at the animal shop on our way to the blacksmith's. The town square should be beyond the marketplace after that."

"Vordin," said Lorenta, a tear escaping her eye, "I went with you and Nodwel. Don't you remember? I was inside the backpack as a spider the whole time. It didn't matter if I was there or not, did it? Here I thought you wanted me along with you two and… You keep saying that I'm part of the group, but I'm not. I'm just this creature that tags along, and no one has the courage to tell me how it really is."

"What? No, Lorenta," Vordin said trying to calm her.

"Out of sight, out of mind," she explained, "That's exactly how it is. I don't matter, because in everyone's eyes, I don't exist. I'm not one of you. I never will be. Even with this new ability The Black Shadow gave me, it makes no difference. I thought things would be different being human during the day and out and about with the rest of you, but it's not. I'm still this monster that no one really wants around."

"Lorenta, I can't speak for the others, but I truthfully consider you a friend. I'm glad that you have stayed with me all this time. In fact, I found myself getting a little frantic when you weren't in the backpack, as it meant I was alone. I don't see you as some sort of monster, please believe me in this," Vordin told her, "I don't know what I would do without you standing by me as you have."

"Really?" said Lorenta, wiping the tear from her cheek.

He took her by the hand and said, "Let's go find Rasindell. We'll find out what we need to know, and then succeed in out quest and become heroes just like in the stories he used to tell us."

"Alright," she said with the beginnings of a smile.

They had continued down the street for awhile in silence, and they had reached the street on which the blacksmith's lay before Lorenta asked, "What does 'happily ever after' mean?"

Vordin replied, "I'm not quite sure what you mean."

"In stories, you know, the princess is rescued by the prince or something like that, and then at the end of the story it's just 'and they lived happily ever after'. How happy can they be if the only story worth telling is that of when they first met and when their love was fresh? There are no stories after, because there is nothing to tell. Shouldn't there be more? If we are to learn about falling in love from these stories, shouldn't there be more about how to keep that love alive? All the stories are about the romance of the first meeting, and all that teaches us is that it is there where all the excitement is and everything after that is dull and uninteresting. Just 'happily ever after'; nothing overly depressing, but nothing worth mentioning either. I've had the same dream twice now, and I'd rather not talk about it. I

<Zaylyn ><Quest For The Sword Fragments And The Hunt For Dranngore><By Katrina Mandrake-Johnston ><Ch 53> < 119 >

just fear that there won't even be a dull 'happily ever after' for me, ever, because of what I am. I guess I'm trying to convince myself that it's not something worth having anyway. Just imagine, if I am to fall in love, that is exactly where it will end, and if there are ugly half-spider children, they will be abandoned with me along with them after my horrible secret is revealed as a result. I don't know, maybe the excitement of the 'happily ever after' is just being saved for another story. But then where are they all? Where are the stories where a husband and wife of twenty years have an adventure with an inspiring romance? If there is a story like that, it's usually because one half of the couple has fallen in love with someone else."

"Lorenta, look around," he told her, "There are many happy couples. I've never seen so much diversity in race here. There are many couples here that have accepted the differences between themselves and found love."

"Yes, but how many are truly happy? 'Happily ever after' sounds so grand, and then when they get to that point, they have no clue of how to adjust. They just become accustom to having the other around and remember that at one time they had exciting passionate feelings for each other, and so they carry on hoping that flame will be somehow rekindled, but it never does."

"Lorenta…" Vordin began.

"Remember that story about the girl who gave so much of herself into each relationship she was in, helping the other to reach his goals, being supportive and paying out of her own pocket to get themselves on their way to a better life? Then as soon as he started to become successful and his life was leading in the right direction, he would leave her. She would be left with nothing. The life she thought she was helping to build was gone and part of her heart had thus withered away. She would be left feeling used up inside, not wanting to start over with a new relationship but at the same time being so determined to be happy and finally have someone to share her life with. She always would have nothing to show for all her efforts. Her money gone, and her hard work all for nothing. This would happen so many times and her heart would break and wither it seemed so often. She was afraid that if and when she did find the perfect man for her, that she would be so used up inside that she wouldn't have anything left of herself to give; that when she finally found the life she wanted, she would be incapable of enjoying it, that only a hollow bitterness would remain. She didn't want to be used by others to get ahead, while she got walked all over and taken advantage of. I don't want that to happen to me, Vordin, and I know it will, or at least something like that. I don't want to be so sad and lifeless like that, and then find the one I'm truly meant to be with, and then have my 'happily ever after' just turn into a dull lonely existence alongside someone who once only long ago had a love for me. Or like the dragon, she didn't even get a boring 'happily ever after'. Her husband, upon discovering her true self, fell to his death. She had to live on knowing that if there had been a way for her to stay with him after that discovery that he would have hated her for it. That's how it will be with me. What kind of life would that be to never be yourself? To have to hide, even from the one you love? I don't want to fall in love and be hated. To be abandoned, knowing his true feelings, and when we have hideous children which look like horrible monsters…"

Lorenta started weeping, and she came to sit on a little wooden stool at one of the stalls in the marketplace. "Is she all right?" the woman at the stall asked.

Vordin nodded, and the woman went back to polishing one of the brass figurines she had on display.

"Hey, hey, where is all this coming from?" said Vordin coaxing her up to continue walking.

When Lorenta had calmed herself a little and they had traveled closer to the town square, he asked, "Is this all because of what happened at Vackiindmire?"

"No, I knew he was a bad choice," she explained, "It just felt nice to be accepted, that's all. To have someone be interested in me, even if it was for the wrong reasons."

"We accept you. We consider you one of us. We're all in this together," he told her once again and this time getting a little irritated with her about this. He thought he saw something that looked like it might be a stage with rows of low benches arranged in a crescent shape in front of it. Vordin now directed Lorenta in that direction.

<Zaylyn ><Quest For The Sword Fragments And The Hunt For Dranngore><By Katrina Mandrake-Johnston ><Ch 53> < 120 >

"Do you really think that? Because somehow I doubt it," she said, a hint of anger showing in her voice, "I disappear into my spider form and then it's like I don't even exist. I've been with all of you since the beginning. Ever since you tried to leave Rasindell's hut without me, I've been there. I've been listening to everything that was happening, all the conversations that went on, but it was as if I wasn't even there. I have to figure out everything on my own secondhand when any decisions are made or information is told to the rest of the group."

Vordin sighed heavily. "Lorenta, you want to know the real truth?" he said to her, "Sometimes I feel as if I'm the one who is just tagging along with the others. That I'm not really contributing anything and that they would probably be better off without me. Yesterday, I learnt that lesson all too well that thinking like that can lead to deadly situations which could have easily been avoided," he explained thinking back to how Weena had convinced him to go with her to the house of the werewolf all in an effort to somehow prove their worthiness to the rest of the group. "You aren't the only one who feels this way. You know, sometimes I think that it wouldn't have even mattered if I had survived my village or not. I feel myself wanting to ask 'What's the point in dragging out the inevitable, when I know we probably are all going to die anyhow?'. But Lorenta, I know not to think like that, and you shouldn't either."

"Vordin, thanks for this. I really needed to have this talk," she told him, "Let's just find Rasindell, okay? I don't want to talk about this anymore."

When they reached the stage, they could see a thin figure wearing a hooded dark grey full-length robe sitting upon a wooden chair in the middle of the platform. Several people were seated on the benches waiting for the next session of storytelling to begin. Lorenta and Vordin also sat within the audience.

"Look at his hand, Vordin!" Lorenta exclaimed in a whisper, "It's nothing but bone. It is just a skeleton beneath that robe. This is not my father. This is not Rasindell. You can clearly see that it is not; that it can't be true."

"I don't know. Let's just wait and see what happens," he told her.

The skeletal figure seemed to come to life and a hollow voice rang out from the bony face beneath the hood. Vordin recognized it as being Rasindell's voice, but it definitely was lacking the edge it had when he was alive.

"A storyteller I be… The spirits, they roam free… Many sights they see… They travel far and wide… Come and listen by my side… Many stories they tell… All of them, I know well… For I, storyteller Rasindell…have yet another story to tell."

***

<World of Zaylyn><Quest For The Sword Fragments And The Hunt For Dranngore><By Katrina Mandrake-Johnston><Ch 54>

CHAPTER 54 = SHADOW RETURNS

The Black Shadow peered over the side of the building from the roof, watching as Vordin and Lorenta left the inn to find Rasindell. He was still pondering whether or not he should go through with what he was planning. Finally, he decided to drop down from the two-story building and absorb the cloak and gloves as his female self had done before. He smoothed back his dark hair and realized how naked he felt without his cloak to wrap about him. He wore only a thin short-sleeved shirt, pants, and leather boots, all of which were black.

He entered the tavern, but was wary about moving any farther into the room. Perhaps he was making a big mistake.

An older man was coming to leave the inn, but as he was passing by Shadow, he stopped, saying, "Same eyes."

"Pardon?" The Black Shadow asked him nervously.

"This woman was just in here. Had the same eyes, such a deep and dark brown they were; almost black. Perhaps you be related somehow?" the man inquired, smiling eagerly with a mouthful of decaying teeth.

<Zaylyn ><Quest For The Sword Fragments And The Hunt For Dranngore><By Katrina Mandrake-Johnston ><Ch 54> < 121 >

Shadow shook his head, wanting this man to leave him alone. He didn't want anything to happen. He wanted to remain in control of himself. He wanted to try to interact with the group. He wanted to pretend he wasn't the horrible monster that he was. He wanted to act and be treated like a normal person.

"Oh, she was a vision of loveliness she was. One I'll never forget. Even in my dreams I could never imagine such a beauty," the old man went on to say. He nudged Shadow in the arm with his elbow. "Look, eh, how practically all the women are swooning over you. Take some advice from an old and single man. Take advantage of your good looks before they wither away," he cackled.

"That's not something that will happen to me," Shadow thought to himself and then told the man, "The true love of one, is far greater a treasure, than to have several passing attractions that never last." The Black Shadow then erased the connection the man had made between his male and female forms and replaced it with a strong acceptance that it had just been a coincidence.

He walked idly up to the counter and ordered a drink. She gave him a friendly smile as she prepared and handed the mug to him. *"She had been so incredibly fearful of me before, knowing who I was. And now, her guard is down, even more so, as it is plain to me that she finds me attractive. I feel as if I am somehow betraying her trust by discarding the appearance of The Black Shadow, as that is their only warning of the danger."* He took a coin from one of his pockets and flipped it onto the countertop.

"So what are we to do then? Just sit here until they return? What if they are unable to find out anything about the sword or about Anthrowst from Rasindell?" asked Candra, "No one else had any luck. What makes you think they'll be able to do any better?"

Dendrox added, "We haven't even considered the possibly that someone else may have already retrieved one or more of the pieces. They could be anywhere, really. If we had found out about the Gem of Enarr from anywhere else, we could have gone on some elaborate quest after the gem just to discover that someone had already beat us to it. The only reason we were able to find it was because we just happened to come in contact with the thief that had retrieved it from wherever it was first hidden away."

"Please don't say that," Weena begged him.

"Well it's true," he explained to her.

"I just don't want to lose hope," Weena told him, "I know how impossible it seems and that there are many factors we aren't even taking into consideration."

This was his opportunity. Shadow stepped forward, coming to sit at the empty table beside theirs as he had done in his female form. "I, ah, heard you mention the name Anthrowst?" he said to them, trying to avoiding the use of the calm melodious tone he often used when speaking as The Black Shadow beneath the hood, and trying to sound as casual as he could. "I know a little about the legend. Can I be of some help?" Shadow offered.

Candra told him bluntly, "Not unless you know where his grave is or about where the pieces of his sword are."

Shadow was beginning to enjoy himself now. With a hint of a smile and staring down into his untouched mug of ale, he said, "Actually, I do happen to know where his grave is said to be. I could take you there," and then he added to make it believable, "for a small fee of course. It is a fair distance from here however."

"No. Classic ploy to lead us into an ambush. It's too easy," Candra said eyeing him suspiciously, "Tell us the location of the grave site, then we'll decide within the next day or so."

This was apparently going to be more difficult than he had first thought. He had come up with an idea of how to introduce himself into the group, but he didn't want to force himself upon them. He wasn't even sure if he could manage to keep them safe when around him. Perhaps this small encounter here within the tavern was enough. He didn't want to push things too far.

"I understand," said Shadow, "If you wish to attempt it on your own, go right ahead. I was planning to head off in that direction myself, and the grave is just slightly out of my way, you see. Just

<Zaylyn ><Quest For The Sword Fragments And The Hunt For Dranngore><By Katrina Mandrake-Johnston ><Ch 54> < 122 >

south of Leekkar there is a trail that will eventually lead you there. If you keep to the left at each junction, you should be able to find it. As for the grave, you'll find the entrance to the crypt at dusk, when the last rays of the sun reflect off its marker. You will see what I mean when you get there."

"Thank-you, we'll look into that then," said Nodwel, "I'm sorry we cannot hire you as our guide, but we have nothing of value to offer. Everything we had is gone."

"I see," he replied, and then making a second attempt he told them, "Well, I'll be traveling alone out that way, and if you don't mind my company? You see, I was going to catch the carriage down to the road to Leekkar and then travel from there. You all are welcome to share the carriage, if you'd like. I'll be heading out in the next few hours."

"There's two more to our party. I doubt there would be enough room. Thank-you for the offer though," Nodwel told him.

No, perhaps I am trying for too much. I should just enjoy the time I have here now," Shadow told himself, and Shadow pulled out a deck of cards, which appeared to have come from his pocket like the coin he had used to pay for his drink. The cards were thin, flat, smooth and flawless pieces of wood with the face of each card burnt into the surface to make each blackened image. "Anyone interested in playing a game with me?" he asked them, although he was expecting a negative reply.

"I will," Weena offered right away to his surprise, and she came to sit at his table.

His face grew flushed, as he remembered how he had been so close to her the night before, his lips against her flesh, the smell of her skin, of how good it had felt to feel the warmth of her body held tightly up against his… and then as his thoughts strayed, the evil inside him swelled remembering… how she had struggled in fear, how her body had grown weak as he drank so deeply, the taste of her blood… "*No!*" he stopped himself as his thoughts were turning dark. That was not what he wanted to remember. It was not what he wanted. He would not let his thoughts become tainted. Not now, not here, not when they were so close, not when he could so easily lose himself, not when he knew that it would start with her. He longed to feel the softness of her skin once more, but he knew that this would only happen if he were to feed again, and that meant she would surely die.

"So, are we playing for money then?" he asked her, trying to focus away from the desires that were starting to surface, "Do you have anything to wager?"

"Well no, we just told you we lost everything," she explained and then thought angrily, "*I have the jewels from returning the scissors, but I'm definitely not going to let Dendrox know that right now.*"

"Just checking," Shadow smiled, "You'd be amazed how many people suddenly come up with money to gamble with when they say they have none to spare at first. So how about I buy you a drink then, and we just play for the sake of doing so?"

Weena suggested, "Why don't I skip the drink and use the money that would have went towards it to play with?"

Dendrox laughed and scoffed, "Do you even know how to play cards?"

"I could get lucky," she told him in defense, and then she added in to test his reaction, "Besides, it's not like we have any other money to put forward toward the group and our quest. I have to try, right?" Dendrox made no sign of guilt whatsoever that he was holding back the money he had made pick pocketing. "*Well at least they were honest about acquiring the gem. They could have just taken off with it, I suppose,*" thought Weena.

Shadow told Weena, "Don't worry, I can teach you. There's no hurry. So what's your name?"

"Weena," she replied, "and yours?"

"Shadow," he said.

"Yeah? Aren't you afraid The Black Shadow might, I don't know, well, take offense or something and come after you with you using such a similar name?" asked Weena.

"Not really," he said with a sly smile, "I've had no problems with using the name so far."

"So with this game, what do I do?" Weena asked, as Shadow idly shuffled the deck.

"Well, there are sixty-three cards in all, and twenty-one different types of cards. So three of each kind. Here," he said handing her the cards, "You might as well familiarize yourself with them." Their hands briefly touched as she accepted them.

<Zaylyn ><Quest For The Sword Fragments And The Hunt For Dranngore><By Katrina Mandrake-Johnston ><Ch 54> < 123 >

With a shy glance she thanked him and proceeded to flip through the deck, but then Shadow realized that ever so often she would look him over out of the corner of her eye.

"The cards are numbered as well," Shadow explained, "Number one is Human, followed by Fire, Bird, Mammal, Reptile, Animal, Wood, Plant, Water, Birth, Dirt, Sea, Air, Force, Stone, Light, Soul, Death, Blood, Bone, and then twenty-one being Life."

"Looks like you know the game pretty well," commented Nodwel with a chuckle.

"Okay, so what then?" asked Weena handing him back the cards. Their hands met once again.

"Candra," said Dendrox getting up from the table, "I think I'm going to take a walk. You want to come with me? There's no sense in sitting around here."

"Well sure," answered Candra, following him to the door, "But it shouldn't take long for Vordin and Lorenta to...," and then she realized that it was because of his feelings for Weena that he wanted to leave.

Shadow continued saying, "The players are dealt nine cards each. Then one player places a card down of their choosing, with a gold piece as it's usually played for money. Then the next player does the same, and the next, and so on. The highest card placed wins the round and all the coins bet and all cards played go into the winner's hand except for the highest card which is discarded. The trick is that you don't have to play a card unless you want to, saving cards until later rounds if a set is not going in your favor. You can only play an equal or higher card than what is displayed. If you cannot play one, or don't wish to, the round goes on without you until a winner for that round is declared. A good strategy is to draw the other players out using smaller cards when you can for a larger win, but in doing so, you also increase your chances of losing an incredible amount if someone has a higher card near the end. Its always good to try to keep track in your mind which cards have already been played in previous rounds. So what do you say? It's actually quite simple."

"I think I have it," answered Weena, "So if I suspect you might have a higher card than me, I can play my highest card right away and only lose a small amount if this is so."

<Zaylyn ><Quest For The Sword Fragments And The Hunt For Dranngore><By Katrina Mandrake-Johnston ><Ch 54> < 124 >

"That's right, but to begin a round, the card played must be ten, which is Birth, or below," he explained, "and all players start a round with nine or more cards, so if someone has less, they pick up new cards until they have a full hand."

"And if you place a card that I am unable to top, you will win the round?" she asked, "It's as simple as that, right?"

"If you cannot play a card, you must put forth a coin into the pile and pick up a new card, then your turn is over and the round continues on as such with the other players until a winner is declared. The number of coins bet on each card can be increased obviously throughout the game as well, but the amount decided upon will stay the same for the duration of a whole round. I'll tell you what," Shadow offered, "If you manage to best me during the first round, I'll pay you what you would have won if you were playing with coin and I'll even buy your two friends here a drink, but you have to play at least two whole games with me after that. Deal?"

"Fine by me," said Asdella, "Don't mind watching the game either, might as well have something to pass the time with until the others return."

Weena inquired, "And by a game you mean what exactly? How is a game ended? For example, can I pull my hand out of the game if say two Life cards are in the discard pile and I know that you have picked up the third into your hand? I cannot possibly win if that happens. I want to know whether or not I will be forced to lose my money until the last card remaining from the deck is drawn up into someone's hand."

"Oh yes, of course, if you're clever enough to watch the cards that well," he chuckled, "You can pull your hand out before a round begins without penalty, but during, you have to place in a coin or whatever amount the bets are set at for the round and pick up a card to end that round as I said before. A game is ended when all cards from the deck are drawn and no one is willing to play forth a round with the cards they have. You catch on quick, and we haven't even begun."

"Thanks," Weena said, feeling herself blush.

"Oh, I should mention that there is an alternate version of the game where all of the cards played in a round are discarded instead of only the top winning card. This is the version usually played when there are only two players, but we'll be playing the original version," he told her, "Myself, I usually play the solitary version."

"And what is that?" Weena inquired.

"Oh, simply three piles of cards with one hand of thirty cards dealt to yourself. Then one card is taken from each pile and placed face up in front of each. From your hand, you then place one card face up to each pile, trying to create a single pile with a highest ranking total. After you have placed your cards, you turn over another card from each pile, and then play from your hand once more, and so on. When all the cards are used, you choose which pile out of the three you think contains the highest added total. If you're right, you win. If not, you lose."

"I see," said Weena.

"Are you sure you two don't want to join in?" Shadow asked Nodwel and Asdella again.

"No, you two go ahead and enjoy yourselves," Nodwel told them, "Asdella, I'm just going to go and check up on Kreasa and her boys. Make sure they're doing all right. I shouldn't be long."

Asdella soon had large mug before her and Weena a small pile of coin.

<World of Zaylyn><Quest For The Sword Fragments And The Hunt For Dranngore><By Katrina Mandrake-Johnston><Ch 55>

CHAPTER 55 =   THE WAY TO ANTHROWST'S GRAVE

***

"The others have been gone quite awhile," Asdella commented.

"Yeah, I'm getting kind of bored with this game," said Weena and then added with a smile, "even though I happen to be winning."

"No, I agree," said Shadow.

<Zaylyn ><Quest For The Sword Fragments And The Hunt For Dranngore><By Katrina Mandrake-Johnston ><Ch 55> < 125 >

Nodwel came down from upstairs asking, "The others not return yet?" He sat back down beside Asdella on the bench at the circular table once again saying, "Kreasa's doing all right. She has a steady head on her shoulders and is dealing with all that has happened as well as is to be expected. She's still a little shaken of course, but she's starting to relax now that she is here."

Candra came back into the tavern alone carrying a rolled up piece of paper. She came to meet them and flattened out the parchment onto the table in front of Asdella and Nodwel. "Weena, come have a look at this," the elf told her.

"Is that a map? Where did you get that from?" Weena asked as she looked it over.

"We stopped over at the equipment shop and Balin let us take a look at his maps," Candra told them.

Shadow thought, "*I see Balin is trying to keep an eye on things too by remaining at the shop beyond what he normally does.*"

"Dendrox was the one who did this," Candra went on to tell them, "He copied out this rough version so we'll have something to follow if we find out any further information. We went up to find Lorenta and Vordin, to see if they had learnt anything from Rasindell, but they didn't find out much from the story he told them. They'll be back along with Dendrox a little later after they pick up a few things. We all added in as much as we could onto this map. Sort of a little record of our adventures so far."

"So Dendrox took the time to draw this?" Weena asked her a little astonished.

"Well, yes, he thought it might help us in our quest," Candra said, furrowing her brow.

"It's just that I hadn't expected…," Weena began and then said, "never mind."

"So, where abouts is this place?" Candra demanded of Shadow.

"It's in the forested area south of Leekkar, I doubt you'd be able to find it on your own though," he explained.

"Yeah, I suspected as much. That's why we've decided to go along with your offer," Candra told Shadow and the rest of them, "We have no other choice, as Lorenta and Vordin came up with nothing except that Anthrowst rescued some outcast troll who he took into his care and became his traveling companion. Apparently the troll was more intelligent that his brethren and questioned their actions, therefore being rejected from the tribe. Anthrowst even taught the creature to speak. So anyway, you are still willing to show us the way to the grave site, right?"

"Sure, it's no problem," answered Shadow, "As I said, I'm heading in that direction anyway."

"And what about transportation?" asked Nodwel, "The horses that draw the carriage were wounded. I'll not have them burdened with eight passengers and I'm sure the carriage driver would not allow such a thing either."

"Why haven't they arranged for a second carriage to make the journey?" asked Weena, "There's certainly a need for it."

"Actually, a new carriage has been built and there are horses that have been made ready to make the journey. All that's left is for them to be hitched to it. The problem is, that no one is willing to take the job. Without anyone willing to become a carriage drriver, there is nothing that can be done with it," Shadow explained and at the same time he sent a message telepathically to Nexzath.

It would be a little suspicious that Nexzath would be conveniently taking a job as a new carriage driver, but Shadow could think of nothing else to convince the group to travel with him. Besides, time was running short, if they had to walk, they might not complete their quest in time. Nexzath had been considering taking this very job anyway, so things were working out perfectly. He would have nothing to worry about traveling through the night, having the protection of The Black Shadow on his side. Vexcindor definitely would become suspicious however, but that couldn't be helped.

Vordin and Lorenta entered the inn, followed by Dendrox. As Nodwel continued to look over the map with discouragement, he gave them a slight nod to acknowledge their arrival. A burlap sack was slung over the thief's shoulder which Weena's attention was immediately drawn to, and she began to wonder what it might contain.

<Zaylyn ><Quest For The Sword Fragments And The Hunt For Dranngore><By Katrina Mandrake-Johnston ><Ch 55> < 127 >

<Zaylyn ><Quest For The Sword Fragments And The Hunt For Dranngore><By Katrina Mandrake-Johnston ><Ch 55> < 128 >

"So you found someone who knows about the grave?" Vordin asked excitedly.

"This fellow here knows it's location. He has offered to take us down, even share his carriage to avoid us the expense, and then show us the way to Anthrowst's grave as he happens to be traveling in the same direction," Nodwel explained.

"Well not all the way," Shadow told them sheepishly, "I do have my own business to attend to. But I'll take you as far as I'm able, direct you along the right path." "*Candra was right in mistrusting me. Not that I'm intending them harm, but I'm appearing far too eager to help them. It's only natural that she would anticipate some sort of ill motive behind my words,*" thought Shadow, "*But as they have nothing else to go on, and I am so far their only lead in finding the grave site, they'll have no choice but to accept my offer.*"

"There are just too many of us for the carriage to accommodate," Nodwel stated, "We appreciate your kindness in wanting to assist us, but we can't ask you to alter your plans on our behalf. We simply cannot ask you to accompany us on foot, delaying and inconveniencing yourself incredibly, and certainly not after you have gone to all the trouble of reserving the carriage for your journey."

"No, wait," said Vordin, "On our way back to the inn, just a few minutes ago, we overheard that a second carriage was being made ready to make a trip down to Vackiindmire."

"Well that's convenient," Asdella grunted, "What are the odds of that?"

"So we are able to take a carriage after all and accept Shadow's offer," said Weena with renewed hope.

"I picked up some food from the market," Dendrox told them, "There's no telling how long it might be until…" he trailed off. It was obvious that he didn't expect any of them to survive this mission. "I ah, got buns sweetened with honey, some sweet and peppery jerked beef, a chunk of cheese which is a little on the tangy side but good, and the apples and carrots I got are really crisp and crunchy. So, we're going with this guy to the grave, huh?"

"*So he bought food with the money he pick pocketed,*" thought Weena, "*Maybe I had misjudged him after all, or maybe it's just because I had said something. But he really does want to save our world in this quest, as do all of us. He could have backed out. I shouldn't blame him for being hesitant. I'm sure we've all had our apprehensions about what's to come.*"

"Let's head out then," suggested Nodwel, "We have enough for the carriage it looks like, right Weena?"

"Oh, yes, I did quite well. There should be enough for the carriage and then some," said Weena speaking of her winnings.

As they were leaving, Asdella unexpected pulled Dendrox aside saying in a hushed voice, "He was letting her win. Either something's amiss, or he's interested in her. I suspect it's the latter. Is this going to be a problem?"

At first Dendrox didn't know what to say. "No, it's fine. I want to get this whole thing over and done with, just like the rest of us."

At the entrance to town, two carriages were waiting just outside. Mantoez was speaking to Koosenor, obviously concerned about the second carriage being operational as the carriage driver was Nexzath.

Weena and Dendrox both recognized Mantoez as being the third carriage driver. His curly hair was an unnatural cherry red, his eyes were bright pink, and he was clearly a member of the fairy folk with all their diversity in sub-races. His short height, not quite reaching four feet, could only be a hindrance when dealing with the horses, and Weena wondered how he was able to manage. Back in Vackiindmire, they had seen him greet Vexcindor and then take over control of the carriage for the morning shift.

"I tell you, I don't like the looks of that one," said Mantoez.

"Mind what you say," warned Koosenor, looking down at the small man, "He'll hear you."

"It's not natural. One should be able to see his face, even with his hood drawn up like that. You know well who this is reminding me of, don't you?" said Mantoez wearing a cross look on his little

<Zaylyn ><Quest For The Sword Fragments And The Hunt For Dranngore><By Katrina Mandrake-Johnston ><Ch 55> < 129 >
round face.

"Exactly why you shouldn't be sayin' anything that might put yourself in danger," replied Koosenor, glancing nervously in Nexzath's direction.

"So I'm just supposed to look the other way?!" he asked angrily, "I shall do no such thing! That man, or whatever he is, is connected somehow to The Black Shadow. What does that say about the safety of the passengers that get into that carriage?"

"There's nothing to be done about it. You know that," Koosenor tried to explain, "The only thing we can do is take extra shifts in order for us to take both carriages safely through to Vackiindmire. I'm sure Vexcindor will make sure anyone desperate enough to travel during the night travels with him instead."

"Extra shifts? Both of us working from dawn to dusk?" Mantoez said not too pleased with the alternative, "Well if that is what it's going to take to ensure that lives are protected, I guess we have no choice. It would only be until we find trustworthy people to take on shifts with the second carriage."

"That will not be an easy thing to do. It's the very reason why the second carriage has so far been delayed from running this long," said Koosenor in dismay.

"Sorry to interrupt," said Shadow as they were clearly ignoring their presence, "I had reserved passage down to Leekkar."

"Yes, that's right," Mantoez nodded to Koosenor, a fierce look upon his face.

"I recognize them from before," Koosenor commented, "You find what you were lookin' for?"

"Hope so," Asdella told him giving a nasty look in Nexzath's direction, "You know about that one?"

"I'd rather not cause any sort of conflict," Koosenor warned.

"I knew it! See, she knows," barked Mantoez, "He's connected somehow to that… that evil thing! The Carriage of Doom it will become known as, it will."

Shadow could feel the sorrow building in Nexzath's heart. *"It wasn't supposed to be this way,"* thought Shadow, *"Things were supposed to get better for Nexzath. He was to hold a job, connect with others in a natural way, not have them shun him because of his odd appearance. Now, because of The Black Shadow, he is becoming even more of an outcast than he was to begin with."*

With a mental apology to Nexzath for causing him further strife, Shadow suggested, "Did you ever think that perhaps that is exactly what he wants you to think? Could it be that The Black Shadow has cursed this poor man into receiving the same treatment he receives himself? The people turning all their hatred for The Black Shadow onto this poor undeserving man?"

To Shadow's dismay, Asdella interjected, "No, he's with that beast, that's for certain. He had joined up with the bandits and then pleaded for his life when The Black Shadow was tearing through their number like paper dolls. He's some sort of disfigured monster and probably made some deal to do The Black Shadow's bidding if he'd cloud his face for him."

It took Shadow a lot of effort, but he was able to remain calm. Perhaps it was because of the occasional glimpse he received now and then that reminded him of Ezmeara that allowed him to tolerate Asdella's harsh words to such an extent. Her hatred of him was just, he could not deny her that.

"That's nonsense," Shadow exclaimed, "Besides, we all can't fit into one carriage. If you are going to reject my help because of some silly superstition, then I'll be happy to carry on alone. There's nothing to worry about. Do you really think there will be some sort of attack in the daylight? We'll be safe. Listen, if it helps matters, I'll take the second carriage."

"I'll come with you," said Weena to Shadow.

"Are you nuts?!" Dendrox shouted at her, "The Black Shadow damn near killed you! You're just going to go off in… He's clearly set this up!"

"I'm not afraid," she said with a scowl, "I can make my own decisions."

"He's worried, I'm sure he didn't mean to yell," Candra explained to her.

"Yes, I'm sorry. I didn't mean to… I just don't want anything to happen to you. Take someone with you for protection then at least," Dendrox pleaded.

<Zaylyn ><Quest For The Sword Fragments And The Hunt For Dranngore><By Katrina Mandrake-Johnston ><Ch 55> < 130 >

"There's no such thing as protection against The Black Shadow," muttered Mantoez grimly, "If that beast wants you dead, you'll be a corpse by morning. There's nothing that can save you."

Dendrox offered, "Weena, I'll come with you then. Maybe…"

"No," Weena snapped at him, "Candra doesn't want me to be helpless. You're worried because you think I am, and you don't want me to get hurt, but what you don't realize is that you're the one who's doing it. Or maybe you do know, and treating me like this makes it easier for you to get rid of me."

Asdella let out a big exasperated groan. "I thought this wasn't going to be a problem," she said narrowing her eyes in Dendrox's direction. "Everyone into the carriages and let's get moving. Enough is enough. Weena, into the second carriage with Shadow, and do it now. I'm coming with you, and so is Vordin. The rest of you into the other, and no arguing."

"Come on, you heard what she said. Time is running short," Nodwel added in, wondering how much longer they actually had and whether or not their time had already run short. *"Lorenta has not received word from the giant spiders since we left Vackiindmire. But does that mean the Killnarin are still underground in the tunnels, or have the spiders been discovered and wiped out before they could get word to Lorenta. Only one of the spiders had made the telepathic connection to her, if that one perishes, we'll be left completely in the dark about the Killnarin's activity. The creatures could well be on their way already,"* Nodwel thought with dread, *"and we are perhaps foolishly still chasing after this damn sword when we could be warning others of the danger, evacuating villages and towns perhaps by sea to safety. But the creatures would eventually spread their evil over our entire world. No one would be safe, not for long."*

<World of Zaylyn><Quest For The Sword Fragments And The Hunt For Dranngore><By Katrina Mandrake-Johnston><Ch 56>

CHAPTER 56 =   THE CARRIAGE TOWARDS LEEKKAR

Nexzath started the carriage in motion after Weena had paid him the fee. Vordin sat opposite Shadow and beside Asdella. Weena found herself becoming more and more attracted to Shadow and was pleased that she had the chance to sit beside him for the journey.

"Why should I feel guilty, or feel any sort of hesitation when it comes to Shadow for that matter? Dendrox has made it clear that he is no longer interested in me. He can't even show me the respect I rightly deserve," thought Weena, *"Shadow is actually interested in what I have to say, appreciates that I am in his company… unlike Dendrox who clearly sees me as a hindrance… just look how he treated me at the house. So what if I didn't know what I was doing, if he had just…"*

Asdella looked Shadow over. He was an incredibly handsome young man. His black hair was combed back away from his face in an appealing way. His smooth youthful skin had a pale and creamy complexion. His inviting dark eyes could hold any woman captivated, definitely making her consider just how wonderful it would be to be kissed by those soft moist lips of his. Shadow's thin black shirt only accentuated the marvelous shape of his upper body. Although it wasn't all that muscular, it could easily entice a woman's interest.

Weena's stomach gurgled loudly. "Sorry, I haven't eaten since yesterday, or no, the day before that, when… when Nexzath had given us the money from The Black Shadow."

Asdella told her, "Kreasa bought us dinner and breakfast when she realized Nodwel had given her everything we had. We would have gotten you a meal too had you not been at the magic shop learning a spell. Nimdor, the magic user of our group, would spend days with his nose in a book at whatever town we were in and that had a new spell for him to learn. He wouldn't eat or sleep on account of some process, we wouldn't even be allowed to talk to him for fear of him losing his concentration. So we all just assumed you were doing the same and thought nothing of it when you didn't return for the night. It was Dendrox that eventually suggested that we go to check on you. Me, Nodwel, and Lorenta were up half the night after that, roaming the streets in search for you. The Black Shadow apparently had just left you out in the open after he had done what he did to you." Asdella glanced over to Shadow at this.

"Perhaps she suspects more than I would like," Shadow thought nervously.

"Anything could have happened to you, Weena, out there in that helpless state," continued

<Zaylyn ><Quest For The Sword Fragments And The Hunt For Dranngore><By Katrina Mandrake-Johnston ><Ch 56> < 131 >

Asdella, "If it hadn't been for Balin, you could have been left to all sorts of danger."

Ashamed of himself, Shadow realized that this was true.

"We had eaten before discovering where you were at the equipment shop," Asdella explained to her, "You should have said something, I'm sure we could have gotten you some food. After such a thing, you should have eaten to help bring your strength back."

"Too bad the bag of food Dendrox got for the trip is in the other carriage," commented Vordin.

"*I could get her something to eat from Shirkint or maybe even Torrnell,*" considered Shadow, "*But if I just happen to come up with a piece of fruit or something out of nowhere… I can't really explain to them that I just happen to be able to transport objects from one place to another instantly. That would arouse too many questions, far too many, as in why don't I just draw in the pieces of the sword from their resting places, meld the sword and its spell together, and transport it and their whole group right to Dranngore. I could maybe get something to Nexzath and then… No, I'm not reading their minds, but I think I know what Asdella is up to. She's trying to discover if what she suspects is true. The name I'm using, Nexzath's involvement, the convenience of the second carriage, possibly the way I was looking at Weena earlier… Asdella knows the guilt I feel, and how it would be the same because of Weena. She's looking for another clue. But once she gets it, then what? Part of me wants them to know the truth. I haven't done anything in order to deceive them except remove my cloak… and hide my fangs in human appearance.*"

"Shadow, I was wondering," Asdella said with the faintest hint of a smile, "you're rather pale, what kind of work do you do? From what I've heard, most of the jobs in Leekkar have to do with the ships coming to the valley for supplies and things like that. You know, ship repairs, transferring goods by boat to the larger ships out in the Ordore'effont Sea, and the like."

His hesitation was enough to give her what she wanted. "Well, I go about my business usually at night, so I don't get much sun, I suppose. I'm actually just running an errand out to Leekkar. I'm usually situated at Shirkint." "*I didn't lie to them,*" thought Shadow, "*but it looks like Asdella is counting on that. I wonder if Ezmeara had told her about that, of how I will never lie unless I absolutely feel the need to.*"

"And what is it you do at Shirkint then?" Asdella interrogated.

Again Shadow hesitated just enough to satisfy her curiosity. "Well, I'm one of those town protectors," he said weakly. "*My victims are usually up to no good in the middle of the night… and most of the time I'm trying to protect the town from myself, so in a way it's true, I guess.*"

With a slight grunt Asdella commented, "Funny, you don't look the part."

"Well, appearances can be deceiving," he answered a little too firmly. "*Damn it, I knew all this would make me say something like that! I might as well just announce out loud exactly who I am!*" "I manage well enough," he added, "Usually, a town protector just patrols the streets at night and reports what they see. The ones that try to handle what's going on by themselves and alone, usually end up a victim themselves."

"Looks like we'll be there soon," commented Vordin, "We have to walk the rest of the way, don't we? Once we get to the road leading to Leekkar?"

"Yes, the carriage doesn't travel to the villages. Perhaps now that there is a second carriage that can be rectified. There used to be one a few years back that made the trip back and forth between them as well as an occasional trip to the towns, but not anymore. Right now the carriage makes but two trips per day, and as it's a long journey, the hours and location of departure vary as well as the drivers. Mantoez and Koosenor tend to try their best to avoid traveling after dark as much as they can and tend to work alternating days in order to do it, where Vexcindor is the only one that will venture out during the night with the carriage. I find that traveling by carriage usually cuts about a third off the time it would take to walk it, well if you're walking at quite a brisk pace. It's about a nine hour ride between the towns," Shadow told them.

"So roughly how long is it going to take us to get to Leekkar then?" Vordin asked him.

"I'd say it's about a five hour walk to Leekkar from the main road, but it will only take us about four to where we will need to be heading into the forest and then it's a fair distance after that to where

<World of Zaylyn><Quest For The Sword Fragments And The Hunt For Dranngore><By Katrina Mandrake-Johnston><Ch 57>

CHAPTER 57 =   ON FOOT TO THE GRAVE SITE PATH

When the carriages had stopped at the junction leading to Leekkar, the passengers continued their journey on foot. Shadow explained that it was a fair distance to where they were headed, but he would let them know when they were near.

Weena purposely lagged behind to walk with Shadow. At first she was delighted, and he returned her flirtatious smiles, but after awhile she began to feel uneasy.

I don't know what it is. I feel nervous around him for some reason. As if something isn't quite right, but I just don't know why. There's just something about him. Maybe it's the way he looks at me sometimes. Most of the time all I see is kindness in his eyes, but ever so often I'll catch a glimpse of something… something almost sinister. I'm sure it's nothing. I'd rather not be caught completely alone in the same place with him though. Perhaps I'm just being foolish, letting my imagination run wild. Maybe it's just because it all seems too good to be true, and for him to show an interest in me over the others, maybe I'm just looking for something to be wrong with it.

"It's just a natural instinct," Shadow told her.

Confused as to what he was talking about, she asked, "What is?"

"The anxiousness you feel," Shadow explained, "It's a natural instinct. It's the fear that the prey feels when it senses the presence of a predator." The corner of his mouth turned up in the beginnings of a wicked smile, exposing the tip of a fang.

Weena could hardly believe her eyes. "It's you!" she whispered in astonishment.

Shadow told her, "I can alter your mind so you forget what you have just discovered, but I do not want to do that. It is better for you to be aware of it and know to be wary. Perhaps it would be wise not say anything to the others."

"No, I won't say anything," Weena assured him, "but I have to know, are we in danger from you?"

"I hope not," he said sincerely, "It would be nice to be able to talk and interact with people without them fleeing in terror. Maybe even have someone I can consider a friend."

"Oh… ah…" Weena fumbled, lost for words. She was still having a hard time visualizing him and the dreaded Black Shadow as being the same. She would have never expected that this young man beside her could have been beneath the hooded cloak. The two didn't connect properly in her mind. She kept trying to imagine Shadow doing the horrible things he had done to the bandits right before her eyes and it just didn't seem possible. *Could he truly be a slave to his own evil? The hunger turning him into something terrible? How can he fight something like that? But he had fought against those evil desires last night when he had held me tightly in his arms. Part of him wanted to kill me, to do to me what he had done to the bandits, but he had managed to hold back in order to spare my life.*

"If you think it best for me to leave, I shall do so. I do not wish to place any of you in danger because of my presence. If you feel you need to warn the others, do so. I will not stop you," he explained.

"And what of the sword piece?" Weena questioned, "If I let the others know the truth, how are we to find it?"

"I will show you the way regardless. I did not mean to pose a threat, or force you to accept me into your group for a short while in exchange for the grave's location," he assured her, and with a halfhearted smile he added, "It was nice to be treated like a normal person, even though it was brief. Please try to understand, Weena, I did not intend to do you harm that night. If I had full control over my actions, I would have never… things, well, they could have been different."

What does he mean that things could be different? Weena wondered, *Is it wrong to admit how good it had felt to be in his arms despite the danger? To be desired so fully? And to know now who he is and what he is… what he is capable of… it just doesn't seem real to look at him now. All I see now is someone so… When I compare how I felt about Dendrox… To think of Shadow now, to remember his touch, how he had wanted to be close, his cheek upon mine, his lips against my skin… to*

<Zaylyn ><Quest For The Sword Fragments And The Hunt For Dranngore><By Katrina Mandrake-Johnston ><Ch 57> < 133 >

imagine what it could have…" She looked away with embarrassment. *"He can hear my thoughts, can't he?"*

Shadow gave a shy smile at this. "We should, ah," and he couldn't help the awkward grin spreading across his lips, "We should probably catch up to the others."

As she nodded in agreement, Shadow thought with a growing dread, *"I desperately hope that what I'm feeling, my attraction to her, is not a result of the evil manipulating its way through in order to finish what it had started. I don't want her to die, not like that. I could have killed her. I almost did. I know there is a strong danger and a very good chance things could go very, very badly, but I don't want to run because of it. I don't want to leave. I want to stay. I haven't felt this happy, this free of myself, for a long time."*

They quickened their pace to join that of the rest of the group.

<World of Zaylyn><Quest For The Sword Fragments And The Hunt For Dranngore><By Katrina Mandrake-Johnston><Ch 58>

CHAPTER 58 = THE BLACK SHADOW QUESTIONED

"So where did the name come from anyhow? The Black Shadow?" Vordin wondered aloud.

"I believe it originates back quite a ways and is all the people could describe him as, as there was nothing else like him, still isn't." said Shadow.

"Yeah, I suppose," Vordin agreed, "Have you heard much about him? I mean, where he came from?"

"I don't think even he knows that," Shadow told him truthfully, "But the name arose because he appeared to be most like a shadow, whether it was through the air, across land, or arising out of the shadows to ensnare his prey from behind. Keep in mind that the language was more primitive back then as well. For him, he was described mostly as things like Evil Shadow, Shadow of Death, Demon Shadow, and so on and so on. I suppose then, out of fear, they started to choose their words more carefully when speaking about him and things like Dark Shadow, Shadow of Night, and Black Shadow started to be used more regularly. The Black Shadow was the one that remained more prominent over the centuries."

"What I want to know," said Asdella bitterly, "is whether he has any weaknesses," and then she said to herself, *"Other than his hunger, but I'd hardly call that a 'weakness'. Ezzy, you damn fool."*

"I don't think he has any. If he were vulnerable to anything, it would definitely come as a surprise to him," answered Shadow, "One thing I do know for certain, is that he never lies. He doesn't need to, as with him the truth tends to be far more frightening than any lie could be."

Candra chuckled saying, "Great, so we ask The Black Shadow if he eventually is going to kill us, and he replies honestly that yes he is, and since we can't really do anything about it, how is this going to help us?"

"He won't lie to us. That's a good thing to know. It really is," said Weena, "This way we can take what he says to be genuine at least." Knowing this, helped to relieve a lot of the fear Weena had been feeling surrounding what had been said to her and also about the sword. She had been dreading that there might be some horrible betrayal on his part at the end of their quest.

Nodwel interjected, "Yes, but I'm sure he'd be sure to leave out just enough of something to have the same effect. Like a damn riddle, if we had only looked a little deeper, we would have discovered the real truth as it had always been there cleverly disguised. His honesty just adds a little more irony to our foolishness and ultimate demise."

Shadow thought to himself, *"Weena, if you were to ask me here and now in front of everyone if I were The Black Shadow, I would say it were so, or say nothing at all, but I would never say otherwise. I know you are aware of this, and yet you make no move to reveal me as such and have no inclination to warn the others of my presence... And it seems neither does Asdella."*

Asdella thought, *"And if he is truly that ancient and is to carry on through the ages to come, what did he want with my cousin? Was he to turn her into some undying monster to stand by his side for eternity?"*

"It's never come to that," thought Shadow, aware of what Asdella was thinking, *"I've never had to*

<Zaylyn ><Quest For The Sword Fragments And The Hunt For Dranngore><By Katrina Mandrake-Johnston ><Ch 58> < 134 >

consider what would come to be. I keep telling myself, that, if I found love, I would cause myself to age with her until her final days, and then unable to pass on in such a manner, I would simply renew my body and carry on as if starting a new life."

He looked to Asdella. Her hatred of The Black Shadow was growing in her, more so now that he had come to walk among them.

"*It would be so very wrong to have denied Ezmeara a natural course of life. It would have been selfish and she would have certainly gone mad. Living forever sounds appealing, but for her to watch all her loved ones, friends and family, grow and change in personality, growing old and dying, while she stayed the same, and with the world around her that she had come to know and understand changing so drastically over time... She might have been able to adapt, but not forever. A few hundred years perhaps, but not forever. Even considering that her family might have somehow come to accept her strange condition of surpassing time, she would have eventually become estranged from her family, and even more so as the generations passing her by increased. And of course there would be the unfavorable connection to me. For us to assume our relationship would have lasted eternally is absurd, the love perhaps could have, but not the spark. We would have become like two members of a family in caring for each other, but not a couple. She however, would have been trapped in the existence I would have given her and forced to watch anyone she falls in love with, wither away while she remained the same. One is meant to watch over their family in spirit form when the time comes to do so, not in body. I know that to deny her eternal life, even if she came to beg for it, that it would have been the right thing to do. But would I have done this? Would I have simply let her live out her life as nature intended? She would have eventually wanted more than I could have given her anyway. She would have eventually craved the normality of everyday life. I know that I probably would have had to let her go long before age took its toll.*"

Aware of how Dendrox felt about Weena, he looked to him thinking, "*But to have love even for a short while, even if it is simply giving it a chance to fizzle out if it is truly destined to, it would be worth it. What is the point of giving up before it even begins, not allowing for the chance that the love may grow? With the right person, love can be achieved eternal, two soul mates coming together. Love is the one thing in life where the expected is not always so. In the end, love and family, the influence you have on others, that is the only thing you can carry with you into spirit form, and therefore the most important part of life. But who am I trying to fool? I've proven time and time again that I am unable to abstain from feeding, that the hunger rules over everything... even love.*"

"Shadow? Are you all right?" asked Weena a little nervously, as he had become distant in his thoughts. Weena feared it may be a sign that the group was in danger.

"So what is he then, some sort of vampire?" asked Lorenta.

"There were vampires once that came to the valley," Shadow told them, "Because of their skin's sensitivity to sunlight, and because the valley is almost completely cast in shadow because of the rock formations, it was sought out by several clans. You'd never know it, because of the magic allowing the light in and for the vegetation and life to thrive as it does, but Dee'ellkka Valley is actually in reality pretty much cast in shadow all the time beneath that magic."

"The Black Shadow mentioned it once, or perhaps I heard it elsewhere," said Vordin, "but he's supposed to be the cause of that."

"Not many are aware of how extensive his influence over the valley is," commented Shadow.

"Well yeah, why wouldn't he want to make this place as appealing as he can?" Asdella scoffed, "This is his own personal feeding ground by the sounds of it."

"*They all know. They are pretending to be unaware, but I do not have to read their minds to know they have figured out the obvious. I did not want to fool them in the first place. It has always been me, I have simply removed my cloak. I am glad that they have not decided to shun me. However, it is most likely because they fear the loss of the grave's location if I leave them. I do not mind their interrogations, I have nothing to hide from them.*"

Shadow replied, trying to keep his tone as calm as possible despite her hurtful words, "I'm sure that's not the reason behind it," and then after a moment's hesitation continued to tell them, "Anyway,

<Zaylyn ><Quest For The Sword Fragments And The Hunt For Dranngore><By Katrina Mandrake-Johnston ><Ch 58> < 135 >
The Black Shadow ended up destroying the vampires that had sought to inhabit the valley."

Asdella interrupted again with the remark, "There, you see, that just proves my point. He couldn't stand to have competition invading his little haven. It was lucky for the people here though, him giving them just one predator to have to deal with instead of many. Although I think they'd be better off dealing with the vampires instead of that beast The Black Shadow. At least with the vampires they would have some chance of defending themselves, have methods of protecting themselves against an attack, hell, even the chance of slaying a vampire. With The Black Shadow there's no hope. He decides who lives or dies. No one is safe; always living in fear."

"Asdella," Nodwel warned in a firm and commanding tone, "I think you've said enough. We all know what The Black Shadow is about. Do you really want to anger him, wherever he is, knowing what he can do to us? So far, he's been helping us on this quest, so let's just keep it that way."

"Yeah, that's what he wants you to believe," snarled Asdella, "And what about the attack on Weena? How did that help us, dwarf?" she sneered, "You'd be singing a different tune if she were dead now, wouldn't you?"

The tension was prominent on the dwarf's brow as he said, "I'd be telling you exactly the same thing, trying to keep the number of our group from declining any further. And it is simply a matter of someone keeping her temper and loose tongue in check."

"Fine, you were saying," she snapped at Shadow with a fierce scowl upon her face.

He had an awful feeling inside. He wanted to bring forth his cloak and wrap it tightly about him, to draw up his hood and escape into himself, but he continued to tell the story. "Maybe it was because when he looked upon the vampires, he saw a little too much of his own monster within himself. He had tolerated their actions for awhile, but with their constant lack of remorse, turning vast numbers of innocents into blood-thirsty creatures like themselves with no concern for the consequences..."

"Like depleting the food supply. Us humans only breed so fast," Asdella remarked with a dry laugh, narrowing her eyes at him with a fierce hatred.

"Asdella," Nodwel warned, once again shooting her an icy glare.

Shadow choked back the emotion that was welling inside him and tried to finish what he had been telling them. "He eventually was forced to take action against them. It was either that or let them spread like some infectious disease across Zaylyn. But in the thrill of the hunt and the killing of those vampires that posed a threat to Zaylyn, The Black Shadow could not stop. Not all the vampires had become a menace; many of them had chosen to feed upon the livestock instead and were trying to peacefully co-exist with the people of Dee'ellkka Valley. Many of them had even called The Black Shadow friend, but he eventually slew them all, and only afterward came to realize what he had done."

"Figures," Asdella commented with a cruel laugh.

Shadow wanted to viciously lash out at her, but her thoughts were filled with the memory of Ezmeara and what had eventually happened to her because he couldn't maintain control over himself. He quickly composed himself, but he began to realize how incredibly painful being around them was going to be for him.

Asdella unexpectedly raised her sword and lunged at Shadow. *Should I let her strike? Allow her to wound me? Look what happened to the people in the street at Shirkint. But for her to strike me, and there to be no injury...*

Shadow smacked the blade aside with his palm as he jumped backwards into a crouch, ready to strike, a low growl rumbling deep in his throat, daring her to approach, his eyes flashing red, his fangs exposed... He was a creature of instinct, and she knew it. A satisfied grin was displayed on the warrior woman's face.

"Is it much farther to the site, Shadow?" she asked in a condescending way.

Shadow, resuming his former appearance and seeing that the others were choosing to ignore what they had just seen, answered, "Not much more, we will be entering the forest soon."

<World of Zaylyn><Quest For The Sword Fragments And The Hunt For Dranngore><By Katrina Mandrake-Johnston><Ch 59>

CHAPTER 59 =   THE FOREST TRAIL

<Zaylyn ><Quest For The Sword Fragments And The Hunt For Dranngore><By Katrina Mandrake-Johnston ><Ch 59> < 136 >

Shadow led the seven of them closer to Leekkar and then headed south into the tree line.

"I don't see any sort of trail. This is the way?" Nodwel asked warily.

Shadow sighed heavily, "If I wanted to harm you, I wouldn't have to bring you all the way out here. I could brutally slaughter all of you from halfway across our world with a single thought if I wished it. I assure you, this is the way to the trail which will eventually take you to the grave."

"And if he's taking us somewhere to feed to some other horrid monster?" Candra whispered to Dendrox, "He didn't exactly specify whose grave he was talking about just now."

Shadow ignored her remark and continued into the trees with the group following reluctantly.

After some distance, they came to an area of trail where five tree stumps had been cut to create seats, each one having a back and armrests. The words 'Rest here, weary traveler' were carved into the trunk of a large tree behind them.

Shadow sat down in one of the seats saying, "I thought this would be the perfect spot to rest for awhile before continuing on, well that is, if you want to." He told himself, "*I have to make it a point not to read their minds, no matter how tempting, otherwise, I won't be allowing myself to experience what they do.*"

"No, this is fine," said Nodwel, "Why don't we have something to eat. Dendrox?"

"Yeah, sure. Who wants what?" asked Dendrox sitting down on the middle stump and opening up the bag.

As Dendrox went about handing out the food, he was surprised to hear Shadow's voice ask, "Is there any of the jerked beef left? If so, I'd like a piece."

He looked up from the bag to see Shadow standing before him. "Ah, yeah, sure. It's just, I didn't think you'd eat, well, food," Dendrox said handing him the meat.

Shadow came to lean up against the thick moss-covered trunk of a nearby tree across from where Weena had seated herself next to Candra. Asdella stood at the opposite side of the five seats glowering at him from behind the end seat where Nodwel was seated. She never let her eyes stray from where Shadow stood, as she occasionally chewed a mouthful from her honey roll.

Lorenta was perched on the armrest of the stump Vordin was seated on next to Nodwel and Asdella. Lorenta gave Shadow the occasional glance now and then to the point where Shadow started to wonder what it was that she could be thinking about, but he didn't intrude into her mind.

"*He is the one responsible for my being created,*" thought Lorenta, "*He even saved Rasindell all those years ago from a Killnarin. It's hard to believe. He has such immense power, and to look upon him now, it's unimaginable.*"

Shadow gradually mustered up enough courage to ask Weena. He took another bite of the dried beef, enjoying its peppery taste, and despite his nervousness, tried to ask her in a nonchalant way, "Hey Weena, I'm going to take a walk around the surrounding area. Do you want to come with me?"

Candra whispered to Dendrox, "She most likely doesn't have a choice in the matter. Just stay calm."

"And who's to say if she will even come back?!" he said to her in a hushed voice with fear, "And if she does, will she still be the same, or return as something else, something like him?"

Shadow's dark eyes looked Weena over, awaiting her reply, as he continued to stand against the tree with his arms folded in front of him. His boots, pants, and short-sleeved shirt were of the purest black, as was his hair, and it contrasted the pale flawless skin of his arms and face. Shadow definitely had a certain dark appeal to him.

"*When he looks at me, it's like I get an excited quiver in my gut, my heart goes all aflutter,*" Weena thought a little nervously, "*First Dendrox, a thief, and now this, the worst choice I could ever possibly make? What is the matter with me? Do I have no sense at all?*"

"Weena?" he asked again, his voice as soothing and inviting as always.

"Yes, sure, of course," she answered him, despite her better judgment.

The others looked to her with worry, but dared not say anything against it.

The two of them wandered into the woods, getting farther and farther away from the others.

<Zaylyn ><Quest For The Sword Fragments And The Hunt For Dranngore><By Katrina Mandrake-Johnston ><Ch 59> < 137 >

He seemed unaffected by the chill breezes that passed over them. The warmer days had finally given way for the colder ones it seemed. The leaves, having turned vibrant colors of red, yellow, and orange, had only recently begun their descent to the ground. This part of the forest appeared to be mostly oak and birch, unlike the western majority being pine and cedar. She gazed longingly at him, almost entranced.

"He's so incredibly handsome, but it's more than just that… and then that night… the touch of his cheek against mine, his lips against my skin… he hadn't meant to…" she thought, and then shuddered as she remembered how his fangs had bitten so deeply into her flesh and the horrible panic and fear for her life she had felt…and she also remembered the incredible passion and longing he had, the waves of pain being turned into pleasure… *"I could have died, but it was my fault really. If I had only stayed away when he had warned me to. It couldn't have been merely about him feeding from me; it was more than that. He could have killed me, but he didn't. It wasn't a painful and vicious attack upon me… I had such a longing, such a desire for him in that embrace… had he not been draining the life out of me, I…"*

Shadow was trying to come up with something to say. He hadn't expected Weena to agree to come with him like this.

Weena stopped him by gently taking hold of his hand. His heart quickened. *"What is she doing?"*

It felt wonderful; the warmth of her hand in his. He wanted to hold her close to him, but he was so very afraid.

Then to his surprise, it was she that drew in nearer and pressed her lips up against his. Her breath was hot upon his face, her lips soft and moist. Her hand ran down the curve of his back as she held him tight against her body. She felt incredible, and as he kissed her, he tried desperately not to let the hunger surface.

"What is she doing?!" he asked himself, *"She knows about the danger!"* but he continued to hug her closely, not wanting to let go.

Without even being aware of it, he slipped into her mind.

"If I'm going to die," Weena thought, her heart breaking with sadness, *"I'd rather have it like this now than later by one of Dranngore's spells or a Killnarin."*

Shadow released her, backing away from her, a pained look on his face.

"What's wrong?" she asked him, moving closer.

"No, please don't," he told her, "Stay away."

"I'm not afraid," she told him, attempting to kiss him once more.

"No, I know what you are trying to do. Please don't," he told her, his voice filled with sorrow.

"Then why are you doing this?! Why string us along like this?! Just destroy Dranngore and the Killnarin yourself! You have the power to do so! Why involve us?! Why endanger our lives?! Tell me why!" she demanded of him, "You're the only one that can mend the sword and its spell. You clearly know exactly where the pieces of the sword are. Why all of this? You can do anything you want! We are like ants beneath your boot! Why do you insist on torturing us?!"

"I don't want to hurt anyone," he tried to explain, "The more I try to stop myself, the worse the repercussions are."

"But why do you insist on attacking people? Why can't you just feed from livestock like those other vampires you spoke of?" she asked him.

"Because I'm not a vampire. I'm something else. Even I don't understand exactly what. And of course I've tried every other alternative there is. There is no escaping. All I know for certain is, that I don't want to be a horrible evil monster anymore, feared and hated by everyone. I am always in fear of what I might do, and I will always be utterly alone. The evil at my core has always made certain of that. Just ask Asdella about her cousin. I loved her, she trusted me, and now she's gone and by own doing. I am an evil creature by nature, and the more I try to deny that, the more firmly it takes control. What you saw with the bandits was a result of that. The thieves that confronted you and Dendrox in the alley, I killed one but managed to spare the other. And in the forest, Kreasa's husband Bren, I spared his life as well before the werewolf finished him off. Two lives saved from my hunger resulted in eleven dead.

<Zaylyn ><Quest For The Sword Fragments And The Hunt For Dranngore ><By Katrina Mandrake-Johnston ><Ch 59> < 138 >

No matter what I do, I can't achieve anything. For a little bit of good, if you can call it that, and for defiance against my evil desires, others are forced to suffer far greater than if I had just given in to what the evil had originally wanted. I can never win it seems. And then, you... because I held back with you... the evil inside me caused for an entire street of people to perish with a single thought back in Shirkint. I tried to stop it, I really did. What should I have done? Was I to hurt you further that night, knowing that I had to go through with it in order to prevent what was to come later if I refused? I can't allow myself to accept that as an option. I can't stop fighting it. I can't let the evil win, otherwise, there will truly be nothing left of me but the monster. What am I supposed to do?" he asked with pleading eyes.

Weena took hold of him in a motherly embrace, his head upon her shoulder as he stared absently into the surrounding forest.

"I can't use such power to solve the problem of the Killnarin. I can't take the risk of letting the evil take control. If my hold over it falters even briefly, I could lose myself to it and cause horrible things to happen, far worse than any Killnarin horde could. I just wish that I could set all that aside, the hunger, the power, the evil, and just live out a normal day, to simply be able to be close to someone without my fear of hurting them."

Weena kissed him gently one last time and said, "Let's head back to the others so we can finish this quest."

<World of Zaylyn><Quest For The Sword Fragments And The Hunt For Dranngore><By Katrina Mandrake-Johnston><Ch 60>

CHAPTER 60 =   THE GARGOYLES

Dendrox was relieved to see Weena return unharmed.

"So where do we go from here?" inquired Nodwel.

"Keep to the left," Shadow instructed, "continuing south."

Shadow remained at the back of the group as they walked in silence. He could sense that they were on edge with having him among them, but he was thankful nonetheless. He knew this was the most he could possibly have hoped for and was grateful. He had never actually walked into this part of the valley, as being able to fly, he never really had the desire to do so. He found it quite enjoyable to experience his surroundings as a human would. He had dulled his senses even further since they had left the area with the stumps, and he hadn't allowed himself even the slightest glimpse into any of their thoughts. He felt as if he were one of them, as if he were included as part of their group, that he was among people that might consider him an ally even if they only partially felt so.

The afternoon was passing them by quickly and after they had traveled quite a distance, they came to yet another fork in the path. This time, however, there were great stone statues standing a little ways into the trees. In this part, the forest floor was thick with vegetation and most of the trail they had been following was overgrown.

"Wow, would you look at those!" Vordin exclaimed, speaking of the gargoyles. He went over to one and yanked away some of the ivy which was partially obscuring it from view. "This is great, just look at the detail. This must have taken years to carve. I always would hear, in the stories Rasindell would tell me, about grand castles overseas that would have countless gargoyles decorating their structure, inside and out. They are meant to protect the castle, thought to have the ability to ward off evil."

Asdella made the snide remark, "I don't know, tell us Shadow. Is it working?"

Shadow found himself letting loose a low threatening growl at this.

"Asdella," Nodwel warned fiercely, "I said that is enough."

"Hey, you know," Vordin commented as he looked over the statues, "It almost looks as if they are pointing to something."

"What do you mean?" Shadow asked coming over to where Vordin was standing. Shadow had become curious and he also wanted to bring himself away from Asdella.

Nodwel grabbed Asdella's arm, hissing at her between clenched teeth, "What the hell is the matter with you?! Why are you trying to provoke an attack?! Are you truly that insane?! He'll kill us all if

<Zaylyn ><Quest For The Sword Fragments And The Hunt For Dranngore><By Katrina Mandrake-Johnston ><Ch 60> < 139 >

that happens! Just don't do anything, you hear me?! He's our only hope of retrieving the sword and later of getting it back together again!"

Shadow helped Vordin to uncover the remaining gargoyles. "I think you're right," smiled Shadow.

Vordin hesitated, a little nervously at first, but continued, "See, this one is looking to this spot of the forest here. This other one is clearly pointing with its claw to the same place, or at least I think it is. Is it?"

"Could be," Shadow commented, "I do not want to look beyond what is here and now, however. Do not ask me to use my powers."

"Oh, I see," said Vordin, not knowing what else to say, "Well this last one is crouched down but is also facing towards this very same spot."

"Don't you think we had better continue on our way to find the sword piece, Vordin?" asked Dendrox, "It's getting late."

"We have to wait until nightfall anyway, Dendrox," replied Shadow, "At dusk, the entrance to the crypt will reveal itself to you. It's not much farther to the graveyard. We should make it there in plenty of time. Just relax. We have time to rest for awhile."

Candra pulled Dendrox aside and whispered to him, "Just relax, he says. Easy for him to say."

Vordin waded about amongst the vegetation, trying to discern exactly where the gargoyles were pointing to, if they were in fact doing so as he thought.

Shadow had been able to drown out their thoughts, but with his heightened sense of hearing, he could clearly hear everything that was being said by everyone.

"Do you think Weena's all right?" Dendrox asked Candra, looking over to Weena who was sitting quietly upon a large boulder by the side of the path. Weena seemed distant, as she idly watched Vordin. He continued to paw through the leaves and shrubs, and ever so often he would check the position of the gargoyles in relation to where he was standing.

"What do you care?" Candra said in a hushed voice, "I thought you're interested in Rinna now. Why are you so overly concerned about whether or not she chooses to foolishly flirt around with The Black Shadow like that? If she refuses to follow commonsense, that's her own fault, right?"

"Damn it, you know it's not like that!" Dendrox shot back to her, out of earshot of the others, "You know how I feel about her. I wanted to keep her out of harm, because I couldn't bring myself to think of anything happening to her. With how we live, you know that she would have to constantly be on guard. Now, it's as if she's trying to put herself in danger to try to prove something. Sure, I'm attracted to Rinna, but nothing happened between us when you left, and I can tell that you've been wondering. When I said Weena was special, I meant it. How I feel hasn't changed. But you know, that with me, she would just be getting herself into something she doesn't really want. What we have, me and you, it's not any kind of life for her. I don't want her to change into something she's not, for her to be accepting things she knows to be wrong as being all right because it's what we do. I want her to be happy. I know that I would never be comfortable in a life of her choosing either, so it's best this way... isn't it?"

"Dendrox, you can't make that decision for her. That is what the problem is. I say, if it's meant to be, so be it. Follow your heart," Candra told him with affection, "I can't bare to have it break, not when you haven't even given it a chance. She doesn't think you to be some heartless criminal, and I know that she would eventually come to know the Dendrox I know, and she couldn't ask for a better man than that."

"I think I might have already lost her, Candra," he said sadly, "I can't do anything right, can I? I only wanted the best for her, that's all."

"Well you are the best, damn it," said Candra, "Don't give up before you even try. Just wait and see how she feels, and for goodness sake, quit trying to get rid of her for her own good or whatever you think you're doing."

"*But look at the way she's looking at him!*" thought Dendrox, "*He's The Black Shadow! What's wrong with her?! It's almost as if she feels some sort of pity for him. She's always putting others*

<Zaylyn ><Quest For The Sword Fragments And The Hunt For Dranngore><By Katrina Mandrake-Johnston ><Ch 60> < 140 >

before herself, even that monster, and even after what he did to her. I don't deserve someone like that, who can be so selfless. But is that what she feels for me? Some sort of pity, because in her eyes she feels I have traveled down the wrong path in life? Does she feel that she is somehow going to save me and turn me into her version of what is proper and acceptable? No, Candra's right, I guess, Weena disapproves of thieving but isn't out to change who we are. It's more that, she wants to try to understand how we go about things and the thoughts and reasons behind them, not confront us in a close-minded defiance. But how can she be okay with what The Black Shadow did to her? …Maybe she isn't. But it's plain to me that she's still fond of him, even with knowing now for sure of who he is. It wouldn't matter to me if she found herself to be attracted to another man despite any feelings she may have for me. It's natural to be drawn to those that interest you. I was to Rinna, still am. Sure, I'll return any flirtatious gestures Rinna throws my way as long as they remain innocent. But in Weena's case, if that creature latches on to her, she'll be in incredible danger, and so much greater than any of us are now. I am also aware that Candra's eyes have lingered a little too long, now and then, when gazing in his direction, but at least I know that she has enough sense not to pursue those desires, no matter how handsome she may find him to be."

Having cleared away much of the forest debris from the place the gargoyles seemed to be pointing to, Vordin was amazed to see what looked to be the surface of a large, smooth and concave, crystal-like object.

Shadow grabbed Vordin with lightening speed, pulling him back.

Lorenta, fearing that he was being attacked, called out in fear, "Vordin!"

"Don't touch it!" warned Shadow, and was disheartened by the incredible look of terror on Vordin's face. "I remember that quite a long time ago… well, I think what you have discovered here might be… I think I'm going to have to start at the beginning," said Shadow, "The gargoyles, the ones that you know, are stone statues, but once there had been similar creatures of flesh and blood. Long ago, a war waged between the gargoyles and the worm-like rock dwelling creatures of which you most likely are unaware even existed. The gargoyles, holed up in their caves and crevices within the mountains, were easy prey for these creatures, as they could erupt from the very rock and devour an unsuspecting gargoyle in a matter of seconds. They were forced to flee time and time again, mountain to mountain, as the numbers of their enemy grew and spread. Eventually, the gargoyles had no choice but to take refuge in the mountain home of a vastly powerful and vengeful sorceress. Once she had discovered the two species trespassing, she cast a horrendous spell, declaring that since they had defiled the sanctity of her mountain, that they would become part of it. The worm-like creatures, as a result, were wiped out of existence, turned to stone as were the flightless gargoyles. The winged gargoyles took flight hoping to escape the radius of her spell, but as their brethren started to drop from the sky like statues, they saw that there would be no escaping. Little know now of the true history behind the massive stone statues we know as gargoyles and most of the ones you see now are man-made. As a last and desperate hope for survival, they had Blandorf, their prince, imprison himself within a magic sphere in hope that it would protect him from the spell's effect. I'm assuming that they had hoped he could later find a way to somehow reverse the spell after it had run its course and dissipated. I think, Vordin, that this is what you have discovered."

"Wow, really?" said Vordin in excitement.

"Whatever you do, do not touch the sphere or you will be captured and held within as well. It appears that the sphere had been placed within a hole in the ground to conceal its location. It's amazing for them to have made it this far, keeping ahead of the spell's reach long enough to end up here. Stand back, and I'll raise it," Shadow instructed Vordin.

The ground shook beneath their feet as the buried object started to rise up, the accumulated dirt over the centuries falling away from it.

Weena observed, *"That would be possible with a Levitation spell. It might even be possible for me to do something like that with years of extensive practice. But with Shadow, he doesn't even have to cast forth a spell. He's not even concentrating, just willing it to happen because it is what he wishes to do. And even with using a spell, for someone to have the strength of mind to even lift something like*

<Zaylyn ><Quest For The Sword Fragments And The Hunt For Dranngore><By Katrina Mandrake-Johnston ><Ch 60> < 141 >

that would be incredible, draining the caster to such exhaustion... I think I am starting to understand why he is reluctant to use his powers to such a great extent. If his evil nature is lying just under the surface as he claims, to let himself relax his control because a certain action had taken more effort to bring forth than usual, he could become very dangerous, or in the least, the spell could take on a vicious nature of its own. I wonder if he even refers to what he can do as being spells. I can't even imagine the power he holds. He can do things so easily, things that would have taken the strongest level of a magic spell to accomplish, and he can do it as if it were nothing. I wouldn't be surprised if he could even take what we are capable of with our spells far beyond what we call the highest level. What he considers a minimal use of his power is awe-striking. Even if anyone else were able to master such superior magical ability, it could only be with one or two spells, not the range he must have."

The glass-like orb that now rested upon the forest floor before them did indeed contain the gargoyle prince. He was curled in the fetal position. Standing, he would have been near six feet tall. His flesh was a deep olive green-grey. His humanoid fingers ended in short claws as did his feet, and at each of his heels he had another claw much like that of a bird's talon. A short thick tail extended from his spine, and an animal skin loincloth hung about his waist. The wings, extending from the shoulder blades of this creature, were jointed in such a way that, if unfurled, it would resemble two arms that were double-jointed at the elbow outstretching themselves. His soft grey wings were currently folded in upon themselves, blanketing his back, the tip of each wing draping up over the opposite shoulder. His head had almost a feline and triangular shape to it, his short pointed ears folding back just above his temples. His large oval eyes were closed and were his most prominent facial feature, as he had a short cat-like nose. His lips were parted and a mouthful of triangular-shaped teeth and long animal-like canines were thus displayed.

"He looks dead," commented Candra.

"No, he is held within a state of limbo, neither dead nor alive, simply existing," said Shadow, "The user enters the sphere, while reciting an activation word of his choosing. It is a little similar to your Shield spell, Weena, in that it acts as a barrier against physical and magical effects. To be able to leave the sphere, the user simply repeats the word and steps out. Now the longer someone is within the sphere, the greater the drain on his body and mind. If anyone stays beyond what they can endure, they are reduced to the state I spoke of and become trapped. As the one inside is the only one that can end the magic of the sphere, it is a terrible thing to have happened. He must have been trying to outlast the duration of the spell cast by the sorceress and failed."

"So what happened to all the really powerful magic users we often hear about in stories and legends?" asked Lorenta, "Like the witch behind the dragon's transformation, the one that became the mother of the Dragonites and Avygons, the human-dragon races. And then also this sorceress with the gargoyles."

"Many met their end as the villain in the heroic adventures you've most likely heard. Power corrupts almost all that gain it," he told her.

Nodwel expected Asdella to make some sort of malicious comment directed at The Black Shadow at this, but she said nothing. Asdella knew well, out of everyone, he was the one who was least likely to abuse his power over Zaylyn. Even though she despised him for the monster he was, in this aspect, she held him in the utmost respect.

"Some of those that did not play the role as some sort of terrible villain," Shadow went on to tell her, "met their end as a result of the ignorance of others, as the people simply would fear the fact that one person could hold that much power, and in turn, would foolishly act against the magic user as a result of that fear. Those that did not fall prey back then, were eventually wiped out through the treachery and greed that resulted through the activity of the wizard's guild within the past two-hundred years. And then again, some simply could not find a suitable apprentice to carry on their knowledge and so their power became lost, or their work would be later found but tossed aside and deemed as being undecipherable by those that simply hadn't been trained to understand it. Even Goranto, the dragon king, he being a very strong magic user, is not around, having been put to sleep under a strong spell. Anyone left, even remotely of power are all in hiding, afraid that a show of their ability might

<Zaylyn ><Quest For The Sword Fragments And The Hunt For Dranngore><By Katrina Mandrake-Johnston ><Ch 60> < 142 >

bring the wizard's guild down upon them. There is another of great power, Glendeana, who would measure as having the magical strength of about a third of my own. She, however, is trapped, imprisoned within an orb much like this one, the magic of the sphere sustaining her life, and even though she is conscious and able to move about within it, she is unable to free herself. I forget who it was that did this to her, as it has been near a thousand years now. I suspect that it might have been Dorlan. I know for certain, however, that I was not the one responsible, but that is what the stories conveniently say, with her being the closest thing to a rival in the apparent struggle for control of our world. Good against evil, so to speak, but it is all just rumor, a very old one. I am glad that Glendeana has remained where she is all this time though. Even so long ago, when I was much more cruel and malicious than I am now, I did not wish to engage in battle with her, and I still feel the same. She could never win, she could never stop me, and the battle would only cause the people and the land to suffer from it. If Dorlan was responsible for imprisoning her, perhaps this is what he was trying to prevent. I sometimes speak with her, visit her as she sits in solitude. She has noticed the changes in me over the centuries, and has been aware of my growing desire to fight against my evil nature and protect the world even in her absence. I offered to free her once, but she agreed that for me to use that much power very likely would trigger the darker side of my being to retaliate, and therefore, she could never trust me to safely do such a thing. If she cannot free herself, I don't suppose anyone can except for me, and so there she remains."

"I'm curious," said Asdella, "Were you able to detect that the gargoyle was here all this time?"

"Actually no," he replied, "His life force is masked within, neither dead nor alive. Unless I had reason to specifically make a search for him in such a bizarre way, I otherwise wouldn't have been aware that he had been removed from our world and left in such a state. With his life force masked and his spirit locked within his body, he was left to be forgotten, even by me."

"Interesting," commented Asdella, and Shadow wondered where she might be going with this.

"It's best, I think, if you all continue on without me," advised Shadow, "I will no doubt only prove to be a hindrance within the group where your attention should be focused elsewhere." He looked to Weena and Dendrox, and then to Asdella and Nodwel. "And besides," he went on to say, "I think I may be the only one able to free him. The gargoyle; he's not an evil creature, but a lot has changed. Continue on in your quest, and I shall stay with him, and if possible, try to help him come to terms with what has happened to his entire race and to become somewhat familiar with what this day and age holds for him."

<World of Zaylyn><Quest For The Sword Fragments And The Hunt For Dranngore><By Katrina Mandrake-Johnston><Ch 61>

CHAPTER 61 = THE GRAVEYARD

"*I don't know what to think anymore,*" Nodwel grumbled to himself, "*If Dranngore can bring down this evil wizard's guild, that would basically make him a hero. And if he succeeds, would that make way for other tyrants to come forth to do their own evil if they stand unopposed by the guild? And will the Killnarin even be able to accomplish Dranngore's wishes or will the creature's instead turn on him with all of Zaylyn following? And if they do turn on him and he is killed by their claws and not the sword we are so desperately searching for, what then? There will be no hope for our world if that happens.*"

The group continued along the path, getting farther and farther into the forest, and just as The Black Shadow had informed them, they soon came to a graveyard. It was fairly large considering its location and appeared to be quite ancient. Surrounding it was a crumbling rock wall. The graveyard was clearly unkempt, the occupants of the graves seemingly long forgotten by time.

Dendrox looked around at the countless tombstones, the many crypts, the few scraggly trees scattered about, the black crows that watched patiently from above in the branches… and fear began to grip him from deep within.

Seeing that he was the only one reluctant to set foot into the graveyard, Candra asked, "Hey, what are you waiting for? Come on, so we can find this place."

He took a step forward, but got an icy chill and hesitated.

<Zaylyn ><Quest For The Sword Fragments And The Hunt For Dranngore><By Katrina Mandrake-Johnston ><Ch 61> < 143 >

"We should probably split up," suggested Nodwel, "The crypt is supposed to reveal itself at dusk by way of some sort of marker. We might be able to locate it beforehand, but I'm betting it will be a brief reflection of the sun's final rays off whatever it is. We'll have a better chance at finding it if we're spread out. If we miss it, we'll be out another day most likely, and it will be one we can't afford to lose. Asdella, you come with me. Weena, Dendrox, and Candra can go together. And Lorenta, can you search around with Vordin?"

Lorenta nodded saying, "We can check off to the left and eventually meet up near the center. Nodwel, if you two head right, doing the same, and the three of them continue straight, we should be able to cover the first half of the graveyard before nightfall, as it doesn't look like it's very far off now."

"Yes, I suppose you would be our best judge in that, being aware because of your changes," commented Nodwel.

"Well, not anymore, but yes," replied Lorenta, "So then just before nightfall, at least one of our groups then will be able to detect where the site is, if it is indeed a brief indication like you suspect. If otherwise, we can easily join up with whomever is closest to it."

"Yes, precisely," smiled Nodwel.

They parted their separate ways, and Candra was left with Dendrox and Weena. Dendrox had yet to step off the trail and pass between the two stone pillars to enter the graveyard. Two small stone gargoyles sat upon the pillars, and they were only about a third of the size of the live one they had seen, but these were much more vicious and demonic looking. They were facing towards the graves which struck Dendrox as being odd.

"*I would have thought them to be facing outwards, as that is what they tend to do, don't they? But then again, here I am imagining them bursting to life and screeching through the air to attack us,*" he thought to himself with a nervous laugh, "*Vordin said they were usually placed to ward off evil, so then, for what reason are they facing inwards? This place gives me the creeps. It just has to be a graveyard at night, doesn't it?*"

"So you coming or what? Don't tell me you're scared or something. I can understand with the wizard we found, sure, but this is completely different, you can't tell me…"

"Damn it, Candra, it's nothing," he interrupted, "It's just this ridiculous nightmare I have sometimes of being in a graveyard with undead horrors attacking me from out of the graves."

"You never told me that before," Candra said with obvious doubt, suspecting that there must be some other reason.

"Yeah, I know, it's stupid," said Dendrox dismissing it, "I'm fine, just a little edgy because of it."

"You're scared. You won't even come in here. What, you think monsters are going to claw their way up through the graves to get at you?" Candra mocked with a cruel laugh, "Ghosts, and zombies, and walking skeletons, eh? It's a nightmare," she said forcefully, "Get over it. This is reality. We have a job to do, and you need to be focused, not babying around in fear because of some foolish nonsense."

"Hey, come on," said Weena, "Don't talk to him like that."

"What?!" she snapped at her viciously, "You know him for a short time and all of a sudden you know everything about him, do you? Shut the hell up! Stop trying to interfere. He knows I'm just joking around. You're scared too, aren't you? I figured as much."

"*Candra's nervous too,*" Dendrox noted, knowing well that her aggressiveness was merely her reaction to it, an attempt to show strength in a time of weakness, "*I'm sure she's worried about The Black Shadow's motives behind all this and whether or not a piece of the sword is even here like he says. We're probably a lot safer now that he left, especially Weena, but then again, as he is aware of pretty much everything, it doesn't really matter if he is physically here or not. I believe what he said about being able to kill a person with a single thought, but then where would the fun be for him in that? Not when he can string a group of people along in a little game, playing with their lives, making them dance like puppets to his every will. When you compare him to a Killnarin, it's a hard choice to choose just which one is the worse evil.*"

"It's going to be dark soon. We should really get going," Weena told them.

<Zaylyn ><Quest For The Sword Fragments And The Hunt For Dranngore><By Katrina Mandrake-Johnston ><Ch 61> < 144 >

Dendrox passed by the pillars into the graveyard to walk beside the two women. He was trying very hard to ignore the thoughts that were creeping out of his imagination to cloud his judgment, and he knew that if either Candra or Weena happened to brush past him, he would surely jump despite his efforts.

As the sun descended below the horizon, the light shone through the eyes of the gargoyles at the entrance, the beams being intensified by something within the statues, and then coming together to strike a small metal disk held by a third tiny gargoyle sitting above the entrance to a plain looking tomb. Everyone came running to meet each other at the indicated site. As with many of the others, an iron gate was positioned at the entrance to this tomb with a short flight of stairs leading down to the burial chamber below.

"*The name is illegible, worn with age, but most likely Anthrowst had requested a false name used upon his burial site, especially if it contained a piece of the sword,*" thought Nodwel, "*Although, the legend of the sword is only about a hundred years old. After returning from the equipment shop, we discovered this when Weena was recovering at the inn from The Black Shadow's attack. This whole place is much, much older than that. What is it he wants us to find here?*" "You know," Nodwel said nervously, "Perhaps we should go back, think this over. Now that we know where it is, we can always return in the morning."

Asdella laughed, "Don't tell me you're frightened, dwarf. You're the one who insisted we not waste any time in this."

"It's starting to get colder at nights now," Vordin commented rubbing at his arms, "I'm freezing all of a sudden."

The moon shone brightly down on them from a cloudless sky, and a thick eerie mist began to roll across the ground.

"Narr?" Nodwel uttered in confusion and amazement.

In the moisture of the air, a humanoid shape had been collecting and forming, and now, it had taken on Narr's distinct appearance, becoming clearer and clearer by the second. Everyone stared in amazement at his shimmering image.

"*I guess Asdella wasn't as crazy as I thought when she said she had been hearing his voice,*" thought Vordin, trying to understand what he was seeing.

"Nodwel? Wait, you can see me?" asked Narr, seemingly just as bewildered as the rest of the group. He held his hands up in front of his face turning them over as he stared in astonishment. "Asdella? You can see me too, right? I'm some sort of ghost like in all those haunted house stories you hear about, aren't I?" He came toward Nodwel and gripped the dwarf's shoulders in a comradely fashion. "How I've missed you, old friend. I've been with you all this time, ever since Dexcsin, but only Asdella could hear me. But look, I'm almost solid now," said Narr grinning, "There's some resistance before my hand passes through to the other side of you, Nodwel."

"Yes, but please don't do that again," begged the dwarf, rubbing at his shoulder where the icy chill of his spirit had phased through him. After Narr had backed away to stand before the group, Nodwel asked, "How is this possible?"

"I don't know," answered Narr, "but I'm glad for it."

"What's that sound," asked Vordin in puzzlement, "It's almost like a hollow rattling sound, I don't know. Do you hear it?"

"Oh, no," said Narr with growing fear, "Get out of here! Go! Go! I'll try to hold them back if I can."

To his surprise, he was able to pick up a fallen tree branch from the ground, and with a panic-stricken expression on his face, he stared off into the mist.

<World of Zaylyn><Quest For The Sword Fragments And The Hunt For Dranngore><By Katrina Mandrake-Johnston><Ch 62>

CHAPTER 62 =   THE CRYPT

"What's going on?" Asdella asked him.

<Zaylyn ><Quest For The Sword Fragments And The Hunt For Dranngore><By Katrina Mandrake-Johnston ><Ch 62> < 145 >

"Me being in this state is no happy coincidence it seems," Narr told them nervously, "I have a feeling we are about to find out what happens when there happens to be a body to go along with whatever spell it is that's allowing me to be like this. Chances are I'm the only spirit around here, which means we're about to encounter a bunch of magically enslaved bodies."

"And you're going to fight them off with a makeshift club?" Asdella asked him in disbelief.

Trying to sound brave, Narr replied, "Well, I was never very good with a sword anyhow, and you all need your weapons. Besides, it hardly matters, I'm already dead, right? I need to protect all of you, if I can."

"No. You can't," Asdella pleaded.

"Have some faith, I'm not completely useless with a weapon," Narr told her in defense.

Asdella explained with real anguish, "No, Narr, what if something happens to you?! What if in this state you can be hurt, your very soul damaged somehow?! I can't let that happen. I can't lose you, Narr, not again!"

Mist had enveloped the area, clouding over and obscuring most everything except for a thirty foot radius.

"Listen, I know what happened to Nimdor, Dimwar, Borin, and well, me, is hard to deal with, but I'm not having you wind up dead too," he told her.

"I can't get the gate open, it's stuck," Candra said in frustration, as she continued to yank at it, "Come on, help me get this open so we can grab the damn sword piece and get out of here before whatever it is out there gets us."

Vordin and Weena came to help her tug at the reinforced iron gate.

Nodwel thought nervously, *"And what if whatever is down there is far worse than what's out here? What if we are the ones meant to release it? Perhaps The Black Shadow means to make us into some sort of undead monsters, as he apparently has become so fond of us. Perhaps he means to bring forth a new band of vampires starting with us, to share in the hunger he suffers."*

"Asdella, go and help Candra and the others. I'm not going to lose you, not like this," Narr pleaded with her.

"And if I lose you forever?" she asked him with tears in her eyes, her voice choked with emotion, "I can't. Not again. Not when I know you're real. Not when I know the others can see you too."

He looked into her eyes saying, "You know that I'm in love with you, Asdella, and the thought of you being hurt is unbearable. If I can, I'm going to protect you, just like I tried when we pulled you back from going after the beast that killed Dimwar. This time," he tried to joke, "you won't be able to bite me, eh?"

"Narr, I'm sorry. I just didn't..." she started to say.

"There's something I've been wanting to do for a very long time and I think this is the closest thing I'm going to get to it," Narr told her, dropping the branch, taking hold of her in his ghostly arms and kissing her long and passionately in that icy embrace.

"Nodwel, Lorenta!" Candra barked, "We could use some help here! Come on, Dendrox!"

Dendrox was staring off into the mist, listening to the sounds that were slowly approaching and trying to determine what it was he was hearing. He knew exactly what it sounded like, but he wouldn't allow himself to believe it. He wouldn't accept the ghost's suggestion as being an option.

"And the fact that it was a ghost that had said it?" Dendrox asked himself, but could not bring himself to do anything but stare off into the night.

The moonlight was especially bright, almost unnaturally so. The white billowing clouds seemed to move about over the ground of their own accord, encircling them, hiding whatever was shambling towards them.

"Asdella," Narr said, holding her as tightly as he could without passing through her, "You need to go. You too Nodwel. I might be able to buy you some time."

"Narr," said Nodwel, as his ghostly friend took up the branch once more, "It, well, it should have been me. You should have been the one to go for help, not me. If only..."

"Hey, come on, what's done is done," Narr smiled at him, "Just be sure to keep Asdella from

<Zaylyn ><Quest For The Sword Fragments And The Hunt For Dranngore><By Katrina Mandrake-Johnston ><Ch 62> < 146 >
pissing off the wrong people, eh, old friend?"

The dwarf nodded and said, "Come on, Lorenta, if the piece is down there, we have no choice."

"Stand back," Lorenta instructed walking up to the gate, and then she tore it from the entrance in a single tug where the three of them could not.

Candra, Weena, and Vordin stared in disbelief.

Nodwel commented, with a smile to Lorenta, "Well, if she was able to pull my entire weight out of the carriage with one arm, what did you expect?"

"Asdella! Dendrox, come on!" yelled Candra, and Dendrox could detect the panic beginning to show in her voice, "Let's go! Come on, hurry!" she barked at the rest of them trying to usher them down the steps to the crypt, but they would not budge.

Asdella came to stand beside Narr, her sword held ready. "Just don't say anything, Narr. I'm not leaving your side, and that's the end of it."

He simply nodded, knowing that it was more than just a display of arrogance.

Dendrox watched in terror as undead horrors began to slowly shuffle towards them from out of the mist.

"It's not real!" he told himself, "It's not possible. It's just the dream. It's not real. I must be dreaming. Weena was in this dream last time. This must be another dream; this time with everyone in it. I just don't recall falling asleep is all."

His eyes were fixated upon the first few members of the increasing horde that was appearing from out of the mist to close in on him.

One of them was a little boy, an elf, his clothing torn and soiled with dirt and dried blood. What was left of his arm dangled at his side. His face was a sickening greenish-grey, his eyes staring blankly.

"This is not what you would find here," Nodwel reasoned despite his fear, "Many of these creatures are recently dead, not hundreds of years old corresponding with the tombs and graves here. On a few, most of their flesh is still intact. Did these others seek the sword as well, only to fail? If so, what was the reason? And a child? Had he been unfortunate enough to play here after dark? Perhaps on a dare as children do? Or is there something else here, something far worse?"

A giant towered above their number, nearly eight feet tall, his race undeterminable. His flesh was heavily decayed, near half of his face on the right side was missing, exposing the bone of his skull. Deep slashes were in his bare arms, his leather jerkin splattered with old blood, and yet he continued to wield a huge and tarnished sword. The stench of the oncoming mob was nauseating.

A skeletal figure wearing a helmet and a broken vest of chain mail came at them wielding a mace and a spiked shield. Narr swung his makeshift club, and to his surprise, sent the bones and metal clattering to the ground with ease.

Vordin was surprised to see a tiny fairy among their number, no bigger than two inches high. Her wings were torn and the vibrant colors they must have had in life were now a dull grey. "It looks as if one of the fairy queen's subjects had also tried to retrieve the sword pieces," thought Vordin, "If they had failed, what made them think that a mere human boy could accomplish the deed? Perhaps it was just out of desperation, or more likely, a cruel joke. They thought a broken leg was hilarious, why not lead us here for much worse?"

Rounding the corner from behind them was a revolting corpse, with slime dribbling from his gaping mouth and insects could be seen clinging to his long scraggly hair. An eye patch was over one eye, while the other stared off into nothingness. A scimitar was clutched in one hand, but the blade had been broken in half. Weena shrieked, but Nodwel easily brought the creature to the ground with his axe.

A skeleton, that was crawling toward them as a result of a missing leg, was dealt a mighty kick by Candra, breaking it apart.

"Do something, Dendrox!" Weena called out to him, "Don't just stand there! Run if you have to!"

A rotting corpse, with humanoid teeth marks all up and down its arm, was reaching for Dendrox. An eye dangled from its socket and the creature's mouth was open exposing its foul teeth. Asdella came to his rescue, slicing the offending arm clean off at the elbow.

<Zaylyn ><Quest For The Sword Fragments And The Hunt For Dranngore><By Katrina Mandrake-Johnston ><Ch 62> < 147 >

"Come on, Dendrox," she grinned, "They're a bunch of pushovers," and with that, she knocked a skeleton to the ground with the hilt of her blade watching it collapse before them.

"Yeah, I guess there's nothing to fear. With them moving so slowly, we can take them all out without them even getting near us," said Dendrox picking up a handful of rocks.

"Might as well take care of them now before we go after the sword," suggested Asdella, "That way we won't have them getting in the way and fouling us up."

Dendrox whipped several rocks at a few of the skeletal figures and watched their bones tumble to the ground below. Suddenly, they didn't seem that frightening anymore. He grabbed another handful and continued to topple them.

Asdella and Nodwel, continued to quickly dispatch the fleshed assailants, while Narr attacked the others. Even Weena, Vordin, and Lorenta joined in, following Dendrox's example and hurling rocks at the bony undead creatures. They were so efficient that they even found themselves having to wait for more of them to make their way out of the mist.

Narr suggested, "Why don't you go down after the sword piece. I can handle anymore that decide to show themselves. I can watch your back easily enough."

Asdella came over to him. "Give me your hand," she demanded.

"What, why?" Narr asked obliging.

Asdella stabbed her sword right through the shimmering image of his hand. "Whoa! Hey! What'd you do that for?!" Narr exclaimed in shock.

"Did it hurt?" Asdella asked him.

"Well, no," he answered, "But, I mean, come on! Why would you do that?! Just so you would know whether or not they could harm me?"

"Yes," she replied plainly, "We shouldn't be long. Thanks Narr."

Narr shook his head in disbelief, watching her race after the others down the steps to the crypt below.

<World of Zaylyn><Quest For The Sword Fragments And The Hunt For Dranngore><By Katrina Mandrake-Johnston><Ch 63>

CHAPTER 63 = ANTHROWST'S TOMB

At the bottom of the stairs, two heavy doors made of stone were shut in place. Nodwel gave them a mighty heave and was able to push them open. Vordin brought his lantern from out of his backpack and opened the metal door of the case. The blackness of the room beyond was illuminated by the glow of the flask, and they all entered. All that was within the small room of the tomb was a large stone sarcophagus.

"Okay, so looks like we all are about to become grave robbers. You all right with that, Weena?" said Candra, a little too condescending.

"Wait a minute, what's that?!" Dendrox asked nervously, watching a shimmering light hovering about in the corner of the room.

The mysterious light grew brighter and larger until they could identify it as being the ghostly figure of a man. "My name is Anthrowst," announced the spirit, "Why have you intruded upon my resting place?"

"We are seeking your sword," Vordin stated bravely.

"And why would you do such a thing? It is for this very reason that my spirit remains cursed, troubled by the knowledge that it was I that created such a terrible weapon. It was intended for good, and I did not consider the damage it could do in the wrong hands. Therefore, I remain here to ensure that it does not leave my tomb."

"But an evil wizard has summoned a whole army of Killnarin into Zaylyn. Our world is doomed if we cannot recover the sword and destroy him with it in order to send the creatures back to where they came from. Please, you must let us take it," Weena pleaded.

Anthrowst furrowed his brow, and staring out from beneath eyebrows that were just as bushy as his large mustache, he looked them over. "I believe that you speak the truth, but I do not think you understand the magnitude of what it is you ask."

<Zaylyn ><Quest For The Sword Fragments And The Hunt For Dranngore><By Katrina Mandrake-Johnston ><Ch 63> < 148 >

"No," said Nodwel, "I assure you we fully understand the incredible risk we are taking, and if there was any other way of accomplishing our mission to save our world, we would have taken it. The sword is our last option, and time is running very short."

"Even if you truly have the potential to succeed in retrieving the sword pieces, manage to mend the sword, and even more amazingly restore the unique spell placed upon the blade, I am sad to say that however noble your intentions may be, and I do believe you in this, unfortunately, you are all to perish here," Anthrowst told them gravely.

"You threaten us, even now?!" Dendrox blurted out, "After we have explained how people are dying and suffering?! We need the sword! It's the only way we can save our world!"

"No, I pose no threat against you, and I truly wish that I am able to help. You see," Anthrowst explained, "the sword was deemed so dangerous that measures have been taken to protect it from being retrieved. Its pieces have been scattered, as you must already know, and I only have information regarding this single piece, the hilt of the sword. You, no doubt, have encountered the walking dead as you approached my tomb?"

"Yes, it wasn't very difficult to battle our way through them," Asdella told him, "They fell easily enough."

"Ah, and that is where your doom lies, in believing this. They only remain slain for a short time before rising again and twice as strong, and they will continue to do so until all that have entered the graveyard are dead."

"So just give us the damn piece so we can get the hell out of here then!" Candra said with frustration, "Where is it?! It's buried with you in here, right?"

"But even if you manage to retrieve the sword piece and escape this graveyard of the damned, you shall not be free," he explained, "The dead will rise up no matter where you are, and pursue you until you are all slain and the piece is returned to its resting place. Only then will their bodies return to their graves and magically be swallowed up by the soil once more. It pains me to know that all of you shall fall this day, but take comfort in knowing that you will become part of this guard against those that would quest for the sword with evil intentions."

Lorenta quickly shut the doors, pressing her back up against it, not knowing what else to do.

"You mean, if we die here, we will become a walking corpse just like those outside?!" Vordin exclaimed in horror.

"They have made their way past your friend outside by now. You may fight, but in the end it will be hopeless. Your souls will at least be free to leave this place. Take comfort in that. I am truly sorry," the specter replied.

The stone doors began to be pushed open, a skeletal arm clawing frantically at them through the opening as more of the undead creatures pushed against the doors in a wild attempt to make their way in.

"Help me hold the door!" Lorenta said in a panic, slamming it shut and snapping the brittle bone of the arm in half. "They are much stronger than before. Apparently Narr did his job a little too well," she laughed nervously.

The broken limb, to their disbelief, was absorbed right through the stone floor. "The arm will return to reform upon its body once more," Anthrowst informed them.

"We'll be safe at least for a time, as long as we don't kill any of them and make them stronger. Perhaps we can somehow subdue them, tie them up, keep them from their weapons, anything," said Nodwel, helping to hold the door along with Asdella, Dendrox, and Candra.

"Unfortunately, the longer they are animated, the stronger they gradually become, and the faster their reanimation once fallen. Slaying them only speeds the process," Anthrowst said to them.

"Is there nothing we can do?!" Weena asked him in fear.

"At least Narr has enough sense to figure out what's happening and stop attacking them," said Asdella.

The doors heaved as something gave them a mighty push.

"It must be that damn giant we saw pushing at the doors along with the rest of these monsters.

<Zaylyn ><Quest For The Sword Fragments And The Hunt For Dranngore><By Katrina Mandrake-Johnston ><Ch 63> < 149 >

We're not going to survive long holding them back," Nodwel said grunting with the strain, "Weena, Vordin, don't just stand there, get the sword piece. We just have to escape these creatures until morning, am I right?"

"Yes," replied Anthrowst, "and I admire your valor, dwarf. But they will arise at the same strength they had achieved at dawn for the following night."

"We can't avoid these things that long, Nodwel!" said Asdella, pushing with all her might against the doors as it was given another forceful shove by the creatures, "Not long enough to find the other two pieces and kill the damn wizard!"

"Is there nothing we can do? There has to be something!" said Candra, the fear and hopelessness showing on her face, "Is there truly no way to stop them?"

"No. The only thing that would end their curse is the Emerald of Enarr," Anthrowst explained sadly, "and that is far from this place, hidden away as another precaution to protect the sword."

"What?!" Dendrox exclaimed in disbelief, "We have it!"

"How is that possible?!" asked Anthrowst with astonishment, "How could you have known that you would need it here?! This is good luck indeed for you. Perhaps your lives will not be forfeit after all."

"We didn't know," said Dendrox, as the doors were almost forced open, "The Black Shadow sent us on a quest to retrieve this very gem."

"Is that so? The Black Shadow has a part in this? If this sword is ever to be truly destroyed and kept from those who would do harm with it, he would be able to do this," Anthrowst commented, "Promise me that my creation will be destroyed once you have accomplished your deed, and please do not fail in your quest, the consequences are so great if you perish. I shudder to think what may happen to Zaylyn if the sword falls into the wrong hands."

The doors were given another mighty heave, and two skeletal warriors clad in chain mail and brandishing short swords burst through into the chamber before the group could force the doors shut again.

Straining with all their might against the doors, they were unable to defend Weena and Vordin who were standing helplessly beside the sarcophagus.

"Weena, no!" Dendrox cried, as he desperately tried to hold the door shut with the others as another massive blow hit it.

Nodwel took up his axe in one hand and, trying to keep most of his strength against the door, tossed it at one of the skeletal warriors. Its bony fingers dropped the rusty sword that it had been raising towards Vordin.

Vordin kicked out at the skeleton's knees, despite his fear, and was pleased to see the bones collapse in on themselves. The ancient warrior, however, simply began to pull itself along the stone floor reaching for him with its bony claw-like fingers. Vordin kicked the skull from its body and rushed over to Dendrox.

"Give me the gem! Quickly!" Vordin said hurriedly, "You have it, don't you?!"

Weena scrambled to pick up Nodwel's axe and found it to be extremely heavy, more so than she had imagined.

"I am not going to die!" she screamed at the horrid vision of death before her. Its bones made a hollow rattling sound in its armour, as it slowly and relentlessly approached her with its deadly weapon.

Dendrox reached into the inside fold of his vest and handed Vordin the gem, shouting, "Weena, get out of the way!"

Instead, she swung the heavy weapon at her attacker with all her might, the weight of the axe pulling itself from her hands as it slammed into the bony ribcage of the skeleton. The bones clattered to the floor along with its armour and so did the axe, Nodwel's weapon sliding across the floor and out of reach.

Vordin and Weena stared in horror as the two piles of bones before them began to magically assemble themselves once more.

"What do we do with the damn gem?!" Weena screamed at the specter, "Tell us now!"

<Zaylyn ><Quest For The Sword Fragments And The Hunt For Dranngore><By Katrina Mandrake-Johnston ><Ch 63> < 150 >

"Why do you keep stalling?! They are much too strong! What are we supposed to do with the gem?!" Vordin shouted at Anthrowst.

The first warrior, now fully intact, swung its blade toward Vordin again. He managed to dodge the blow, and it collided with the stone wall of the chamber next to Dendrox, breaking free a huge piece of rock. The creature, however, instead of turning on Dendrox, kept its focus on Vordin.

"We're not going to be able to hold the door much longer!" yelled Candra, "Every blow is getting stronger by the second!"

The second skeleton swung its weapon toward Vordin as well, perhaps aware that he was now in possession of the gem.

To everyone's surprise, Lorenta attempted to hold both doors closed with her forearm, while in one quick and graceful fluid motion with her free hand, she grabbed hold of the skeletal sword arm of the warrior with incredible strength. In doing so, she was able to stop the creature from completing an attack that would have surely killed Vordin, while still miraculously continuing to maintain her hold upon the doors with the help of the others.

The skeleton struggled within her grip but remained firmly held by her. The first warrior approached again with its blade, and Lorenta gave it a mighty kick which sent it flying across the room to shatter against the wall.

"I'm not sure," Anthrowst finally said, "There should be some sort of recess where the gem would fit into place."

"Find it quickly!" urged Lorenta, "I am stronger than all of you, but this creature is gaining advantage over me by the second, and if I fall victim, the doors will surely open!"

The skeleton Lorenta had broken apart was already half formed, and Weena gave it another vicious kick to scatter its bones yet again before frantically helping Vordin to search the sarcophagus.

"It must be here somewhere, but where?!" shouted Vordin shaking.

The scattered bones of the warrior were quickly reforming up from the floor. Lorenta struggled to hold back the other skeleton as its weapon began to bear down on her, her strength failing, and the doors were on the verge of being thrown open to release a horde of undead monsters into the room.

"Here!" Vordin exclaimed, as he found a small indentation at the base of the sarcophagus just large enough to fit the emerald.

He frantically fumbled with the gem.

He could hear Lorenta's panicked cry, as her hold began to slip terribly, and he could hear the scraping sound of the doors being forced open as the undead creatures now gave one long continuous push against the doors while his companions continued to uselessly strain against them in a futile attempt to hold the horde back.

Vordin placed the gem within the recess, feeling as though his heart would leap from his throat in fear.

The sound of bones clattering to the stone floor and the soft thud of fleshy corpses dropping to the ground were a welcome relief as he turned to look upon his fellow companions.

"We did it! We're alive!" Weena exclaimed in sheer delight.

"Well done, my friends! Please, take the sword piece," said Anthrowst with a smile, "I bid you good luck in your ventures for the other two pieces. Please find a way of destroying it when you have saved Zaylyn from this terrible fate you speak of. My traveling companion, a troll named Steren, was entrusted with the other pieces. He should still be alive, as trolls have been known to live near three hundred years at times. I suspect he will have made his home somewhere near the mountains, but as the troll clans have rejected him, he will not be among their numbers. Destroy the sword, and let my soul rest easy knowing that my creation will do no harm."

Anthrowst dipped his hands into the sarcophagus, passing right through the lid, and he phased the hilt of his sword through to place upon the surface of the stone lid.

<World of Zaylyn><Quest For The Sword Fragments And The Hunt For Dranngore><By Katrina Mandrake-Johnston><Ch 64>

CHAPTER 64 = ASDELLA, NODWEL, AND NARR

<Zaylyn ><Quest For The Sword Fragments And The Hunt For Dranngore><By Katrina Mandrake-Johnston ><Ch 64> < 151 >

Vordin was the one to take the sword piece and tuck it safely within his backpack. Then the group came up out of the tomb. The strange thick mist had vanished, and the moon still shone brightly down upon them from the clear night sky above.

"Narr?" Asdella called out, watching the remainder of the undead be magically absorbed into the ground to return to their resting places, the curse being ended. "Narr?" she called again, and this time with panic, her voice wavering with emotion. She searched frantically with her eyes into the darkness of the graveyard around them.

Nodwel had never seen this side of her. She always portrayed a certain hardness about her, in her manner and way of speaking; even in times of weakness it was always there beneath the surface. Now, she seemed so frail, so weak, so vulnerable, so afraid, that it made Nodwel's heart ache for her.

"Narr?" she called again, but then added with anger, "Answer me, damn it!"

"Asdella," Nodwel said softly.

"Do you see him?" she asked him, with such a desperation and with such anguish behind her watery eyes.

"There's a chance that he didn't make it. That he has passed on with the others," Nodwel tried to explain.

"No, he's here!" said Asdella, with the aggressiveness the dwarf knew all to well coming back into her voice, "Narr wouldn't leave us! He's here somewhere! The undead creatures were just animated corpses without souls. Their spirits had left them long ago. Anthrowst said that if we perished our spirits would be free to leave this place. In his case, he is merely choosing to remain in his tomb until the sword is taken care of. Anthrowst remained unaffected by the gem. Narr is here somewhere! He would never leave us! The creatures couldn't hurt him! I made sure of it, you saw! My blade passed right through him."

"I know," said Nodwel, "but you have to consider that perhaps his energy had become depleted in his efforts, or perhaps that the creatures were able to injure him after all in some other way than just physically, or perhaps, Asdella, that Narr accomplished what he had wished in helping to defend us in the battle and has now passed on being satisfied. He died, Asdella, you know that it could never carry on like that, with him in that state. You know you could have never continued to live your life like that forever, trying to hold on to him and what it could have been."

"Yes I could!" she screamed at him, the tears streaming down her cheeks, her teeth bared in an angry grimace as she raised her sword towards him, "I could hear him! I could see him within my mind! I could sometimes even feel his touch! He's not gone!" and she took a swing in his direction.

Nodwel, anticipating her reaction, took up his axe to defend himself. "Asdella!" he said firmly, "You know what I say is true."

"No!!" she screamed at him, "His spirit is still here! There has to be some way of reviving him. I don't care. I can't lose him! Not when everything else has been taken away from me!" and her sword clashed against the shaft of his axe.

"Should we do something?" Weena asked nervously, "She could kill him. What do we do?"

"I think we should just move back a ways and not get involved in this," Dendrox said bringing the others to a relatively safe distance, "You can always use your Shield spell on him, right Weena? It looks like Nodwel has enough skill to hold her off long enough for her to blow off some steam."

The dwarf blocked another slash from her sword.

"Yeah, I can always shoot her with one of my arrows if I need to, and Weena has her Heal spell," Candra added.

"And if my magic doesn't work?" Weena asked, shocked at their relaxed attitude toward the situation, "You can't rely on me like that. Magic doesn't even work that way. It's not a simple fix to life's problems. You have no idea of what must go into a spell. The... oh, never mind."

Asdella grunted in another forceful swing of her blade, which Nodwel easily dodged.

"I can save him! He's still here!" she screamed at the dwarf, and to his relief she collapsed to her knees saying sadly, "I thought maybe that was what the emerald was for. It was the gem of a necromancer. It was the only reason I could think of at the time for The Black Shadow to want it. He

<Zaylyn ><Quest For The Sword Fragments And The Hunt For Dranngore><By Katrina Mandrake-Johnston ><Ch 64> < 152 >

could have brought my cousin back to life, but he didn't. He has the power, I know he does. I thought maybe because he didn't want to bring her back with his own power, that maybe he was going to use the gem instead to do it. He is incredibly lonely, and he feels the guilt because of what he did to her, I reasoned that this must be his plan."

"So then what has this got to do with Narr?" Nodwel asked her.

"Do you think I would let that monster bring her back to life just so he could eventually break down and slaughter her a second time?!" she said fiercely with hatred, "I would never let him do that!" She stood and looked into Nodwel's kindly brown eyes. "Had this been his plan, I was going to bring back Narr with it instead."

"And if he was to return as some horrid thing? A mere shell of who he once was? Would you still have done this to him?" Nodwel questioned softly, "Asdella, you had more than enough time with him. Don't taint his memory with this kind of madness."

"You don't understand! I have nothing now!" said Asdella, "The Black Shadow; it's all his fault. He killed my cousin! Then when I was taken as a slave to be brutalized and raped by horrid and vicious men, The Black Shadow came and he could have rescued me and the other women, but he just left us, left me, to continue that torture! It's his fault I have been reduced to this cold heartless shell of a woman. Even with the Killnarin, he could easily stop them, but he instead sends us out to do it. If I recall, he saved Vordin from one of the beasts," she said accusingly, "The Black Shadow didn't lift a finger when we all were dying at Dexcsin, and I know he knew exactly what was happening to us. He didn't save Yarin, did he? He didn't rescue Borin down in the tunnels either. What makes Vordin so damn important then? Why should he be allowed to live while everyone else was left to die?!"

"Asdella, don't talk like that. Vordin has nothing to do with it! Don't you dare take your anger out on him!" said Nodwel threateningly.

"It could instead be Lorenta that he's protecting," Asdella commented, "She's always with Vordin. The Black Shadow helped create her. She's his daughter in a way. The Black Shadow could have stopped the Killnarin. He could have saved Narr. He owes me that! He could have at least allowed me to have that, to have something good after all he's caused me. He probably thinks healing my shoulder earlier in the forest can make up for everything," she said bitterly, "He thinks he can walk among us and have us forget what he really is. I suppose he suspects us to pity him because he is occasionally reluctant to admit just how evil a creature he really is. I wonder what would happen if his precious little Vordin and his oh so special Lorenta were truly in danger of being slain."

"Asdella, don't you dare think of taking some sort of revenge out on them!" Nodwel barked at her, "You take your problems directly to The Black Shadow if you are so eager to do so, but you leave them out of it!"

"That is the only vengeance possible against The Black Shadow, you fool!" she yelled into his face, "The only thing that can truly hurt him, is to hurt the ones he cares about! Don't you realize that?! I would just be following his own example, doing what he's done to me, what he does to others, now wouldn't I? I'm not going to attack Vordin and Lorenta if that is what you are dreading, dwarf, but I do deserve to have Narr returned to me. Don't you dare try to tell me otherwise."

"But Asdella…" Nodwel began and found himself to be lost for words.

"I can allow myself to be happy with him," she tried to explain, "I realize that it is a little late for me to admit my love for him, now that he is dead, but I can accept that. He's not gone, and we can be happy together. I know now, that I am not losing my mind, as you all could hear and see him."

"Asdella?" said Dendrox, "Why don't we start heading back along the trail? If I were him, I'd be scouting on head in order to help us in the quest."

She looked him over and finally agreed, "Yes, you're probably right. Otherwise, he would have said something to me. I'm not expecting to see his image again, if that is what you are thinking. I know it was clearly the result of the spell, but I should still be able to hear him!"

"No, we understand," said Dendrox, "but we should hurry if we are to have any hope of finding this troll."

"And how are we to find him?" asked Candra, "He's somewhere near the mountains, yes, but the

<Zaylyn ><Quest For The Sword Fragments And The Hunt For Dranngore><By Katrina Mandrake-Johnston ><Ch 64> < 153 >
search could take years and still we could come up empty-handed."

"Perhaps Narr has gone on to discover that for us," added in Weena.

"Don't patronize me!" Asdella snapped at her, "You may think that you're smarter than everyone else here, but you really have no clue at all!"

"I haven't received any word from the giant spiders," said Lorenta, "So that is a good sign. It hopefully means we still have time to retrieve the sword."

Asdella said to her, "Yes, and I remember that The Black Shadow conveniently altered your entire being in order to so generously give you the ability to stay human during the day. What do you suppose happened to your little mind link, eh?"

"You have it all wrong!" Weena dared to say, "Shadow's not like that! He truly is trying to help us!"

"Once again, you are so clouded to the real truth, you make me sick!" remarked Asdella, "Sure, there is a small part of him that is on our side. What you fail to realize is, that that part of him is just as much a victim to his evil as anyone else. The larger evil in him has a hand in everything he does, and probably without him even being aware of it. What he considers a good deed, is in fact simply being allowed to occur because it helps to lead into an even bigger act of evil later. Do you see why I am reluctant to so foolishly give him my trust, to let my guard down, as that is what the evil side of him would love to have happen, to increase the pain and shock of the betrayal. You're as big a fool as my cousin was, if you think otherwise, Weena," and, glancing briefly over to Dendrox before returning her icy gaze back to her, Asdella then said, "And you're a bigger fool than I was with Narr, if you can't see what's right before your eyes. Let's go find this damn troll then."

<World of Zaylyn><Quest For The Sword Fragments And The Hunt For Dranngore><By Katrina Mandrake-Johnston><Ch 65>

CHAPTER 65 =   TO LEEKKAR IN THE DARK

They followed the path back the way they came, with Vordin holding his magical lantern high to light their way.

When they returned to where they had discovered Blandorf, the last live remaining gargoyle, thick broken pieces of the sphere were scattered about on the ground.

"Looks like the gargoyle left with The Black Shadow," commented Nodwel.

Weena said, "Well at least now with Nexzath and Blandorf, he won't be alone."

"Unless he kills them," added in Asdella, "He killed off the vampires he spoke of, and they would have been the closest thing to whatever he is."

"I think we better get to Leekkar as soon as possible. I don't much like roaming around in the dark like this with who knows what lurking about," commented Dendrox.

"The wolf-beast Kreasa spoke of could well be out here somewhere," added Nodwel.

Weena thought with dread, *"Yes, and they don't know that Vordin and I just happened to make him angry enough to come hunt us down. Shadow was the only one protecting us from him. Now that Asdella has berated him into abandoning us..."*

"You know how at Dexcsin, there was a central well for the whole village?" said Candra, "Well, I mean, I know there were only a handful of people living there, but what was to stop someone from poisoning the well? If Dranngore was so eager to get rid of everyone to access the tunnels, why didn't he just do it that way?"

"He had called it 'practice' for the creatures, remember?" Lorenta told her.

"I actually had asked Shadow about the well on our way back to meet the rest of you, when we were at the tree stumps. I was curious, especially where the water was shared between the spider colony as it was," said Weena, "He said that in the villages here in the valley, that their wells are enchanted by purifying spells."

"At Nilnont too," added in Vordin, "An ancient force of good was supposed to have done it, along with many other things. It was probably the woman trapped in the orb The Black Shadow spoke of."

"Actually, no, at first yes, but Shadow said that once she became trapped, she no longer could maintain and recast her spells. Shadow has been the one keeping her spells active for her," replied

<Zaylyn ><Quest For The Sword Fragments And The Hunt For Dranngore><By Katrina Mandrake-Johnston ><Ch 65> < 154 >
Weena.

"I suppose he needs to keep his food supply contented and provided with clean water," remarked Asdella.

"Asdella, I've had just about enough from you," Weena said angrily, "You just won't give anyone a chance, no matter what they do. I wouldn't be surprised if you've driven him off completely with all you've said and done."

"And did you happen to ask him why the villages and towns here are so small? Why there are only a few hundred people scattered about in places that probably all put together wouldn't add up to any other town anywhere else?"

"I did ask him that," she answered solemnly, "He wouldn't exactly say."

"I thought so. You know the answer then, don't you?" said Asdella.

"But if everyone gives up on him, when he's trying to make such an effort, what do you think will happen then?" Weena tried to reason with her.

"My cousin said the same thing. You have it wrong," Asdella told her, "I haven't given up on him. If he can truly fight the evil, then it would be all the better for Zaylyn, but I cannot forgive him for the things he's done and I cannot ignore him for the creature that he really is. I showed you all that on the way here from the carriage. Did you think he wanted to confirm his identity like that to us? You saw how little it took to bring the demon to the surface, and that was with him holding it back."

"She's right though, Asdella," said Nodwel, "There isn't any way I can think of for us to find the troll Anthrowst spoke of. Our only hope is if The Black Shadow guides us, and chances are, he's left us."

"Then we find some other way," barked Asdella.

Nodwel muttered to himself, *"Damn it, Asdella, your arrogance has most likely helped to destroy our entire world!"*

With his heightened night vision, Nodwel was soon able to detect the torch lights at Leekkar as they were burning high and brightly as beacons within the dark.

"The village isn't far off," Nodwel announced to them, as they neared its location. As they came to the road, they were surprised to see a carriage coming to meet them.

<World of Zaylyn><Quest For The Sword Fragments And The Hunt For Dranngore><By Katrina Mandrake-Johnston><Ch 66>

CHAPTER 66 = NEXZATH AND BLANDORF

They soon could see that it was Nexzath driving the carriage and coming to meet the light of their lantern. He stopped alongside the group, coming from the direction of Leekkar.

Before anyone could say anything to him, they heard the flap of wings above them and felt the rush of wind as the gargoyle descended from the air to stand before them. They watched in wonderment as his outstretched wings collapsed and folded in on themselves to collect against his back like a velvety grey cloak. His animal skin loincloth had been replaced by a pair of brown pants that had the back cut out of them to allow for his tail.

"I don't know about this Nexzath. She wants me to wear gloves, some sort of shirt over my front and arms, and a hooded cloak down over my wings, and even some sort of footwear, as well as these pants?" said the gargoyle with irritation, "Shadow thinks it's for my own good somehow, but I don't know if all this is really necessary. Besides, as soon as I take flight, I won't be fooling anyone. I suppose she'll want me to avoid flying whenever we are around large groups of people too. To hinder a gargoyle's ability to take to the sky whenever he pleases is well... well it's just wrong."

"Blandorf, these are the ones Shadow was telling you about," Nexzath said to him.

"I thought as much," commented Blandorf with a toothy grin, his moss-green eyes sparkling in the moonlight.

"So where is Shadow? Did he send you two to guide us to the other pieces of the sword?" asked Weena with renewed hope, "You know where the troll named Steren is, the one that had been a friend of Anthrowst's?"

"Actually, no," Blandorf answered, hesitating awkwardly, "We are here of our own accord."

<Zaylyn ><Quest For The Sword Fragments And The Hunt For Dranngore><By Katrina Mandrake-Johnston ><Ch 66> < 155 >

"Shadow left. Something apparently had made him greatly concerned," said Nexzath. A long forked tongue came forth from out of the darkness of the hood to waver up and down, testing the air, and then it was drawn back again.

"She was talking to me, and then as a 'he', took flight and headed out to sea. Shadow was apparently keeping a watchful eye over your group as The Black Shadow is capable of doing so from afar. She said simply 'What if Asdella is right?', and then as a 'he', he said that he needed to consult a higher power of good or something along those lines and pretty much that you would be left to your own devices until he knew the truth. I have no idea where he could have been going, as the Ordore'effont is quite large and he gave no real clue as to his destination or even of when he would return."

"So he has abandoned us?!" Weena wailed in desperation, "He's left us to perish in this impossible quest?!"

"Who is this 'she' you keep referring to?" inquired Vordin.

"Oh, Shadow," replied Blandorf, "I know, it is quite confusing, not really knowing which one to use when referring to The Black Shadow."

"What do you mean?" asked Vordin.

"Yes, what exactly are you saying?" added in Asdella, wondering if Ezmeara had even known about this part of The Black Shadow. If not, what else had he kept from her?

"Oh, I hadn't realized that you were unaware. I thought you would have known. Nexzath, you don't suppose she would be angry with me for saying as such, do you?" asked Blandorf a little nervously.

"I'm sure if he wanted otherwise, he would have stopped the words before they could have been said," answered Nexzath and then replying to Vordin's question said, "The Shadow you know, the male part, is only half of his entire being. The other half is female, having her own separate body and personality to a degree but sharing the same mind. Only one half can come forward at a time while the other resides at the back of the mind observing things secondhand. It was a lot for me to absorb as well, but it became clearer when I saw the transformation and spoke to the female Black Shadow myself."

"The Black Shadow is also a woman?" Candra asked in disbelief, "How is that possible?"

"It just is," replied Nexzath.

"*So Shadow was never an ordinary man once,*" thought Weena, "*He was never an innocent cursed with this evil as I came to believe, and trying to somehow achieve his former self. I had come to think of him as a vampire of sorts, even though he said he wasn't one, and I started to believe that he had once been a mortal and therein lay his compassion for us. I suppose such magical power could have been achieved throughout the incredible expanse of years he is said to have lived, but it isn't that. And he is alive, of that I'm sure, he's not some undead creature. So he really is some extraordinary being, but can he really be as evil as everyone believes? Can pure evil be truly at the root of everything he does, no matter what it is he is intending, as it is at the nature of his very being?*"

Asdella grunted saying, "Makes sense I guess. In stalking and luring his prey, what better than to appear as the opposite sex? My cousin had not known about this other half, I suspect, for this very reason. Even I found his appearance to be strangely alluring, despite what I knew about him."

"First of all, I should thank Vordin for discovering my prison as he did," said Blandorf calmly, and Vordin nodded. "So which one of you is Asdella?" asked Blandorf.

"I am," she replied fiercely.

"What exactly did you say?" questioned Blandorf, his voice taking on a threatening tone, "Or I suppose it could have even been something you thought that sent him off like that."

"What does it matter?" barked Asdella, stepping forward to confront the gargoyle face to face, "I suppose you have joined with that foul creature, The Black Shadow, and find nothing wrong with the evil he inflicts upon our world?" and she raised her sword toward him with a sneer.

Blandorf merely laughed boldly into her face and took hold of the blade. Despite her firm grip, determination, and force exerted to hold her blade steady, he simply moved it aside and held it away from him.

<Zaylyn ><Quest For The Sword Fragments And The Hunt For Dranngore><By Katrina Mandrake-Johnston ><Ch 66> < 156 >

"What do you suppose you are to do with that, eh? A gargoyle's skin cannot be pierced or cut by a mere blade, nor much else. You mean to duel me in battle, do you? And what would you be trying to prove with such a foolish act?"

Weena told them, "Asdella said something about how the evil rules over him completely and even the deeds he considers to be good are driven by the evil to allow for further evil to be accomplished later."

Blandorf growled at Asdella, pushing her blade which she gripped so tightly backwards in her hands and thus sending the warrior sprawling to the ground with her sword clattering down beside her.

"And so you want him to stop striving for good and embrace the evil inside him?! Are you mad?!" Nexzath asked her in astonishment, his tongue flicking forward briefly, "You said that all his efforts are for nothing and instead are just allowing for greater evil to take place without him knowing it?! Why would you say such a thing?!"

"It most likely is so, what of it?!" snapped Asdella getting to her feet, glaring at the both of them fiercely.

Blandorf, his temper waning, said to Asdella angrily, "I did not want to return to this world to simply watch it be destroyed! Shadow is now so unsure of himself, that he is probably too afraid to do anything to help in retrieving the sword or in way of restoring it, because he will feel that the evil inside him is at the root of his motives."

"But this is the reason why we have come here to meet them, is it not? We suspected as much," said Nexzath.

"But now we know it for certain," growled the gargoyle, "Do you really wish to have Zaylyn be at the mercy of these Killnarin, Asdella? Shadow has shown no intention of harming our world, even shown reluctance to feed from its people. If anything, he has done more than his share in benefiting our world, and even now in order to save us from this awful threat. When my people were alive, The Black Shadow was much darker and much more savage than he is now. I am aware of his struggle against himself, and if I can help him in that struggle, I shall."

"And I suppose as your skin cannot be pierced, that you are safe from him," said Asdella.

"No, his fangs are the only thing I know of that can pierce the skin of my kind," he informed her, "We were not immune to his attacks long ago and neither am I today. Many of my kind met their end in the bellies of our enemies, swallowed up whole, but we also fell prey to The Black Shadow as did the other races inhabited here."

"Perhaps The Black Shadow went to speak with the woman trapped within the orb he spoke of," suggested Vordin.

"Could be," commented Lorenta, "So you two are offering us your help then?"

"I can take you to Torrnell," replied Nexzath, "Blandorf has offered to fly along the mountain range in search of the troll. You are certain he has the other pieces?"

"It was what we were told," said Nodwel, "If not, hopefully, he will at least know where to find them."

"Elf, you are the kind that has heightened vision, like myself?" asked Blandorf.

"Yes, I do," Candra told him, "and my name is Candra."

"Very well," said the gargoyle, "You shall ride with me in search for the troll once we arrive near the mountains."

Candra was about to say something about how unwilling she was to be precariously situated so high above the ground and so carelessly putting her life in the hands of this creature, but Dendrox quickly hushed her. Instead Dendrox informed him, "She can't see as well during the dark, perhaps someone with night vision would be better."

"The dwarf?" he laughed, "We wouldn't even make it off the ground. My wings and strength can only endure so much."

"Then perhaps you should carry on alone without Candra's additional weight on your shoulders," Dendrox suggested, "Is it really so necessary that she accompany you?"

"She will be safe enough and an extra pair of eyes from above will aid us greatly in our search.

There is also a certain matter I feel I need to discuss with her, something of the utmost importance."

"Blandorf, no. Just let it be. It is best she doesn't know about your farfetched theory," Nexzath warned him.

"And if it can help us in some way?" Blandorf questioned, "I'll let the elf decide for herself. We should be on our way. It should be daylight by the time we reach the mountains, so there shouldn't be any problem that way. It's a shame, Candra, that you lost the darkness vision your ancestors once had. I heard that their kind once lived below ground, able to navigate their tunnels and chambers with ease, much like the many different kinds of cave dwelling dwarves of long ago. In that aspect, they were most like the gargoyles. I'm sure there are still many colonies that follow the old ways, but I am also sad to see that the traditions and knowledge of the past are slowly fading out of its people."

Nexzath got down from his seat and opened the carriage door for them to enter.

"I'll be flying on ahead of the carriage," Blandorf went on the say, "Shadow said something about a dragon and a band of trolls up around Torrnell. If there happens to be trouble, I'll return to warn you, and perhaps we will therefore be able to avoid an unwanted encounter."

Blandorf's wings unfolded, and with a massive upward thrust of his legs and a forceful push downwards against the air with his wings, he lifted off into the air to glide and beat his wings in flight.

Feeling that they had no other choice but to travel with these two strange creatures that had allied themselves with The Black Shadow, they entered the carriage and seated themselves for the journey. They were relieved that this carriage was slightly wider than the other and thus allowed them some added comfort in their exhaustion. Several members of the group found themselves dozing off now and then as the carriage made its way toward Torrnell.

CHAPTER 67 =   OFF TO MEET BLANDORF

They arrived at the main road between Shirkint and Vackiindmire around dawn. After the short journey north, they soon arrived at the road leading to Torrnell, later coming to a halt just outside the village and completing their journey in a third of the time it would have taken them on foot. The horses were clearly in need of a rest after traveling the distance so quickly as they had done.

"You won't have time to stop here at the village, unfortunately," Nexzath told the group, and the horses continued to pull the carriage along the dirt road of the village at a slow trot. "I'll take you to the outskirts of the village," he told them, "You should continue on your way as soon as possible with what you have already. I mustn't leave the carriage, so I will not make the journey with you. Blandorf, however, will do what he can. He'll be landing closer to the mountains, so you should meet him there as soon as you can. I'm sure he'll be able to locate you when you approach."

As Candra peered out the window of the carriage, she could see that, although much larger, the layout of the village reminded her of Dexcsin in a way. The houses that they were passing by, however, were similar to the ones in Shirkint, having two houses, one on top of the other and a spiral staircase leading to the top home. Each building was much wider and shorter than the ones at Shirkint though, and Candra suspected that the homes within were only one level.

They eventually came to pass by the general store and the village well. They could hear a flock of sheep bleating in the distance to the south, and several people could be seen carrying large baskets filled with a variety of different vegetables coming in from the crop fields on the outskirts of the village.

Candra recognized one of the men standing outside the next building they were passing as being the one she had seen at the blacksmith's at Vackiindmire, the one whom Candra had learnt to be the butcher here at Torrnell. A cross look was upon his face and Candra could overhear him say, "Our livestock not enough now?! Damn dragon now be rippin' my roof apart to be takin' what I have in my shop!"

A young woman came up to him to say, "Then you see why I am so persistent in having something done against the beast. Why won't anyone listen to me?!"

"Dea, you've been told. To take action against the dragon would cause more trouble than our village could handle. It be best to let it alone," he answered her with irritation, "Now you best be off, I

<Zaylyn ><Quest For The Sword Fragments And The Hunt For Dranngore><By Katrina Mandrake-Johnston ><Ch 67> < 158 >

have work to do."

"I thought as much," Dea commented angrily and stormed off toward the general store.

The carriage passed by several other shops and houses until Nexzath brought the horses to a halt at the edge of the village. "Here we are," said Nexzath, "Good luck to you."

"A serpent-shape shifter. We heard something about them. Is that what you are?" inquired Dendrox as they all exited the carriage.

"No," answered Nexzath plainly, "I am simply who I am, and I have yet to discover anyone else like me. Blandorf is waiting, you should hurry."

"Very well then. Thank-you for your help. We'll be on our way," said Nodwel bidding him farewell.

"Wait a minute," said Weena coming up to Nexzath, "What exactly do you look like under that hood?"

"I understand your curiosity," replied Nexzath, "but is it really so important? I am the same person regardless of my appearance, am I not? I know well the reaction one has when I am looked upon. I do not care to see it again. Farewell in your quest. I wish you luck."

Lorenta pulled Weena aside, urging her to follow the rest of them away from the village and to head across the grassy plain in the direction of the mountain range. Lorenta knew exactly how Nexzath felt in that regard and knew Weena's curiosity, no matter how innocent, would only bring him pain.

"Weena?" Lorenta asked her as they hurried after the others, "Rasindell once mentioned how Dee'ellkka Valley is one of the most unnatural places he had ever seen. Do you also find this to be so? The mountains and cliffs surrounding the valley is what I am most curious about. I know The Black Shadow allows light into the valley, but for the formations to be so high and ridged, and to be so all enclosing, do you think he is also responsible for the very landscape as well?"

"Well, I don't really know," answered Weena.

Lorenta told her, "Dendrox mentioned something along those lines after showing us the map he had drawn; that he found it odd. Mountains usually have a gradual incline according to what Rasindell had taught me, flat terrain gradually becoming more rocky over quite a distance before reaching what could be called a mountain."

"No, I do understand what you mean. It's almost as if someone has cut all the jagged tips off numerous mountains and hilltops and placed them all in a row to create a wall of some sort," said Weena, "It only took me a few hours to come over from one side to the other and into the valley."

"Exactly, and that's also what the cliffs appear to be: walls. Three high rock walls completely enclosing the valley," said Lorenta, "I'm sure the others are aware of it, but what I want to know is why. The Black Shadow must have altered the land as well."

"Perhaps it was to provide protection for the people here," Weena weakly suggested.

"It was clearly done a long time ago when he was a creature with evil fully in his heart. I think it might have been to purposely blanket the valley in shadow. Do you think so? Perhaps even he has forgotten the reason behind that action, but it has me curious," said Lorenta, "Even the window at The Old Scabbard Inn at Shirkint was blackened. Do you remember how odd that had seemed? And it just happens to be the one place The Black Shadow has become known to frequent. The Killnarin thrive in darkness, so maybe there is a chance that he also does. In a way, I too was linked to darkness, my power to change coming only then. I have to admit, although I enjoy having my human form during the day, it has me a little nervous, especially after what Asdella said about all The Black Shadow's actions being evil in some way no matter how beneficial they might seem. Even though I was raised by Rasindell, he was the one responsible for my creation. And even before that, Rasindell was rescued by The Black Shadow and now so has Vordin. What does all that mean, if his actions are only done to serve evil? And if so, why are we even continuing after the sword?"

Weena replied, "We have no choice but to quest for the sword. It's our only sliver of hope. The alternative would be just to sit idly by. I don't think any of us could simply do nothing."

"And if we are then responsible for something worse to occur, if and when we succeed?" Lorenta questioned, her voice trembling slightly.

<Zaylyn ><Quest For The Sword Fragments And The Hunt For Dranngore><By Katrina Mandrake-Johnston ><Ch 67> < 159 >

"I don't think you are meant for evil, Lorenta, nor do I think that Vordin or your father were saved to accomplish some terrible deed," Weena told her matter-of-factly.

"Thank-you, Weena," Lorenta said with a smile, and then after a several moments, lost in thought, she said, "All my new ability has done is allow myself to further deny who I really am, pretending as if the spider part of me doesn't exist. Perhaps that is why he gave me the power to change during the day. In a way, he desires to hide his true self and be accepted as I do. Perhaps he merely wanted to see if I would choose to remain in human form, as I have, or continue to revert back to my spider form, accepting that my true identity is to be both."

The group continued in silence for quite some time, and as they neared the base of the closest mountain, Blandorf dropped out of the sky to greet them.

"Candra, my beauty!" exclaimed the gargoyle with a sly smile across his lips, "Grab hold across my shoulders up onto my back and let's go find this troll, shall we?" As he waited for her, he stretched out his wings, full span, and twitched his tail back and forth behind him.

"I'd rather not," replied Candra.

"What, you afraid I might drop you?" Blandorf chuckled, "I promise, I'll deliver you back to your friends safe and sound."

"It's our only chance, Candra, unfortunately," added in Nodwel.

"Yes, I know," she said nervously and walked reluctantly over to the gargoyle.

She took hold, her fingers interlocking across his chest, one arm under his muscular bicep and the other over his shoulder.

"Mind the wings and hold on tightly. The lift off is probably what you'll find to be the most difficult," explained Blandorf, "but once we're in the air, it shouldn't be as hard for you, as you'll be able to use your legs to secure your position as well."

Dendrox had never seen her wear such a fearful expression in all his life, and before he could say even a single word to her, they were gone. Dendrox watched as the gargoyle beat his wings against the wind flying north to search the distance between where the group was situated and the Ordore'effont Sea.

"I suppose we better start heading south then, although I don't see how we can be of any use," breathed Nodwel.

<World of Zaylyn><Quest For The Sword Fragments And The Hunt For Dranngore><By Katrina Mandrake-Johnston><Ch 68>

CHAPTER 68 = CANDRA AND THE GARGOYLE

As Blandorf's powerful wings beat against the air, Candra held onto him as tightly as she could, her legs straddling the small of his back, her cheek pressed against the smooth greenish-grey skin of his muscular shoulder.

"How are you doing?" asked the gargoyle, "You know, you can loosen up on that death grip you have there. I'm not going to let you fall. Can you see well enough from where you are?"

"No," she said, her voice incredibly shaky.

"Listen," he chuckled, "If you do happen to slip off for whatever reason, I'll be able to catch hold of you in a second."

"Long before I hit the ground?" Candra asked uneasily.

"Yes, of course. I'm starting to enjoy having you pressed so closely against me. You should fly with me more often," he chuckled, "Come on, it's all right. Look how the morning light shimmers over the water ahead. You'll miss everything with your face buried like that."

Candra lifted her head up, feeling the chill air rush against her face. She could see the Ordore'effont Sea to the north, the mountain range to their left, and below them the wind rustled the high grasses of the field in such a way that it gave the appearance of great rolling waves. They were much higher up than she had hoped they were. Blandorf then flew even higher, nearing the highest peaks of the mountains, and Candra could see the land stretching out beyond on the other side of the mountainous wall. The sea was indeed beautiful under the sun's rays and she suspected it would be

<Zaylyn ><Quest For The Sword Fragments And The Hunt For Dranngore><By Katrina Mandrake-Johnston ><Ch 68> < 160 >
even more spectacular under the moonlight.

"Why are we so high?" called out Candra beside Blandorf's ear over the blare of the wind.

"I thought I'd get you used to flying first before searching for the troll. The higher we are, the greater chance of you overcoming your fear," he told her, "And if you happen to fall, it gives me more time to grab hold of you before you hit the ground." She gripped him tighter. "It was just a joke, Candra, relax," he chuckled.

"Yes, but it was the truth," she added nervously.

"Time for some real flying then, I think," Blandorf said and turned his wings inward, plummeting downward into a dive.

Candra shrieked in terror, but Blandorf continued to swoop through the air performing several spins and dives, until finally gliding down gently to land by the water's edge far to the north.

Candra's legs trembled incredibly as she came to sit upon the gravelly beach.

"I told you that you would be all right. There's nothing to fear. Not when you're with me," he smiled widely, folding his wings against his back and coming to sit beside her.

"So how are you able to fly? Surely your wings alone cannot support such weight, can they?" she asked him, looking the gargoyle over in wonderment.

"Ah, good question. The answer would be no, the most my wings could do naturally would be to allow me to glide from one place down to another. You see, the winged gargoyles are born with the magic of flight, as are most of the dragon species, and winged fairy folk, and so on. Many species are born with magic at their core. I even think there might be a type of elf that is born with the ability to cast certain Natural magic spells and definitely true for several different kinds of fairy folk. When I was growing up, there was this one gargoyle who was born with these gnarled stumps where his wings should have been. It didn't really matter very much to him, as not all gargoyles have wings. You see, although he was wingless, he still had the magic of flight within him. He used to be able to leap incredibly high into the air as a result of it, as he bounded from rock to rock in the games we all used to play as children."

"It must be hard for you to have lost everyone as you have," said Candra, feeling for him.

"Well, if it hadn't been for Vordin and Shadow, I'd still be locked away. My father was killed protecting his people, eaten by one of those foul worms. As the prince, it was I that led my people to what I thought was safety at the mountain the sorceress inhabited. I am still responsible for them, and if there is a way to restore even a few of them, I must try. But it has been so long. If only I had been able to outlast the spell and had been able to emerge from the orb, I might have been able to rescue them somehow... save them while the spell was still fresh. It may be far too late to attempt anything now. I must accept that things did not happen in such a way back then, and that I am here now and therefore must carry on as best as I can. These mountains have been home to my kind for a very long time. I suspect that the trolls that inhabit them now have taken over our old tunnels and chambers. From what I've heard, trolls are very violent and greedy creatures. I can see how they have resorted to plundering the village of Torrnell rather than fending for themselves. If we avoid the larger underground passages where the tribes are most likely situated, we should be able to find the troll we're looking for. As a child, I used to explore the mountains with several of the other children, and we used to find all sorts of great hiding places. Together, we should have no problem finding him."

"You said something earlier. That there was something you wanted to tell me," Candra said to him, "What was it?"

"Oh, maybe Nexzath was right. Perhaps it is best if I say nothing at all," he replied.

"No, you can't say that," snapped Candra, "You have to tell me what it was now. I can't just forget about it."

"It's about The Black Shadow. Are you sure?" he questioned.

"Yes, yes, of course," said Candra.

"I am able to sense the emotions of others," he told her, "Didn't you find it odd that I was told the names of everyone in your group except for yours? What he feels about Weena is a mixture of... well, it's rooted between the hunger, and a familiarity and hope that she could have a better understanding of

<Zaylyn ><Quest For The Sword Fragments And The Hunt For Dranngore><By Katrina Mandrake-Johnston ><Ch 68> < 161 >

who he is because of what happened, his attack on her, and because he had spared her life. It's so very hard to explain in words. But for him to avoid speaking of you, has me very suspicious."

"What do you mean?" asked Candra, "I don't understand."

"It was in the female that I sensed it briefly. Which makes me believe what I suspect even more so," explained Blandorf.

"I still don't know what you mean," Candra told him.

"The female would have a better understanding of how the male version of The Black Shadow really feels. His avoidance, I suspect, is because he fears his evil may take hold and infect his thoughts of you," Blandorf went on to say.

Candra gave the gargoyle a confused look and said, "What exactly are you saying? I thought he was interested in Weena. Are you saying that he merely feels some sort of connection to her because he fed from her? Why is he all of a sudden coming after me?"

"No, it's always been you, and I can see why. His hunger has nothing to do with what he feels for you, and his denial of this, is his way of keeping it that way," Blandorf told her.

"So what am I to do?" Candra asked him nervously.

"Nothing," he replied, "I merely thought you should know. Because of this, you may be able to have influence over him where we cannot."

"Yes, I see," said Candra, "but do you really think I am safe around him?"

"I suspect safer than the rest of us at the moment," said Blandorf, "He will be aware of our conversation just now, however, and of what I believe to be true regarding yourself."

"You mean he can truly hear what we are saying right now from wherever it is he took off to?" she asked him, finding it a little hard to believe.

"He can be aware of pretty much everything, if he wishes it, I suppose… of our every action and most likely even our very thoughts, if he decides to or we give reason for him to pry into our minds," he told her, "It's a little hard to accept, I know. It makes me feel extremely vulnerable to know something like that, knowing that there is no escaping him no matter how far you run."

"Do you think he will restore the sword for us if we manage to get the pieces?" she asked.

"Before, I would have said yes, definitely," he told her, "But now, he is so uncertain of himself, I couldn't tell you one way or another. He wanted you to complete your quest, so all there is left, is to continue to do so. You think we should begin our search for the troll then?"

Candra nodded, and the two of them stood. Blandorf outstretched his wings, with Candra marveling at the display. She took hold as she had done before, and with a downward thrust of his wings, he leapt up into the air once more.

<World of Zaylyn><Quest For The Sword Fragments And The Hunt For Dranngore><By Katrina Mandrake-Johnston><Ch 69>

CHAPTER 69 = CANDRA AND BLANDORF'S SEARCH

Candra peered over the gargoyle's shoulder, as they soared through the air.

"So if we avoid the major entrances to the tunnels, it should narrow our search incredibly. If I remember correctly, there should be a little nook coming up. Could be the troll. Could be some other creature. Could be empty. We'll have to go on foot to know for sure."

Blandorf flew toward the mountains until landing in a rocky and forested area. "It's up higher," he told her, folding and collecting his wings against his back, "There had been a bit of a trail leading to it, but I see that everything is pretty much overgrown now. I'm amazed I can even recognize anything anymore, the way things have changed. Where tiny shrubs once were, now great and sturdy trees stand. The rock of the mountain face is pretty much the same though. I'm certain that this is the place. Follow me."

Blandorf hiked up through the vegetation with ease, and Candra struggled to match his pace. "What am I doing?" thought Candra, "Agreeing to ride on the back of a gargoyle so high above the ground, and now following him to a dark and dreary cave? Normally, I'd have Dendrox with me at least. But it wouldn't really make a difference whether Dendrox was with me or not. I'm totally vulnerable when it comes to Blandorf and his abilities, aren't I? I can't explain it, but oddly, I really do

<Zaylyn ><Quest For The Sword Fragments And The Hunt For Dranngore><By Katrina Mandrake-Johnston ><Ch 69> < 162 >
feel safe around him."

"Candra, I found it!" he called out with delight, "Quickly, get up here and let's see what we can find."

"It's a little steep," she replied, her feet sliding over the loose rocks in her climb as she tried to balance with her hands in almost a crawl.

Blandorf made his way down to her and offered her his hand. She hesitated, staring a moment at the olive green-grey color of his skin and the pearly white of his short claw-like nails.

"Come on, I'll help you up. Just watch your footing," he said, a hint of nervousness to his voice.

"*I wonder if he can truly sense my uneasiness,*" Candra said to herself. She looked up over his broad and bare muscular chest to his face. The gargoyle's waning smile, beneath his flat cat-like nose, displayed his sharp triangular-shaped teeth and long canines. His large moss-green eyes looked back to her softly in almost a pleading manner and with obvious affection.

"Candra? What's the matter? Come on, it's all right. I'll help you balance your way to the top," Blandorf told her, gently moving his hand a little closer.

She finally accepted and took hold of his hand, making her way to where the cave entrance was situated. It appeared as if it had been cut into the rock and not a natural formation. Blandorf sat down upon a boulder, his tail wrapping around the rock to rest at his side.

A little suspicious, she asked him, "So what exactly is this place? Some sort of tunnel?" She came to sit upon one of the rocks by the entrance as well.

"The Ganairsh made most of these tunnels throughout the mountains. This is one of them, but it doesn't go very far and doesn't connect to anything," he told her.

"Ganairsh?" Candra questioned.

"Large worm-like creatures that used to prey on my kind," he explained.

"The Black Shadow told us about them. I didn't know what they were called though. Sorry, I didn't mean to…" Candra trailed off and then added, "I just didn't realize that they were as large as that to make such a tunnel as this."

"That's alright," he replied, "Our skin can't be pierced very easily, meaning the young Ganairsh were no threat to our numbers. It was the larger ones that were able to devour us whole, and eventually, as they began to increase and concentrate their attacks on us, they soon drove us from our homes. This war with the creatures, if you can call it that, went on for several generations. They would attack so suddenly that we had no choice but to eventually flee from place to place and over the years we continued to retreat almost across the entire mountain range. We couldn't determine when or where an attack would come upon us. The king, my father, was swallowed in mid flight as he tried to lead the survivors to safety after the last major attack. I didn't know what to do. I did the best I could and ended up dooming both my clan and the Ganairsh as well in bringing my people to what I thought was safety."

"I'm sorry," Candra told him, "Do you really think there is a chance of reversing the spell after all this time?"

"I'm going to try, but I doubt I'll be able to. I'm not about to let that task consume and waste what's left of my life however," he told her.

"Well no. I agree," said Candra, "And usually, the answers a person seeks end up surfacing when they least expect it. Search when you can, but you shouldn't run yourself into the grave because of it."

"So you see any of those half-dragons yet?" Blandorf asked her. Candra nodded, and he went on to say, "Yeah, when Shadow took me to Shirkint at the inn there, I saw one. She made me bundle up in a hooded cloak with gloves and with cloth swatches tied around my feet and even made me keep my tail hidden up within the folds of the cloak. If Shadow expects me to do that every time I go anywhere, forget it. But anyway, this half-dragon, a Dragonite was what I think she called him, I had never seen one before. They even have tails, although the one I saw had it hidden down his pant leg. Looked ridiculous, I say. Why bother?"

"I suppose in order to appear more human," said Candra, "They are often called human-dragons, and I suspect the reason for that is to remind those that they are in fact part human. Dendrox and me, we met two half-breeds that were part Dragonite, so that proves that at least a few have accepted their

<Zaylyn ><Quest For The Sword Fragments And The Hunt For Dranngore><By Katrina Mandrake-Johnston ><Ch 69> < 163 >
race as being somewhat normal."

Blandorf chuckled, "I doubt anywhere else but in Shirkint though. That's about the only place I've seen that embraces half-breeds and other oddities so openly. If Shadow had not chosen Shirkint to be his home from time to time, I don't think it would remain as such."

"What do you mean? I do know that the people there are almost afraid to breathe for fear of him. We came into contact with the thieves guild, and what a spineless group that was," she commented.

"He mentioned that," said Blandorf, "They found out you had some sort of connection to him, didn't they?"

"Well, yes, but for them to act so carelessly? How can they even call themselves a guild of thieves? They're all talk," said Candra.

"Not quite so," Blandorf explained, "You see, since Shadow has been striving to find some spark of good within himself, he's been feeding on the undesirables that come into the town if he can find them. Therein lies the guild's desperate attempt to befriend you, because of your favorable connection to him. I'm assuming they overdid it a little."

"Yeah, even making a point to mention her family members," she commented, remembering how open Rinna had been.

"There, you see, trying to deter an attack on them as well. But you see, I'm sure they knew that being in his favor could also backfire and cause just the opposite to happen. I guess they were willing to take that risk. The guild was tiny, wasn't it? Only a handful of members?" he asked, and Candra nodded. "I'm sure it wasn't always that way. The few that remain probably know very well what happens when something is done to interfere with the way The Black Shadow runs Shirkint."

"Every one of them was a half-breed; the two Dragonites ones I spoke of and a couple of shape-shifters," Candra mentioned.

"Ah, yes, The Black Shadow has a soft spot for half-breeds. I suspected that the remaining members of the guild were as such, as it works in favor for their survival. And for this new race of human-dragons, I guess it helps that they happen to be fairly intelligent, otherwise, I'm sure they would be treated with the same reproach that the Garcs and goblins receive, perhaps even more so. But anyway, as I was saying, it was a surprise to see this Dragonite I saw. The dragons were still ruled by their king when I was here last and long before these human-dragons came to be. Goranto's brother, Baracken, would have never allowed such a mixing of the blood, and because it being with a human, that would have surely enraged him even further. Goranto himself, I could see accepting what has come to be, even though many of his subjects, I'm sure, would have sided with his brother in his rejection of the human-dragons. I suppose, in a way, it's fortunate that Baracken and Goranto have disappeared. Goranto is supposed to be sealed up somewhere by a spell, and Baracken was apparently slain by some human wizard. That, I don't believe for a second, that such a powerful dragon prince was defeated by a single little wizard, but as it's been a little over two hundred years, I'm told, since it was supposed to have happened, perhaps there is some truth to it."

"Do you think we should go in there?" Candra asked him nervously, speaking of the cave, "It's awfully dark."

"I'll keep you safe, come on. There's no need to worry. Us gargoyles, we can see in the dark almost as well as we can see in the daylight," he said with a warm smile, and he gently took her by the hand. "You know," Blandorf said leading her into the darkness of the cave, with the daylight quickly fading behind them as they continued to make their way along the rock corridor, "Being able to read a person's emotions is far better an ability than being able to hear a person's thoughts, I say. Shadow can do both, but he blocks it out most of the time, well the emotion reading part at least. I don't blame him either. To have to live with what the hunger forces him to do and then feel everyone's pain wherever he goes as well as hearing their thoughts... That's exactly what the evil inside him enjoys, so there is more to him blocking it out for the most part, as best as he can. You see with me, I can read a person very well in only a short time. I suppose that is why both Shadow and myself connected so easily. We didn't have to take the time to explain things verbally, well, for the most part. And besides, you know what it is that I often find most of all? So many people aren't even aware of how they truly feel about

<Zaylyn ><Quest For The Sword Fragments And The Hunt For Dranngore><By Katrina Mandrake-Johnston ><Ch 69> < 164 >

something anyway, and even their thoughts are often betraying or clouding themselves from realizing the underlying truth."

Candra said, "It's obvious you are able to read much deeper than simple emotions like happy, sad, and the like, is that right?"

"Yes, much deeper, and probably more so than anyone else in my clan could too," he told her, "That's why it's hard to explain it in words when I look into someone. It's almost as if I am able to feel what they do to an extent."

Candra inquired, "So then what exactly is it that you sense from The Black Shadow?"

"It's hard to say. It's actually quite frightening being able to feel the evil desires trying to bubble forward in him and then his frantic and desperate attempts to push them back down and ignore them, praying with such a hopelessness that he doesn't act upon them. I do believe though that there is a piece of him that desires good despite his evil nature. But that part of him is... I guess the best way to describe that feeling to you, would be for you to imagine yourself trapped in a deep pool of, I don't know, mud or something like that, and that you are frantically trying to keep yourself from drowning in it. There's a strong undertow pulling you under as you struggle so helplessly. You struggle and struggle so greatly and for so long, feeling yourself slipping now and then as you desperately try to stay afloat. There is no ending to this, and the suction is constantly trying to pull you under, and at some times it pulls at you stronger than others. You find yourself wanting to just give up in that exhaustion to stay afloat and with the constant struggle to not suffocate in that all consuming blackness. He now has become tired with all of this; all this constant teetering on the edge of his evil and the fading goal of the good he is trying to achieve. And in that frustration, I fear he may soon give in to that evil. Asdella has done nothing but make him choke on his decent into that darkness, while Nexzath and now myself have been trying to help him pull himself free. Asdella has him believing that there was never a piece of good within him at all in the first place and what he thought was there was merely a cleverly disguised tool that his evil is using to concoct more elaborate and fiendish plots with which to amuse himself. You see, for such a creature, with what seems like unlimited power, to always know the outcome of his actions, even being able to manipulate any outcome to his very whim, able to make everyone around him dance like puppets to do whatever he desires... A being like that would eventually become so bored with the way things were that he would have to trick his own self away from what he was doing to be able to have any sort of excitement in life. You can see how he has now so easily come to doubt and mistrust his own motives to such an extent. Asdella has just helped that suspicion to grow to the verge of chaos. If that sliver of good sinks to the bottom and stays there until it is allowed to drown out, I don't think there will be any going back for him."

"And you were able to feel all this from him?" asked Candra as they slowed their pace.

"I was able to sense more from him than from anyone else before. It was as if I were instead experiencing his emotions firsthand and perhaps even some of his thoughts as if they had been my own. It was overwhelming, to the point where I could barely sense anything else but what I found within him," he explained.

She asked, "Well, do you think he can ever separate himself from the evil?"

They came to a halt within the darkness of the tunnel and Blandorf went on to say, "That is what he is trying to do. To not have to worry about his evil lashing out on its own despite his efforts to control it. The hunger, unfortunately, is a different matter, one that he can never escape," Blandorf told her, "I asked him to, ah... I couldn't take being swarmed with what he felt, with what... with what it made me feel in return when he... I had to finally ask him to block out his emotions from me. When he fed, it... I just couldn't take it, and then through him feeling what his victims... I couldn't let his evil infect me as well, manipulating my sense of right and wrong. It was as if I was losing myself and no longer able to tell where my mind ended and his began. It was as if his mind was swallowing me up, devouring me in that all-consuming evil. All there was for me to do was to grab hold of that drowning sliver of good in him in order to try to pull myself from his mind, to bring myself back to my surroundings and my own thoughts. If that part of him hadn't been there as a kind of beacon in that horrible darkness... I've never been that frightened in all my life."

<Zaylyn ><Quest For The Sword Fragments And The Hunt For Dranngore><By Katrina Mandrake-Johnston ><Ch 69> < 165 >

Candra felt a water droplet land on the skin of her arm, and it took her a moment before she realized that it had been a tear. She decided that she had better change the subject, and since she had been wanting to know the answer for a very long time, she asked him, "So can you tell me what it is that I feel for Dendrox?"

"Yeah, sure," Blandorf said, quickly composing himself and continuing along the passage once more, "You love him. You love him as you would a brother, but that love is much deeper than that, as if he were an inseparable part of you. You therefore act accordingly."

"You mean about Weena," Candra said sheepishly.

"I don't see anything in here. I think we should just go back, take to the sky, and search somewhere else," he suggested and began to guide her through the dark back the way they had come. "When it comes to Weena, you feel that you need to also accept her, to see and feel what he does for her in order to understand and be all right with their affections toward each other," said Blandorf.

She said defensively, "I just don't want to see him hurt."

"Yes, I know, and in turn you would feel his heartbreak when it is there, perhaps more so than he would because the two of you are so close. But, Candra, it's not up to you to choose his mates for him, now is it?"

"Yes, I know that," she replied with irritation.

"It's hard to change how you feel despite what your mind tells you though, isn't it?" he said matter-of-factly, "And what of yourself? Is it that you are so concerned with his happiness, that you have neglected your own? I'm sure Dendrox would react in the same way you have, to anyone you become attracted to. But is it really fair to deny yourself this?"

"I haven't really found myself drawn to anyone before. My relationships in the past, well, they've been hollow, pretty much meaningless other than a passing interest. I do want more than that though. I've come to realize this with Weena and Dendrox, that feelings cannot, should not, be tossed aside for the pursuit of treasure or even out of fear for their own safety. I know that sounds selfish, but I cannot bring myself to part with her, whether it be for Dendrox's sake or my own. Besides, when Dendrox tried to separate from her to try to protect her from harm, she got herself into such incredible danger with The Black Shadow that it was simply unbearable. She's better off with us, even if we have to take extra precautions and because of her our own lives are put at risk. She's trying to accept our way of life, and I'm willing to embrace her pursuit into the magical arts."

With a bit of a laugh, he told her, "I'm glad you have come to terms with this, but again, it is not about you. It is what Dendrox decides and how Weena feels in return. We were talking about you, not them, weren't we? That you should not concern yourself with their relationship so much that it hinders your own ability to have one."

"But I don't feel anything for anyone, and besides, it's not as if I have the time to think about that with everything that's going on right now," she said to him.

"Weena and Dendrox seem to have found the time, and I'd say they are better off for it, especially at a time like this when all our lives could be cut very short," the gargoyle commented.

"You're right," she admitted, "I don't want to be alone. Perhaps this is why I've been so intrusive, so afraid that Dendrox might replace my affections for Weena's."

"You know that would never happen. He's proven that to you, or so he feels he has," Blandorf told her.

Candra fell silent in thought. "Yes, I suppose you're right. Still, I feel I've been cast aside in a way," admitted Candra, "But I do believe that I would gladly accept affections from another, whereas before I would have purposely disregarded them. Before I simply would do so because I felt, that since I had Dendrox, that he was all I needed. Unfortunately, I don't really feel attracted to anyone. The Black Shadow has to be the most handsome and attractive man I've ever met or even seen, and yet, there was nothing more than a physical desire."

"Yes, I already know how you feel about The Black Shadow in that regard, and I am glad for it. I wouldn't want you to be put in danger because of him," he told her squeezing her hand a little tighter with the thought.

<Zaylyn ><Quest For The Sword Fragments And The Hunt For Dranngore><By Katrina Mandrake-Johnston ><Ch 69> < 166 >

"But you said that he definitely has an interest in me?" Candra asked with worry, "Doesn't that put me in danger?"

"No, you know, I think with him it's more than simply a desire. I believe he would feel the same about you whether in male form or not. Now that I think about it, it might even be similar to what I've felt in the connection he's formed with Nexzath and also with myself now. I'm not sure exactly what it is he truly feels for you, as he has made it a point to even shadow it from himself. It's strong, whatever it is, and I'm certain that you might have the ability to sway his actions, perhaps more so than I or Nexzath could."

"But how?" she asked with confusion.

"I don't really know, but if he ever turns, deeply embracing his evil, it's those he feels most strongly about that are going to suffer the most. That means me, Nexzath, you, most likely Weena, and definitely Asdella, and then I'm sure the rest of your group would soon follow, and as well as most of the people in Shirkint that he has come to know," Blandorf told her gravely.

<World of Zaylyn><Quest For The Sword Fragments And The Hunt For Dranngore><By Katrina Mandrake-Johnston><Ch 70>

CHAPTER 70 = HAIL OF ARROWS

Once again, Blandorf took flight with Candra's arms tightly wrapped diagonally across his chest, with one arm over his shoulder and her other arm beneath his other as before. With her body awkwardly positioned between his wings, which extended from his shoulder blades, she rested her head beside his as she had done earlier, but this time the tension had faded from her form.

"Where to now?" she whispered beside his ear.

"There's a few other places that might prove worth checking, but he could be anywhere really. Do you know much about trolls?" he asked her.

"No," she answered.

"Great, me either," he grunted with a chuckle.

"Well, maybe we should keep an eye out for a water source, a stream or something like that," Candra suggested, "If I were him, I'd want fresh water nearby."

"You see, that's the problem, so would the others, which means that's not where we would find him, as he was an outcast and is even more so now after his involvement with Anthrowst for so long. Besides, these underground passages have plenty of water sources available for those that know what to look for, well at least when they were home to the gargoyles they did. But with the damage the increasing number of Ganairsh caused, and these trolls that now inhabit the mountains, and not to mention the passage of time, I can't really be a better judge. I wish I could."

He dove in closer to the treetops saying, "There was a small passageway into the rock face somewhere around here, if I remember correctly. Maybe we'll luck out and see a campfire he's made, eh? But do trolls even bother cooking their food? I don't think they have the intelligence or patience to do so; it's less than a Garc. So basically, with a troll, if they can't smash it or scream at it in order to get a flame to ignite, then I assume it would be too difficult for them."

"Steren was far more intelligent than the rest and exiled because of it, or so we were told," said Candra, "And then, with his time spent by Anthrowst's side, learning to speak and most likely many more skills, and probably growing accustomed to cooking his food, it's well possible that we could see a campfire near his home."

"Looks like there might have been a landslide, the entrance to the passage I mentioned is clearly blocked. There's no point in landing. We should continue to search farther south, I suppose," Blandorf said to her, and with a massive beat of his wings, he rose to a higher altitude.

After some time had passed, Candra noticed that there was a young boy walking through the grassy fields below them near the base of the mountain range. As they grew closer to his location, the boy began to run, and they could hear him shrieking in terror.

"Something's wrong," said Blandorf descending lower out of the sky to glide over the landscape, "He's in some sort of trouble. I'm going to try to help him, if I can."

<Zaylyn ><Quest For The Sword Fragments And The Hunt For Dranngore><By Katrina Mandrake-Johnston ><Ch 70> < 167 >

"No, wait!" Candra told him as they closed in toward the boy, "He's running from you!"

"What?" he said in disbelief, turning his head to look at Candra with a puzzled look across his face. He too, however, was coming to this same realization.

Before she could repeat what she had said, the boy had seized up a large rock in his hand and hurled it at Blandorf's head. It found it's mark, purely by luck, and the gargoyle's shoulder slammed hard into the ground below as he fell, gouging a trail into the soil behind him. Candra was thrown from his back with the impact. The boy continued to run, and eventually he turned to scramble along a trail leading into the trees that continued up the side of the mountain.

Blandorf lay on his side upon the ground, the knee high grasses flattened beneath him. His wings were outstretched beside him. His eyes were closed. Candra had taken the force of the fall mostly to her hands and knees, but the wind had still been knocked out of her when her torso hit against the dirt.

"*I can't blame the kid. If I had seen Blandorf swooping down behind me like an eagle after its prey, I would have probably done the same,*" she told herself, "*I guess things have changed a little more for him than he realized. I mean, no one here has even seen a live gargoyle in several hundred years it seems. And then, like an idiot, I had to distract him like that, didn't I? If only I had kept my mouth shut, he probably would have seen the rock coming.*"

Candra hurried over to Blandorf, and knelt beside him. "Blandorf?" she called, "Are you all right?" When he didn't answer, she grabbed at his shoulder and shook him fiercely. "Blandorf! Damn it, wake up!" she shouted at him with fear in her voice.

He groaned, but didn't move. She came to cradle his head in her lap. A purplish discoloration was forming over his right eye where he was struck. She ran her fingertips gently along his temple.

"I don't know what to do," she told him. "Please wake up," she begged.

He groaned again, and this time put a clawed hand up to his forehead. His eyes opened to look up to Candra. He asked her hurriedly with worry, "Are you okay? You're not hurt, are you?"

"Never mind me," she said with relief to see him awake, "What about you? Are you all right?"

"Yeah, I think so," he replied, "I guess Shadow was right about hiding my appearance and being cautious about who sees me when flying. I know the people must now be unfamiliar with seeing a gargoyle about, and they never were overly friendly to begin with around us, but am I really so monstrous to look at? Am I really so frightening?"

"It takes some getting used to, I have to admit, but no, at least not the way I see you. Besides, I don't need to answer, do I? You can already read me, can't you?"

"Yes," he smiled, "More so than you have come to realize I think. Thank-you, Candra."

Blandorf got up from the ground, his wings stretching up toward the sky as he tried to gain his balance. Candra stood asking him, "Your wings, they're not damaged, are they?"

"No, I think I'll be able to fly. It's just that I still feel a little bit dizzy. Maybe it would be best to wait awhile, just to be sure. I don't want to put you in danger," he explained.

A few moments later, they noticed a group of five men coming out from the trees where the boy had gone up the mountain trail.

"What's going on?" Blandorf asked her.

Candra, using her enhanced distance vision, could see that they were all armed with bows and arrows. "They're armed. They must be coming after us, believing we meant to attack the boy," said Candra.

"Well, tell them otherwise!" Blandorf shouted with worry, and then wincing from the pain it had caused him, brought a hand up to where his head still throbbed.

"I don't think they'll listen. It doesn't look like they're in the mood to talk," she said nervously and reached for her bow.

"No, wait! You can't fire at them!" Blandorf tried to reason.

"They mean to kill us! Of course I'm going to defend myself!" she snapped back.

The group released a hail of arrows towards them as they stood helpless. Blandorf brought his wings forward, stretching them out before them like a cocoon in order to shield Candra from the piercing shafts of wood and metal. Blandorf winced, grunting in pain, as the arrows slammed into the

<Zaylyn ><Quest For The Sword Fragments And The Hunt For Dranngore><By Katrina Mandrake-Johnston ><Ch 70> < 168 >
velvety membrane of his wings. They did not pierce his skin, but where they struck him, Candra could see the dark welts of the wounds forming beneath.

"We need to get out of here," Blandorf said, with fear for Candra's safety more than he was for his own.

"What do we do?" she asked, as she watched in horror as another hail of arrows struck his wings in front of her and she heard him cry out from the pain.

He grabbed her in his arms, holding her tightly to his chest. Blandorf turned in the direction of the mountains, and keeping Candra's body protected with his own, his back exposed toward their assailants, he opened his wings and leapt up into the air in an attempt to flee into the mountains. More arrows were released towards them, many of them striking him in the back and his side, until they were finally able to escape out of range.

The narrow footpath, where they came to land, was strewn with bright autumn leaves. The sunlight filtered down on them through the treetops.

"Are you injured very badly? Maybe we should just rest here a moment," she suggested.

"Yes," he grunted, holding his side where the discoloration of the bruising was most prominent and, like the injuries to the membrane of his wings, had already begun to clearly show.

He kept his wings outstretched and held high, obviously as it was much too painful for him to collapse and fold them against his back. "Where were you struck exactly? Is this where it hurts the most, on your side here?" she asked, her eyes looking into his with worry.

"Feels like pretty much everywhere, actually," he tried to laugh, but winced at the pain it caused him, "I'll be all right, Candra. I heal quickly. Don't worry. In a few days there won't be a mark on me."

"But are you sure you're all right? Maybe you should sit down for awhile. With that blow to the head and all, it might be best," she suggested helping to ease him down to the rocky ground.

He rested his head upon her lap, and as she rested her hand gently over him in an attempt to comfort him, he closed his eyes and tried his best to block out the pain he was in.

<World of Zaylyn><Quest For The Sword Fragments And The Hunt For Dranngore><By Katrina Mandrake-Johnston><Ch 71>

CHAPTER 71 = BLANDORF AND CANDRA

It was an hour before Blandorf announced, "I need to get you back to the rest of the group. Perhaps they were able to find something. We're not having any luck in finding this damn troll anyhow. They most likely haven't traveled too far on foot, so we'll be able to meet up with them fairly quickly then."

"Are you sure you're up to it?" she asked him with concern and helped him up to stand.

"I don't have a choice in the matter, do I? I'm your only way of getting back to them, and Zaylyn is counting on that sword being found," he told her, folding his wings up to blanket his back and grimacing at how sore it felt to do so, "I don't think I'll be able to take having you against my back though, if that's all right."

"No, of course. Whatever you feel is best," Candra replied and came to stand before him.

She had thought nothing of it at first, until she came to realize that she had become especially aware of how close he was to her. She was simply to put her arms tightly around him to secure her grip in flight, and he was to do the same, but Candra found herself feeling a little too eager to do so than she felt she ought to. Looking into his eyes, she stepped closer. Hesitating at first, she then slowly put her hand around his waist in order to eventually wrap her arms about his chest. As she raised her other hand, meant to be positioned up over his shoulder, she found herself hesitating once again.

Blandorf placed his hand about her waist, but the other he raised up to gently caress her cheek as he looked her over affectionately.

She parted her lips slightly, feeling that she perhaps should say something, but she was lost for words. Instead Candra moved her arm up to finally come to rest upon his shoulder, letting her hand glide up over the smooth hairless skin of his muscular chest.

The arm he had about her waist pulled her in closely against him, and he ran his fingers softly from

<Zaylyn ><Quest For The Sword Fragments And The Hunt For Dranngore><By Katrina Mandrake-Johnston ><Ch 71> < 169 >

her cheek along the line of her jaw and down to her collarbone resulting in giving her an excited shiver. The corner of Blandorf's mouth turned up in a mischievous little grin at this.

He drew in closer, clearly wanting to kiss her, but then it was he that hesitated this time, merely putting both his arms about her waist and resting his cheek against hers. He closed his eyes and whispered, "We can turn back now if you wish. What is it that you truly want?"

A silence fell between them. Candra was aware that he was able to sense what she was feeling, but even she was uncertain of what it was she so unexpectedly felt here with him. In that next moment, his lips, soft and moist, were upon hers, as they held each other in a sensual embrace. With each touch, each caress, the more passionate their kisses grew.

He stopped and asked her with a sly grin, "Should we head back to the others now?"

With a smile she shook her head. "How are your injuries?"

"They're feeling better by the minute," he told her, lifting the quiver up over her head and placing it beside them on the ground. She removed her bow from her shoulder and did the same with it.

With a mischievous little grin across his lips, he unfurled his wings in a magnificent display and then lowered her down to the forest floor where he continued to kiss her and eventually began to remove her clothing.

Soon he was holding her naked form tightly against him in a warm embrace, as he ever so slowly flapped his wings in time with the increasing waves of intensifying pleasure that they were experiencing.

<World of Zaylyn><Quest For The Sword Fragments And The Hunt For Dranngore><By Katrina Mandrake-Johnston><Ch 72>

CHAPTER 72 = BLANDORF AND ASDELLA

When Candra and Blandorf finally came gliding down out of the sky to join up with the rest of the group farther south, they could tell that Asdella had apparently been having a heated argument with Weena.

Asdella snapped at her, "So, Weena, you still think Shadow is so great, do you? That I am continuously slandering his good side somehow? I see that you are still referring to him as merely Shadow instead of The Black Shadow, pretending that he is not the monster he really is. Blandorf," she said deciding that he was to be dragged into their discussion, "Tell me, who fell prey?"

The gargoyle remained silent. "Come on," Asdella demanded, "You were with him for more than an entire night, since late afternoon the day before, right? Apparently, before he sent us to travel to the graveyard on our own, his last feeding had been from Weena. He would have fed since then. Who was it that fell prey?!"

"He, ah," Blandorf began, clearly not wanting to talk about it, "Nexzath was with us. Shadow, well, he... he seemed to double over in pain. He had a look of fear and panic on his face, and his eyes seemed to glow with a reddish light, his fangs exposed as he tried to endure the pain. He managed to say something about going too long without feeding, and yes, that it was your friend here who had been the last. He warned us not to follow, but we did. I carried Nexzath upon my back and by the time we reached him..." he trailed off.

"Yes, go on. She needs to hear this. I think all of us do," Asdella said with a satisfied grin.

"Yes, I suppose you are right. It was just before dusk. He had attacked the carriage traveling to Vackiindmire. At first we were too much in shock to do anything. I mean, I had heard the stories long ago, but to actually see it! Even Nexzath, who had accompanied him a few times to try to help him hold back and not kill those he fed from, had never seen him in that state. It was as if the Shadow we had just been conversing with only just before was gone and had been replaced by some savage and malicious beast. The door to the carriage had been torn from its hinges. What was left of one dwarf was strewn across the ground, his body having been ripped to pieces as The Black Shadow fed." He hesitated, and Candra knew that this was what he had been telling her about earlier; of how he had been aware of what The Black Shadow felt during those moments, the good and the evil, the desire to tear into their flesh, and being able to feel the victims pain and terror. "The second dwarf, who had decorated himself with ribbons and what not for whatever reason, he started to run upon our arrival,

<Zaylyn ><Quest For The Sword Fragments And The Hunt For Dranngore><By Katrina Mandrake-Johnston ><Ch 72> < 170 >

which had been a mistake as it merely drew The Black Shadow's attention. We watched as he leapt at him with lightening speed, and then the screams that followed..." Blandorf trailed off, "They were unbearable to hear. We didn't know what to do. We tried calling out to Shadow, begging him to stop, begging him not to slaughter them. All reason was seemingly gone, his actions appearing to be driven purely by evil. We feared that he would soon turn on us as well. I grabbed hold of Shadow, not knowing what else to do, while Nexzath stood between him and his prey. The elf and carriage driver cowered behind Nexzath as I struggled to hold Shadow back. I knew what we were doing was useless, but all we could do was hope our efforts would somehow make him realize what he was doing and for him to gain control of himself. He tore loose from my grip and, with a vicious growl, pushed Nexzath aside. We managed to stop him, but not before he killed the elf. The carriage driver was spared. We were able to at least save one life."

Asdella explained with hatred, "And because you saved him, The Black Shadow's hunger will intensify even further in his next feeding. Don't you understand, you've made things worse!"

"And what would you have us do?!" Blandorf shouted at her, "Just stand by and do nothing while he kills? That would be awful! How can you even justify that in your own mind? Even The Black Shadow himself knows he cannot simply allow that to happen! You're saying for us not to even try?! We risked our own lives to save that man! How dare you?!"

"And who are you to decide whether that man's life is worth all the lives it will cost for that rescue? Is his one life worth all the people he will eventually kill as a result of that intensified hunger?" Asdella snarled at him.

"If it came to that, I would sacrifice my own life, as would Nexzath I'm sure, in order to prevent more lives being lost," he told her, "Can you say the same? Would you stand between The Black Shadow and his prey in order to save someone else?"

"I would have. Had he only waited, had I only run faster, had I not been so afraid to follow, had I not been so hesitant... I would have given my life for hers, for my cousin. If it meant Ezmeara would have lived instead of me, I would have. She gave her life in order to prevent him from feeding from many; her one life to save numerous others. And what did that do? Absolutely nothing! He still can't stop himself! He can't fight his evil, he can't go against his very nature; it's impossible! And then you," she snarled with disgust at Weena, "Do you really think your life is worth that of all the people he must have killed as a result of sparing you?"

There were tears in Weena's eyes now. She asked, "Blandorf, who was the carriage driver?"

"I don't know, some half-elf with blonde hair," answered the gargoyle.

"It's different when it's someone you know, isn't it? You remember the dwarf and elf at that first table at The Old Scabbard Inn, don't you? And then the dwarf that later joined them, the one who encountered the imp and the fairies? They are all dead now, and looks like Koosenor was almost a victim as well. What do you think of your precious Shadow now, eh?"

"You have no idea how much trouble you've caused, Asdella," Blandorf snarled at her, "No, wait, you do, don't you? All this because of your cousin?" *"and because you felt he should have rescued you from being abused,"* Blandorf thought to himself remembering what he had seen within Shadow, *"I'd never say it to your face, but he left you there for your own good, as to have saved you then would have strengthened the already tedious connection between you two and the evil would have done far worse because of it. You should be thankful the evil had been satisfied then with just letting things be as they were with you. I don't think he could have held on to the good in him as long as he has, if he had become responsible back then for the countless horrors that would have followed and knowing that they were directed upon the cousin of his beloved."* "You have such hatred directed at The Black Shadow, trying to have some sort of vengeance, and if your cousin was here right now, I'm sure she'd slap you right in the face! He told me about Ezmeara! It's all about you, isn't it? You don't even care that you are undoing what she was trying to help him do. It's even what she died for, and all you care about is the pain her death has caused you. You care about nothing else except how things are going to affect you and you alone. ...I can't be here right now. I'm afraid in my anger I might do something I might regret. Candra, the last place I can think of where the troll might be is near the base of the

<Zaylyn ><Quest For The Sword Fragments And The Hunt For Dranngore><By Katrina Mandrake-Johnston ><Ch 72> < 171 >

mountain just a little farther south from here. I told Nexzath that I would meet him at Vackiindmire later this afternoon. He wanted to leave the carriage there so he could come join us in our search. However, I think it's best if I leave for the town now," he said glowering over at Asdella.

Leaving them behind, Blandorf took to the air.

"Great, Asdella! Thanks a lot!" Candra snapped at her, "We could have used his help, you idiot! Don't you see the damage you've done?! And Blandorf is merely trying to help! How dare you try to take your anger out on him, you bitch!"

Asdella merely rolled her eyes at Candra in response.

"*All those words, had they all been for nothing?*" thought Weena, remembering how she had spoken with Shadow alone in the woods earlier, "*Had he even meant what he had said? No, he had been sincere. I'm sure of it. But to go and attack people so soon after? How could he just go and...*"

"The gargoyle thought the troll would be somewhere in this area," said Nodwel, "so I suggest we head out and really start concentrating our search from here on, as we have lost our advantage from above."

<World of Zaylyn><Quest For The Sword Fragments And The Hunt For Dranngore><By Katrina Mandrake-Johnston><Ch 73>

CHAPTER 73 = STEREN THE TROLL

As they all continued south, Dendrox caught up to Candra and asked her, "So, what was it like flying? You looked absolutely terrified when you left."

"Oh, I eventually got used to it. It was amazing being able to soar over the landscape like that. It was really beautiful," she told him, her mind clearly occupied by something else.

"Candra, are you all right?" Dendrox questioned, "I mean, I didn't know what to think when he just took off with you like that. I didn't even know if I'd ever see you again."

"Yes, I know," she said to him, "I'm sorry."

"Candra, what's the matter? Why won't you look me in the eye? I've never seen you like this. Candra, he didn't hurt you, did he?"

"No," she told him, but still seemed distant, "No, of course not. I'm fine. I just need a little time alone is all, okay?"

"Well sure, that's fine," he told her, "Candra, I was really worried about you," and the tension showed in his voice, "I'm glad to see you back in one piece."

"Yeah, thanks," she said to him plainly, and she then walked quickly ahead of him.

Weena came to ask him, "So is she okay? Did something happen to her?"

"Don't know," he replied, "but it's probably good that that creature has left us for the moment."

"Dendrox, listen, I have something to tell you," Weena said reluctantly.

"What is it?" he asked her, looking longingly into her sparkling blue eyes.

She untied and handed him the little cloth pouch about her waist. "There are jewels inside," she told him and then added, "Or at least that's what I was told. I, ah, stole the scissors from your pouch and returned them for the reward. I knew I shouldn't of taken such a risk, but..."

"I know," he interrupted her, "I saw that the message about them had disappeared. I asked Balin when I was looking over the maps about it and found out they had been returned," he grinned at her.

As the group traveled in silence for a fair distance, Candra's attention was later distracted for a moment by something glistening far up near the top of a bare rock wall a little way up the mountain. "I see something," Candra announced to them all, "I think we better go check it out."

"What is it?" Dendrox came to ask her.

"Right there," she said pointing toward the light, "The sunlight is reflecting off something there, you see it?"

"No, I don't," he answered, straining to see what she was talking about.

"Well, it's there," she stated, "Come on, then."

Dendrox followed her up the mountain through the trees and over the jagged rocks, as did everyone else. "*Blandorf should be here,*" thought Candra, "*If this really is the place where the troll is,*

<Zaylyn ><Quest For The Sword Fragments And The Hunt For Dranngore><By Katrina Mandrake-Johnston ><Ch 73> < 172 >

he should be with us when we find it after all the effort he put into the search. When it had been just the two of us, it... To see him among the group again, looking so different compared to everyone else, so unlike the man inside I have come to see him as... Being aware of their reactions to him... and if Dendrox knew of our strange attraction, what would he think of it? It's not as if Blandorf can just openly walk among others within a town or city without drawing everyone's attention to him, to us. Perhaps our lives, Dendrox's and mine, are destined to head in a different direction. Did we really believe we could both live the life of a thief forever? Perhaps Weena was the first step in us coming to realize that."

They came to stand now upon a wide trail at the base of the rock wall Candra had seen. Looking up at the sheer surface, she asked, "Alright, now what? It was somewhere up there that I saw it. Without Blandorf, I don't think we'll be able to reach it."

"I had that rope I picked up at Dexcsin," said Nodwel, "but it got left on the floor of the chamber back in the spider tunnels. Even if we still had it, I doubt it would make any difference, where it's such a steep incline."

"We wait for the gargoyle to return then," said Asdella.

"It's your fault he's left!" Candra snapped at her.

"We have to find another way," said Vordin, "We can't afford to waste anymore time when the Killnarin could spring into action at anytime."

"You're right, but what else is there to do?" commented the dwarf.

Dendrox suggested, "If we can somehow find a way up and around to where we could maybe lower someone down to search the rock for what Candra saw, but without a rope of some sort, that would also prove to be difficult."

Vordin turned to Lorenta saying, "Remember that man, the magic stealer? He said you possessed some sort of magic. He spoke as if your whole being radiates magic."

"That's probably just because I'm able to transform," she told him.

"No, but you said the giant spiders also told you something along those same lines, that you might be able to put that magical energy to use in other ways like for the mind linking ability, right?" said Vordin, "Maybe that's not all you can do. You just assume you are retaining your spider abilities from before, but what if that is not all? You didn't know that you could partially transform yourself to bite the magic stealer and the bandit leader like you did, and the potency of your venom was incredibly strong. Perhaps you are able to scale the wall. Have you ever tried?"

"Well no," she answered, "but even if I could, the weight is too great. My size increased, so even in spider form I would be too large."

Vordin repeated, "But have you ever tried?"

"Well no," she said again.

"So go ahead and make the attempt then," he told her.

"Alright, I'll give it a try," said Lorenta, "Stand back a bit then."

Her body became aglow with the magical green light as the flames burst forward, lapping over her form. Her arms and legs split in two, each piece turning into a fuzzy grey spider leg as the flames subsided.

Vordin exclaimed, "There, see, like this you might be able to scale the wall and retrieve the piece as well. All you have to do is try. You'll have a better chance, a better hold against the rock face, than any of us with the extra limbs."

"If you say so. I doubt this is going to work though," she told him, but she placed her legs against the rock wall and started to climb.

"I'm doing it!" she called out to them, "I had no idea I was able to do this! I'll have the sword piece, if that is what it is, and be back down in no time at all!"

They heard a noise; something crashing through the brush. Lorenta quickly changed her limbs from spider back into human and dropped down from the short height she had achieved.

"Hide," Lorenta whispered, "Whoever it is will see only me, probably only heard me, and will not continue to search for any others."

<Zaylyn ><Quest For The Sword Fragments And The Hunt For Dranngore><By Katrina Mandrake-Johnston ><Ch 73> < 173 >

"But you're the only one who can get the piece," Vordin whispered hurriedly, "and what if something terrible happens to you?"

"Just do it, now," Lorenta commanded fiercely.

The others scrambled into the vegetation, deciding that retrieving the sword piece had to take priority. They all knew that, with Lorenta's strength and abilities, her decision was mostly made in order to distract whomever it was long enough for the others to continue their search.

A net was thrown out over Lorenta, and a large troll, standing near eight feet, emerged from the trees. He had long black scraggly hair and two yellowy-brown tusk-like teeth that jutted out from his lower jaw. The light brown skin of his thick and heavy brow shadowed his dark eyes. He twitched his large wide nose as he sniffed at the air, and the black claw-like nails of his hand, partially clad in a black glove, came up to scratch at one of his pointed ears prominently positioned at the sides of his broad head.

Despite the fact that he was a troll, he wore regular clothing; a pair of boots, black pants and a long-sleeved shirt, with even a short grey hooded cloak that only came to hang just below his shoulders. A thick piece of twine was around his waist and also another was wrapped diagonally across his chest where he had tied on various trinkets. He appeared to behave more like a goblin would than a barbaric troll or even a green-skinned Garc.

"What is he going to do with her?" Vordin whispered.

"Maybe we should attack him," suggested Asdella, "kill him before he has a chance to do anything to her and then we can just grab the sword piece unopposed and be off with it."

"We don't even know if what Candra saw is a piece of the sword, and Steren was entrusted with both of the remaining pieces, remember?" whispered Vordin, "Lorenta might be able to learn something from him. Do you always have to use violence to try to solve all our problems?"

Steren sniffed at the air once again, gazing about the forested trail. He then made his way over to Lorenta within the net and dragged her away with him.

<World of Zaylyn><Quest For The Sword Fragments And The Hunt For Dranngore><By Katrina Mandrake-Johnston><Ch 74>

CHAPTER 74 =   THE SWORD PIECES

Steren took Lorenta and locked her within a makeshift cage made of thick tree branches and rope. She did not struggle and allowed herself to be placed within, knowing that she could easily escape by use of her superior strength or even by transforming into her spider form and slipping through the bars.

"So your name is Steren? You are the troll that was a friend to Anthrowst?" she asked him.

"Me is," he said gruffly and sat down upon a large fallen tree within his makeshift campsite. There were the remains of a campfire and the skins of several small animals that were stretched out between several long skinny poles in order to dry.

"So Anthrowst, he decided to break the sword into pieces and hide them within different locations in the valley?" she questioned.

"It not," he replied, "You not trick me. Last piece not in valley. I hide so not even me know."

Disheartened, Lorenta inquired, "How did you manage to do that?"

"Piece is lost," he laughed, "No one find it now."

"What do you mean?" she asked with tension in her voice, "What happened to it?"

"I give it to merchant ship," Steren explained, "Me say take away to different place and no tell me where. Ship takes piece in cargo. But one pirate, his ship hunt outside Seedelle Bay and take cargo from many different ship. Maybe yes sword piece taken, maybe no. Later many ship find pirate, crush ship, treasure sink to bottom. Maybe sword piece on bottom of sea or maybe in hidden treasure place. No one know. Sword is lost, Zaylyn safe."

Lorenta breathing a heavy sigh decided she might as well keep him talking in hope of learning something more. "So how did you come to have the sword pieces in the first place? What was it that happened?"

"Anthrowst friend to me," he went on to say, "Other trolls not same, me smart. Other trolls eat, fight, smash, no think; not same like me. Other troll only take, no give. When me small, other trolls no

<Zaylyn ><Quest For The Sword Fragments And The Hunt For Dranngore><By Katrina Mandrake-Johnston ><Ch 74> < 174 >

friend; throw rocks, hurt me, no let eat food. Anthrowst save, teach me. Me help. Have great adventures with Anthrowst. One day he get sick. He break sword, give me pieces. Then one day he not wake up. Me no let sword hurt. You stay. Me hide sword again so no one find. Later me let you go."

"So one of the sword pieces is hidden up somewhere in the rock wall I was at, isn't it?" said Lorenta.

He glowered at her saying, "Sword is wrong, it no help, evil want grab it, hurt world. You want for good? No matter, evil take away, hurt world. You no can have."

Lorenta added, "But what if we destroy the sword afterward? After we've used it? That is what Anthrowst wants, isn't it? These creatures called Killnarin, the only way to rid them from our world is to kill the wizard who summoned them here. So many people have already died because of them and so many will follow if we are unable to stop him."

The troll shook his head. "You can no destroy sword, only break, spell only break. Hide so no one find."

"But if it were possible?" she asked him, "What then?"

"You no find last piece," he told her, "You no put together. I hide piece again. You sleep now."

Having said this, Steren pulled the hood up over his head and leaned back to rest his back against the bark of the tree behind him. He closed his eyes.

"*Trolls are partially nocturnal,*" Lorenta remembered from Rasindell's stories, "*Similar to cats in a way, I suppose.*"

With what Vordin had suggested earlier, she decided to try something else instead of making an obvious escape. It was approaching the time when she would have to molt, renewing the outer skeleton of her spider form. She wondered if perhaps it were possible for her to do the same while remaining in human form. She highly doubted such a thing could be possible, but she decided that there could be no harm in trying.

"What are we supposed to do?" asked Vordin, "What if she's in trouble?"

Weena assured Vordin, "As soon as she transforms back into a spider, she'll be able to make her escape unseen. He has no idea that she can shape-shift like that."

"But what happens then? If she turns back into spider form, he will definitely come looking for us thinking she escaped. He doesn't seem to be an evil creature. He is merely trying to protect the sword from being made whole and falling into the wrong hands."

"We wait for her or the gargoyle, whoever shows up first," said Nodwel.

Lorenta had been gone a little over an hour before she came out of the trees to join them, most of the time having been spent in her effort to perform her molt.

"Where's the troll?" Nodwel asked.

"Did you kill him?" asked Asdella.

"No," she glared at her, "I was able to molt in my human form. He won't be able to tell the difference, thinking that I am merely asleep. By the time he realizes that all that remains of his captive is an empty shell, we'll be long gone with the sword piece. There's a chance that the other piece of the sword was lost at sea, however, something about a pirate."

"I guess Leekkar is our next destination then," commented Nodwel.

<World of Zaylyn><Quest For The Sword Fragments And The Hunt For Dranngore><By Katrina Mandrake-Johnston><Ch 75>

CHAPTER 75 = THE BLACK SHADOW RETURNS

As they made their way across the grassy fields with the hilt and blade tip of the sword within Vordin's backpack, Vordin said to Lorenta, "You know, if it weren't for you, we wouldn't have been able to retrieve either of the pieces."

Realizing that this was indeed true, she smiled at him saying, "Yes, I guess you're right, at the graveyard and here. Thanks Vordin."

A smile crept over Candra's lips as she looked up to the sky to see Blandorf's massive wings

<Zaylyn ><Quest For The Sword Fragments And The Hunt For Dranngore><By Katrina Mandrake-Johnston ><Ch 75> < 175 >

gliding through the air as he brought Nexzath upon his back down to meet them. Dendrox looked to her with a curious suspicion, not knowing what to think. However, he watched that pleasant smile turn into a look of terror, and as he looked back up to the sky, he saw it too.

Behind the gargoyle, a dark shape was speeding through the air after him and Nexzath. Candra could see that Blandorf was frantically trying to increase his speed even though his wings and body had not completely healed.

An awful thought crossed the elf's mind, "*The Black Shadow... he sees and hears everything. He knows about me and Blandorf, and what has happened between us. If Shadow secretly craves my affections as Blandorf thought he might, he could be out to kill us both! Have we finally pushed him over the edge with what we've done?! Blandorf must be coming to warn us, but even he knows how useless that would be. We are all helpless against The Black Shadow.*"

As Blandorf landed and Nexzath released him, the gargoyle rushed over to Candra, his wings still outstretched behind him. "Shadow's returned!" he said frantically with fear in his eyes, "Something's wrong. He's..."

The Black Shadow slammed into the ground a little distance away from them, in a landing that shook the ground. His black form raised up to stand before them. He hadn't bothered to bring forth his cloak. His eyes were glowing, burning a deep blood red, and a low and vicious growl rumbled from within his throat.

"Shadow?" Weena called out nervously.

A malicious sneer crept across his lips exposing his pearly white fangs. The fingers of his right hand, along with his glove, like liquid, elongated into long needle-like claws. He chuckled a cruel laugh and said in a calm and melodious voice, "Come now, Asdella. You so eagerly wanted a fight, didn't you?"

"Asdella, don't. He's not the same," Blandorf warned her, "He'll kill you."

Shadow grinned, and the ground shook and began to crack releasing scalding vents of steam. "Come on, what are you waiting for?!" he snarled.

Together, Vordin and Lorenta slowly started to back away from him.

Asdella suddenly cried out in horrible pain, raising her left arm up in astonishment and terror. Blandorf pulled Candra closer to his side with fear, and Nexzath also drew nearer to his winged friend. The flesh of Asdella's forearm began to bubble as she continued to scream in agony, the skin and muscle of her arm dripping away from the bones like melting wax.

"Please stop!" Weena wailed, tears streaming down her cheeks.

Asdella ran at The Black Shadow, lunging at him blindly in horrible mind-searing pain. "That's better," he chuckled, and he took her pain away.

Asdella stopped, looking in disbelief at her useless skeletal forearm dangling at her side with only a few strands of tissue remaining to hold the bones in place. She snarled and swung her sword at him with all her might.

With an evil laugh, he leapt at her, slashing the long claws of his hand viciously across her face, leaving three bloody lines as a result. And as she cried out in sheer agony, an unseen force appeared to take hold of her in both body and mind, crushing Asdella in that relentless embrace until a terribly frightened wailing shriek finally escaped her lips. Then her body was sent limply sprawling to the ground.

"Asdella!" Nodwel cried out, fearing that she may have been killed.

"Stop! Please stop!" begged Weena, "Why are you doing this?!"

"I need to know the truth," he growled, "If I can bring myself to kill you all now, I will know that I am indeed an evil creature with no hope of going against it."

Blandorf whispered to Nexzath, "Get on my back, quickly, it's us he'll lash out at first, once he's finished with Asdella." As Nexzath quietly took hold of him, Blandorf offered Candra his hand saying, "Come with us. I'll try to take you both."

"I can't leave Dendrox," she told him, "The third piece was lost at sea in a pirate raid. Go, I'll be all right."

<Zaylyn ><Quest For The Sword Fragments And The Hunt For Dranngore><By Katrina Mandrake-Johnston ><Ch 75> < 176 >

Snarling, Shadow sent an invisible force to slam into Candra which threw her backwards to land hard on her back and away from Blandorf's outstretched hand.

"Candra! No!" Dendrox cried out.

The gargoyle looked to Shadow in horror. "No, don't. Please, don't hurt her!" he pleaded desperately.

Shadow watched the elf pick herself up from the ground, a low growl rumbling deep in his throat. Candra made her way back to Blandorf, as Shadow watched her intensely with blood red eyes.

"See," she whispered nervously in a trembling voice to Blandorf, "He could have killed me just then, but he didn't. Go. If I can do some good here, I will, otherwise, we're all dead anyhow, right?"

Blandorf nodded, the concern for her growing in his eyes, and then he took to the air. To Candra's relief, Shadow let Blandorf and Nexzath flee.

Asdella stirred on the ground, moaning in pain as she tried to pull herself up. Shadow let out a vicious snarl in her direction, and Candra called out, "Asdella, for goodness sake, stay down, damn it!" and for once she actually listened. Candra started to slowly edge her way over to The Black Shadow.

"Candra, what are you doing?!" Dendrox exclaimed in fear.

"We need him to fix the sword," she replied.

"Are you insane?!" he snapped back at her in disbelief.

Candra walked over to stand before The Black Shadow. "I… I don't need to say anything, do I? You can look into my mind, into my heart? I understand what it is you're trying to do here. In a way it's similar to what I did to Weena when I lashed out at her in the forest, one of the underlying reasons being to discover if I was even capable of doing such a thing. But please, just look into me; see things through my eyes and see what exactly it is you're doing here. Look into me and see that my intentions are genuine. See what me and Blandorf spoke about. See that we both believe that there is still hope for you; that all is not lost. Isn't that what you're trying to prove here? To discover if that part of you that you feel is good even exists?"

His eyes grew brighter, making Candra even more fearful for her life than she already was, and he snarled, "The evil in me wants Asdella dead and it always has. Even now I can still feel it pushing at me to rip her apart."

He looked over to Asdella, watching her continue to writhe in agony as she clutched at her mutilated arm with the blood from her wounds trickling down her face. The redness of his eyes slowly began to fade as he said, "And yet, Asdella still lives. I gave the evil an opportunity to claim what it so desperately desired, and yet Asdella is still alive, all of you are," he told Candra looking back to her once again, "Even now, I want to slaughter all of you, but yet nothing happens. Tell me, what can that mean? I went to see Glendeana and she agreed with Asdella… that the evil rules my every thought, my every action, that I am a creature of the purest evil through and through. But if this is so, why haven't I killed you all yet? I can feel my evil wanting to. Right now, there is no hunger to cloud my judgment, I made sure of that before I came here," and he smiled wickedly at this for a brief moment before he asked her solemnly, "There is no reason why you all should remain standing here safe from harm, if I fully am purely evil, is there?"

"Then what we believe," Candra dared to say, "What you believed… It must be true. A part of you must desire to be free of the torment you cause others," she nervously tried to reason with him.

Candra watched the claw-like fingers of his glove retract back to normal. She watched as his cloak formed up and out of his clothing to hide his face beneath its hood and to drape over his shoulders to flow about him. She took a step backwards. The glow to his eyes had dimmed incredibly, but it still had not vanished completely.

The elf then let out a shriek of terror as The Black Shadow wrapped his arm about her waist and leapt up into the air with her and out of sight.

"Candra?" uttered Dendrox, unable to believe that she was no longer standing there, that she was gone again and this time most likely would never return.

<Zaylyn ><Quest For The Sword Fragments And The Hunt For Dranngore><By Katrina Mandrake-Johnston ><Ch 76> < 177 >

CHAPTER 76 = CANDRA, THE BLACK SHADOW, AND BLANDORF

Asdella stood cradling what was left of her arm, The Black Shadow obviously having taken her pain away once more. Nodwel stared at it in disbelief as he tried to think of some way or anything he might be able to say to comfort her. Then to his great surprise and horror, the bones of the skeletal hand clenched into a fist.

"It's…" the dwarf stammered, "It's just like what we saw at the graveyard!"

"Which tells you who it was that had a hand in helping Anthrowst place such a spell to help keep his tomb protected against those searching for the sword, doesn't it? I suspect that this part of me will always be like this from now on. It doesn't hurt anymore. It just feels strange, very strange," she said unclenching her bony fist once more.

Blandorf came out of the sky, this time without Nexzath. "Candra!" he said frantically, "Where is she?!" He looked over to the two warriors and at Asdella's arm not knowing what to think of it. He folded his wings over one another as usual to blanket his back like a cape, the tips of his wings draping over his shoulders. "Where's Candra?!" he asked again, his fear growing as he looked to everyone.

"She's gone," Dendrox said in a hushed and pained voice.

"No! What do you mean?!" Blandorf shouted, grabbing Dendrox by the shoulders.

"She's gone. The Black Shadow flew away with her," he told him.

"You let her go with him?!" he shouted almost in a growl, "How could you let her go with him?!" he said shaking Dendrox in anger and frustration, and gripping him harder until it finally made Dendrox cry out. "I'm sorry. I didn't mean to… I don't know my own strength sometimes," Blandorf said releasing him, "But she is in grave danger, more than you know! How could you let her go?!" he wailed, his tail swinging back and forth in anguish.

"She's nothing to you. Why do you care so much?" Dendrox inquired with suspicion, "Have you done something to put her in more danger than she already is? Because, I warn you, if you have…" Dendrox threatened, "If you've done anything to harm her… or have made it so harm will find its way to her in some way…"

"I thought maybe because of how he felt about her," Blandorf said sheepishly, "that she would somehow be safe."

"Ah," Asdella laughed, "The Black Shadow has fallen for her, hasn't he? I knew Weena was merely a tasty snack. Let me guess. You said something to try to talk her away and out of his grasp, tried to convince her to stay away from him, right?"

"It's a little more complicated than that. I have to find her," he told them, the panic showing in his eyes.

"You know The Black Shadow won't let you find them unless he wants you to," Asdella said to him, "Don't even bother, you'll be uselessly flying around for hours. Besides, if the two of you have angered him, with him in that psychotic state, Candra most likely is dead already."

"Don't say that!!" Dendrox screamed at her, "You heartless bitch!! You got what was coming to you! Candra doesn't deserve to have anything bad happen to her!"

"Dendrox!" Weena shouted at him, "How can you say that?! Look at her! Look at what he did to her arm! How can you say she deserves this?! How can you justify that?!"

"He doesn't mean it," Blandorf explained with irritation.

"Can you find her? Rescue her?" Dendrox asked looking up into the face of the gargoyle with pleading and desperate eyes.

"I'll try, but Asdella is right. I will never find them unless he wishes it to be so," he explained, and opening his wings, took to the air.

***

Shadow took Candra north to Shirkint to land just outside the town wall. There his body changed shape, and as the hood was lowered, Candra saw a woman now standing before her.

"Perhaps it is his female half as well that is feeling rejected by our actions," Candra wondered, *"The Black Shadow appeared to Blandorf in his female form from the moment he released him from the*

<Zaylyn ><Quest For The Sword Fragments And The Hunt For Dranngore><By Katrina Mandrake-Johnston ><Ch 76> < 178 >

orb. Why else would that be so, unless she held some attraction to him."

"I am but one being, Candra," Shadow said to her, "I always have been. There is no real distinction between my halves. My form usually just corresponds to whatever my thoughts and desires are, if I let it, and occasionally my form is determined by the thoughts and desires of others when I choose to let it do so. Come with me to the inn. I need to speak with you."

The Old Scabbard Inn was empty. "Where is everyone?" Candra asked nervously, as there wasn't even anyone at the counter.

"I've sent them away," she replied plainly, "Come, sit with me."

***

By the time the group had crossed over the field in the direction of Leekkar, they saw that Nexzath had come to meet them with the carriage along the road just on the outskirts of the forest.

"Get in," Nexzath told them solemnly, "I'll take you to Leekkar." A long forked tongue slipped out from beneath his hood to waver a moment in the air before returning to the shadows of his hidden face. "I see that Candra is not among you. I take it Blandorf did not return in time then. I am truly sorry."

No one dared say anything more and entered the carriage.

***

Within the tavern, they sat at the circular table in the corner, and Shadow asked her, "Are you aware that it is normal for a gargoyle to claim more than one mate at a time?"

"No, I didn't," Candra replied nervously.

"It is a natural course of action when they are able to feel another's emotions so freely," she explained, "It leaves little room for jealousy or false thoughts when one is able to sense exactly how one feels for another. If one loves another to a different degree than their chosen mate, it is clearly known and is accepted as such without a grave feeling of betrayal, or the feeling that their emotions have been mislead. Basically, if a gargoyle senses affection in another and feels the same, they will embrace it. When and if that feeling fades in either person, they simply move on."

"So what are you saying?" Candra asked with a lump in her throat.

"Nothing really," she answered plainly, "It is something you need to be aware of however. If he comes to love another to an equal or lesser degree, he will see nothing wrong with it. He won't see the reason behind the pain it will cause you because he will believe you to clearly understand and be aware of how he feels for you without doubt and despite how he may feel about anyone else. With his kind there is no hiding one's true feelings, whether they are acted upon or not."

"Are you attracted to him?" Candra asked, fearing the answer.

"Yes," Shadow said to her, "but that is beside the point and not the reason why I am trying to explain this to you. This is about you and him, and has nothing to do with how I may feel. He is completely aware of my attraction to him through his ability to sense it. I am not about to interfere out of some sort of jealousy, if that is what you are fearing. But should he ever grow to have feelings in return, he will continue to be aware of mine. I would be unable to tell him otherwise, unable to deny how I feel for him, as he would be able to sense my true feelings. And I have to say, that honestly, I would not refuse him but welcome any sign of affection he wishes to give. With him, with gargoyles, anything done to act upon a feeling of affection is beside the point and not of any major significance. There is no sense of betrayal as a result in this. The emotion of love is either present in the person or it isn't, and they are constantly aware of any feelings that their mate may hold for another."

"I see," said Candra.

"He expects you to act in a similar manner to a certain degree. He will know instantly if you become attracted even in the slightest to another and will probably accept it, as long as you don't compare, or judge, or feel you must trade one love for another. As long as you can keep your feelings separate and unique to each individual in nature, you'll be fine. It would be over between you two with that very first thought of discarding him for another. Not that I'm saying you would or should, but I'm explaining to you that if you ever did, that you would not be able to hide your desires from him. With Blandorf's kind heart, he probably would even encourage you to act upon it if it is truly what you wish,

<Zaylyn ><Quest For The Sword Fragments And The Hunt For Dranngore><By Katrina Mandrake-Johnston ><Ch 76> < 179 >

in order for you to find a greater happiness, whether it be with or without him. There would be no point in you trying to deny those emotions you might develop for another for his sake, as he would already know how you truly feel about everything," Shadow explained, "Do you understand? If this ever happens, you must be clear on how it will affect him."

"Yes, I think I do," replied Candra, "Actually, Dendrox would often try to convince himself into this reasoning as well, stating that there was no reason to feel guilty about finding Rinna attractive because his feelings for Weena were clear in his mind and therefore he found nothing wrong with returning innocent flirtations with her."

"It's not the same as that," Shadow said, letting out a breathy sigh.

"No, I know. I understand," Candra assured her, and finding her courage, inquired, "But didn't you say, that if Blandorf ever came to love another to an equal or lesser degree? Isn't that what you said? You're saying that what he feels for me is as strong as that, strong enough to be called love?"

"Perhaps I should not have said as much," Shadow commented sheepishly.

"And if he ever came to have feelings for you as well, that it would not, could not, be greater than what he feels for me?" she said feeling somewhat triumphant.

"I'm afraid that it would actually only be to a far lesser degree if he did. In his eyes you would always come first before any others that he chooses to acknowledge," Shadow replied with a hint of jealousy.

"And there isn't anyone else?" Candra asked, "A gargoyle to take her place by his side should the spell be reversed, awakening them from being stone."

"As in a relationship that merely came to an end because of the spell? Someone that would eventually come to take her place as his queen, now that he is his father's successor?" Shadow questioned, "No, there is not. His relationships in the past with other gargoyles have never lasted long enough for it to come to that, nor had any of the emotions felt been strong enough to be of any note."

"That's right, I forgot that he is in fact a prince," Candra commented, "Aren't there any other gargoyles, ones that were unaffected by the spell? Surely he would be happier with one of his own kind."

"Do not think that way," Shadow snarled, "Your race has nothing to do with how he feels," and then calming herself, she went on to say, "And no, the clans scattered across Zaylyn all came together to form one in those desperate times and to make their homes in the safety of Dee'ellkka Valley. That is until they began to fall prey to the Ganairsh."

Candra nervously asked, "And what is it you feel when you look at me? Blandorf said that it was strong whatever it was he sensed."

"Merely a desire to be near you," was her answer, and she broke eye contact, "to befriend you if you will let me, and if you wish to accept my affections, I would gladly offer them to you."

"Interesting," commented Candra, "I've actually come to discover quite a lot about myself because of everything that's been going on with Dendrox and Weena. So what is it then that you expect from me?"

"Nothing. Nothing at all. Just to know that you are aware of how I feel about you is satisfaction enough. But most of all, it's the peace of mind it brings for me to be able to admit this without fear of the evil manipulating or corrupting it and with knowing that it does in fact stem from a part of me that is good and is able to remain pure above the rest. I have come to a new realization in this. There is stillness within me now where there had not been before."

"Alright. That's fair enough," she decided, "and you feel now that you can keep yourself from turning on others?"

"Unless the hunger takes hold, but yes," said Shadow.

"So what would you like to do?" Candra inquired with a smile that was on the verge of being slightly mischievous, "We could go about town and have a look at what the shops have to offer. That's about as normal as I can think of, and it might be fun just the two of us girls."

An astonished look came across Shadow's face, and then she said smiling, "Yes, I'd like that very much."

<Zaylyn ><Quest For The Sword Fragments And The Hunt For Dranngore><By Katrina Mandrake-Johnston ><Ch 77> < 180 >

CHAPTER 77 =   DENDROX AND BLANDORF AT LEEKKAR

***

Dendrox stared absently out the window of the carriage, watching the dirt road passing quickly by under the wheels.

"*Candra knows what she's doing, doesn't she? She's capable of working a situation in her favor most often enough, not to mention all the times she's done it to me. She'll do her best to talk him down, try to reason with him. But can he even be reasoned with? Will he even bother giving her a chance to talk? He practically killed Asdella, mutilating her,*" he thought to himself.

Nodwel had wrapped his light brown undershirt around the bone of her undead arm to hide it from view and merely wore his leather jerkin over his wide and hairy chest. Dendrox looked to Asdella. She was also staring absently out the window beside her on the other side of the carriage wearing a blank expression on her face. He looked to her arm cradled in her lap and then returned his gaze to the road below the wheels.

"*I shouldn't have said such a thing to Asdella,*" he admitted to himself, "*but then again, if she had just kept her mouth shut all those times, if she just had stopped trying to push him over the edge like that, all of this could have been avoided and Candra would be safe as well... But there's something else, isn't there? That gargoyle, it's absurd to think that there could possibly be anything between them. Can Candra really be attracted to that creature? Is it just a cry for help, an attempt to show me that she feels I've been neglecting her in a way because of Weena? No, that's not it. I really do think she sees something in him... And then, Blandorf said The Black Shadow has some sort of interest in Candra. If he knew that, why would that damn gargoyle still pursue her knowing he was putting her in such danger because of it?! Shadow will most likely kill her out of jealousy! It should be him to suffer The Black Shadow's wrath, not her... But then, Blandorf did keep referring to Shadow as a 'she'. What can that mean?! That the female side has an interest in him as well? Why else would Shadow choose his female form to speak with him? So then Candra has been left to face two sides of jealousy coming at her!*" Dendrox thought with even greater fear and hopelessness.

Weena watched Dendrox in silence, seeing the worry vex him so terribly now, more so now than when Candra had been taken the first time. Even though Weena had seen the kinder side of Shadow, she had seen the evil in him take action as well. Dendrox's worry was undoubtedly justified, as was her own fear for Candra with knowing how fiercely the hunger would grip Shadow if it suddenly decided to take hold.

"*In jealousy over me, Candra practically killed Weena out of the hurt it has caused her,*" Dendrox thought to himself, "*If I had known, I... I don't know what I would have done. I mean, she even came and kissed me afterwards to discover what it was she really felt for me. Can Candra truly feel she can somehow identify with The Black Shadow in what he did back there to Asdella? And then with Candra and Blandorf, when he offered to take her away from there with him and Nexzath, Shadow separated them with that blast of force that almost sent Candra flying! And yet, Candra stayed because of me, because she really felt she could somehow save others in this... even if it meant she had to risk sacrificing her life to do it. It is so unlike Candra to do something like that, at least it was before all of Zaylyn became held in jeopardy and also since she met Weena. I don't blame Blandorf and Nexzath for wanting to flee, as The Black Shadow apparently tends to first turn most viciously on those he's closest to. And yet, later on his own, Blandorf returned for Candra knowing this, that he was putting his life in grave danger to do so. It is very clear to me now what it is that's going on. I don't even know if I could actually bring myself to do the same for Weena, although I'd like to say that I would. I'm not as brave as all that. If I was, I would have tried to stop Candra from being taken by The Black Shadow, wouldn't I?*" Dendrox choked back the horrible gut-wrenching feeling that his thoughts were bringing him.

"*Ha!*" he said to himself, trying to force out a chuckle, "*And Candra tries to lecture me in her bizarre reverse way on how difficult it will be for Weena to follow or even be associated with us in our lifestyle. I definitely think her walking hand in hand with a gargoyle will make us stand out in a crowd* much more than anything Weena could do or say to slip us up in something we are trying to do. As for the sword, Candra's right; we need The Black Shadow to mend the sword and its spell, when and if we get all the pieces in time. Does she really think she can calm that evil and malicious beast in him long enough for that? And that is if it is even at all possible. The Black Shadow can read thoughts and probably her emotions as well. If she doesn't have an ulterior motive other than the sword… if she says, thinks, or probably even feels something the wrong way… And if what I suspect about her and Blandorf is true… or even about The Black Shadow and the gargoyle… What if Candra decides to try to seduce the male Shadow into submission, and he senses something is amiss? Or even if it succeeds and she becomes trapped there by his side… He killed Asdella's cousin even though he said he loved her. Candra, wherever you are, be safe."

Nexzath brought the horses to a halt once they reached the village of Leekkar. "I'm returning to Vackiindmire for the time being. The horses are in dire need of a good rest. As it is, I'll be returning well into the night as it is a fair distance to travel and I don't want to be pushing them anymore like I have been. Besides, Vackiindmire needs to be warned of the danger as soon as possible," he told them as they exited the carriage.

"Yes, good idea," commented Nodwel, "If the Killnarin make their next move, with Vackiindmire so close…"

"Yes, that too," Nexzath broke in, "But I meant about The Black Shadow." Nexzath turned the horses about and started off back down the road.

"Let's go see what we can find out at the tavern. Maybe we'll get lucky and only need to loosen a few tongues with ale instead of coin," commented Asdella, "Or I guess I could scare them into telling us what we want to know with this arm of mine now, eh?" She moved the bones of her hand within the bundle of cloth, listening to the hollow rattling sound it made as the bones collided with each other.

A large figure came forward from out of the shadow of a nearby building. "Dendrox?" he said solemnly, "I need to speak with you."

It was Blandorf. He had donned the clothing Shadow had acquired for him earlier. A light brown hooded cloak was draped up over his head and shoulders and was almost floor length as was necessary to conceal his wings. He had the same brown pants he had worn earlier on, the ones that had been cut to allow for his thick tail extending from the base of his spine, and the cloak also helped to keep it partially hidden as well. As his wings could fold in on themselves to blanket his back like a cape of their own anyway, one could barely tell they were even there beneath the cloak. Thick pieces of black cloth had been wrapped and tied with twine around his feet, hiding his clawed toes and the large talon that curved downward from the back of each heel. Large suede gloves were over his hands and clawed fingers, and like Shadow had done for Nexzath, his face beneath the hood had been concealed in shadow. The front half of a leather jerkin had been strapped over the greenish-grey color of his chest like a bib, tied around his waist and also with crisscrossing straps across his back. This allowed for unrestricted movements of his wings beneath the cloak if he had to suddenly take flight. Two sleeves had also been attached to the jerkin to conceal the flesh of his muscular arms.

Dendrox stepped up to Blandorf and replied with an unpleasant edge to his voice, "Yes, hello."

"You know?" asked Blandorf, knowing well that he did.

"You're, ah, involved with Candra?" Dendrox asked him uncomfortably.

"For as long as she dares to hold those feelings in her heart, I suppose," answered Blandorf, "I know where mine lie."

"And what of The Black Shadow? If the female offered you herself, her power, what would happen to Candra then?"

"She already has," Blandorf informed him, "I would not take it, if it meant I would lose Candra."

"But that jealousy you've caused! She could most likely die because of it, if she even is still alive right now! And what of the male Shadow? You stole Candra away when you knew of his interest in her, didn't you? When you knew he would know exactly what was going on between you two! How could you put her in danger like that?!"

"Because I love her!" he snapped back at him and then apologetically said in a defeated voice, "I could think of nothing else but that. I'm sorry. I'm so sorry."

"So what are you doing here? You couldn't find them?" Dendrox asked firmly.

"Asdella's right," he sighed, "I won't be able to find them until The Black Shadow wishes it. He's able to cloud minds; I could be looking right at them and not even see them. But the reason why I've come is because, while I was flying, I saw something in the bay. There was a legend my people used to tell about a sea creature, a serpent, that inhabited the waters of the Ordore'effont Sea and occasionally entering Seedelle Bay. I'm sure what I saw had to be that ancient beast. I watched it come near the little boating dock near Shirkint where the boats coming into the bay from the larger ships come to get supplies if they don't go all the way down to Leekkar. I thought maybe if you can't find out any information here, that we could perhaps check there as well. Maybe someone there has heard something, and if we're lucky, we maybe can catch a glimpse of the sea creature while it still remains in the bay."

"I doubt we'll have the time," answered Nodwel.

"I could go," said Vordin excitedly, "I probably won't be of much use here anyway."

"Don't you see? We're just drawing out the inevitable. This has always been a lost cause," stated Nodwel, "We just haven't realized it; so desperately fooling ourselves into thinking there could be some sliver of hope left."

"Don't say that," said Lorenta, "Please don't say that."

"Candra's gone, probably dead, and look at Asdella! How can you think we can find the last piece, when it most likely is at the bottom of the sea in the belly of a sunken pirate ship?" the dwarf said coldly.

"We found the other two," Lorenta told him, "I'm not about to simply give up. After all those who have died, you are just going to give up?"

"This isn't some little adventure story like you hear in a bedtime story! Even though it does happen to be a quest for a magical sword. This is real, don't you understand that? It's all so very real! I can't deceive myself any longer into thinking our efforts to retrieve this sword will make any sort of difference," said Nodwel, "It's just too hard to put the reality of it aside, in an effort to give myself false hope."

"And if there is a chance we are able to succeed, what then? You give up now, you make that failure a certainty. I would rather die trying to play the role of a hero than that of a coward," said Vordin courageously.

"Yes, you're right; we need to try regardless. I don't want to give up either, no matter how hopeless I know it to be," Nodwel told him. "So what about that mind link I saw you and Lorenta attempting," he asked them, "Do you think it will work? If you run into trouble, Vordin, do you think you can get word to us through Lorenta?"

"Unless The Black Shadow has conveniently destroyed it," grumbled Asdella, "Probably both our link to the giant spiders and the link they created to each other."

"If Vordin wants to go, I'll take him," offered Blandorf, "My wounds are completely healed now, much faster than I had expected."

Dendrox pulled him aside and whispered, "What wounds? What are you talking about?" He now was fearing that Candra may have been attacked by him and that she had merely been playing along long enough to escape.

"We were attacked," Blandorf explained, "I forgot how frightening my appearance can be to others and we were attacked. I shielded Candra from their arrows with my wings and body."

Dendrox didn't know what to say. "*So this is what is in store for us if we do get out of this alive? Never mind the added attention because of his presence; we run risk of being hunted down by monster hunters because of him in addition to any bounties we might cause to be put out on us? It will be an added danger to Weena as well. We would have to be constantly on guard everywhere we go and in everything we do, no matter if our intentions are law abiding or not. No wonder Candra wouldn't look me in the eye. If she really does care for this creature, she knows what that will bring for us.*"

<Zaylyn ><Quest For The Sword Fragments And The Hunt For Dranngore><By Katrina Mandrake-Johnston ><Ch 77> < 183 >
Blandorf glanced to him with a pained look. With Dendrox's realization at how greatly the gargoyle's intrusion into their lives would affect them, Blandorf felt the animosity towards him growing quickly within the thief. Blandorf called out to Vordin, "We should depart fairly quickly. Grab hold, onto my back, and we'll be off."

***

<World of Zaylyn><Quest For The Sword Fragments And The Hunt For Dranngore><By Katrina Mandrake-Johnston><Ch 78>

CHAPTER 78 =   THE BLACK SHADOW AND HOATAM

Candra and Shadow went about the shops, all the time with Candra trying to make her feel at ease in doing so. They tried on dresses, sampled sweets at the marketplace, and pawed over interesting trinkets they discovered among the various shops. The two of them casually chatted about the gargoyles and their origins, and also briefly about the dragon king and his brother, as well as various other things. The most important thing was that Shadow was smiling, expressing her joy at Candra's company.

Candra wondered if the male version of The Black Shadow would eventually start to emerge. He had already admitted to her that there was an attraction. There was no need for him to hide within his female form. *"Is he choosing to stay in female form for Blandorf's sake? But then again, it doesn't really matter what form The Black Shadow is in, does it? He is but one being; the physical appearance is basically an afterthought. Is he in female form because he wishes to be, or his body simply reacting to what I want? I certainly can't be more at ease with him as a woman, that's for sure,"* thought Candra.

As the two women were strolling absently down an oddly vacant street, a middle-aged man came to follow them.

"Long time no see," Hoatam said from behind them, making them stop and turn to face him, "I see you have found a new friend. It's been awhile since I have tasted pretty young elf flesh," he grinned, "Let me guess, you must be Candra, am I right?"

"How do you know my name?" she said demanding an answer.

"Oh?" he chuckled, "Don't you know who I am? I guess that whiny blue-robed girl Weena and that whelp of a boy didn't bother to even warn you. How unfortunate."

Shadow let out a low threatening growl which rumbled deep within her.

"Temper, temper," he laughed. "Let that viciousness boil, release the beast within," he dared her, "You won't do it. You'd sooner slaughter her than you would me. Isn't that right? So afraid to attack, so afraid of what that desire for revenge might bring. How pathetic," he laughed, "I'm unstoppable."

"Shadow, who is this man?" Candra asked in confusion and with growing fear.

"So tell me, Shadow, you protected the boy from being hunted down, I believe Vordin was his name, and you even went as far as to put some sort of barrier up to keep me from entering the inn to get at Kreasa and her boys. What is it that you think you are trying to do? You're going soft, and here I thought you to be the ultimate challenge."

"Weena went back there with Vordin. The guild warned us about that house and how lucky we had been. If I had known she would have gone back there on her own… it's all my fault, isn't it? If only I hadn't pushed her so," thought Candra. "You're the werewolf," the elf stated, "aren't you?"

"Don't interrupt, mortal," he snarled at her.

"You are nothing but a weak and insignificant worm, Hoatam," Shadow growled at him, "Human like the rest of them."

"Ha! One that has proven to be the biggest threat to the all mighty Black Shadow! Even the all powerful sorceress Glendeana couldn't stand up to you, not like I have!" he announced triumphantly.

"You are but a despicable coward, embracing borrowed power as if it were your own," she said, her words dripping with hatred.

"But it is my own," he laughed mockingly, "You know well what I have done. I killed the last. Brought the beast to murder her own kin at Dexcsin," he grinned widely, "You won't let her species die. I will never let her go or her unborn children. I alone have come to stand unopposed in my power, even bringing you to everlasting defeat."

<Zaylyn ><Quest For The Sword Fragments And The Hunt For Dranngore><By Katrina Mandrake-Johnston ><Ch 78> < 184 >

"What is he talking about?" Candra questioned with curiosity.

"Silence!" barked Hoatam.

"He is merely a host. The wolf inside him is a spiritual being which needs to bond with another to survive. This foul monster of a man hunted their kind within their hosts nearly to extinction, until he discovered the true nature of their being. The pregnant female that he had separated from her host, out of fear that her children would die along with her, had no choice but to accept Hoatam's offer to bond with her in a desperate hope that they would live…"

"Yes, yes," he cut her off, "And hoping that she would be able to postpone their births while she so feebly attempted to devise a plan. She hoped that I would not discover how to infect others, imprisoning her children within them and allowing others to gain power under my ultimate rule," Hoatam finished telling Candra with a mocking smile to The Black Shadow, "And I suspect that it is only a matter of time before they are ready to be born into another. So, tell me Shadow? Are you just going to let me feast upon this pretty little elf as you did that wimpy stable boy, Thorin, you had grown so fond of?"

"I did not let you!" Shadow said through clenched teeth, her fangs now visible to those around her, the illusion hiding them failed, and her dark eyes were beginning to flash red.

"Oh, poor thing," he laughed heartily, "Did you have your thoughts elsewhere when I was tearing him apart? Too preoccupied with satisfying your own hunger to come to his rescue?"

Shadow stared intensely upon him with a fierce loathing and clenched her hands into fists as a fierce and unearthly growl resounded from within her that made the very air around them tremble.

"She's going to lose it!" Candra thought with dread and despair, *"All hope will be lost! What The Black Shadow did to Asdella was nowhere near what he needed to determine what indeed could be found outside his core. If there is hope for Shadow to rise above the evil, this will determine it. She will either snap, letting the rage and sorrow take her over, or find herself in that confusion and step aside from it in order to save this innocent wolf being this man has enslaved. I know what it is like to balance on that fine line. I fell into the darkness when I tortured and slaughtered the two men that murdered my father. I lost myself that day. It changed me forever. I fear that whatever creature emerges in her, freeing itself in order to destroy him and in doing so this spectral wolf Shadow is trying so hard to protect, that there will be no turning back for her. The good will sink to the bottom of her subconscious and suffocate into nothingness as Blandorf feared. Shadow must also know this to be true and is why she has apparently been avoiding the werewolf all this time."*

"What are you waiting for?" he goaded, "So let's see you stop me. Send the elf away to safety. Run! Hide away! Admit that I have surpassed you; that you fear what I am able to do, that I can hurt you so easily whenever I wish the more you try to associate with the people here. Ha! With Thorin, you didn't even make a move to stop me until he was almost completely devoured, vanishing away his remains. Tell me," he laughed, "As you held what was left of his dying and bleeding body, were you able to resist finishing him off? I'm sure you would have held the power to heal his wounds, perhaps even make him whole again, and yet he is gone, with you wallowing in sorrow and never showing your female side until only yesterday. I never knew I could hold such power over you, Shadow, and it feels wonderful!" he gloated and, turning to Candra, asked, "Shall I prove it to her once again, Candra? Bring her to the point where all she can bring herself to do is to savor what I left of your flesh like some ravenous animal?"

"I did no such thing to Thorin, and you shall not have her or anyone else!" Shadow told him.

"Don't make me laugh. Such idle threats; they mean nothing to me. And what's this I find? Denial, is it? How pathetic. I shall leave you to your little games for now," he said dismissing her with a wave of his hand in front of her grimacing face, "Go. Play at being human. I will eventually get my claws into Kreasa and her boys as soon as they leave the protection of the tavern, and anyone else I please for that matter."

Shadow stared intensely into Hoatam's eyes as if she were trying to glare right through him and she gripped at Candra's wrist.

"What's the matter?" Hoatam chuckled, "Still can't make sense of my thoughts, can you? Too

<Zaylyn ><Quest For The Sword Fragments And The Hunt For Dranngore><By Katrina Mandrake-Johnston ><Ch 78> < 185 >

many souls all jumbled up together? Such a shame," he laughed, grinning widely, "Go, run along."

Shadow leapt up into the air to land upon the roof of a nearby building, pulling Candra by the arm along after her. Shadow sat down upon the reddish-brown shingles of the roof as she stared blankly in front of her.

"Are you all right?" Candra asked with concern.

"Thorin… What was Hoatam saying? I did no such thing! I returned too late; after he was slain. I couldn't sense him anywhere. All that remained was blood and little pieces of mangled flesh. It was Thorin's. There was no mistaking that. What did Hoatam mean when he said part of his body simply vanished? Could I have done something back then, without even being aware of it? No… no, with him I would have known. Hoatam is just playing with my emotions in this. He's lying! It's all a game to him!"

"Shadow, you resisted the temptation to lash out at him. You see what this means? You can be certain that Blandorf and I spoke the truth, that Asdella was wrong about you. Perhaps Glendeana, the woman in the orb you spoke of, maybe she just wanted you to discover this on your own," Candra suggested, "Perhaps she said you were still an entirely evil being merely to see how hard you would fight to prove her wrong."

Shadow just continued to stare absently at the rooftop, and a tear rolled down her smooth pale cheek. Candra came to kneel down beside her. She put a hand to her shoulder, cautiously at first, and then coaxed her gaze away from the roof to look at her. Shadow's dark haunting eyes, accentuated by her long lashes, held Candra captivated for a few moments before the elf could find herself once more.

"Shadow, what about the sword? Can you still say that what you intend for us to do with it is beneficial?"

Shadow nodded and told her, "Bring me the pieces and I will make it whole once more, but for nothing more will I use my powers to do in this quest. I will have nothing more to do with it other than to destroy the sword afterwards as Anthrowst had hoped to do. I have caused enough harm already. I do not want to be responsible for any more." She embraced Candra tightly, whispering into her ear, "Without you, without Nexzath and Blandorf, I would be completely lost now to the evil. You three, with the past efforts of Ezmeara and Thorin, are the real heroes in rescuing Zaylyn from a fate far worse than what the Killnarin and Dranngore could have brought. Thank-you, thank-you so much."

"But the hunger," Candra said nervously, with Shadow's lips so close to her throat, "What about that? Now that you seem to be able to more easily subdue your more malicious tendencies, will you be able to stop yourself from killing when you feed?"

Shadow gripped her tighter. "That is something I will have to continue to strive for," Shadow whispered, now sounding slightly lethargic, "Why, are you willing to offer yourself to me to test that?"

Candra felt the gentle cool touch of Shadow's soft moist lips upon her skin and felt the unexpected excitement that it brought. Candra felt the warmth of her breath and the seemingly everlasting stillness between them in that single moment… and then Shadow pushed her away, gasping in the realization of how eager she had suddenly become to taste her, to feel Candra's life's blood flowing into herself in that embrace, to relish in the desires she was capable of invoking in Candra as she fed… "I'm sorry," Shadow stammered, "I need to get you back to the others… back to Blandorf."

<World of Zaylyn><Quest For The Sword Fragments And The Hunt For Dranngore><By Katrina Mandrake-Johnston><Ch 79>

CHAPTER 79 = THE RED CLAW TAVERN

***

After Blandorf and Vordin had left them, Asdella said to them all, "So, I guess we should look around for this place Koosenor told us about. Some tavern run by two women, remember? The Red Claw I think he said it was. It's getting late anyway. We should probably make arrangements for the night. I, for one, can't take going through another night without sleep; I just don't have the stamina."

"I agree," commented Nodwel.

"Nodwel, Weena," said Asdella, "you both are coming with me to The Red Claw. Lorenta and

<Zaylyn ><Quest For The Sword Fragments And The Hunt For Dranngore><By Katrina Mandrake-Johnston ><Ch 79> < 186 >

Dendrox, see what you can find out elsewhere." Dendrox was glad to see Asdella take charge of the group in this moment, as Nodwel's attempts at leadership had apparently worn far too thin.

As they wandered through the dirt streets, they saw that it was fairly similar to Torrnell in design. There were two homes to every house, a wooden staircase at the side of each building leading up to the top home. There were cobblestones however laid down in the central hub of the village where the well was situated and the smell of sea water and fish assaulted their nostrils on the breeze when it was there.

Asdella found the tavern easily enough just north of the village well. Dendrox slipped a small gem into Weena's hand and whispered, "In case the remaining coin you have isn't enough." Weena nodded and headed with Asdella and Nodwel in the direction of The Red Claw, a building with a lobster's claw painted upon the sign that swung in the chill breeze over its door.

Dendrox peered over the edge of the well and said to Lorenta, "You think there's anything down there? Like how there was at Dexcsin, I mean."

Lorenta also peered over the side into the blackness. "Could be," she replied, "Dendrox, I... you don't think I will ever become like that do you?"

"Like what? What do you mean?" he asked her.

"Like The Black Shadow," Lorenta answered, "I... I keep seeing similarities in him. For example, how he can flow his clothing about him like a black liquidly substance into a desired form. My entire body in turn does the same when I make a transformation. And in my dream, I see myself dressed in a black hooded cloak holding a half spider, half human child. I thought it was about me, about my own acceptance of my spider half, or even about what my future might bring in having my own offspring, but now I'm not so sure. What if there is a deeper meaning? The Black Shadow himself warned me against acknowledging that connection. Perhaps my dream in a way was doing the same. The villagers in my dream were burning me alive as I remained trapped within a building. Seeing my own face behind the guise of The Black Shadow, is that an attempt to realize my fears about where my life truly stems from? That I am a child of The Black Shadow? I am here, I exist in this world, because an evil being wished it to be, and if he is truly completely evil, what does that say about me? What evil desire resulted in my creation and for what ultimate purpose am I meant for? Vordin noted that it was I that made it possible for the two sword pieces to be collected. What if this quest is what I was intended for, and if so, would it really be so wise to continue with it? Maybe Nodwel is right after all in that we should stop."

"I'm sure that it is not so. The Black Shadow may have had a hand in your creation, but it was Rasindell that raised you, right? You are his daughter and your own person," Dendrox told her.

"That's what The Black Shadow said as well," commented Lorenta, "But what about what Asdella said, that the spell effecting the graveyard had to have come from The Black Shadow? The gem, it was supposed to have come from the necromancer Enarr. Where do you suppose he could have gotten such a power? You know what I suspect? That The Black Shadow, in his quest to spare his victims, endowed Enarr with the ability to manipulate the dead in hope that Enarr could find a way to bring those Shadow had killed back to life without tapping into his own stronger powers himself. I also suspect that The Black Shadow is responsible for Rasindell's curse, for him to remain in this world to recite the legends of Zaylyn."

Dendrox looked up and was surprised to see Etor from the thieves' guild come out of the butcher shop across from them. He was still dressed in the brown long-sleeved shirt and black vest and pants he had worn when Dendrox had seen him last.

"Thanks sis," Etor called back into the shop, and as he was about to close the door behind him, he added, "Hey, Anota, I'm going over to the tavern to go check on Denonta. After what happened, he's pretty shaken and that's saying a lot for our father, eh? He kept assuring us that to work at The Old Scabbard during midday was the safest shift of them all, even more so than Gulair and Colex, that Ondaff always took from late evening to early morning when all the..." Etor now noticed that it was Dendrox standing over by the well.

"You! What are you doing here?!" he exclaimed in a mixture of anger and fear. He called back to his younger sister, "Anota, close up now and get home, don't worry about losing your job, I'm sure he'll

<Zaylyn ><Quest For The Sword Fragments And The Hunt For Dranngore><By Katrina Mandrake-Johnston ><Ch 79> < 187 >
understand the urgency."

"What's the matter?" asked Lorenta, as Etor came over to them with his grey eyes fixated on Dendrox in a threatening glare.

"What did you do, Dendrox?!" Etor practically snarled at him, "My father, Deckbar, he works at Shirkint at the inn. He's ever so careful not to do anything to draw the attention of The Black Shadow, as am I, as is my entire family! What did you do?! Why are you here in Leekkar?! What have you brought down upon us?! What did you tell him?! You've put my family in jeopardy?! We did nothing to the two of you at the guild! We did everything you wanted; everything The Black Shadow wanted! What did you do?!"

"Nothing, I swear!" Dendrox replied.

"My father one minute was at The Old Scabbard, and the next, he found himself instantly back home," Etor told him, "It can only be The Black Shadow's doing. Who's this?"

"Lorenta," said Dendrox.

"Be thankful he's still alive," Lorenta told him, "The Black Shadow is losing his grip over himself. Everyone is in danger. He nearly killed all of us."

"What?!" Etor exclaimed, running his fingers through his dark blonde hair in an attempt to hide his nervousness, "He usually doesn't bother with those that stay out of his way. But yes, you're right. My father is still alive. Chances are The Black Shadow retreated to the inn to be in a familiar place and just didn't want anyone else around."

"You really think so?" asked Dendrox.

"It's what I'd like to believe," said Etor.

"How long ago was it that your father appeared?" asked Lorenta.

"Not long. Why? Where's your friend, the elf?" he asked narrowing his eyes.

"Taken by The Black Shadow," answered Dendrox.

"I see," said Etor, "Then I suppose there is no harm in making sure you have somewhere decent to sleep. My youngest sister is part owner at The Red Claw. Funny story involving Zindle in how that came to be. I'm sorry about Candra. Don't worry, I'll make sure Denonta gets you properly seen to. Just don't forget the favor. So what is it that you're doing in these parts?"

"Looking for a broken piece of sword," Lorenta explained to him, "It was in with the cargo of a ship that had been raided by pirates."

Etor chuckled. "You've come to the right place then. I'd watch yourself. Around here, a girl shouldn't go anywhere unescorted, more so than anywhere else with the lot Leekkar usually gets comin' in from the ships."

"I can look after myself well enough," Lorenta told him, "I'm stronger than I look."

"Oh, yeah?" Etor said with a growing smile as he walked them toward the tavern, "Me too. You wouldn't be able to guess, but these scrawny little arms of mine have inhuman strength. So you a half-breed of some sort? You don't look it."

"A shape-shifter," she replied a little nervously.

"I'm part elf, part Dragonite," Etor told Lorenta, "but then you'd see that for yourself to look at either of my little sisters." He pulled back the sleeve of his shirt to reveal patches of flesh-colored scales randomly scattered along the tan-colored flesh of his arm. "All human-dragons have these random sprays of scales. You see one before?" he asked her, and Lorenta nodded. "Yeah, bald, oddly-colored eyes and skin, claws, tail… Being only half, I guess I lucked out with just inheriting the scales."

Etor opened the door to The Red Claw and ushered the two of them inside. From the door he called out to his youngest sister, "Hey Denonta! Make sure these two are shown some hospitality, would ya?"

"Where are you going?" Lorenta asked him, having enjoyed the extra attention he was beginning to show her.

"Don't worry, I'll be right back. Just have to run and let Anota and my father know not to worry, and that we're out of danger," he told them.

<Zaylyn ><Quest For The Sword Fragments And The Hunt For Dranngore><By Katrina Mandrake-Johnston ><Ch 79> < 188 >

"Whoa, wait a minute," Dendrox stopped him, "What are you talking about?"

"Well, The Black Shadow got what he wanted, didn't he? I said I was sorry 'bout Candra. It's obvious that, because of it, he has no reason to bother with us," said Etor closing the door.

The woman Etor had addressed as being his sister, stood six feet tall with her straight golden-brown hair in a ponytail that fell to mid back. Her eyes had a slight slant to them and were such a brilliant green that they almost glowed. Her skin was a dark tan color on the verge of being tangerine. Denonta tapped her large clawed hands upon the countertop as she eyed the two of them suspiciously.

"Another favor for my brother, eh?" she said with irritation, "Sindeana ain't goin' ta like this. I keep doin' him these favors, I'm goin' ta eventually have to be havin' words with her, which is somethin' I'd rather not be doin'. But that's between him and me, ain't it? Just tell me what is it you be wantin' and I'll see what I can do." Dendrox nodded in acknowledgement of this.

"Dendrox! Over here!" Nodwel called out from a smoky corner of the tavern.

The two of them had to pass by several rough and unruly looking characters before they could eventually join their companions at the table. "Remember that group that me and Candra ran into at Shirkint where we got Enarr's item from?" Dendrox said to them choosing his words carefully, "Turns out the sister of one of them is part owner of this place. But most importantly, something happened at The Old Scabbard Inn which means Shadow is most likely there... but there's no telling what happened to Candra."

"Yeah, well, we asked around," Nodwel informed them, "about anything from roughly a hundred years ago when the sword piece would have been in transit, and well, there was only one pirate of real note around that time. Unfortunately, the last this pirate was heard of, his ship was sinking to the bottom of the sea. It's lost if it was still on board, and if not, we have no leads and no time if we did. I could use a few more mugs of ale, I think. Asdella, you want another?"

Dendrox let out a breathy sigh and then said, "Me too. There's nothing we can do now."

Etor joined them soon after and arranged for them to be provided with drinks and lodgings for the night at the inn when they had need of it. He struck up a conversation with Lorenta again, and slowly he came to learn about the hardships they had been through.

Dendrox, however, in the meantime, had continued to prod the local patrons for any bit of information he could. No one provided him with anything of note except for one man Dendrox spoke to. The man had gotten himself quite drunk and had been rambling on about how he had lost his leg.

"I used t' be a fisherm'n," the man had told him, "Now I be crew on this 'ere ship. But this 'ere leg o' mine," he had said propping his wooden leg up on the chair beside him, "A damn thing I'll never be gettin' used to, it be. Y' know, a blasted sea monster did this 'ere, it did! I ain't lyin' neither. I sees you be thinkin' I is," he had slurred, waving a bony finger in Dendrox's face, and then continued saying, "But I ain't. Sea monster comes and eats m' catch, rips m' nets and even part of me boat! Completely ruined my life that beast did. So of course I try to kill the creature with dis harpoon I gots, and what'd it do? It bites m' leg clean off and dives back down in ta the depths. Damn near bled to death sinkin' on what was left of me boat. If I hadn't been rescued by them pirates shortly aft'r with all them there healin' magic things..." He had then belched a foul stench into Dendrox's face and then commented with a laugh, "It be a girl captain, I kid you not. She killed some big shot pirate who raped some friend of 'ers and killed 'er father by throwin' 'im overboard to drown he did. She no doubt was to be meetin' the same fate aft'r he had his way with 'er. But the clever little whip caught him by surprise, she did. The crew didn't really know what t' do aft'r that as the captain had just finished killin' his first mate for protestin' 'bout somethin' or another. So the crew made the girl the new captain since she had dispatched the old. It be a joke really just until they were ta reach shore. Turns out she be a far bett'r captain than d' old, treated the crew with more respect that's for sure, even got 'em all a bit of treasure on the way. Incredible brain in that head of 'ers. Cunnin' as a fox, I say. She made sure the loot was split 'tween the crew too, not like that greedy bastard that'd no sooner look at ya than stab y' in the back."

"That's a little hard to believe," Dendrox had commented.

The man had waved him closer and whispered, "Real reason be The Black Shadow. When the

<Zaylyn ><Quest For The Sword Fragments And The Hunt For Dranngore><By Katrina Mandrake-Johnston ><Ch 79> < 189 >

crew be playin' 'round s'if she be the captain, he came, landed right on the deck he did, and had words with 'er. No one dare challenge her since then but one, and he got snatched from the ship so fast by that black monster… But that's beside the point. You see, given the chance, that girl's proven to be the best pirate 'round these parts of late. The Black Shadow merely got her foot planted in the right direction, basically gettin' Soolina a crew and a ship as a result."

***

<World of Zaylyn><Quest For The Sword Fragments And The Hunt For Dranngore><By Katrina Mandrake-Johnston><Ch 80>

CHAPTER 80 = SEARCH FOR THE FINAL FRAGMENT AND GALORPH

Blandorf landed, and Vordin, very shaken, released his grip from around the gargoyle. At the water's edge there was a small log cabin, and as they continued on foot, they could see a middle-aged man relaxing on the porch in a rocking chair.

"Hello," Vordin said to the man when they arrived at the water's edge in front of the cabin, "I was wondering if you could maybe help us. Do you know anything about a pirate, say around a hundred years ago, that used to plunder the waters near the valley?"

"Ha, you'll have to be more specific than that boy," the man replied.

"It's about a insignificant piece that might have been taken along with the rest of the cargo in an attack by this pirate. It's a broken fragment of sword. A troll would have been the one to arrange for the sword to be on the first ship," said Blandorf.

"Yes, that's right," added in Vordin.

"Can't say I have," he told them, "My name's Bockair. Not many bother t' come this way anymore on foot. You'll probably have better luck down at Leekkar. That place frequents a lot of folks that might know a story or two that could help you. Try the tavern; that'd be your best bet. It's called The Red Claw."

"We've just come from Leekkar," commented Blandorf with frustration, "Have you ever seen anything unusual in the water?"

Bockair chuckled, coming down from the porch to join them. "Follow me," he told them leading them out onto the wharf, and then, pointing to the water where a dark shape was forming up beneath the surface, he said, "You mean like that? That'll be one of the reasons why not many come this way much anymore."

A dark blue serpent-like head rose silently and gracefully out of the water to tower above the three of them. Vordin and Blandorf both stared in awe and wonder. "Her name's Galorph," Bockair told them.

"Yes, I know," Blandorf told the man, still staring in amazement at the massive creature before them, "I always wondered if the stories were true. Such an ancient and graceful creature… and I… I can feel her. Vordin, it's amazing!"

"She's not going to hurt you, boy; you look an awful fright," Bockair chuckled.

The sea serpent made a low bleating noise which ended in a high-pitched whistle. She bent her large head down to where they were standing, and as her huge amber eyes gazed upon Vordin, she released a breath of air from her nostrils that almost sent Vordin falling over backwards.

"I think she likes you!" laughed the gargoyle.

Galorph nudged Vordin with her snout and knocked him sprawling. "What's she doing?!" Vordin exclaimed in a panic.

"Relax," Bockair told him, "Looks like she wants to make friends with ya, probably even share a bit of her treasure as an offering of friendship as she usually does. It's a rare and special occasion, this. Y' should be very proud. It's just shiny junk she finds as she swims out and about in the water. Occasionally, she'll come across somethin' that can fetch some coin, and if she is willing t' part with it, it helps ta pay for the odd sheep she's partial to as an alternative meal to the massive amounts of fish she eats out there in the Ordore'effont. It's not often one gets t' befriend such a magnificent creature as she is, and I, myself, greatly cherish that honor she has so graciously extended to me. You'd be surprised at just how clever she is too. Go on, she wants ta take you t' view her little treasure horde."

<Zaylyn ><Quest For The Sword Fragments And The Hunt For Dranngore><By Katrina Mandrake-Johnston ><Ch 80> < 190 >

"She does, Vordin. It's safe," Blandorf assured him.

"What… what do I…" Vordin started to ask just before Galorph opened her mouth and gently picked him up in it. Vordin shrieked in horrible fear as she swam side-winding through the water at an incredible speed all the way to the opposite side of the bay where she entered a narrow cave like passage in the high rock cliff. She set Vordin down on the narrow shelf of rock within the cave, where above the water line, she kept her collection of shiny bits of metal and other colorful objects. Galorph gave Vordin another nudge with her snout that sent him toppling.

Vordin pawed through the trinkets scattered about on the rock floor, merely to keep the sea serpent pleased with his actions. Then a thought came to him. "*If the sword piece was indeed lost at sea, chances are she might have found it. It could well be here as it has no value as a piece of treasure, but the metal might have sparked her interest*." Vordin continued to sift through the items, this time with purpose in a search for the middle piece of the sword's blade.

***

<World of Zaylyn><Quest For The Sword Fragments And The Hunt For Dranngore><By Katrina Mandrake-Johnston><Ch 81>

CHAPTER 81 =   THE SWORD OF ANTHROWST

"Hey, somethin's wrong with Lorenta," Etor told them, as she winced in pain and held her head.

"The Killnarin," she said with dread, "They're leaving the spider tunnels."

"What do you mean? Those creatures you told me about?" asked Etor, "What do we do?"

"We make our way to Shirkint, I suppose," said Asdella.

"Yes," agreed Dendrox, "If Candra is there and we can somehow get The Black Shadow to help us…"

"We've failed," said Nodwel, "I'd like to return to Shirkint as well though. We can help make our stand against the creatures there. Kreasa and her boys are there as well; they should be warned. Failick, the centaur we spoke to, he may have come up with some sort of defense plan with his friend who owns the magic shop there."

"This is real, isn't it?" said Etor, "We'll do our best to rally the people of the village against these beasts if they decide to attack here."

Lorenta winced again, this time crying out in searing pain. After a moment, she managed to say, "It was Vordin… at least I think it was. He has the sword… or at least that's what I thought he said."

"What?!" Weena exclaimed in disbelief, "Then let's go!"

"We'll never get to him in time," Nodwel told her, "We still have to get the sword back together and only The Black Shadow can do that. Then, there is the matter of finding out where this despicable creature of a man even is in order to kill him with it. What if the sword doesn't even do what we think it does?"

"There's a way to be certain of that," Etor told them reluctantly, "Dendrox, you remember what we purposely didn't mention back at the guild? Well we have something that… I don't know, gives information about things we want to know about. It's how we were able to monitor your connection to The Black Shadow and your activities to a point within Shirkint. We mostly use it to identify what's of value and worth stealing, finding out the origins of an object and whether it has any magical properties. I've most likely forfeited my life by telling you this, but I do believe you. Take my ring, with it you'll be able to access the guild's inner most chambers. It is a large plain white slab of stone. Place the sword upon it and wait to see what results."

Asdella, pulling back the cloth around her skeletal arm, gripped the bones around her empty mug. The thick glass shattered as she squeezed. "Interesting," Asdella chuckled, "Anthrowst said the undead creatures increased in strength the more the night progressed. Looks like it's the same for mine now."

"Yes, I definitely believe your story," Etor told them staring in astonishment at Asdella's hand, "Wait here for me. You need to get to Shirkint quickly, right? I have something that will help you." He then shook his head saying, "I can't believe I'm doing this. I'm most likely going to be kicking myself later for doin' somethin' like this."

Etor left the tavern, and when he finally returned, he held five bottles of thick brown liquid. "We

<Zaylyn ><Quest For The Sword Fragments And The Hunt For Dranngore><By Katrina Mandrake-Johnston ><Ch 81> < 191 >

should probably go outside first, just to be safe," he told them and handed one of the bottles to each of them.

Once outside he explained, "Okay, now what these bottles contain is a highly potent potion of speed. You probably won't find this in such a great quantity or quality anywhere else. It's worth… well, pretty much priceless, but if our world is truly in danger, now is the time for it. Plus, I still have a full bottle of the stuff left over, so all is not lost. Now what you do, is you take a small swallow at first, let your body adjust, then take another, and another, and so on. You'll know when you've hit your top speed and after that only take another swallow when you feel the effects starting to wear off. If you take it all at once, you'll most likely send your heart into… well, you'll die."

***

As Blandorf walked with Vordin along the path that would eventually lead them to the main road and up to Shirkint, The Black Shadow and Candra came out of the sky to land before them.

"I have the sword pieces," Vordin said triumphantly, "All of them!"

"Candra, I… is everything all right?" Blandorf asked her.

"Yes, I think so," she replied glancing over to Shadow.

The female Black Shadow lowered her hood and said to Vordin, "Give me the pieces."

He looked nervously to Candra and Blandorf, and then back to the captivating vision of beauty that The Black Shadow was. "It's okay, Vordin," Blandorf told him, "There's a stillness now in her."

"*Like the stillness before a storm?*" Vordin thought with worry.

"It's all right, Vordin. Give her the sword," Candra said to him, "She can differentiate now between the evil and the good she is trying to do. All of her actions are not ruled by the evil. We can trust her…" and then Candra hesitated before adding, "It's just the hunger that remains strong."

"But, what…" Vordin stammered, not knowing what to do.

Shadow held her hand out to her side and the hilt suddenly appeared. The next pieces were taken from his backpack in the same manner, and in this way, the sword was magically made whole once more. Shadow handed the Sword of Anthrowst to Vordin. "I'll remain at The Old Scabbard for the time being. I'll destroy the sword afterwards for you, if and when you succeed in your quest," she told them and then vanished before their eyes.

"What's that?" Vordin asked, looking down the road at what appeared to be a blurry mass flowing over the ground to approach them.

They stared in wonder until the mass began to draw nearer and slowed until they could recognize the individual figures as being their companions. Dendrox immediately grabbed Candra and squeezed her so tightly in a heartfelt embrace that she could barely breathe.

"Is that the sword?!" Nodwel asked in disbelief, "It's been made whole?" Vordin nodded, marveling at the iridescent shimmer along the length of the blade. "Do we know where the wizard is then?" asked the dwarf with growing hope.

"Not yet," said Candra, "But I'm sure we will before the Killnarin make their next move."

"It's too late," Asdella told her, "They've already left the tunnels and are headed to wherever it is they are going, whether it be to enact Dranngore's plan or one of their own."

"No!" gasped Candra, "There is something I need to do first then, back at Shirkint."

"Me too," said Dendrox, "Give me the sword, Vordin. I want to find out exactly what using this sword is going to do. Don't worry, Candra, I'll explain on the way into town. Come on, Vordin."

"What should I do?" asked Weena timidly.

"We need to find where this wizard is going to be and fast. Where's this damn wizard's guild supposed to be situated?! The last of the sun's rays are gone now, and with the Killnarin roaming about stronger than ever, all we can really do that might possibly be of some help is to warn the people of Shirkint," Nodwel grumbled with frustration and desperation.

"Can we trust him? How eager did Etor seem for us to return to the guild? And with his ring?" Candra asked as she followed quickly after Dendrox in the direction of the Sinva's home and the thieves' guild below it, "What if we are so blindly walking into a trap after all we've done to get the

<Zaylyn ><Quest For The Sword Fragments And The Hunt For Dranngore><By Katrina Mandrake-Johnston ><Ch 81> < 192 >

sword? All the precautions taken to break the sword, to ensnare the pieces so they couldn't be retrieved… And here we have the sword whole and with its spell fully intact..."

"No, you're right," admitted Dendrox with a chill, "How could we be so blind? What were we thinking in dropping our guard? Even if Etor's intentions are genuine, there's no excuse for us having that kind of disregard. We need to be extremely careful in this. We were so concerned about whether using the sword will cause something terrible to happen, that we were just about to go into an unknown situation and probably end up handing it over to who knows who. Etor could even be the one being deceived, not realizing the bigger picture if there even is one. The question is, do we trust him or The Black Shadow?"

"No, we turn around Dendrox, and we trust Shadow," said Candra.

"But how do we…" he began.

"No, we trust The Black Shadow! To doubt her now in such a tedious time… The Killnarin are a delightful alternative to what could come. What small measure we've seen of Shadow's evil, what we've seen of the Killnarin… all that is nothing compared to what could be, Dendrox. We take the sword and finish this quest. And we trust that the good in Shadow is able to remain strong."

"Okay, Candra," Dendrox said uneasily, "Whatever you think is right. You know I'll follow."

"I need to get to the magic shop," Candra told him as they hurried down the streets of Shirkint.

Blandorf, at Candra's instruction, had gone to sit with The Black Shadow within The Old Scabbard Inn. Candra had tried to reason with him that they could finish the quest without him and that Shadow needed him to be there with him should his hold over himself start to falter. Blandorf obliged in order to please her, despite his concern.

Weena stood by the town entrance beside Lorenta and Vordin as she waited for the others to return. Nodwel and Asdella had gone to quickly speak with Failick about the approaching Killnarin and what was to be done about them should they attack Shirkint. Despite the fact that they had the sword, the two warriors knew well that the chance they could still fail was great.

Weena glanced over the message board to pass the time and a curious expression crossed her face. "I'm going to go speak with Balin," she told them, "He should be there this time of night, right? It's just shortly after dusk. I need to ask him about something. I won't be long."

When everyone came to meet shortly after, Weena announced, "I know where the guild is! I know where Dranngore will be!"

"What? How?" asked Vordin.

"The red-headed young girl Dranngore used to speak to the Killnarin with, the one the giant spiders showed Lorenta," Weena explained, "Well look here on the board; she wasn't chosen by Dranngore at random. I spoke with Balin further about it. If we're right, it looks very likely that this girl is related to one of the wizards at the guild, or at least that's what Balin came to suspect. Anyway, he was told that if anyone came forward with information on her whereabouts, that a message was to be sent to a remote location halfway up one of the mountains. It definitely looks like we have discovered where the wizard's guild is. I know roughly which mountain it is, and if we didn't have these potions, we definitely wouldn't be able to make it in time. We'll have to divvy what's left of them in order to have enough for Vordin and Candra."

"Wait for me then. I need to make sure Kreasa is all right before we leave," said Nodwel, and he rushed over to the inn.

His heart fell when he stepped into the abandoned room of the tavern. The dwarf frantically ran up the stairs to the second floor and to the room where he had last left Kreasa and her two young sons.

When Kreasa answered the door, she embraced him saying, "Nodwel, you're alive! The werewolf, he's found us! He can't enter the building. The Black Shadow himself came and told us as much, early last night. He even took me to one of the windows here on the second floor to show me what that foul beast looks like in his human form. Hoatam, that's the werewolf's name, he looked up at me and The Black Shadow from the street below with such a viciousness. Can The Black Shadow really be trying to protects us? And now, now, everyone from the inn has mysteriously vanished except for us. What's

<Zaylyn ><Quest For The Sword Fragments And The Hunt For Dranngore><By Katrina Mandrake-Johnston ><Ch 81> < 193 >
going on?!"

"Kreasa," said Nodwel, "We have the sword and The Black Shadow is here somewhere within the inn."

"Should we flee? We don't dare leave here!" Kreasa told him with anguish.

"Blandorf, he is here with The Black Shadow. If there is trouble with either creature, the werewolf or The Black Shadow, he may be able to help. He's a gargoyle..."

"A gargoyle?" Kreasa interrupted in disbelief.

"Yes, but you need not be afraid. I'll try to return as quickly as I can," he told her, "Keep your children safe."

"Weena?" Candra said to her, "I have something for you. Come over here for a minute."

Curious, Weena obliged. To her surprise, the elf held out her ring to her. "My mother's ring?" Weena said looking to Candra in confusion.

"I know I should have probably asked first, but I had it enchanted," Candra told her, "I asked the woman what I could possibly get for a ring, she gave me a list of various spells, and I tried to pick what I thought would be best for you." Weena was lost for words.

"Where'd you get the incredible fee that must have cost?" inquired Dendrox.

"Rinna," Candra replied, "I felt she needed to contribute for various reasons and that Weena was owed to receive that contribution for various reasons as well." Dendrox knew what she meant by this.

"What spell?" asked Weena.

"No, there's only one charge in it, and in order to ensure that it will be there for you only when you desperately need it, I can't reveal it to you," the elf explained.

"Let's go," said Nodwel coming out of the inn, "Vordin, I think you should be the one to take the sword for now. It was you that the quest was first bestowed upon."

Vordin and Candra were instructed on how to take the doses of the potion in order to reach maximum speed and maintain it. Then, in a blur of speed, the group departed for the mountains and the wizard's guild.

<World of Zaylyn><Quest For The Sword Fragments And The Hunt For Dranngore><By Katrina Mandrake-Johnston><Ch 82>

CHAPTER 82 = THE WIZARD'S GUILD

As the last doses of the potion began to wear off, the group slowed to a stop about a third of the way up the mountain trail.

"I hope this is the right mountain, Weena," Nodwel said looking about with concern.

"It is. I'm sure of it," she answered.

"Maybe the Killnarin haven't arrived yet," suggested Vordin.

"No, there's no chance of that," said Nodwel, "If this is where they were destined, we would have seen them."

"You mean we've come all this way, and the Killnarin have instead decided to go off on their own agenda?!" Candra said in dismay.

"Unless Weena has led us up the wrong mountain," Asdella grumbled.

"No, this is the one!" Weena insisted, "The chambers of the wizard's guild must have been built right into the mountain face. There should be an opening of some sort; probably disguised."

"The Killnarin," said Dendrox, "Remember Candra? The wizard, the one who was turning invisible that we found?"

"The arrogant pest we picked up in our travels into Dee'ellkka Valley whose disappearance led us to be slaughtered at Dexcsin?" said Asdella bitterly, "What of him?"

"Well remember, Candra? I didn't find any tracks of any kind made by his attacker; there was only trampled vegetation to be found," Dendrox explained.

"He was turning invisible to escape from the beast, right? He may have been doing this merely in order to see where his attacker was coming from," suggested Weena, "The Invisible spell is able to conceal footprints, even hide any shadows that might be cast. It's almost as if what or who the spell is

<Zaylyn ><Quest For The Sword Fragments And The Hunt For Dranngore><By Katrina Mandrake-Johnston ><Ch 82> < 194 >
cast upon is brought into a slightly different plane of existence for a short time, well maybe not as far as to say that, but at least removed enough to…"

"Your point?" snapped Asdella rudely, holding up her skeletal forearm in the moonlight and watching as she clenched and unclenched the bones of her hand.

"Well, he may have been casting the spell to be able to see the Killnarin if the beast had turned itself invisible as well is all," Weena explained, "Maybe he wasn't casting it to hide."

"I couldn't see any tracks made by the creatures after returning to Nilnont either, Dendrox," commented Vordin, "or at Dexcsin come to think of it."

"So even if that was the case with the wizard, it seems their ability to conceal their movements comes naturally to them," said Nodwel, "Even if they came this way, we wouldn't be able to tell."

"Unless Dendrox is able to find something out of the ordinary," remarked Candra.

"In the dark? By the light of Vordin's lantern alone?" Dendrox laughed, "Come on, Candra, that's expecting a little too much of me, isn't it?"

"Let's just continue up the trail and find the wizard's guild," said Lorenta, already heading up the rocky path, "It's where Dranngore would have sent them if they are still under his control."

"There's been no further word from the spiders?" Dendrox inquired.

"No, they returned to secure their tunnels once the Killnarin had vacated. The Killnarin were headed north last they saw of them, so chances are they made their way here."

Just then, they felt a slight tremor in the rock beneath them. "The Black Shadow?" Vordin questioned.

"No," Candra told him, "He's back at Shirkint with Blandorf. Although I'm sure that it would not really make any difference where he is to be able to do that, he said he would play no further part in this." *It was the right thing to do in leaving Blandorf with Shadow, wasn't it?* she asked herself, *"I know he's dangerous, but Blandorf will be safe, won't he? Here I am referring to Shadow as a 'him' when I know damn well that probably some time after I had left them that Blandorf's presence would have eventually brought out the female in Shadow whether or not Shadow had intended her to surface or not."*

"You know what?" said Weena hurrying after Lorenta and waving at the others to follow, "I bet it's a superior Blast spell being cast, or more likely several of them being cast all together at once to cause such a tremor. The Killnarin must be battling the guild. They're here, and I'm sure Dranngore must be as well in order to witness the guild's destruction."

"But is that such a terrible thing?" added Nodwel, clambering up the trail by the lantern light, "The wizard's guild is an evil organization. You said it yourself, Weena. They've enslaved and killed countless people in their quest for power, am I right? The Killnarin with their high magic resistance might be the only thing able to bring them down."

"We can't let the Killnarin run free all over Zaylyn. We find Dranngore and worry about what is to happen when the time comes," said Asdella helping the dwarf to steady himself in his climb.

"And if the Killnarin are here and Dranngore isn't, what then?" asked Dendrox, "If I were him, I'd stay clear of the battle; safe and sound somewhere else. And remember, he did send that girl to speak to the Killnarin instead of addressing them in person."

No one made a reply as they all were dreading this at the back of their minds as well.

"I don't know what to think. I don't know what it is I feel," Candra said to herself as she continued to hike up the trail with the others, *"And when Shadow was so close to me, I… And what of Dendrox? Do I intend to drag him into all this, and for what exactly? Is it best to just let things be? Leave Blandorf with Shadow, as it is clear he intends to stand by him? But can I really give him up as I probably should? The thought gives me… I don't think I can. Do I just accept his affections when there is a passing chance to do so when our paths happen meet? And knowing of Shadow's feelings for him, can I just let that be? I suppose I shouldn't dwell upon it, as an easy solution for her would be simply to eliminate the competition, meaning me. But she made it clear that she felt there wasn't one and that even Blandorf wouldn't see it as there being one… I'm so confused, and I can't deny what it was I felt when I was so close to Shadow, a longing I can't quite explain. Can I simply accept things as*

<Zaylyn ><Quest For The Sword Fragments And The Hunt For Dranngore><By Katrina Mandrake-Johnston ><Ch 82> < 195 >

they are, just simply feel what it is I happen to be feeling at any given moment and then simply leave it at that instead of trying to make sense of it? And my greatest fear is that my emotions are no longer even my own. Are my emotions being manipulated, and if so, do I really want to know and have them cease to be?"

When the group arrived at the trail's end, halfway up the mountain, they could see the mouth of a large cave and that a tunnel extended for what looked to be quite a ways into the rock of the mountain.

"I wonder why Blandorf didn't mention this?" thought Candra, "We certainly must have flown past it. The wizard's guild is supposed to be a little over two hundred years, formed around the time when the dragon king was placed under a spell and his brother was apparently killed by the wizard that founded the guild. The human-dragons came to be shortly after their disappearance. Blandorf's kind were turned to stone before this, possibly three hundred years ago or perhaps even more. The rest of Zaylyn had forgotten true gargoyles for a much longer time before that, as they all fled to Dee'ellkka Valley and merely became myth and legend to the other parts of the world. Shadow told me how they were hunted down like demons. How they were often shackled and stoned to dead after capture. In some parts of Zaylyn, they were netted and burned alive. Others would hire wizards to perform torturous spells upon the gargoyles they had captured, making them suffer horribly for days or even months at a time before their deaths. The worst was the poisoned food. Whole crops would be tainted with poison by the people and on occasion the livestock would be poisoned as well; all in an effort to wipe the gargoyles out of existence. After watching his father be stoned to death by some heartless townsfolk, it actually was one of Blandorf's ancestors that had rallied the clan leaders together in order to flee to the safety of the valley."

"Candra, you all right?" Dendrox asked her.

"Oh, yeah, fine," she told him. "It doesn't look large enough for it be the lair of a dragon, and besides, I'm sure Blandorf would have told me about this, had this cave been here when the gargoyles were," Candra said to herself, "Gargoyles live twice as long as any of us do... humans, dwarves, elves... even goblins, Garcs, and centaurs... most likely even the human-dragons and a few of the fairy folk, I suppose. What will that mean for us? And then The Black Shadow, I can't imagine what it must be like for him; to live eternally and watching everything and everyone fade away while remaining the same? And yet, at the same time having the power to change that, forever tempted to give someone life eternal to match his own and be forever vexed with whether it would be right to do such a thing regardless of what his own feelings might be. If I were in his place, I would grant it to everyone I ever cared about and that way I would never be left alone in the passing of time. But then I would have to end up granting it to everyone, as anyone I give such a gift to would want it for those they cared about as well. But I suppose nature's plan solves that problem on its own, doesn't it? The love and company of the offspring are meant to replace that of the ones that have passed on in their old age. And even then, it does not matter if the body ceases in its ability to house its spirit, as our loved ones will continue to stand beside us despite that, and they will know our hearts and inner most feelings and whether our thoughts be bad or good, I suppose. I know my father is watching over me, standing beside me in everything I do. I know he weighs heavily on my conscience in things I know I shouldn't be doing and is probably ashamed of the more unsavory thoughts I've had in the past. But he knows what my mistakes have taught me, and that despite everything I've done, everything thought, and everything said, my heart really is trying to remain kind and good. And I know that all those times when I had survived by pure luck alone or even because of a funny feeling in my gut, that he must have had something to do with it... or even my mother... all of my ancestors are watching over me and guiding me through life with their love and hoping that I will make the right decisions to become a good person and that I will follow and be true to my heart's desire in my quest for happiness."

"Come on, Candra," Nodwel told her, "We're going in."

"Maybe it's best if I go first," suggested Lorenta, "I could hold the lantern to light the way as Vordin has the sword, and to put him in harm's way..."

"Yes, fine Lorenta," Nodwel told her, "Let's get in there before it's too late. We've hesitated

<Zaylyn ><Quest For The Sword Fragments And The Hunt For Dranngore><By Katrina Mandrake-Johnston ><Ch 82> < 196 >

enough already," and then Nodwel thought to himself, "*And to give Asdella the sword now, or even me for that matter, might jeopardize the entire mission should we be attacked. The sword must only be used to serve its purpose; nothing else. If using the sword is even the right thing to do.*"

The group made their way warily into the blackness of the corridor illuminated by the lantern held in Lorenta's outstretched arm.

<World of Zaylyn><Quest For The Sword Fragments And The Hunt For Dranngore><By Katrina Mandrake-Johnston><Ch 83>

CHAPTER 83 = DRANNGORE

Soon they could see a short and wiry man standing before a large double door that was closed to the events happening in the chamber beyond. His wispy brown hair was all askew, appearing almost as if it were electrified with a static charge. His grey robes were tattered and soiled with mud around the bottom edge. On either side of him, a glowing orb about the size of a fist, much like what Candra and Dendrox had seen in Rinna's little treasure horde, had been placed into a little metal cuplike recess set into the rock of the corridor. He had not heard them approach, and ever so often, he would let out a giggly squeal of delight as he listened to the explosive magical energy clearly failing in the guild's attempts to battle the Killnarin and at the occasional gurgling scream that could be heard.

"You pitiful creature," Asdella snarled, startling the little man into a shriek of fright, "You shall pay for what you have done!"

"Who... who are you? What are you doing here?" the man stammered in fear.

"You are Dranngore, are you not?!" Nodwel bellowed, adjusting his grip on the handle of his battle-axe in a threatening manner.

"Wait, how do you know my name?" asked Dranngore in a trembling voice, "Who are you people... and my word, what has happened to your hand woman?!"

"Everyone's dead because of you!" Asdella said between clenched teeth, the fury boiling within her, "Everyone at the village of Dexcsin, everyone at Nilnont, my friends, the man I loved. Now it's your turn, you sniveling little worm!" and she raised her sword in her fleshed sword arm, preparing to run at him.

"Wait don't!" Candra yelled at her, grabbing hold of her shoulder.

"I just want to wound him a little," Asdella replied, "Make him suffer first before we end his miserable waste of a life."

"No, Asdella," said Nodwel, eyeing the wizard suspiciously, "We must kill him with the sword to send back the Killnarin. We can't take the chance. We can't make a single mistake. Not after coming so far."

A hardness came over Dranngore's icy blue eyes, his fear diminishing and his mouth twisting in anger at them. "Yeah, you heard right," Asdella barked, "We mean to stop you; to ruin all your plans. We have the Sword of Anthrowst. What do you think of that?!"

"That's not possible. The sword is lost; broken. You cannot stop the Killnarin," he told them, and then he grinned as another blood-curdling scream was heard coming from beyond the doors. "One of them send you?" he chuckled.

"No, The Black Shadow sent us actually," smiled Dendrox.

Dranngore looked to him, his face falling with fear for a second, and then smiling said, "You lie."

Vordin held the sword up to the light where the blade's shimmering incandescence could plainly be seen. Dranngore's face fell once again in fear, and he then grimaced in anger. "So it's true," Dranngore snarled, "You've come to stop me. You've come to rescue the wizard's guild. You've come to ensure that they remain strong in their deeds and continue to do so unopposed. You would serve such an evil monster as The Black Shadow in this? What do you have to gain by accomplishing this evil deed?"

"Evil?!" Vordin shouted at him, his tears starting to flow, "You are the one who is evil!"

"Am I?" he laughed, "Seems to me that I am the only one putting a stop to the wizard's guild and their evil ways. In most eyes, that would make me a hero."

"You and your Killnarin slaughtered my entire village... killed my parents," yelled Vordin, his arm

<Zaylyn ><Quest For The Sword Fragments And The Hunt For Dranngore><By Katrina Mandrake-Johnston ><Ch 83> < 197 >
trembling with emotion as he held Anthrowst's sword out towards him.

"Yes, I see," replied Dranngore, "but please wait. Let me explain. All is not lost."

"What do you mean? Speak now, and make it quick," commanded Nodwel, "I warn you, I do not have a lot of patience."

"I can undo all the damage they have done," Dranngore grinned at them, "I take it you are from one of the villages that were destroyed by the beasts, right? Well you can have them back, everyone you have lost."

"You lie!" snapped Candra.

"No. No, I don't," he assured them with a wide grin, "Everyone that has fallen prey to the Killnarin can be restored to life. Everyone slain prior to the wizard's guild of course, as that has been my goal all along."

"I don't believe you. You're just wasting our time; trying to save your pathetic life," snarled Asdella.

"The network of chambers and tunnels is extensive, and it seems even the Killnarin are having quite some difficulty in bringing the wizards in there to their deaths. If you really believe you will be doing the right thing in killing me now in order to save those foul men and women, then do so. I'm sure they'll kill you, your reward being in that they will deliver you a quick death instead of the long and painful one sentenced to those that dare invade their precious guild uninvited," he told them, "Listen well. If you kill me with that sword, yes, you will expel the Killnarin from our world, but you will also be condemning all those people in the villages that the Killnarin attacked to certain death, where they could have otherwise been saved. I understand that your friends were among their number. It's all a matter of time, isn't it? Let the Killnarin accomplish what they were meant for, and I will send the creatures back myself and restore the damage they have done. The wizard's guild will be destroyed; their evil finally brought to an end and all will be well."

"You can really bring everyone back?" Vordin asked, his voice wavering.

"We've seen what the guild is capable of," commented Weena, "Maybe it wouldn't be so bad. I mean, were we really sent to save the guild? We were merely sent to stop the Killnarin. If Dranngore means to send them back anyway... Are we seriously expected to murder him?"

"How are you planning to do this?" Candra questioned him.

"Does it matter? All you really have to know is that I am the most powerful one here. Can any of you bring forth a whole army of Killnarin into our world and focus them as well as is humanly possible upon a specific path as I have done? But I am not about to undo all the damage they have caused for nothing. I, for one, do not really care whether the people are revived or not. But, I can see you clearly are so greatly concerned about them. I am willing to undergo such a lengthy and strenuous task for you, but you must answer a riddle in order to gain this favor of me. If you kill me now, you will be condemning all the lives that have been lost to remain that way forever. I say it's more than a fair trade, don't you think?"

"Ask your riddle," said Nodwel.

"What?! He's clearly stalling!" Candra yelled at him.

"You've been tainted by The Black Shadow. You have no say in this," Asdella told her flatly.

"Excuse me?! I have not! How dare you?!" Candra snapped back at her.

"Ask your riddle, Dranngore," Nodwel said again in a defeated voice.

"Kill him! Don't give in to what he wants! He clearly is manipulating you! Don't you see it?!" Candra tried to reason with them.

"We've all lost our friends in this, Candra. If there's a chance to get them back... We have to try, don't you see?" Nodwel told her disheartened.

The wizard wore a smug expression on his bony face. Weena could see the enormous magical toll that his plan for revenge had taken on Dranngore. If he were truly able to send the Killnarin back, she wondered if he would even survive such a cost that it would take to his body and mind to do so.

Vordin looked to Dranngore. "Ask your riddle," he said to him, lowering the sword.

"Vordin, give me the sword!" Candra demanded fiercely.

<Zaylyn ><Quest For The Sword Fragments And The Hunt For Dranngore><By Katrina Mandrake-Johnston ><Ch 83> < 198 >

"No!" he replied with a glare.

"Dendrox..." Candra began.

"No, Candra," Dendrox dared to say to her, "Yarin... all those people... Nodwel's right. And... and maybe Asdella is too."

"What, that I'm The Black Shadow's minion now? Come on, Dendrox, you don't really..." Candra trailed off as Dendrox broke her gaze.

"Just that the gargoyle's involvement with him might have, well, clouded your judgment a little," replied Dendrox.

Dranngore watched the group with delight. "Shall I ask my riddle then? Who will be the one to answer?" he asked them with an overzealous grin.

"I'm really good at solving them, so I guess I will," Vordin answered thinking, *That's all I did, solving puzzles and riddles, for most of my time growing up. Who knows, maybe all that time spent wasn't a waste of time after all.*

Dranngore's smile faltered a little at this, but he asked, "What has a head, four legs, but only one foot?"

"What kind of strange animal is that?!" exclaimed Weena, "How are we supposed to know the answer to that?! Maybe Candra's right."

"No, I know it," Vordin told them, "It's a bed. The head of the bed, the foot of the bed, and the four legs beneath."

A fearful look came across Dranngore's face.

Asdella tone was calm and menacing as she said to him, "Your riddle has been answered, and it was a pathetically easy one by the way. I have a riddle for you, now. What's long and sharp, made of metal and can cut through a despicable wizard like butter? Candra is right, I see it now too. He cares only for his revenge. It has consumed him. All that matters is that his precious Killnarin remain in this world long enough to complete their task. His own life is meaningless compared to the revenge he craves. The guild has already taken away his life, denied him who it was he wanted to be. I know this well. The real question here is whether we let him have his revenge. I don't really care what happens to the damn wizard's guild. He is the one responsible for everyone's death, and he needs to pay. It just happens that we can accomplish both our own vengeance and send the Killnarin back as well in having the means to do so."

Locked in Asdella's fierce and unmerciful gaze, Dranngore's fear was plain to see. He said to them, "But that of course was just the first riddle."

"So ask another then," Vordin said with frustration, raising the sword in his direction once more.

"Okay then," Dranngore said slightly relieved, as his Killnarin army continued their massacre beyond the doors, "My back is arched. If you point me in the right direction and release me, I can cause death without touching my victim." He wore a triumphant grin now, obviously pleased with himself as he looked upon the puzzled faces within the group.

Vordin's mind was racing, his emotions clouding his train of thought. Then he looked to Candra and the answer started to come to him. "It's a bow," he told Dranngore, "It's back is arched and when the bow is aimed with an arrow and released it can kill. The bow, however, never touches the victim, it's the arrow that does."

Dranngore let out a wavering laugh. "You're too smart for your own good," he commented, "And now for the third and final riddle..."

"Enough!" snapped Asdella, and a loud crash and a horrified scream was heard coming from beyond the doors. "Can you bring them back?" she snarled at him.

"Yes, but you must answer my riddle first," replied Dranngore.

"Fine, go ahead then," said Vordin with determination.

"Here it is then," Dranngore said nervously, "Most of the time, I'll show you disappointment. If I show you beauty, I'll show how it withers away."

Candra suspected that he was merely saying anything he could think of to pass off as an unsolvable riddle in order to ensure that there was enough time for his Killnarin to finish their task.

<Zaylyn ><Quest For The Sword Fragments And The Hunt For Dranngore><By Katrina Mandrake-Johnston ><Ch 83> < 199 >

Asdella held the wizard in an unwavering gaze. Vordin found himself struggling. He couldn't think of anything that would fit. The others seemed to be stumped on this one as well.

"I don't..." Vordin started to weep, "I can't... I've failed."

"Oh, that's too bad," Dranngore rejoiced with relief.

"It's a reflection," stated Asdella. An astonished look came across Dranngore's face, as he could see that this answer could very well fit his riddle and could think of nothing he could say to dispute it. "What, didn't think the barbarian to have a brain? I wasn't always so," Asdella told him.

"*Don't they see through his lies? Surely Dendrox must,*" thought Candra.

"The... the final riddle is for you to tell me what they all have in common," Dranngore said hurriedly, "If you want me to do this task for you..."

"Restore my arm as proof then," Asdella snarled.

"Ah, what... I, ah," Dranngore stammered, "I don't think I can. That's different."

Vordin mind was desperately trying to put the pieces together. "*A bed and a bow both have wood components. But then how does the reflection fit in?*"

"It's death," said Asdella.

"What? What do you mean?" Dranngore said, his voice thick with fear.

"The answer to your damn riddle. Even you didn't know the answer to your own question, did you? It's the only relation I can think of; the bed being a place of death, the bow causing death, and to see the first two together reflects to others a vision of their own mortality," said Asdella letting her sword clatter to the stone floor and grabbing up the magical sword from out of Vordin's weak grasp, "So, Dranngore, I don't think you can do anything at all, can you? All this time stalling, and you haven't even bothered to fire off one measly little spell in your defense. Maintaining your hold over the Killnarin is taking every last bit of your magical stamina, isn't it? You are just stalling until the creatures complete their task, aren't you?"

"In Rasindell's past, when he encountered a Killnarin, the wizard who had summoned it was killed right after it killed the woman it was meant to attack," Vordin remembered aloud.

"That would explain why he is hiding behind these doors here like a coward. And also why he used the girl to speak to the Killnarin instead of confronting them himself," stated Asdella.

"Wait, how could you possibly know about that?" asked Dranngore.

"So he's not in control of the Killnarin," said Nodwel, "If they come through those doors, they'll kill him as well, and then there will be no hope of us sending the creatures back with the sword if that happens. Once they're done with the guild, they'll eventually find their way out to us as well."

"The sword won't undo what the Killnarin have caused to happen. Everyone killed will stay dead. It will only vanish the creatures from our world back to where they belong. It will only reverse the spell that summoned them and every other spell he's cast as well," stated Weena.

"Exactly," said Dranngore, "No need to be so hasty," he added nervously.

<World of Zaylyn><Quest For The Sword Fragments And The Hunt For Dranngore><By Katrina Mandrake-Johnston><Ch 84>

CHAPTER 84 = DRANNGORE'S DEFEAT OF THE WIZARD'S GUILD

Someone was banging frantically on the two doors behind Dranngore. "Please! Let me out!" they heard a man's voice cry out, "Everyone else is dead! Please, Dranngore, I know it's you! Open the doors! Call them off! We were wrong! Is that what you want to hear, damn it?! Call them off if you even can, you maniac! Open the doors! Ah! No!" They heard him pound on the door a few more times before they heard something large and heavy land before the doors where a wet crunching sound was later heard. The Killnarin, to the group's relief, then bounded away from the doors howling in triumph as it headed farther and farther away from them.

Dranngore was ecstatic as he stared down at the pool of blood seeping under the doors to collect on the rock floor of the corridor. He turned to the group gleaming with sheer joy. "Ha! It matters not whether you've answered correctly or not, fools! The Killnarin have slain all the wizards, do you hear?! Do you hear that I have won?! They are all defeated!"

Snarling in anger, Asdella lunged at him with Anthrowst's sword. She stared in disbelief as the

<Zaylyn ><Quest For The Sword Fragments And The Hunt For Dranngore><By Katrina Mandrake-Johnston ><Ch 84> < 200 >
sword stopped in mid thrust.

She looked to Dranngore in astonishment, as he loudly and boldly let out a shrill laugh right into the warrior woman's face. "Did you think I would come unprepared? That I would leave myself vulnerable to an attack from one of my Killnarin should one of them decide to take a swipe at me before their task was complete?"

"It's a Shield spell," Weena explained, "A powerful one. A higher level Shield spell will last much longer and be far stronger than what you've seen with my weak one. It'll be a short while until it dissipates. Until then we can't get to him."

"It doesn't matter," Asdella said with frustration, "I'll be ready to skewer him as soon as it does."

"Oh, it matters not what you do now, as my vengeance has been fulfilled. The boy was right; the Killnarin would have eventually turned on me as well given enough time," he told them, "Go ahead, kill me and send them back. My task is complete. I shall die with my life fulfilled and content. My name will become legend as it is I who have defeated the entire wizard's guild."

"And who is there to tell this story?" Lorenta asked him, "Do you really think we shall say anything about it, if that kind of recognition is what you truly desire? Everyone is dead. No one will know it was you who did this unless you bring the villagers and our friends back to life."

"You are all fools, except for maybe your warrior woman here and the elf. You really believe a mere human can hold such power as to raise the dead? If you truly wanted to defeat the all mighty Dranngore and foil his plans, you should have struck me down much earlier," he laughed at them, "The weak are manipulated so easily. I care not for fame, just for the knowledge that each member of the wizard's guild will forever remember that it was I, Dranngore, who defeated them. They shall forever know the shame and guilt of their actions against me, even in death, for I have proven them wrong."

"You evil, selfish little man. It may be true that the souls of the guild shall be tormented as you say, but so shall you. You will suffer for your evil deeds," Nodwel said, glaring at him with loathing.

"Ha! How so? Spoil my revenge?" he mocked, "Too late! Physically torture me until I die? The Killnarin will destroy you, long before I am dead."

"So cast another spell," Asdella dared him, "You're too weak, aren't you? You don't even have the guts to try, as you will collapse from exhaustion."

He closed his eyes and cast another spell. "Damn it, Asdella! He just renewed the Shield spell and at a pretty powerful level it looks like" Weena yelled at her, "He must have used a magical item the first time!"

"You continue to threaten me?!" Dranngore shouted at Asdella, and then a malicious grin spread across his lips, "You know how Anthrowst's sword works. Don't you dare threaten me, bitch! If I live, my Killnarin will rule and all of Zaylyn will become their gruesome playground. If I die by their claws or by some other means other than that sword, the same fate awaits Zaylyn. And it won't be long now as I have relinquished my hold on them in order to cast this second Shield spell myself. The true question is, do I hate the world enough to kill myself now or even wait for the Killnarin to do it? One prick from this poison needle of my ring," he said holding it out for all to see, "and all your hopes shall end. It matters not if you kill me with the sword even a second after, as you well know. It will be the poison that first lays claim on my life, whether the poison works in a single instant or takes years to complete its task. The magic in the sword will be useless to you, unless it makes the first cut. Answer one final riddle for me."

"What?! Are you serious?!" Candra exclaimed in disbelief.

"I care not for if the world lives or dies, as my death is upon me either way. I have decided to have some fun in my last moments, and that is all. You, boy, are the one who must answer and save Zaylyn from a horrible demise. I advise that you hurry, as my Killnarin are hungry for more bloodshed. I am connected to them, and I feel them approaching quickly, you have but a few minutes before all of our lives are ended here by them. They are far too strong now for any of you to defeat without the use of the Sword of Anthrowst," he told them, "My riddle for you is this... Siblings torn, a blackened heart fueled by jealousy and turned to thievery, and wizards sitting upon a stolen throne while they reap the magical rewards of another."

<Zaylyn ><Quest For The Sword Fragments And The Hunt For Dranngore><By Katrina Mandrake-Johnston ><Ch 84> < 201 >

The Shield spell was beginning to dissipate, the duration of his spell coming to an end with time, and a wicked grin began to spread across Asdella's lips.

"No, wait... I..." Dranngore stammered, watching in horror as the protection of his spell faded into nothingness.

Asdella thrust the sword into Dranngore's thin and wiry frame.

The wizard collapsed, the ground awash with his life's blood as he lay dying in pain and with a fearful and helpless look in his eyes.

"It's been done. The magic of the sword has been activated, hasn't it?" Weena said urgently, pleading with the others, "Let me heal him, please! We can't just let him die now; murdered by us in this awful quest?!"

"Yes, please," Dranngore begged weakly, outstretching his pale bloodied hand towards Weena, "Help me. Don't let me die."

"Don't you move, Weena," barked Asdella.

"No, this is wrong! He doesn't have much time. We have no right to deem ourselves his executioner!"

Asdella whipped the sword around to threaten Weena with it. She stared in horror at the bloodied blade, defensively raising up her hands in front of her. "I don't care if the Killnarin have already been sent back or not! He suffers! He is to be slain with the sword, Weena," Asdella snarled at her, "And besides, I'm not going to open up those doors until I know they're gone for certain. This foul man dies, slow and painful."

Weena felt the frustration build up inside her, and she hadn't intended to, but in that moment, in Asdella's defiance against her, the symbols and their names began to flash through her mind... and a bout of steam shot out from her hands to strike Asdella. She had not been harmed to everyone's relief. Weena was extremely astonished by what had just taken place, as was everyone else, but Weena quickly seized the opportunity and rushed forward past Asdella, intent on casting her healing spell upon Dranngore.

"I'm not going to be part of this. I'm not going to be responsible for another's death like this," Weena cried out and started to make an attempt to cast the magic.

To her horror, Asdella thrust the sword into Dranngore again and again, over and over, as he lay there, making him cry out in agony until he was finally dead.

The warrior woman wore a triumphant grin upon her face, as she stared down coldly at Weena who was kneeling beside his body.

"I'm sorry, Weena, but it had to be done," Candra said softly.

"We should search the chambers beyond, to see if it actually worked, to see if the Killnarin are still about," said Dendrox solemnly.

The Sword of Anthrowst was torn from Asdella's hand by an unseen force and hovered before them in mid air for a few moments before melting into a silvery puddle upon the rock floor of the corridor.

"I guess this is The Black Shadow's way of telling us that we have succeeded," said Vordin, but he did not at all feel victorious.

<World of Zaylyn><Quest For The Sword Fragments And The Hunt For Dranngore><By Katrina Mandrake-Johnston><Ch 85>

CHAPTER 85 =   THE DRAGON ARISES

As the group wandered through the chambers and passageways of what had been the wizard's guild, they found that they had indeed succeeded in ridding their world of the Killnarin. Dranngore as well had succeeded in eliminating the wizard's guild. It was only when they reached the inner sanctum of the mountain and discovered a small room that was completely bare except for a large glowing crystal resting upon a metal table, that they realized this was where the guild's power came from and allowed them to steal the magical energy and life force of those they had enslaved.

"We have to destroy it," Weena told them, "Can't you see, it's continuing to collect power, even now."

<Zaylyn ><Quest For The Sword Fragments And The Hunt For Dranngore><By Katrina Mandrake-Johnston ><Ch 85> < 202 >

Asdella stepped up to the crystal and picked it up in her skeletal hand. Her hand had been getting increasingly stronger as the night progressed. She squeezed, and the crystal shattered. The glow subsided, and Weena smiled.

Weena suspected that this had been Asdella's way of trying to make amends with her for what had happened with Dranngore, and Weena was all too aware that it very well could have been a bout of flame that had erupted and lashed out toward Asdella had she been able to continue with her studies of the spell. It frightened her at how easily the spell was connecting within her, and only with a single reading, which was unheard of.

As they were leaving the room, the mountain began to tremble. The group hurried themselves out of the mountain and into the night air. There they beheld an awful sight. Something appeared to be erupting out of the very rock high above them. They watched as a massive black dragon freed himself from his prison, his stolen crystal no longer used against him by the wizard's guild to subdue him. The beast beat his leathery wings, soaring high into the night sky, illuminated by the moonlight, and eventually the dragon disappeared out of sight as he flew over the mountains and away from the valley.

"Dranngore's riddle," said Candra, "It was about the dragon king, Goranto, and his evil brother, Baracken: siblings torn. The crystal must have been his, used to amass a greater magical power in order to battle against Goranto: a blackened heart fueled by jealousy turned to thievery. Once he defeated the king and could take his place, that's when the wizard must have somehow used his own crystal against him in order to continuously drain his energy and keep him in such a powerless state. Wizard's sitting upon the stolen throne while they reap the magical rewards of another. Isn't that what Dranngore meant by his riddle?"

"And so?" asked Asdella plainly.

"Well, from what Blandorf and Shadow told me," said Candra, "most likely, he'll rally the dragons under him to do his bidding and will now stand unopposed by his brother. There's a very good chance that he'll try to kill all of the Dragonites, and their existence will probably spur his already fierce loathing of the humanoid races."

"The Avygons are half dragon as well," added in Lorenta, "I'm sure, wherever they are, that they won't be safe from his hatred either."

"No one will be," stated Candra, "He'll lead the dragons to kill us all, only allowing for a few to live as their servants."

Asdella snarled, "We should never have destroyed that crystal, Weena."

"We urgently need to return to Shirkint, and for more reasons than one," Nodwel told them all with dread.

****

NEXT = WORLD OF ZAYLYN = BOOK # 3

Awakening Of The Dragon King Goranto

****

I hope you enjoy my novels as much as I enjoy writing them.   See website to leave feedback

<< *** >>   See website for order information and special features   << *** >>
****

(World of Zaylyn website =   http:// www.webspawner.com/users/worldofzaylyn)

****

Awakening Of The Dragon King Goranto
By *Katrina Mandrake-Johnston*
World of Zaylyn

Baracken is no longer kept at bay. The wizard's guild, using the dragon's own crystal against him, had kept him subdued while they used its power to drain the magical energy of others for themselves. Now that Dranngore has eliminated the guild with his Killnarin and the group has destroyed the crystal not knowing what would come of it, Baracken, the evil brother of the dragon king, has been set free. With Goranto ensnared long ago under a spell, Baracken can now claim the throne and rule over the dragons of Zaylyn. All human-dragons would surely perish and so would countless others.

Dea, from the village of Torrnell, decides to take the matter of the dragon there into her own hands. Will she succeed in stopping its attacks upon her village?

Did Hoatam, the werewolf, speak the truth when he said that Thorin's half-devoured body mysteriously vanished? Will Hoatam finally succeed in creating other werewolves to become his followers? Will Nodwel be able to escort and protect Kreasa and her sons on their way back to Dexcsin with the werewolf so eagerly hunting them down?

To Dendrox and Candra's horror, they discover that it just so happened that Cranok, their home village, was home once to the wizard that had started the wizard's guild and imprisoned Baracken. This was where the dragon was first headed in his reign of terror, and the two thieves start to greatly fear for the safety of Dendrox's parents.

Goranto is the only one who can possibly stand against Baracken and unite the dragons in continued peace with the humanoid races of Zaylyn and not terrorize and dominate over them in superiority as his brother wishes to do. The group feels they have no other choice but to find a way to awaken the dragon king, Goranto, and therefore stop Baracken.

Lure-va = self

Dae-mond = don't want

Doanda = peaceful

Zool-va = will care for / protect

Tooc-cut = feel pain for

Shee-va = happy

Dae-kruntie = frustrating / irritating

Nick-ca-lore = bring to / draw forth

Blicka = small amount

Creat-tah = skill

Creat-tore = strength / willpower

Seblortee = deep love / chosen mate

Dis-calunt = confuse / cloud mind / lost

Baskeynea = birth / create

Satoot = speed pregnancy

Blin-d-dorseca = mixing of body / breed / create offspring

Sem-black-art = mend / make whole / return to former state

Black-core = electric

Nu-door-ta = blend in surrounding / hide in among

Me-ca-tore = intelligence

Plend-da-oats = purify / rid bad / make safe

Sam-blor = large amount

May-licka = see image / dream

Comb-blat = stop movement

Soon-da-blust = force / explode

Kai-na = want

Do-la = you

Gru-lund-deey = beautiful / admire / respect

Coke-ca = open / push out

Minst-da = expand to another / inclusive

Miy = outside self / body / personality

Ploonda = close / bring in

Zordniea = choke / stop breath

Zoulpla = separate state

Med-ta = sleep / rest

Soon-ga = levitate / rise up / fly

Drat-tone = hurt

Bin-drost = hate

Diy = inside self / spirit

Sooc-gadoingt = closeness / love / feelings for

Brur-down = come / being called / follow

Cac-coon = collected / focused

Doon-da = cold

Dan-dost = heat

Black-ca-ist = shock / strike / affect aggressive

Pleck-ca-d-own = grab / touch / seize

Soose-sa-in = change state / freeze / melt / evaporate

Sam-dose-ca = hide from eyes

Printed in the United States
By Bookmasters